ISBN 978-1-331-07836-4
PIBN 10141981

# 1 MONTH OF
# FREE
# READING

## at

## www.ForgottenBooks.com

By purchasing this book you are eligible for one month membership to ForgottenBooks.com, giving you unlimited access to our entire collection of over 700,000 titles via our web site and mobile apps.

To claim your free month visit:

www.forgottenbooks.com/free141981

English
Français
Deutsche
Italiano
Español
Português

# www.forgottenbooks.com

**Mythology** Photography **Fiction**
Fishing Christianity **Art** Cooking
Essays Buddhism Freemasonry
Medicine **Biology** Music **Ancient**
**Egypt** Evolution Carpentry Physics
Dance Geology **Mathematics** Fitness
Shakespeare **Folklore** Yoga Marketing
**Confidence** Immortality Biographies
Poetry **Psychology** Witchcraft
Electronics Chemistry History **Law**
Accounting **Philosophy** Anthropology
Alchemy Drama Quantum Mechanics
Atheism Sexual Health **Ancient History**
**Entrepreneurship** Languages Sport
Paleontology Needlework Islam
**Metaphysics** Investment Archaeology
Parenting Statistics Criminology
**Motivational**

*" Sir," said* Dr. Johnson, *" let us take a walk down Fleet Street."*

# TEMPLE BAR

## 𝔄 𝔏𝔬𝔫𝔡𝔬𝔫 𝔐𝔞𝔤𝔞𝔷𝔦𝔫𝔢

### FOR TOWN AND COUNTRY READERS.

### VOL. XXXVII. MARCH 1873.

LONDON:

RICHARD BENTLEY & SON, 8, NEW BURLINGTON STREET.

NEW YORK: WILLMER AND ROGERS.

LONDON:
PRINTED BY WILLIAM CLOWES AND SONS,

# CONTENTS.

# TEMPLE BAR.

DECEMBER 1872.

## The New Magdalen.

### By WILKIE COLLINS.

### Chapter IX.

#### NEWS FROM MANNHEIM.

LADY JANET'S curiosity was by this time thoroughly aroused. Summoned to explain who the nameless lady mentioned in his letter could possibly be, Julian had looked at her adopted daughter. Asked next to explain what her adopted daughter had got to do with it, he had declared that he could not answer while Miss Roseberry was in the room.

What did he mean? Lady Janet determined to find out.

"I hate all mysteries," she said to Julian. "And as for secrets, I consider them to be one of the forms of ill-breeding. People in our rank of life ought to be above whispering in corners. If you *must* have your mystery, I can offer you a corner in the library. Come with me."

Julian followed his aunt very reluctantly. Whatever the mystery might be, he was plainly embarrassed by being called upon to reveal it at a moment's notice. Lady Janet settled herself in her chair, prepared to question and cross-question her nephew—when an obstacle appeared at the other end of the library, in the shape of a man-servant with a message. One of Lady Janet's neighbours had called by appointment to take her to the meeting of a certain committee which assembled that day. The servant announced that the neighbour—an elderly lady—was then waiting in her carriage at the door.

Lady Janet's ready invention set the obstacle aside without a moment's delay. She directed the servant to show her visitor into the drawing-room, and to say that she was unexpectedly engaged, but that Miss Roseberry would see the lady immediately. She then turned to Julian, and said, with her most satirical emphasis of tone

and manner, " Would it be an additional convenience if Miss Roseberry was not only out of the room, before you disclose your secret,
but out of the house ?"

Julian gravely answered, " It may possibly be quite as well if Miss
Roseberry is out of the house."

Lady Janet led the way back to the dining-room.

" My dear Grace," she said, " you looked flushed and feverish when
I saw you asleep on the sofa a little while since. It will do you no
harm to have a drive in the fresh air. Our friend has called to take
me to the committee meeting. I have sent to tell her that I am
engaged—and I shall be much obliged if you will go in my place."

Mercy looked a little alarmed. " Does your ladyship mean the
committee meeting of the Samaritan Convalescent Home? The
members, as I understand it, are to decide to-day which of the plans
for the new building they are to adopt. I cannot surely presume to
vote in your place?"

" You can vote, my dear child, just as well as I can," replied the
old lady. " Architecture is one of the lost arts. You know nothing
about it ; I know nothing about it ; the architects themselves know
nothing about it. One plan is no doubt just as bad as the other.
Vote, as I should vote, with the majority. Or as poor dear Dr.
Johnson said, ' Shout with the loudest mob.' Away with you—and
don't keep the committee waiting."

Horace hastened to open the door for Mercy.

" How long shall you be away ?" he whispered confidentially. " I
had a thousand things to say to you, and they have interrupted us."

" I shall be back in an hour."

" We shall have the room to ourselves by that time. Come here
when you return. You will find me waiting for you."

Mercy pressed his hand significantly and went out. Lady Janet
turned to Julian, who had thus far remained in the background, still,
to all appearance, as unwilling as ever to enlighten his aunt.

" Well ?" she said. " What is tying your tongue now? Grace is
out of the room ; why don't you begin ? Is Horace in the way ?"

" Not in the least. I am only a little uneasy "——

" Uneasy about what ?"

" I am afraid you have put that charming creature to some incon-
venience in sending her away just at this time."

Horace looked up suddenly with a flush on his face.

" When you say ' that charming creature,' " he asked sharply, " I
suppose you mean Miss Roseberry ?"

" Certainly," answered Julian. " Why not ?"

Lady Janet interposed. " Gently, Julian," she said. " Grace has
only been introduced to you hitherto in the character of my adopted
daughter "——

"And it seems to be high time," Horace added haughtily, "that I should present her next in the character of my engaged wife."

Julian looked at Horace as if he could hardly credit the evidence of his own ears. "Your wife!" he exclaimed, with an irrepressible outburst of disappointment and surprise.

"Yes. My wife," returned Horace. "We are to be married in a fortnight. May I ask," he added, with angry humility, "if you disapprove of the marriage?"

Lady Janet interposed once more. "Nonsense, Horace," she said. "Julian congratulates you, of course."

Julian coldly and absently echoed the words. "Oh, yes! I congratulate you, of course."

Lady Janet returned to the main object of the interview.

"Now we thoroughly understand one another," she said, "let us speak of a lady who has dropped out of the conversation for the last minute or two. I mean, Julian, the mysterious lady of your letter. We are alone, as you desired. Lift the veil, my reverend nephew, which hides her from mortal eyes! Blush, if you like—and can. Is she the future Mrs. Julian Gray?"

"She is a perfect stranger to me," Julian answered, quietly.

"A perfect stranger! You wrote me word you were interested in her."

"I *am* interested in her. And, what is more, you are interested in her, too."

Lady Janet's fingers drummed impatiently on the table. "Have I not warned you, Julian, that I hate mysteries? Will you, or will you not, explain yourself?"

Before it was possible to answer, Horace rose from his chair. "Perhaps I am in the way?" he said.

Julian signed to him to sit down again.

"I have already told Lady Janet that you are not in the way," he answered. "I now tell *you*—as Miss Roseberry's future husband—that you too have an interest in hearing what I have to say."

Horace resumed his seat with an air of suspicious surprise. Julian addressed himself to Lady Janet.

"You have often heard me speak," he began, "of my old friend and schoolfellow, John Cressingham?"

"Yes. The English consul at Mannheim?"

"The same. When I returned from the country I found among my other letters, a long letter from the consul. I have brought it with me, and I propose to read certain passages from it, which tell a very strange story more plainly and more credibly than I can tell it in my own words."

"Will it be very long?" inquired Lady Janet, looking with some alarm at the closely written sheets of paper which her nephew spread open before him.

Horace followed with a question on his side.

"You are sure I am interested in it?" he asked.   "The consul at Mannheim is a total stranger to me."

"I answer for it," replied Julian, gravely, "neither my aunt's patience nor yours, Horace, will be thrown away if you will favour me by listening attentively to what I am about to read."

With those words he began his first extract from the consul's letter.

* * *  "'My memory is a bad one for dates. But full three months must have passed since information was sent to me of an English patient, received at the hospital here, whose case I, as English consul, might feel an interest in investigating.

"'I went the same day to the hospital, and was taken to the bedside.

"'The patient was a woman—young, and (when in health) I should think, very pretty.   When I first saw her she looked, to my uninstructed eye, like a dead woman.   I noticed that her head had a bandage over it, and I asked what was the nature of the injury that she had received. The answer informed me that the poor creature had been present, nobody knew why or wherefore, at a skirmish or night attack between the Germans and the French, and that the injury to her head had been inflicted by a fragment of a German shell.'"

Horace—thus far leaning back carelessly in his chair—suddenly raised himself and exclaimed, "Good heavens! can this be the woman I saw laid out for dead in the French cottage?"

"It is impossible for me to say," replied Julian.   "Listen to the rest of it.   The consul's letter may answer your question."

He went on with his reading:

"'The wounded woman had been reported dead, and had been left by the French in their retreat, at the time when the German forces took possession of the enemy's position.   She was found on a bed in a cottage by the director of the German ambulance'"——

"Ignatius Wetzel?" cried Horace.

"Ignatius Wetzel," repeated Julian, looking at the letter.

"It *is* the same!" said Horace.   "Lady Janet, we are really interested in this.   You remember my telling you how I first met with Grace?   And you have heard more about it since, no doubt, from Grace herself?"

"She has a horror of referring to that part of her journey home," replied Lady Janet.   "She mentioned her having been stopped on the frontier, and her finding herself accidentally in the company of another Englishwoman, a perfect stranger to her.   I naturally asked questions on my side, and was shocked to hear that she had seen the woman killed by a German shell almost close at her side.   Neither she nor I have had any relish for returning to the subject since.   You were quite right, Julian, to avoid speaking of it while she was in the room.

I understand it all now. Grace, I suppose, mentioned my name to her fellow-traveller. The woman is, no doubt, in want of assistance, and she applies to me through you. I will help her; but she must not come here until I have prepared Grace for seeing her again, a living woman. For the present, there is no reason why they should meet."

"I am not sure about that," said Julian, in low tones, without looking up at his aunt.

"What do you mean? Is the mystery not at an end yet?"

"The mystery has not even begun yet. Let my friend the consul proceed."

Julian returned for the second time to his extract from the letter:

"'After a careful examination of the supposed corpse, the German surgeon arrived at the conclusion that a case of suspended animation had (in the hurry of the French retreat) been mistaken for a case of death. Feeling a professional interest in the subject, he decided on putting his opinion to the test. He operated on the patient with complete success. After performing the operation he kept her for some days under his own care, and then transferred her to the nearest hospital—the hospital at Mannheim. He was obliged to return to his duties as army surgeon, and he left his patient in the condition in which I saw her, insensible on the bed. Neither he nor the hospital authorities knew anything whatever about the woman. No papers were found on her. All the doctors could do, when I asked them for information with a view to communicating with her friends, was to show me her linen marked with her name. I left the hospital after taking down the name in my pocket-book. It was "Mercy Merrick."'"

Lady Janet produced *her* pocket-book. "Let me take the name down too," she said. "I never heard it before, and I might otherwise forget it. Go on, Julian."

Julian advanced to his second extract from the consul's letter:

"'Under these circumstances, I could only wait to hear from the hospital when the patient was sufficiently recovered to be able to speak to me. Some weeks passed without my receiving any communication from the doctors. On calling to make inquiries I was informed that fever had set in, and that the poor creature's condition now alternated between exhaustion and delirium. In her delirious moments the name of your aunt, Lady Janet Roy, frequently escaped her. Otherwise her wanderings were for the most part quite unintelligible to the people at her bedside. I thought once or twice of writing to you and of begging you to speak to Lady Janet. But as the doctors informed me that the chances of life or death were at this time almost equally balanced, I decided to wait until time should determine whether it was necessary to trouble you or not.'"

"You know best, Julian," said Lady Janet. "But I own I don't quite see in what way I am interested in this part of the story."

"Just what I was going to say," added Horace. "It is very sad, no doubt. But what have *we* to do with it?"

"Let me read my third extract," Julian answered, "and you will see."

He turned to the third extract, and read as follows:

"'At last I received a message from the hospital informing me that Mercy Merrick was out of danger, and that she was capable (though still very weak) of answering any questions which I might think it desirable to put to her. On reaching the hospital I was requested, rather to my surprise, to pay my first visit to the head physician in his private room. 'I think it right,' said this gentleman, 'to warn you, before you see the patient, to be very careful how you speak to her, and not to irritate her by showing any surprise or expressing any doubts if she talks to you in an extravagant manner. We differ in opinion about her here. Some of us (myself among the number) doubt whether the recovery of her mind has accompanied the recovery of her bodily powers. Without pronouncing her to be mad—she is perfectly gentle and harmless—we are nevertheless of opinion that she is suffering under a species of insane delusion. Bear in mind the caution which I have given you—and now go and judge for yourself.' I obeyed, in some little perplexity and surprise. The sufferer, when I approached her bed, looked sadly weak and worn; but, so far as I could judge, seemed to be in full possession of herself. Her tone and manner were unquestionably the tone and manner of a lady. After briefly introducing myself, I assured her that I should be glad, both officially and personally, if I could be of any assistance to her. In saying these trifling words I happened to address her, by the name I had seen marked on her clothes. The instant the words 'Miss Merrick' passed my lips a wild vindictive expression appeared in her eyes. She exclaimed angrily, 'Don't call me by that hateful name! It's not my name. All the people here persecute me by calling me Mercy Merrick. And when I am angry with them they show me the clothes. Say what I may, they persist in believing they are my clothes. Don't you do the same, if you want to be friends with me.' Remembering what the physician had said to me, I made the necessary excuses and succeeded in soothing her. Without reverting to the irritating topic of the name, I merely inquired what her plans were, and assured her that she might command my services if she required them. 'Why do you want to know what my plans are?' she asked suspiciously. I reminded her in reply that I held the position of English consul, and that my object was, if possible, to be of some assistance to her. 'You can be of the greatest assistance to me,' she said, eagerly. 'Find Mercy Merrick!' I saw the vindictive look come back into her eyes, and an angry flush rising on her white cheeks. Abstaining from showing any surprise, I asked her who Mercy Merrick was? 'A vile woman, by her own confession,' was the quick reply. 'How am I to find her ?' I inquired next. 'Look for a woman in a black dress, with the Red Geneva Cross on her shoulder; she is a nurse in the French ambulance.' 'What has she done?' 'I have lost my papers; I have lost my own clothes; Mercy Merrick has taken them.' 'How do you know that Mercy Merrick has taken them?' 'Nobody else could have taken them—that's how I know it. Do you believe me or not?' She was beginning to excite herself again; I assured her that I would at once send to make inquiries after Mercy Merrick. She turned round, contented, on the pillow. 'There's a good man!' she said 'Come back and tell me when you have caught her.' Such was my first interview with the English patient at the hospital at Mannheim. It is needless to say that I doubted the existence of the absent person described as a nurse. However, it was possible to make inquiries, by applying to the surgeon, Ignatius Wetzel, whose whereabouts was known to his friends in Mannheim. I wrote to him, and received his answer in due time. After the night attack of the Germans had made them masters of the French position, he had entered the cottage occupied by the French ambulance. He had found the wounded Frenchmen left behind, but had seen no such person in attendance on them as the nurse in the black dress, with the red cross on her shoulder. The only living woman in the place was a young English lady, in a grey travelling cloak, who had been stopped on the frontier, and who was forwarded on her way home by the war correspondent of an English journal."

"That was Grace," said Lady Janet.

"And I was the war correspondent," added Horace.

"A few words more," said Julian, "and you will understand my object in claiming your attention."

He returned to the letter for the last time, and concluded his extracts from it as follows:

"'Instead of attending at the hospital myself I communicated by letter the failure of my attempt to discover the missing nurse. For some little time afterwards I heard no more of the sick woman whom I shall still call Mercy Merrick. It was only yesterday that I received another summons to visit the patient. She had by this time sufficiently recovered to claim her discharge, and she had announced her intention of returning forthwith to England. The head physician, feeling a sense of responsibility, had sent for me. It was impossible to detain her on the ground that she was not fit to be trusted by herself at large, in consequence of the difference of opinion among the doctors on the case. All that could be done was to give me due notice, and to leave the matter in my hands. On seeing her for the second time, I found her sullen and reserved. She openly attributed my inability to find the nurse to want of zeal for her interests on my part. I had, on my side, no authority whatever to detain her. I could only inquire whether she had money enough to pay her travelling expenses. Her reply informed me that the chaplain of the hospital had mentioned her forlorn situation in the town and that the English residents had subscribed a small sum of money to enable her to return to her own country. Satisfied on this head, I asked next if she had friends to go to in England. 'I have one friend,' she answered, 'who is a host in herself—Lady Janet Roy.' You may imagine my surprise when I heard this. I found it quite useless to make any further inquiries as to how she came to know your aunt, whether your aunt expected her, and so on. My questions evidently offended her; they were received in sulky silence. Under these circumstances, well knowing that I can trust implicitly to your humane sympathy for misfortune, I have decided (after careful reflection) to ensure the poor creature's safety when she arrives in London by giving her a letter to you. You will hear what she says; and you will be better able to discover than I am whether she really has any claim on Lady Janet Roy. One last word of information, which it may be necessary to add, and I shall close this inordinately long letter. At my first interview with her I abstained, as I have already told you, from irritating her by any inquiries on the subject of her name. On this second occasion, however, I decided on putting the question.'"

As he read those last words, Julian became aware of a sudden movement on the part of his aunt. Lady Janet had risen softly from her chair and had passed behind him with the purpose of reading the consul's letter for herself over her nephew's shoulder. Julian detected the action just in time to frustrate Lady Janet's intention by placing his hand over the last two lines of the letter.

"What do you do that for?" inquired his aunt sharply.

"You are welcome, Lady Janet, to read the close of the letter for yourself," Julian replied. "But before you do so I am anxious to prepare you for a very great surprise. Compose yourself, and let me read on slowly, with your eye on me, until I uncover the last two words which close my friend's letter."

He read the end of the letter, as he had proposed, in these terms:

"'I looked the woman straight in the face, and I said to her, 'You have denied that the name marked on the clothes which you wore when you came here was your name. If you are not Mercy Merrick, who are you?' She answered instantly, 'My name is'"——

Julian removed his hand from the page. Lady Janet looked at the next two words and started back with a loud cry of astonishment, which brought Horace instantly to his feet.

"Tell me, one of you!" he cried. "What name did she give?"

Julian told him:

"GRACE ROSEBERRY."

## Chapter X.

### A COUNCIL OF THREE.

For a moment Horace stood thunderstruck, looking in blank astonishment at Lady Janet. His first words, as soon as he had recovered himself, were addressed to Julian:

"Is this a joke?" he asked, sternly. "If it is, I for one don't see the humour of it."

Julian pointed to the closely written pages of the consul's letter. "A man writes in earnest," he said, "when he writes at such length as this. The woman seriously gave the name of Grace Roseberry, and when she left Mannheim she travelled to England for the express purpose of presenting herself to Lady Janet Roy." He turned to his aunt. "You saw me start," he went on, "when you first mentioned Miss Roseberry's name in my hearing. Now you know why." He addressed himself once more to Horace. "You heard me say that you, as Miss Roseberry's future husband, had an interest in being present at my interview with Lady Janet. Now you know why."

"The woman is plainly mad," said Lady Janet. "But it is certainly a startling form of madness when one first hears of it. Of course we must keep the matter, for the present at least, a secret from Grace."

"There can be no doubt," Horace agreed, "that Grace must be kept in the dark, in her present state of health. The servants had better be warned beforehand, in case of this adventuress or madwoman, whichever she may be, attempting to make her way into the house."

"It shall be done immediately," said Lady Janet. "What surprises me, Julian (ring the bell, if you please,) is, that you should describe yourself in your letter as feeling an interest in this person."

Julian answered—without ringing the bell.

"I am more interested than ever," he said, "now I find that Miss Roseberry herself is your guest at Mablethorpe House."

"You were always perverse, Julian, as a child, in your likings and dislikings," Lady Janet rejoined. "Why don't you ring the bell?"

"For one good reason, my dear aunt. I don't wish to hear you tell your servants to close the door on this friendless creature."

Lady Janet cast a look at her nephew which plainly expressed that she thought he had taken a liberty with her.

"You don't expect me to see the woman?" she asked, in a tone of cold surprise.

"I hope you will not refuse to see her," Julian answered quietly. "I was out when she called. I must hear what she has to say—and

I should infinitely prefer hearing it in your presence. When I got your reply to my letter, permitting me to present her to you, I wrote to her immediately, appointing a meeting here."

Lady Janet lifted her bright black eyes in mute expostulation to the carved cupids and wreaths on the dining-room ceiling.

"When am I to have the honour of the lady's visit?" she inquired, with ironical resignation.

"To-day," answered her nephew, with impenetrable patience.

"At what hour?"

Julian composedly consulted his watch. "She is ten minutes after her time," he said—and put his watch back in his pocket again.

At the same moment the servant appeared, and advanced to Julian, carrying a visiting card on his little silver tray.

"A lady to see you, sir."

Julian took the card, and, bowing, handed it to his aunt.

"Here she is," he said, just as quietly as ever.

Lady Janet looked at the card—and tossed it indignantly back to her nephew. "Miss Roseberry!" she exclaimed. "Printed, actually printed on her card! Julian, even MY patience has its limits. I refuse to see her!"

The servant was still waiting—not like a human being who took an interest in the proceedings—but (as became a perfectly bred footman) like an article of furniture artfully constructed to come and go at the word of command. Julian gave the word of command, addressing the admirably constructed automaton by the name of "James."

"Where is the lady, now?" he asked.

"In the breakfast-room, sir."

"Leave her there, if you please; and wait outside within hearing of the bell."

The legs of the furniture-footman acted, and took him noiselessly out of the room. Julian turned to his aunt.

"Forgive me," he said, "for venturing to give the man his orders in your presence. I am very anxious that you should not decide hastily. Surely we ought to hear what this lady has to say?"

Horace dissented widely from his friend's opinion. "It's an insult to Grace," he broke out warmly, "to hear what she has to say!"

Lady Janet nodded her head in high approval. "I think so too," said her ladyship, crossing her handsome old hands resolutely on her lap.

Julian applied himself to answering Horace first.

"Pardon me," he said, "I have no intention of presuming to reflect on Miss Roseberry, or of bringing her into the matter at all. The consul's letter," he went on, speaking to his aunt, "mentions, if you remember, that the medical authorities of Mannheim were divided in opinion on their patient's case. Some of them—the physician-in-chief being among the number—believe that the recovery of her mind has not accompanied the recovery of her body."

"In other words," Lady Janet remarked, "a madwoman is in my house, and I am expected to receive her!"

"Don't let us exaggerate," said Julian, gently. "It can serve no good interest, in this serious matter, to exaggerate anything. The consul assures us, on the authority of the doctor, that she is perfectly gentle and harmless. If she is really the victim of a mental delusion, the poor creature is surely an object of compassion, and she ought to be placed under proper care. Ask your own kind heart, my dear aunt, if it would not be downright cruelty to turn this forlorn woman adrift in the world, without making some inquiry first?"

Lady Janet's inbred sense of justice admitted—not over-willingly—the reasonableness as well as the humanity of the view expressed in those words. "There is some truth in that, Julian," she said, shifting her position uneasily in her chair, and looking at Horace. "Don't you think so too?" she added.

"I can't say I do," answered Horace, in the positive tone of a man whose obstinacy is proof against every form of appeal that can be addressed to him.

The patience of Julian was firm enough to be a match for the obstinacy of Horace. "At any rate," he resumed, with undiminished good temper, "we are all three equally interested in setting this matter at rest. I put it to you, Lady Janet, if we are not favoured, at this lucky moment, with the very opportunity that we want? Miss Roseberry is not only out of the room, but out of the house. If we let this chance slip, who can say what awkward accident may not happen in the course of the next few days?"

"Let the woman come in," cried Lady Janet, deciding headlong with her customary impatience of all delay. "At once, Julian—before Grace can come back. Will you ring the bell this time?"

This time Julian rang it. "May I give the man his orders?" he respectfully inquired of his aunt.

"Give him anything you like, and have done with it!" retorted the irritable old lady, getting briskly on her feet, and taking a turn in the room to compose herself.

The servant withdrew, with orders to show the visitor in.

Horace crossed the room at the same time—apparently with the intention of leaving it by the door at the opposite end.

"You are not going away?" exclaimed Lady Janet.

"I see no use in my remaining here," replied Horace, not very graciously.

"In that case," retorted Lady Janet, "remain here because I wish it."

"Certainly—if you wish it. Only remember," he added, more

obstinately than ever, " that I differ entirely from Julian's view. In my opinion the woman has no claim on us.'

A passing movement of irritation escaped Julian for the first time. "Don't be hard, Horace," he said, sharply. "All women have a claim on us."

They had unconsciously gathered together, in the heat of the little debate, turning their backs on the library door. At the last words of the reproof administered by Julian to Horace, their attention was recalled to passing events by the slight noise produced by the opening and closing of the door. With one accord the three turned and looked in the direction from which the sounds had come.

## CHAPTER XI.

### THE DEAD ALIVE.

JUST inside the door there appeared the figure of a small woman dressed in plain and poor black garments. She silently lifted her black net veil, and disclosed a dull, pale, worn, weary face. The forehead was low and broad ; the eyes were unusually far apart; the lower features were remarkably small and delicate. In health (as the consul at Mannheim had remarked) this woman must have possessed, if not absolute beauty, at least rare attractions peculiarly her own. As it was now, suffering—sullen, silent, self-contained suffering—had marred its beauty. Attention and even curiosity it might still rouse. Admiration or interest it could excite no longer.

The small thin black figure stood immovably inside the door. The dull, worn, white face looked silently at the three persons in the room.

The three persons in the room, on their side, stood for a moment without moving, and looked silently at the stranger on the threshold. There was something, either in the woman herself or in the sudden and stealthy manner of her appearance in the room, which froze, as if with the touch of an invisible cold hand, the sympathies of all three. Accustomed to the world, habitually at their ease in every social emergency, they were now silenced for the first time in their lives by the first serious sense of embarrassment which they had felt since they were children, in the presence of a stranger.

Had the appearance of the true Grace Roseberry aroused in their minds a suspicion of the woman who had stolen her name, and taken her place in the house ?

Not so much as the shadow of a suspicion of Mercy was at the bottom of the strange sense of uneasiness which had now deprived them alike of their habitual courtesy and their habitual presence of mind. It was as practically impossible for any one of the three to doubt the identity of the adopted daughter of the house, as it would be for you who read these lines to doubt the identity of the nearest and dearest relative you have in the world. Circumstances had fortified Mercy behind the strongest of all natural rights—the right of first possession. Circumstances had armed her with the most irresistible of all natural forces—the force of previous association and previous habit. Not by so much as a hair's breadth was the position of the false Grace Roseberry shaken by the first appearance of the true Grace Roseberry within the doors of Mablethorpe House. Lady Janet felt suddenly repelled, without knowing why. Julian and Horace felt suddenly repelled, without knowing why. Asked to describe their own sensations at the moment, they would have shaken their heads in despair and would have answered in those words. The vague presentiment of some misfortune to come had entered the room with the entrance of the woman in black. But it moved invisibly; and it spoke, as all presentiments speak, in the Unknown Tongue.

A moment passed. The crackling of the fire and the ticking of the clock were the only sounds audible in the room.

The voice of the visitor—hard, clear, and quiet—was the first voice that broke the silence.

"Mr. Julian Gray?" she said, looking interrogatively from one of the two gentlemen to the other.

Julian advanced a few steps, instantly recovering his self-possession. "I am sorry I was not at home," he said, "when you called with your letter from the consul. Pray take a chair."

By way of setting the example, Lady Janet seated herself at some little distance, with Horace in attendance standing near. She bowed to the stranger with studious politeness, but without uttering a word, before she settled herself in her chair. "I am obliged to listen to this person," thought the old lady. "But I am *not* obliged to speak to her. That is Julian's business—not mine." "Don't stand, Horace! You fidget me. Sit down." Armed beforehand in her policy of silence, Lady Janet folded her handsome hands as usual, and waited for the proceedings to begin, like a judge on the bench.

"Will you take a chair?" Julian repeated, observing that the visitor appeared neither to heed nor to hear his first words of welcome to her.

At this second appeal she spoke to him. "Is that Lady Janet Roy?" she asked, with her eyes fixed on the mistress of the house.

Julian answered, and drew back to watch the result.

The woman in the poor black garments changed her position for the first time. She moved slowly across the room to the place at which Lady Janet was sitting, and addressed her respectfully with perfect self-possession of manner. Her whole demeanour, from the moment when she had appeared at the door, had expressed—at once plainly and becomingly—confidence in the reception that awaited her.

"Almost the last words my father said to me on his death-bed," she began, "were words, madam, which told me to expect protection and kindness from you."

It was not Lady Janet's business to speak. She listened with the blandest attention. She waited with the most exasperating silence to hear more.

Grace Roseberry drew back a step—not intimidated—only mortified and surprised. "Was my father wrong?" she asked, with a simple dignity of tone and manner which forced Lady Janet to abandon her policy of silence, in spite of herself.

"Who was your father?" she asked, coldly.

Grace Roseberry answered the question in a tone of stern surprise.

"Has the servant not given you my card?" she said. "Don't you know my name?"

"Which of your names?" rejoined Lady Janet.

"I don't understand your ladyship."

"I will make myself understood. You asked me if I knew your name. I ask you, in return, which name it is? The name on your card is 'Miss Roseberry.' The name marked on your clothes, when you were in the hospital, was 'Mercy Merrick.'"

The self-possession which Grace had maintained from the moment when she had entered the dining-room, seemed now for the first time to be on the point of failing her. She turned and looked appealingly at Julian, who had thus far kept his place apart, listening attentively.

"Surely," she said, "your friend, the consul, has told you in his letter about the mark on the clothes?"

Something of the girlish hesitation and timidity which had marked her demeanour at her interview with Mercy in the French cottage, reappeared in her tone. and manner as she spoke those words. The changes—mostly changes for the worse—wrought in her by the suffering through which she had passed since that time, were now (for the moment) effaced. All that was left of the better and simpler side of her character asserted itself in her brief appeal to Julian. She had hitherto repelled him. He began to feel a certain compassionate interest in her now.

"The consul has informed me of what you said to him," he answered kindly. "But, if you will take my advice, I recommend you to tell your story to Lady Janet in your own words."

Grace again addressed herself with submissive reluctance to Lady Janet.

"The clothes your ladyship speaks of," she said, "were the clothes of another woman. The rain was pouring when the soldiers detained me on the frontier. I had been exposed for hours to the weather—I was wet to the skin. The clothes marked 'Mercy Merrick' were the clothes lent to me by Mercy Merrick herself while my own things were drying. I was struck by the shell in those clothes. I was carried away insensible in those clothes after the operation had been performed on me."

Lady Janet listened to perfection—and did no more. She turned confidentially to Horace and said to him, in her gracefully ironical way, "She is ready with her explanation."

Horace answered in the same tone, "A great deal too ready."

Grace looked from one of them to the other. A faint flush of colour showed itself in her face for the first time.

"Am I to understand?" she asked with proud composure, "that you don't believe me?"

Lady Janet maintained her policy of silence. She waved one hand courteously towards Julian, as if to say, "Address your inquiries to the gentleman who introduces you." Julian, noticing the gesture and observing the rising colour in Grace's cheeks, interfered directly in the interests of peace.

"Lady Janet asked you a question just now," he said; "Lady Janet inquired who your father was."

"My father was the late Colonel Roseberry."

Lady Janet looked indignantly at Horace. "Her assurance amazes me!" she exclaimed.

Julian interposed before his aunt could add a word more. "Pray let us hear her," he said in a tone of entreaty which had something of the imperative in it this time. He turned to Grace. "Have you any proof to produce," he added in his gentler voice, "which will satisfy us that you are Colonel Roseberry's daughter?"

Grace looked at him indignantly. "Proof!" she repeated. "Is my word not enough?"

Julian kept his temper perfectly. "Pardon me," he rejoined, "you forget that you and Lady Janet meet now for the first time. Try to put yourself in my aunt's place. How is she to know that you are the late Colonel Roseberry's daughter?"

Grace's head sank on her breast; she dropped into the nearest chair. The expression of her face changed instantly from anger to discouragement. "Ah," she exclaimed bitterly, "if I only had the letters that have been stolen from me!"

"Letters," asked Julian, "introducing you to Lady Janet?"

"Yes." She turned suddenly to Lady Janet. "Let me tell you how I lost them," she said, in the first tones of entreaty which had escaped her yet.

Lady Janet hesitated. It was not in her generous nature to resist the appeal that had just been made to her. The sympathies of Horace were far less easily reached. He lightly launched a new shaft

of satire—intended for the private amusement of Lady Janet
"Another explanation!" he exclaimed, with a look of comic resignation.

Julian overheard the words. His large lustrous eyes fixed themselves on Horace with a look of unmeasured contempt.

"The least you can do," he said, sternly, "is not to irritate her.
It is so easy to irritate her!" He addressed himself again to Grace,
endeavouring to help her through her difficulty in a new way. "Never
mind explaining yourself for the moment," he said. "In the absence
of your letters, have you any one in London who can speak to your
identity?"

Grace shook her head sadly. "I have no friends in London," she
answered.

It was impossible for Lady Janet—who had never in her life
heard of anybody without friends in London—to pass this over
without notice. "No friends in London!" she repeated, turning to
Horace.

Horace shot another shaft of light satire. "Of course not!" he
rejoined.

Grace saw them comparing notes. "My friends are in Canada,"
she broke out impetuously. "Plenty of friends who could speak for
me, if I could only bring them here."

As a place of reference—mentioned in the capital city of England
—Canada, there is no denying it, is open to objection on the ground
of distance. Horace was ready with another shot. "Far enough off,
certainly," he said.

"Far enough off, as you say," Lady Janet agreed.

Once more Julian's inexhaustible kindness strove to obtain a hearing for the stranger who had been confided to his care. "A little
patience, Lady Janet," he pleaded. ; "A little consideration, Horace,
for a friendless woman."

"Thank you, sir," said Grace. "It is very kind of you to try and
help me; but it is useless. They won't even listen to me." She
attempted to rise from her chair as she pronounced the last words.
Julian gently laid his hand on her shoulder and obliged her to resume
her seat.

"I will listen to you," he said. "You referred me just now to the
consul's letter. The consul tells me you suspected some one of taking
your papers and your clothes."

"I don't suspect," was the quick reply, "I am certain! I tell
you positively Mercy Merrick was the thief. She was alone with me
when I was struck down by the shell. She was the only person who
knew that I had letters of introduction about me. She confessed to
my face that she had been a bad woman—she had been in a prison—
she had come out of a refuge"——

Julian stopped her there with one plain question, which threw a doubt on the whole story.

"The consul tells me you asked him to search for Mercy Merrick," he said. " Is it not true that he caused inquiries to be made, and that no trace of any such person was to be heard of ? "

"The consul took no pains to find her," Grace answered angrily. " He was, like everybody else, in a conspiracy to neglect and misjudge me."

Lady Janet and Horace exchanged looks. This time it was impossible for Julian to blame them. The farther the stranger's narrative advanced, the less worthy of serious attention he felt it to be. The longer she spoke, the more disadvantageously she challenged comparison with the absent woman, whose name she so obstinately and so audaciously persisted in assuming as her own.

"Granting all that you have said," Julian resumed, with a last effort of patience, " what use could Mercy Merrick make of your letters and your clothes ? "

"What use ?" repeated Grace, amazed at his not seeing the position as she saw it. " My clothes were marked with my name. One of my papers was a letter from my father, introducing me to Lady Janet. A woman out of a refuge would be quite capable of presenting herself here in my place."

Spoken entirely at random, spoken without so much as a fragment of evidence to support them, those last words still had their effect. They cast a reflection on Lady Janet's adopted daughter which was too outrageous to be borne. Lady Janet rose instantly. "Give me your arm, Horace," she said, turning to leave the room. "I have heard enough."

Horace respectfully offered his arm. " Your ladyship is quite right," he answered. " A more monstrous story never was invented."

He spoke in the warmth of his indignation, loud enough for Grace to hear him. " What is there monstrous in it ? " she asked, advancing a step towards him defiantly.

Julian checked her. He too—though he had only once seen Mercy —felt an angry sense of the insult offered to the beautiful creature who had interested him at his first sight of her. "Silence ! " he said, speaking sternly to Grace for the first time. " You are offending— justly offending—Lady Janet. You are talking worse than absurdly —you are talking offensively—when you speak of another woman presenting herself here in your place."

Grace's blood was up. Stung by Julian's reproof, she turned on him a look which was almost a look of fury.

"Are you a clergyman ? Are you an educated man ?" she asked. " Have you never read of cases of false personation, in newspapers and books ? I blindly confided in Mercy Merrick before I found out what

her character really was. She left the cottage—I know it, from the
surgeon who brought me to life again—firmly persuaded that the
shell had killed me. My papers and my clothes disappeared at the
same time. Is there nothing suspicious in these circumstances? There
were people at the hospital who thought them highly suspicious—
people who warned me that I might find an impostor in my place."
She suddenly paused. The rustling sound of a silk dress had caught
her ear. Lady Janet was leaving the room, with Horace, by way of the
conservatory. With a last desperate effort of resolution, Grace sprang
forward and placed herself in front of them.

"One word, Lady Janet, before you turn your back on me," she
said, firmly. "One word, and I will be content. Has Colonel Roseberry's letter found its way to this house or not? If it has, did a
woman bring it to you?"

Lady Janet looked—as only a great lady *can* look, when a person
of inferior rank has presumed to fail in respect towards her.

"You are surely not aware," she said, with icy composure, "that
these questions are an insult to Me?"

"And worse than an insult," Horace added warmly, "to Grace!"

The little resolute black figure (still barring the way to the conservatory) was suddenly shaken from head to foot. The woman's eyes
travelled backwards and forwards between Lady Janet and Horace
with the light of a new suspicion in them.

"Grace!" she exclaimed. "What Grace? That's my name. Lady
Janet, you *have* got the letter! The woman is here!"

Lady Janet dropped Horace's arm, and retraced her steps to the
place at which her nephew was standing.

"Julian," she said. "You force me for the first time in my life to
remind you of the respect that is due to me in my own house. Send
that woman away."

Without waiting to be answered, she turned back again, and once
more took Horace's arm.

"Stand back, if you please," she said quietly to Grace.

Grace held her ground.

"The woman is here!" she repeated. "Confront me with her—and
then send me away, if you like."

Julian advanced, and firmly took her by the arm. "You forget
what is due to Lady Janet," he said, drawing her aside. "You forget
what is due to yourself."

With a desperate effort, Grace broke away from him, and stopped
Lady Janet on the threshold of the conservatory door.

"Justice!" she cried, shaking her clenched hand with hysterical
frenzy in the air. "I claim my right to meet that woman face to
face! Where is she? Confront me with her! Confront me with
her!"

While those wild words were pouring from her lips, the rumbling of carriage wheels became audible on the drive in front of the house. In the all-absorbing agitation of the moment, the sound of the wheels (followed by the opening of the house door) passed unnoticed by the persons in the dining-room. Horace's voice was still raised in angry protest against the insult offered to Lady Janet; Lady Janet herself (leaving him for the second time) was vehemently ringing the bell to summon the servants; Julian had once more taken the infuriated woman by the arm, and was trying vainly to compose her—when the library door was opened quietly by a young lady wearing a mantle and a bonnet. Mercy Merrick (true to the appointment which she had made with Horace) entered the room.

The first eyes that discovered her presence on the scene were the eyes of Grace Roseberry. Starting violently in Julian's grasp, she pointed towards the library door. " Ah !" she cried, with a shriek of vindictive delight. " There she is !"

Mercy turned as the sound of the scream rang through the room, and met—resting on her in savage triumph—the living gaze of the woman whose identity she had stolen, whose body she had left laid out for dead. On the instant of that terrible discovery—with her eyes fixed helplessly on the fierce eyes that had found her—she dropped senseless on the floor.

## How they used to tell Stories.

THERE is a very numerous class of persons who anxiously and persistently inquire as to the relations between themselves and the future, and these persons are called, by people who do not anxiously and persistently inquire into anything, infidels.

The non-inquirers were despised even by orthodox Johnson. When some one remarked that Foote was an infidel, Johnson contemptuously replied, "He is an infidel as a dog is an infidel; he has made no inquiry into the subject." There are a good many Christians who are at best so, because they found themselves so, and have made no further inquiry into the matter.

There was a time when orthodoxy reigned alone, and had no opposing doxy to contend with. There was no heterodoxy to be put down in blood, or to triumph over the anguish of the vanquished right thinkers. Happy time!

Now people have often amused themselves with thinking of the various characters in past ages whom they would most wish to see. One would recall Socrates, another would fain look upon the great Julius, a third has had a curiosity to see what manner of man Judas could have been, a fourth turned his thoughts to her whose beauty took the mind prisoner, and would have summoned that superb and strong-minded Judith to be looked upon for a minute or so. Charles Lamb would have liked to have had Guy Faux face to face with him, and his delight would have been uncontrollable if he could have spent half an hour at the *Boar's Head* in Eastcheap with Shakespeare once more in the flesh, and Falstaff made a real personage for the nonce. These are good selections, and a thousand equally good might be easily made. We should be glad to see any of the individuals above named, still gladder to see all of them together; but there is not among them the particular personage on whom we should especially desire to look. *He* is of quite another quality.

Who he was, we know not. What he was, we are entirely ignorant of. Whence he came, whither he went, who was his father, what place he held in the world—all these were matters of which we are profoundly ignorant. We only know what he did, and what has come of the doing.

The man whom we have the greatest curiosity to behold is that disturbing personage who was the projector, inventor, and perfecter of the first Ism!

What Ism? What do we mean by Ism? Well, we mean the first

doubter when there was nothing doubtful. In these days, when everything is made to seem doubtful, and is necessarily so, since a hundred opposite things are daily preached, and each preacher holds the other ninety-nine to be liars—or, at the best, fools—doubt is getting permanently enthroned in the hearts of men. But there was a season when the world was in its prime, and young Time, as Mr. Moore informs us, told his first birthdays by the sun, when Truth shone bright and unmistakable as the sun itself. At that period there must have existed the man who first hinted that things were really not what they seemed to be, and that people must neither believe their eyes nor take upon trust anything that was told them.

That man was the inventor of Isms. The contemporaries to whom he communicated his naughty thoughts were like ground of diverse quality into which seed is cast. In them sprouted the germs of all the Isms that have since come up in crops or in single stalks. Thence came all the religions, or non-religions, that have since existed. My friend, if you smiled scornfully when the last prelate whom you saw in the pulpit, puzzled you extremely by the riddle which he made worse confounded by trying to explain, you may thank, for your lack of full faith, the inventor of the first Ism.

Nay, the bishop himself would not have had the task of confusing his hearers by explanations which rendered more and more obscure what was once perfectly clear, if it had not been for the first doubter. That inventor of incredulity is the father of Isms. We put upon his shoulders the weight of all the consequences that have ensued. We should have preferred to live in the times before Doubt was born. Since that is not possible, and Doubt has become our yoke-fellow, let the blame lie upon the head and shoulders of Doubt's father. A pretty burthen he has to bear! He is the real Atlas, and he groans under the burthen. Alcides himself is hardly equal to the task of vicarious portership.¹

Consequently, the projector of the first Ism is the remarkable personage we should most care to look upon. No man has accomplished a work so fruitful in consequences; but he has modestly withdrawn from human research, and we look for him in vain. ·

Like all story-tellers, he came from the East. As stories come thence westward they seem to deteriorate. So do words. The "deuce" of our western world was a beneficent divinity of the Eastern regions. Even the cherub who stood to grasp any intruder who should endeavour to cross the threshold of Paradise is now said to have furnished the root of our vulgar word "to grab."

When Banier vulgarised the old mythology the process was equally depoetising. Jupiter, launching his bolts from the clouds above Olympus, is a sufficiently heroic figure; but when we are told that the old story is a myth, and that Jupiter was a country squire who lived on the top of a hill, kept uproarious house, and was a terror to all the country round, we are uneasy under the bathos. We prefer the original story of Juno to the one which makes of her a farmer's wife, with a couple of peacocks on her lawn. We can better understand the figurative story of Actæon who was devoured by his own hounds. He was depoetised by the ancients themselves. From them we learn that Actæon was one of those rogues, so common in our own days, who live beyond their incomes, cheat their creditors, pay a shilling or two, or promise to pay a shilling or two, for every pound they owe, and would feel very much surprised if they found themselves classed by honest men in the category of thieves, of whom they are really the very worst sort. Actæon was of this family; he kept a pack of hounds when he could hardly keep a terrier, and being ruined in consequence, literally went to the dogs.

The story of Amphitryon is the one which has least suffered in coming from the East; but, in fact, it cannot be said to have altogether come out of the Eastern boundary. The story suffers as it is told on the stage here in London; but the Amphitryon of the Theban story is almost as good as the hero of the Hindoo story in which he was to be originally found. Jupiter took the place of Amphitryon in the household of the latter, at bed and board. In the earlier story there is a more graceful fancy.

The Egyptians claim Amphitryon for their own. They extol the dinners he gave at Memphis, and they say, or said, that his son Hercules was the last-born of the gods. But the original Amphitryon was a Hindoo gentleman.

The Hindoo name of the hero has gone out of memory. He was not a great personage, like the more classical hero. He was a handsome stalwart fellow, who had a pretty little wife, who used to make him frantic with jealousy at her very gracious way to any young fellow who paid her a compliment on her beauty. The Hindoo kept his temper and a stick. The latter once got the better of his temper. He so applied it to the shoulders which he would have done better to have kissed, that he left his wife insensible, and he swore by his great gods that he would never keep house with her again.

The angry husband strode away from the scene of domestic disturbance. There had been watching him a deity of those sunny skies, from a rosy little cloud. Descending in the latter to the ground, and lightly tripping on to the firm-set earth, he gave himself a shake or two, the last of which shook him into the shape of the handsome, stalwart, but no longer angry-looking, husband. Immediately afterwards the coquettish little wife was wonderfully surprised to find herself on a seat in her garden, with her husband at her feet, confessing himself to be a brute, and wondering how he could even say a hasty word to the choicest of women and the very pearl of wives.

"Well, this is something new," cried the little woman.

"But it shall be lasting," exclaimed the imaginary husband.

And so it appeared to be for at least a considerable period. The new household was cited as the happiest in the land; and if a husband made an observation that was not in accordance with his wife's feelings, the husband of the aforesaid little woman was pointed out to him as a model to be followed. A son was born in that household, and there were fireworks enough let off in honour of the little stranger to have set the world afire. On the following morning, as the father was going out of doors, there met him on the threshold the original husband. They stood, not merely face to face, but nose to nose. The confusion that ensued is not to be described. The stupor and astonishment of the little wife at the sight of a couple of husbands is not to be expressed. After a world of disputing, the lady exclaimed, "Let us all go to the Brahmin; he will settle the question." And they went.

"Look here," said the arbitrator, "you are troublesome people, all of you, but the affair must be arranged at once. Let plaintiff and defendant kiss the lady's lips, and he who gives the loudest smack is the true man."

The little woman put up her coral lips, which the real husband kissed, as he stooped down to them, with a report as of half a dozen revolver chambers at once.

"Not bad, my man," said the Brahmin. "The other fellow will find it hard to do better."

That other fellow, however, looked in the lady's eyes as they smiled on him, murmured something as he bent his head to her lips which seemed (as we are informed) like "rosebuds steeped in dew," and straightway placed his lips to hers. At that moment the world shook with a thunder as of the whole artillery of the skies, and the spectators shouted the Hindoo phrase for "This is the real Simon Pure."

"You are the sons and fathers of asses," roared the Brahmin. "None but a deity ever saluted in that fashion."

As he said it the divinity was seen rising in his rosy cloud, and laughing merrily as he looked down over the side of it. The husband was told it was only a dream. As the late husband's son sat down with them at breakfast his present father remarked it was the funniest dream he had ever had.

And now à *propos* to breakfasts.

It has been a favourite subject with many essayists to treat of our imported enjoyments. As we take our seat at the breakfast table we remember the essay in which we were first told that, to furnish the board, ships had crossed the seas from all quarters of the compass. The tea that reached our lips had made its first start from China, and perhaps the cup came with it. The Mediterranean had yielded up those appetising little fish for our delight, and Indian elephants had been civil enough to contribute the handles to the knives. Each meal, indeed, is said to have come from a long way off, and that originally a long time ago. The very bread descends, we are informed, from the original corn that once grew wild in the plains of Central Tartary. We must thank Lucullus and Asia Minor even for our cherries. There is indeed a champagne which is made of home-grown gooseberries, but that gooseberry itself is of a foreign ancestry. It has worked itself into the champagne legend, as some incidents in the stories of our country have connected themselves with others in narratives of different countries. It becomes as difficult to say which is the older, the gooseberry or the grape, as it is to decide whether, after all, the Amphitryon story went from Egypt to India or came from India to Egypt. We know that Cinderella was a born African, though she belongs to the legendary lore of Europe. Sometimes the beginning of a story is in one hemisphere and the ending of it in another; just as a man who falls sick of a fever in Europe gets well with the bark that comes to him from South America.

We question whether young people would care to know that " the Sleeping Beauty" is, after all, only a bit of natural history popularised. One has sympathies with the young prince who makes his way through the sleepers and comes to her who slumbers and makes sleep beautiful. When she awakes, the very earth is glad, for marriage and fruitful happiness come of it. We feel, however, as if sympathy had been duped when we are told, with a sort of mocking laugh, that all this only interprets the fact that the beautiful but somnolent Earth is stirred to love and gladness by the touch and breath of the great awakener, young. Spring. Some such double meaning lies beneath the descent of Proserpine to the realms of darkness and her return to the surface of the earth again. The child of Ceres performs this feat every year, and she is garnered up at harvest home, without the clowns knowing anything of her story. As for that marvellous legend of St. Ursula and her eleven thousand virgins being only the Lady Moon and her very numerous daughters, we have no doubt of its being so, but we are rather sorry to hear it.

In an erudite introduction to a book called ' Tales of the Teutonic Lands,' the pedigree of many a well-known story is narrated. When we have read it the question naturally suggests itself, " Who was the original story-teller ?" Among persons long since passed away, he is the one whom we should somewhat care to see. Since his time all writers of romance (which includes history and a good deal of science) have been only his imitators. The world has contained only adapters of that truly original's first stories. They have sometimes disguised them, as Gipsies dye their stolen children in walnut-juice, that their parents may not recognise them. This simile has been accounted very witty. Sheridan has the credit of being the genuine parent of it, but a score of men used it before he did ; and as the Gipsies came from the East, perhaps the simile came with them, even as Pythagoras came, leaving behind him his original name of Buddha Ghooroos ! At all events, it was one of our many good things said before us, and we take what is our own wherever we have the good luck to find it.

In the Elysian Fields, will all the felonious adapters of the original legend-maker be able to look him in the face ? Will they approach him with a general *peccavimus?* And will the Great Romancer's brow darken, or will he receive and dismiss them with a " Bless you, my children ?"

One thing is quite sure, namely, that neither the great original's fame, nor the stories which he told and which have been stolen from him, would have survived, had it not been for the patient labour, and the love they took in the labour, on the part of such grave scholars and gay narrators as the compilers of the book we have named, Messrs. Cox and Jones. To have collected and digested and set forth for public instruction and amusement such a mass of legend (and this volume is only a part of the mountain of measure) would seem to warrant that they must be almost as venerable as Methuselah. With what awful emotion would the stoutest man among us entertain the thought that in their duality of compound author may lie hidden the proto-narrator of the legendary world !

That first of romancers could not have told his stories more grace-fully or more picturesquely than they are told here. One of the prettiest is that of ' Frithjof and Ingebjorg.' These were playfellows, though the latter was the King of Norroway's daughter, and the boy was only a Thane's son. While yet children they became fellow pupils of Hilding, who taught them " the wisdom of men and the knowledge of the gods." When we hear that the two increased in beauty as they grew, we begin to suspect what the end of it will be. Meanwhile, after study with the sage, they played together among the hills. Now and then the boy would take the little maid in a boat far out to sea, and if the wind drove the spray in sheets upon them, In-gebjorg would only clap her hands for joy ; she had no fear where Frithjof was. They tarried long with their tutor, and youth and maiden still sat together to listen to his lessons ; but now, if Hilding spake of Freyja's golden hair, the youth would smooth Ingebjorg's tresses and think that Freyja's could not be half so beautiful ; and if the philosopher told of Frigga's lovely eyes, the Thane's son would look into those of the King's daughter, and feel that the whole world could not match them for a sweet blue loveliness. Then, among the stories which Hilding told them, was one of Baldur's death, one of those stories in which personages take the place of facts—real or supposed. Baldur the radiant, supremely beautiful, the beloved of gods and men, son of Odin "Allfather," so wise and sweet of words that the gods kept silence in Asgard when he spake, lives a life of inexpressible happiness with Nanna, his soft-eyed wife, in their palace of Bridin-blick, till the thought comes upon him that he must die, and then there is sorrow in Asgard and over all the earth. Even Odin's wise ravens could not see what might ensue, which is the less to be wondered at as they knew only the past and the present. Accordingly, Allfather, with his ravens, his wolves, and his steed Sleipnir, make swift descent into the pale kingdom of Death, where pitiless Hel holds sway. The scenery and properties of the restless goddess are novel and wonderful enough to stir the heart-pulses of a stage-manager. Through grandeur and mystery, and beauty and horrors, Odin makes his way, till he comes to a chamber where he sees a table spread, a cup full of mead, and a golden bed. After much ado he learns that all is prepared for the coming of Baldur the Beautiful. Odin rushes back with the unpleasant news, which is no sooner promulgated than the whole universe, earth and skies, gods and men, things animate and things inanimate, make oath that nothing in them or of them shall ever do injury to the beloved son of Odin. In very sport they assail him in a hundred ways, each of which would be mortal but for their oath. But Baldur had a sharpsighted enemy named Loki, who had been overlooked; and Loki found a twig of mistletoe which had no more taken the oath than himself. Whereupon this shabby fellow made an arrow-point of the mistletoe twig, and with wicked application of the same Baldur was killed outright. The whole universe was in despair, and when the ship bearing his body crossed the lone seas to the shores of the lurid Lady Hel, Thor's hammer flashed across the sky, and his chariot wheels rattled forth thunder. Nevertheless, Baldur was irrevocably dead. Yet Hel, not being so implacable as she was said to be, consented to ransom him at the cost of a universal downpouring of tears. Forthwith gloom, decay, mourning, finally weeping, became general, and at the end thereof Baldur reappeared in gladness, and beauty, and radiancy; and we have only to express thereon our wonder that all the gods, even the two ravens, knew that it was written that Baldur should return. They needed not to have been in such a turmoil about it. He has died a thousand times since and has come back. He died this year on the 21st of September, and he will assuredly return on next 21st of June. For this was how Hilding taught them of the 'Death of Summer Time.' The mode of instruction has since been changed, but there is another fashion which prevails now much the same as it did then. The Thane's son and the young Princess fell mutually in love. The youth, indeed, did not make her an offer, but simply told Ingebjorg "that she should be his wife some day," and it made her glad; in truth, she wished no better lot. But his Majesty the King was in a furious passion, and roared out *Mésalliance!*—or would, if he had known French and it had been fashionable to speak it. Frithjof made as many sensible remarks as might have overcome a dozen unreasonable men; but King Bela was as obstinate as a score of unreasonable men. Whether Love ultimately prevailed over the sternly stupid Majesty of Norroway, we are not going to say. There is some exquisite story-telling before the *finale* is reached, and certainly we shall not be indiscreet enough to say whether or not the last scene is a gorgeous temple with a fragrant altar, and troups of maidens clad in bridal white following Ingebjorg clad in an ermine robe, and Frithjof looking about him with an air of "this is the happiest day of my life." At such a ceremony Baldur's presence would be desirable, and we do find a remark to the effect that the temple was lightened all about with the shining of the gods. So it may be, that some extraordinarily felicitous event was going on there in the "sweet summer tyde."

# 𝔄 Reminiscence of the American 𝔅ar.

## A DEFENCE FOR MURDER.

### By EDWIN JAMES.

"IF the Attorney-General desires to read any affidavits in answer to this application on the part of the sheriff, the court is now prepared to hear them," was the announcement made from the bench.

The District Attorney then rose and read a series of affidavits, substantially to the following effect :—That the prisoner, George Lewis, was in his custody to await his trial upon a true bill found against him for the wilful murder of Mr. Amasa Watson, at Princetown, in the state of New Jersey. That the deponent (the sheriff) had, since the prisoner had been in his custody, caused inquiries to be made into his history and antecedents, and had found, and now stated on his information and belief, that the said George Lewis was engaged at the time of the alleged murder in keeping a notorious gambling house in the city of New York; that he believed him to be a dangerous and desperate character; that he had been convicted in the state of California of uttering forged United States Government Bonds to the amount of $100,000, and was thereupon sentenced to ten years' imprisonment in the gaol of San Francisco; from which prison he made his escape, and effected such escape by bribing the warders of the gaol, and afterwards strangling the watchman who guarded the exterior of the said gaol at night time. That it is reported and believed that the said George Lewis has committed more than one murder in the said state of California. That after he had been committed to the custody of this deponent he seized one of the watchmen who was engaged to guard him in his cell by the throat, and attempted to strangle him, with the intention of making his escape from prison, as he had done before in the state of California. That in consequence of such conduct, he (the sheriff), in order to secure him with safety, had him chained by the ankles and the wrists to the floor of his cell, leaving him sufficient liberty to stand erect, but preventing him from approaching the door or window. That he (the sheriff) believed that the said George Lewis now intends and contemplates effecting his escape if possible, and that he would resort to any means, however desperate, to effect such object; because this deponent found secreted in a hole which had been made in the wall of his cell two large files and a screw-driver, which are now produced and shown to this court, and which covered with the paper now also produced, and on which the following note is written:

"At the risk of my life, I put the things you want through the window. Try after twelve o'clock. I will keep him out till one," and which is in the handwriting of a female, but is unknown to this deponent. That after finding the said note and the files, the said George Lewis was thrown down on the floor of his cell, and an examination made by this deponent and his assistants, when it was discovered that the chains which fastened him had been completely filed through, and could have been knocked off with the greatest facility.

The affidavits concluded with a statement that the sheriff went in personal and bodily fear of the prisoner, and that unless he was allowed to imprison him in the manner he had done, he would not be responsible for his detention and appearance at the trial.

Startling and surprising as were these allegations, the only person who listened to them with indifference was the prisoner. "Can you answer them?" asked his counsel anxiously. "If you can, we will prepare an affidavit forthwith."

"The statement about California," he whispered, "is all a lie."

"Can you deny the statement of your attempt at escape?" we asked.

"I shall not deny it now," he replied; "of course I'd get out if I could," and we could obtain no more from him.

"Do the counsel for the prisoner intend to present any affidavits in reply to those which have been read?" asked the judge.

The court granted some minutes for consultation with our client, and that resulted in our declining to read any affidavit in reply.

The argument then proceeded upon the facts as they appeared, and at its conclusion the prisoner was remanded; the decision was adjourned, and the judge, accompanied by a surgeon selected by him, proceeded to the cell to examine it, and to view the manner in which the prisoner was confined by the sheriff.

We awaited with some anxiety the result of this examination. It occupied more than an hour, and during that interval a tall, coarse-looking man pushed his way through the audience to the table where the counsel sat, and, addressing me, asked whether he could see George Lewis, and if he would again come into court? I recognised him as one of the men who had called at my office in New York, and paid me the money for the defence. I replied that in all probability Lewis would be again brought into court to hear the decision upon the motion.

"I must see him," said he; "I must see him. And I must have his signature to this," taking from his pocket-book a printed paper.

After an absence of an hour the judge returned, and gave a decision to the effect that the cell in which the prisoner was confined was an unfit and improper place to imprison a man who was not convicted of any crime; that the manner of confining him was cruel and inhuman; and the sheriff was directed to imprison him in a larger compartment of the gaol, that his chains should be immediately removed, and that if the sheriff feared escape he was empowered by the court to employ a sufficient number of watchmen effectually to secure the accused.

Thus ended the application, and the prisoner was remitted to custody. He had been brought into court to hear the judgment—and before he was removed he was accosted by his friend from New York, and an angry altercation ensued between them.

"No, I won't sign that. You want to rob me of the bonds. You have thirty thousand dollars of mine now—you owe me fifteen thousand dollars from the bank, I gave you. You know how I got into this trouble, but you had not the courage to do it," said Lewis, in a whisper, but with a determined manner. His lip quivered, and he grasped the back of the chair, from which he had risen, with his huge hands.

The man's hand was upon his revolver, and any where but in the court blood would have been shed before such a quarrel subsided.

" You won't sign it, then ?" in a loud, menacing tone, demanded the stranger.

"No, never !" replied Lewis; "never !" And with an imprecation he reiterated, "Never! You shall never keep the bonds. Give them to me, or " (with another imprecation) "you shall stand here beside me. You shall not keep them. I will bury them. You have robbed me before."

" Then," said the stranger, " I will "——

The dialogue was suddenly interrupted by the officer of the sheriff coming up, taking Lewis by the arm, and requesting him to accompany him to the gaol below.

The Attorney-General then placed the depositions in the hands of the prisoner's counsel, accompanied with a notice that the trial was appointed for the 12th of December next.

The documents were voluminous, and had been taken with great care. The testimony had been gathered from every witness who could throw any light upon the dark and mysterious transactions of that fatal night, and presented a mass of facts strongly implicating the accused—demanding explanation, and satisfactory evidence in rebuttal. The case presented by the testimony was substantially the following:

There was a large hotel on the banks of the Passaic, much frequented by visitors from New York and Philadelphia; and it was deposed that a Mr. George Lewis had registered his name in the book, and had sojourned there for some days previous to the discovery of the murder. The entry in the book described him as "a merchant," resident in New York. He lived at the hotel, not merely expensively, but extravagantly, indulging in luxuries—hiring carriages and horses; and was accompanied by a lady—a Mexican or Californian—of very remarkable beauty, who displayed at the table d'hôte a profusion of costly jewelry, and attired herself in that peculiar style which by some is designated the height of fashion, and by others the acme of vulgarity and bad taste. The test of hotel respectability was achieved by the punctual payment of the bill when presented, and the lady and gentleman had secured the respect and confidence of the host, and the attention of the fraternity of coloured waiters, so essential to personal comfort in a large American hotel.

Mr. Lewis, whose real avocation demanded his nightly attendance in New York, was much absent, and passed only a few hours during the day in the society of his wife.

On the evening the murder was committed, it appeared from the depositions that he had hired at the hotel a waggon and one of the best and fastest horses which the stable afforded. He was absent all that night, and returned with it about noon of the following day. It was observed that the horse had been little cared for, and had been recklessly and cruelly driven, and it was asserted by the stableman as his opinion, "had not seen the inside of a stable since he was taken away."

A negro boy deposed, that on the morning of the 6th, before it was quite light, under a shed at the end of a long lane near the railway station he had seen a horse and waggon standing, the horse fastened to one of the timbers which supported the shed, "shivering all over with the cold, and that the waggon was covered all over with snowy slush and mud." Under the porch of a chapel on the road from Princetown to the hotel some children at play from the village school had found a hat, and inside the hat five skeleton keys and a small dark lantern; and the hat had been identified as that worn by Mr. Watson when he left his cottage on the Saturday morning.

The skeleton keys had been taken by the constabulary to the hotel, and a very remarkable statement was made with reference to them by a gentleman who was an inmate at the time.

A violent quarrel had occurred between the lady who was believed to be the wife of Lewis, and himself; loud shrieks from her room for help brought to the scene the proprietor, waiters, and guests. She had been cruelly beaten, and Lewis, to escape the angry remonstrances of those who had interfered for her protection, hurried down the stairs, and in his haste to leave the hotel put on a coat then hanging in the hall, the property of one of the guests, and left his own upon the same frame. During the evening, the owner of the coat, missing his own, and believing it had been taken by mistake, put on the coat left by Lewis, and in one of the pockets discovered a bunch of very peculiar-looking keys. They were shown to the proprietor and placed in the bureau. Lewis returned and found them there. He appeared much disconcerted, and, taking them from the office, made some hurried explanation that they had been made in California and fitted some large boxes or trunks in which he kept valuable property, and that no person could open the locks but with those keys. The lady vehemently corroborated this statement, and although the story was not implicitly believed at the moment, no suspicion was then aroused.

When the keys were brought by the officer to the hotel with the hat of the deceased, and distinctly identified as those which had been found in the pocket of Lewis's coat, he was at once arrested and lodged in the gaol at Trenton.

Search was made in the apartments occupied by Lewis and the lady, and the latter placed under the surveillance of the local police. No property lost by the deceased could be traced to their possession; but in a small valise found in the lady's wardrobe a little piece of torn paper with the name "James Talman" written upon it was discovered, and this, as it afterwards transpired, was the most damning and conclusive evidence of his guilt.

"Talman" was a dealer in wood, and supplied the deceased. With the large amount of bonds and money stolen on the night of the murder from the safe several vouchers and receipts were also abstracted, and this piece of paper was one of them. It was identified by Talman as having been given by him to Mr. Watson three days before the murder, and in its original form was a receipt, and was proved to have been kept by him in the safe.

Upon these depositions the prisoner was committed for trial, and a true bill found upon an indictment for murder.

The partners of Lewis in the gambling-house in New York came punctually to my office at the time arranged at the last interview. Their tone and manner were evidently altered, and they evinced little disposition to assist him in his defence. From what had occurred when they met in the court at Trenton it was obvious that no good feeling existed between them. Lewis charged them with having in their possession a considerable amount of property—how obtained was as yet to be developed.

"Have you brought the witnesses down to give the testimony, as you agreed at our previous interview?" I asked.

"No; we don't mean to take any more trouble about it," answered the elder gentleman, the one who had met him in the court-house at Trenton. "He has got himself into the trouble, and he must get himself out of it."

"Will you not bring the witnesses down here to make their statements, as you arranged to do?" I asked.

" No, I shall have no more to do with the matter.   If he gets convicted, that's his business, not mine," said he, and was about to leave
my office.

" Before you go, sir," I remarked, " it might be as well that you
should see the depositions which are upon that table.   You were
anxious to learn the description of the bonds which were taken after
the murder.   They are all set forth there—the amount, the numbers,
the denomination, and all the particulars.   They amount to seventy-one
thousand dollars ; and I see by an advertisement in the *New York
Herald* of this morning that notice is given of the loss, and a caution
to bankers and brokers against negotiating them.   I am not your
counsel, and should decline, after what has occurred, to act for you ;
but it is evident that the bonds can be traced to your possession.   You
have said that Lewis has got himself into this trouble, and must get
himself out of it ; but in doing so *you* may be got into it.   You now
refuse him your assistance.   You know that he is a determined man.
He charged you in the court, and in my presence, with having the
possession of bonds which I presume must be those set forth in the
depositions.   Your position is one of some danger in this business.
You have, I presume, your own counsel ; I should recommend you to
consult him "——Before I had concluded the sentence they both left,
saying, as they closed the door, that they would call again in a few
days.

One of the most acute and experienced of the New York detectives
was already upon their track ; the scent was burning and lay well.
From bank to bank ; from the offices of brokers known to negotiate
and purchase securities obtained from questionable sources, he was
hunting them.   Plans had been laid to obtain an interview with them
upon the following day, on the pretence that a capitalist was prepared
to make a large advance upon the missing bonds and ask no questions.   An offer had been made by one of their emissaries to Lewis in
Trenton gaol, that if he would divulge in whose hands he had placed
certain bonds it should be much to his advantage with reference to
the serious charge upon which he was imprisoned ; but in vain.   Lewis
knew nothing of any bonds, and the trap to entice the gamblers to
the office of the capitalist, though temptingly baited, was as warily
shunned.   The steamer which sailed for California upon that evening
carried, as a part of its freight, the two gentlemen who had honoured
me with their confidence, and most probably the bonds which had
found their way, by some mysterious agency, from the safe of the
murdered man into their possession.

I remember a former Chief Justice of the common pleas, now
deceased, once telling how a very shrewd attorney upon his circuit,
much employed in the defence of prisoners, invariably got all his
clients convicted ; and there never was an exception where the client

had become possessed, either by honest or dishonest means, of property real or personal.

He died wealthy, and after his death it was suggested, that whenever he received a retainer, and had his first interview with his client in the prison, an assignment of all his property to himself, in trust for the client's wife and children, in the event of a conviction, was very strongly recommended and generally accomplished. Questions and controversies as to the disposal of the property thus assigned were less likely to arise in the event of the conviction of the assignor than upon his acquittal.

So with the friends and partners of Mr. Lewis. After the interview in the court at Trenton it was clear that property had been intrusted to them by the accused, which they either had already appropriated, or intended to appropriate, to their own use, and that their interest would be more served by the conviction of their *confrère* than by his being free and demanding an account from them at a future day. And thus vanished at once all hope of the promised testimony to establish the presence of the accused in the city of New York on the night of the murder; and thus also vanished the two gentlemen, who, it was now evident, were cognizant of all the particulars attending the crime, perhaps instigated it, and who, so far as was yet ascertained, were the only persons who had derived any benefit by its commission.

The accused was pacing the mean compartment which had been allotted to him by the order of the court when I entered. I had read the depositions, and had conferred upon them with the counsel at Trenton, who was acting with me for the defence, and we proceeded to the gaol together. My coadjutor was a man of much intelligence, and skilled in the practice of the defence of criminals. He had seen Lewis several times since my interview with him, but could never obtain one word from him, and truly enough observed, that the testimony contained in the depositions, the prejudice which had accumulated against the prisoner, and his refusal to give any explanation to his counsel, or to suggest the line of defence he wished to be adopted, rendered the case one of the most difficult he had ever undertaken.

" Mr. Lewis, we have now come to see you, and have brought the depositions, which we have both carefully considered. We propose to read them to you and take your suggestions as to any evidence which can be produced at the trial, to answer and explain them," said Mr. Langham—for that was the name of the counsel. And that gentleman then read the testimony.

It occupied nearly two hours; during which time Lewis walked up and down the room, smoking his cigar, assuming an air of careless indifference, beneath the surface of which, a restless feverish anxiety was at work; and he stood still when the various statements, forcibly and conclusively tending to fix guilt upon him, were narrated by his counsel. He stood still—knocked the ash from his cigar against the wall, and paced the room again with a more hurried step. He saw and felt how every circumstance was weaving itself link by link into a chain, and binding him with its python folds from head to foot—and binding him beyond the hope of extrication; he saw and felt how he was tracked and traced, and how every step, which he had vainly thought was shrouded in an impenetrable veil of darkness and mystery, was exposed and brought into the light of day; he saw and felt how his presence in New York at an early hour of that morning, effected at the risk of his life, instead of being his safe-guard from detection, only accumulated the proof of guilt; and when the counsel had concluded, he stood amazed and silent—threw his cigar with violence upon the floor, and with affected composure drawing a chair near him and seating himself, said,

" Is all that really there ? "

" It is indeed," said the counsel, " and I am informed that some additional depositions have been made since these were given to us, and that we shall receive them this evening. They have traced some of the bonds," he added, " and found a list of them *in your hand-writing*. Some men in New York obtained an advance of money upon them, and gave some paper containing the amount and numbers of the bonds, pledged for that advance."

" Bah ! how can they prove my handwriting ? They are all " (with an oath) " —— lies," ejaculated the prisoner.

" It may be so," replied the counsel; " but you have written notes since you have been here to the sheriff's daughter. She has been arrested for assisting you in your endeavour to escape, and has con-fessed that she did so, and that she wrote the note read to the court from the affidavits, and has given to the Attorney-General four notes written by you in pencil to her. They have compared the handwriting, and it is sworn to be the same."

" Then these " (with a deep curse) " scoundrels in New York have *squealed* upon me," said the prisoner, and clenched his powerful hands and struck the chair upon which the counsel sat, so violently, that the blow almost dislocated the legs and arms of that crazy piece of furniture. " By God they have squealed ! "

" If you mean by that," said I, " that they have betrayed any con-fidence you placed in them, and given information against you, it is very probable ; for you will remember one of them made a threat in the court-house, when you refused to sign some paper he brought, which I could not then understand. They have sailed for California, and the bonds have been advertised ; and the detectives were in pur-suit of them before I left New York."

" Yes," more in soliloquy than addressing us, said he. " They wanted to rob me, and because I would not let them they have squared it with the detectives and gone." He lit another cigar, threw himself back in his chair, put his feet upon the table, muttered some internal imprecations and asked when he should see us again.

"Your trial is fixed for next Monday; this is Thursday," said the counsel. "Do you intend to furnish us with any evidence, or the names of any witnesses you desire to have produced, or any suggestions for the cross-examination of those witnesses who, you now know, will be brought against you in support of the prosecution?"

"Not now," he answered sullenly; "I will see you again;" and we retired.

"I guess this ain't a very satisfactory position for counsel to be placed in," quaintly observed Mr. Langham, as we walked from the gaol to his office. "I guess he don't realise his position."

"I am quite sure he does not realise ours," I observed, and we then decided to send a clerk with a copy of the depositions to the prisoner, accompanied by a letter requesting him to read them, and to furnish his counsel with instructions as to the course he wished to be pursued on the trial, without delay.

Until the very morning appointed for the trial our client had made no communication to his counsel. It has been truly remarked by a great jurist that on the part of an advocate, to enable him to fulfil his duty in an adequate manner, two endowments are necessary: appropriate information in all its plenitude, and the ability, experience, and zeal necessary to turn it to full account. We were about to embark upon a judicial investigation, in which the life of the accused was at stake, without any testimony, without any explanation of any one of the mass of evidentiary facts arrayed against him, and, when combined, presenting an irresistible inference of guilt; but so it was, and there was no help for it.

. On the morning of the trial we sought another interview with our client. We found him in the same sullen mood in which we had left him some days since. We asked him if he had read the depositions which had been sent to him; he answered "No."

"Are we, then, to go into court without your furnishing us with any suggestions whatever for your defence?" we asked.

"I have nothing to say. Let us wait and see what they prove on the first day, and we can then get up our case," said he, as he was brushing his clothes and preparing for his appearance in court; and we left him.

On the morning of Monday the trial commenced.

Criminal procedure, as administered in the state of New Jersey, is very analogous to that of England. In that state the civil law is not codified, as in most of the other states of the Union; the common law of England, as it existed when the American colonies were an appanage of the British crown, regulates their jurisprudence. The forms of indictment are the same, the rules as to the admission of evidence the same, and the decisions of the English courts upon all cognate subjects are authorities in both the civil and criminal courts.

The statutes of the state legislature define the offences and prescribe the punishment; but the trial, the empanelling and qualification of the jurors, are modelled entirely upon the English system.

In a very lucid and elaborate speech the Attorney-General opened the case for the prosecution. Every fact was arranged in its due order and importance, and five hours were occupied in its delivery. The almost breathless attention of the vast audience was never intermitted for one moment, and at the conclusion of a most logical and argumentative speech the Court adjourned to the following morning.

We now knew from that statement the testimony which was to be adduced against us, and the order in which it was arranged. The identity of the prisoner and his presence in the village upon the night of the murder were to be proved by one witness only—an old negro, who was an assistant in a barber's shop; a creature of rather weak intellect, but subtle and cunning as the negro frequently is, and familiarly known as "Looney Johnson."

The Attorney-General relied upon substantiating by Mr. Johnson's testimony that the accused was seen in the village about ten o'clock, that he was observed by the witness standing opposite the door of the deceased's shop, afterwards looking into the shop window, and again seen standing near the porch of a chapel at the corner of the road leading to the cottage where the deceased resided.

The witness was pointed out to us in the court, and certainly appeared to be an extraordinary individual. He quickly perceived that he was observed by the prisoner's counsel, and seemed to be as much interested in taking his survey of us as we were of him.

It is not easy to form any judgment of the age of such a gentleman from outward appearance. He was a very dark specimen of the African; the small-pox had left its vestiges upon his features, which, though disfigured, wore a kind and benevolent expression; and when your eye was fixed upon him closely they relaxed into a broad grin, which he evidently had no power of controlling. A sly humour twinkled in his eye.

He sat at the extreme end of one of the low benches which stretched across the crowded court, the observed of all observers. He seemed to have spread himself to his largest dimensions; either arm, extended at right angles to his body, was supported by the back of the bench; his long legs were thrust out as far as they could go, and he leaned back upon the form with a dignified and nonchalant air.

His attire was striking and characteristic. It was the very depth of one of the coldest of American winters, and the bitter north wind, blowing the sleet against the shivering windows of the court-house, made us all desire as much warmth as we could possibly obtain, while Mr. Johnson, by the costume he had adopted, evinced a total disregard of the thermometer.   A pair of linen pants, with very demonstrative blue stripes, fitted so closely to his figure that it seemed miraculous how he had ever got into them, and being in them, it seemed more miraculous still how he could get out of them, if he ever has.   A vest, the material of which must at one time have been of a bright yellow colour, had, by age, like port wine, or by frequent ablution, lost its natural tint, encased his form from his throat to the pit of his stomach. If ever the vest had been made to fit the human form, it must have been for a person of much larger symmetry than Mr. Johnson.   A blue surtout coat, small in contrast with the vest, completed his attire.

It was whispered amongst some of the witnesses that the District Attorney had borrowed the garment from a popular Methodist minister in the village, of whose congregation Mr. Johnson was a somewhat distinguished member.   A shirt collar of very considerable proportions, hardened or stiffened to excess, encircled by a bright scarlet cravat, approximated so closely to the lobe of either ear, that it evidently was either dangerous or uncomfortable for Mr. Johnson to move his head at any angle to his body; the effect of this unpleasant state of things being to impress a superficial observer with the idea that Mr. Johnson was an individual of a disagreeable and stuck-up affected manner, and of a haughty and imperious demeanour; both of which suppositions would have been erroneous, and quite inconsistent with Mr. Johnson's idiosyncrasy.

The witness was now directed by the court to take the stand, and the oath was administered.   Every eye was upon him, and in spite of all cries of "Order," and in defiance of the vigorous hammering of the gavel with which every American judge is provided on the bench, the audience clambered upon the seats, and stood upon the tables and benches, to obtain a glimpse of Mr. Johnson and to catch every sentence of his narrative.

He detailed in a somewhat confused manner the facts as they had been stated to the jury by the Attorney-General.   The direct examination was long, minute, and tedious; large maps and diagrams of the *locus in quo* were affixed upon the walls of the court, and his attention was directed by the examining counsel from time to time to the different localities where he persisted he had seen the accused. The examination occupied the attention of the court until mid-day, the time at which, in the rural districts of the state of New Jersey, it is the habit of the judges to take a "recess" for dinner; it being understood that, upon the reassembling of the court the cross-examination was to be proceeded with.

My learned coadjutors and myself, from the closest watching of the testimony and the manner in which it was given, had not failed to observe that in many respects the mental organisation of the witness was deficient. He had a most indefinite and confused notion of chronology; his idea of mensuration and distance was very inaccurate; all application of time and the hour to any event or transaction he was detailing was treated with supreme indifference.

Punctually at one o'clock the judge re-entered the court, and behind him came Mr. Johnson and resumed his seat. His demeanour evidenced self-satisfaction. He had dined at the same table with the judge, the jury, the counsel, and the witnesses; his testimony had been the topic during dinner of animated conversation, and it was whispered in the court-room that after dinner he had fortified himself against any attack of dyspepsia by more than one libation of very hot rum-and-water. However that might have been, and although his head presented the same stiff, immovable, and uncomfortable appearance as before dinner, he seemed to be greatly pleased with himself and everybody and everything about him.

"How long have you lived at Princeton, Mr. Johnson?" was the first question put to the witness upon cross-examination.

"Don't know, boss. Wasn't raised there, though."

"Where were you raised?"

"Don't know, boss, 'xactly. Mother used to say I was raised in Varginny," was the answer.

"Now, never mind, sir, what your mother used to say. I want to know."

"But I had to mind what my mother used to say, boss, I tell ye. You didn't know my mother, boss, did ye? She split my head with a dipper one day because I didn't mind. Hee! hee! hee!" interjected the irrepressible witness.

"Stop," said the judge, "you must answer the counsel's question; he has a right to test your recollection and your accuracy. And you are not to tell us anything your mother knows, but only what you know yourself."

"Yes, boss, all right; but mother knew a precious sight more than I know. Did you know my mother, boss?" The witness concluding with thus interrogating the judge.

"Stop," again said the judge. "Don't examine me. Now, attend to the counsel's question."

"All right, boss; but if he don't know my mother, I don't want him to say nuffen about her," grumbled the witness.

"Now," the counsel resumed, "where were you raised, and how long have you lived at Princeton?"

"Guess I was raised down south. Mother "——

"Stop," thundered the judge, for his patience was sorely tried. "Stop, you're talking about your mother again. Stop,"

"Guess I couldn't be raised without a mother, boss, could I? Hee! hee! hee!"

"You are not asked about your mother at all," explained the judge, in a tone of kind remonstrance. "You are asked if you know where you were raised? If you do know, say so; and if you do not, then say you do not."

"I don't want no lawyer to say nuffen against my mother," *sotto voce*, in the ear of the judge, mumbled the witness.

"The counsel has not said anything about your mother, nor against her. Now attend, and answer the counsel's question," said the judge.

"Now, Mr. Johnson, for the fourth time I ask you where you were raised, and how long you have lived at Princeton?" asked the counsel.

"My sister told me down in old Varginny—when mother died—that "——

"Stop," said the counsel. "I ask you if *you* knew where you were raised? Never mind what your sister told you, nor when your mother died."

"Perhaps," said the judge, addressing the examining counsel, "you might as well postpone this portion of the cross-examination, and proceed with something else. It seems difficult, if not impossible, to obtain a distinct and satisfactory answer from the witness at present. Try something else."

The counsel conceded with reluctance, remarking that such a course very much deranged the system of cross-examination which he had purposed to submit the witness to, and then resumed his questions.

"Now, Mr. Johnson, what is your occupation at Princeton?"

"What do you say, boss?"

"What is your occupation? How do you get your living?" asked the counsel.

"My living, boss? My living ain't nuffen," said the witness.

"Where do you live?"

"Live with Mr. Stearnes, the barber; tain't no living no how. Lather the customers and brush 'em; they give me a few cents, the best on 'em, sometimes a gennelman will give me ten cents. Ain't many gennelmen down there, boss! Hee! hee! hee!" was the reply.

"At what time did you first see the man who you say was Mr. Lewis, on that Saturday night?" inquired the counsel.

"Guess it was the night time, boss."

"But what time of the night?" asked the counsel.

"Guess it was dark, boss."

"But what time? What o'clock was it?"

"Don't know nuffen about the time, boss."

"Where did you first see him upon that night?   Look at that map on the wall, and show the jury where you first saw him," said the counsel.

This was cruel.   The witness in vain endeavoured to turn his head in the direction of the map on the wall; the shirt-collar upon each side effectually prevented it.   Despite the solemnity of the investigation the effect of his struggles to survey the map was so irresistibly ludicrous that the audience, unable to control that which at first was a general titter only through the court, gave way to loud and uproarious laughter.

"Why don't you look at the map and answer the counsel's question?" interrupted the judge, who had not observed the witness's dilemma.

The witness gave a stolid vacant stare at the judge, but did not move.

"Get up and go to the map," said the judge.   "Get up, and show the counsel where you saw him."

"What map, boss?"

"There—that map hanging on the wall."

The officer of the court led the witness from the stand, and placed him in close proximity to the map.

"Now," said the counsel, "point out upon that map the spot where you say you first saw Mr. Lewis on that night."

After his eye had wandered over the large area of paper for some minutes, the witness dabbed his finger upon a green coloured spot, and said, "Here, boss, here.   I saw him here.   Hee! hee!"

"Why, that is the Cemetery.   Do you mean to swear you saw him in the Cemetery?"

"Guess I do, boss—see him and the old dog too," replied the witness.

"Saw who in the Cemetery?" quickly retorted the counsel.

"Why, old Mr. Watson and his dog.   Knew the old dog well, he often come to our store, carrying his master's basket," said the witness.

"You are asked where you saw the man you say was Lewis on the Saturday night, and where you first saw him?" impatiently inquired the counsel.

"Oh, Lewis!   Guess I see him.   Know I see him."

"Where?" repeated the counsel.   "Show the jury where you saw him.   Point to it on the map."

"Guess I see him in Princeton."

The judge: "Do you know Mr. Watson's store?"

"Guess I do.   Lathered him for years, boss," was the reply.

The judge: "Now, where was the man you say was Lewis that night?   Where did you see him?"

"Standing by the chapel, boss.   Up here."

"How was he dressed?" asked the counsel.

"Dressed in black," said the witness.

"How tall was he?" by the counsel.

This seemed to puzzle him. He twisted his hat about, and then looked into it, and then twisted it again.

"Guess he was about twelve foot."

"What! do you mean twelve feet high?" said the counsel.

"Guess he was—'bout twelve foot."

A slight sensation pervaded the audience.

"Why, how tall are you?" asked the judge.

"Guess mother said father was twelve foot."

"Now never mind your mother. How tall do you think you are?" inquired the judge.

"'Bout twelve foot. Guess I'm twelve foot, boss," said the witness.

"How far is the chapel where you have said you saw him from Mr. Watson's store?" was the next question.

"About two mile, I guess, boss."

"Two what? Why, the whole village is not a quarter of a mile long, is it?" peevishly said the counsel.

"Guess it is," said the witness.

"Is what?" asked the counsel.

"Quarter of a mile long, boss."

"Did you drink anything at your dinner?" asked the judge, looking very seriously at the witness.

"Yes, boss; drank water though."

"Nothing more?" said the judge.

"No, boss, nuffen at the dinner,"

"Did you drink anything after dinner?" inquired the counsel.

"What do you say, boss?"

"Did you drink anything after your dinner, and before you came into court?" repeated the counsel.

"I didn't pay for nuffen, boss," and he twisted his hat about and looked askance at the jury, and then lifted his eyes and gazed up on the ceiling, the white portions of his eyes looking as large as billiard balls.

"You are not asked if you paid for anything, Mr. Johnson. You are asked if you drank anything?" repeated the counsel.

"That ain't nuffen to him, boss, is it?" (appealing to the judge).

"I see him drink at dinner all the time. Hee! hee!"

"Mr. Sheriff, take this witness into your custody, and produce him in court to-morrow morning," said the judge. "I shall adjourn the cross-examination. See that he gets nothing to drink."

"Why, boss, I ain't had my tea yet. The District Attorney told me this child should have plenty to eat and drink when he came from Princetown "—— said the witness.

"I think you have had too much to drink," replied the judge as he was closing his note-book.

"No, not too much, boss. A gennelman gib me three glasses of rum-and-water—it ain't hurt me," the witness muttered as he left the stand with the sheriff.

The court then adjourned until the morrow. When the audience had left, the counsel for the prisoner had the opportunity of conferring with him.

"Well, they have not done much the first day—have they, counsellors?" observed Lewis.

"Not much at present. The jury will not place much reliance upon the testimony of Mr. Johnson, and it seems that they have no other evidence of your being seen near the store of Mr. Watson upon that night," we observed.

"Do you wish to give us any instructions relative to the proceedings of to-morrow?" one of the counsel asked.

"None," in the same sullen tone as he had before adopted, was the response.

The lady who had passed at the hotel as the wife of Lewis had been, since his arrest, under the close surveillance of the local police. She had been threatened with arrest and indictment as accessory before and after the murder. Efforts had been made to induce her to divulge the facts connected with the possession of the valise in which the fragment of the receipt had been found. She was importuned with promises and intimidated with threats, but in vain.

When Lewis absconded from California after his escape from prison, he left there a wife and child. The wife having heard of his arrest upon the charge of murder, started immediately for New York, and I found a telegram, addressed to me as his counsel, on my return from the court to the hotel, announcing her arrival in that city.

The rumour of her unexpected presence was not long upon its journey to the ears of the Mrs. Lewis who was still sojourning at the *Passaic Hotel*. She came to Trenton, under the care of the police, to obtain an interview with the prisoner. It was denied by the sheriff, and she then determined to seek an opportunity of speaking to him in court upon the following day. Such was her first impulse, but the wounded vanity of the woman was aroused, and she decided upon a course which would render the escape of her paramour impossible. She had loved him and risked much for him; she had been the victim of his passion and his depravity; she had shielded him more than once from detection; she had implored him to pause in his career of guilt; in the dark crimes he had made her participate she had been faithful and loyal as woman only can be; she had sacrificed honour, reputation, hope, for one who had treated her with inhumanity and used her as an implement of crime and disgrace. In the dearest point a woman can be wronged, she suffered. Despair, guilt, inevitable ruin closed in upon her. She struggled hard, but the one passion overmastered all; she found solace in revenge. He had deceived her, and she would now betray him; though it cost his life, she would betray him. And with wild eye, haggard cheek, and faltering tongue, the woman transformed to fiend stood before the District Attorney in his office, and asked permission to make a statement in the case of murder now being tried against George Lewis.

The prisoner had been placed by the sheriff in the cell in which I originally found him, upon the excuse—for it was nothing else—that the larger compartment in the gaol was required for the use of some wretched debtors who had recently been consigned to his custody. He had sent for me at a late hour.

"I wish," said he (after I had entered, and taken my seat beside him upon the filthy mattress whose acquaintance I had made on my first interview), "to make a full statement to you of the whole of this case. There is no chance for me, I see plainly. I care not for conviction, nor for death. They have determined to convict me; but that I should be discovered by such a set of country" (with an oath) "fools, is all that worries me. They think they have got me fast, and so they have; but I care not for life—no, not that for it," and he threw the butt of his cigar into the corner of the cell—" not *that* for death to-morrow morning. Look at me; do you think I do?"

He stood erect, and drew himself to his utmost height. His cheek was pallid and his lips compressed with inward rage and mortification, but fear was a stranger to his thoughts.

' The lion lies with his head reclined upon his paws in his captor's pitfall. He sees the rifle levelled at him, but stirs not; the indignity of his capture has subdued him. In the jungle he would have bartered his life dearly; lured to a grave, he resigns it sullenly.

We were alone. A candle on the table lent but little light to the gloom of the miserable place; the deep snow obstructed all air from the small orifice at the window; and the heavily-ironed door had been barred and bolted on the outside by the express direction of the sheriff when the counsel was admitted to this midnight interview. He placed one of his hands—and such a hand!—upon my shoulder, and in a determined and deliberate tone thus addressed me:

"If you think you can be any good as my counsel, do; but I am sure you don't. I have no witnesses now. Those" (with an oath) "villains swore they would see me through it, that they would hire the testimony in New York to prove an alibi; they have robbed me of all the money and bonds, and gone; they planned the whole job, but were afraid to do it."

He paused and looked at me for a reply. I made none.

" And now I'll tell you all," said he.

"Tell me enough to make some defence for you," said I. "I would rather not hear more."

"No; I'll tell you all. Listen to me. Old Watson had been spotted for months. I knew well the amount of money and bonds he had in his safe. Mrs. Lewis had been on his track. She went on the cars (train) with him to New York often on the Monday. She would have had his parcel once, but the one she was to put into his bag was the wrong colour; he had changed the paper after she had made up the package to be slipped into his valise. That old dog was in her way when she went into his store. She took poisoned cake for him many times, but he was too smart. The night *I fixed* him was a dark night, snow falling gently. I meant to shoot him, but the place was too quiet. I stood opposite his door when he came out. The old nigger was right. When he got under the wall of the cemetery I crossed over to him and seized him by the collar, and put the lantern in his face; he was too scared to make any noise. I turned him round and shoved his head against the wall, and held him with this hand here (pointing to his throat). The dog flew at me and tore my pants, and bit me all down the legs. After I had held him a little time he fell forward against me, and I took him up and pitched him over the wall into the graveyard; he was as quiet as a baby, and I heard no noise after he fell in there. His hat fell off, and when he fell on me he knocked off mine. I threw mine over instead of his. The dog stood by his hat and would not let me come near it. I tried to get him away, but could not; he howled and barked, and jumped up the wall looking after his master. I caught him by the throat and held him on the ground; he struggled hard with me for some time and I choked him. I then pitched him over after the old man. He groaned afterwards several times. I took the basket with the key and went to the store, and got the bonds and bills, about seventy-thousand dollars in all. I drove as hard as I could, and put the keys and the hat under the porch of the chapel, and intended to return and take them—they were gone. The bonds I took to New York. I jumped on the cars of the mail train; it did not stop, but they threw on the mail bags. I was in New York at half-past two o'clock, and the play was going on at the Faro table. I put five thousand dollars in the bank, when we had a run of luck against us. All the other I left with —— and —— to be melted. They have robbed me of all. I brought the valise down to the *Passaic Hotel*, and Mrs. Lewis burnt all the papers in the fire-place in her bedroom. She knew of the murder, and waited for me outside the village when I went on the Friday night to old Watson's store to see the safe. If the bonds had been there then I had the gags all ready to put on him, and should not have hurt him if he had made no noise."

He paused, and I sat amazed at the cool recital of such horror.

"Look here," said he, resuming, "where that" (with an oath) "old dog bit.me;" and he took off his coat and showed me his arms.

A loud knock at the door and the sheriff's voice announced, as he opened it, that the gaol was about to be closed, and thus the interview terminated.

Upon a condition exacted from the District Attorney, that she should not be required to appear as a witness against the prisoner, his mistress had made a full and unreserved statement of all the facts connected with the crime, and how much she really knew was disclosed in the confession made by the prisoner to his counsel.

For ten days the trial proceeded. The testimony as it appeared in the depositions came out in stronger force. The counsel—without a witness, without the means of explaining any of the facts which pressed so powerfully against the prisoner—contested to the last, and a charge from the judge, leaving no hope of a verdict in their favour, resulted in a conviction of "Murder in the first degree." Amid the breathless silence of the crowded audience that verdict was pronounced. No one heard it with so much unconcern as the prisoner; and with gesture and manner more defiant than he evinced on his entering the court, he passed through the avenue formed by the gazing spectators and returned to his lonely cell, never to leave it until his march to death.

The really dramatic portion of this case commenced after the trial had ceased, and after the prisoner's conviction. Then began a series of declarations and intrigues on the part of the prisoner; his stern refusal to listen to religious teaching, and a belief in the powers of darkness to assist him in escaping from his doom, such as were rarely heard of in the criminal annals of any country. Efforts were made to obtain a new trial—a procedure allowed in every state of the Union—but in vain; and the prisoner, upon the refusal of the application, was sentenced to death with the usual solemnity.

Upon the morning when his spirit was to be sent upon its unknown career, the prisoner walked before the sheriff with firm and unfaltering step, and stood motionless under the rude beam which had been erected in the little garden behind the gaol. The bright sunlight of a cold, crisp, frosty morning streamed down upon the platform where the malefactor gazed for the last time, with vacant, careless stare, upon all that surrounded him.

By the combined strength of eight men hired for the purpose by the sheriff, and the application of ill-adapted machinery, after a painful and violent struggle

. . . . . . "It was done—
The spirit was gone;
For weal or for woe, 'twas known only to One."

# Henry Murger.

## By WALTER BESANT.

THE Prophet of Bohemia. We sing of the man who first enlightened the world on the lives of those that wait upon hope and struggle in the path of Art against an adverse fortune ; who, while he tore down the veil and showed the truth, at the same time raised a cloud of illusion which permits the youthful imagination to hear only the laughter and to ignore the pain. It is only when one becomes older that the suffering shows more clearly than the joy—the days of privation are seen to be more numerous than the days of feasting.

> " Aimons et chantons encore,
> La jeunesse n'a qu'un temps."

How glorious—in a perennial round of champagne, flowers, and song ; roaming in the wood with Rosette, and filling an empty purse with a poem ! Ragged, perhaps, at times, and a little hungry, but still in what goodly company—with how noble a fellowship ! And then the future all before you—the future of fame and success ! Let us see what they are—the imaginary and the real Bohemia.

Alfred de Musset, Alfred de Vigny, and Henry Murger form a sort of literary triad, which may be studied together. Utterly unlike each other, they present occasional points of contrast which are too striking to be overlooked. In former numbers of TEMPLE BAR (Nov. 1870, and March 1872) I endeavoured to give sketches of the first two. They represent the influences of the first third of this century on young men well-born, well-educated, and highly trained. We have to do, so far as the third is concerned, with a mere child of the people, pitchforked into the ranks of literature, but never representing in the smallest degree the voice of the people. It is not a problem which we have to solve. There is no mystery ; only a simple, sad life to tell, mistaken in its aims, bankrupt in its aspirations, ruined by its follies. The miserable necessities of a grinding poverty were its excuse ; the impatience which a weak will could not resist, that impatience which longed to enjoy before the period when fortune fixed its time of enjoyment, was the fatal rock on which it split. Alfred de Musset led no happy life, but he pursued at least a high standard of art ; Alfred de Vigny was a disappointed man because he rated his own powers too high ; poor Murger was wretched because he failed to see that Art must be everything—that genius must love his mistress all in all, or not at all. He loved other

things as well, and so in the lute the rift widened till the music was
mute.

Let me first, with permission of the many who know his book so
well, recall some of the incidents in the career of that prince of
Bohemians, the imaginary Rodolphe.  You will see why, as we go on.

The Rodolphe of the ' Scènes de la vie de Bohême,' when we first
meet him, is a young man of two or three and twenty.  His face is
almost hidden by a profusion of beard, his forehead, by way of compensation, being only relieved from absolute baldness by half a dozen
hairs carefully drawn across it in a vain endeavour to personate their
departed brethren.  He is dressed in a black coat, out at elbows and
" gone " under the arms, in trowsers which might be called black, and
boots which had never been new, because he always bought them
secondhand.  We find him in the Café *Momus*, Rue Saint-Germain-
l'Auxerrois.  We talk literature and art; we drink; we make the
acquaintance of three other congenial spirits, Messieurs Colline,
Schaunard, and Marcel, and we plunge into Bohemian life.  Rodolphe,
poet and *littérateur*, is the editor of *The Scarf of Iris*, a journal not
entirely unconnected with the millinery and drapery interests, in fact,
a journal of fashion.  Later on we find him connected with the
*Castor*, an organ of public opinion devoted mainly to advance the
great hatting cause.  Rodolphe's three friends, one of them an artist,
one a musician, one a philosopher, scholar, private tutor, are, like himself poor, ragged, out at elbows.  They are afflicted with a Gargantuan
hunger.  When funds come in their first thought is food; they go
out and eat; they go on eating till there is nothing left in the locker,
then they go back to their customary short commons with the
resignation of philosophers and the hope of youth.  Rodolphe falls in
love with Louise.  He talks to her in what the author calls the
poetry of love.  Louise only understands the *patois* of love, so they
hardly comprehend one another, and his first flight of the heart is a
failure.  He is turned out of his lodgings by an impatient proprietor,
and lives for a time like the sparrows, *sub Jove*, sleeping in the
branches of a tree.  Like the sparrows too he is always hungry.
An uncle, an uncle of romance, a really useful piece of domestic
furniture, finds him out at this juncture, and relieves his wants.  The
uncle is a manufacturer of stoves; has for a long time been meditating
a work on chimneys.  In his nephew he sees one who can do for him
what education and nature have entered into a conspiracy to prevent
him from doing himself—write the book.  He locates him in a fifth
floor; gives him materials, furnishes the list of chapters, provides
him with food, and takes away all his clothes except a Turkish
dressing-gown, in order that he may not run away.

The work progresses slowly, far too slowly for the uncle's impatience.  In the agonies of composing the chapter on ' Smoky Flues,'

Rodolphe discovers from the papers that he has won a prize of three hundred francs (twelve pounds) at a certain Academy of Floral Games. He is rich, he is a capitalist; he tears himself from his drudgery and escapes back to Bohemia and his friends and the editorship of the *Castor*. He lives, as do all his friends, in the cheapest room at the top of the house; he can seldom afford the luxury of fire and not always that of candles, so he goes to bed and stays there. His bed is insufficiently supplied with blankets; so he lies between the mattresses; his expenses from day to day are not, as may be imagined, enormous; and provided only he can weather what he calls the " Cape of Storms," that is to say the first or fifteenth of the month, when the bills come in, he is tolerably happy. His time is chiefly spent with his friends at the Café *Momus*, to the grief and indignation of the pro- prietor, for all the other customers are driven away by the four Bohemians, who drink little and eat nothing. Driven to desperation, the landlord draws out at last a list of his grievances and presents it to them himself. This unique bill of charges sets forth how M. Rodolphe, who always came first, was accustomed to seize the papers and keep them all day; how, because M. Rodolphe was editor of the *Castor*, they never ceased bawling for the *Castor*, till that paper was also taken in by the café; that accomplished, they left off asking for it; how Rodolphe and Colline were in the habit of keeping the *trictrac* table to themselves from ten in the morning till twelve at night, the other votaries of the game having nothing to do but to gnash their teeth; how M. Marcel had so far forgotten what was due to a public establishment as to bring his easel there, and make appointments with models of both sexes; how M. Schaunard was talking of bringing his piano and giving a concert of his own works; and how he received visits at the café from a young lady named Phémie, who came without a bonnet; how they actually made their own coffee in the establish- ment; and how they, lastly, instigated the waiter to send a love letter, the composition of which was clearly traceable to the pernicious influence of M. Rodolphe, to the old and faithful wife of the pro- prietor. The artists compromise matters by conceding the minor points, such as a bonnet to Phémie and the coffee to the establish- ment, and continue to frequent the Café *Momus*.

Then they all fall in love. Rodolphe's passion for Mimi may be read in the 'Scènes,' chapter fourteen; nothing more faithful, more real, than this sketch of a girl torn from her lover—from his empty stove and meagre dinners—by the attractions of velvet and silk, plenty to eat and drink, and warmth:

> " When the purse is empty—isn't it so, my dear?—
>     Farewell love, and good-bye 'tween me and thee.
> You will leave me lonely, with never an idle tear;
>     Go, and soon forget me—isn't it so, Mimi?

"Comes to the same, you see; for after all, my dear,
  Happy days have dawned and died for me and thee:
Not too many, 'tis true: best things are ever, here,
  Shortest and soonest over—isn't it so, Mimi?"

Six years pass; the friendship of the four knows no diminution, their worldly prospects no improvement. Then a change. One of them takes advantage of political disorders, and gets made an ambassador. Sublime impudence of the novelist! Rodolphe and Marcel succeed at last. Then Mimi comes back—poor frail Mimi, a skeleton, pale, worn, emaciated—comes back to seek help and shelter by that Bohemian hearth where her only happy days were spent, with the only man who was ever really kind to her. They pawn their things to keep the life in her. But she dies. Then the band of Bohemians is broken up; they go into society; they take their places in the world; they become respectable, staid, and *successful*. Marcel the painter pronounces the funeral oration over the past. "We have had," he said, "our time of carelessness and youth; it has been a happy time, a time of romance and thoughtless love; but this prodigality of days, as if we had an eternity to throw away, must have an end; we can no longer live outside the skirts of society; our independence, our liberty, after all, are doubtful advantages. And are they real? Any *crétin*, idiot, illiterate ass, is our master, at the price of lending us a few francs. . . . It is not necessary,'in order to be a poet, to wear a summer paletôt in December; we can write poetry just as well in warm rooms and on three meals a day. Poetry does not consist in the disorder of existence, in improvised happy days, in rebelling against prejudices which we can less readily overturn than we can upset a dynasty, and which rule the world. Whatever we say or do, this is certain, that to succeed we must take the beaten path. Here we are, thirty years of age, unknown, isolated, disgusted with ourselves. Up to the present this existence has been imposed upon us; it is no longer necessary; the obstacles are destroyed which prevented our leaving this life. It is finished."

It seems almost as stupid to give the life of Rodolphe in a magazine article as it would be to give the life of Martin Chuzzlewit. I do so only because in the book is written the early life of its author, because every character, except perhaps that of Marcel the artist, stands out clear and distinct from the canvas, and is an evident portrait of an early friend. I do not know the original of Colline, but a Parisian friend writes to me as regards Schaunard the ragged musician. "There still exists," he says, "in the Rue Hautefeuille, close by the École de Médecine, right in the Quartier Latin, an old *brasserie*, black with smoke, fitted up with wooden tables, called the *Brasserie Andler*, after the name of its proprietor, an honest and enormously big Swiss. Thither used to resort about the years 1858–60 the chiefs of the Realistic School, with their apostle Champfleury, and their high priest the painter Courbet. It was something like the Café *Momus*, although not quite so ragged and out-at-elbows. As a student at this period, I used to frequent this café, and made the acquaintance there of the wreck of Henry Murger's old band of friends. The only celebrity remaining there was poor Schaunard, or at least he whom Murger took for his type of a Bohemian musician. His real name was Schaun; he was then about forty years of age, and had an intelligent and open front, regular features, and a moustache *à la mousquetaire*. He had not *fait son chemin;* he was however considered *très-fort* in musical composition."

The name of the real Rodolphe was Henry Murger. He was born in the year 1822, at the foot of Mont Blanc, his father being of very poor and humble station. When he was still an infant he was brought to Paris, where his father got a place as *concierge* or porter. His boyhood was passed in the streets and in the court of the hotel. Education he had little or none: only the simplest rudiments of learning, such as a poor man could afford to give his son: no Latin, no Greek, none of that education, most useful of any, which boys at a great school communicate to each other. When he was thirteen or fourteen years old he got noticed by M. Étienne de Jouy, who lived in the hotel. It does not appear clearly how far De Jouy, then a very old man, interested himself in the boy. But he took some care of him, it is clear, because he obtained for him his first situation. Intercourse with this old adventurer could not fail of being singularly useful to a lad of genius and imperfect education. Old De Jouy was a man whose history ought to be written. He knew Voltaire by heart when he was a child; he had a commission and lost a finger fighting the Moorish pirates at thirteen; fought the English under Tippoo Sahib at twenty; rescued a Hindoo girl from suttee, nearly getting killed in the process; got put into prison for trying to snatch a Cingalese girl from a convent; escaped in an open boat and was picked up at sea; came back to help tear down the Bastille; fought in the revolutionary army; prison again as *suspect;* married an English girl; prison again for that; turned royalist; and took to writing, getting another dose of prison from his own friends in 1819. One may fancy the old man pouring his pernicious Voltairean doctrines into the ears of the bright-eyed boy who sat listening to the revelations of new worlds.

When he was sixteen, De Jouy placed him in the household of Count Tolstöi, one of the great Russian House of Ostermann Tolstöi, as private secretary. One of Murger's biographers has discovered that the cook of the Count had four times as large a salary as the private secretary, and has a bitter fit of sneering thereat. It seems to me a very simple thing. A cook is a most important functionary. He exercises exceedingly delicate duties, and he must be a man of the greatest skill and experience, while young Murger had nothing to do but to read and copy. Surely this kind of sneer is very absurd. And it is always happening. Whenever the life of a man of genius is written, somebody discovers that when he was sixteen, and had five shillings a week, the footman had ten; and then we lift up our hands in pity and disgust. The secretaryship did the boy a great deal of good. Count Tolstöi made him read all the best French writers—those of the nineteenth century only—so that Murger remained to his last day as ignorant of the writers before Chateaubriand as he was of Chinese. His three years of this work made him a writer as well as a reader, and when he left the Count at the age of nineteen or twenty he obtained at once a post on ' Correspondance de Journaux de Departements.' To be sure it was not a great thing—fifty francs a month, eight hours a day, twopence an hour—but it was a beginning; it launched him into the sea of literature, and placed him among the struggling mob of young writers, painters, dramatists, poets, and novelists which formed his land of Bohemia. " It was a bad generation," says Pelloquet, "one which was old before its time; one without enthusiasm yet without experience; one overflowing with vanity yet without self-respect; which opposed its petty irony to every kind of enthusiasm: which allowed the magnificent heritage of 1830 to perish in its hands."

In other words, the lofty enthusiasm of the Romantic school was dying out, and as yet nothing had arisen to take its place. We need not, however, look for high aims and devotion to art in Henry Murger and his school.

Murger tells us something of his own struggles in a letter:—

" Possessing some tincture of orthography we worked at our sheet, where our prose was occasionally paid for at the rate of eight francs an acre—something like the price of English pears. The founder of our journal, in which prudence compelled us to refrain from putting ' The conclusion to-morrow,' disappeared one day. He owed us for many an acre of copy. We began by tearing our hair, a distraction which nature no longer permits me; then we agreed to pass the bankruptcy over to the account of profit and loss.

" Nevertheless, three months afterwards—it was a Saturday and the last day of Carnival—while we were regretting the impossibility of keeping the feast, comes an official letter, in which we were invited, as creditors of the journal, to receive twenty-five per cent. of our claims. Think of it! Never were poor recipients more happy."

He got literary promotion and was put on the staff of the *Corsaire*, edited the *Moniteur de la Mode*, just as Rodolphe edited the *Echarpe d'Iris*; contributed verses in the style of Alfred de Musset to the *Artiste*, and wrote novelettes and sketches, among others the famous ' Scènes de la vie de Bohême.' And at last people discovered that

there was a man among them who had opened a new vein; and
success, of its kind, came to him.

He is spoken of by those who knew him in his younger days as a
singularly modest and unassuming man, prematurely bald, with great
sweetness of expression; always good-natured in his conversation,
quick of temper but easily appeased, and entirely without malice. He
used to make his appearance in the office of the *Corsaire* bathed with
perspiration, as if he had been running through the streets, and sit
down to write a chapter of his 'Scènes,' for which he was paid at the
rate of a louis a chapter—not much more than a penny a line. Not
that he was a rapid writer; on the contrary, he would spend days and
weeks over a single chapter, touching and retouching, but his ideas
flowed freely. He was always in somewhat delicate health, the effect
of many dissipations, which he condemned, but had not the courage to
resist.

Among his friends were Fanchéry, poor Gérard de Nerval, Champfleury, Nadar, Beaudelaire, Pelloquet, and others who have since made
some kind of mark in literature, small though it be with some of them.
Some of them used to assemble either in that Café *Momus*, where
Rodolphe first met his friends, or in that other *brasserie* in the Quartier
Latin of which we have spoken. On the site where once stood the
Café *Momus*, is now a confectioner's shop, so that the Bohemians of
the present day, however anxious to keep up old associations, must go
elsewhere to hold their *réunions*.

In one of these early years, his friend Pelloquet tells how he went
to pay him a visit. He found him ill in bed, alone. The room
almost bare of furniture; the bed without curtains or hangings, ill
furnished with covering. As he lay there, this poor young Bohemian,
his visitor remarked that his eyes constantly turned with longing to
a certain shelf, where reposed a black velvet domino and a pair of
soiled kid gloves. Soiled kid gloves and a velvet domino. They
ought to have been carved upon his tombstone, for they give a sort of
key-note to his life. In sickness and in health; in poverty or in
funds, he was always looking at the velvet domino and the soiled kid
gloves. To the young man, entirely ignorant of society, never having
penetrated into the circles of social order and domestic happiness,
the *bal de l'opéra* probably appeared to be the highest attainable
form of human enjoyment. Music was there, at any rate, with warmth,
lightness, and society; with bright eyes, and with forgetfulness of the
" acres of copy " which had to be written before his rent was paid. When
the last illusions of youth were gone there remained the habit. Henry
Murger's ideas of "pleasure" probably never altogether changed.

It is noteworthy that the ' Scènes ' were written at the early age of
six-and-twenty. In it he touched the highest point of his genius.
He never got any further. Later on, when he wrote the ' Dernier

rendezvous,' his style is deepened, his fire fiercer, but he never wrote anything so good, so faithful, and so complete. It is as real as Defoe, and ten times more *spirituel.* A vein of youthful gaiety runs through it from beginning to end; not the gaiety of careless acquiescence, but of hope. The ragged artists only regard their life as *en parenthèse.* Better days are coming. Marcel shows at last, how the life of Bohemia is only an episode in the career of a man possessed of genius but destitute of friends. This point has been entirely overlooked by his critics. They seize on the scenes in the book, and neglect its obvious moral. Yet in Marcel's words the moral lies clear and distinct. But the stern moralist is quick to seize an opportunity; so he points the finger of scorn at the young fellows; shows how they are at their wits' end for the next day's dinner; how they practise all kinds of expedients; declaims at their grovelling and material life; at their gigantic feasting when money comes. in, at their want of prudence and foresight. Very well, they do eat and drink enormously when they can; they do lack foresight; their life is shabby, poor, and mean. Very true indeed. But suppose our moralist, who is generally fat and well liking, with a balance to his credit, were condemned to a few years of privation; what if he were so far reduced as to be sometimes actually hungry? Is it not reasonable that a young fellow of five and twenty, with a really obtrusive twist, and with barely enough to eat, should look upon abundance as a thing specially desirable and altogether lovely? Nobody finds fault with Homer when he describes the [great banquets, dwelling with delight on the meat upon the spit, the long tables, and the zealous attendants. The poet is probably one of those who had but a nodding acquaintance with roasted mutton and broiled venison; but he had recollections, and he rolled them over under his tongue. So with poor Murger. Starving men dream of banquets; thirsty men of fountains; your hungry genius of Belshazzar's feast. Moreover, if an unexpected windfall put him in possession of funds, he does not waste his wealth in paying debts, but calls his friends together and gives them a lordly dinner. Who will care for saving a few paltry francs out of this miserable present, when he looks forward to a great and solid future? Not for these things do we blame Murger's artists.

Rodolphe and Marcel went back to society; Murger stayed in Bohemia. He never had the courage to give up his old habits, perhaps, because he was always in money difficulties, he never had the means; so he was always on the outskirts of the world, always looking for better things, singing gaily:

"Just as a gipsy wanderer
Roams at his own sweet will
So I on the highway of Art
Am aimlessly wandering still.

> Just as a gipsy wanderer,
>     Nothing but hope at his back;
> Penniless else is my pocket,
>     Nothing but hope in my pack."

Yet he made his name; was put on the *Revue des deux Mondes*; wrote more novels and sketches, all exactly alike; brought out two or three plays, but failed of making a real dramatic success.

As the years go on and he passes to the thirties, he ceases to sing of youth, and betakes him to regretting the past:

> "Hast thou forgot, Louise, Louise,
>     That night in the garden grey,
> When, like the blossoms on the trees,
>     Your hands in my hands lay?
> Our parted lips refused a word;
>     Our knees all trembling met;
> The willows o'er us hardly stirred;
>     Say thou rememberest yet.
>
> "Canst thou forget, Marie, Marie,
>     The day we changed our rings?
> The golden sun lies on the lea;
>     The lark above us sings.
> The brooklet prattles down the glade
>     Beside us as we lie;
> Marie! though springs and roses fade,
>     Let not this memory die.
>
> "Canst thou forget, Christine, Christine,
>     The room with roses gay,
> So near the sky, so small, so mean,
>     Our April and our May?
> And when, one night, the moonbeams bright
>     Fell on thy cheek and breast,
> 'Unveil,' they cried, 'thy beauty's pride:'—
>     Canst thou forget the rest?
>
> "Ill ending hath my poor Marie;
>     And fond Louise is dead;
> Christine, the fragile, on the sea
>     To sunnier skies is fled.
> Alas! Louise, Marie, Christine,
>     Down with the years are borne;
> The past a ruin that hath been;
>     I left sometimes to mourn."

The old loves are gone and can return no more. Or they come back and find the heart dead and cold, the flame extinct:

> "I saw a swallow yestere'en,
>     The bird that brings the flowers;
> I thought of one who loved me when
>     She had her idle hours.

Pensive I gaze on this old sheet
  Time-worn, dusty, wan;
The calendar of that brief year,
  When first our love began.

"No, no! my youth cannot be dead,
  For I remember yet;
And if outside your footsteps strayed,
  My heart would bound, Musette—
Musette, the faithless! why, again,
  It leaps up still, in truth.
Come back and share once more my fare—
  Bread, with the mirth of youth.

"Why, see; the very chairs, the same
  That loved your face so fair,
Only at mention of your name,
  Put on a brighter air.
Come back, my sweet, old friends to greet,
  In mourning for you still:
The old arm-chair, the great glass where
  Your lips have drunk their fill.

"The white dress that became you so,
  Put on, my eyes to please;
On Sundays, as we used to do,·
  We'll wander 'neath the trees.
And in the arbour, as of yore,
  We'll drink the white wine clear,
To bathe thy wing ere yet it spring
  In full song to the air.

    *     *     *     *     *     *

"Well; she remembered; yestermorn,
  When carnival was done,
To her old nest the bird was borne;
  Musette has come and gone.
My arms flew wide, but yet I sighed;
  My heart was so estranged.
It was Musette; 'twas I; but yet—
  We both were, somehow, changed."

Like most men brought up in the midst of great cities, Murger was passionately fond of the country. A few years before his death he found a little thatched cottage at Marlotte, that village in the Forest of Fontainebleau where the artists love to find subjects for their easels. Thither he went at the first breath of spring, trying to revive his youth among those quaint interminable alleys, all alike save for the play of the cross lights. Among those he used to wander, thinking, we may suppose, of his faded illusions, of the better fortunes of that imaginary Rodolphe, his own *umbra*. Perhaps in those latter days the black domino and soiled kid gloves were forgotten, put into a pocket. But at all times they represented that sort of gaiety which he could describe and *convey*, though he never seems to have felt it. For he was never a light-hearted man, never of bright and happy disposition: latterly, irritable, perhaps from the contrast between his conception of life and his execution; morose and sensitive to the highest degree. Something always jarred; he was never in tune with nature.

The great charge always thrown in his teeth is that he failed in his promise. This seems to me a short-sighted and imperfect way of putting it. He was a man who had the rare faculty of accurately describing. He told what he knew, not adding to the details of reality, but setting them off with the bright and happy touches of genius. He knew, unfortunately, only one kind of life. He described this perfectly, inimitably. As he knew nothing else, he went on describing it. But when he attempted to go beyond what he knew, as in 'Madame Olympe,' or the 'Victime de bonheur,' he appears to me to be vague, commonplace, and insipid. On the other hand, no one can read the stories of Francine, Hélène, Marianne, so full of sympathy and sorrow, without feeling that they are real stories, only put into shape by the artist. Because they are true, they are lifelike.

I cannot persuade myself that he has done much harm. None but a very youthful mind could be attracted by the life which he describes. His scenes are so full of misery and poverty; we see present always before us the yearning eyes with which the poor artists gaze upon the world of respectability and plenty. Their *amourettes* are so sad and so full of bitter results; their surroundings are all so mean and sordid. No one can be hurt by the story of Rodolphe. At the same time his books are absolutely, totally, incredibly devoid of moral sense or religious principle. I believe that Murger never had either. Perhaps his father, the *concierge*, was too busy looking after the lodgers to inculcate morals or religion. Perhaps the Voltairean De Jouy was too busy repeating the works of his master, which he perhaps still had by heart. His obvious fault, that on which everybody fixes, is, of course, his inability to see anything in life but youth. Youth means joy, health, love; if money goes with it, it means flowers, expeditions to Ville d'Avray and Asnières, with champagne. When youth goes there is nothing left. One might as well die at once as grow old. Life only has twenty years in it—between eighteen and thirty-eight. So, getting close to that turning point when, with men of his "persuasion," the years bring nothing but dust and ashes, he wrote those melancholy verses of his, of which the reader may take the following as a translation, for want of a better:—

"Whose steps are those? who comes so late?"
"Let me come in; the door unlock."
"'Tis midnight now; my lonely gate
I open to no stranger's knock.

" Who art thou?  Speak."  " Men call me Fame;
 To immortality I lead;"
" Pass, idle phantom of a name."
 " Listen again, and now take heed:

" 'Twas false.  My names are Love and Youth!
 Why, God himself is young and true."
" Pass by; the girl I thought all truth
 Has long since laughed her last adieu."

" Stay, stay; my names are Song and Art.
 My poet, now unbar the door."
" Love's dead.  Song cannot touch my heart,
 My girl's pet name I know no more."

" Open then now; for see, I stand,
 Riches my name—with gold—with gold—
Gold and your girl in either hand."
 " Too late; the past you still withhold."

" Then, if it must be, since the door
 Stands shut till first my name you know,
Men call me DEATH.  Delay no more;
 I bring the cure of every woe."

" 'Tis DEATH?  Ah! guest so pale and wan,
 Forgive the poor place where I dwell;
An ice-cold hearth, a broken man,
 Stand here a welcome thee to tell.

Welcome at last; take me away;
 Whither thou goest let me go;
Only permit my dog to stay,
 That e'en for me some tears may flow."

Lines very sickly and morbid, are they not?   But at the same time,
in one so *real* as Murger was, they no doubt expressed a mood which
more than once clouded his brain.   To show that he was not always
moaning over himself and his ruined aspirations, take the following,
which I have rendered as faithfully as is in my power:

" It was Saturday saying to Sunday,
 'The village is still and asleep;
By the clock it is twelve, and for one day
 Rouse up, your own watches to keep.
I am tired of my trouble and labour,
 I must rest for a week from my care;
Your hour is striking, my neighbour.'
 Quoth Sunday, 'My friend, I am here.'

" He awoke, and the night lay behind him,
 The night in its royal array:
The spangles of stars seemed to blind him;
 He rubbed his dull eyes as he lay.

He yawned as he dressed, like a mortal,
 ' And then, when his toilette was done,
He knocked at the dark Eastern portal,
 To wake up his comrade, the Sun.

" He climbed to the top of the mountain,
 He gazed on the village beneath ;
No sound but the drip of the fountain,
 ' 'Tis as still,' murmured Sunday, ' as death.'
He crept down the hillside, and going
 Pit-a-pat, to the village he came ;
To the cock whispered, ' Friend, by your crowing,
 Don't tell the good people my name.'

" But 'tis Sunday; 'tis Sunday; behold him,
 With the spring, with the sweet month of May ;
The almond, as if to enfold him,
 Hangs out a white robe on each spray.
Every flower its eyelid uncloses ;
 In the garden an Eden is born ;
The violets sing to the roses ;
 The proud oak unbends to the thorn.

" On the edge of his nest, just awaking,
 The thrush gives a welcome of song
To the swallows their homeward way taking
 From the south, where they've lingered so long.
In his plumage of spring, flying proudly,
 The goldfinch gleams bright in the trees,
So glad that he cannot too loudly
 Fling song after song to the breeze.

" He has come, he has come, and gift-laden ;
 His hands full of treasures for all ;
And a ribbon is here for the maiden,
 And here, for her sister, a doll.
There is nothing but singing and laughter ;
 Uncorking of bottles and flasks ;
And see, there is more yet ; for after
 There follow the music and masks.

" Oh ! rest for the peasants, and ease ;
 They may ask of each other, and tell—
' Thy father is better, Therese ?'
 ' And the little one, Robin, is well ?'—
' Fine weather for vines and for dressing '—
 ' The fairest of seasons and best.'
And to all Sunday comes with his blessing—
 Save only the piper—of rest."

The end to a life of many privations, much dissipation, and much disappointment, came very early. He had his ten years of a very fair success, and lived so much out of the world, that he hardly knew he was successful; he was *décoré* in 1860—a doubtful honour for one like him. He died in 1861, before completing his thirty-ninth year.

It was perhaps time, because youth was gone for him, and wealth had not come. His heart must have sunk when he reflected on the men who had succeeded and himself who had failed—on the sermon which he put into Marcel's mouth fourteen years before.

He had complained of languor and faintness for some time. The winter killed him. He died in a hospital after a fortnight's illness, his last moments of work being spent in revising his poems; Mimi the faithful, for Rodolphe had his Mimi who loved him, attended on him to the last. After passing all his life as a Voltairean and an infidel, he died *en bon chrétien*, with a priest at his bedside. All literary Paris attended his funeral, whither also, out of respect for their *sacer vates*, came the whole of the Pays Latin. The day was foggy and cloudy— a fitting time for the funeral of one whose life had been a long succession of rainy days. And then the critics wrote tearful notices of him —those bright and sympathetic notices which they do so well in France. If he had been an Englishman they would have had his life all written out ready for use, to be pulled down and printed, dry and hard, on the day after his death. His life, with all its embarrassments, disappointments, and miseries, may be taken as a bitter contrast to Marcel's sermon, which he wrote at six-and-twenty. Who would desire such a life? Is it not better to be " respectable," when respectability means comfort, ease, dignity, and a decent income?

He died, and we pity him. Why? Is it not because he lets us see his heart? He was a sympathetic man; so, because he can feel the struggles of others, we too feel for him. And then one fancies that the hand of fate was upon him. In his early lack of education, his isolation from the real world, his entranced absorption in the present, his exaggerated idea of the world of pleasure, we see so many snares and pitfalls, into all of which he tumbles and falls by turns. He should have been taken into that quiet domestic life in which poor France, so much decried in these evil days, is so rich. There he would have found peace and a wider world. But his guardian angel was asleep when he wanted help; so he blundered, naturally enough. What are they about—these guardian angels—that they let things turn out so badly?

## Poor Pretty Bobby.

### By RHODA BROUGHTON.

"YES, my dear, you may not believe me, but I can assure you that you cannot dislike old women more, nor think them more contemptible supernumeraries, than I did when I was your age."

This is what old Mrs. Wentworth says—the old lady so incredibly tenacious of life (incredibly as it seems to me at eighteen) as to have buried a husband and five strong sons, and yet still to eat her dinner with hearty relish, and laugh at any such jokes as are spoken loudly enough to reach her dulled ears. This is what she says, shaking the while her head, which—poor old soul—is already shaking a good deal involuntarily. I am sitting close beside her arm-chair, and have been reading aloud to her; but as I cannot succeed in pitching my voice so as to make her hear satisfactorily, by mutual consent the book has been dropped in my lap, and we have betaken ourselves to conversation.

"I never said I disliked old women, did I?" reply I evasively, being too truthful altogether to deny the soft impeachment. "What makes you think I do? They are infinitely preferable to old men; I do distinctly dislike *them*."

"A fat, bald, deaf old woman," continues she, not heeding me, and speaking with slow emphasis, while she raises one trembling hand to mark each unpleasant adjective; "if in the year '2 any one had told me that I should have lived to be that, I think I should have killed them or myself; and yet now I am all three."

"You are not *very* deaf," say I politely—(the fatness and baldness admit of no civilities consistent with veracity)—but I raise my voice to pay the compliment.

"In the year '2 I was seventeen," she says, wandering off into memory. "Yes, my dear, I am just fifteen years older than the century, and *it* is getting into its dotage, is not it? The year '2— ah! that was just about the time that I first saw my poor Bobby! Poor pretty Bobby."

"And who *was* Bobby?" ask I, pricking up my ears, and scenting, with the keen nose of youth, a dead-love idyll; an idyll of which this poor old hill of unsteady flesh was the heroine.

"I must have told you the tale a hundred times, have not I?" she asks, turning her old dim eyes towards me. "A curious tale, say what you will, and explain it how you will. I think I *must* have told you; but indeed I forget to whom I tell my old stories and to whom I do not. Well, my love, you must promise to stop me if you have heard it before, but to me, you know, these old things are so much clearer than the things of yesterday." ·

"You never told me, Mrs. Hamilton," I say, and say truthfully; for being a new acquaintance I really have not been made acquainted with Bobby's history. "Would you mind telling it me now, if you are sure that it would not bore you?"

"Bobby," she repeats softly to herself, "Bobby. I daresay you do not think it a very pretty name?"

"N—not particularly," reply I honestly. "To tell you the truth, it rather reminds me of a policeman."

"I daresay," she answers quietly; "and yet in the year '2 I grew to think it the handsomest, dearest name on earth. Well, if you like, I will begin at the beginning and tell you how that came about."

"Do," say I, drawing a stocking out of my pocket, and thriftily beginning to knit to assist me in the process of listening.

"In the year '2 we were at war with France—you know that, of course. It seemed then as if war were our normal state; I could hardly remember a time when Europe had been at peace. In these days of stagnant quiet it appears as if people's kith and kin always lived out their full time and died in their beds. *Then* there was hardly a house where there was not one dead, either in battle, or of his wounds after battle, or of some dysentery or ugly parching fever. As for us, we had always been a soldier family—always; there was not one of us that had ever worn a black gown or sat upon a high stool with a pen behind his ear. I had lost uncles and cousins by the half-dozen and dozen, but, for my part, I did not much mind, as I knew very little about them, and black was more becoming wear to a person with my bright colour than anything else."

At the mention of her bright colour I unintentionally lift my eyes from my knitting, and contemplate the yellow bagginess of the poor old cheek nearest me. Oh, Time! Time! what absurd and dirty turns you play us! What do you do with all our fair and goodly things when you have stolen them from us? In what far and hidden treasure-house do you store them?

"But I did care very much—very exceedingly—for my dear old father—not so old either—younger than my eldest boy was when he went; he would have been forty-two if he had lived three days longer. Well, well, child, you must not let me wander; you must keep me to it. He was not a soldier, was not my father; he was a sailor, a post-captain in his Majesty's navy, and commanded the ship *Thunderer* in the Channel fleet.

"I had struck seventeen in the year '2, as I said before, and had just come home from being finished at a boarding-school of repute in those days, where I had learnt to talk the prettiest *ancien régime* French and to hate Bonaparte with unchristian violence from a little ruined *émigré maréchale*; had also, with infinite expenditure of time, labour, and Berlin wool, wrought out 'Abraham's Sacrifice of Isaac and 'Jacob's First Kiss to Rachel,' in finest cross-stitch. Now I had bidden adieu to learning; had inly resolved never to disinter 'Télémaque' and Thompson's 'Seasons' from the bottom of my trunk; had taken a holiday from all my accomplishments, with the exception of cross-stitch, to which I still faithfully adhered—and indeed, on the day I am going to mention, I recollect that I was hard at work on Judas Iscariot's face in Leonardo da Vinci's 'Last Supper'—hard at work at it, sitting in the morning sunshine, on a straight-backed chair. We had flatter backs in those days; our shoulders were not made round by lolling in easy chairs; indeed, no *then* upholsterer made a chair that it was possible to loll in. My father rented a house near Plymouth at that time, an in-and-out *nooky* kind of old house—no doubt it has fallen to pieces long years ago—a house all set round with unnumbered flowers, and about which the rooks clamoured all together from the windy elm tops. I was labouring in flesh-coloured wool on Judas's left cheek, when the door opened and my mother entered. She looked as if something had freshly pleased her, and her eyes were smiling. In her hand she held an open and evidently just-read letter.

" 'A messenger has come from Plymouth,' she says, advancing quickly and joyfully towards me. "Your father will be here this afternoon.'

" '*This afternoon!*' cry I, at the top of my voice, pushing away my heavy work-frame. 'How delightful! But how?—how can that happen?'

" 'They have had a brush with a French privateer,' she answers, sitting down on another straight-backed chair, and looking again over the large square letter, destitute of envelope, for such things were not in those days, "and then they succeeded in taking her. Yet they were a good deal knocked about in the process, and have had to put into Plymouth to refit, so he will be here this afternoon for a few hours."

" 'Hurrah!' cry I, rising, holding out my scanty skirts, and beginning to dance.

" 'Bobby Gerard is coming with him,' continues my mother, again glancing at her despatch. 'Poor boy, he has had a shot through his right arm, which has broken the bone, so your father is bringing him here for us to nurse him well again.'

I stop in my dancing.

" 'Hurrah again!' I say brutally. 'I do not mean about his arm; of course I am very sorry for that; but at all events, I shall see him at last. I shall see whether he is like his picture, and whether it is not as egregiously flattered as I have always suspected.'

"There were no photographs you know in those days—not even

hazy daguerreotypes—it was fifty good years too soon for them. The picture to which I allude is a miniature, at which I had stolen many a deeply longingly admiring glance in its velvet case. It is almost impossible for a miniature not to flatter. To the most coarse-skinned and mealy-potato-faced people it cannot help giving cheeks of the texture of a rose-leaf and brows of the grain of finest marble.

" 'Yes,' replies my mother, absently, ' so you will. Well, I must be going to give orders about his room. He would like one looking on the garden best, do not you think, Phœbe ?—one where he could smell the flowers and hear the birds ?'

" Mother goes, and I fall into a meditation. Bobby Gerard is an orphan. A few years ago his mother, who was an old friend of my father's—who knows ? perhaps an old love—feeling her end drawing nigh, had sent for father, and had asked him, with eager dying tears, to take as much care of her pretty forlorn boy as he could, and to shield him a little in his tender years from the evils of this wicked world, and to be to him a wise and kindly guardian, in the place of those natural ones that God had taken. And father had promised, and when he promised there was small fear of his not keeping his word.

" This was some years ago, and yet I had never seen him nor he me ; he had been almost always at sea and I at school. I had heard plenty about him—about his sayings, his waggeries, his mis-chievousness, his soft-heartedness, and his great and unusual comeliness ; but his outward man, save as represented in that stealthily peeped-at miniature, had I never seen. They were to arrive in the afternoon ; but long before the hour at which they were due I was waiting with expectant impatience to receive them. I had changed my dress, and had (though rather ashamed of myself) put on everything of most becoming that my wardrobe afforded. If you were to see me as I stood before the glass on that summer afternoon you would not be able to contain your laughter ; the little boys in the street would run after me throwing stones and hooting ; but *then*—according to the *then* fashion and standard of gentility—I was all that was most elegant and *comme il faut*. Lately it has been the mode to puff oneself out with unnatural and improbable protuberances ; *then* one's great life-object was to make oneself appear as scrimping as possible—to make oneself look as flat as if one had been ironed. Many people *damped* their clothes to make them stick more closely to them, and to make them define more distinctly the outline of form and limbs. One's waist was under one's arms ; the sole object of which seemed to be to outrage nature by pushing one's bust up into one's chin, and one's legs were revealed through one's scanty drapery with startling can-dour as one walked or sat. I remember once standing with my back to a bright fire in our long drawing-room, and seeing myself reflected in a big mirror at the other end. I was so thinly clad that I was transparent, and could see through myself. Well, in the afternoon in question I was dressed quite an hour and a half too soon. I had a narrow little white gown, which clung successfully tight and close to my figure, and which was of so moderate a length as to leave visible my ankles, and my neatly-shod and cross-sandaled feet. I had long mittens on my arms, black, and embroidered on the backs in coloured silks; and above my hair, which at the back was scratched up to the top of my crown, towered a tremendous tortoise-shell comb; while on each side of my face modestly drooped a bunch of curls, nearly meeting over my nose.

"My figure was full—ah! my dear, I have always had a tendency to fat, and you see what it has come to—and my pink cheeks were more deeply brightly rosy than usual. I had looked out at every upper window, so as to have the furthest possible view of the road.

"I had walked in my thin shoes half way down the drive, so as to command a turn, which, from the house, impeded my vision, when, at last, after many tantalising false alarms, and just five minutes later than the time mentioned in the letter, the high-swung, yellow-bodied, post-chaise hove in sight, dragged—briskly jingling—along by a pair of galloping horses. Then, suddenly, shyness overcame me—much as I loved my father, it was more as my personification of all knightly and noble qualities than from much personal acquaintance with him—and I fled.

"I remained in my room until I thought I had given them ample time to get through the first greetings and settle down into quiet talk. Then, having for one last time run my fingers through each ringlet of my two curl bunches, I stole diffidently downstairs.

"There was a noise of loud and gay voices issuing from the parlour, but, as I entered, they all stopped talking and turned to look at me.

"'And so this is Phœbe!' cries my father's jovial voice, as he comes towards me, and heartily kisses me. 'Good Lord, how time flies! It does not seem more than three months since I saw the child, and yet then she was a bit of a brat in trousers, and long bare legs!'

"At this allusion to my late mode of attire, I laugh, but I also feel myself growing scarlet.

"'Here, Bobby!' continues my father, taking me by the hand, and leading me towards a sofa on which a young man is sitting beside my mother; 'this is my little lass that you have so often heard of. Not such a very little one, after all, is she? Do not be shy, my boy; you will not see such a pretty girl every day of your life—give her a kiss.'

"My eyes are on the ground, but I am aware that the young man rises, advances (not unwillingly, as it seems to me), and bestows a kiss, somewhere or other on my face. I am not quite clear *where*, as I think the curls impede him a good deal.

VOL. XXXVII.

"Thus, before ever I saw Bobby, before ever I knew what manner of man he was, I was kissed by him. That was a good beginning, was not it?

"After these salutations are over, we subside again into conversation—I sitting beside my father, with his arm round my waist, sitting modestly silent, and peeping every now and then under my eyes, as often as I think I may do so safely unobserved, at the young fellow opposite me. I am instituting an inward comparison between Nature and Art: between the real live man and the miniature that undertakes to represent him. The first result of this inspection is disappointment, for where are the lovely smooth roses and lilies that I have been wont to connect with Bobby Gerard's name? There are no roses in his cheek, certainly; they are paleish—from his wound, as I conjecture; but even before that accident, if there were roses at all, they must have been mahogany-coloured ones, for the salt sea winds and the high summer sun have tanned his fair face to a rich reddish, brownish, copperish hue. But in some things the picture lied not. There is the brow more broad than high; the straight fine nose; the brave and joyful blue eyes, and the mouth with its pretty curling smile. On the whole, perhaps, I am not disappointed.

"By-and-by father rises, and steps out into the verandah, where the canary birds hung out in their cages are noisily praising God after their manner. Mother follows him. I should like to do the same; but a sense of good manners, and a conjecture that possibly my parents may have some subjects to discuss, on which they would prefer to be without the help of my advice, restrain me. I therefore remain, and so does the invalid.

## CHAPTER II.

"FOR some moments the silence threatens to remain unbroken between us; for some moments the subdued sound of father's and mother's talk from among the rosebeds and the piercing clamour of the canaries—fishwives among birds—are the only noises that salute our ears. Noise we make none, ourselves. My eyes are reading the muddled pattern of the Turkey carpet; I do not know what his are doing. Small knowledge have I had of men save the dancing-master at our school; a beautiful new youth is almost as great a novelty to me as to Miranda, and I am a good deal gawkier than she was under the new experience. I think he must have made a vow that he would not speak first. I feel myself swelling to double my normal size with confusion and heat; at last, in desperation, I look up, and say sententiously, 'You have been wounded, I believe?'

"'Yes, I have.'"

"He might have helped me by answering more at large, might not he? But now that I am having a good look at him, I see that he is rather red too. Perhaps he also feels gawky and swollen; the idea encourages me.

"'Did it hurt very badly?'

"'N—not so very much.'

"'I should have thought that you ought to have been in bed,' say I, with a motherly air of solicitude.

"'Should you, why?'

"'I thought that when people broke their limbs they had to stay in bed till they were mended again.'

"'But mine was broken a week ago,' he answers, smiling and showing his straight white teeth—ah, the miniature was silent about *them!* 'You would not have had me stay in bed a whole week like an old woman?'

"'I expected to have seen you much *iller*,' say I, beginning to feel more at my ease, and with a sensible diminution of that unpleasant swelling sensation. 'Father said in his note that we were to nurse you well again; that sounded as if you were *quite* ill.'

"'Your father always takes a great deal too much care of me,' he says, with a slight frown and darkening of his whole bright face. 'I might be sugar or salt.'

"'And very kind of him, too,' I cry, firing up. "What motive beside your own good can he have for looking after you? I call you rather ungrateful.'

"'Do you?' he says calmly, and without apparent resentment. 'But you are mistaken. I am not ungrateful. However, naturally, you do not understand.'

"'Oh, indeed!' reply I, speaking rather shortly, and feeling a little offended, 'I dare say not.'

"Our talk is taking a somewhat hostile tone; to what further amenities we might have proceeded is unknown; for at this point father and mother reappear through the window, and the necessity of conversing with each other at all ceases.

"Father staid till evening, and we all supped together, and I was called upon to sit by Bobby, and cut up his food for him, as he was disabled from doing it for himself. Then, later still, when the sun had set, and all his evening reds and purples had followed him, when the night flowers were scenting all the garden, and the shadows lay about, enormously long in the summer moonlight, father got into the post-chaise again, and drove away through the black shadows and the faint clear shine, and Bobby stood at the hall door watching him, with his arm in a sling and a wistful smile on lips and eyes.

"'Well, we are not left *quite* desolate this time,' says mother, turning with rather tearful laughter to the young man. 'You wish that we were, do not you, Bobby?'

" ' You would not believe me, if I answered 'No,' would you?' he asks, with the same still smile.

" ' He is not very polite to us, is he Phœbe?'

" ' You would not wish me to be polite in such a case," he replies, flushing. " You would not wish me to be *glad* at missing the chance of seeing any of the fun?'

"But Mr. Gerard's eagerness to be back at his post delays the probability of his being able to return thither. The next day he has a feverish attack, the day after he is worse; the day after that worse still, and in fine, it is between a fortnight and three weeks before he also is able to get into a post-chaise and drive away to Plymouth. And meanwhile mother and I nurse him and cosset him, and make him odd and cool drinks out of herbs and field-flowers, whose uses are now disdained or forgotten. I do not mean any offence to you, my dear, but I think that young girls in those days were less squeamish and more truly delicate than they are nowadays. I remember once I read 'Humphrey Clinker' aloud to my father, and we both highly relished and laughed over its jokes; but I should not have understood one of the darkly unclean allusions in that French book your brother left here one day. *You* would think it very unseemly to enter the bedroom of a strange young man, sick or well; but as for me, I spent whole nights in Bobby's, watching him and tending him with as little false shame as if he had been my brother. I can hear *now*, more plainly than the song you sang me an hour ago, the slumberous buzzing of the great brown-coated summer bees in his still room, as I sat by his bedside watching his sleeping face, as he dreamt unquietly, and clenched, and again unclenched, his nervous hands. I think he was back in the *Thunderer.* I can see *now* the little close curls of his sunshiny hair straggling over the white pillow. And then there came a good and blessed day, when he was out of danger, and then another, a little further on, when he was up and dressed, and he and I walked forth into the hayfield beyond the garden—reversing the order of things—*he*, leaning on *my* arm; and a good plump solid arm it was. We walked out under the heavy-leaved horse-chestnut trees, and the old and roughed-barked elms. The sun was shining all this time, as it seems to me. I do not believe that in those old days there were the same cold unseasonable rains as now; there were soft showers enough to keep the grass green and the flowers undrooped; but I have no association of overcast skies and untimely deluges with those long and azure days. We sat under a haycock, on the shady side, and indolently watched the hot haymakers—the shirt-sleeved men, and burnt and bare-armed women, tossing and raking; while we breathed the blessed country air, full of adorable scents, and crowded with little happy and pretty-winged insects.

"'In three days,' says Bobby, leaning his elbow in the hay, and speaking with an eager smile, 'three days at the furthest, I may go back again; may not I, Phœbe?'

"'Without doubt,' reply I, stiffly, pulling a dry and faded ox-eye flower out of the odorous mound beside me; 'for my part, I do not see why you should not go to-morrow, or indeed—if we could send into Plymouth for a chaise—this afternoon; you are so thin that you look all mouth and eyes, and you can hardly stand, without assistance, but these, of course, are trifling drawbacks, and I daresay would be rather an advantage on board ship than otherwise.'

"'You are angry!' he says, with a sort of laugh in his deep eyes. 'You look even prettier when you are angry than when you are pleased.'

"'It is no question of my looks,' I say, still in some heat, though mollified by the irrelevant compliment.

"'For the second time you are thinking me ungrateful,' he says, gravely; 'you do not tell me so in so many words, because it is towards yourself that my ingratitude is shown; the first time you told me of it it was almost the first thing that you ever said to me.'

"'So it was,' I answer quickly; 'and if the occasion were to come over again, I should say it again. I daresay you did not mean it, but it sounded exactly as if you were complaining of my father for being too careful of you.'

"'He *is* too careful of me!' cries the young man, with a hot flushing of cheek and brow. "I cannot help it if it make you angry again; I *must* say it, he is more careful of me than he would be of his own son, if he had one.'

"'Did not he promise your mother that he would look after you?' ask I, eagerly. 'When people make promises to people on their death-beds they are in no hurry to break them; at least, such people as father are not.'

"'You do not understand,' he says, a little impatiently, while that hot flush still dwells on his pale cheek; "my mother was the last person in the world to wish him to take care of my body at the expense of my honour.'

"'What are you talking about?' I say, looking at him with a lurking suspicion that, despite the steady light of reason in his blue eyes, he is still labouring under some form of delirium.

"'Unless I tell you all my grievance, I see that you will never comprehend,' he says sighing. 'Well, listen to me and you shall hear it, and if you do not agree with me, when I have done, you are not the kind of girl I take you for.'

"'Then I am sure I am not the kind of girl you take me for,' reply I, with a laugh; 'for I am fully determined to disagree with you entirely.'

"'You know,' he says, raising himself a little from his hay couch

and speaking with clear rapidity, 'that whenever we take a French
prize a lot of the French sailors are ironed, and the vessel is sent into
port, in the charge of one officer and several men; there is some slight
risk attending it—for my part, I think *very* slight—but I suppose
that your father looks at it differently, for—*I have never been sent.*'

"'It is accident,' say I, reassuringly; 'your turn will come in good
time.'

"'It is *not* accident!' he answers, firmly. 'Boys younger than I
am—much less trustworthy, and of whom he has not half the opinion
that he has of me—have been sent, but *I, never.*  I bore it as well as
I could for a long time, but now I can bear it no longer; it is not,
I assure you, my fancy; but I can see that my brother officers, knowing how partial your father is to me—what influence I have with him
in many things—conclude that my not being sent is my own choice;
in short, that I am—*afraid.*'  (His voice sinks with a disgusted and
shamed intonation at the last word).  'Now—I have told you the sober
facts—look me in the face,' putting his hand with boyish familiarity
under my chin, and turning round my curls, my features, and the
front view of my big comb towards him,) 'and tell me whether you
agree with me, as I said you would, or not—whether it is not cruel
kindness on his part to make me keep a whole skin on such terms?'

"I look him in the face for a moment, trying to say that I do not
agree with him, but it is more than I can manage.  'You were right,'
I say, turning my head away, 'I *do* agree with you; I wish to heaven
that I could honestly say that I did not.'

"'Since you do then,' he cries excitedly—'Phœbe! I knew you
would, I knew you better than you knew yourself—I have a favour to
ask of you, a *great* favour, and one that will keep me all my life in
debt to you.'

"'What is it?' ask I, with a sinking heart.

"'Your father is very fond of you'——

"'I know it,' I answer curtly.

"'Anything that you asked, and that was within the bounds of possibility, he would do,' he continues, with eager gravity.  'Well, this
is what I ask of you: to write him a line, and let me take it, when I
go, asking him to send me home in the next prize.'

"Silence for a moment, only the haymakers laughing over their
rakes.  'And if,' say I, with a trembling voice, 'you lose your life
in this service, you will have to thank me for it; I shall have your
death on my head all through my life.'

"'The danger is infinitesimal, as I told you before,' he says, impatiently; 'and even if it were greater than it is—well, life is a good
thing, very good, but there are better things, and even if I come to
grief, which is most unlikely, there are plenty of men as good as,
better than I, to step into my place.'

" ' It will be small consolation to the people who are fond of you that someone better than you is alive, though you are dead,' I say, tear-fully.

" ' But I do not mean to be dead,' he says, with a cheery laugh. ' Why are you so determined on killing me? I mean to live to be an admiral. Why should not I?'

" ' Why indeed?' say I, with a feeble echo of his cheerful mirth, and feeling rather ashamed of my tears.

" ' And meanwhile you will write?' he says, with an eager return to the charge; ' and *soon?* Do not look angry and pouting, as you did just now, but I *must* go! What is there to hinder me? I am getting up my strength as fast as it is possible for any human creature to do, and just think how I should feel if they were to come in for something really good while I am away.'

So I wrote.

## CHAPTER III.

" I OFTEN wished afterwards that my right hand had been cut off before its fingers had held the pen that wrote that letter. You wonder to see me moved at what happened so long ago—before your parents were born—and certainly it makes not much difference now; for even if he had prospered then, and come happily home to me, yet, in the course of nature he would have gone long before now. I should not have been so cruel as to have wished him to have lasted to be as I am. I did not mean to hint at the end of my story before I have reached the middle. Well—and so he went, with the letter in his pocket, and I felt something like the king in the tale, who sent a messenger with a letter, and wrote in the letter, ' Slay the bearer of this as soon as he arrives!' But before he went—the evening before, as we walked in the garden after supper, with our monstrously long shadows stretching before us in the moonlight—I do not think he said in so many words, ' Will you marry me?' but somehow, by some signs or words on both our parts, it became clear to us that, by-and-by, if God left him alive, and if the war ever came to an end, he and I should belong to one another. And so, having understood this, when he went he kissed me, as he had done when he came, only this time no one bade him; he did it of his own accord, and a hundred times instead of one; and for my part, this time, instead of standing passive like a log or a post, I kissed him back again, most lovingly, with many tears.

" Ah! parting in those days, when the last kiss to one's beloved ones was not unlikely to be an adieu until the great Day of Judgment, was a different thing to the listless, unemotional good-byes of these stag-nant times of peace!

" And so Bobby also got into a post-chaise and drove away; and we watched him too, till he turned the corner out of our sight, as we had watched father; and then I hid my face among the jessamine flowers that clothed the wall of the house, and wept as one that would not be comforted. However, one cannot weep for ever, or, if one does, it makes one blind and blear, and I did not wish Bobby to have a wife with such defects; so in process of time I dried my tears.

"And the days passed by, and nature went slowly and evenly through her lovely changes. The hay was gathered in, and the fine new grass and clover sprang up among the stalks of the grass that had gone; and the wild roses struggled into odorous bloom, and crowned the hedges, and then *their* time came, and they shook down their faint petals, and went.

"And now the corn harvest had come, and we had heard once or twice from our beloveds, but not often. And the sun still shone with broad power, and kept the rain in subjection. And all morning I sat at my big frame, and toiled on at the 'Last Supper.' I had finished Judas Iscariot's face and the other Apostles. I was engaged now upon the table-cloth, which was not interesting and required not much exercise of thought. And mother sat near me, either working too or reading a good book, and taking snuff—every lady snuffed in those days: at least in trifles, if not in great things, the world mends. And at night, when ten o'clock struck, I covered up my frame and stole listlessly upstairs to my room. There, I knelt at the open window, facing Plymouth and the sea, and asked God to take good care of father and Bobby. I do not know that I asked for any spiritual blessings for them, I only begged that they might be alive.

"One night, one hot night, having prayed even more heartily and tearfully than my wont for them both, I had lain down to sleep. The windows were left open, and the blinds up, that all possible air might reach me from the still and scented garden below. Thinking of Bobby, I had fallen asleep, and he is still mistily in my head, when I seem to wake. The room is full of clear light, but it is not morning: it is only the moon looking right in and flooding every object. I can see my own ghostly figure sitting up in bed, reflected in the looking-glass opposite. I listen: surely I heard some noise: yes—certainly, there can be no doubt of it—someone is knocking loudly and per-severingly at the hall-door. At first I fall into a deadly fear; then my reason comes to my aid. If it were a robber, or person with any evil intent, would he knock so openly and clamorously as to arouse the inmates? Would not he rather go stealthily to work, to force a *silent* entrance for himself? At worst it is some drunken sailor from Plymouth; at best, it is a messenger with news of our dear ones. At this thought I instantly spring out of bed, and hurrying on my stock-ings and shoes, and whatever garments come most quickly to hand—with my hair spread all over my back, and utterly forgetful of my big comb, I open my door, and fly down the passages, into which the moon is looking with her ghostly smile, and down the broad and shallow stairs.

"As I near the hall door I meet our old butler, also rather dishevelled, and evidently on the same errand as myself.

"'Who *can* it be, Stephens?' I ask, trembling with excitement and fear.

"'Indeed, ma'am, I cannot tell you,' replies the old man, shaking his head, 'it is a very odd time of night to choose for making such a noise. We will ask them their business, whoever they are, before we unchain the door.'

"It seems to me as if the endless bolts would never be drawn—the key never be turned in the stiff lock; but at last the door opens slowly and cautiously, only to the width of a few inches, as it is still confined by the strong chain. I peep out eagerly, expecting I know not what.

"Good heavens! What do I see? No drunken sailor, no messenger, but, oh joy! oh blessedness! my Bobby himself—my beautiful boy-lover! Even *now*, even after all these weary years, even after the long bitterness that followed, I cannot forget the unutterable happiness of that moment.

"'Open the door, Stephens, quick!' I cry, stammering with eagerness. 'Draw the chain; it is Mr. Gerard; do not keep him waiting.'

"The chain rattles down, the door opens wide, and there he stands before me. At once, ere any one has said anything, ere anything has happened, a feeling of cold disappointment steals unaccountably over me—a nameless sensation, whose nearest kin is chilly awe. He makes no movement towards me; he does not catch me in his arms, nor even hold out his right hand to me. He stands there, still and silent, and though the night is dry, equally free from rain and dew, I see that he is dripping wet; the water is running down from his clothes, from his drenched hair, and even from his eyelashes, on to the dry ground at his feet.

"'What has happened?' I cry hurriedly. 'How wet you are!' and as I speak I stretch out my hand and lay it on his coat sleeve. But even as I do it a sensation of intense cold runs up my fingers and my arm, even to the elbow. How is it that he is so chilled to the marrow of his bones on this sultry, breathless, August night? To my extreme surprise, he does not answer; he still stands there, dumb and dripping. 'Where have you come from?' I ask, with that sense of awe deepening. 'Have you fallen into the river? How is it that you are so wet?'

"'It was cold,' he says, shivering, and speaking in a slow and strangely altered voice, 'bitter cold. I could not stay there.'

"'Stay where?' I say, looking in amazement at his face, which, whether owing to the ghastly effect of moonlight or not, seems to me ash white. 'Where have you been? What is it you are talking about?'

"But he does not reply.

"'He is really ill, I am afraid, Stephens,' I say, turning with a forlorn feeling towards the old butler. 'He does not seem to hear what I say to him. I am afraid he has had a thorough chill. What water can he have fallen into? You had better help him up to bed, and get him warm between the blankets. His room is quite ready for him, you know—come in,' I say, stretching out my hand to him, 'you will be better after a night's rest.'

"He does not take my offered hand, but he follows me across the threshold and across the hall. I hear the water drops falling drip, drip, on the echoing stone floor as he passes; then upstairs, and along the gallery to the door of his room, where I leave him with Stephens. Then everything becomes blank and nil to me.

"I am awoke as usual in the morning by the entrance of my maid with hot water.

"'Well, how is Mr. Gerard this morning?' I ask, springing into a sitting posture.

"She puts down the hot water tin and stares at her leisure at me.

"'My dear Miss Phœbe, how should *I* know? Please God he is in good health and safe, and that we shall have good news of him before long.'

"'Have not you asked how he is?' I ask impatiently. 'He did not seem quite himself last night; there was something odd about him. I was afraid he was in for another touch of fever.'

"'Last night—fever,' repeats she, slowly and disconnectedly echoing some of my words. 'I beg your pardon, ma'am, I am sure, but I have not the least idea in life what you are talking about.'

"'How stupid you are!' I say, quite at the end of my patience. 'Did not Mr. Gerard come back unexpectedly last night, and did not I hear him knocking, and run down to open the door, and did not Stephens come too, and afterwards take him up to bed?'

"The stare of bewilderment gives way to a laugh.

"'You have been dreaming, ma'am. Of course I cannot answer for what you did last night, but I am sure that Stephens knows no more of the young gentleman than I do, for only just now, at breakfast, he was saying that he thought it was about time for us to have some tidings of him and master.'

"'A dream!' cry I indignantly. 'Impossible! I was no more dreaming then than I am now.'

"But time convinces me that I am mistaken, and that during all the time that I thought I was standing at the open hall-door, talking to my beloved, in reality I was lying on my bed in the depths of sleep,

with no other company than the scent of the flowers and the light of
the moon.   At this discovery a great and terrible depression falls on
me.   I go to my mother to tell her of my vision, and at the end of
my narrative I say,

"'Mother, I know well that Bobby is dead, and that I shall never
see him any more.   I feel assured that he died last night, and that he
came himself to tell me of his going.   I am sure that there is nothing
left for me now but to go too.'

"I speak thus far with great calmness, but when I have done I break
out into loud and violent weeping.   Mother rebukes me gently, telling
me that there is nothing more natural than that I should dream of a
person who constantly occupies my waking thoughts, nor that, considering the gloomy nature of my apprehensions about him, my dream
should be of a sad and ominous kind; but that, above all dreams and
omens, God is good, that He has preserved him hitherto, and that, for
her part, no devil-sent apparition shall shake her confidence in His
continued clemency.   I go away a little comforted, though not very
much, and still every night I kneel at the open window facing
Plymouth and the sea, and pray for my sailor boy.   But it seems to me,
despite all my self-reasonings, despite all that mother says, that my
prayers for him are prayers for the dead.

## Chapter IV.

"Three more weeks pass away; the harvest is garnered, and the pears
are growing soft and mellow.   Mother's and my outward life goes on
in its silent regularity, nor do we talk much to each other of the
tumult that rages—of the heartache that burns, within each of us.
At the end of the three weeks, as we are sitting as usual, quietly
employed, and buried each in our own thoughts, in the parlour,
towards evening we hear wheels approaching the hall door.   We
both run out as in my dream I had run to the door, and arrive in
time to receive my father as he steps out of the carriage that has
brought him.   Well! at least *one* of our wanderers has come home,
but where is the other?

"Almost before he has heartily kissed us both—wife and child—
father cries out, 'But where is Bobby?'

"'That is just what I was going to ask you,' replies mother
quickly.

"'Is not he *here* with you?' returns he anxiously.

"'Not he," answers mother, 'we have neither seen nor heard anything of him for more than six weeks.'

"'Great God!' exclaims he, while his face assumes an expression of
the deepest concern, 'what *can* have become of him? what *can* have
happened to the poor fellow?'

" ' Has not he been with you, then?—has not he been in the *Thunderer ?*' asks mother, running her words into one another in her eagerness to get them out.

" ' I sent him home three weeks ago in a prize, with a letter to you, and told him to stay with you till I came home, and what can have become of him since, God only knows!' he answers with a look of the profoundest sorrow and anxiety.

" There is a moment of forlorn and dreary silence; then I speak. I have been standing dumbly by, listening, and my heart growing colder and colder at every dismal word.

" ' It is all my doing!' I cry passionately, flinging myself down in an agony of tears on the straight-backed old settle in the hall. ' It is my fault—no one else's! The very last time that I saw him, I told him that he would have to thank me for his death, and he laughed at me, but it has come true. If I had not written *you*, father, that accursed letter, we should have had him here *now*, this *minute*, safe and sound, standing in the middle of us—as we never, *never*, shall have him again!'

" I stop, literally suffocated with emotion.

" Father comes over, and lays his kind brown hand on my bent prone head. ' My child,' he says, ' my dear child,' (and tears are dimming the clear grey of his own eyes), " you are wrong to make up your mind to what is the worst at once. I do not disguise from you that there is cause for grave anxiety about the dear fellow, but still God is good; He has kept both him and me hitherto; into His hands we must trust our boy.'

" I sit up, and shake away my tears.

" ' It is no use,' I say. ' Why should I hope? There is no hope! I know it for a certainty! He is *dead*' (looking round at them both with a sort of calmness); ' he died on the night that I had that dream—mother, I told you so at the time. Oh, my Bobby! I knew that you could not leave me for ever without coming to tell me!'

" And so speaking, I fall into strong hysterics and am carried up-stairs to bed. And so three or four more lagging days crawl by, and still we hear nothing, and remain in the same state of doubt and un-certainty, which to me, however, is hardly uncertainty; so convinced am I, in my own mind, that my fair-haired lover is away in the land whence never letter or messenger comes—that he has reached the Great Silence. So I sit at my frame, working my heart's agony into the tapestry, and feebly trying to say to God that he has done well, but I cannot. On the contrary, it seems to me, as my life trails on through the mellow mist of the autumn mornings, through the shortened autumn evenings, that, whoever has done it, it is most evilly done. One night we are sitting round the little crackling wood fire that one does not yet need for warmth, but that gives a cheerfulness to the room and the furniture, when the butler Stephens enters, and going over to father, whispers to him. I seem to understand in a moment what the purport of his whisper is.

" ' Why does he whisper ?' I cry, irritably. 'Why does not he speak out loud ? Why should you try to keep it from me ? I know that it is something about Bobby.'

" Father has already risen, and is walking towards the door.

" ' I will not let you go until you tell me,' I cry wildly, flying after him.

" ' A sailor has come over from Plymouth,' he answers hurriedly ; ' he says he has news. My darling, I will not keep you in suspense a moment longer than I can help, and meanwhile pray—both of you pray for him !'

" I sit rigidly still, with my cold hand tightly clasped, during the moments that next elapse. Then father returns. His eyes are full of tears, and there is small need to ask for his message ; it is most plainly written on his features—death, and not life.

" ' You were right, Phœbe,' he says, brokenly, taking hold of my icy hands ; ' you knew best. He is gone ! God has taken him !'

" My heart dies. I had thought that I had no hope, but I was wrong. " I knew it !" I say, in a dry stiff voice. ' Did not I tell you so ? But you would not believe me—go on !—tell me how it was—do not think I cannot bear it—make haste !'

" And so he tells me all that there is now left for me to know—after what manner, and on what day, my darling took his leave of this pretty and cruel world. He had had his wish, as I already knew, and had set off blithely home in the last prize they had captured. Father had taken the precaution of having a larger proportion than usual of the Frenchmen ironed, and had also sent a greater number of Englishmen. But to what purpose ? They were nearing port, sailing prosperously along on a smooth blue sea, with a fair strong wind, thinking of no evil, when a great and terrible misfortune overtook them. Some of the Frenchmen who were not ironed got the sailors below and drugged their grog ; ironed them, and freed their countrymen. Then one of the officers rushed on deck, and holding a pistol to my Bobby's head bade him surrender the vessel or die. Need I tell you which he chose ? I think not—well " (with a sigh) " and so they shot my boy —ah me ! how many years ago—and threw him overboard ! Yes— threw him overboard—it makes me angry and grieved even now to think of it—into the great and greedy sea, and the vessel escaped to France."

There is a silence between us : I will own to you that I am crying, but the old lady's eyes are dry.

" Well," she says, after a pause, with a sort of triumph in her tone, " they never could say again that Bobby Gerard was *afraid!*

"The tears were running down my father's cheeks, as he told me," she resumes presently, "but at the end he wiped them and said, 'It is well! He was as pleasant in God's sight as he was in ours, and so He has taken him.'

"And for me, I was glad that he had gone to God—none gladder. But you will not wonder that, for myself, I was past speaking sorry. And so the years went by, and, as you know, I married Mr. Hamilton, and lived with him forty years, and was happy in the main, as happiness goes; and when he died I wept much and long, and so I did for each of my sons when in turn they went. But looking back on all my long life, the event that I think stands out most clearly from it is my dream and my boy-lover's death-day. It *was* an odd dream, was not it ?"

## Quacks of the Eighteenth Century.

THE quacks of the present day are sufficiently numerous, and meet with enough success to cause astonishment to every thinking person ; but, compared with their predecessors of the eighteenth century, they pale into insignificance. It may not be uninteresting to the reader to have brought before him a few of the men who traded upon the credulity of our forefathers in the days of Anne and the three Georges, the days of Addison, Pope, and Johnson. When we consider their numbers, their ignorance, and the impudence of their pretensions, we find it almost impossible to understand the success they met with, and the way they were spoken of and patronised by the highest in the land. Cobblers, tinkers, footmen, and tailors (some not able to read their own advertisements), assumed the title of doctor, and pretended to be able to cure every known disease. They advertised particulars of their wonderful cures, and by the use of scraps of Latin or doggerel rhymes, or by claiming to be " seventh son of a seventh son," or an " unborn doctor," secured the patronage of the lower orders. They put forward the most extraordinary assertions, as inducements for the public to confide in their medical ability. One asserted that " he had arrived at the knowledge of the green and red dragon, and had discovered the female fern seed ;" another stated that " he had studied thirty years by candle-light for the good of his countrymen ;" whilst a third, by heading his bills with the word

" TETRACHYMAGOGON,"

ensured their being read by crowds of people, of whom the majority when sick would go to no other but this learned man. The poverty and ignorance of the lower classes may explain the success these quacks met with amongst them ; but what are we to think when we find them patronised by the nobility, and even called in to the aid of suffering royalty ?—when we find them receiving titles from an English sovereign and being honoured with the thanks of the House of Commons ?

The strange fact that these quacks found so many people to trust in them is well considered by Dr. Pearce, Bishop of Rochester, in No. 572 of the *Spectator :* " The desire of life is so natural and strong a passion that I have long since ceased to wonder at the great encouragement which the practice of medicine finds among us. Those who have little or no faith in the abilities of a quack will apply themselves to him, either because he is willing to sell health at a reasonable profit or because the patient, like a drowning man, catches at every twig, and hopes for relief from the most ignorant, when the most able physicians give him none.    Though impudence and many words are as necessary to these itinerary Galens as a laced hat to a merry-andrew, yet they would turn very little to the advantage of the owner if there were not some inward disposition in the sick man to favour the pretensions of the mountebank.    Love of life in the one and of money in the other creates a good correspondence between them."

One of the most pertinacious advertisers in the early part of the century was Sir William Read.    Originally a tailor, he became oculist to Queen Anne and afterwards to George the First.    From Queen Anne he received the honour of knighthood.    Though so ignorant that he could hardly read, yet, by an unusual amount of impudence and by the use of a few scraps of Latin in his advertisements, he obtained a great reputation for learning, and such an amount of patronage as enabled him to ride in his own chariot.    When travelling in the provinces he practised (" by the light of nature ") not only in small towns and villages, where the ignorance of the inhabitants might be supposed to favour his pretensions, but also in the principal seats of learning.    In one of his advertisements he calls upon the vice-chancellor, university, and city of Oxford, to vouch for his cures. He advertised in the *Tatler* that he had been " thirty-five years in the practice of couching cataracts, taking off all sorts of wens, curing wry necks, and *hair* lips, without blemish, though never so deformed." His wife assisted him, and after his death, which occurred at Rochester, on the 24th of May, 1715, carried on his business.

In those days, as at present, the quacks advertised testimonials from. grateful patients.    These are referred to in the *Spectator :* " Upon this a man of wit and learning told us, he thought it would not be amiss if we paid the *Spectator* the same compliment that is often made in our publick prints to Sir William Read, Dr. Grant, Mr. Moore the apothecary, and *other eminent physicians,* where it is usual for the patients to publish the cures which have been made upon them, and the several distempers under which they laboured."*

The Dr. Grant here referred to was a celebrated advertising quack.    Commencing life as a tinker, he afterwards, though very illiterate, became a Baptist preacher in Southwark, then turning quack, he eventually became oculist to Queen Anne.    Speaking of Read and Grant, a writer in the *Grub Street Journal* says :

" Her Majesty, sure, was in a surprise,
Or else was very short-sighted,
When a tinker was sworn to look after her eyes
And the mountebank Read was knighted."

* The *Spectator* follows this up with some humorous testimonials from persons who have been cured of jealousy, spleen. selfishness, and other distempers by reading certain numbers of that periodical.

Dr. Grant had his portrait engraved on a copper-plate, from which copies were printed for distribution.   Of this portrait the same writer says:

> " A tinker first his scene of life began;
> That failing, he set up for cunning man;
> But wanting luck, puts on a new disguise,
> And now pretends that he can mend your eyes.
> But this expect, that like a tinker true,
> Where he repairs one eye he puts out two."

Mr. Moore the apothecary, was known as the " Worm Doctor," because of a celebrated worm-powder that he sold.   In one of the numbers of the *Tatler* a London tradesman advertises that he had been cured of rheumatism by Mr. Moore, of the Pestle and Mortar, Abchurch Lane.   Moore and his worm powders will be handed down to posterity, since they form the subject of one of Pope's poems, of which one distich runs—

> " Vain is thy art, thy powder vain,
> Since worms shall eat e'en thee."

Early in the century flourished Dr. Tom Saffold, who use to publish his bills in verse, thus:

> " Here's Saffold's pills, much better than the rest,
> Deservedly have gained the name of best;
> A box of eighteen pills for eighteenpence,
> Though 'tis too cheap in any man's own sense."

Specimens of his poetical powers were also placed on his doorpost. Dr. Case, who afterwards lived in the same house, erased the verses of his predecessor and substituted two lines of his own:

> "Within this place
> Lives Doctor Case."

He is said to have gained more by this couplet than Dryden did by all his works.

The following elegy appeared on the death of Dr. Saffold:

> " Lament, ye damsels of our London city,
> Poor unprovided girls, though fair and witty;
> Who masked would to his house in couples come
> To understand your matrimonial doom;
> To know what kind of man you were to marry,
> And how long time, poor things, you were to tarry.
> Your oracle is silent; none can tell
> On whom his astrologic mantle fell;
> For he when sick refused the doctor's aid,
> And only to his pills devotion paid.
> Yet it was surely a most sad disaster
> The saucy pills at last should kill their master."

To understand some allusions in the above the reader must be reminded that nearly all these quacks pretended to a great skill in astrology, and joined the business of fortune-telling with that of selling drops and pills.

The sterner sex were not, however, allowed to monopolise the field of quackery. One of the best known characters of the last century was Mrs. Mapp the Bone-setter, who, after leading a wandering life for some time, settled down at Epsom, then a place of fashionable resort. The remarkable strength with which she was endowed, together with such knowledge as she had acquired from her father (himself a bone-setter), mainly contributed to the success which, in many cases, undoubtedly attended her operations. She journeyed to town twice a week in a coach-and-four, and, at the *Grecian Coffee House*, operated on her town patients, carrying their crutches back to Epsom as trophies of her skill. During one of these visits she was called in to the aid of Sir Hans Sloane's niece, and the success which she met with on this occasion became the talk of the town. A comedy called 'The Husband's Relief, or the Female Bone-setter and the Worm Doctor,' was brought out at the theatre in Lincoln's Inn Fields. Mrs. Mapp attended the first performance, accompanied by Ward and Taylor, two quacks, who will be noticed presently. A song in her praise was sung, of which one verse runs—

> " You doctors of London, who puzzle your pates
>    To ride in your coaches and purchase estates ;
>    Give over, for shame, for your pride has a fall,
>    And the Doctress of Epsom has outdone you all."

Many remarkable cures effected by her are noted in the public journals of the day, and there is no doubt that she was in the receipt of a very large income. The following extract from the *Grub Street Journal*, of the 19th of April, 1736, will give the reader a sufficient insight into her brief married life: " We hear that the husband of Mrs. Mapp, the famous bone-setter at Epsom, ran away from her last week, taking with him upwards of a hundred guineas, and such other portable things as lay next to his hand. Several letters from Epsom mention that the footman, whom the fair bone-setter married the week before, had taken a sudden journey from thence with what money his wife had earned, and that her concern at first was very great, but as soon as the surprise was over, she grew gay, and seems to think the money well disposed of, as it was like to rid her of a husband." At this time she was at the height of her prosperity; in December of the next year she died, " at her lodgings near Seven Dials, so miserably poor that the parish was obliged to bury her."

Dr. Ward, one of the quacks mentioned as accompanying Mrs. Mapp to the Lincoln's Inn Fields Theatre, was the son of a drysalter in Thames Street.   He became a footman, and it is said that whilst travelling with his master on the continent he obtained from some monks those receipts by which he afterwards made his "Friar's Balsam" and other nostrums.   He began to practise physic about 1733, and for some time combated the united efforts of wit, learning, argument, and ridicule.   The *Grub Street Journal* attacked him in a well-written article, showing the mischievous effects of his "pill," giving instances of fatal results from its use, and pointing out its probable principal ingredient.   He replied, giving copies of depositions made before certain magistrates to show that these fatalities arose from other causes.   He also inserted in his reply several testimonials to his wonderful success.   The controversy went on for some time, no doubt much to Ward's profit.   One of his detractors finishes an article with the following warning to the public:

> "Before you take his drop or pill
> Take leave of friends and make your will."

Praised by General Churchill and Lord Chief Justice Reynolds, he was called in to prescribe for George the Second.   The king recovering in spite of his attentions, Ward received a solemn vote of thanks from the House of Commons, and obtained the privilege of driving his carriage through St. James's Park.   He died in 1761, leaving his statue, by Carlini, to the Society of Arts.

Dr. Taylor, or the Chevalier Taylor, as he called himself, was a quack oculist, whose impudence was unparalleled, as his memoirs written by himself will testify.[*]   Dr. Johnson, in a conversation with his friend Beauclerk, talking of celebrated and successful irregular practisers in physic, said: "Taylor was the most ignorant man I ever knew, but sprightly; Ward the dullest.   Taylor challenged me once to talk Latin with him.   I quoted some of Horace, which he took to be part of my own speech.   He said a few words well enough."   *Beauclerk.*—"I remember, sir, you said that Taylor was an instance how far impudence could carry ignorance."   It was said of Taylor that five of his coach-horses were blind in consequence of their master having exercised his skill upon them.

About this time there practised in Moorfields a quack who advertised himself as the "Unborn Doctor."   A writer of the time speaks of him as the "stuttering Unborn Doctor," and relates that a gentleman having asked him to explain his title, he replied, "Why, you s—s—ee, sir, I w—w—as not b—born a d—d—doctor, and s—s—so I am an u—u—u—unborn doctor."

We may mention here Dr. Hancock, who recommended cold water and stewed prunes as a universal panacea.   There was also the pro-

---

* He published his travels in 1762, in which he styled himself "Opthalminator Pontifical, Imperial, Royal," &c.

G 2

prietor of the Anodyne Necklace, the wearing of which for one night would enable children to cut their teeth without pain, even though they had previously been on the brink of the grave. These necklaces had a good sale at the really moderate price, considering their effect, of five shillings each.

We must not pass over the gentleman who thus introduces himself in the *Evening Post* of August the 6th, 1717 : " This is to give notice that Doctor Benjamin Thornhill, sworn servant to His Majesty King George, *seventh son of the seventh son*, who has kept a stage in the rounds of West Smithfield for several months past, will continue to be advised with every day in the week, from eight in the morning till eight at night, at his lodgings at the *Swan Inn*, in West Smithfield, till Michaelmas, for the good of all people that lie languishing under distempers, he knowing that *Talenta in agro non est abscondita* — that a talent ought not to be hid in the earth. Therefore he exposes himself in public for the good of the poor. The many cures he has performed *has* given the world great satisfaction, having cured fifteen hundred people of the king's evil, and several hundreds that have been blind, lame, deaf, and diseased. God Almighty having been pleased to bestow upon him so great a talent, he thinks himself bound in duty to be helpful to all sorts of persons that are afflicted with any distemper. He will tell you in a minute what distemper you are troubled with and whether you are curable or not. If not curable he will not take any one in hand if he might have five hundred pounds for a reward."

Of foreign quacks who have resided in England we may mention Dominicetti, Katerfelto, and Cagliostro. Dominicetti in 1765 set up medicated baths in Cheyne Walk, Chelsea, which, although they made a considerable sensation for a time, do not seem to have secured the lasting favour of the public, for in 1782 Dominicetti became bankrupt. Katerfelto, an ex-Prussian soldier, practised in England during the great prevalence of influenza in 1782. To the sale of his nostrums he added the attractions of legerdemain, and electric and microscopical exhibitions. Cowper, in his ' Task' alludes to him :

> " And Katerfelto, with his hair on end
> At his own wonders, wondering for his bread."

The " arch-quack" Cagliostro, whose story is told by Carlyle, favoured England with his presence from 1785 to 1787. He lived in Sloane Street, Knightsbridge, where he did a good trade in Egyptian pills at thirty shillings the drachm.

In 1780 Dr. Graham opened a house in the Adelphi Terrace as the Temple of Health. His rooms were stuffed with glass globes, marble statues, medico-electric apparatus, figures of dragons, stained glass, and other theatrical properties. The air was drugged with incense, and the ear was charmed with strains of music from a self-acting organ.  Here he lectured on the beneficial effects of electricity and magnetism, and explained according to his advertisements "the whole art of enjoying health and vigour of body and mind, and of preserving and exalting personal beauty and loveliness ; or, in other words, of living with health, honour, and happiness in this world for at least a hundred years."  One of the means to this end was the frequent use of mud baths at a guinea each ; and on certain occasions he might be seen up to his chin in mud, accompanied by the priestess of the temple, otherwise Vestina, the Goddess of Health.  This "goddess" was Emma Lyons, previously a domestic servant, afterwards the wife of Sir William Hamilton and the *friend* of Lord Nelson.  Dr. Graham removed to Schomberg House in Pall Mall, where he opened the Temple of Health and Hymen.  Here he had his celestial bed, which he professed cost sixty thousand pounds.  One night in this bed secured a beautiful progeny, and might be had for one hundred pounds.  For a supply of his Elixir of Life he required one thousand pounds in advance.  A Prussian traveller who was in England at the time described this temple, with its vari-coloured transparent glasses, its rich vases of perfumes, half-guinea treatises on health, and divine balm, at a guinea a bottle.  Magneto-electric beds were on the second-floor, and might be slept in for fifty pounds a night.  Each bed rested on six massy transparent columns.  The perfumed drapery was of purple, the curtains of celestial blue.

Graham spared no expense to attract visitors.  He had two footmen in gaudy liveries and gold-laced hats to stand at the entrance.  His rooms at night were brilliantly lighted.  With an admittance fee of five shillings his rooms were crowded by people anxious to see this magnificent show and to hear the lecture of the quack or his assistants.  One of his advertisements informs us that "Vestina, the rosy Goddess of Health, presides at the evening lecture, assisting at the display of the celestial meteors, and of that sacred vital fire over which she watches, and whose application in the cure of diseases she daily has the honour of directing.  The descriptive exhibition of the apparatus in the daytime is conducted by the officiating junior priest."  This priest was a young medical man, afterwards Dr. Mitford, and father of the celebrated authoress.

Graham's expenses were very large, and when the public ceased to patronise him and his receipts fell off, the Temple of Health was closed, and the whole of the "properties" were sold by auction in 1784.  Graham died poor in the neighbourhood of Glasgow.

# Talleyrand.

## By the Author of 'Mirabeau,' 'Danton,' etc.

The chain of being begins with the animalcule and expands into the elephant: so it is with the chain of events. No action or accident of our lives is insignificant; the most trivial may be the germ of our destiny. When a child at nurse Talleyrand had a severe fall. What event could possibly be more inevitable or commonplace in a child's history? It was not commonplace, however, in this child's history. But for that fall he would have been simply a noble of *l'ancien régime*: profligate, indolent, voluptuous, an unit amongst his herd; expiating his sins at last in the obscurity of exile, or more probably beneath the knife of the guillotine; and thus he would have dropped out of the world leaving no trace behind, and history would have known him not. What that fall made of him and did for the world is to be found in the annals of four revolutions.

Charles Maurice de Talleyrand-Périgord, eldest son of the Comte de Talleyrand, was born in Paris in the year 1754. The Comtes de Talleyrand were descended from a younger branch of the sovereign counts of Périgord, one of the most ancient and illustrious families of France, and whose haughty motto, *Ré que Dieu,** they bore.

The father of Charles Maurice was a soldier, his mother a lady-in-waiting at Court. In the very hour of his birth the infant was consigned to the care of a nurse, who removed him at once to her home in a distant part of the country, where he was reared very little differently to her own peasant children. This was the fashionable way of disposing of infantine encumbrances in those days; their advent was a disagreeable accident which condemned the fine ladies to a month's seclusion; but with that the trouble ended, the accident was given into the hands of some peasant nurse, and was thought of no more until it was of an age to be trained for a soldier, or a priest, or a courtier, as the case might be.

When scarcely a twelvemonth old, he was lamed for life by a fall. Eleven years passed away, during which time the fond mother had not only never seen her offspring, but was even ignorant of the accident that had befallen him. About this period his uncle, the Bailli de Talleyrand, a naval captain, returned to France after an absence of many years. Being desirous of seeing his nephew, he made a journey to the remote village to which the boy had been exiled. It was in the depth of winter that he undertook this expedition, and the snow lay

* God alone is our king.

thick upon the ground. As he neared the place he met upon the road a blue-eyed, fair-haired boy, dressed like a peasant, to whom he offered some silver to guide him to Mother Régaut's (the nurse's name was Régaut). Delighted·at the thought of the promised reward, the boy eagerly undertook the service, but he was very lame, and could not keep pace with the horse, so the good-natured *bailli* lifted him into the saddle. His wonder and consternation may be imagined when, upon arriving at the cottage, he was informed that in his poor little lame guide he saw the nephew he had come to seek. Not another hour did Charles Maurice remain beneath that roof: the *bailli* took the boy back with him to Paris. Such was the childhood's days of the future great European diplomatist, who was destined thereafter to hold the destinies of France within his grasp.

From the village he was transplanted to the College D'Harcourt, where, all ignorant as he was when he entered it, he soon carried away the first prizes, and became ultimately one of its most distinguished scholars. His mother now paid him an occasional visit, but as she was always accompanied by a surgeon, who pulled and cauterised, and tortured the boy's leg, her visits were more terrible than pleasing. But all the pulling, and cauterising, and torturing effected no good— the lameness was incurable. The head of the house of Talleyrand must be a soldier—such was the tradition of the family, and it had never yet been departed from. A cripple could not be a soldier. It was announced to him that his birthright would be transferred to his younger brother.

" Why so ?" asked the boy.

" *Because you are a cripple,*" was the cruel answer.

Whatever of good might have existed in his original nature those words crushed out ; the flavour of their bitterness lingered in his heart unto the last days of his life. From the hour in which they were spoken his disposition gradually changed ; he became taciturn, callous, and calculating ; a cynic, a heartless debauchee, sparing neither man nor woman that stood in the path of his interest or his pleasure. He had not been spared, why should he spare others? It was not for nothing he earned thereafter the title of *le diable boiteux*.

Being a Talleyrand, as he could not be a soldier, he must be a churchman. From the College d'Harcourt he was sent to St. Sulpice and afterwards to Sorbonne to complete his studies. He made no secret of his dislike for the profession he was thrust into, and testified his utter unfitness for it by a life of gambling and debauchery. In 1773 he was received into the church. Thereafter he was known as the Abbé de Périgord, and proved a most admirable addition to the dissolute and atheistical clergy of the age.

In that same year he was presented at Court, and became an *habitué* of Du Barry's boudoir. One evening, at one of her gay assemblies, while a number of young gallants were amusing the lady by the recital of scandalous stories, and their own amorous adventures, the Abbé was observed to be silent and melancholy.

"Why are you so sad and silent?" demanded the hostess.

"*Hélas madame la comtesse, je faisais une réflexion bien mélancolique; c'est qu'à Paris il est plus facile d'avoir des femmes que des abbayes.*"

The King was so charmed with this *bon mot* when it was repeated to him, that he at once presented the witty *abbé* with a very handsome benefice! From this dates his rise in the church.

In 1780 he was appointed agent-general of the French clergy, a post which placed in his hands the entire administration of the ecclesiastical revenues, and which he filled with consummate ability. But, as though in constant protest against the wrong that had been done him, and the uncongenial profession to which that wrong had consigned him, the immorality of his life was as flagrant as ever; his profane epigrams were repeated in every drawing-room; his scandalous love adventures were in every mouth.

Although Louis the Fifteenth and his mistress held a licentious wit to be an admirable recommendation for church preferment, Louis the Sixteenth was quite of an opposite opinion, and when the bishopric of Autun, for which the Abbé had long been intriguing, fell vacant (1788), it was only after a lapse of four months, and at the dying request of the Comte de Périgord, who probably felt a late compunction for the wrong which had been done to his son, that the King reluctantly bestowed upon him the coveted dignity.

Here is his portrait sketched by a contemporary at this period: "Picture to yourself a man thirty-three years of age, handsome figure, blue and expressive eyes, nose slightly *retroussé*, complexion delicate almost to pallor. In studying the play of his features we observe upon his lips a smile, sometimes malignant, sometimes disdainful. Studious of his personal appearance, a coquet in his ecclesiastical toilet, but frequently changing the costume of his order for that of the laity, irreligious as a pirate—performing mass with an unctuous grace—the Abbé Périgord finds time for all; he appears sometimes at Court, but oftener at the Opera. He reads his breviary, the 'Odes of Horace,' and the 'Memoirs of Cardinal de Retz'—a prelate whose qualities he greatly esteems. If he meets Narbonne, Lauzun, Boufflers, Segur, and the Bishop of Châlons in the house of Madame Guimard, he will sup with them. Ordinarily fond of his bed, he will at a need pass two or three nights consecutively in hard work. Assailed by creditors, closing his doors to the importunate, never promising without restrictions, obliging through circumstances, sometimes through egotism; greedy of renown, more greedy still of riches; loving women with his senses, not with his heart; calm in critical positions; haughty to the great, suave to the humble; pausing in a work upon finance to write a *billet doux*; neither vindictive nor wicked; an enemy to all violent measures, but knowing, if necessary, how to use them."

Another contemporary thus epigrammatically describes him: " He dressed like a coxcomb, thought like a deist, and preached like a saint."

At the assembling of the States General he at once espoused the popular side. Like Mirabeau, his own order had rejected him; from them he had nothing to hope; distinction in any path of life rather than in the church was preferable to his taste; while, with the ambitious spirit that animated all, whether gentle or plebeian, in that age, everything seemed possible to him in the new order of things which was at hand. No proof of the utter effeteness of the *ancien régime* is so conclusive as the strange phenomenon of so many of its own body helping to destroy it. La Fayette, Mirabeau, and Talley- rand, all three of the noblest of the aristocracy, pioneered its destruc· tion before Robespierre, Marat, or Danton were heard of. On the 15th of June, 1789, after the nobles and the clergy had demurred to deliberate in the same chamber with the *tiers état*, Mirabeau proposed that the latter without further delay should declare itself " the repre- sentatives of the French people." On the 22nd of June, seven days later, thanks to the unwearied zeal of the Bishop of Autun, a majority of the clergy joined the *tiers état*. In his very first speech he pro- posed and carried that the States General should henceforth be fused into the National Assembly, the title already assumed by the representa- tives of the people, and that its discussions should be unrestricted.*

A little later, and La Fayette gave the signal for the destruction of the Bastille and created the National Guard. The noble radicals began their work bravely!

Day by day the principles of the Bishop advanced more and more, and day by day he became more and more popular; he was a member of the Cordeliers and the Feuilletons; his speeches on finance were everywhere the theme of the highest laudation; but his crowning act was to carry the motion for the surrender of all ecclesiastical property to the use of the nation. Long and stormy was the debate, but on the 2nd of November the decree was passed. Early in 1790 he brought forward a manifesto to advocate the abolition of all privileges, to advo- cate church reform, and a vast plan of public education. On the 16th of February in the same year he was named President of the Assembly, a post which even Mirabeau could not attain until one year later.

After a short deliberation, he gave in his hearty adherence to the Act called 'Civil Constitution of the Clergy,' consecrated new bishops to replace those who, from scruples of conscience or the fear of Papal thunders, had refused the oath, and was, on the 1st of May, 1791,

---

* The electors, in sending their representatives to the States General, had restricted the discussion and action to certain subjects.

excommunicated by his Holiness the Pope for his pains. Having of late looked rather towards political than ecclesiastical preferment, the Bishop's course of action was immediate and decisive; he availed himself of the opportunity to cast off his irksome fetters, at once seceded from the church, and was thereafter known simply as M. de Talleyrand.

But his sagacity foresaw and prophesied to what events were hastening. Writing to a lady friend, he says, "If the prince depends upon the affection of the people, he is lost; if the people are not guarded against the character of the prince, I foresee terrible misfortune—torrents of blood flowing through years to efface the enthusiasm of a few months. I foresee the innocent and the guilty involved in the same destruction. . . . . Mirabeau believes with me that we are marching too quickly towards a republic. What a republic! composed of thirty millions of corrupted souls. I fear that having attained to that, the fanatics will only begin to light their torches, the anarchists to erect their scaffolds. Who knows how many amongst us may escape the fire or the *lanterne?* I must arrange my affairs in such a manner that I shall not be without resources whatever happens."

The political creed of Mirabeau and Talleyrand was the same; both were of the party of order; both advocated the principles of constitutional monarchy and rational freedom; but with those points all similarity between the two men disappears. The one would have martyrised himself to have enforced those principles: the other would not have imperilled his fortunes for an hour to have maintained any principles. Upon his death-bed Mirabeau sent for Talleyrand, as the man by sympathy and creed the most fitted to be the repository of his plots and secrets. But with that mighty genius was swept away the last bulwark of order, and so cautious and calculating a man as the ex-bishop was not the one to oppose the invading forces of mob rule.

Twice in the year 1792 was he sent on diplomatic service to London—the second time arriving with an autograph letter from Louis the Sixteenth to George the Third. But the excesses of the revolution were every day rendering its principles more unpopular in England, and the letter, like every other act of the unfortunate monarch, being supposed to have been dictated, produced no effect. The object of the mission was to conclude an alliance between France and England; but while the negotiations were actually pending came the news that the King was deposed—news which at once terminated diplomatic relations between France and all foreign countries.

Except by Fox and the Whigs, Talleyrand was received but coldly in this country. When presented at St. James's, the Queen disdainfully turned her back upon him. "She did right," he said afterwards, "*for her Majesty is very ugly.*"

Upon his return to Paris he found that the revolution had so far outstripped him that France was no longer a safe abode for any man of birth and position. He lost no time in obtaining a passport from Danton and in returning to London for the third time. A paper which implicated him as having been in secret correspondence with the Court being found in the iron chest, a decree of accusation was pronounced against him by the Convention, and his name was included in the list of *émigrés*. Until 1794 he resided in London. Here he mingled with the *émigrés* with a view, possibly, to future contingencies that might happen to the Bourbons, and was well received in certain circles, particularly that of Lansdowne House. In general society he was noted as cold in manner, silent, sententious, formal, scrutinising; but amongst the more genial few this mask was cast aside, and he was the wit and polished man of the world. In the January of the year last named he received, under the Alien Bill, an order of expulsion as a Jacobin. In a letter addressed to Lord Granville he declared that his residence in England had no reference to politics—he had sought there simply an asylum. The letter remained unanswered and unnoticed.*

From England he sailed for the United States of America. At Washington he was well received, and, longing to revenge himself upon the English Government, he actively associated himself with the Anti-Anglican party. But he soon grew weary of his new home, and was about to set sail for the East Indies † when he received the news of Robespierre's downfall and of the growing desire of France for a settled government. He at once determined upon returning to his native land.

The most active of his friends in Paris was Madame de Staël, who was deeply attached to him, and through whose intercession with Joseph Marie Chénier he ultimately obtained his recall. It was in the latter part of 1795 that he once more returned to Paris. The Reign of Terror had passed away, and the Reign of Society had once more

* There is every reason to believe that the English Government was perfectly justified in expelling him. When pleading in the Convention for the reversal of Talleyrand's accusation, Chénier made a declaration to the effect that he had found among Danton's papers a correspondence which indicated that the exile had been an accredited agent and spy of the Republic during the whole time of his sojourn in England. It is true that the correspondence was never produced, but that he obtained his passport from Danton under some such conditions is a conjecture well warranted by the character of the latter; that Talleyrand to a certain extent fulfilled those conditions is equally in harmony with his own character.

† The vessel in which he was to sail was never heard of from the time in which she left the shores of America. Had he been a passenger on board her Napoleon might never have reigned, and how different from what it is might have been thirty years of European history! Another instance of the gravity of so-called insignificant events.

taken its place. To the clubs had succeeded the *jeunesse dorée*. Freed from the horrible phantom, the bloody realities of the guillotine, the Parisians were once more *gai* and *sans souci*. There were no distinctions of rank, no grand seigneurs, no rich people, no artificial ceremonies —everybody lived together in a happy state of equality, their homes the parks, the promenades, and the public gardens.

Upon his arrival Talleyrand was everywhere welcomed as a wit and a gentleman, was elected a member of the National Institute, where he delivered two admirable lectures upon the commercial relations between England and America, and three weeks afterwards was named Minister of Foreign Affairs'. In the Directory, which was composed of Carnot and Barthélemy, Red Republicans—and of Lareveillière-Lepaux, Rewbell, and Barras, moderates, Talleyrand attached himself to Barras; and when Pichegru, a, Robespierrean at the head of the Assembly, was conspiring for the triumph of the extreme party, he it was who planned the *coup d'état* by which Barras seized upon Pichegru and Barthélemy and put Carnot to flight. But the advantage thus gained was only temporary; the constant defeat of the French arms by the Allies put the Directory in bad odour, and Talleyrand, attacked by the violent republicans as a noble and an *émigré*, resigned his appointment.

Talleyrand first met Napoleon during the latter's visit to Paris after the Peace of Campo Formio. Upon his return from the Egyptian campaign, Napoleon's ambition was to become one of the Directory. But his age was a prohibition that could not be surmounted. From their first meeting, Talleyrand had assiduously cultivated the friendship of the great general in whose daring genius and iron will he foresaw the best ruler for France. The Directory was weak and divided; at any moment mob rule might rise again triumphant; a despotic genius alone could create strength and order out of the chaos to which all things had been reduced by the Revolution. "*When society is powerless to create a government, government must create society,*" was one of his profoundest maxims. And to carry out this maxim he now devoted all the powers of his subtle genius.

The Directory would not admit Napoleon among its members; therefore the Directory must be destroyed. The first step was to gain over Siéyès, who had succeeded Pichegru as the head of the Five Hundred, and who had also succeeded Rewbell in the Directory; Siéyès gained over Ducos, and, by a pre-arranged plan, both resigned; the casting vote remained with Barras, a weak obstacle in the hands of Talleyrand; a body of troops overawed the malcontents, and—the Directory was no more.

Three consuls were appointed—Buonaparte, Ducos, and Siéyès.* The arch-plotter was rewarded with the portfolio of the foreign minis-

* The two latter were afterwards succeeded by Cambacérès and Lebrun.

try, and from that time firmly attached himself to the fortunes of the man whose elevation he had secured. The confirmation of the consulship for life, and the founding of the Order of the Legion of Honour, were chiefly indebted to his exertions. In the debate upon the latter, he spoke these profoundly true words : " The present age has created a great many things, but not a new mankind ; if you would legislate practically for mankind, you must treat men as what they have always been and always are. . . . In reorganising human society, you must give it those elements which you find in every human society."

The treaties of Lunéville and Amiens were among the first and most successful of those diplomatic triumphs with which his fame as a minister is chiefly associated. But there appears to have been nothing Machiavellian about his mode of conducting negotiations ; on the contrary, he is said to have always spoken in an open straightforward manner, never arguing, but always tenaciously sticking to the principal point. Napoleon said that " he always turned round the same idea."

About the same time he was reconciled to the Church of Rome. The Pope wrote him an autograph letter, containing a dispensation that enabled him to marry. The lady was one Madame Grandt, whom he had first met during his exile in London, and who afterwards openly lived with him in Paris. Napoleon, expressing himself somewhat scandalised at the immoral connection, commanded that he should either marry her or cease to live with her. Accordingly, upon the arrival of the dispensation, the marriage was celebrated with as much privacy as possible. The lady was very beautiful, but far from clever. Several stories are told of her *bêtise;* the best known is the following : Having read Defoe's ' Robinson Crusoe,' she was one day introduced at dinner to Sir George Robinson ; thinking him to be the veritable Crusoe whose adventures she had been reading, she puzzled him exceedingly with questions about his shipwreck and the desert island, winding up the absurd scene by asking particularly after his man Friday ! When surprise was expressed at his choice of a wife, Talleyrand replied, " A clever wife often compromises her husband, a stupid one only compromises herself." But Madame Talleyrand was not always stupid. When Napoleon, in congratulating her upon her marriage, expressed a hope that the errors of Madame Grandt would be sunk in Madame Talleyrand, she replied, " In that respect I cannot do better than follow the admirable example of your Majesty."

After Napoleon's coronation there gradually arose between him and his great minister a coldness which, in the course of time, grew upon the former into an intense dislike. It is impossible, in so brief an article, to more than glance at, without attempting to explain, the causes of this change. In the first place, Talleyrand was opposed to the marriage with Marie Louise ; in the second place, he was opposed to his master's schemes of universal conquest, for his sagacity forewarned him that one serious reverse would crumble his vast empire into dust. Such counsels excited only the indignation of a man drunk with victory.

Was Talleyrand implicated in the murder of the Duc d'Enghien, and in the scheme of the Spanish invasion? These are "historic doubts" that have been much discussed by historians and biographers. At Elba, Napoleon distinctly declared that those, the worst deeds of his life, were counselled by his foreign minister; but Napoleon is not an undeniable authority; besides, at that time he was posing himself as a hero of virtue before the eyes of Europe, and was desirous of shifting the burden of his crimes unto other shoulders. Such an act of impolitic and useless bloodshed was utterly opposed to the cold calculating character of the diplomatist, which, with all its vices, contained nothing of cruelty or vindictiveness.* With the Bourbons he always desired to be on good terms; another reason which argues equally against his participation in either act. During the Spanish war, however, Napoleon wrote him several confidential letters couched in a strain which scarcely bears out his, Talleyrand's, assertion that he had strongly opposed the expedition. The most probable solution of the doubts, and that most consonant with his character, may be that, although emphatically averse to both those acts of lawless power, he closed his eyes and passively submitted to the inevitable.

Created Prince of Benevento, enormously rich, and broken in health, Talleyrand availed himself of the rupture with his Imperial master to resign his office. He did not however entirely retire from diplomacy, but continued from time to time to superintend several important negotiations. "*It is the beginning of the end!*" he said to Savary when he heard the news of the burning of Moscow, and the subsequent disasters of that terrible campaign. But although he foresaw that the star of Napoleon was setting fast, he was not guilty of the cold-blooded tergiversation that has been imputed to him. His urgent counsel was, "Peace with Russia at any price." When the Allies were marching upon Paris his advice was that the Empress should remain in Paris as the only means of saving the dynasty. But Joseph Buonaparte decided the question by producing a letter from his brother, in which it was commanded that in the event of such a crisis as that in which they were then involved Marie Louise should at

---

* Amongst all the unsparing insults and opprobrium that Napoleon heaped upon his minister's head, in that terrible quarrel between them which preceded the latter's resignation, no reference was made to this shameful deed. Surely in that hour of ungovernable rage and malice the Emperor would not have forgotten this the blackest accusation that he could have hurled against him? For a full account of this celebrated scene see Sir Henry Bulwer's 'Historical Characters.'

once retire into the provinces.* *"Now what shall I do?"* he said to Savary. *" It does not suit every one to be crushed under the ruins of an edifice that is overthrown!"*

From that hour Talleyrand became the arbiter of the destinies of France. The Emperor Alexander, who took up his abode at the house of the Prince, said: *" When I arrived in Paris I had no plan —I referred everything to Talleyrand ; he held the family of Napoleon in one hand, that of the Bourbons in the other—I took what he gave me."* *" It must be either Buonaparte or Louis the Eighteenth,"* was his counsel. The result of the conference was a proclamation refusing to treat with any member of Napoleon's family. This at once destroyed the plan that had been mooted of a regency under Marie Louise, and secured the accession of the Bourbons.

" How did you contrive to overthrow the Directory, and afterwards Buonaparte himself?" inquired Louis. " Mon Dieu, Sire! I have done nothing for it—*there is something inexplicable in me that brings misfortunes upon all those who neglect me."* At all events, Talleyrand did good service to his country in pressing forward a constitution to limit the power of that King of whom, and of the family, he truly said, that in their exile *they had learned nothing nor forgotten nothing.*

Created Grand Almoner and Minister of Foreign Affairs, the Prince was despatched to the congress at Vienna, with secret instructions to endeavour to sow discord between the Allies, and thus break up the bond of hostility so inimical to the interests of France. But the escape of Buonaparte from Elba scattered all these plots to the winds.

Napoleon made overtures to win back Talleyrand to his cause, but neither interest nor inclination swayed the diplomatist in that direction ; the Emperor had repeatedly and grossly insulted him, added to which he knew that both France and Europe were surfeited with war, and that, irresistible as was the storm for the time, it could not last. So he retired to Carlsbad on pretence that his health required the waters.

The Hundred Days passed away ; but Louis had determined upon the minister's disgrace. Talleyrand knew this, and, preferring to take the initiative, waited upon the King at Ghent, the day after Waterloo, to request permission to remain at Carlsbad. " Certainly, M. de Talleyrand, I hear the waters are excellent," was the reply. But His Majesty could not so easily rid himself of the obnoxious diplomatist. The Duke of Wellington informed him that if he wished for the influence of England he must have a man at the head of the government in whom England could confide. The party of the Constitutional Legitimists, through Guizot, demanded that a cabinet should be formed

* Napoleon wrote thus : *" If Talleyrand wishes the Empress to remain in Paris it is to betray her . . . beware of that man !"* Was this merely an ebullition of gall ? Was it a suspicion founded upon certain premises ? *Or was the warning warranted by ascertained facts ?*

with M. Guizot at the head; so on the day after the polite dismissal at Ghent, M. de Talleyrand received a mandate to join the King at Cambrai. But he had his revenge in refusing to form a ministry until the King signed a proclamation, the pith of which was an acknowledgment of the errors of his late reign.

To the fallen party Talleyrand behaved with the utmost clemency, providing numbers of those who wished to quit France with money and passports, and reducing the proscription list to half the original number.

He retained the premiership of France until the 24th of September, 1815. But his government was weak, the King hostile. The Emperor Alexander had declared that the Tuileries could expect nothing from St. Petersburg while M. Talleyrand remained at the head of affairs,* added to which the minister foresaw the mischievous effects that would accrue from the violent Royalist reaction that was at hand, and preferred tendering his resignation to encountering the coming storm.

From 1815 to 1830 he took no active part in politics, unless it was to protest against the Spanish war, and to utter a defence of the liberty of the press. Much of his time was spent at Valençy upon his estate. In Paris his drawing-room vied in magnificence, and in the brilliancy of its society, with the royal palaces—being a second and almost greater court. Here, paying homage to the great diplomatist, assembled all the beauty, all the wit, all the riches, and all the intellect of the Restoration. But he was no longer the gay *abbé*, the *petit-maître* of Du Barry's boudoir, with whom every woman was in love. The picture of him drawn by Lady Morgan in 1816 is not an attractive one.

"Cold, immovable," she writes, "neither absent nor reflective, but impassible; no colour varying the livid pallor of his face, no expression betraying his impenetrable character. For the moment one could not tell whether he were dead or living; whether the heart beat or the brain throbbed no mortal observer could verify; from the soul of that man the world is disdainfully excluded; if one might hazard a conjecture after what we have seen, it is to recognise in him the enigmatical sphinx who said 'Speech was given us to conceal our thoughts.' Neither the most tender love, the most devoted friendship, nor any community of interests would make that face, which can only be compared to a book in a dead language, speak."

Another writer, pursuing the same theme, says, "To baffle his penetrating sagacity, you must not only not speak, but not think. It was not only by his language that he concealed his thoughts, but by his silence."

On account of the numerous *bons mots* and epigrams that claim

* The Emperor Alexander conceived an inveterate dislike to Talleyrand for the neglect that Russian interests received at his hands during the congress at Vienna.

him for parent Talleyrand is commonly thought to have been a brilliant conversationalist and a flippant wit. Lamartine, however, has given us quite a different picture in the following passage: "A taste for lively sallies and epigrams has been attributed to him which he did not possess. He was, on the contrary, slow, careless, natural, somewhat idle in expression, always infallible in precision. His sentences were not flashes of light, but condensed reflections in a few words."

On the first day of the revolution of July he made no sign. On the third he sent his secretary to St. Cloud to see if the King were still there. Upon being informed of the departure for Rambouillet, he dispatched a paper to Madame Adelaide at Neuillet, containing these words: "Madame can put every confidence in the bearer, who is my secretary." "When she has read it," he said to the secretary, "let it be burned or brought back to me; then tell her that not a moment is to be lost—Duc d'Orleans must be here to-morrow; let him take the title of Lieutenant-General of the Kingdom, which has been already accorded to him; the rest will come."

Upon the accession of Louis Philippe he undertook the embassy to St. James', and obtained the recognition of England for the new Sovereign. Thus did he for the fourth time change the dynasty of France! His last diplomatic labours were to tide over the Belgian difficulties and to assist in the formation of the quadruple alliance.

The end was coming fast. To gratify his family, but not from personal conviction, he consented to make his peace with the church. During his last hours his rooms were filled with the flower of Parisian society. Louis Philippe himself visited his deathbed. Those last hours are well described in the following quotation: "M. de Talleyrand was seated upon the side of his bed, supported in the arms of his secretary. It was evident that death had set his seal upon that marble brow; yet I was struck with the still existing vigour of the countenance. It seemed as if all the life which had once sufficed to furnish the whole being was now contained in the brain. From time to time he raised up his head, throwing back with a sudden movement the long grey locks which impeded his sight, and gazed around; and then, as if satisfied with the result of his examination, a smile would pass across his features and his head would again fall upon his bosom. He saw death approaching neither with shrinking nor fear, nor yet with any affectation of scorn or defiance."

He died on the 17th of May, 1838, aged 84.

"He possessed a mixture of the firmness of Richelieu, knowing how to select a party, the finesse of Mazarin, knowing how to elude it; the restlessness and factious readiness of the Cardinal de Retz, with a little of the magnificent gallantry of the Cardinal de Rohan," says a French writer; thus connecting him, by comparison, with all his great predecessors in statecraft.

Guizot thus sums up his character : "Out of a crisis or a congress he is neither skilful nor powerful. A man of court and of diplomacy, not of government, and less of a free government than any other ; he excelled in treating by conversation, by an agreeableness of manner, by the skilful employment of his social relations with isolated people ; but authority of character, fecundity of talent, promptitude of resolution, power of eloquence, sympathetic intelligence with general ideas and public passions, all these great means of acting upon mankind at large he entirely wanted. . . . Ambitious and indolent, flattering and disdainful, he was a consummate courtier in the art of pleasing and serving without servility ; supple and amenable to the highest degree when it was useful to his fortunes ; always preserving the air of independence ; an unscrupulous politician, indifferent to the means and almost to the end, provided that it secured his personal success ; more bold than profound in his views, coldly courageous in peril, adapted for the grand affairs of an absolute government ; but in the great air and the great day of liberty he was out of his element, and was incapable of action."

Talleyrand could neither love nor hate ; he was a passionless man ; he never committed a cruel or vindictive action, and never a purely motiveless generous one. Every thought, feeling, plan of his nature revolved round one great centre—SELF. He could not, as a great statesman, have created a broad, comprehensive scheme of government ; his own petty interests ever dwarfed his ideas. In him the reasoning faculty was largely developed, the imaginative not at all ; he trusted to no deductions, to no speculations that were not rigidly derived from his own personal experiences : hence his views, although wonderfully correct, were never all-comprehensive. He understood mankind sectionally ; he could almost infallibly foresee how each section would act *singly ;* but of that "touch of nature that makes the whole world kin "—of those subtle links that can mass mankind as a whole, and by which all great rulers have swayed their worlds, he knew nothing. Because no process of mathematical reasoning, no experience, however extended, can deduce them ; their existence can only be revealed by the inspiration of those creative faculties of the mind that revealed to Shakespeare a Macbeth and a Hamlet.

He worked for the greatness of France, because upon the greatness of France depended the greatness of Talleyrand. He was purely a cynic—the well-being of mankind never for a moment entered into his calculations. To him the world was a chess-board—mankind the pieces ; he ranged his kings and his queens, his bishops and his generals, and played them one against the other ; when the game was exhausted and the sovereign was encompassed by enemies beyond all hope of escape, he cried "Checkmate," and began the game afresh. It was said of him, "Like a cat, he always falls upon his feet ; cats do not follow their masters, they are faithful to—*the house.*"

His vices were those of the age in which he was educated; his licentiousness, his cynicism, his scepticism, his selfish contempt for mankind, were learned in the boudoir of Du Barry. In reason and in action, he was of the nineteenth century; in thought and feeling, he was of the *ancien régime*. His liberalism had been learned in the school of Voltaire; he accepted the advance of political ideas as a necessity, but with no sympathy. "The thoughts," he said, "of the greatest number of intelligent persons in any age or country are sure, with few more or less fluctuations, to become in the end the public opinion of their age or community." And he always yielded to public opinion.

While attached to any government, he served it faithfully and zealously; and in all his tergiversations he scrupulously retained the outward forms of decency, reserving to himself a respectable excuse for his defection: "*I have never kept fealty to any one longer than he has himself been obedient to common-sense,*" he said.

The most brilliant of his talents was a marvellous and almost prophetic foresight, in proof of which I extract the two following quotations from his writings. The prophecy contained in the first is rapidly coming to pass; that contained in the second has just been wonderfully fulfilled:

"Upon the side of America, Europe should always keep her eyes open, and furnish no pretence for recrimination or reprisals. America grows each day. She will become a colossal power, and the time may arrive when, brought into closer communion with Europe by means of new discoveries, she will desire to have her say in our affairs, and put in her hand as well. Political prudence then imposes upon the government of the Old World to scrupulously watch that no pretext is given her for such an interference. The day that America sets her foot in Europe, peace and security will be banished for many years."

"Do not let us deceive ourselves; the European balance that was established by the Congress of Vienna will not last for ever. It will be overturned some day; but it promises us some years of peace. The greatest danger that threatens it in the future are the aspirations that are growing universal in central Germany. The necessities of self-defence and a common peril have prepared all minds for Germanic unity. That idea will continue to develop until some day one of the great powers who make part of the Confederation will desire to realise that unity for its own profit. Austria is not to be feared, being composed of pieces that have no unity among themselves. It is then Prussia who ought to be watched; she will try, and if she succeeds all the conditions of the balance of power will be changed; it will be necessary to seek for Europe new bases and a new organisation."

# Marryat.

WHEN it is remembered what the condition was of nine-tenths of the vagabonds and adventurers who landed in England under the banner of Duke William, we are the more surprised that any person should be proud of being descended from them.

To be sure, some of the least scrupulous and most lucky acquired lands, whereby those exceptional vagabonds became respectable. They were "gentle," "noble," anything that a man can be who is "spacious in the possession of dirt." We will hope that the Norman Marryat— "De Maryat," if you please—was one of the exclusive tenth who had something more than ruffianly qualities to boast of. Probably he had a Christian name. For other distinction he was, perhaps, called after the village from which he was lured by the sound of the great bastard's trumpet and the lying of the duke's recruiters.

Be this as it may, the Marryats took root in this land. They took a good deal of the land also. They earned honour by knightly service. They married heiresses, and manifested some peculiarity by disembowelling their wives!

Of course we mean their deceased wives. The custom, peculiar to the family—so we are told—must have been carried beyond limits that could be tolerated. Else, why, in the reign of our second Edward, did the Bishop of Bath and Wells excommunicate a young Marryat for subjecting the departed wife of his bosom to this "fancy"? Perhaps it was the bishop who was fanciful.

After being a crusading, chivalrous, and flourishing race, the Marryats changed with political changes. One of them danced before Queen Elizabeth at Cambridge. But this young fellow, John, fought abroad as well as he danced at home. He was as happy in love as in war, for he married the shy heiress of a Puritan sire, and became by that marriage not only a progenitor of Puritanical descendants, but the direct lineal ancestor of the author of 'Peter Simple,' "whom no one," says his daughter, in a recently published biography, "would have suspected of being of Puritanical descent."

However, there was a very mixed blood in the veins of *our* Marryat —Norman, Saxon, Cavalier, Puritan. His mother, Caroline von Geyer, was born in America, the daughter of a German gentleman. His father was a well-to-do squire of Wimbledon, Surrey. Chivalry had not died out from his father's breast, who, when he was a West India proprietor and a member of Parliament, was the chief agent in passing a bill for the abolition of slave-grown sugar. He had fifteen sons and daughters; and when he died, Campbell wrote twelve lines, by way of threnodia, which we rejoice to think were *not* inscribed upon the good man's tomb.

As Marryat "learned with facility," the master was rash who declared that he would be nothing but a dunce, because he forgot as fast as he learned. He was decidedly what we should now call a "bad boy," and was flogged, accordingly, often. Yet he took pains in a droll way. He was a delicate lad, with a head that seemed disproportionate to his attenuated body. He once found some difficulty at getting some of his lessons into that head in the usual way. He was then a pupil at Ponder's End. Perhaps the name was suggestive. At all events, the master was astonished, on entering the school, to see the wrong end of Master Marryat in the air. He was standing on his head, and was trying to achieve his task in that novel position for a student. But he was much oftener on his feet, running away from school, till his sire was weary of spending money in recapturing him. His last escapade was caused by an injury to his honour. He was disgusted with having to wear the clothes of an elder brother, who had grown too big for them. Nothing remained, but to send him to sea. In 1806 Master Fred, then fourteen, was shipped on board the fighting *Impérieuse*, under the fighting captain, Lord Cochrane. This meant daily peril of life, and Marryat was delighted at the prospect.

In that famous time, when this one ship was sufficient to embarrass a whole French army, by cutting off their supplies by sea and by pitching shot into their ranks as they showed themselves on the coast, the crews scarcely knew, for three years, what it was to be at rest from engaging with enemies afloat, cutting out (in boats) hostile vessels moored under batteries, in seemingly safe harbours, or varying the turbulent tenor of their ways by storming forts, or executing other perilous exploits, on land. Men and officers dropped to sleep in the midst of their triumphant celebrations of victory, and were awakened to achieve fresh glory by the voice of their familiar friend, the gun. In that fighting period the powder got so burnt into their faces that years could not remove it.

It is certain that this perilous and bloody time was thoroughly enjoyed; yet Marryat accused England of being naturally blood-thirsty, and not inclined to see anything glorious in a battle that was not gained by much loss of life. This was rather the official view. Cochrane was exceedingly careful of his men's lives; but as he reaped successes without commensurate slaughter of his officers and crew, the Admiralty would not promote the one nor praise the other. Of his own life and limbs Mr. Midshipman Marryat was by no means careful. In an engagement in the Bay of Arcajou he was struck down, and was afterwards laid out for dead, and for burial in the water. But he revived just in time. An unsympathising officer looked down on the body, and, for the funeral oration, said that *there* was a cock that had done crowing and a chap that had cheated the gallows. The wounded boy could scarcely speak for fainting, but he wagged his young tongue to the rather bold tune of "You're a liar."

In the heat of action he did not even know when he was badly wounded. On one occasion he received three wounds; the worst of the three was in the stomach, and that was precisely the one of which he knew nothing till the fight was over. Yet it was a bayonet wound; but the bayonet had thrust into the wound a part of the middy's shirt, which plugged it, and stooped all bleeding. When he afterwards undressed in his cabin and pulled off his shirt, away came the piece, which had not been torn from it, and which was in the wound. The blood then flowed, and the young fellow learnt how badly he was wounded. The wounds he received and the dangers he incurred never affected otherwise than beneficially his finer nature. There was aboard his ship another midshipman, named Cobbett, who was Marryat's bitterest enemy. Cobbett once fell overboard; Marryat plunged immediately after him, and held up the fellow, who had brutally treated him from the first moment of Marryat's joining, till a boat reached them and took in both rescued and rescuer. In a letter the noble young middy wrote to his mother he referred to this incident, and added, "From that moment I have loved the fellow as I never loved friend before. All my hate is forgotten. I have saved his life." It should be added, that he saved many other lives under similar circumstances. On one occasion he leaped from the poop of the vessel, which was going seven knots an hour, to save a poor seaman who had fallen overboard. The attempt failed, and Marryat himself was nearly lost. He was nearly two miles astern of the ship, and had been half an hour in the water before a boat reached him and took him in. In some of these attempts he was on the point of drowning; and he described the sensation as that of being rather tenderly and comfortably wrapped up in liquid green fields. He ran much greater peril in much less dangerous localities. After long uninterrupted service, he was, in 1813—then a lieutenant of a year's standing— dancing at a ball in Barbadoes, when he broke a bloodvessel. He was consequently invalided.

After rest came the Peace of 1815, which left Marryat further leisure for many things; among others may be mentioned his falling in love, and his marriage in 1819, with a knight's daughter. In 1820 he was afloat again, in command of the *Beaver*, which acted as a sort of sea-sentinel, cruising round and round St. Helena till the imperial prisoner in that island died, 1821. Marryat took the portrait of the ex-emperor, as he lay, with hands crossed above the crucifix on his breast: a picture which has been engraved both in France and England. The Captain attended the funeral, brought home the news of

Napoleon's death, and in August of the same year was employed in escorting the remains of poor Queen Caroline to Cuxhaven.

Subsequently he wrote a pamphlet against the impressment of seamen: this, too, at a time when it might have marred his professional prospects. For nearly three years (1823–6) he was actively engaged in the difficult but not inglorious Burmese war. He fought like a hero, made sketches as if he had been a professional draughtsman, and had a way of his own in picking up valuable trifles; it could not have been instinct; he probably acted upon information. When prisoners of rank fell into his power he caused them to be stripped, and had their bodies subjected to being carefully felt by the hands of some of his sailors. If they felt anything like a hard tumor it was immediately lanced, and the suppuration was in the form of a valuable jewel. Marryat no doubt knew that when a Burmese wanted to secure that sort of property he made an incision in his skin and thrust the precious stone beneath it. He had an eye here to his own interests, as the old bumboat woman had who was upset with him and a midshipman, when the Captain's gig went over in Falmouth Bay. The old woman was as much at home in the water as if she had been born a mermaid. She playfully struck out and held up the Captain, who, being able to hold himself up, bade her help to rescue the boy. The old lady stoutly refused; she wouldn't demean herself to save a mere middy when she might have the glory of saving the captain!

When the latter was again out of harness he set up his home at Brighton, where there was a court of mingled etiquette and free-and-easiness. At "receptions" it was the custom to kiss Queen Adelaide's hand, and King William kissed each lady on either cheek. The Fitzclarences made fun of the ceremony, and would, with consummate vulgarity, ask of the groups of ladies among whom they stood, "Well, has dad bussed you yet?" His Majesty himself, as is well known, was not punctilious on points of ceremony. At one of the royal evening parties King William remarked that Mrs. Marryat often looked at the clock and then spoke to the Captain. At last he asked the lady the reason for this proceeding. She briefly stated that Captain Marryat and herself were engaged to a second evening party at that hour. "Then, why don't you go?" said the king. The lady had to explain to him that etiquette compelled them to stay in the room till their majesties had retired. "Oh, d—— it!" exclaimed the religious and gracious king, "come along o' me, and I'll smuggle you out."

Marryat manifested the straightforwardness of his character when he stood candidate for the Tower Hamlets. He depended for success on his pamphlet against impressment, but he was questioned by an elector as to the equally serious question of flogging. The elector remarked that he had a son fit for the sea, and he was himself of an age at which he might go afloat, and he wished to know the Captain's

sentiments. Marryat might easily have evaded a dangerous answer,
but he replied, with the most disagreeable frankness, that if father and
son ever served under him, and he could not otherwise keep them from
offending against the law of the navy, he would order them both to be
flogged. He, of course, lost his election.

But life is full of compensations. Marryat found some in literary
work and success. Before he gave up the command of the *Ariadne*
he had written 'Frank Mildmay, or the Naval Officer,' in which there
are many reminiscences of his own life. For this first attempt Mr.
Colburn gave him £400. By the time he had written 'Japhet in
Search of a Father,' he could command three times that sum. Later
still there was increase of honorarium; yet Marryat called his work
"slavery,". and protested that the idea of Heaven was rendered tenfold more delicious to him by his conviction that no publisher would
ever be allowed to enter into the joys of Paradise. That he was a good
story-teller there is no gainsaying. Whatever he undertook to do he
did it with earnestness. Wide were the extremes of his " doing." At
one time leading an assault while cannon in front of him volleyed and
thundered; at another time by the bedside of his boys or girls, invent-
ing stories to which they listened till the voice of the speaker gently
monotoned them into slumber. ·

During Marryat's visit to America, in 1837–9, he displayed some of
the best traits in his character. He expressed all his opinions fearlessly, and found that the Americans liked him all the better for it in
time. At one period, indeed, he was hung in effigy, and copies of his
books were burnt, simply because, on British ground, in Canada, he
had described Captain Drew's cutting out of the *Caroline* as a gallant
action. He brought home furs and skins, with which he decorated his
London house and filled it with fleas. When he betook himself again
to literature, and contributed 'Joseph Rushbrook' to the *Era* newspaper, he was thought to have injured the dignity of authorship by
writing in a weekly newspaper. He was consoled by the resulting sum
paid into his bankers. His own estimate of the literary man was not
a high one. Like Congreve, Marryat seemed to think that a professional author and gentleman could not be identical. The profits of
the one, however, enabled him to .play the higher line of character
more successfully than he could otherwise have done, and perhaps
ill health may account for some of his peculiarities. Warm-hearted,
he was soon offended. "No one," says his daughter, "could have
decided, after an absence of six months, with whom he was friends and
with whom he was not." One of his friends said of him, "If he had
no one to love, he quarrelled for want of something better to do. He
planned for himself and everybody, and changed his mind ten times a
day." After he turned farmer, in Norfolk, he laid aside the sailor, and
dressed the new character as if he were about to play Hawthorn, in

'Love in a Village.' At times, indeed, he was like nobody but himself. Out with his dog and his gun he wore an eyeglass of very odd fashion. A strip of whalebone surrounding a plain piece of crystal was stuck through a hole cut in the brim of his hat, and so arranged as to hang down in front of his right eye. With the exception of his linen, we are told that the garments he usually wore were scarcely worth the consideration of the poorest man in the village; and yet the delicacy of his everyday life is vouched for; but it is admitted that his humour too often bordered on a want of refinement.

The fact is, Marryat was an excessively passionate man; but he was not so at home. And that might well be, as he described his Norfolk home in 1844: "My children are good, my household do their duty; we have no quarrelling or discontent among ourselves, and I have plenty of employment that interests me, as there is profit and loss attending it." His household could not have been an extravagantly dear one to keep, for he says that a single music lesson by a master from Norwich would cost him more than it did to feed his whole household for a week. With doubtful farming, he followed literature for the benefit chiefly of the young. It is curious to find the author of 'Peter Simple,' on being invited to write a story in the 'Novel Times,' declining, on the strange ground that his name would do the paper more harm than good. Perhaps he grew afraid of criticism; this is the more probable, as he was so anxious to protest that he did not care a jot for it. We do not know what the practice of reviewers and art-critics may be now. They were evidently of the no-better-than-they-should-be class if Marryat was justified in saying in a letter to a friend: "I believe I am a proud sort of person for an author, as I neither dedicate to great men nor give dinners to literary gentlemen; and dogs will snap if they are not well fed." This sounds ill, and indeed there are many passages in his letters that should not have been printed. It is easy to see who is meant in the Lady M—— of the following passage from one of his letters: "Lady M—— going to be married! I did not think she was such an Irish jackass. I'd as soon go to church with a paint-pot." There was as little truth in the report as in the Captain's comment. Another singularity is to be found in the fact that, with all the money he made by his novels, he complained in his later days of being in want of it. Probably the cost of being a gentleman-farmer absorbed the profits of authorship. Be this as it may, in 1845 ill health brought his literary career, save some work for children, to a close. The last novel in which he had a hand was 'Valeria,' now forgotten. Of this he was the author as far as down to a part of the third volume. Symptoms of the illness which became fatal to him manifested themselves; Marryat gave up the work, which was finished by another hand.

Thenceforth the athletic form began to waste away. He who up to this period, with his weight of fourteen stone, could have leaped a ditch or cleared a railing with the agility of a man of five and twenty, began to fade out of existence. In the prime of his manhood and in the full vigour of his intellect the disease which overcame him manifested itself. He ruptured a blood-vessel, and lessened two stone weight by it. He could spare the latter, but the loss of blood was irreparable. He lay on a mattress on the ground during the summer of 1848, uncomplainingly wasting away; often cheerful, oftener wandering in his mind. The frequent rupture of internal blood-vessels, and the consequent increasing weakness, reduced the once powerful man to the mere shadow of his former self. He might have said, as Cornelia's spirit said to Paulus:

"En sum quod digitis quinque levatur onus."

Early on an August morning of 1848, his family who were about him heard him murmur a sentence of the Lord's Prayer. As he finished it he gave a short sigh, a shiver passed through his frame, and he was gone.

# Roots.

---

It was a glorious evening as my young philosophical friend and I settled ourselves down for a quiet talk in the long grass on the top of Farewell Point. The sun was sinking behind the dark mountains on the mainland, sending a ten-mile path of gold across the smooth sea to the rocks beneath our feet. The last breath of air had died away, and the great Pacific was gradually sullenly heaving, till it wearied itself into a dead calm, "Just like" (said my young friend) "a tempestuous woman recovering from a fit of hysterics." Even the murmuring *pohutikawas* had ceased to wail their dirges over the sleepy water, and there was no sound but the distant growl of the long swell on some more exposed point, the note of a lively parson-bird,* imitating the accents of some member of his congregation with most reprehensible facetiousness, and the splash of the frivolous dancing mullet ·in the still harbour. Peace, calm, rest, everywhere; yet what so jarring as a scene like this when one is heavy at heart? I had got out of bed the wrong side this morning, as the nursemaids say. In the first place a cutter had arrived at daylight, bringing the news of the failure of poor Jean Haynes's run on the Kaiwarra, involving the loss of three hundred pounds my good man had lent him to start with; *consequently* my good man thought fit to find fault with my wild unsystematic way of educating the children; *consequently* (that being almost my only purpose and pleasure in life) I retorted that they were the only children I knew who looked on learning as a pleasure, *consequently* my worthy sister-in-law was set on to me, to lecture me on everything in general, and the conventionalities and the training of children in particular; *consequently*, in my desperation, I came out with a speech that would have made her hair stand on end, had it not been trained in far too orthodox a manner to dream of doing anything of the kind; *consequently* both she and my good man preached a joint sermon upon my innate wickedness; *consequently* I rushed into the bush and made my way up to Farewell Point in a very sore frame of mind. What an old fool I must be to let these continuous petty troubles make life so unbearable to me! How slow some people live! Here am I, after forty years of humdrum life amongst humdrum people, not yet able to fit myself into their groove, and still as sensi-

* The *tui* is called "the parson-bird," partly because he has two white feathers hanging from under his throat, partly because he always has a great deal to say for himself—at least, so say irreverent wood-cutters,

tive about being misunderstood and unappreciated as a morbid child. Well, well! We people with imaginations must pay for the pleasure of dreaming I suppose. But still it is terrible to have to force one's mind into an unnatural shape, not for a day, but for a life; to be taught constantly that all one's most innocent impulses have a sin lurking at their root; to hear that all thoughts that do not run in a certain groove are contraband. Bah! I know now what my young friend meant by saying that machine-made good people sent many of their fellow-creatures to the devil.

My young friend appeared to have guessed my thoughts to some degree, for, after looking quizzingly into my troubled face, he struck up the following remarkable doggrel :

" Oh, would I were a vegetable,
    A cabbage, or a cauliflower !
Unconscious and unfidgetable,
    I'd dream away life's bitterest hour.

To stop my thinking, I would be
    A demmed, cold, damp unpleasant body ;
I'd be a monk, I'd be a she,
    I'd swamp my brains in whisky-toddy.

Oh, theirs must be a happy life,
    To have no brains or botheration,
And when the time comes for the knife,
    Be ate with placid resignation.

Their gentle state my "——

" Where on earth does that nonsense come from ?" interrupted I crossly.

"That nonsense," replied he gravely, "was written by me some years ago, at a time when I had so addled my poor little brains with speculating that I was beginning to prepare myself for suicide or madness. The verses themselves will tell you what a state of despairing idiotcy I was reduced to. It was just at the time when I was entering upon my present phase, and hadn't got accustomed to its worries."

" What phase do you call that ?"

" Well, I don't know a name for it in English, for we English always affect to be rather ashamed of it; but the Germans call it something that sounds like *Sturm und Drang.* It is a disease arising from a sudden increase in the vitality of the spirit, which is apt to seize the young male of the human species between the ages of sixteen and twenty-four. Its chief symptoms are a wild desire to get back to what is natural, to find out the cause of everything, to reduce everything to first principles, to seize on generalities. A tendency to find no religion lofty enough, no political system perfect enough. Exalted but vague ambitions and ideals, great earnestness, restless but purposeless energy ; and lastly, owing to the soul being literally born a second time, a babyish power of realising the infinite mystery and wonder of the most commonplace things, which makes the cool matter-of-course view of the rest of the world in general infinitely exasperating.

"A young man in this phase (take myself as an instance) always puts me in mind of a child seeing the moon for the first time, realising its awful wonder, and being intensely hurt and vexed with the dulness of grown-up people who are not in the least struck with the solemn unexplainable mystery of the spectacle."

"Do you believe that most people go through this phase of second childhood on entering life?"

"A great many more than we suppose, to a greater or lesser extent. I never," said he, smiling, "see a remarkably fat, respectable, comfortable-looking old gentleman, who talks nothing but farming, three per cents., or ultra-Conservative politics, without thinking to myself, 'My good old friend, there was a time when you were a sentimental republican at heart, and wrote poetry in secret.'"

"What is the next phase to be?" asked I, laughing.

"God only knows," replied he. "Some subside in a very short time into mere jolly worldly take-it-easy cynicism; some rush into frantic religion; some remain on the same stilts all their life, and run their course in this world with an extra portion both of bitterness and pleasure; while others, though retaining their lofty ideals to the end, are strong enough to take the world as it is, and to turn their energy to whatever fraction of the great work may lie in their path, and lie down at last in peace, having contributed their mite to the happiness of their fellow men."

"Well," said I, "it seems that after enjoying two or three years of this mental stomach-ache people become pretty much what they were before. What's the good of it?"

"People are *not* quite the same as they were before—after it; their few years of *Sturm and Drang* are the heating in the furnace which qualifies the metal; their effect, however invisible, is never quite lost. After the sharp miseries of conception the twice-born young soul rushes, with a titanic strength and energy unknown before, to the groove best suited for it. And the marks of this fiery second birth remain for ever. Ay! take a deep dive in your unconventional way into the depths of some character apparently bound entirely by conventional laws and inbred prejudices, and then you will startle into life a keen recollection of the days of wild beautiful ideas, and the terrible ordeal of doubts. That mind can never quite narrow itself again to the limits of mere *ignorant* prejudice. Even its fierce fanaticism has something distinctive about it. It is the bigotry of earnestness, not of mere dull conceited ignorance. You ask me what is the purpose of this ordeal. No man can tell God's reasons, but it seems to me as if, in order to prevent us becoming mere bundles of conventional instincts and inherited prejudices, He had ordained that a large proportion of us, on entering manhood, should have suddenly and rudely the whole of our past education and its influences torn from our souls for a space, forcing us back to refreshing nature and naked first principles on all subjects."

"That's rather fanciful," said I.

"It don't seem so to me," replied he, "because I think it is the key to the vastly superior progress of some nations over others. Chinamen—most Orientals—even Roman Catholic Europeans, drop behind in the race, simply because they have lost the knack of, or discountenance, this wild fermentation of mind at the beginning of manhood. There could be *no improvement* if all were orthodox, as it is called, on every subject. Wherefore let not the world be too hard on us mad young Berserkirs; one in a hundred of us does good to his kind."

"And you call yourself a Conservative, you twisting young eel!" cried I. "What rejoicing among the angels of my party there would be if they could have heard that last declaration of your opinion!" .

"You old silly," answered he, impudently, "what I said don't compromise my British Conservatism in the least. I am a Conservative, and a staunch one, simply because, after going through a good many countries, this blessed New Zealand included, I have come to the human and fallible conclusion that the British constitution is, or was, the best in the world. I am a staunch Conservative, but of course no opponent to what I believe to be progress. I simply say, what you Liberals call progress, i.e., an advance towards democracy, I believe to be a step in the wrong direction in the nineteenth century, whatever it may be in the twenty-fifth."

Political conversations are, holds my young friend, newspaper articles without their good English, so we become silent by mutual consent, and gaze dreamily at the gorgeous sunset. The sea had turned to a pale dull oily grey, the torn fragments of summer cloud were changing their gorgeous golden and scarlet hues for modest pink and white, and of the fierce radiance that so lately inflamed the sky nothing remained but a deep fiery glow behind the blackening hills, marking the wake of the day.

My young friend, with his face between his hands, was gazing northward across the sleeping ocean as if his eyes could almost reach the lovely islands of the tropics, murmuring to himself a wild old South Sea poem:

"Lay me down on the deck, my lad, with my face towards the bow.
  They say there is land in sight; but my eyes are failing now.
  Young though I be, my course is run. It seems so hard to die,
  With the fresh sea sparkling round me, and the land I love so nigh.

You say the land's rising quick, Bill, but I know that I shall not last
I'm going soon, for already the pain of this cursed wound is past.
It was not the whale, poor betch, she never 'ud do one harm,
But ye see my foot slipped, and that thundering lubber Jem, he jogged
    my arm.
I'd like to see Tahiti, with its flowers and fruit, once more,
With its wild blue mountains rising up from the palm-trees on the shore,
The trees 'neath which I've lain and spent so many happy hours,
While the wild girls lolled around and rigged my head with their bright
    wild flowers;
Sleeping, and sucking cocoa-nuts, and kissing, the livelong day.
I knows they weren't always faithful, Bill, but they never axed for pay.
You mind a lass called Nita, the last time as we was there,
Tall and strong, with glistening eyes, and coal-black rippling hair?
I loved her true, and when I left I promised to come again,
And now I shall never see her more.    It 'll give the poor lass pain.
I'd like to see—but what matter now?    I know that I'm going fast.
I'll be signing my mark in another ship's books before this watch
    is past;
To-morrow, Bill, you'll launch me away to my home in the deep blue sea.
I'll have a glorious grave, indeed, the whole of the ocean free!
I'll deck myself out with the small coral-fish, those ones with a brilliant
    blue,
And them, you know, like butterflies, all of a golden hue;
And I'll choose a patch of silvery sand in the coral to lay my head,
There isn't a king in the wide, wide world, will have such a lovely bed.

    \*       \*       \*       \*       \*       \*

You say that the land is nigh, but my eyes are failing now,
Lay me down on the deck, my lad, with my face towards the bow."

"If that ballad," say I, "wasn't coarse, and so very rough in expression, it would be rather fine."

"And yet," replied he, "if you eliminated its coarseness and polished its expression you would take away its reality, and consequently its pathos.    It is that wild, coarse, misty ignorance of the poor dying whaler, contrasting, yet blending, with his innate, strange, poetic feeling, that gives it at once its sadness and its truth."

"You are very tiresome about poetry," cried I.    "You are ridiculously sentimental about any doggerel ballad, but when I give you some lofty spiritual poetry to read, such as Newman's 'Dream of Gerontius,' or Myers' 'St. Paul,' you fly into a tumult of rage and scorn, rave of their base prurient materialism and their windy nonsense in one breath, and parody them with a merciless vandalism of which you ought to be ashamed."

"Because they try to do something above their powers.    They try to soar above humanity, and consequently sink below it.    To get beyond (as they fancy) their earthiness they work themselves into a religious ecstasy, which requires to be fed by a tangible, materialistic, and often prurient idea of spiritual things; mix this with a proper leaven of windy wordy nonsense, and you have a religious poem of the kind you have mentioned. So, as no one can write superhuman poetry to please me, I content myself with poems breathing the beauties of humanity, of which we all know something, taking perhaps for my type of perfection Hood's 'Bridge of Sighs.',"

"But, surely," say I, "for all your sneering, this kind of ecstatic religious fervour does us good, by raising our thoughts from the sordid earth to a sense of the reality of higher things ?"

"Sordid earth, indeed !" retorts he, scornfully. "You people who use that argument seem to be possessed by an idea that God placed you in the world just to prove that you were a great deal too good for it. Leave such notions of the vileness of God's work to shallow-pated young priests and vain ecstatic young ladies. Why try to raise ourselves above the earth (if it be possible) while there is higher divinity, vaster beauty, in the everyday life around us than our little souls can take in in a lifetime, in spite of its tangibility ?"

"And so, most inconsistent of young persons, you who rave against the deification of man in all existing religions are as great a humanity worshipper as any !" cried I triumphantly.

"With a slight difference," answered he drily. "I love and try to learn from my brother, whom I do know, but don't for a moment assume that he is a likeness of God, whom I don't know."

"I think," said I, branching off, "that you carry your humanity worship almost too far. You love even its imperfections. None of your beloved characters in poetry and prose are by any means faultless. A perfect saint you don't love half as much as a good-hearted sinner, as long as he has no meanness about him. You take after your great idol, the cynical Thackeray, who would go a mile out of his way to find a hole in the coat of any man with an appearance of respectability, and handled a good-for-nothing Bohemian with the loving tenderness of a mother with her first baby."

"A soulless godless world calls Thackeray a bitter cynic, chiefly because they do not understand him, partly because he is an undying reproach to their hypocritical shams and heathen selfishness. They would have said the same of One whom Thackeray worshipped, had they lived in those days. He was no mere coldblooded disbeliever in the constancy and honour and generosity of mankind because he did not possess them himself; his bitterness sprang from an earnest love of the virtues he daily saw counterfeited and neglected. A cynical heartless remark, that in many circles, both high and low, would pass without notice or comment, struck bitter anger and sorrow into his more loving sensitive soul. Still worse, when time after time he, an earnest lover and seeker of what is good and noble, rushed eagerly at the appearance of it, and found he had grasped a sham. And thus he, not unlike the great Master that he served, learnt to pour out all his warm love and forgiveness to the simple warmhearted sinner, and to hold the more sinless, but hypocritical and self-complacent Pharisee, in loathing and disgust.

"And they say he was a disbeliever in human goodness!—he who revelled in the simple, manly, boyish purity of a character like Clive Newcome's until we are infected with his enthusiasm, hardly knowing why; he who loved and believed in goodness so much that he could dwell fondly over the rather insipid virtues of Amelia! Who but a man with an *intense* love and faith in human goodness and nobility could have drawn Warrington? A sketch dim, misty, imperfect, yet, owing to the warm intensity of its creator's feeling, a living picture, before which we can remain for ever with the tears in our eyes and a love in our hearts which seem almost absurdly wasted upon a mere phantasm of a writer's brain.

"And how beautiful, how almost piteous, is his triumphant exultation when, having drawn the faults, and even meannesses, of some lifelike human character, as scrupulously and sternly as though he were forced to it by some spell, he seizes on some little trait of warm, noble, human feeling! I tell you that man was no mere sour caviller, but more like one who, having his perceptions of good and evil sharpened by some purer spiritual atmosphere, was grieved and angered by our meanness, yet loved and worshipped all that was noble in our nature from the bottom of his great sore heart."

"You are an idolater," cried I, "and moreover, a polytheist; for you nearly blew me into space yesterday for saying I did'nt care for Dickens. How many more demigods am I to put into my calendar?"

"Bulwer Lytton and Charles Kingsley will do for the present," answered he laughing: "but you mustn't suppose that because I pitched into your feminine lack of appreciation of humour yesterday you are to put that delightful literary acrobat, Dickens, on to the same pedestal with my sublime Thackeray. I have studied Dickens unceasingly since I was ten years old, and yet the only *personal* feeling I have got towards the author is gratitude for having given so many hours of great pleasure and amusement. I never learnt anything from him; my inner self was never touched and changed by any of his words. To put it shortly, I read Dickens for his books and Thackeray for himself.

"In one sense Dickens's writing is a most charming literary *tour de force*. When his delightfully grotesque creations are sent for a time into the background, and the author himself comes forward and tries to be didactic or sentimental, I skip; for when he is didactic he is provokingly bumptious; when he uses sentiment he elaborates it artificially till I can't swallow it. His Nells and Smikes wont draw water into my eyes after the first reading.

"With Thackeray it is different. Call it a literary fault, if you will;

he himself is the most interesting character in all his books. In every work he seems to say, 'Here am I, with a living world round me. I will paint a small fragment of it exactly as I see it. I claim for my pictures no merit of invention, only the merit of being true to life. Reader, let us go hand in hand and talk and think over their faults and virtues together.'

"And it is his intuitive knowledge of when to let a picture speak for itself that gives him such a power of pathos. . It is its terrible simplicity of narration, its hideous commonplaceness (I don't know if you understand what I mean), that makes the description of that poor blackguard, Rawdon Crawley's, discovery of his wife's deceit so undyingly touching. The story of the catastrophe, is told without a comment. And then, when poor Rawdon, crushed, wild, and broken-hearted, goes to his prim, shallow, respectable brother, to tell him, the latter naturally begins the conversation with the presupposed idea that Rawdon has come to borrow money of him. There is something awfully cruel in this simple truth. The contrast between the utter despair of Rawdon's mind and the petty irritation of that of his obtuse brother, is rendered more ghastly by its natural commonplaceness. And the next touch, when even the shallow despicable Pitt is really moved with awe and pity at the great grief he finds himself in the presence of, derives its beauty from its truth to nature. And then, poor Rawdon goes to Macmurdo, to ask him to act as his second, and the goodnatured, Epicurean, jolly old soldier, sympathises with him as far as a man of his kind, who has led his kind of life, can—and that is not far. Again a contrast—horribly cruel, horribly simple and natural. You feel that poor Rawdon's ignorant untrained soul is alone for the first time with a great agonising grief, and the whole picture is so horribly lifelike, that you find yourself saying, 'Poor fellow! poor fellow!' with a choke in your voice, ay, though you read it fifty times."

"And yet," said I, "you profess to disbelieve in a devil. You! you! with your horrible power of realising the misery of things, from the squashing of a wasp to the breaking of a heart? Why, your mind has greater necessity for a devil than any I know."

"So a devil is necessary to me, is it?" answered he a little grimly. "Well, well, you are touching a great truth. 'The Devil,' like many another dogma, holds his place in men's minds because he fills a gap they dislike. I tell you there is a conviction growing daily in my mind that all religious theories and dogmas spring from or are connected with *one* want. Theories in all creeds of falls of man, redemptions, future rewards and punishments, extinction, devils, sins, and so on, *ad libitum*, spring from the same source. If I were asked to define what is a religion, as shortly as possible, I should say, 'An attempt to account for the origin, purpose, and nature, of what we then call *pain* as comfortably to ourselves as possible.' What matter if these explanatory dogmas that we console ourselves with lead to perpetual contradictions, blasphemies, and absurdities? Better that, says the conceit of human nature, than to own such mysteries beyond our reach. Oh, that insufferable, ignorant, self-importance of man! Making all his religious theories contain one word for God and two for himself!

"Man! man! you blind mole! study nature; learn all you can of the universe around you; and if you do this, not merely as a schoolboy learns Latin lines by heart, but make your mind deduce from what you see, you will learn some lessons. You will find out the extremely narrow limits of human knowledge—man's insignificance in the universe; you will find that every commonplace thing, traced back, is an utterly insoluble mystery. And having once realised these bitter things, you will get a feeling of God's utterly unreachable, ungrasp-able magnitude, that you never felt before. And from this last convic-tion comes peace of mind at last. From the bitter lesson of your own small worth and importance, and that of his inconceivable unintel-ligible power, you will get a 'faith,' a childish, fatalistic trust, that will make your previous miseries of doubt, and longings for revelation concerning your existence and destiny, seem like a laughable dream. You will cry, as I do now, 'Fool that I am, that know the narrow limits of my mind, that can realise that *every* simple thing around me is a mystery beyond my reach; that can feel from these things how inconceivable He is, and yet can flinch from blindly trusting that little atom, myself, and all my destiny, to Him! Shall I, in my foolish conceit and ignorance, cry for a knowledge that He has seen fit to deny to my race, and keep waiting for a revelation till I make an artificial one to comfort myself with?' Well, well! this religion won't come in our time, as I said to you the other day; so let us go back to the Devil, and the reasons why I can't believe in him. I believe that he was born (like many another article of faith) out of that absurd pre-sumption that our notions of right and wrong are divine, not merely in the sense of being intended by God for us, but in the sense of being *applicable to God himself and his actions*. In this wise. Man said, 'There is a God,' and the highest thing he could conceive being (as it is to this day), a perfect man, he created him in the spiritual image of man, with a man's ideas of good and evil. But here a difficulty pre-sented itself. If God was a being with our notions of justice and mercy, and also all-powerful over the universe, how came what man calls pain and sin? A theory of a Devil, that is to say, an antagonistic power of evil, apparently solved the difficulty. I say apparently, because really, it leaves the problem nearly where it was; for it is just as monstrous to believe that a Supreme Being with our notions of justice and mercy, and having almighty power, would allow an evil spirit to gratify his cruelty on us, as to believe that He does it himself. The disciples of Zoroaster, avoided this difficulty by making the good spirit and the evil one of equal power. But such a theory, besides being contrary to the teachings of the simplest natural science (don't sneer), is utterly repugnant to our feelings—more terrible than even the coldest blankest rationalism."

" What you call science, is liable to err," said I.

"So it seems is religion," replied he drily; "for I never met a religious man of *any* creed, who did not think that all religions but one were more or less false. When will religious people learn this evident but humiliating truth :

'If it were not for the merest accident of birth,
    You might have been high priest to Mumbo Jumbo?'

But there is this to be said, that, if they did realise fully this truth, it would take half the power for good out of their religion. Depend upon it, that a little bigotry, a little narrowmindedness, is a good and useful thing. *If men were not thoroughly convinced of the absolute truth of the creed they hold, what power (except in a few exceptional cases) would it have to direct their actions?* And so, though I don't believe in the Devil, because I think I see his human origin; because his existence seems to be a blasphemy against God, because all nature (of which man is part), denies a divided power, I see, that like many another human dogma, he is useful in the great work of improvement, and could not be dispensed with, at present, without harm."

" I don't yet quite understand your standpoint on these subjects," said I; " you are continually on both sides of the hedge. You take some so-called revealed fact out of a religion, pull it to pieces, show its human origin, the contradictions, and blasphemies it leads to, give a lot of reasons which prevent you from believing in it, and then coolly turn round and say it is good for men to believe in, &c."

" What," cried he, " would you have me put myself on the level of the lowest form of missionary, and say, for instance, ' I do not believe in the tenets of Hinduism ?—I feel sure they are not God's truth, therefore Hinduism cannot have benefited mankind, and most likely has done it harm ?' Away with such blasphemy—for blasphemy it is. Are we to deny that the world and all it contains have a Divine origin? Are we to say that the many religions of the earth are here in defiance of His will? I, the sceptic, at least, believe so firmly in God's great all-pervading power, as to feel convinced that all around me is made by Him with a purpose, whether I know it or not; have faith enough in Him to feel convinced that these religions, whose tenets I cannot believe in, are part of his great developing plan, the end of which I cannot even guess at. And holding this trusting fatalistic faith in Him, how can I dare to look at any portion of His work, and in my insignificant human knowledge say, ' I know better, this ought not to be ?'

> ' Nay, friend, think not that I am one of those
> Who calmly claim omniscience, and suppose
> That God Almighty, scarcely knows the worth
> Of this or that existing on the earth,
> And cry, ' False creeds I cannot bear to see,
> Because I'm sure that God agrees with me.'

" Well, that's all very well," said I, "but it seems to me that this extreme humility and perfect trust that you not unnaturally triumph in must lead to sheer fatalism, and from that to simple indifference. If the mass of mankind believed, as you do, that the whole world, with its good and evil contents, was a great plan, in which they were merely automata, they would simply put their hands in their pockets and loaf away their lives without a purpose, and all improvement, humanly speaking, would come to an end."

" Well," answered he, coolly, " haven't I told you so often before ?—(not that fatalism *always* produces indifference, but it, at any rate, seems to be the natural consequence of it). But now you will see why I am always on both sides of the hedge, as you call it. This conviction of the uselessness of my negative creed to mankind forces me to see the good of religions, and to understand, *from the deficiencies* of my own scheme, how and why they produce virtue. And then, you see, my firm conviction that we are all part of God's plan of improvement, makes me believe that the narrow-minded man, who deems that his opinions alone are God's truth, is doing His work, shows me how his very narrowness and fanaticism are of good use, while none the less are men of the school to which I belong working in the same scheme by opposing his want of liberality. I might go on for ever on this theme. As in nature, so in men, opposing forces producing results. I cannot imagine a greater evil for mankind than the sudden loss of the superstitions and fallacies that they now believe in, excepting the utter destruction of that puny whisper in favour of greater liberality that is now always affecting their hearts, if not their heads.

" Yes, I am continually on both sides of the hedge. Confirmed sceptic though I be, the invariable conclusion that all my speculations lead to is the superior power for good of almost any religion (that is to say, any scheme that professes to throw light on mysteries beyond the reach of human investigation), over the noblest, purest form of what is called scepticism. The very humility, the want of assumption of knowledge of the latter, makes it unattractive to men and powerless to direct their actions ; the very perfection of its trust in God tends to fatalism and indifference.

" Is it not strange how extremes meet ? The stronghold of a pious

Romanist is his blind faith, that of the sceptic his complete trust in God. The slur so often cast against the former is his toleration of pious frauds; and here am I, the sceptic, with all my contempt for dishonesty of thought, forced into a respect for their utility, both by my conscience and senses. Ay! I respect pious frauds. Though the presumption, and superstition, and uncharitable exclusiveness of every religion move me with pity, with horror, with contempt, I cannot shut my eyes to the fact that the good that they do far out-weighs the evil—far outweighs the good that could be done by a negative humble creed like mine. And in them I see the finger of God leading mankind on the march towards greater purity and virtue in the manner best suited to them. Who am I that I should not bow my head and say, It is good?"

"Then why." asked I, rather stupidly, "if you feel the worthless-ness of your belief as compared to religion, don't you leave it?"

"Why?" cried he, opening his eyes and half laughing. "Why, how can I leave my creed unless it leaves me? Belief ought to be a matter of conscience, not compulsion. Ah, well! You orthodox people never can appreciate our only virtue—a sacred fearless un-bribable honesty of thought. Supposing I (if it were possible to me, which I don't believe,) were to force or persuade myself to believe anything because I knew it would be good and pleasant for me to believe it, my conscience would tell me that I was committing a great crime—a moral suicide. But come; it is as dark as pitch, and if we don't want to be drowned or break our necks we had better be getting homewards."

And so we scrambled home in silence through the murmuring forest, occasionally lighted by weird moon flashes through the shiver-ing trees. for the land breeze had sprung up, pondering each over our own thoughts. And as I thought over all he had said, I could not help being struck by the glorious loftiness of the position from which he judged the world, by his power in seeing good in what he hated, but still more by the uselessness of this position—useless except in the negative way of mitigating bigotry and partisanship on all sides. Would he. too, some day, buckle on the armour of life and come down to fight in God's cause on one side or another?

Time will show.

# The Wooing o't.

A NOVEL.

---

## CHAPTER XVI.

THE London season was at the spring-tide, in the fullest flood, when Trafford found himself once more in the Albany.

Lord Torchester had never got further than the great metropolis, having been swept into the social maelstrom, where he found an excellent place assigned him—and Trafford was much struck and amused by the increase of self-possession and worldly tact which the young earl appeared to have acquired, even in the short space of four or five weeks. He had begged Trafford to join him, and was very pleased to see him; but he evidently had not a disengaged moment, and Trafford, for whom London had none of the charms it possessed for his cousin, quickly determined to seek somewhere else for the change of scene and thought he felt he must have.

A great friend of his, an artist, as yet scarcely known (for Geoffrey Trafford had many dear friends in Bohemia), was about to start for Bordeaux, intending to sketch among the picturesque old towns of Aquitaine, and then to push on to the Pyrenees. Trafford proposed to accompany him so far. There was a good deal of the artist in his nature, and he was an immense favourite among the pleasant, careless, ready-witted knights of the brush and the pen; who declared him to be a good fellow though unavoidably a fine gentleman, and as ready to rough it in any of their expeditions as the poorest among them. But first he must see Lady Torchester and Bolton. His aunt, on the occasion of his dining with her the day after his arrival, had been surrounded by a large party of her own peculiar people. He had therefore, no opportunity of executing his self-imposed mission.

The stamp of the busy season was nowhere more visible than in the vicinity of Lincoln's Inn. Hansom cabs writhed and twisted through the tortuous approaches, coming out into its comparative quiet from beneath mysterious archways, and depositing anxious-looking clients, pale lawyers, florid country gentlemen—doomed flies on the edge of that web of courts which spreads its meshes between the so-called " Fields " and Chancery Lane. The dusty heated faces that looked out from under those terrible horsehair wigs, which at once proclaim and punish the limbs of the law, were visibly in need of sea baths and fresh air, as the owners thereof whisked from one court to another, the tails of their gowns fluttering behind them.

In a large, quiet, cool back room, on the ground floor of a large dull house on the south side of the above-named fields—a vast house, every room of which was crammed with clerks and papers, and where the scratching of pens ceased not from morn till eve in the everlasting task of wrapping up the sense of facts in a mist of words—in this cool, big, back room, enthroned in state, sat Mr. Bolton, head of the great firm of Bolton and Lee, a prince among solicitors, a depository of aristocratic secrets—from whose penetrating eye no client's little weaknesses were hidden. He was dictating a letter to a doughy looking clerk, who took down his utterances in shorthand. As he spoke, another youth entered with a slip of paper, at which Mr. Bolton glanced, and saying shortly, " In five minutes," continued his letter to the end. Whereupon the doughy looking clerk vanished, and shortly after Mr. Geoffrey Trafford was ushered in.

" Very glad to see you," said Bolton, shaking hands with him cordially. " When did you return? I began to be afraid you would never come back."

" I arrived a few days ago," said Trafford, drawing a chair in front of Bolton's table.

" Can't say you are looking the better of your stay in Paris; though you seem to have done the state great service. I suppose you have seen the Countess, and received the ovation she had prepared for you? You certainly have been the salvation of her son."

" Nothing of the kind, I assure you," said Trafford, impatiently. " I did nothing, could do nothing. The luck of the family was in the ascendant, and Torchester is a free man. Yes, I dined with my aunt on Tuesday, and was glad to see her so cheerful and content. I am going out of town again next week, so I thought I would have a talk with you, and hear what you have been doing."

" Quite right, Mr. Trafford. By the way, your last from Paris gave me great pleasure. Though you commit yourself to nothing, I could see the promise of a political career. I have my eyes open for the first chance of a seat. I had a talk with our honest Mudborough representative; but I am sorely afraid you are too liberal for that constituency."

" I think I am," said Trafford, absently.

" By the way, I have put all your available capital into Oldham and Garret—you gave me carte blanche."

" I have no doubt you have done well," returned Trafford, thoughtfully. " I suppose there is nothing left "——

"Except the Riversdale Farms," interrupted Bolton, " and though they are underlet they bring in a trifle over four hundred a year."

" One would not starve on that," said Trafford.

"Starve! My dear sir! your fortune is before you. Why, you will be able to reckon on eight per cent. for your capital; so there is a very decent income to begin upon. Enough to start you on some career free from carking cares, and needing only to think of success."

Trafford rose, and walked to the window without speaking, and then turning with his pleasant smile to Bolton, exclaimed, " I am really not worth the trouble you take. Yet I feel rather ashamed of having done nothing but hunt and shoot and fish, for these twenty-five years past. I suppose I have followed my vocation, and for the life of me I cannot find another. I have not a mission of any sort, and I have a strong conviction that England will pull through all her difficulties without my help."

" She would be all the better for the help of an honest, intelligent, well-educated gentleman, to counterbalance the crowd of officious, self-interested demagogues who force themselves to the front to pick up what they can."

" Yet if I do join the 'crushing crowd,' Bolton, I fancy I shall be a bit of a Radical."

" Be something," said the energetic old gentleman emphatically. " I was brought up a Tory, and I lean to that faction, but were I a young man I should be a Liberal. Whatever one's likings or pre-judices, we must go with the spirit of the times, or be thrown out of the race altogether."

" To tell you the truth," rejoined Trafford, " I want to do some-thing, be interested in something, and get rid of this infernal sense of self and isolation that hangs round me like a winding-sheet." He stopped abruptly at the sight of Bolton's astonished expression of countenance as he listened to such an unwonted outburst from the usually calm debonair Trafford. " I mean, I am rather sick of my-self," he continued, laughing. " I suppose I have caught the trick of tall talking from my French acquaintance."

" My dear young friend, you are not well ; you had better see Dr. Saville. Now I look at you, you are looking thin and haggard ; not half the man you were two months ago."

" Pooh ! nonsense ! Seriously, Bolton, I am resolved to make my-self a place, but I am going to run over to St. Petersburg first. Nothing to be done here during the winter, and St. Petersburg is one of the few places I don't know."

" Come, Mr. Trafford, no looking back, once you have put your hand to the plough."

" But I haven't put my hand to it. Then the Countess wants me to take Torchester in hand and convey him away somewhere north, where his cousin, Miss Wallscourt, is staying ; the heiress that is to be, towards whom the pious Countess' feelings are somewhat tinged with the old leaven. But if she thinks that because I was ready to mar one marriage I am willing to make another, she is much mistaken. From henceforth my revered cousin must manage his love affairs himself. He will be all right now."

"I suppose so. But, my dear Mr. Trafford, I always thought the young lady in question would exactly suit you. Lady Torchester ought to remember the Earl has come in to a highly improved and improvable estate; while you—well, you would undoubtedly be the better of an heiress-wife. You know Miss Wallscourt?"

"Yes—that is, I knew her as a child and a very young girl, a pretty and uncommonly self-willed little thing. She must be one or two and twenty now. No, Bolton, my fancies do not lead that way; I don't care for matrimony. I'll tell you what I'll do. I will amuse myself and make up my political mind till Christmas, and then I'll come into residence in this huge market and do something. I will! not to please you only; to please myself.

"If you begin in that spirit, you will succeed. But an heiress is not to be despised; such an heiress, well bred, well born, a family connection, no objectionable blood ties, sufficient good looks, et cetera, to do away with a mercenary air—eh?"

Trafford took up his hat and rose lazily. Leaning his arm on the chimneypiece, he remarked,

"I begin seriously to doubt whether education and civilisation, and all the other botherations, do one any good; I mean in the sense of enjoyment. A well-to-do savage in a country full of game has a far jollier life of it than I have, for instance. He can indulge his natural tastes, and not be cribbed, cabined, and confined, with here a barrier of rank and there a rampart of duty, debts to oneself, to one's tailor, to society, and the Lord knows what besides. I think I would go back to North America, were it not for having tasted that fatal tree of knowledge, which somehow spoils the flavour of other fruit."

"Pooh! nonsense! My young friend, you have always permitted me to assume the character of your mentor, so I must tell you, your nonsense is not even original. There is no occupation more exhilarating than the struggle to get the better of one's fellow-creatures. Throw yourself into the battle, and we shall hear no more of such thin philosophy. I cannot help thinking, Mr. Trafford," looking keenly at him, "that you are not well, or—or something."

Trafford laughed good-humouredly. "I am well enough, old friend," he said. "I only want work, I suppose, and as you have plenty, I will take myself away."

"Where are you going?"

"To dine with Lady Torchester. She wants a tête à tête dinner, as I start to-morrow. When we met on Tuesday 'twas in a crowd. Good-bye, Bolton, and many thanks for your fatherly care of self and belongings."

"Keep me informed of your movements," said Mr. Bolton, rising and shaking his young friend's hand, "and don't throw away the 'goods the gods provide.'"

"*Au revoir,*" returned Trafford, and closed the door on his mentor.

\* \* \* \* \* \*

At the early hour of seven that evening Geoffrey Trafford sat at dinner with his aunt in the handsome but sombre dining-room of The Beeches.

"I am afraid my hours are uncomfortably early for you, Geoffrey," said the Countess. "Had I thought, I should have said dinner at eight."

"My dear aunt, I have dined well at all hours, from eleven till nine; seven is, I think, sensible. I should be shocked had you changed your hour for me."

"When do you start to-morrow?—Barnes, Mr. Trafford will take a little more fish."

"Thanks. We talk of catching the steamer at Gravesend about two to-morrow."

"The steamer! By what route do you travel then?"

"By steamer to Bordeaux."

"Rather an uncomfortable mode of progress!"

"Not to an old salt like myself. No, thanks" (fowl offered); "lamb."

"Was Paris very full of English?"

"They were as thick as leaves that fall in Vallambrosa."

A pause, during which Lady Torchester longed for the dessert and uninterrupted confidence.

"Will you not take champagne, Geoffrey?"

"Dear Lady Torchester, no. It would be sacrilege to mix any other vintage with your incomparable Burgundy. I saw Bolton to-day. He was inquiring particularly for your ladyship. What a capital fellow he is!"

"Yes," returned the Countess slowly, doubtfully. "Poor dear Lord Torchester had the highest possible opinion of him. But is it not sad to see a man of his age so absorbed in the things of this life? It is curious that neither Mr. Badger nor Mr. White, both very enlightened men—Torchester's tutors—you remember Mr. Badger I am sure?—neither of them liked Mr. Bolton. They thought—I do not know exactly what they thought, but they did not like him."

"No, I fancy not," said Geoffrey, accepting a segment of iced pudding.

"He certainly is a hopeless heathen in some ways, but you could not have a sounder adviser. I am sure I owe him an unlimited amount of gratitude for all sorts of good services."

At last dessert was put on and they were alone.

"Now, my dear Geoffrey, I quite long to hear all details. I had such a hurried talk with you when you were here with all those people. When you went over first how did Torchester receive you?"

"Not very cordially. He evidently thought my visit boded interruption to his plans," replied Geoffrey, his heart beating a little faster than he expected at this much-wished-for opening, which he meant to use in Maggie's service, while he remembered that it was just a week that very evening since, by such a tremendous effort of self-control, he had bid her good-bye with but indifferent composure. "I soon saw I could do very little with him, and I much fear my efforts, though guarded, earned me his hearty disgust," added Trafford, laughing as he remembered the *tête à tête* he had so ruthlessly interrupted.

"I am sure, Geoffrey, Torchester is warmly attached to you, and he ought to be. I will always believe that you did somehow save him. I am sure, but for you, this Miss Grey would now be my daughter-in-law."

As the Countess spoke an idea flashed across Trafford's mind. "Could it be that a half-unconscious preference for me decided her against so tempting an offer?" but he put away the thought.

"Miss Grey certainly would have been your daughter-in-law by this time but for herself," he replied gravely, "and I do not know another woman who would have acted as she did. Think of the temptation, to even a girl of good position! Torchester was of age—perfectly his own master—a few words, a moment's time, would have changed her from a penniless dependent waif to a peeress of England—to a social position which the commonest good sense and good conduct would have made all her own. Even you would not have turned your back on your son's wife, and every one must feel that Torchester is just the sort of fellow to stand by the woman who bears his name."

"You are quite quite right," cried the Countess eagerly. "Then why did the young lady let him escape? Perhaps she had not understanding—education enough—to see all these advantages?"

Trafford shook his head and helped himself to some more strawberries. "She has quite brains enough to comprehend it all. Torchester owes his failure, I mean his escape, to three reasons: first, she was not a tinge in love with him"——

"Yet," interrupted the mother, "my boy is certainly attractive."

"No doubt. But though younger a little in years, Miss Grey has been matured in the school of adversity, and looks on your boy *as* a boy. Then she had a strong idea it would make you miserable—this I encouraged; and thirdly, I could see she very wisely thought that when Torchester cooled down enough to count the cost of his whim, he might think it rather expensive. But my first reason includes all the rest."

"She must be an uncommonly high-minded young woman," said Lady Torchester, with measured approbation.

"I suppose she is," returned Trafford, musingly. "But my dear aunt, don't you think it argues a low standpoint of morality when we are roused to admiration by a girl following her own natural healthy instinct for happiness in her own class, instead of standing on tip-toes to snatch that which is far above, out of her reach? Miss Grey has shown soundness of heart and mind."

"Which are sufficiently rare to be extremely valuable. Is she pretty, Geoffrey? Of course poor Torchester thought so, but it does not therefore follow."

"She is scarcely pretty; yet your son showed very good taste," said Trafford, smiling, and answering the real question. "She is very fair and gentle; you might easily pass her in a crowd; but if you looked at her once you would be sure to look again. There is a quiet harmonious grace about her I cannot quite describe. I fancy it is the result of never *seeming*; her great charm is her wonderful naturalness and earnestness—she "——

"My dear Geoffrey," interrupted the Countess, with the faintest tinge of suspicion, "you appear to take a very deep interest in this young person."

"I do indeed," said Trafford with disarming frankness and self-possession, looking straight into his aunt's eyes. "And more, I want *you* to take an interest in her. She is rather unfortunately placed; an orphan, a true-hearted, right-minded girl, utterly dependent on an uncle and aunt sufficiently burdened already, and living with a terrific female—this Mrs. Berry—low, ignorant, idiotic, on the point of marriage with a French blackleg."

"I am sure I should be very happy to be of any use to her," said Lady Torchester, kindly, "if you would point out the way. And how did you manage to find out all this, Geoffrey? You must surely have become very intimate with my son's *innamorata?*"

"You see," replied Trafford, with excessive candour, "when I found the sort of girl she was I ventured to speak of you, and then she frankly told me that my cousin was safe, as far as she was concerned; so we became great friends, and I gathered what I have told you partly from conversation, partly from observation. I am sure, my dear aunt, you are too true a woman not to believe that there are men to be found who would gladly help a girl they like and respect without a shade of personal feeling in the matter."

"They are to be found," said Lady Torchester, "but they are not numerous; if however they exist anywhere it will be among the Traffords, for though not brilliant personages, they have ever been true and loyal gentlemen. Now what can I do for this young lady?"

Trafford paused, considerably puzzled, and smiling to himself at the Countess's bit of simple family pride. "It is easier to say, 'Do something' than to define what the 'something' is to be," he said, at

length. "I suppose Miss Grey wants to do something, or be something, that will enable her to earn her bread—she has nothing, you
know."

"And what can she do?"

"Oh! I can hardly tell. She speaks French very well, and I
think she plays, and I fancy she would read aloud pleasantly. She
would be the very thing for some crotchety dowager who had married
off her daughters and wanted a nice kindly companion"—and as he
said this Trafford groaned in spirit at the idea of consigning dear
bright Maggie to such a fate; but it was the best he could do for her.

"I suppose she might suit a crotchety dowager like myself, eh,
Geoff?" said the Countess good-humouredly.

"The cap does'nt fit you in the least," rejoined Trafford.

"Well, I really do not want a companion yet; and besides, think of
the danger of her coming in contact with Torchester! It is not to
be entertained for a moment! However, I will see what I can do;
and "——— a pause as though for an effort—"suppose I were to write
to her?"

"It would be by far the best plan, and exceedingly kind!" cried
Trafford.

"But how could I write to her? It would be a difficult letter,"
urged Lady Torchester.

"Not at all, my dear aunt, if you just think. Say—oh! say that
you have heard so much of her from your son and nephew, and understanding that she is not quite settled with Mrs. Berry, you would be
happy to be of use if she would inform you how you could serve her—
something just to open communications."

"That would be very vague, and rather in the character of a *carte
blanche*. Nevertheless"—noticing the earnestness of her favourite
nephew's countenance—"I *will* write, and try to do something for
your *protégée*. Surely she must have some wonderful charm, to interest
Torchester as a lover and you as a friend!" and Lady Torchester rose
as she spoke.

"Once you take the affair into your hands neither of us need trouble
ourselves further. May I not waive ceremony, and be permitted to
accompany you to the drawing-room at once?"

"Certainly, if you care to do so," returned the Countess, flattered
by the wish; and the cosy *tête à tête* was prolonged by an open window,
which permitted the odours of the garden to penetrate the room.

Trafford had said his say and gained his point, and now became a
most sympathetic listener to Lady Torchester's plans and projects
respecting her son, who was the ocean to the river of her thoughts.
Tea proved a pleasant interruption; and after the servants left the
Countess sipped hers in thoughtful silence.

Suddenly, as though speaking to herself, she remarked, "I fancy she would make Mr. Blackmore an excellent wife. He would be quite perfect if he had a wife. Her father was an artist, you say?"

"Whose?" asked Trafford, considerably bewildered. "Maggie's?"

The familiar name dropped with fatal readiness from his lips—he would have given the world to recall it; but Lady Torchester was too engrossed by her own thoughts to heed him, so he escaped.

"Do you mean Miss Grey's father?" repeated Trafford. "Yes, I believe he was. And who may Mr. Blackmore be?"

"Oh! he is the curate at Mount Trafford. Such a pious, earnest, admirable man; but he ought to marry. If you and Torchester are out of the way I shall certainly ask Miss Grey to stay with me; and if I think her worthy of him I shall invite Mr. Blackmore to meet her."

"Worthy of him! Oh! Eros, hear her!" But Trafford's spoken reply was a calm assurance that Miss Grey was, he felt sure, admirably suited to be a clergyman's wife; and then he wrote her address in Paris for his aunt.

"How long do you think of staying among the Pyrenees, Geoffrey?"

"Six weeks, perhaps; certainly not more than two months. I shall want to see Bolton again early in August."

"Then I hope you are going to Craigmurchan Castle?"

"Lady Macallum asked me in a general way yesterday, but I am not sure. Why? do you wish me to go?"

"Because if you go, Torchester will; and though it is not consistent with my views to plan worldly projects, still I think it is desirable that Margaret Wallscourt and my son should have an opportunity of meeting. She is not in town this season, on account of the deaths in the family; but I imagine she will be at the Macallums."

"Well, I have promised Tor to join him at the shootings he has taken, or is going to take, which are within a drive of Craigmurchan. But remember, my dear aunt, that in your or Torchester's matrimonial designs I shall meddle no more. Take my advice: put your trust in Providence, and leave your son alone."

"Such advice from *you*, Geoffrey, is indeed a rebuke," said the Countess, with a grave smile.

"An unintentional one."

"But, Geoffrey, do you not think Margaret exactly the right wife for my son?"

"I cannot possibly say. I have not seen her since she was first in long frocks. If I meet her in Scotland you shall have my opinion."

After a little more talk, Trafford bid Lady Torchester good-night.

"The braw moon glistened o'er" roadway and hedgerow, villa and cottage, as Trafford drove rapidly and mechanically back to town. Thank God he had interested the Countess in his young friend; for of course, from henceforth, Maggie was only to be his *protégée*; a good little girl, to be helped, but nothing to him, personally. No, no;

he had had enough of that folly, and too much for a man of his age and experience. It was time he should take a more practical view of life; all pleasant things, somehow, were wrong and enervating; so he would see about politics, and write a pamphlet, by Jove! On what? *Noblesse oblige*—'The Obligations of Rank?' Pshaw! it had been done a dozen times already. How well even these roadside boxes look in the moonlight! "Not a fortnight ago that moon looked on me and Maggie in the Bois de Boulogne. What a delicious evening that was! I would give a year or two to have it over again! How sweet and young and calm she looked; but I never could come out of it so well a second time. I half wish I had had a kiss—just one to remember. Bah! what folly! What a queer imbroglio one's brain is at times! Maggie's kisses, I suppose, are reserved for some blessed Blackmore; these rascal curates get the pick of everything. Hollo! you fellows, do you want the whole of the road?" This was shouted savagely at some carters, whose waggons, piled perilously high with cabbages, were drowsily proceeding townwards.

And so, battling with himself, Geoff Trafford reached his chambers. He glanced through his letters—a vague unacknowledged hope that perhaps that predicted difficulty which was to drive Maggie to him for counsel and help had come! But no. Then he hoped Lady Torchester's letter would find her in Paris, but of course it would. Mrs. Berry could never get away suddenly; otherwise, thought Trafford, "I should be afraid, for her sake, to acknowledge I possessed a further clue to her."

So he turned over the invitation cards which had already begun to pour in upon him; but loathing all in his inmost soul, sought refuge in his club, where he did find relief and oblivion—in congenial sporting talk.

*       *       *       *       *       *

The next day, in a magnificent flood of sunshine, and with a delicious breeze just dimpling the water, Trafford set out on his travels.

His artist friend was in the highest, the most contagious good spirits. He had sold a couple of pictures unusually well; he had paid his most pressing debts, and for him life had not a cloud. He had a mind, he told Trafford, to winter in Spain, and bring back a wealth of sketches.

There were few passengers besides themselves—and those foreigners; the fare was good, the weather fine; and under these favourable conditions Trafford managed to become more like himself again. It was quite a relief to get rid of that haunting picture of Maggie— slender, brown-haired, bending over her work, or turned slightly from his glance at times, or meeting it fully and frankly when his talk roused her special interest, with her clear, soft, honest grey eyes; or that varying smile—so bright, at times so sad, or a tinge contemptuous. And then there was a composed despondent expression he knew so well, with the head turned away, showing the pretty white young throat and small ear. It was a positive relief to keep these visions at bay—to feel the power of resistance increase; though they would come still. And so the good ship sped away, and the friends reached their destination. Then ensued several weeks of pleasant wandering, during which few letters reached the wanderers. And Trafford almost hoped his folly and weakness were quite cured.

CHAPTER XVII.

THE same evening that lit up the picturesque streets of the Black Prince's capital, to the admiration of Trafford and his friend, was lowering with a heavy oppressive heat over our heroine's original quarters in Beverly Street. Yet an unwonted air of cheerfulness and animation pervaded the chemist's house.

There was no card in the fanlight over the front door, yet the dingy drawing-room was evidently occupied by the family.

The back parlour was encumbered with corded boxes, an open portmanteau, a plethoric hamper, while, though late, the table was loaded with materials for a most substantial tea, and over all beamed —yes, beamed!—Aunt Grey. The corkscrew curls were a shade less wiry, the tightly-closed lips were a trifle relaxed, as she fussed to and fro.

Jemima was putting the last touches to a bonnet of high pretensions, while the worthy chemist was seated at table, partaking of the good things over which his eldest daughter presided.

"I cannot fix this ribbon any way," exclaimed Jemima, impatiently. "I must say Maggie was a wonderful help where there was anything to do up; she would twist this into shape in no time."

"Don't talk nonsense," said Mrs. Grey, sharply. "You have no perseverance. Maggie ain't cleverer than her neighbours."

"When did you hear from Maggie last?" asked Mr. Grey—his mouth full of poached egg and toast.

"I can hardly tell—oh, about three weeks ago," said Bell.

"You have written to her, I suppose?" returned her father.

"No, indeed, there has been no time," put in Mrs. Grey.

A loud ring and small knock at the front door interrupted her.

"Whoever is that?"

"It's only Dick playing tricks," said Jemima.

And the next moment the youth she named rushed in, exclaiming, "Here's Maggie back again, bag and baggage, in a cab!"

"Don't tell ridiculous stories," said his mother, undisturbed.

"It is true, though! You come and see."

Jemima dropped her work and rushed into the hall, while Bell called after her that she was a fool to mind him. But another sound caught Mrs. Grey's ear; she stood still for an instant to listen, and then followed her daughter. A general hubbub of voices ensued, then all came crowding into the room together with Maggie—the veritable Maggie in their midst—very pale and weary looking, with a travelling bag in her hand, and crowned by a wide-brimmed grey straw hat.

" Maggie, my dear," cried Uncle John, kindly, " I am truly pleased to see you. We were just speaking of you."

" Dear, dear uncle "—a hearty hug and kiss—" how well you are looking! I am so glad to see you—my aunt, too! You all look as bright as possible."

" And what on earth has brought you back so sudden?" cried Aunt Grey, not unkindly. " Why there's no end to the changes."

" Oh," said Maggie, " I have a long story to tell. Mrs. Berry (who has been engaged for some time to a Frenchman) started with me from Paris on Thursday last, intending, she said, to go to London to see her lawyer, and have matters arranged previous to her marriage. When we landed at Dover Monsieur de Bragance, her intended, to my surprise, met us on the pier. Mrs. Berry said she was not well enough to go on to town, so we went to an hotel. She was out nearly all day yesterday; went out again early this morning; and when she returned informed me she was married to Monsieur de Bragance, and as her dear husband did not like me, that she was reluctantly obliged to send me away; that she herself was about to accompany him back to the Continent, and that I had better put my things together and take the next train up to town. Then she cried a good deal, and kissed me; gave me five pounds and my travelling expenses, begged me to go and see Mr. Dunsford, and tell him what a grand marriage she had made. So I packed her things and my own, took first train I could get after—and here I am."

" Well, I never!" sighed Mrs. Grey, sitting down suddenly, as if she was unable to stand up against such tidings.

" What a mad—unprincipled—idiotic person!" said Uncle Grey, energetically, as he stirred his tea with some violence. " Well, my dear, you are very welcome here, and we must take better care who we let you go to in future."

" Oh!" cried Maggie, her colour returning quickly and vividly under the influence of a warm atmosphere and the concentrated attention of five pairs of eyes. " I shall not trespass on your kindness and my aunt's long; for I shall be able to find something to do much more easily now."

" My dear girl, there's nothing but changes," began Mrs. Grey, with unusual good humour, when Dick broke in boisterously,

"Now, Maggie, you shall guess who we're expecting in to tea." .

Maggie looked round as she untied her hat, and very naturally guessed, "Tom?"

"Tom, indeed!" with derision. "Try again; two more guesses."

"I cannot possibly guess—unless," with a glance at her aunt's unusually benignant face, "it is Mr.—Mr.—oh! the gentleman who used to come in and talk science with my uncle."

"No, no," chorussed Dick, Bell, and Jemima, with loud laughter.

"Don't worrit," cried Mrs. Grey. "Maggie will be glad to get off her things and have a cup of tea. How could she ever guess? John is come back; came more than a month ago, and was going off to-morrow to have a look at Paris and see you. It is lucky after all you did come to-day."

"John! dear cousin John come back!" cried Maggie, breathless with astonishment, and feeling a certain glow of comfort in her desolation—for it *had* been a day of utter desolation.

"That he has," said the proud father. "Come back, to be the stay and support of his parents and family—a prosperous man, I am happy to say, and worthy of it."

"Yes, I must say he has behaved very handsome," put in Mrs. Grey; "but there, Jemmy, go up with Maggie to my room and let her put off her cloak. Here, I'll make fresh tea."

While Maggie made her simple toilet Jemima poured forth a volume of revelations, which may be epitomised. Things had been very gloomy with the chemist and his family before John arrived, but the active colonist had exercised the magic of energy, common sense, and a judicious outlay of capital. He had seen all pa's creditors. He had rowed Tom "awful," and got Tom a berth as surgeon of a passenger ship to Australia with a captain he knew, and he was to sail to-morrow; indeed Jemima opined that Tom was downright afraid of John. She believed John was awfully rich, and he was going to buy a business for pa somewhere down in the country, where they would be quite among the gentry, but for her part she did not want to leave London. There was a young fellow, a chum of Tom's—Maggie must remember him—Fred Banks—rather wild, but so handsome and dashing, and so desperately fond of her (Jemima), that it was hard lines having to give him up, and——

Here Mrs. Grey's voice was heard calling shrilly and vociferously from the bottom of the stairs, "Come down, can't you? Don't stay all night there chattering."

"I can tell you John was uncommon cross when he found you were away," said Jemima significantly, as they went downstairs. "Oh, they have come in; I see their hats."

Maggie's head ached, and she felt utterly bewildered; yet through all she was conscious of an ardent curiosity to see what John was like.

She remembered him with sincere affection and gratitude, and that queer half cousinly half lover-like letter she had received from him in Paris—nearly forgotten as it had been in the joys, the griefs, the excitement of the intervening time—came back to her mind with a sudden vivid flash, now that she was so completely isolated, and reduced at one blow to the original elements of her life. Perhaps John would be a friend she could love, something to help her to banish the memories she fought so hard against. These ideas darted, after the Will-o'-the-Wisp fashion of intuitive thought, through her brain, while Jemima struggled with the door handle—locks being chronically disordered in houses of Mr. Grey's pattern—and then it opened. The room seemed crowded; all the party, save one, were seated round the table; Tom, with an air of having been tamed, next his mother, while on the hearth-rug, with his back to the fire-place, stood a tall, large man, with high broad shoulders and a quantity of rough dark red hair, a short thick beard of the same colour a shade or two lighter, and copious moustaches. This individual's elbows were resting on the mantlepiece, thus dragging open his waistcoat, displaying a grey flannel shirt, a light blue tie with long ends, one of which hung loose, and a white linen collar. His eyes were light and small, but quick and keen, and although everyone was talking, his accents rose above all; he was exclaiming in an energetic drawl, if so contradictory a description can be accepted, "It is a d——d shame."

There was a sudden silence as Jemima and her companion entered. John Grey's sharp eyes fixed themselves eagerly on our heroine, who, in her turn, gazed appalled at this altered and enlarged edition of "Cousin John." He was a thousand times uglier, and, to her eye, more repulsive, than her least favourable recollections depicted him! The pause, however, was but momentary, for the next instant, pushing Jemima roughly aside, and exclaiming, "Is this little Maggie?" "Cousin John," without the smallest hesitation, took her in his arms, nearly lifted her off the ground, and gave her a huge kiss!—a kiss so redolent of tobacco, and a suspicion of brandy, that Maggie's dismay was complete.

"Here's your tea, Maggie," called Aunt Grey. "Sit down here."

"May I not sit by my uncle? It used always to be my seat?" asked Maggie, as she shook hands with Tom, and niched herself in between her uncle and Jemima. "I was so surprised, so pleased, John, to hear you had come back," she added, anxious to atone for her own guilty feelings. "Was it a sudden thought?—you said nothing of it in the letter you wrote me last January?"

"Well, it was and it wasn't. My partner wanted to establish an agency over here, so he made me come; as I was a London man, he thought I would manage better than him; and I never was so taken aback as when I found you were away, wandering about with this infernal humbug of a widow."

Maggie looked up, startled at his language. Could this be shy silent "Cousin John," who hated and feared his stepmother, and now stood there as though monarch of all he surveyed?

"I am sure if I had met you in Paris, Maggie, I should not have known you. You are quite a tip-topper."

"Nor should I have known you, John, I'm sure. You have grown so much, and have got quite old-looking. Has he not, uncle?"

"Yes; he is a strapping fellow," said the father proudly. "Take some more beef, my dear?"

"Here Dick—Bell—some of you—cut Mag some more beef;" and John seized her plate, without paying any attention to her decided refusal. "You must be famished, and cut up into the bargain. Here, Tom, shove yourself up a little higher;" and John seated himself opposite his cousin, whom he regarded critically and with undisguised scrutiny, from the neat frill of lace which finished her black silk dress at neck and wrists, to the little white hands that were crumbling her bread in some confusion. "Why, you look as if you had come out of a bandbox instead of a train. You might be an heiress, from your turn-out!"

"Oh," cried Tom, "you forget that Maggie's bargain with the widow included her old clothes; so you needn't wonder at her finery," and that amiable youth looked to Jemima for appreciation.

"Hold your tongue, you blockhead," said his elder brother angrily.

"Quite true, Tom," replied Maggie unmoved; "and a very good bargain it was for me. Her left-off garments were very nice."

"Bravo, Mag, you are a trump!" cried John, enchanted with her coolness. "But as I was saying when you came in, it was a d——d shame to turn you adrift without due notice or nothing, and such a shabby tip as five pounds."

"You mustn't expect every one to be as open-handed as yourself," said Mrs. Grey, with transparent flattery.

"Still, I owe Mrs. Berry a great deal," said Maggie kindly. "She has given me many advantages, and I am sure I shall find some employment as a governess or companion very soon."

"Well, we will see about that," said Cousin John significantly.

"You must have had lots of fun," cried Bell. "Used you to go everywhere with Mrs. Berry?"

"Not everywhere, but to a great many places, particularly in Paris I am very sorry not to be there when you go" (civilly to John), "for I might have been some use to you. You are going over to-morrow, are you not?"

"I am not sure about it."

Bell and her mother exchanged glances.

"You see," continued John, "I have a good deal to look after. There is my own business first, before everything; then the governor here has got everything into a precious muddle—I'll be hanged if I ever saw anything like it. The missis" (a nod to his stepmother) "is out 'o sight the best man of business of the two. He is quite unfit for London; and I think I am on the scent of a good concern down in the country—proprietor dead—and widow wants to part with it. It will suit the governor to a T, if he will only sharpen up a little—and Dick will soon be a help to him. I expect they will pay me a good percentage!"

"I feel quite bewildered," said Maggie. "You seem to me, John, like some magician come to lift every one out of the Slough of Despond, with a sort of 'Hey Presto!'"

John laughed long and loud, enchanted with this echo of his own opinion.

"You see," he returned, "I have been accustomed to put my shoulder to the wheel, and it's a deuced rusty wheel I couldn't turn; so I hope I shall make them keep their heads above water for the rest of their time. I am going to ship off Tom here to-morrow."

Whereat Mrs. Grey put her handkerchief to her eyes.

"And Maggie," asked Jemima, "did you learn to play and sing?"

"To play, yes—not to sing."

"Come now, do play us something, like a dear," cried Bell. "I would so like to hear, if you really can."

"Indeed I am so very tired I should like to go to bed," urged Maggie, who felt completely worn out, and longing for solitude and a good cry.

"Oh, you can stay up a little while," said Jemima. "It is ever so long since we heard a note of music, though I do play sometimes." So saying she opened an old-fashioned upright piano, and began to jingle a noisy galop.

"Oh, Jemimy!" cried Maggie, stopping her ears. "It is frightfully out of tune. I really couldn't touch it."

"Set you up!" laughed Bell.

"There—there," said Cousin John, impatiently. "Don't bother any more; don't you see Mag is tired out? She has turned as pale as a ghost."

"Well, get away with you, and settle Maggie's old room the best way you can for her. We will make it better to-morrow; but I have heaps to do still before I go to bed, and I cannot spare the 'gurl.'"

Maggie therefore said "Good-night," took a candle and sallied into the hall. There the sight of her large box struck her with dismay. Turning to the parlour again she said, "I must ask some one to help me up with my box. "Come along, I'm your man," said Cousin John. "Is this it?" He seized it, heaved it on his shoulder in the most porter-like fashion, and went away rapidly aloft, Maggie following.

"Your old quarters," he said, pausing at the door of one of the garrets. "Yes," returned Maggie. He pushed the door open and set down his burden. "What a shame to put you in this desolate hole." (He did not offer to give up his own room to her.) "Do you remember how I found you crying here the day after my father brought you from Altringham?"

"I do—I do, indeed," sighed Maggie, full of self-reproach; "and how good you were to me!"

"You were always a little trump," returned Cousin John, shaking her hand and gripping it painfully tight. "Come, Mag, you must pay the porter," and he stooped to kiss her again.

"Oh no, John!" cried Maggie; for this was more than she could bear. "I hate kissing any one."

"Don't, if you don't like, then," said John, shortly, and tramped away downstairs.

\*          \*          \*          \*          \*          \*

Maggie's waking next morning was a shade more cheerful than her falling to sleep. It is true her eyes felt stiff and sore from the long fit of weeping which ensued on finding herself alone and in the dark. But "balmy sleep" had done its usual beneficent work, and she was physically refreshed. All was as yet quiet. The light which came through her uncurtained window was faint, so she lay still and pondered over the sudden transformation scene which had been enacted yesterday. The ingredients of the dull aching pain that pervaded her whole being, as if a positive poison had been introduced into every nerve of her system, were numerous and complicated; but the largest proportion, perhaps, was due to the sense of having fallen back into bondage and dependence—to a position which seemed to cut her off from all that made life worth having. The place she held with Mrs. Berry was certainly humble enough; still, she had grown to be of importance to her patroness, and feeling this, she felt at home. Mrs. Berry was commonplace, ignorant, ill-bred, but she had been kind to Maggie, and, still more, dependent on her; and oh! what glimpses of delight did she not owe to that foolish deluded woman!

In the dim dawn of that foggy morning, through the duskiness of that sordid, miserable garret, the light, and glitter, and perfume of "the ball," the culminating glory of her life, came back with all the fairy loveliness which memory lends her revivals of joy.

This and the like of it had passed away from her for ever! Never again would such a voice as Trafford's hold pleasant converse with her, or ask her for a waltz with that veiled earnestness she understood so well; and then the waltz itself, and that startling but delightful dinner, and ramble in the Bois de Boulogne! Oh, she must not think of it. She wished she had not gone. What madness and folly to remember all this! Even alone, in the faint dawn, she blushed for herself. It was so shameful to be thus fascinated by a man who, beyond all doubt, considered her beneath him socially, even if she were not too ill-educated and insignificant to attract him personally. And yet, come what might, he *did* like to be with her and to talk to her; he took some special interest in her, and at any rate spared her all foolish compliments or insolent love-making. Yet what could hold Geoffrey Trafford back from doing as he liked? He could have only thought of her as a pleasant, good little girl; something higher than a housemaid. "While I allow this man to fill up my heart—no, not my heart, my fancy," she said indignantly to herself. "What a shame! I will put him away and trample out such weakness. I have my own life to live, independent of him. Why should I let a shadow spoil it? And I am sure it does not promise to have so much brightness that I can afford to be unnecessarily miserable. Oh, how I wish I could fall in love with Cousin John!—I would try hard, if he were anything like what I expected—that would cure me. But he is so—so very dreadful!"

At this point of her reflections the voice of Mrs. Grey was heard, as if from her chamber, shouting shrill instructions to "the gurl"; and distant slamming of doors echoed from below.

"I must get up," said Maggie to herself. "I suppose they will breakfast early because Tom is going away." The interval of dressing was also busily employed, but by more practical cogitations. First, there was poor Mrs. Berry, now La Comtesse de Bragance. Maggie could have cried to think of her alone, and in the power of that sneering French devil. Yes, she must make her way to see Mr. Dunsford, and ascertain if anything could be done to help her, for the time would soon come when she would want help; and then it would surely not be selfish in her to mention her own wants, for Mrs. Berry told her in her hurry yesterday that he would give her a character; and she must lose no time in endeavouring to find employment. She was quite sure her aunt did not want to take her away into the country, and London was the place for such a quest as hers.

When Maggie came down Mrs. Grey and "the gurl" were the only members of the family afloat. Her aunt's curls were not yet released from their nocturnal prison of papers; a dingy dressing-gown, a knitted woollen "crossover" tied behind, a face that had evidently bent over the smoky beginnings of the kitchen fire, and was further blurred by occasional tear-drops, removed with the back of the hand or the ever-ready and grimy duster—this sounds like a very unattractive exterior. Yet never had Aunt Grey seemed so lovely to Maggie before. Her hard features had softened into a wistful expression, her keen eyes were dimmed with natural moisture, for her precious boy—the one bloom, the one tenderness, of her rugged character—was about to leave her and plunge into the darkness of an unknown world.

"Maggie, would you mind dusting the parlour and putting it straight? You see" (with a pathetic snuffle) "poor Tom wants his breakfast early to go to the Docks, and John will expect everything in order, though it was the middle of the night."

In deep amazement at her aunt's change of tone towards her step-son, Maggie exclaimed with alacrity, "Yes, to be sure I will. Give me the duster; and don't fret about Tom, aunt, though of course it is very hard to part with him. Think what a good opening this situation is for him."

"Opening, indeed!" returned Mrs. Grey in a mysterious tone of dissatisfaction. "He is that clever that he'd soon have made an opening *here* if he had had a chance; but never mind—you go upstairs, my dear."

So Maggie went, and soon imparted a new aspect to the room, which looked quite revived, when "the gurl" came slowly in, with an alarming jingle—a heavily-laden tray in her outstretched hands, and the table-cloth in a tight roll under her arm.

"If you leave those things I will lay the breakfast-table," said Maggie briskly, she was so thankful to be busy.

"I'm sure, 'm, I am ever so much obliged to you," said "slavey," and vanished.

The process of "laying the cloth" was not quite completed when a heavy shuffling was heard in the passage, and then John's voice shouted down the kitchen stairs, "I say, why the deuce haven't you brought my boots up? I left them in the hall last night on purpose to remind you; but you have no more head than "—— (unintelligible grumble), and enter John, without a collar, in a pair of highly objectionable leather slippers, rubbed a dirty white, through one of which the brown toe of a woollen sock was distinctly visible.

"Maggie!" he cried, not abashed—that did not seem possible—but a little put out. "Why, I thought we should not see you these hours. You looked so dead-beat last night, I thought you'd want twenty-four hours' sleep at least. Come, let's have a look at you. You don't seem as if you had had rest enough yet."

"Oh, I am all right this morning," she returned, extricating her hand from his grasp.

"And are you doing that d——d stupid girl's work here? By Jove, it is too bad!"

"Why?" asked Maggie, still busying herself about the table. "You know I am no stranger here; and it would ill become me to sit idle in Uncle Grey's house."

"You are a regular little brick; you always were," continued John, taking up a position on the hearth-rug, whence he gazed admiringly on his cousin, wondering dimly what it was that made her such a dainty creature, different from all other women he had ever met.

"And you are glad to see cousin John once more?"

"Indeed I am," replied Maggie, hastily furbishing up her gratitude to stimulate her cordiality. "I should be very good for nothing if I were not."

"Did you get the letter I wrote to you—let me see—last January?"

"Yes, I did," returned Maggie, smiling, as she remembered that famous epistle, and sighing to think of how and why her ideas had developed so largely since. "I got it in Paris."

"And why didn't you write?"

"I did. I did, indeed; but not immediately."

"Hum! More interesting employment—or amusement?"

"Employment, plenty. Mrs. Berry did not let me eat the bread of idleness, though she was very good."

"At any rate, you've not learned to be a fine lady. It does one's heart good to see you bustling about."

"Yes," said Maggie, irresistibly impelled to put him down. "I have so far learned to be fine, that I don't like to see gentlemen—specially young gentlemen—in their slippers, and without their collars, in the morning."

"Why, that's a downer for me! Well, Mag, I wish you would make that lazy, ill-conditioned, stupid girl bring me my boots."

"Poor thing, why abuse her? Think of all she has to do. No, cousin John, kind old friend as you are, I will *not* look after *your* boots, though I will gladly lay my uncle's breakfast-table. Go, get them yourself, and then dress, like a good boy."

She spoke with a pleasant smile and pretty little nod. But John did not like it. His overweening estimate of himself was "roughed" by her remarks, and he went sulkily out of the room. At the door he stumbled over the desired boots, and went moodily away to "dress," as his cousin—his intended *protégée*—little Mag, who was to be lifted out of her Cinderella condition by the might of his will, had told him.

The family now came dropping in. Tom last—or last but one, if we count the reappearance of John in a slightly improved toilet; and the conversation became general, if the universal clatter, in which no one listened to the other, can be so dignified. Tom, whose spirits were wild from the sense of being out of debt and danger, little heeded his mother's tears. The prospect of new scenes and amusements left little room for regret. Dick was unfeignedly pleased at the departure of his brother. Jemima slightly regretted it: it looked like separation from the fascinating Fred Banks. The father, wrapped up in his eldest son, was indifferent.

"Well, John," asked the head of the house, "will you go over to Paris to-night?"

"I am not quite sure. I'll see Tom off, and then make up my mind."

"I thought you were quite determined?" said Mrs. Grey.

"You were wrong, then."

"Is it not unusual for a ship to start on Sunday?" asked Maggie.

"Not at all," replied cousin John. "Sailors like it; and Tom, we had better be off soon—she'll be out of dock, I'm thinking, early."

"Dear, dear," said the mother; "don't they wait for passengers at Gravesend? Mightn't Tom go down to-morrow?"

"If you choose to stand his rail fare, and mine, there and back; for remember, I'll see him on board; and it will take the change out of a couple of sovereigns."

John spoke in what seemed to Maggie—fresh from intercourse with Trafford, and even De Bragance, whose insolence was always polished —a savage tone.

"If his mother wishes to keep him with her another day"—— began the kind old chemist.

"D—— it, governor," interrupted John, roughly. "You had better recollect whether you have any money to spare, or any you can call your own."

Maggie instinctively drew nearer to her uncle, as if to protect him, and looked in his face to see how he bore such insolence. It pained her to see the distressed guilty look that stole over his gentle worn countenance; and she could not keep her eyes from flashing a glance of angry remonstrance straight into her cousin's, as he sat opposite. John sat on for a while, unmoved by looks or silence—for the sublime disapprobation of the general benefactor had rather an intimidating effect on the company. And then, with a kindly smile in his eyes— and Maggie admitted to herself that he had a pleasant honest smile— exclaimed disrespectfully, but genially,

"Never mind, old boy. You are going to make a lot of tin, you know, in the new business, and pay me cent per cent."

Mr. Grey smiled a somewhat sickly smile; and Maggie saw how hard it is to skin over the wounds which hasty words inflict.

"Oh! we had better be off," cried Tom. "Where's the use of waiting?"

"Better bear the wrench at once, aunt," said Maggie kindly; "it would be just as bad to-morrow. You see he is quite happy, naturally, to go away into the world."

And then every one rose—and for twenty minutes or so confusion dire reigned throughout the entire establishment. Parcels left at the top of the house were remembered spasmodically. Boxes were fastened and then reopened, to receive some article of the last necessity. Dick was eagerly despatched for a cab, and then franticly recalled—and Maggie thought of the similar *bouleversement* which distinguished her own and Mrs. Berry's departure more than two years before.

At last the three young men departed. Mrs. Grey retired downstairs, and quiet once more was restored.

It was not quite so dreadful that Sunday as Maggie anticipated. John did not return till tea-time; and after the early dinner Mrs. Grey went up to her room. The young ladies, with Dick, went out to walk, and Maggie had a long confidential talk with her uncle.

The evening was well disposed of by going to hear a popular preacher, and Maggie, after her long absence from England, enjoyed the service in a genuine English church.

"I must make my way to the City to-morrow," said Maggie, after supper, addressing her aunt, "I want to see Mr. Dunsford, Mrs. Berry's solicitor, and I do not like to go quite alone; will you allow Bell or Jemima to come with me?"

"*I* will go with you. I am the proper person to go," said cousin John, resolutely. He had not escorted the young ladies to church, preferring avowedly to stay at home and smoke.

"Thank you," returned Maggie, seeing there was no escape. "If you can spare the time; but you are so busy."

"I shall manage it," said John.

\*          \*          \*          \*          \*          \*

Monday was a dark day with a drizzling rain; just enough to make the streets slippery and unpleasant. And Maggie, with a sinking heart, prepared to accompany cousin John to Mr. Dunsford's office. She could not help fancying that highly respectable man of business would somehow hold her responsible for Mrs. Berry's matrimonial follies; on two or three occasions he had written to her on Mrs. Berry's affairs, and always conveyed the idea that he looked to her as a sort of brains-carrier. On the whole, she was rather glad cousin John had offered to go with her, for whatever his faults, he would let no mortal man brow-beat him, or anything belonging to him, she felt sure. Her gladness, however, was a little damped when, after an elaborate toilet, John sallied forth like a bridegroom out of his chamber, and certainly, on that day, rejoicing, to run his course. His trousers, of a large check pattern in light and dark shades of brown, conveyed the painful impression of being conspicuously patched on the knees; moreover, a broad brown stripe down the outsides further distinguished them. A brown and blue speckly waistcoat, well opened, to show a reckless display of white shirt-front, a light blue satin tie with long ends drawn through a massive gold ring, and a bran new dark blue frock coat, which hung straight down from his shoulders, innocent of any sartorial art to make it fit the bend of the back, completed his costume.

He was in the act of removing the silver paper from a glossy hat when Maggie came in.

"Well," said John, looking at her admiringly; "I hope I am got up smart enough to please you? You must not think I have no clothes to wear."

"Oh, no! I am sure you are very smart indeed," cried Maggie, a little touched by his simple vanity, and despairing of any reformation in his taste.

"That's right," he returned, evidently pleased at her verdict. "And now come along; if it was not for your black dress, we might be taken for a bride and bridegroom."

So saying he marched off, leaving her to follow.

The streets being rather slippery, cousin John insisted on piloting his cousin from the corner where the 'busses passed to the step of one of those vehicles, by grasping her upper arm tightly in his large strong hand, till the tender flesh and veins felt crushed and sore.

"You hurt me, pray let go my arm," she urged, and the next moment found herself nearly lifted into the 'bus. It was with a sensation almost of thankfulness that she observed John compelled to sit at the door while she found a place at the other end.

It was a long journey, however, and before it was more than half accomplished, the shifting company had changed frequently, and enabled cousin John to place himself next his fair *protégée*.

"I say, what a delicate concern you are, Maggie! You can't bear to be touched. I hope you hav'n't turned cantankerous—you didn't use to be."

"Indeed I am not," smiling pleasantly; "but you really did hurt me; you don't know how hard you hold."

"Do I?" said John, with a complaisant laugh—like all men of his stamp, he was quite proud of his physical strength. "I must remember you are a tender article in future."

Maggie shook her head, in token of declining conversation at the pitch required in an omnibus, and John found a congenial spirit in an opposite neighbour, a stout man, regardless of his H's, with whom he shouted a profound discussion on the increase of the bank rate and its probable effect upon railway stock.

On arriving at Mr. Dunsford's office they found that gentleman had not yet come in, and a weary interval of waiting ensued.

John fretted at being kept, yet would not hear of leaving Maggie alone; he walked about the room, and read the prospectuses of insurance and other companies, which hung framed and glazed upon the wall; he drummed upon the window, and looked at his watch. "What hours for a fellow to keep! He can be no great man of business, not to be at his office by eleven. I have fifty places to go to, and I'll be late for them all."

"Then pray leave me here! do not wait," said Maggie, who felt painfully nervous at the idea of the coming interview, and was still more unnerved by John's impatience.

"No, I shall not leave you to be humbugged and bullied by this lawyer fellow. Why, you are as pale as a ghost at the idea of it! What a little coward you are," sitting down beside her; "and yet you have a sort of pluck, too."

"A very curious sort, I am afraid. Still, I am not quite a coward."

"Mr. Dunsford will see you now," said a clerk, looking into the dingy room in which they were incarcerated.

John Grey jumped up and led the way, and Maggie came trembling after.

Deep and dire was Mr. Dunsford's anger when Maggie, with no small difficulty, managed to inform him of poor Mrs. Berry's fatal marriage. Though a cool self-contained man of business, he could not refrain from muttering the word "idiot," under his breath.

"And when did this precious marriage take place?"

"On Saturday," said Maggie, almost tearful at the magnitude of the misfortune; while cousin John, who had not removed his hat, stood with his hands in his pockets, looking out sharply for an opportunity of interfering, and watching Maggie's distressed face.

"And pray why didn't you write and let me know what was going on, Miss Grey? From all I have known of you—your letters, and the way you kept Mrs. Berry's accounts—I really thought you a very sensible conscientious person. You ought to have let me know."

"But, Mr. Dunsford, I could not possibly interfere. I begged and implored of Mrs. Berry not to commit herself too far until she had consulted you, and she promised me faithfully she would not. We were coming to London to see you and have everything properly settled, when we met the Count at Dover, and that morning she went out with him; I had not the most remote idea she was gone to be married; but I begin to think now they must have settled it all before the Count left Paris."

"Highly probable," said the lawyer, drily.

"The young lady is a trifle green, sir," put in John.

Mr. Dunsford looked at him over his spectacles, but made no reply.

"I am surprised Mrs. Berry has not written to you," said Maggie.

"She waited to let you break the news. Where is she and her precious Count to be found?"

"I have not an idea. She said she was going back to the Continent with her husband, and that she would write to me."

"She is sure to write to me," rejoined Mr. Dunsford, "as all her property is in my hands, and Monsieur will want to finger some of it before long. However, when she gives me a chance to tell her so, I will wash my hands of her. I had a great respect for poor Mr. Berry (who always seemed a sensible man till he met her), and I promised him to take care of her as far as I could; but now I shall certainly wash my hands of her."

"Oh! pray do not say that, Mr. Dunsford!" cried Maggie, imploringly. She will want your help sorely yet. Monsieur de Bragance will spend her money, and ill-treat her, and leave her to die or starve— if he cannot kill her safely. You must try and keep back a little of her money for her. After all, she is only silly—not wicked."

"Wickedness is seldom so severely punished as folly," said the lawyer, coolly; "and I must say I hoped greatly that you would have helped to keep her straight."

"I tried all I could," returned Maggie, unconsciously clasping her hands; "but, you see, I was too insignificant to have much influence, though she was very, very kind to me."

"And how the deuce," exclaimed John, "could you expect a widow with well lined pockets to mind such a chit as this?"

"Perhaps not—perhaps not," said Mr. Dunsford, looking kindly at Maggie. "But from all I can gather, I believe you were a very pleasant and useful companion; and I hope my very foolish client did not fail to acknowledge your services properly."

"Ay! to the extent of a 'fi-pund' note and her blessing," put in John; "though she was sent adrift in the middle of a quarter, were'nt you Mag?"

"Oh, John! Mrs. Berry and I were on those terms "——

"She had a right to cheat you, I suppose," interrupted John. "I leave it to you, sir, if this was fair."

"Not handsome treatment, by any means, and I am afraid I can do you no good."

"Thank you," said Maggie hesitating; "I think perhaps you could; for as I must endeavour to find some other employment, and I cannot apply to Mrs. Berry until I know where to find her, perhaps you would'nt mind—that is—you would be so good as to let me refer to you? You might say that I lived with Mrs. Berry, and that she was satisfied, and all that."

"I have no objection to do so. I shall be very happy also to mention you to my daughter, who might possibly hear of something to suit you."

"You are very good," replied Maggie gratefully; adding in a timid voice, as if half afraid to obtrude her poor little affairs upon so great a man, "Would you advise me to put an advertisement in the *Times?*"

"This young lady is so desperate independent she ca'nt bear to stay even for a week or two with her own uncle," said John facetiously, adding, with an air of insufferable patronage, "If she would only wait a bit I think I know a place that would suit her exactly."

" Every one knows their own wants and wishes best," returned Mr. Dunsford, rising. " I dare say an advertisement might bring you some chance, but I would not advise your putting it in until the end of August, when people are returning to town. Meantime I will mention you to my daughter, and a—— leave me your address."

Maggie had written it on a card and gave it to him.

" Ah! Beverly Street," he said; " the same place where Mrs. Berry found you—very well. I shall not forget, good morning."

" Now John, I can release you, and I am sure I am so much obliged to you," said Maggie, as they found themselves in the street, a narrow little dusky street near Doctors Commons.

" Never mind, you'll want something to eat, so come along; we'll look for a cake shop or a luncheon bar, or something."

" Oh no! thank you. I could'nt eat anything; just show me where I shall find an omnibus, that's all I want."

" But I say you *must* have something! It will be all hours when you get back, and I'd like to see the missus order up anything for *you* after dinner's gone. No, no Mag! you sha'nt starve while you are with me; besides, I want to eat myself."

He was still kind and considerate for her, while she, ingrate that she was, could not keep out of her memory and her heart another voice—oh! how different in tone and accent!—a voice so soft, so varied in modulation, with a ring of power in it; and which had addressed almost the same words to her scarce four weeks ago! But she felt she was in cousin John's hands, she must do what seemed good in his eyes. So they went into a huge cake shop at the top of Ludgate Hill, with a dusty floor strewn with flakes of pastry and fragments of buns, where at a grimy little marble table, all stained with rings of porter and drops of sherbet, she strove diligently to consume a veal-and-ham pie. While John, with much satisfaction, devoured two, and washed them down with a glass of brandy-and-water.

" I don't feel at all inclined to let you go," said John, as he came out of the cake shop triumphant. " What a pity we didn't tell them not to expect us back, we might have dined somewhere and gone to the theatre."

" I do not think that would quite do, John!"

" Why'not?—not proper? Why you and I are like brother and sister, ain't we, Mag?"

" Oh yes indeed," cried Maggie, delighted to accept the relationship. " I am sure no brother could be kinder and truer than you are, dear John."

" Well, as you must go, here's a 'bus—take care of yourself—good-bye," and with a squeeze of the hand that left Maggie's tingling, John turned and was lost in the crowd.

# TEMPLE BAR.

JANUARY 1873.

## The New Year.

### BY JOHN SHEEHAN.

#### I.

WHO flies to our earth on the wings of the morning,
  A lone silver star on her beautiful brow,
A wreath of green holly her bright locks adorning,
  Her mantle of moonlight flecked o'er with the snow?

#### II.

'Tis Time's latest born!  Let us welcome and bless her;
  Our best wassail bowl we will crown for her now;
By the Yule-log's still lingering glow we'll caress her,
  And kiss her all round 'neath the mistletoe bough.

#### III.

Shall this be a moment of silence and sorrow,
  To grieve as Fate rings out our years ebbing fast;
All doomed, young and old—e'en the youngest to-morrow—
  Like the now vanished year, to be things of the past?

#### IV.

Shall we mourn o'er false friends, or o'er true ones departed,
  Loves slighted, hopes blighted, past folly, and strife,
Ambition's wild game, and review, broken hearted,
  The fields won and lost in the Battle of Life?

V.

Oh no! for of hope 'tis the day-spring, the season
　　Life's ills to forget, and life's joys to renew;
Life's wrongs to forgive, and remember with reason
　　If some there be false, there are more that are true.


VI.

Oh ring out, ye joy-bells, to chasten and cheer us,
　　The heart-searching chimes to fond memory dear:
From steeple or tower your best peal of the year is
　　The Old which rings out, and rings in the New Year!


VII.

In the crisp air ring forth our New Year's celebration!
　　A happy New Year may she be to us all;
A New Year of peace to a tempest-toss'd nation;
　　A New Year of hope to the land of the Gaul!


VIII.

The great German land, who her wanton invader
　　Hurled back, and maintained her inviolate Rhine—
May a New Year of still fairer laurels o'ershade her;
　　Civic Freedom arise! May those laurels be thine!


IX.

To the mighty Republic, whose children inherit
　　Our language and laws, our religion and blood,
Speed o'er the Atlantic! God's increase, young Spirit,
　　Breathe o'er her, and still may He say "IT IS GOOD!"


X.

Bounteous Heaven, endow with just laws those who need them,
　　With increase, hope and peace! Equal blessings with these
Vouchsafe to our own classic Motler of Freedom,
　　Enthron'd midst her honours, and riches and ease:

### XI.

Let a New Year of Thought and Heart-Progress beam on her,
   Her conscience awakening, and humbling her pride;
May she blush for, at last, her sole stain of dishonour—
   Her millions who still in the darkness abide.

### XII.

To the hoarse roaring gulf waves, dear England, oh hearken!
   Which divide rich and poor, and part knowledge from crime.
MENE! TEKEL! UPHARSIN.   The gulf is a dark one!
   Proud land, bridge it o'er!   Be thy warning in time!

# The New Magdalen.

## By WILKIE COLLINS.

### CHAPTER XII.

#### *Exit* JULIAN.

JULIAN happened to be standing nearest to Mercy. He was the first at her side when she fell.

In the cry of alarm which burst from him, as he raised her for a moment in his arms, in the expression of his eyes when he looked at her death-like face, there escaped the plain—too plain—confession of the interest which he felt in her, of the admiration which she had aroused in him. Horace detected it. There was the quick suspicion of jealousy in the movement by which he joined Julian; there was the ready resentment of jealousy in the tone in which he pronounced the words, "Leave her to me." Julian resigned her in silence. A faint flush appeared on his pale face as he drew back while Horace carried her to the sofa. His eyes sank to the ground; he seemed to be meditating self-reproachfully on the tone in which his friend had spoken to him. After having been the first to take an active part in meeting the calamity that had happened, he was now to all appearance insensible to everything that was passing in the room.

A touch on his shoulder roused him.

He turned and looked round. The woman who had done the mischief —the stranger in the poor black garments—was standing behind him. She pointed to the prostrate figure on the sofa, with a merciless smile.

"You wanted a proof just now," she said. "There it is!"

Horace heard her. He suddenly left the sofa and joined Julian. His face, naturally ruddy, was pale with suppressed fury.

"Take that wretch away!" he said. "Instantly! or I won't answer for what I may do."

Those words recalled Julian to himself. He looked round the room. Lady Janet and the housekeeper were together, in attendance on the swooning woman. The startled servants were congregated in the library doorway. One of them offered to run to the nearest doctor; another asked if he should fetch the police. Julian silenced them by a gesture, and turned to Horace. "Compose yourself," he said. "Leave me to remove her quietly from the house." He took Grace by the hand as he spoke. She hesitated and tried to release herself. Julian pointed to the group at the sofa and to the servants looking on. " You have made an enemy of every one in this room," he said, " and you have not a friend in London. Do you wish to make an enemy of *me ?* " Her head drooped ; she made no reply ; she waited, dumbly obedient to the firmer will than her own. Julian ordered the servants crowding together in the doorway to withdraw. He followed them into the library, leading Grace after him by the hand. Before closing the door he paused, and looked back into the dining-room.

" Is she recovering ? " he asked, after a moment's hesitation.

Lady Janet's voice answered him. " Not yet."

" Shall I send for the nearest doctor ? "

Horace interposed. He declined to let Julian associate himself, even in that indirect manner, with Mercy's recovery.

" If the doctor is wanted," he said, " I will go for him myself."

Julian closed the library door. He absently released Grace ; he mechanically pointed to a chair. She sat down in silent surprise, following him with her eyes as he walked slowly to and fro in the room.

For the moment his mind was far away from her, and from all that had happened since her appearance in the house. It was impossible that a man of his fineness of perception could mistake the meaning of Horace's conduct towards him. He was questioning his own heart, on the subject of Mercy, sternly and unreservedly, as it was his habit to do. " After only once seeing her," he thought, " has she produced such an impression on me that Horace can discover it, before I have even suspected it myself ? Can the time have come already, when I owe it to my friend to see her no more ? " He stopped irritably in his walk. As a man devoted to a serious calling in life, there was something that wounded his self-respect in the bare suspicion that he could be guilty of the purely sentimental extravagance called " love at first sight."

He had paused exactly opposite to the chair in which Grace was seated. Weary of the silence, she seized the opportunity of speaking to him.

" I have come here with you as you wished," she said. " Are you going to help me ? Am I to count on you as my friend ? "

He looked at her vacantly. It cost him an effort before he could give her the attention that she had claimed.

" You have been hard on me," Grace went on. " But you showed me some kindness at first ; you tried to make them give me a fair hearing. I ask you, as a just man, do you doubt now that the woman on the sofa in the next room is an impostor who has taken my place ? Can there be any plainer confession that she is Mercy Merrick than the confession she has made ? *You* saw it ; *they* saw it. She fainted at the sight of me."

Julian crossed the room—still without answering her—and rang the bell. When the servant appeared, he told the man to fetch a cab.

Grace rose from her chair. "What is the cab for?" she asked sharply.

"For you and for me," Julian replied. "I am going to take you back to your lodgings."

"I refuse to go. My place is in this house. Neither Lady Janet nor you can get over the plain facts. All I asked was to be confronted with her. And what did she do when she came into the room? She fainted at the sight of me."

Reiterating her one triumphant assertion, she fixed her eyes on Julian with a look which said plainly, Answer that if you can. In mercy to her, Julian answered it on the spot.

"So far as I understand," he said, "you appear to take it for granted that no innocent woman would have fainted on first seeing you. I have something to tell you which will alter your opinion. On her arrival in England this lady informed my aunt that she had met with you accidentally on the French frontier, and that she had seen you (so far as she knew) struck dead at her side by a shell. Remember that, and recall what happened just now. Without a word to warn her of your restoration to life, she finds herself suddenly face to face with you, a living woman—and this at a time when it is easy for any one who looks at her to see that she is in delicate health. What is there wonderful, what is there unaccountable, in her fainting under such circumstances as these?"

The question was plainly put. Where was the answer to it?

There was no answer to it. Mercy's wisely candid statement of the manner in which she had first met with Grace, and of the accident which had followed, had served Mercy's purpose but too well. It was simply impossible for persons acquainted with that statement to attach a guilty meaning to the swoon. The false Grace Roseberry was still as far beyond the reach of suspicion as ever, and the true Grace was quick enough to see it. She sank into the chair from which she had risen; her hands fell in hopeless despair on her lap.

"Everything is against me," she said. "The truth itself turns liar, and takes her side." She paused and rallied her sinking courage. "No!" she cried resolutely, "I won't submit to have my name and my place taken from me by a vile adventuress! Say what you like, I insist on exposing her; I won't leave the house!"

The servant entered the room, and announced that the cab was at the door.

Grace turned to Julian with a defiant wave of her hand. "Don't let me detain you," she said. "I see I have neither advice nor help to expect from Mr. Julian Gray."

Julian beckoned to the servant to follow him into a corner of the room.

"Do you know if the doctor has been sent for?" he asked.

"I believe not, sir. It is said in the servants' hall that the doctor is not wanted."

Julian was too anxious to be satisfied with a report from the servants' hall. He hastily wrote on a slip of paper: "Has she recovered?" and then gave the note to the man, with directions to take it to Lady Janet.

"Did you hear what I said?" Grace inquired, while the messenger was absent in the dining-room.

"I will answer you directly," said Julian.

The servant appeared again as he spoke, with some lines in pencil written by Lady Janet on the back of Julian's note. "Thank God we have revived her. In a few minutes we hope to be able to take her to her room."

The nearest way to Mercy's room was through the library. Grace's immediate removal had now become a necessity which was not to be trifled with. Julian addressed himself to meeting the difficulty the instant he was left alone with Grace.

"Listen to me," he said. "The cab is waiting, and I have my last words to say to you. You are now (thanks to the consul's recommendation) in my care. Decide at once whether you will remain under my charge, or whether you will transfer yourself to the charge of the police."

Grace started. "What do you mean?" she asked angrily.

"If you wish to remain under my charge," Julian proceeded, "you will accompany me at once to the cab. In that case I will undertake to give you an opportunity of telling your story to my own lawyer. He will be a fitter person to advise you than I am. Nothing will induce *me* to believe that the lady whom you have accused has committed, or is capable of committing, such a fraud as you charge her with. You will hear what the lawyer thinks, if you come with me. If you refuse, I shall have no choice but to send into the next room and tell them that you are still here. The result will be that you will find yourself in charge of the police. Take which course you like; I will give you a minute to decide in. And remember this: if I appear to express myself harshly, it is your conduct which forces me to speak out. I mean kindly towards you; I am advising you honestly for your good."

He took out his watch to count the minute.

Grace stole one furtive glance at his steady resolute face. She was perfectly unmoved by the manly consideration for her which Julian's last words had expressed. All she understood was, that he was not a man to be trifled with. Future opportunities would offer themselves of returning secretly to the house. She determined to yield—and deceive him.

"I am ready to go," she said, rising with dogged submission.

"Your turn now," she muttered to herself as she turned to the looking-glass to arrange her shawl. "My turn will come."

Julian advanced towards her, as if to offer her his arm, and checked himself. Firmly persuaded as he was that her mind was deranged—readily as he admitted that she claimed, in virtue of her affliction, every indulgence that he could extend to her—there was something repellent to him at that moment in the bare idea of touching her. The image of the beautiful creature who was the object of her monstrous accusation—the image of Mercy as she lay helpless for a moment in his arms—was vivid in his mind while he opened the door that led into the hall, and drew back to let Grace pass out before him. He left the servant to help her into the cab. The man respectfully addressed him as he took his seat opposite to Grace.

"I am ordered to say that your room is ready, sir; and that her ladyship expects you to dinner."

Absorbed in the events which had followed his aunt's invitation, Julian had forgotten his engagement to stay at Mablethorpe House. Could he return, knowing his own heart as he now knew it? Could he honourably remain, perhaps for weeks together, in Mercy's society, conscious as he now was of the impression which she had produced on him? No. The one honourable course that he could take was to find an excuse for withdrawing from his engagement. "Beg her ladyship not to wait dinner for me;" he said. "I will write and make my apologies." The cab drove off. The wondering servant waited on the doorstep, looking after it. "I wouldn't stand in Mr. Julian's shoes for something," he thought, with his mind running on the difficulties of the young clergyman's position. "There she is, along with him in the cab. What is he going to do with her after that?"

Julian himself—if it had been put to him at the moment—could not have answered the question.

---

Lady Janet's anxiety was far from being relieved when Mercy had been restored to her senses and conducted to her own room.

Her mind remained in a condition of unreasoning alarm which it was impossible to remove. Over and over again she was told that the woman who had terrified her had left the house, and would never be permitted to enter it more. Over and over again she was assured that the stranger's frantic assertions were regarded by everybody about her as unworthy of a moment's serious attention. She persisted in doubting whether they were telling her the truth. A shocking distrust of her friends seemed to possess her. She shrank when Lady Janet approached the bedside. She shuddered when Lady Janet kissed her. She flatly refused to let Horace see her. She asked the strangest questions about Julian Gray, and shook her head suspiciously when they told her that he was absent from the house. At intervals, she hid her face in the bedclothes, and murmured to herself piteously, "Oh! what shall I do? What shall I do?" At other times, her one petition was to be left alone. "I want nobody in my room"—that was her sullen cry—"Nobody in my room."

The evening advanced and brought with it no change for the better. Lady Janet, by the advice of Horace, sent for her own medical adviser.

The doctor shook his head. The symptoms, he said, indicated a serious shock to the nervous system. He wrote a sedative prescription; and he gave (with a happy choice of language) some sound and safe advice. It amounted briefly to this: "Take her away, and try the sea-side." Lady Janet's customary energy acted on the advice without a moment's needless delay. She gave the necessary directions for packing the trunks over night, and decided on leaving Mablethorpe House with Mercy the next morning.

Shortly after the doctor had taken his departure, a letter from Julian, addressed to Lady Janet, was delivered by private messenger.

Beginning with the necessary apologies for the writer's absence, the letter proceeded in these terms:

"Before I permitted my companion to accompany me to the lawyer's office, I felt the necessity of consulting him as to my present position towards her.

"I told him—what I think it only right to repeat to you—that I do not feel justified in acting on my own opinion that her mind is deranged. In the case of this friendless woman, I want medical authority, and, more even than that, I want some positive proof, to satisfy my conscience as well as to confirm my view.

"Finding me obstinate on this point, the lawyer undertook to consult a physician accustomed to the treatment of the insane, on my behalf.

"After sending a message, and receiving the answer, he said, 'Bring the lady here—in half an hour; she shall tell her story to the doctor instead of telling it to me.' The proposal rather staggered me; I asked how it was possible to induce her to do that. He laughed, and answered, 'I shall present the doctor as my senior partner; my senior partner will be the very man to advise her.' You know that I hate all deception—even where the end in view appears to justify it. On this occasion, however, there was no other alternative than to let the lawyer take his own course—or to run the risk of a delay which might be followed by serious results.

"I waited in a room by myself (feeling very uneasy, I own) until the doctor joined me after the interview was over.

"His opinion is, briefly, this:

"After careful examination of the unfortunate creature, he thinks that there are unmistakably symptoms of mental aberration. But how far the mischief has gone, and whether her case is, or is not, suffi-ciently grave to render actual restraint necessary, he cannot positively say, in our present state of ignorance as to facts.

"'Thus far,' he observed, 'we know nothing of that part of her delusion which relates to Mercy Merrick. The solution of the diffi-culty, in this case, is to be found there. I entirely agree with the lady that the inquiries of the consul at Mannheim are far from being conclusive. Furnish me with satisfactory evidence either that there is, or is not, such a person really in existence as Mercy Merrick, and I will give you a positive opinion on the case, whenever you choose to ask for it.'

"Those words have decided me on starting for the Continent, and renewing the search for Mercy Merrick.

"My friend the lawyer wonders jocosely whether *I* am in my right senses. His advice is, that I should apply to the nearest magistrate, and relieve you and myself of all further trouble in that way.

"Perhaps you agree with him? My dear aunt (as you have often said) I do nothing like other people. I am interested in this case. I cannot abandon a forlorn woman who has been confided to me to the tender mercies of strangers, so long as there is any hope of my making discoveries which may be instrumental in restoring her to herself—perhaps, also, in restoring her to her friends.

"I start by the mail train of to-night. My plan is, to go first to Mannheim, and consult with the consul and the hospital doctors; then to find my way to the German surgeon, and to question *him;* and, that done, to make the last and hardest effort of all—the effort to trace the French ambulance and to penetrate the mystery of Mercy Merrick.

"Immediately on my return I will wait on you, and tell you what I have accomplished, or how I have failed.

"In the meanwhile, pray be under no alarm about the reappearance of this unhappy woman at your house. She is fully occupied in writing (at my suggestion) to her friends in Canada; and she is under the care of the landlady at her lodgings—an experienced and trust-worthy person, who has satisfied the doctor as well as myself of her fitness for the charge that she has undertaken.

"Pray mention this to Miss Roseberry (whenever you think it desirable), with the respectful expression of my sympathy, and of my best wishes for her speedy restoration to health. And once more forgive me for failing, under stress of necessity, to enjoy the hospitality of Mablethorpe House."

Lady Janet closed Julian's letter, feeling far from satisfied with it. She sat for a while, pondering over what her nephew had written to her.

"One of two things," thought the quick-witted old lady. "Either the lawyer is right, and Julian is a fit companion for the madwoman whom he has taken under his charge, or, he has some second motive for this absurd journey of his which he has carefully abstained from mentioning in his letter. What can the motive be?"

At intervals during the night that question recurred to her ladyship again and again. The utmost exercise of her ingenuity failing to answer it, her one resource left was to wait patiently for Julian's return, and, in her own favourite phrase, to "have it out of him" then.

The next morning Lady Janet and her adopted daughter left Mablethorpe House for Brighton; Horace (who had begged to be allowed to accompany them) being sentenced to remain in London by Mercy's express desire. Why—nobody could guess; and Mercy refused to say.

CHAPTER XIII.

*Enter* JULIAN.

A WEEK has passed. The scene opens again in the dining-room at Mablethorpe House.

The hospitable table bears once more its burden of good things for lunch. But, on this occasion, Lady Janet sits alone. Her attention is divided between reading her newspaper and feeding her cat. The cat is a sleek and splendid creature. He carries an erect tail. He rolls luxuriously on the soft carpet. He approaches his mistress in a series of coquettish curves. He smells with dainty hesitation at the choicest morsels that can be offered to him. The musical monotony of his purring falls soothingly on her ladyship's ear. She stops in the middle of a leading article and looks with a care-worn face at the happy cat. "Upon my honour," cries Lady Janet, thinking, in her inveterately ironical manner, of the cares that trouble her, "all things considered, Tom, I wish I was You!"

The cat starts—not at his mistress's complimentary apostrophe, but at a knock at the door which follows close upon it. Lady Janet says, carelessly enough, "Come in;" looks round listlessly to see who it is; and starts, like the cat, when the door opens and discloses—Julian Gray!

"You—or your ghost?" she exclaims.

She has noticed already that Julian is paler than usual, and that there is something in his manner at once uneasy and subdued—highly uncharacteristic of him at other times. He takes a seat by her side, and kisses her hand. But—for the first time in his aunt's experience of him—he refuses the good things on the luncheon-table, and he has nothing to say to the cat! That neglected animal takes refuge on Lady Janet's lap. Lady Janet, with her eyes fixed expectantly on her nephew (determining to "have it out of him" at the first opportunity) waits to hear what he has to say for himself. Julian has no alternative but to break the silence, and tell his story as he best may.

"I got back from the Continent last night," he began. "And I come here, as I promised, to report myself on my return. How does your ladyship do? How is Miss Roseberry?"

Lady Janet laid an indicative finger on the lace pelerine which ornamented the upper part of her dress. "Here is the old lady, well," she answered—and pointed next to the room above them. "And there," she added, "is the young lady, ill. Is anything the matter with *you*, Julian?"

"Perhaps I am a little tired after my journey. Never mind me. Is Miss Roseberry still suffering from the shock?"

"What else should she be suffering from? I will never forgive you, Julian, for bringing that crazy impostor into my house."

"My dear aunt, when I was the innocent means of bringing her here I had no idea that such a person as Miss Roseberry was in existence. Nobody laments what has happened more sincerely than I do. Have you had medical advice?"

"I took her to the seaside a week since, by medical advice."

"Has the change of air done her no good?"

"None whatever. If anything, the change of air has made her worse. Sometimes she sits for hours together, as pale as death, without looking at anything, and without uttering a word. Sometimes, she brightens up, and seems as if she was eager to say something— and then, Heaven only knows why, checks herself suddenly as if she was afraid to speak. I could support that. But what cuts me to the heart, Julian, is, that she does not appear to trust me and to love me as she did. She seems to be doubtful of me; she seems to be frightened of me. If I did not know that it was simply impossible that such a thing could be, I should really think she suspected me of believing what that wretch said of her. In one word (and between ourselves) I begin to fear she will never get over the fright which caused that fainting fit. There is serious mischief somewhere—and try as I may to discover it, it is mischief beyond my finding."

"Can the doctor do nothing?"

Lady Janet's bright black eyes answered, before she replied in words, with a look of supreme contempt.

"The doctor!" she repeated disdainfully. "I brought Grace back last night in sheer despair, and I sent for the doctor this morning. He is at the head of his profession; he is said to be making ten thousand a year—and he knows no more about it than I do. I am quite serious.

The great physician has just gone away with two guineas in his pocket. One guinea for advising me to keep her quiet; another guinea for telling me to trust to time. Do you wonder how he gets on at this rate? My dear boy, they all get on in the same way. The medical profession thrives on two incurable diseases in these modern days—a He-disease and a She-disease. She-disease—nervous depression; He-disease—suppressed gout. Remedies, one guinea if *you* go to the doctor; two guineas, if the doctor goes to *you*. I might have bought a new bonnet," cried her ladyship indignantly, " with the money I have given to that man! Let us change the subject. I lose my temper when I think of it. Besides, I want to know something. Why did you go abroad?"

At that plain question Julian looked unaffectedly surprised. " I wrote to explain," he said. " Have you not received my letter?"

" Oh, I got your letter. It was long enough, in all conscience— and, long as it was, it didn't tell me the one thing I wanted to know."

" What is the ' one thing '?"

Lady Janet's reply pointed—not too palpably at first—at that second motive for Julian's journey which she had suspected Julian of concealing from her.

" I want to know," she said, " why you troubled yourself to make your inquiries on the Continent *in person?* You know where my old courier is to be found. You have yourself pronounced him to be the most intelligent and trustworthy of men. Answer me honestly— could you not have sent him in your place?"

" I *might* have sent him," Julian admitted—a little reluctantly.

" You might have sent the courier—and you were under an engagement to stay here as my guest. Answer me honestly once more. Why did you go away?"

Julian hesitated. Lady Janet paused for his reply, with the air of a woman who was prepared to wait (if necessary) for the rest of the afternoon.

" I had a reason of my own for going," Julian said at last.

" Yes?" rejoined Lady Janet, prepared to wait (if necessary) till the next morning.

" A reason," Julian resumed, " which I would rather not mention."

" Oh!" said Lady Janet. " Another mystery—eh? And another woman at the bottom of it, no doubt? Thank you—that will do—I am sufficiently answered. No wonder—as a clergyman—that you look a little confused. There is perhaps a certain grace, under the circumstances, in looking confused. We will change the subject again. You stay here, of course, now you have come back?"

Once more the famous pulpit orator seemed to find himself in the inconceivable predicament of not knowing what to say. Once more

Lady Janet looked resigned to wait—(if necessary) until the middle
of next week.

Julian took refuge in an answer worthy of the most commonplace
man on the face of the civilised earth.

"I beg your ladyship to accept my thanks and my excuses," he said.

Lady Janet's many-ringed fingers mechanically stroking the cat in
her lap, began to stroke him the wrong way. Lady Janet's inexhaustible patience showed signs of failing her at last.

"Mighty civil, I am sure," she said. "Make it complete. Say,
Mr. Julian Gray presents his compliments to Lady Janet Roy, and
regrets that a previous engagement—Julian!" exclaimed the old lady,
suddenly pushing the cat off her lap, and flinging her last pretence of
good temper to the winds—"Julian, I am not to be trifled with!
There is but one explanation of your conduct—you are evidently
avoiding my house. Is there somebody you dislike in it? Is it Me?"

Julian intimated by a gesture that his aunt's last question was
absurd. (The much-injured cat elevated his back, waved his tail
slowly, walked to the fireplace, and honoured the rug by taking
a seat on it.)

Lady Janet persisted. "Is it Grace Roseberry?" she asked next.

Even Julian's patience began to show signs of yielding. His manner
assumed a sudden decision, his voice rose a tone louder.

"You insist on knowing?" he said. "It is Miss Roseberry."

"You don't like her?" cried Lady Janet, with a sudden burst of
angry surprise.

Julian broke out, on his side: "If I see any more of her," he
answered, the rare colour mounting passionately in his cheeks, "I
shall be the unhappiest man living. If I see any more of her, I
shall be false to my old friend who is to marry her. Keep us apart.
If you have any regard for my peace of mind, keep us apart."

Unutterable amazement expressed itself in his aunt's lifted hands.
Ungovernable curiosity uttered itself in his aunt's next words.

"You don't mean to tell me you are in love with Grace?"

Julian sprang restlessly to his feet, and disturbed the cat at the
fireplace. (The cat left the room.)

"I don't know what to tell you," he said, "I can't realise it to
myself. No other woman has ever roused the feeling in me which
*this* woman seems to have called to life in an instant. In the hope of
forgetting her I broke my engagement here; I purposely seized the
opportunity of making those inquiries abroad. Quite useless. I think
of her, morning, noon, and night. I see her and hear her, at this
moment, as plainly as I see and hear You. She has made *her*-self a
part of *my*-self. I don't understand my life without her. My power
of will seems to be gone. I said to myself this morning, ' I will
write to my aunt; I won't go back to Mablethorpe House.' Here I

am in Mablethorpe House, with a mean subterfuge to justify me to my own conscience. 'I owe it to my aunt to call on my aunt.' That is what I said to myself on the way here; and I was secretly hoping every step of the way that She would come into the room when I got here. I am hoping it now. And she is engaged to Horace Holmcroft—to my oldest friend, to my best friend! Am I an infernal rascal? or am I a weak fool? God knows—I don't. Keep my secret, aunt. I am heartily ashamed of myself; I used to think I was made of better stuff than this. Don't say a word to Horace. I must, and will, conquer it. Let me go."

He snatched up his hat. Lady Janet, rising with the activity of a young woman, pursued him across the room, and stopped him at the door.

" No," answered the resolute old lady, " I won't let you go. Come back with me."

As she said those words she noticed with a certain fond pride the brilliant colour mounting in his cheeks—the flashing brightness which lent an added lustre to his eyes. He had never, to her mind, looked so handsome before. She took his arm, and led him to the chairs which they had just left. It was shocking, it was wrong (she mentally admitted), to look on Mercy, under the circumstances, with any other eye than the eye of a brother or a friend. In a clergyman (perhaps) doubly shocking, doubly wrong. But, with all her respect for the vested interests of Horace, Lady Janet could not blame Julian. Worse still, she was privately conscious that he had, somehow or other, risen, rather than fallen, in her estimation within the last minute or two. Who could deny that her adopted daughter was a charming creature? Who could wonder if a man of refined tastes admired her? Upon the whole, her ladyship humanely decided that her nephew was rather to be pitied than blamed. What daughter of Eve (no matter whether she was seventeen or seventy) could have honestly arrived at any other conclusion? Do what a man may— let him commit anything he likes, from an error to a crime—so long as there is a woman at the bottom of it, there is an inexhaustible fund of pardon for him in every other woman's heart. " Sit down," said Lady Janet, smiling in spite of herself; " and don't talk in that horrible way again. A man, Julian—especially a famous man like you— ought to know how to control himself."

Julian burst out laughing bitterly.

" Send upstairs for my self-control," he said. " It's in *her* possession—not in mine. Good morning, aunt."

He rose from his chair. Lady Janet instantly pushed him back into it.

" I insist on your staying here," she said, " if it is only for a few minutes longer. I have something to say to you."

"Does it refer to Miss Roseberry?"

"It refers to the hateful woman who frightened Miss Roseberry. Now are you satisfied?"

Julian bowed, and settled himself in his chair.

"I don't much like to acknowledge it," his aunt went on. "But I want you to understand that I have something really serious to speak about, for once in a way. Julian! that wretch not only frightens Grace—she actually frightens Me."

"Frightens you? She is quite harmless, poor thing."

"'Poor thing!'" repeated Lady Janet. "Did you say, 'poor thing'?"

"Yes."

"Is it possible that you pity her?"

"From the bottom of my heart."

The old lady's temper gave way again at that reply. "I hate a man who can't hate anybody!" she burst out. "If you had been an ancient Roman, Julian, I believe you would have pitied Nero himself."

Julian cordially agreed with her. "I believe I should," he said quietly. "All sinners, my dear aunt, are more or less miserable sinners. Nero must have been one of the wretchedest of mankind."

"Wretched!" exclaimed Lady Janet. "Nero wretched! A man who committed robbery, arson, and murder, to his own violin accompaniment—*only* wretched! What next, I wonder? When modern philanthropy begins to apologise for Nero, modern philanthropy has arrived at a pretty pass indeed! We shall hear next that Bloody Queen Mary was as playful as a kitten; and if poor dear Henry the Eighth carried anything to an extreme, it was the practice of the domestic virtues. Ah, how I hate cant! What were we talking about just now? You wander from the subject, Julian; you are, what I call, bird-witted. I protest I forget what I wanted to say to you. No, I won't be reminded of it. I may be an old woman, but I am not in my dotage yet! Why do you sit there staring? Have you nothing to say for yourself? Of all the people in the world, have *you* lost the use of your tongue?"

Julian's excellent temper, and accurate knowledge of his aunt's character, exactly fitted him to calm the rising storm. He contrived to lead Lady Janet insensibly back to the lost subject, by dexterous reference to a narrative which he had thus far left untold—the narrative of his adventures on the Continent.

"I have a great deal to say, aunt," he replied. "I have not yet told you of my discoveries abroad."

Lady Janet instantly took the bait.

"I knew there was something forgotten," she said. "You have been all this time in the house, and you have told me nothing. Begin directly."

Patient Julian began.

## Chapter XIV.

### COMING EVENTS CAST THEIR SHADOWS BEFORE.

"I WENT first to Mannheim, Lady Janet, as I told you I should in my letter; and I heard all that the consul and the hospital doctors could tell me. No new fact of the slightest importance turned up. I got my directions for finding the German surgeon, and I set forth to try what I could make next of the man who had performed the operation. On the question of his patient's identity he had (as a perfect stranger to her) nothing to tell me. On the question of her mental condition, however, he made a very important statement. He owned to me that he had operated on another person injured by a shell-wound on the head, at the battle of Solferino, and that the patient (recovering also in this case) recovered—mad. That is a remarkable admission; don't you think so?"

Lady Janet's temper had hardly been allowed time enough to subside to its customary level.

"Very remarkable, I dare say," she answered, "to people who feel any doubt of this pitiable lady of yours being mad. I feel no doubt —and, thus far, I find your account of yourself, Julian, tiresome in the extreme. Get on to the end. Did you lay your hand on Mercy Merrick?"

"No."

"Did you hear anything of her?"

"Nothing. Difficulties beset me on every side. The French ambulance had shared in the disasters of France—it was broken up. The wounded Frenchmen were prisoners, somewhere in Germany, nobody knew where. The French surgeon had been killed in action. His assistants were scattered—most likely in hiding. I began to despair of making any discovery, when accident threw in my way two Prussian soldiers who had been in the French cottage. They confirmed what the German surgeon told the consul, and what Horace himself told *me*, namely, that no nurse in a black dress was to be seen in the place. If there had been such a person, she would certainly (the Prussians informed me) have been found in attendance on the injured Frenchmen. The cross of the Geneva Convention would have been amply sufficient to protect her: no woman wearing that badge of honour would have disgraced herself by abandoning the wounded men before the Germans entered the place."

"In short," interposed Lady Janet, "there is no such person as Mercy Merrick?"

"I can draw no other conclusion," said Julian, "unless the English doctor's idea is the right one. After hearing what I have just told you, he thinks the woman herself is Mercy Merrick."

Lady Janet held up her hand, as a sign that she had an objection to make here.

"You and the doctor seem to have settled everything to your entire satisfaction on both sides," she said. "But there is one difficulty that you have neither of you accounted for yet."

"What is it, aunt?"

"You talk glibly enough, Julian, about this woman's mad assertion that Grace is the missing nurse, and that she is Grace. But you have not explained yet how the idea first got into her head; and, more than that, how it is that she is acquainted with my name and address, and perfectly familiar with Grace's papers and Grace's affairs. These things are a puzzle to a person of my average intelligence. Can your clever friend, the doctor, account for them?"

"Shall I tell you what he said, when I saw him this morning?"

"Will it take long?"

"It will take about a minute."

"You agreeably surprise me. Go on."

"You want to know how she gained her knowledge of your name, and of Miss Roseberry's affairs," Julian resumed. "The doctor says, in one of two ways. Either Miss Roseberry must have spoken of you, and of her own affairs, while she and the stranger were together in the French cottage; or the stranger must have obtained access privately to Miss Roseberry's papers. Do you agree so far?"

Lady Janet began to feel interested for the first time.

"Perfectly," she said. "I have no doubt Grace rashly talked of matters which an older and wiser person would have kept to herself."

"Very good. Do you also agree that the last idea in the woman's mind when she was struck by the shell, might have been (quite probably) the idea of Miss Roseberry's identity and Miss Roseberry's affairs? You think it likely enough? Well! what happens after that? The wounded woman is brought to life by an operation, and she becomes delirious in the hospital at Mannheim. During her delirium the idea of Miss Roseberry's identity ferments in her brain, and assumes its present perverted form. In that form it still remains. As a necessary consequence, she persists in reversing the two identities. She says she is Miss Roseberry, and declares Miss Roseberry to be Mercy Merrick. There is the doctor's explanation. What do you think of it?"

"Very ingenious, I dare say. The doctor doesn't quite satisfy me, however, for all that. I think"——

What Lady Janet thought was not destined to be expressed. She suddenly checked herself, and held up her hand for the second time.

"Another objection?" inquired Julian.

"Hold your tongue!" cried the old lady. "If you say a word more I shall lose it again."

"Lose what, aunt?"

"What I wanted to say to you, ages ago. I have got it back again —it begins with a question. (No more of the doctor! I have had enough of him!) Where is she—*your* pitiable lady, *my* crazy wretch —where is she now? Still in London?"

"Yes."

"And still at large?"

"Still with the landlady, at her lodgings."

"Very well. Now, answer me this! What is to prevent her from making another attempt to force her way (or steal her way) into my house? How am I to protect Grace, how am I to protect myself, if she comes here again?"

"Is that really what you wished to speak to me about?"

"That, and nothing else."

They were both too deeply interested in the subject of their conversation to look towards the conservatory, and to notice the appearance at that moment of a distant gentleman among the plants and flowers, who had made his way in from the garden outside. Advancing noiselessly on the soft Indian matting, the gentleman ere long revealed himself under the form and features of Horace Holmcroft. Before entering the dining-room, he paused, fixing his eyes inquisitively on the back of Lady Janet's visitor—the back being all that he could see in the position he then occupied. After a pause of an instant, the visitor spoke, and further uncertainty was at once at an end. Horace, nevertheless, made no movement to enter the room. He had his own jealous distrust of what Julian might be tempted to say at a private interview with his aunt; and he waited a little longer, on the chance that his doubts might be verified.

"Neither you nor Miss Roseberry need any protection from the poor deluded creature," Julian went on. "I have gained great influence over her—and I have satisfied her that it is useless to present herself here again."

"I beg your pardon," interposed Horace, speaking from the conservatory door. "You have done nothing of the sort."

(He had heard enough to satisfy him that the talk was not taking the direction which his suspicions had anticipated. And, as an additional incentive to show himself, a happy chance had now offered him the opportunity of putting Julian in the wrong.)

"Good heavens, Horace!" exclaimed Lady Janet. "Where do you come from? And what do you mean?"

"I heard at the lodge that your ladyship and Grace had returned last night. And I came in at once, without troubling the servants, by the shortest way." He turned to Julian next. "The woman you were speaking of just now," he proceeded, "has been here again already—in Lady Janet's absence."

Lady Janet immediately looked at her nephew. Julian reassured her by a gesture.

"Impossible," he said. "There must be some mistake."

"There is no mistake," Horace rejoined. "I am repeating what I have just heard from the lodge-keeper himself. He hesitated to mention it to Lady Janet for fear of alarming her. Only three days since this person had the audacity to ask him for her ladyship's address at the seaside. Of course he refused to give it."

"You hear that, Julian?" said Lady Janet.

No signs of anger or mortification escaped Julian. The expression in his face at that moment was an expression of sincere distress.

"Pray don't alarm yourself," he said to his aunt, in his quietest tones. "If she attempts to annoy you or Miss Roseberry again, I have it in my power to stop her instantly."

"How?" asked Lady Janet.

"How, indeed!" echoed Horace. "If we give her in charge to the police we shall become the subject of a public scandal."

"I have managed to avoid all danger of scandal," Julian answered; the expression of distress in his face becoming more and more marked while he spoke. "Before I called here to-day I had a private consultation with the magistrate of the district, and I have made certain arrangements at the police-station close by. On receipt of my card, an experienced man, in plain clothes, will present himself at any address that I indicate, and will take her quietly away. The magistrate will hear the charge in his private room, and will examine the evidence which I can produce, showing that she is not accountable for her actions. The proper medical officer will report officially on the case, and the law will place her under the necessary restraint."

Lady Janet and Horace looked at each other in amazement. Julian was, in their opinion, the last man on earth to take the course —at once sensible and severe—which Julian had actually adopted. Lady Janet insisted on an explanation.

"Why do I hear of this now for the first time?" she asked. "Why did you not tell me you had taken these precautions before?"

Julian answered frankly and sadly.

"Because I hoped, aunt, that there would be no necessity for proceeding to extremities. You now force me to acknowledge that the lawyer and the doctor (both of whom I have seen this morning) think, as you do, that she is not to be trusted. It was at their suggestion entirely that I went to the magistrate. They put it to me whether the result of my inquiries abroad—unsatisfactory as it may have been in other respects—did not strengthen the conclusion that the poor woman's mind is deranged. I felt compelled in common honesty to admit that it was so. Having owned this, I was bound to take such precautions as the lawyer and the doctor thought necessary. I have done my duty—sorely against my own will. It is weak of me, I dare say—but I can *not* bear the thought of treating this afflicted creature harshly. Her delusion is so hopeless! her situation is such a pitiable one!"

His voice faltered. He turned away abruptly and took up his hat. Lady Janet followed him, and spoke to him at the door. Horace smiled satirically, and went to warm himself at the fire.

"Are you going away, Julian?"

"I am only going to the lodge-keeper. I want to give him a word of warning in case of his seeing her again."

"You will come back here?" (Lady Janet lowered her voice to a whisper). "There is really a reason, Julian, for your not leaving the house now."

"I promise not to go away, aunt, until I have provided for your security. If you, or your adopted daughter, are alarmed by another intrusion, I give you my word of honour my card shall go to the police-station—however painfully I may feel it myself." (He, too, lowered his voice at the next words.) "In the meantime, remember what I confessed to you while we were alone! For my sake, let me see as little of Miss Roseberry as possible. Shall I find you in this room when I come back?"

"Yes."

"Alone?"

He laid a strong emphasis, of look as well as of tone, on that one word. Lady Janet understood what the emphasis meant.

"Are you really," she whispered, "as much in love with Grace as that?"

Julian laid one hand on his aunt's arm, and pointed with the other to Horace—standing with his back to them, warming his feet on the fender.

"Well?" said Lady Janet.

"Well," said Julian, with a smile on his lip and a tear in his eye, "I never envied any man as I envy *him!*"

With those words he left the room.

## CHAPTER XV.

### A WOMAN'S REMORSE.

HAVING warmed his feet to his own entire satisfaction, Horace turned round from the fireplace, and discovered that he and Lady Janet were alone.

"Can I see Grace?" he asked.

The easy tone in which he put the question—a tone, as it were, of proprietorship in "Grace"—jarred on Lady Janet at the moment.

For the first time in her life she found herself comparing Horace with Julian—to Horace's disadvantage. He was rich; he was a gentleman of ancient lineage; he bore an unblemished character. But who had the strong brain? who had the great heart? Which was the Man of the two?

"Nobody can see her," answered Lady Janet. "Not even you!" ·

The tone of the reply was sharp—with a dash of irony in it. But where is the modern young man—possessed of health and an independent income—who is capable of understanding that irony can be presumptuous enough to address itself to *him*? Horace (with perfect politeness) declined to consider himself answered.

"Does your ladyship mean that Miss Roseberry is in bed?" he asked.

"I mean that Miss Roseberry is in her room. I mean that I have twice tried to persuade Miss Roseberry to dress and come downstairs —and tried in vain. I mean that what Miss Roseberry refuses to do for Me, she is not likely to do for You "——

How many more meanings of her own Lady Janet might have gone on enumerating, it is not easy to calculate. At her third sentence, a sound in the library caught her ear through the incompletely-closed door, and suspended the next words on her lips. Horace heard it also. It was the rustling sound (travelling nearer and nearer over the library carpet) of a silken dress.

(In the interval while a coming event remains in a state of uncertainty, what is it the inevitable tendency of every Englishman under thirty to do? His inevitable tendency is to ask somebody to bet on the event. He can no more resist it than he can resist lifting his stick or his umbrella, in the absence of a gun, and pretending to shoot if a bird flies by him while he is out for a walk.)

"What will your ladyship bet that this is not Grace?" cried Horace.

Her ladyship took no notice of the proposal; her attention remained fixed on the library door. The rustling sound stopped for a moment. The door was softly pushed open. The false Grace Roseberry entered the room.

Horace advanced to meet her, opened his lips to speak, and stopped —struck dumb by the change in his affianced wife since he had seen her last. Some terrible oppression seemed to have crushed her. It was as if she had actually shrunk in height as well as in substance. She walked more slowly than usual; she spoke more rarely than usual, and in a lower tone. To those who had seen her before the fatal visit of the stranger from Mannheim, it was the wreck of the woman that now appeared, instead of the woman herself. And yet, there was the old charm still surviving through it all; the grandeur of the head and eyes, the delicate symmetry of the features, the unsought grace of every movement—in a word, the unconquerable beauty which suffering cannot destroy, and which time itself is powerless to wear out.

Lady Janet advanced, and took her with hearty kindness by both hands.

"My dear child, welcome among us again! You have come down-stairs to please me?"

She bent her head in silent acknowledgment that it was so. Lady Janet pointed to Horace: "Here is somebody who has been longing to see you, Grace."

She never looked up; she stood submissive, her eyes fixed on a little basket of coloured wools which hung on her arm. "Thank you, Lady Janet," she said faintly. "Thank you, Horace."

Horace placed her arm in his, and led her to the sofa. She shivered as she took her seat, and looked round her. It was the first time she had seen the dining-room since the day when she had found herself face to face with the dead-alive.

"Why do you come here, my love?" asked Lady Janet. "The drawing-room would have been a warmer and a pleasanter place for you."

"I saw a carriage at the front door. I was afraid of meeting with visitors in the drawing-room."

As she made that reply, the servant came in, and announced the visitors' names. Lady Janet sighed wearily. "I must go and get rid of them," she said, resigning herself to circumstances. "What will *you* do, Grace?"

"I will stay here, if you please."

"I will keep her company," added Horace.

Lady Janet hesitated. She had promised to see her nephew in the dining-room on his return to the house—and to see him alone. Would there be time enough to get rid of the visitors and to establish her adopted daughter in the empty drawing-room before Julian appeared? It was a ten minutes' walk to the lodge, and he had to make the gatekeeper understand his instructions. Lady Janet decided that she had time enough at her disposal. She nodded kindly to Mercy, and left her alone with her lover.

Horace seated himself in the vacant place on the sofa. So far as it was in his nature to devote himself to any one he was devoted to Mercy. "I am grieved to see how you have suffered," he said, with honest distress in his face as he looked at her. "Try to forget what has happened."

"I am trying to forget. Do *you* think of it much?"

"My darling, it is too contemptible to be thought of."

She placed her work basket on her lap. Her wasted fingers began absently sorting the wools inside.

"Have you seen Mr. Julian Gray?" she asked suddenly.

"Yes."

"What does *he* say about it?" She looked at Horace for the first time, steadily scrutinising his face. Horace took refuge in prevarication.

"I really hav'nt asked for Julian's opinion," he said.

She looked down again, with a sigh, at the basket on her lap—considered a little—and tried him once more.

"Why has Mr. Julian Gray not been here for a whole week?" she went on. "The servants say he has been abroad. Is that true?"

It was useless to deny it. Horace admitted that the servants were right.

Her fingers suddenly stopped at their restless work among the wools: her breath quickened perceptibly. What had Julian Gray been doing abroad? Had he been making inquiries? Did he alone, of all the people who saw that terrible meeting, suspect her? Yes! His was the finer intelligence; his was a clergyman's (a London clergyman's) experience of frauds and deceptions, and of the women who were guilty of them. Not a doubt of it now! Julian suspected her.

"When does he come back?" she asked, in tones so low that Horace could barely hear her.

"He has come back already. He returned last night."

A faint shade of colour stole slowly over the pallor of her face. She suddenly put her basket away, and clasped her hands together to quiet the trembling of them, before she asked her next question.

"Where is"—— She paused to steady her voice. "Where is the person," she resumed, "who came here and frightened me?"

Horace hastened to reassure her. "The person will not come again," he said. "Don't talk of her! Don't think of her!"

She shook her head. "There is something I want to know," she persisted. "How did Mr. Julian Gray become acquainted with her?"

This was easily answered. Horace mentioned the consul at Mannheim, and the letter of introduction. She listened eagerly, and said her next words in a louder, firmer tone.

"She was quite a stranger, then, to Mr. Julian Gray—before that?"

"Quite a stranger," Horace replied. "No more questions—not another word about her, Grace! I forbid the subject. Come, my own love!" he said taking her hand, and bending over her tenderly, "rally your spirits! We are young—we love each other—now is our time to be happy!"

Her hand turned suddenly cold, and trembled in his. Her head sank with a helpless weariness on her breast. Horace rose in alarm.

"You are cold—you are faint," he said. "Let me get you a glass of wine!—let me mend the fire!"

The decanters were still on the luncheon-table. Horace insisted on her drinking some port wine. She barely took half the contents of the wine-glass. Even that little told on her sensitive organisation; it roused her sinking energies of body and mind. After watching her anxiously, without attracting her notice, Horace left her again to attend to the fire at the other end of the room. Her eyes followed him slowly with a hard and tearless despair. "Rally your spirits," she repeated to herself in a whisper. "My spirits! Oh, God!" She looked round her at the luxury and beauty of the room, as those look who take their leave of familiar scenes. The moment after, her eyes sank, and rested on the rich dress that she wore—a gift from Lady Janet. She thought of the past; she thought of the future. Was the time near when she would be back again in the Refuge, or back again in the streets?—she who had been Lady Janet's adopted daughter, and Horace Holmcroft's betrothed wife! A sudden frenzy of recklessness seized on her as she thought of the coming end. Horace was right! Why not rally her spirits? Why not make the most of her time? The last hours of her life in that house were at hand. Why not enjoy her stolen position while she could? "Adventuress!" whispered the mocking spirit within her, " be true to your character. Away with your remorse! Remorse is the luxury of an honest woman." She caught up her basket of wools, inspired by a new idea. "Ring the bell!" she cried out to Horace at the fire-place.

He looked round in wonder. The sound of her voice was so completely altered that he almost fancied there must have been another woman in the room.

"Ring the bell!" she repeated. "I have left my work upstairs. If you want me to be in good spirits, I must have my work."

Still looking at her, Horace put his hand mechanically to the bell and rang. One of the men-servants came in.

"Go upstairs, and ask my maid for my work," she said sharply. Even the man was taken by surprise; it was her habit to speak to the servants with a gentleness and consideration which had long since won all their hearts. "Do you hear me?" she asked impatiently. The servant bowed, and went out on his errand. She turned to Horace with flashing eyes and fevered cheeks.

"What a comfort it is," she said, " to belong to the upper classes! A poor woman has no maid to dress her, and no footman to send upstairs. Is life worth having, Horace, on less than five thousand a year?"

The servant returned with a strip of embroidery. She took it with an insolent grace, and told him to bring her a footstool. The man obeyed. She tossed the embroidery away from her on the sofa. "On second thoughts I don't care about my work," she said. "Take it upstairs again." The perfectly-trained servant, marvelling privately, obeyed once more. Horace, in silent astonishment, advanced to the sofa to observe her more nearly. "How grave you look!" she exclaimed, with an air of flippant unconcern. "You don't approve of my sitting idle, perhaps? Anything to please you! I hav'nt got to go up and down stairs. Ring the bell again."

"My dear Grace," Horace remonstrated gravely, "you are quite mistaken. I never even thought of your work."

"Never mind; it's inconsistent to send for my work, and then send it away again. Ring the bell."

Horace looked at her, without moving. "Grace!" he said, "what has come to you?"

"How should I know?" she retorted carelessly. "Didn't you tell me to rally my spirits? Will you ring the bell? or must I?"

Horace submitted. He frowned as he walked back to the bell. He was one of the many people who instinctively resent anything that is new to them. This strange outbreak was quite new to him. For the first time in his life he felt sympathy for a servant, when the much-enduring man appeared once more.

"Bring my work back; I have changed my mind." With that brief explanation she reclined luxuriously on the soft sofa cushions; swinging one of her balls of wool to and fro above her head, and looking at it lazily as she lay back. "I have a remark to make, Horace," she went on, when the door had closed on her messenger. "It is only people in our rank of life who get good servants. Did you notice? Nothing upsets that man's temper. A servant in a poor family would have been impudent; a maid-of-all-work would have wondered when I was going to know my own mind." The man returned with the embroidery. This time she received him graciously; she dismissed him with her thanks. "Have you seen your mother lately, Horace?" she asked, suddenly sitting up and busying herself with her work.

"I saw her yesterday," Horace answered.

"She understands, I hope, that I am not well enough to call on her? She is not offended with me?"

Horace recovered his serenity. The deference to his mother implied in Mercy's questions gently flattered his self-esteem. He resumed his place on the sofa.

"Offended with you!" he answered, smiling. "My dear Grace, she sends you her love. And, more than that, she has a wedding-present for you."

Mercy became absorbed in her work; she stooped close over the embroidery—so close that Horace could not see her face. "Do you know what the present is?" she asked in lowered tones; speaking absently.

"No. I only know it is waiting for you. Shall I go and get it to-day?"

She neither accepted nor refused the proposal—she went on with her work more industriously than ever.

"There is plenty of time," Horace persisted. "I can go before dinner."

Still she took no notice: still she never looked up. "Your mother is very kind to me," she said, abruptly. "I was afraid, at one time, that she would think me hardly good enough to be your wife."

Horace laughed indulgently: his self-esteem was more gently flattered than ever.

"Absurd!" he exclaimed. "My darling, you are connected with Lady Janet Roy. Your family is almost as good as ours."

"Almost?" she repeated. "Only almost?"

The momentary levity of expression vanished from Horace's face. The family-question was far too serious a question to be lightly treated. A becoming shadow of solemnity stole over his manner. He looked as if it was Sunday, and he was just stepping into church.

"In OUR family," he said, "we trace back—by my father, to the Saxons: by my mother, to the Normans. Lady Janet's family is an old family—on her side only."

Mercy dropped her embroidery, and looked Horace full in the face. She, too, attached no common importance to what she had next to say.

"If I had not been connected with Lady Janet," she began, "would you ever have thought of marrying me?"

"My love! what is the use of asking? You *are* connected with Lady Janet."

She refused to let him escape answering her in that way.

"Suppose I had not been connected with Lady Janet," she persisted, "Suppose I had only been a good girl, with nothing but my own merits to speak for me. What would your mother have said, then?"

Horace still parried the question—only to find the point of it pressed home on him once more.

"Why do you ask?" he said.

"I ask to be answered," she rejoined. "Would your mother have liked you to marry a poor girl, of no family—with nothing but her own virtues to speak for her?"

Horace was fairly pressed back to the wall.

"If you must know," he replied, "my mother would have refused to sanction such a marriage as that."

"No matter how good the girl might have been?"

There was something defiant—almost threatening—in her tone. Horace was annoyed—and he showed it when he spoke.

"My mother would have respected the girl, without ceasing to respect herself," he said. "My mother would have remembered what was due to the family name."

"And she would have said, No?"

"She would have said, No."

"Ah!"

There was an undertone of angry contempt in the exclamation which made Horace start. "What is the matter?" he asked.

"Nothing," she answered, and took up her embroidery again. There he sat at her side, anxiously looking at her—his hope in the future centred in his marriage! In a week more, if she chose, she might enter that ancient family of which he had spoken so proudly, as his wife. "Oh!" she thought, "if I didn't love him! if I had only his merciless mother to think of!"

Uneasily conscious of some estrangement between them, Horace spoke again. "Surely, I have not offended you?" he said.

She turned towards him once more. The work dropped unheeded on her lap. Her grand eyes softened into tenderness. A smile trembled sadly on her delicate lips. She laid one hand caressingly on his shoulder. All the beauty of her voice lent its charm to the next words that she said to him. The woman's heart hungered in its misery for the comfort that could only come from his lips.

"*You* would have loved me, Horace—without stopping to think of the family name?"

The family name again! How strangely she persisted in coming back to that! Horace looked at her without answering; trying vainly to fathom what was passing in her mind.

She took his hand, and wrung it hard—as if she would wring the answer out of him in that way.

"*You* would have loved me?" she repeated.

The double spell of her voice and her touch was on him. He answered warmly, "Under any circumstances! under any name!"

She put one arm round his neck, and fixed her eyes on his. "Is that true?" she asked.

"True as the heaven above us!"

She drank in those few commonplace words with a greedy delight. She forced him to repeat them in a new form.

"No matter who I might have been? For myself alone?"

"For yourself alone."

She threw both arms round him, and laid her head passionately on his breast. "I love you! I love you!! I love you!!!" Her voice rose with hysterical vehemence, at each repetition of the words—then suddenly sank to a low hoarse cry of rage and despair. The sense of her true position towards him revealed itself in all its horror as the confession of her love escaped her lips. Her arms dropped from him; she flung herself back on the sofa cushions, hiding her face in her hands. "Oh, leave me!" she moaned, faintly. "Go! go!"

Horace tried to wind his arm round her, and raise her. She started to her feet, and waved him back from her with a wild action of her hands, as if she was frightened of him. "The wedding-present!" she cried, seizing the first pretext that occurred to her. "You offered to bring me your mother's present. I am dying to see what it is. Go, and get it!"

Horace tried to compose her. He might as well have tried to compose the winds and the sea.

"Go!" she repeated, pressing one clenched hand on her bosom. "I am not well. Talking excites me—I am hysterical; I shall be better alone. Get me the present. Go!"

"Shall I send Lady Janet? Shall I ring for your maid?"

"Send for nobody! ring for nobody! If you love me—leave me here by myself! leave me instantly!"

"I shall see you when I come back?"

"Yes! yes!"

There was no alternative but to obey her. Unwillingly and forebodingly, Horace left the room.

She drew a deep breath of relief, and dropped into the nearest chair. If Horace had stayed a moment longer—she felt it, she knew it—her head would have given way; she would have burst out before him with the terrible truth. "Oh!" she thought, pressing her cold hands on her burning eyes, "if I could only cry, now there is nobody to see me!"

The room was empty, she had every reason for concluding that she was alone. And yet, at that very moment, there were ears that listened, there were eyes waiting to see her.

Little by little the door behind her which faced the library and led into the billiard-room was opened noiselessly from without, by an inch at a time. As the opening was enlarged, a hand in a black glove, an arm in a black sleeve, appeared, guiding the movement of the door. An interval of a moment passed, and the worn white face of Grace Roseberry showed itself stealthily, looking into the dining-room.

Her eyes brightened with vindictive pleasure as they discovered Mercy sitting alone at the farther end of the room. Inch by inch she opened the door more widely, took one step forward, and checked herself. A sound, just audible at the far end of the conservatory, had caught her ear.

She listened—satisfied herself that she was not mistaken—and, drawing back with a frown of displeasure, softly closed the door again, so as to hide herself from view. The sound that had disturbed her was the distant murmur of men's voices (apparently two in number) talking together in lowered tones, at the garden entrance to the conservatory.

Who were the men? and what would they do next? They might do one of two things: they might enter the drawing-room, or they might withdraw again by way of the garden. Kneeling behind the door, with her ear at the keyhole, Grace Roseberry waited the event.

# Reminiscences of Winchester College.

## By FRANK BUCKLAND.

IT is now thirty-three years ago since, a frightened and trembling lad, in the month of August, 1839, I found myself standing underneath the gateway of William of Wykeham's noble college at Winchester, duly entered as a Scholar thereof by the nomination of Dr. Shuttleworth, then Warden of New College, Oxford, afterwards Bishop of Chichester. In those days there was no railway to Winchester, and I went from Oxford to Winchester in a four-horse coach, the driver of which wore most wonderful top-boots and a marvellous coat with gigantic buttons. I had great respect for this coachman, as he once brought my Father a semi-dead crocodile, in the coach boot, from Southampton. My Father turned the dead crocodile into the pond in the middle of the quadrangle, at Christchurch, to revive him; but he refused to be revived, so I rode about upon him, Waterton fashion, and somehow I always associated the Southampton coachman with a crocodile. I recollect perfectly well that he once told me he had driven my mother to school to Southampton, and this made me think him very old. Soon after we had driven over Folly Bridge on our road to Winchester, crossing the Thames at Oxford, and were ascending the Bagley Wood Hill on the Abingdon Road, the rest of the passengers began to complain about a nasty unpleasant smell, which apparently proceeded from the luggage on the top of the coach. A bluebottle fly first appeared from out of Bagley Wood, then another, until a perfect swarm of flies soon followed the coach, hovering and buzzing over the luggage. The passengers were mostly Oxford boys, going to Winchester, and there was a strong idea among them that somehow or other I knew from whence this odour proceeded. I knew perfectly well the cause of the smell, but I said nothing. The "governor," then canon of Christ Church, had kept a haunch of venison for me to take as a present to the head master, Dr. Moberly; he had kept it so long hanging up in the larder at Christ Church, that it had become very "exalted" indeed; nevertheless he packed it up, thinking to make it last anyhow as far as Winchester. His experiment failed, and the other boys punched my head on the top of the coach, and were very near throwing me and my venison overboard altogether.

We Oxford lads arriving at Winchester, all went down to the college together, and put on our gowns for the first time. Our gowns were made of cloth, the like of which I never since beheld, and our hats were taken away, as no Winchester boys, except præfects, wear hats. It is rare to find a Winchester man now with a bald head, and even now I never wear a hat if I can possibly help it.

Immediately after chapel the old stager boys all came round the new arrivals to examine and criticise them. I perfectly recollect one boy, H——, to whose special care my poor confiding mother had entrusted her innocent unsuspecting cub, coming up to me with a most solemn face, and asking me if I had brought with me my copy of the school book 'Pempe moron proteron'? I said I had not. "Then," says he, "you must borrow one at once, or the Doctor," i.e. Dr. Moberly. the head master, "will be sure to flog you to-morrow morning, and your college tutor, one of the præfects, will also lick you." So he sent me to another boy, who said he had *lent* his 'Pempe moron proteron,' but he passed me on to a third, he on to a fourth; so I was running about all over the College till quite late, in a most terrible panic of mind, till at last a good-natured præfect said, "Construe it, you little fool." · I had never thought of this before. I saw it directly: *Pempe* (send) *moron* (a fool) *proteron* (further); so the title of this wonderful book after all was, ' Send a fool further.' I then went to complain to H——; he only laughed, and shied a Donnegan's lexicon at my head. I dodged it like a bird, so he made me pick it up and bring it to him again, like a retriever dog. I then had to "run for another shot," and he winged me this time; so I shall never forget the translation of *Pempe moron proteron.*

The beds in " chambers " (as the sleeping apartments are called) are, I believe, as old as William of Wykeham himself; they are made of very thick oak planks, and there is a hollow for the bed clothes, after the style of the beds for fox-hounds in kennels. I was glad enough to turn in after this long and anxious day. I dreamed of home, and calculated how big some young ducks I had left in the outhouse at home would be when the holidays came round. They were *my* ducks. I had bought them as "squeakers" on Port Meadow, with my pocket money, and my father had promised that if I was a good boy at my lessons I should cut their heads off when I came home, on the wood block in the tool house, with the gardener's hatchet. It was made a great treat to my brother and myself to cut a duck's head off while my dear old Father held the duck's legs—but he was not dressed for the occasion in his canonical robes.

In the midst of my dreams I imagined that an eruption of Mount Vesuvius had suddenly taken place. I felt myself flying through the air, and then experienced a most tremendous crack on the back of my head; in fact I was "launched." I afterwards ascertained that all new boys were "launched" the first night after arrival. The process of "launching" is in this wise: when the innocent is fast asleep, dreaming of home and mother, two boys catch hold of one side of the bottom of the mattress and two of the other, and at the signal

"Launch!" run the bed out in the middle of the room with the boy in it; they then cut away like rabbits to their own beds, while the wretched "junior," has to rearrange his bed as well as he can, and tumble in again, frightened out of his wits. There is, however, a little mercy shown, for it is considered unfair to launch the same boy twice in the same night, particularly as he has, in the course of a day or two, when he is beginning to be able to sleep again (for "launching" made me sleep with one eye open) to be initiated into another College mystery.

A few nights afterwards I dreamt I was wandering on the sea shore, and that a crab was pinching my foot. Instantly awakening, I experienced a most frightful pain in my great toe. I bore it for a while, until at last it became so intense that I had to jump up with a howl of agony; all was quiet, but the pull continued, and I had to follow my toe and outstretched leg out of bed. I then found a bit of wetted whipcord tight round it; but the whipcord was so ingeniously twisted among the beds that it was impossible to find out *who had* pulled it. I returned to bed as savage as a wounded animal. The moment I was settled, the boys all burst into a shout: " Toe fit tied!" " By Jove, what a lark!" This barbarous process is called " toe fit tie " because there is a line in Prosody which begins, " To fit ti, ut verto verti." Hence the origin of this Winchester custom.

The latest arrival in College is called " junior in chambers," and in my time "junior in chambers" had a precious hard time of it. He had to get up at " first peal," i.e. when the chapel bell rang—and this was awfully early in the morning—call all the boys in the room, light the fire, put out the præfects' washing apparatus, &c. The Winchester fires were large faggots burnt upon " dog-irons." It requires great art to make a faggot light quickly, and the burning sticks were awkward to handle. No tongs were allowed; so when a boy first took office he had a pair of " tin gloves " given him; i.e., one of the seniors took the red hot end of a bit of stick, and blowing it to keep it alight made a mark down all the fingers and round the wrists; after he had received his " tin gloves " woe be to the boy who managed the faggots clumsily, for he instantly was formally presented with another pair of " tin gloves." The " junior in chambers " had also to clean the washhand basins, and they were only cleaned before chapel time on a Sunday morning. We had to do this out in the open, at two water-taps, which were called " conduit." I'll be bound to say that very few Winchester boys *now* know how to clean basins properly. The secret is to use salt. But " cleaning basins " was terrifically cold work for our fingers on frosty mornings, especially if we had chapped hands; and what with " tin gloves " and salt, this was often the case. We also had to mark the basins. I wonder if any of my readers know how to mark indelibly a common white washhand basin with initials of the owner. Well, it is a Winchester secret. If you rub the basin hard with the pipe part of an ordinary drawer key, you will wear off the white enamel of the basin and lay bare the brown part of the structure. One boy, F——, now a judge in India, was wonderfully clever at marking basins. He used to be let off cricket to mark basins, and he used to sit by the "tap" working away at the basins, like a cobbler. How I envied him! For I even now hate cricket. I had quite enough of it as a fag at Winchester. The "junior in chambers" had also to clean the knives. There were no American knife-cleaners in those days; but we cleaned the knives by rubbing them up and down quickly between the cracks between the stones of the College court. I could now walk to my favourite knife-cleaning place just by the College chapel door; it is on the west side.

It was also the duty of "junior in chambers," as well as other "fags," to make coffee for the præfects. There is a great art in making coffee. The coffee must be mixed with cold water, it must then be put on the "dog-irons" till large bubbles come to the surface; these must be broken one by one with a piece of stick; a piece of the skin of a sole must then be put into the coffee, it must be allowed to boil up again, and then a small cup of cold water thrown in and the coffee allowed to settle. The juniors used to take pride in making coffee, and I recollect once, when there was a "coffee match," I got the second prize, and will now back myself to make coffee against anybody, even professed cooks. We used also to make plum-puddings; but we never began them till very late at night, and we thought the master, Dr. Wordsworth (now Bishop of St. Andrews) had gone to bed and would not come his rounds that night. I used to roll the dough with the towel roller that was behind the door. The biggest licking I ever got in my life was for making a *heavy* plum-pudding; and to this day I would not undertake to make a plum-pudding, as I shall never forget that licking.

The præfects, when not particularly busy with their books, instituted bolstering matches among the juniors. A bolster, properly arranged, is a very formidable weapon, and the great object was to skin one's adversary's nose. This is done by a well directed blow which brings the rough edge of the bolster on to the bridge of the nose. I recollect on one occasion having a fierce battle with a lad who has since died, holding a high official appointment. In the middle of the fight we heard a key put in the door. By Jove! it was Dr. Wordsworth, coming the rounds! I was into bed in a moment, and though panting like a hunted fox, pretended to be fast asleep. Dr. Wordsworth put the light of the lantern he carried right into my eyes, but I never moved a muscle, because I knew perfectly well that if I had been caught my name would have been "ordered" for a flogging the next morning, while I should have most certainly have got a "tunding" with a ground-ash- stick from the præfects for being such a fool as to be caught by the master.

I had not been long at Winchester before I was appointed to be "rod maker." The rods consist of four apple twigs; these are tied fast into four grooves at the top of a light wooden handle. It requires some skill to make a rod properly, as the twigs are apt to shift. round under the string, and thus get loose; and if a rod were not properly made, and if it broke when the master was using it, I think the manufacturer was entitled to one cut from a rod made by some one else. The præfects used to buy the ground-ashes from Bill Purvis, the under cook. They were sapling ashes, with the roots on. The legend was, that Purvis used to boil them with the mutton to get the grease into them, and then put them up the big college chimney to toughen; and, by Jove! they were tough as whalebone!

Unless a boy had twenty juniors, i.e., twenty boys below him in the school, he was not allowed to "think." The præfects, when they wanted anything, used to cry "Junior! Junior!" and the junior boy in the school had to run instantly. The præfect would say, "Where is so-and-so?" The junior would answer, "Please, I *thought* so-and-so." "Have you got twenty juniors?" "No." "Then you must have three clows for thinking." "Clows" are boxes on the ear; they don't hurt much; but we boys found out the proper way to shift one's head, so that the clows did not hurt.

Altogether, we juniors had a pretty hard time of it; but it was wonderful good training; it made one so awfully sharp and certain about little things. The edict against "thinking" was good; it made one find out for certain, or else say "I don't know." We were never whacked for "not knowing," only for "thinking." Many people about are always "thinking"; they should have been at Winchester. A few "clows" administered to them when juniors would have done them much good.

I once made a tremendously lucky hit. I was very nearly at the bottom of a class before Dr. Wordsworth. A senior boy was construing a passage in the first Georgic, describing a man rowing up stream with oars:

"Non aliter quam qui adverso vix flumine lembum
Remigiis subigit : si brachia forte remisit,
Atque illum in præceps prono rapit alveus amni."

None of the boys could construe the word "*atque*." The ordinary meaning of "*atque*" is "and." I thought to myself, if I left off rowing when pulling against stream, it is common-sense that the boat would immediately carry me down stream. I was a long way down the class, and when my turn came to answer as to what was the English of *atque*,

I jumped up boldly and sung out, "*Atque*, immediately." "Good boy," says Dr. Wordsworth, "take their places"; and if I recollect right I took twenty-two places at one leap, and marched in triumph from the bottom to within two of the top of the class.   I have a strong idea that when school hour came I got a licking from two or three boys for knowing what the English of *atque* was.   There was one consolation, however.   The next day I was set on in Dr. Wordsworth's new edition of the Greek grammar, of which he was especially fond, and which we boys, who knew the *old* Greek grammar pretty well, hated with all our hearts.   I had to interpret something connected with the formation of the aorists of some horrible Greek verb. I never could understand Greek grammar, and I never shall; knowing nothing about these aorists, præterpluperfects, and things of that kind.   So Wordsworth's Greek grammar *atque*—immediately— sunk me, like a stone round my neck, to my old position at the bottom of the class, and, if I recollect right, two places lower than from where I started.

We boys were very fond of recording maltranslations.   I recollect one of my own.   Dr. Moberly had "put me on" to translate a passage which I confess I had never looked at.   I was pulled up short at the words "*Numinis Idæi*," which ought to mean, "of the god of Ida."   I translated it, "of the Numidean Ideus."   I also recollect one boy, whose name was Salmon—of course I cannot forget that name— translating

"Aspice bis senos lætantes agmine cycnos" (*Æn.* i. 393,)

which ought to be, "behold two hundred swans."   He translated it, "Behold two old swans."   The following translation is also a legend among Winchester boys :

"Silvestrem tenui musam meditaris avenâ " (*Ecl.* i. 2,)

which, being properly interpreted, would read as follows : " *Meditaris*, thou art playing; *silvestrem musam*, a rustic song; *tenui avenâ*, on your slender flute."   The following very different version, however, was given by the unfortunate boy, thus: " *Tenui*, I held; *silvestrem musam*, my woody muse; *meditaris arenâ*, on the shores of the Mediterranean."   Other maltranslations, from the records of public schools, are given in that admirable little book, ' The Art of Pluck." " *Et tu, Brute*," "You brute, you." " *Mala duces avi domum*," which ought to be, "Thou art taking her" (Helen) "home under bad auspices," was rendered thus: "Thou bringest apples to the house of thy grandfather."   " *Ite, capelli*," "Go it, you cripples." " *Terra mutat vices*," "The earth changes her shift."   The author of ' The Art of Pluck' then proceeds to observe: "From which examples is seen, first, how simple words, which cannot be construed wrong so far as grammar concerneth, may yet be turned by fit attention to a wrong meaning; how, secondly, a complex sentence so turned to a wrong meaning may yet be further improved in wrongness by bad grammar, as happened with Mr. Thomas ——, of —— College, who. when he had construed '*Hannibal Alpes transivit summâ diligentiâ*,' ' Hannibal passed over the Alps on the top of a diligence,' was straightway reproved by the examiner as having construed wrong; whereon he yet improved the wrongness by bad grammar, construing thus: 'The Alps passed over Hannibal on the top of a diligence'; and again, by worse grammar: 'A diligence passed over Hannibal on the top of the Alps.'" I only recollect one Greek maltranslation. It was this: καὶ ἐξελθὼν ἔξω ὁ Πέτρος ἔκλαυσε πικρῶς, which should be, "And Peter went out and wept bitterly." The undergraduate, whose brain was crammed by the coach to the utmost, translated it, "And Peter went out and slammed the door violently." I have lately heard one in Portuguese that really took place. A certain lad received extra pay on board ship as being a great linguist. The ship was disabled, and put into a Portuguese harbour with a broken mast. The interpreter did not know a word of Portuguese, and was puzzled how to get out of the mess. Some one said, "All right; all you have to do is to speak English and put an 'o' at the end of every word." So when the Portuguese ship carpenter came on board, the interpreter boldly went up to him and said, "Look-o here-o, we-o want-o new-o mast-o ship-o." The puzzled carpenter answered, "*Non intendi*," i.e. "I don't understand." The captain roared out to the interpreter, "What does he say?" The interpreter very sharply answered, "Oh, he says you can't have it under *ten days*." "Oh, confound him!" said the captain, "that won't do for me. What fools these Portuguese are!"

The passenger by the train from Winchester to Southampton, if he looks out of the window just as he passes Winchester station, will see a hill on the downs, surrounded by a ditch and a valley and a rampart. This is St. Catherine's Hill, or, as we boys called it, "Hills." At certain seasons of the year we were marched on to these hills before breakfast. The custom was to keep line, while the præfect of Hills "whipped in" with a ground-ash, as we ascended the hill. When we got within the remains of the old earth fortification which forms a kind of crown to the hill, we broke up. Many of the boys played football or cricket. For my own part, I never did either; my great delight was to dig out field mice, and at that time there were a great lot of field mice on " Hills." They make long burrows through the turf of the downs, and then into the chalk itself. There are certain signs by which the experienced "mouse-digger" can tell whether the mouse is in the hole or not, but, for the benefit of the little mice, I shall not give the present Winchester boys this knowledge: let them acquire it for themselves. Having discovered a hole with a mouse in it, the next process is to pass down it a flexible stick, and this showed where the hole had taken a turn.  We then dug down to this turn, and passing the stick further up the burrow, dug down to it again.  In about three diggings I generally managed to get the mouse, but the last part of these engineering operations had to be conducted with very great care, as the mouse generally made a bolt for it.  Little pick-axes used to be sold at a certain shop in Winchester; we called these "mouse-diggers."  During the holidays I was initiated into the noble art of fox-hunting by my uncle, Thomas Morland, Esq., who kept the Berkshire hounds at Sheepstead, near Abingdon.  He was then very particular about having the fox earths stopped.  Acting, therefore, upon my experience in the matter, I took very good care to stop all the mouse earths that were within a reasonable distance of the one on which I was operating.  The consequence of this and other precautions was, that I was looked up to by the other boys as the most experienced mouse-digger in the College.  I also tried to set the fashion of eating these field mice as we caught them.  On some mornings we were fearfully hungry on the top of these hills (we went there before breakfast).  I used to skin the mice, run a bit of stick through them, and roast them in front of a fire which I made out of sticks collected from a fence which divided " Hills " from a ploughed field.  This hedge belonged to one Farmer Bridger, who complained to the warden about our burning his hedge, so I had to take the mice home and cook them in College.  A roast field mouse—not a house mouse—is a splendid *bonne-bouche* for a hungry boy; it eats like a lark.  Mice cooked in College were not nearly so good as mice cooked on " Hills."

The præfects, that is, the senior boys, were not required to go on the hill, they were allowed to wander about the water meadows below, and each præfect was permitted to be accompanied by the junior boy he chose to invite.  Now, I was then a good hand at trapping and snaring anything, and it soon got about that I knew how to wire trout.  My skill was put to the test, and after that I very seldom went on the hill again—which I regretted, because I was fond of mouse-digging—as I had to wire trout for the præfects' breakfasts.  The guardian of these meadows was a funny old fellow, who lived in a wretched cabin close by a certain weir, and we boys knew him as " Waterman."  When, therefore, we started on our trouting expeditions, the first thing to do was to send out scouts to " mark down " Waterman, and generally a decoy party was sent out *without* any wires; their duty was to poke about and pretend to look for trout, while myself and the real poachers were at work quite in an opposite direction.  The wires I used were the finest pianoforte wires, and there is great art in making the noose and passing it over the trout's head.  We did not do much harm after all, for the water was so clear and the trout so artful, that we never caught very many.

"Waterman," though, once very nearly caught me; but I gave him a tremendous chase across the meadows and through the various water-courses, and ultimately had to swim the river to get away from him. The sleeves of our college gowns acted as pockets, and I had two trout in one sleeve and one in another. When swimming the river the fish in my sleeves came to life again, and I had a hard job to land myself and my fish.

Rat-hunting was a celebrated sport of us boys. There was a mill which adjoined our playground, which we called "Meads." The miller used to catch the rats in the mill and let them down in a round wire rat-trap (how well I recollect that trap!) out of a little porthole window in the mill, by means of a string. We then turned the rats out one at a time in the middle of the cricket ground, and gave them a due amount of law; when they had got their proper distance "the hounds" were laid on. "The hounds" were not allowed to use sticks or stones, but had to catch the rat by the tail : a very difficult operation, I can assure you, and the rats bite fearfully if you do not know how to handle them. You should twist them round and round the moment you get a hold on the tail. If a rat showed particularly good sport he was kept to hunt again on an off-day when the miller had no rats.

I was also, I am-sorry to say, very fond of wiring cats. There was a grating in a certain iron door named "Moab." (The reader must know that " Moab " was the place where some marble basins and washing accommodation had been erected for the use of the boys; we christened it Moab, on account of the passage, " Moab is my wash-pot.") The cats used to come through the grating at " Moab " gate, but they were very artful and used to push the wires on one side. The first cat I caught was the " sick-house " cat. Now " sick-house " was the hospital for the boys, and " Mother " was the kind-hearted old matron who looked after it. Of course I let " Mother's " cat go free, and " Mother " never found me out, though I think she always suspected me.

There were a great many jackdaws in the college tower. The bell-ringer's name was " Dungee," the under porter's, " Joel "; College porters from time immemorial at Winchester, have been called by the names of the minor prophets in succession. Dungee and Joel taught me to ring bells, and I was very fond of going to assist. When the young jackdaws were fit to take, Dungee, Joel, and myself used to collect them out of the holes in the tower. We reared them and let them fly when they were properly fledged. The mother jackdaws used frequently to come to feed their young when we boys were in school at lessons. We used to get up early in the morning to catch lob-worms to feed the jackdaws. I frequently tried a plan to catch the Winchester rooks. It is this: roll up a piece of brown paper in the shape of a cone, place a piece of cheese at the far end of it, then put plenty of birdlime or pitch inside; the bird puts his head into the cone, the birdlime sticks to his feathers; he attempts to fly, and tumbles about in a ridiculous manner. I confess I was not very successful at this fun; the Winchester rooks seemed to have imbibed some of the learning of the place.

Though we were very fond of rat-hunting and mouse-digging, yet we did not have much to do with fire-arms. When dining last year at the regular Wykehamist dinner an old brother Wykehamist told me that he well recollected in his time that Dr. Gable once suddenly called upon all the boys to parade their Ainsworth's Dictionaries. One lad brought up his dictionary with fear and trembling. Dr. Gable found it would not open; he therefore made the boy open it, when it was discovered that the leaves had been beautifully glued together, and it had been converted into a case for a brace of pistols. This same boy's "Scob" (or school-box) was then searched, and instead of the proper amount of classical books that *should* have been there the Doctor found a brace of live ferrets eating a fowl's head.

A great deal has been said and written about the cruelty of "fagging," and more especially of "tunding," at Winchester. As in almost every case under dispute, there are two ways of looking at this matter. Kept within bounds, "tunding" is an excellent institution, but of course may be sometimes very much abused, particularly if the præfect happen to have a bad temper. The boys of this generation would be a great deal better for a little judicious "tunding." I lately had a page boy who could work well if he liked; one day, after a series of omissions, such as not cleaning the monkeys' night-cage when they were in their day cage—not feeding the parrot—omitting to brush clothes—boots not ready—the room where I cast fish left untidy, &c., always "thinking" (see my definition of thinking above)—I called him up and said, "Now, John, I'm going to give you a present of fifty pounds." The boy's face brightened up, and he said, "Oh, thank you, sir." "It's not in money, though, John," said I. "I'm going to give you a jolly good hiding, and that will be worth fifty pounds to you."

All I can say in concluding these remarks is, that the jolly good hidings and the severe fagging I got as a lad at Winchester have been of the utmost value to me in after life, and therefore I should be very sorry to see "fagging" and "tunding" altogether done away with at Winchester. God bless the dear old place, and all Wykehamists, past, present, and future, is the sincere wish of

FRANK BUCKLAND,
*Inspector of Salmon Fisheries.*

# A Vagabond Heroine.

## By MRS. EDWARDES,

### AUTHOR OF 'ARCHIE LOVELL,' 'OUGHT WE TO VISIT HER?' &c.

## CHAPTER I.

### THE WINE IN THE GRAPE-FLOWER.

SPAIN or Clapham?

A brand-new Clapham villa, all dust, dullness, and decorum, with " Mr. Augustus Jones" upon the brand-new door-plate. A drawing-room, like one's life, oppressively stiff and uninteresting, dining-room to match, husband to match, everything to match. Fine Brussels carpets beneath one's feet; a sun possessing the warmth and cheeri-ness of a farthing rushlight over head. Servants to wait upon one and consume one's means; a brougham, perhaps, bearing the Jones coat of arms and liveries; indisputable respectability, indisputable appearance—value, how much of solid good to oneself?—well-main-tained. Amusement, pleasure, play, the quick-coursing blood, the jollity, the " go " of existence, nowhere.

So much for Clapham.

And Spain? Spain, just across the Pyrenees there ; Spain, from whence the warm wind blows on Belinda's face at this moment: what of that alternative? An uninteresting husband to start with—so much in common have futurity's chances both ; but not a stiff, not a dull one. A genial little human creature in the main is Maria José de Seballos, wine merchant and commission agent of Seville; un-burthened, 'tis true, by superfluity of intellect, but light of step in waltz and cachuca, and singing tenor love-songs passably ; his swarthy fingers too beringed, his swarthy locks too bergamotted, for the very finest taste ; his diet overtending, somewhat, towards garlic ; and still, if but by virtue of his Spanish picturesqueness, less vulgar far than Mr. Augustus Jones of Clapham? What would life be by his side?

In the first place, thinks Belinda sagely, life, did one marry the little Sevillian, need not of necessity be passed at his side at all. Maria José would naturally have to look after his agency business, travel to distant countries for wine orders, take his pleasure, as Spanish gentlemen do, in club or café, leaving his wife free—free in a flat in a Seville street ; no appearance to keep up, no respectability ; a tiled floor instead of Brussels carpet beneath one's feet ; not a hope of

brougham or liveries this side heaven—but free!  The good warmth-
giving sun of Spain overhead, a hundred sweet distractions of dance
and *tertulia* to count the days by, bull-fights, theatres, and music for
one's Sundays : enjoyment, in short, the rule, not the exception of
life, and with only Maria José, who, after all, stands comparison with
Mr. Augustus Jones right well, for drawback.

Belinda crosses her arms, shakes her head philosophically, yawns a
little, then casts herself full-length on the turf, in one of those
attitudes of delicious southern laziness which Murillo's beggar children
have made familiar to us, and gazing up through the branches of the
cork-trees at the intense smalt blue of the sky above, begins to
meditate.

Sunburnt as a maize-field in June, unshackled bodily and mentally
by rule as any young *Gitana* who roams the mountains yonder,
through what contradictory whim of fortune came Belinda O'Shea by
this high-sounding name of hers ?  A name reminding one of the
musk and millefleurs of boudoirs, of Mr. Pope's verses, china teacups,
rouge, pearl powder, artifice !  She will be seventeen in a month or
two, but possesses few of the theoretic charms assigned by poets and
novel-writers to that age.  Her hands and feet are disproportionally
large for her slender limbs ; her waist is straight, but formless ; her
gait and gestures are masculine—no, not that either: to eyes that
can read aright the girl is as full of potential womanly grace as is the
grape-flower of wine ; and still I dare not call her "feminine," as
people of the north or of cities understand the word.  She can play
*paume*, the national Basque fives or rackets, with any *gamin* of her
stature in St. Jean de Luz ; in the excitement of the sport will show
hot blood like her comrades, occasionally, indeed—say at some dis-
puted point of a set match—will be tempted into using a very mild
*gamin's* expletive or two ; she can row, she can swim, she can whistle.
But through her great dark eyes, poor forsaken Belinda, the softest
girlish soul, still looks out at you with pathetic incongruity ; and
though her vocabulary be not choice, she possesses heaven's great gift
to her sex, a distinctly, excellently feminine voice.  Of her possible
beauty at some future time we will not now speak.  She is in the
chrysalis or hobbledehoy stage, when you may any day see a skinny
sallow ugly-duckling of a girl turn into a pretty one, like a transformation in a Christmas piece.  Eyes, mouth, feet, hands—all look too big
for Belinda at present ; and as to her raiment—her tattered frock, her
undarned . . .  No, I must really enter a little upon the antecedent's
of my heroine's life before I make known these details, in all the
disgraceful nakedness of fact, to the public.

To begin with, the blood of earls and kings (Hibernian kings) runs
in her veins.  Her mother, the Lady Elizabeth Vansittart, fifth
daughter of the Earl of Liskeard, at the romantic age of forty-one fell

in love with and married a certain fascinating Irish spendthrift, Major Cornelius O'Shea, whom she met accidentally at a Scarborough ball; endured the neglect, and worse than neglect, of her handsome husband for the space of two years; then, happily for herself, poor soul, died, leaving Cornelius the father of one baby daughter, the Belinda of this little history.

Why Major O'Shea, an easy-tempered, easy-principled soldier of fortune, no longer himself, in the freshest bloom of youth—why O'Shea in the first instance should have been at the pains to woo his elderly Lady Elizabeth no one could tell, except that she *was* Lady Elizabeth, and that interest, that *ignis fatuus* of ruined men, might be supposed to lie dormant in the Earl her father's family. Whatever his motives, whatever his matrimonial disappointments, the Major, even his best friends allowed, behaved himself creditably on his wife's death: wore a band that all but covered his hat, swore never again to touch a card or dice-box (nor broke his oath for three weeks), and wrote a letter, full, not only of pious, but of well-worded sentiment, to his father-in-law, from whom, despite many touching allusions to the infant pledge left behind by their sainted Elizabeth, he received, I must say, but a curt and pompous dozen lines in reply. Then, his duties as a widower discharged, Cornelius cast about him to see how he should best perform those of a father. The sum of three thousand pounds, Lady Elizabeth's slender fortune, was settled inalienably on the child. "Me little one is not a pauper entirely," O'Shea would say, with tears in his good-looking Irish eyes. "If Providence in its wisdom should be pleased to sign my recall to-morrow, me angel Belinda would have her mother's fortune to stand between her and starvation." And so, till she had reached the age of seven, "me angel Belinda" was indifferently boarded, at the rate of about forty pounds a year and no holidays, in a Cork convent. Then O'Shea brought his face and lineage once more to the marriage-market, on this occasion winning no faded scion of nobility, but the still-blooming widow of a well-to-do London lawyer, and Belinda for the first time since her birth had to learn the meaning, bitterer than sweet, poor little mortal, in her case, of the word "home."

No young child, it may be safely asserted, was ever unhappy in a community of cloistered nuns. Screen a flower as persistently as you will from the wholesome kisses of sun and light, and if some straggling breath of heaven chance to reach it, not a poor distorted colourless petal but will assert nature in spite of you. Bring women's hearts to a state of moral anæmia by all the appliances priestly science can command, then let little children come near them, and from each pale vestal will blossom forth the instincts of maternity still. If Belinda had never known the exclusive passion of a mother's love she had known what at seven years of age is probably to the full as welcome—

petting and attention without limits. Before she had been a week under the roof of her father and his new wife the cold iron of neglect, sharper to a child's sensitive nature than any alternation of harshness and affection, had entered her soul.

The second Mrs. O'Shea was a woman whom all the ladies of her acquaintance called "sweet"—you know the kind of human creature she must be? A blonde skin, the least in the world inclined to freckles, blonde hair, blonde eyelashes, eyes of a dove, voice of a dying zephyr. A sweet little woman, a dear little woman, an admirably well-dressed, and what is more, a *well-conducted* little woman, but . . . not fond of children. Nothing could more beautifully befit her character and the occasion than her conduct towards her small step-daughter. "I should never forgive myself if the poor darling grew up without regarding me as a mother," said Mrs. O'Shea, not wholly forgetful, perhaps, that the poor darling could call the Earl of Liskeard grandpapa. "And though the Major is so sadly indifferent on the *most vital* of all subjects, I feel it my duty to bring her at once under Protestant influences." But the Protestant influences established—a grim London nurse in a London back nursery; the discovery made, too, that obdurate aristocratic connections were in no way to be softened through the child's agency—and Belinda, on the score of love, could scarce have fared worse had she been one of the gutter-children whom she watched and envied through the prison-bars of her window down in the court below.

Had she been ornamental, the balls of life might have broken differently for her; a rose-and-white, flaxen-curled puppet, sitting beside another rose-and-white, flaxen-chignoned puppet in a brougham, being scarcely less attractive, though on the whole more troublesome, than a good breed of pug. But she was very far indeed from ornamental; a skinny, dark-complexioned child, with over-big eyes looking wistfully from an over-small face, and hair cropped close to the head, *coupé a rasoir*, according to a French fashion often adopted for the younger children in some Irish convents. And so, all fortuitous accidents working together and against her, Belinda was left to starve; her small body nourished on the accustomed roast mutton and rice pudding of the English nursery, and her soul—eager, fervent, hungry little soul that it was—left to starve!

She tried, impelled by the potent necessity of loving that was in her, to love her nurses. But Mrs. O'Shea's was a household in which, notwithstanding the sweetness of the mistress, the women servants shifted as perpetually as the characters in a pantomime. If Belinda loved a Sarah one month, she must perforce love a Mary the next, and then a new Sarah, and then a Hannah. She tried, casting longing eyes at them from her iron-barred prison windows, to love the neighbouring gutter children—happy gutter children, free to make the most of such grimy fractions of earth and sky as fate had yielded them. She tried—no, effort was not needed here : with all the might of her ardent, keen-strung nature, Belinda, throughout those early years of isolation and neglect, loved her father.

Little enough she saw of him. O'Shea had come into a fortune of some thirty or forty thousand pounds by his second marriage, and was spending it like a man—(" like a monster," Mrs. O'Shea would declare piteously, when the inevitable day of reckoning had overtaken them. Would she ever have consented to a brougham and men-servants and Sunday dinners—Sunday dinners! with her principles!—if she had known that Major O'Shea was a pauper, not worth the coat he was married in?) Occasionally, twice in three months perhaps, the fancy would strike Cornelius to lounge, his pipe in his mouth, into the child's nursery for a game of romps. Occasionally, after entertaining some extra fine friends at dinner, perhaps he would bid the servants bring Miss O'Shea down to dessert, chiefly, it would seem— but Belinda was happily indiscriminative—for the opportunity her presence afforded of airing his connection with the Earl of Liskeard's family ; on a few blissful Sundays throughout the year would take her out, clinging to his hand, happy to the verge of tears, for a walk through the parks.

This was all—the sole approach to parental love that brightened Belinda's lonely child's life; and as years went on even this scant intercourse between O'Shea and his daughter lessened. Difficulties multiplied round the man ; truths of many kinds dawned upon the poor pink-and-white fool whose substance he had wasted. Recriminations, long absences, cruel retrenchments of expenditure, falling off of fair-weather friends—all followed in natural sequence. And then came the crash in earnest ; Belinda's pittance their only certain support for the future. The house in May Fair must be exchanged for one in Bayswater ; the house in Bayswater must give place to lodgings ; the lodgings, from elegance, so-called, must sink to respectability ; respectability to eighteen shillings a week, no extras, and dirt and discomfort unlimited. Belinda, instead of roast mutton and rice pudding, must eat whatever cold scraps chanced to be over from yesterday's meal, and no pudding at all; instead of yawning over French verbs or thrumbing scales on the piano, must run errands, mend clothes, crimp chignons, plait false tresses, and generally make herself the milliner, lady's maid, and drudge of her stepmamma, Rose.

Barring the hair-dressing duties, which, seeing the straits to which they were reduced, goaded her to desperation, I should say the change of fortune affected the girl's spirits but lightly. Children of a certain age rather like catastrophes that cut them adrift from all old landmarks, so long at least as the catastrophes wear the gloss of newness. Belinda, by temperament, craved for change, movement, action of any kind, and of these she had far more in Bohemia than Belgravia. She had also more of her father: not a very desirable acquisition, one would say, viewing matters with the eyes of reason; but Belinda, you see, viewed them with the eyes of love—enormous difference!

Cornelius descended the ladder of life with a philosophic gentlemanly grace that added the last drop of bitterness to Mrs. O'Shea's cup. It was not his first experience of the kind, it must be remembered; and so long as abundant alcoholic resource fail not, 'tis curious with what ease men of his stamp get used to these little social vicissitudes. O'Shea had worn a threadbare coat, had frequented a tavern instead of a club, had drank gin-and-water instead of claret and champagne, before this, and fell back into the old well-greased groove of insolvency, almost with a sense of relief.

Belinda, who could see no evil in what she loved, thought papa's resignation sublime.

His dress, from shabbiness degenerated to something worse; his nose grew redder, his hours and his gait alike more uncertain. In Belinda's eyes he was still the best and dearest of fathers, the most incomparably long-suffering of husbands. "Rose must have her chignons crimped, must put on her pearl-powder and her silk dresses, just as if we were rich still," the girl would think, with the blind injustice of her age, "while papa, poor papa, wears his oldest clothes and broken boots—yes, and will sing a song at times to his little girl, and be gay and light-hearted through it all." And the wisdom of the whole world would not have convinced her that there could be courage, of a kind, in Rose's crimped chignon and silk dresses, and cowardice— that worst cowardice which springs from apathetic despair—in her father's greasy coat and broken boots and gin-and-water jovialty.

The truth was this: Cornelius knew that his last trick was made; Rose, that she had the possibility of one still in her hand—a certain Uncle Robert, crusty, vulgar, rich, "living retired" in his own villa at Brompton. Very different would Belinda's story have turned out had this uncle chanced to be an aunt. The old lady never lived who could resist the blandishments of Cornelius O'Shea when he willed to fascinate. Upon the coarse, tough heart, the hardened unbelieving ears, of Uncle Robert, the Irishman's sentiments, repentance, touching allusions even to honour and high lineage, were alike wasted. Rosie had chosen to throw herself away upon a scoundrel; don't talk to him about birth; Uncle Robert called a man a gentleman who acted as a gentleman. Rosie, poor fool, had made her bed and must lie upon it—for Uncle Robert's language was no less coarse than his intelligence. Still, let her come to want, let the scoundrel of a husband decamp, take his worthless presence to any other country he chose, and keep there, and the door of Uncle Robert's house would never be closed against his sister's child. And as the old man had not another near relation upon the face of the earth, Mrs. Rose knew pretty well that, O'Shea's disappearance once encompassed, not only would the door of Uncle Robert's house, but a fair chance of a place in Uncle Robert's will, stand open to her.

A last card, I repeat, was yet to be played by Mrs. O'Shea. She played it well; with that instinctive knowledge of male human nature that you will find in the very shallowest feminine souls. Uncle Robert was a democrat to the backbone; tittle-tattle from the bloated " upper ten " must consequently be tasteful to him, were it but as proof of his own Radical theories; and Rose would prattle to him by the hour together, about her ladyship's card debts and his Grace's peccadilloes, and her poor dear O'Shea's intimate connection with the aristocracy. Uncle Robert was as proud of his purse, as any self-made man in England. Nothing swelled him with the righteous sense of solvency like the sight of another's pauperism; still, for *his* niece to have appeared discreditably dressed before the servants, a poor relation, in all the galling indecency of a merino gown or mended gloves, would have exasperated the old man beyond measure. So Rose took excellent care to do her pauperism genteelly. In the most becoming little bonnet, the most scrupulously neat silk dress—" the last of all my pretty things, Uncle Robert. Ah, if you knew—can we poor women help being foolish?—if you knew how dreadful it is to one to give up the refinements of life!"—in the most becoming attire, I say, that woman could wear, this simple creature would pay her humble, tearful, conciliatory visits to the Brompton villa, and seldom return without a crisp piece of paper, never entirely empty-handed, to the bosom of her family.

At last, one fine spring morning, came an overture of direct reconciliation, couched in the plainest possible language, from Uncle Robert's own lips. Let Major O'Shea betake himself to America, one of the colonies, anywhere out of England that he chose, solemnly swearing to keep away during the space of two years at least, and Uncle Robert promised not only to receive back his niece to preside over his house and sit at the head of his table, but to pay O'Shea the sum of three hundred pounds before his departure. Enough, surely, to last, if the man had a man's heart within his breast, until such time as he could gain a decent independence for himself by work.

Cornelius was absent from home, that is to say from their dingy lodgings, for the time being, when this occurred; had been absent more than a fortnight, heaven knows on what mission—I believe he called it the " Doncaster Spring Meeting," to his wife and daughter. He returned late that same evening, rather more hiccoughing of speech than usual, and with just sixpence short for the payment of his cab hire in his pocket.

Rosie broke the news of her uncle's proffered generosity, as O'Shea

sat drinking his hot gin-and-water after supper, Belinda mending a
very torn stocking with very long stitches, at his side.

"Of course it is impossible," sighed Mrs. O'Shea, with tears in her
meek eyes. "I feel it a duty to mention the proposal, if only to show
the Christian spirit of *my* relations; but of course, such a separation
would be impossible."

"Impossible, Rosie!" cried O'Shea, his soddened face brightening.
Of so fine and discursive a nature was the creature's hopefulness, that
the bare mention of three hundred pounds, and of being rid of his
domesticities, sufficed to inspire him with the visions of a millionaire.
"Who talks of impossible? Am I the man, d'ye think?—is Cornelius
O'Shea the man—to let his own paltry feelings stand between his family
and prosperity?"

And in less time than it has taken me to write, husband and wife
had made up their minds heroically to the sacrifice. The details were
not difficult to agree upon. Cornelius would seek his fortune in
America, "the best country on earth for a man of resolution and
ability"; poor semi-widowed Rose take refuge at Brompton; Belinda,
with the hundred and twenty pounds a year derived from her mother's
fortune, might be considered independent. She should be sent to some
moderately expensive boarding-school for the next two years, the term
of her father's banishment, and Uncle Robert had considerately said
that she might look upon his house as her home during the Midsummer
and Christmas holidays.

Belinda independent, Cornelius put upon his legs and offered his
freedom, and Rose restored to a pew in church, fine clothes and livery
servants—what a touch of the magician's wand was this!

Next day was Sunday. Major O'Shea dyed his whiskers, which he
had suffered to grow grey under the cold shade of poverty, brushed up
his coat, put on a pair of lavender gloves, and lounged away the afternoon in the park, his hat as rakishly set on his head, his whole air as
jaunty, as in the palmiest days of his youth. Madame, after duly
attending morning service—for was it not her first duty, said Rose,
her eyes swimming, to offer thanksgiving for her own and her dear
O'Shea's good fortune?—Madame, after attending morning service,
betook herself to Brompton, and employed the remainder of the day
in talking over events and planning a thousand agreeable domestic
comforts for herself with Uncle Robert. Belinda, poor little fool,
cried herself white and sick with passionate grief. She did not want
respectability or boarding schools, or a home in the holidays. She
wanted all she loved on earth, her worthless old father, and was to
lose him.

"We really have very different ways of showing our affection,"
said Mrs. O'Shea, when she returned, well dressed, blooming, full of
hope in the future, and found the child crouched down, dinnerless,

dirty, her face disfigured and swollen with tears, beside a fireless hearth. "I suppose I shall suffer more than any one else by your papa's absence, but I do *what is right*. I do not embitter the thorny path of duty still more to his feet"—Rosie had always a fine florid style of metaphor of her own when she tried to talk grand—"by useless tears and lamentations."

From that night on, until the hour of final separation, scarcely more than a week, Belinda kept her feelings better under control. She worked a little purse in secret, upon which you may be sure many a salt tear fell, put in it all her slender hoard of pocket-money, and pushed it into her father's not unwilling hand on the day of his departure, instinct telling her what kind of gift would to Cornelius be the welcomest token of filial love. When the supreme moment of parting had arrived she clung to him, shivering, tearless, dumb; while Rosie, whose only feeling was one of cheerful relief, cried almost to the verge of unbecomingness, and uttered every imaginable wifely platitude about the heartrending cruelty of the situation, and the dreadful, dreadful pain that her devotion to duty and to her husband's interests was costing her.

Then came the removal to Brompton: fine rosewood and mahogany; excellent dinners; City friends; Uncle Robert's vulgar, purse-proud talk—all, it would seem, very tasteful to Mrs. O'Shea. And then, less than a twelvemonth after Belinda felt the last kiss of her father's lips, came a New York paper, directed in a strange hand, to Uncle Robert, and containing the bald announcement of Cornelius O'Shea's death. The poor little girl, away at a second-class Brighton boarding-school, was summoned home in haste; the blinds of the Brompton villa were drawn decently close for four days and partially lowered on the fifth, or imaginary funeral day; Rosie, for the second time in her life, veiled her sorrow under the most bewitching weeds. Uncle Robert talked about the mysterious ways of Providence, kept the corners of his mouth well down before the servants, and ere a week was over had made a new will, leaving every shilling he possessed at the unconditional disposal of his dear niece Rose.

O'Shea, in short, in dying had committed by far the best action of his half-century of life, and everybody in the house knew it; everybody but Belinda. Nature has compensations for us all: gives a neglected little daughter to love, to mourn, even a Cornelius O'Shea. Fiercer than ever grew Belinda's rebellion now against Uncle Robert's smart furniture, dinners, butler; all of them bought, she would say, her dark eyes flashing fire through their tears—bought with papa's life. If they had not driven papa away from England he had not died, nor she been desolate. Let them send her away—anywhere on the face of the earth that was *not* Brompton. Yes, she would go to school abroad; to Boulogne, Berlin, as they chose. Only—

pathetic stipulation for her age—let her remain away until she was
old enough to see after herself in life unaided, and let her have no
holidays. And a charmingly opportune chance of gratifying the
girl's perverse fancies was not long in presenting itself. Sedulously
reading through the educational column of the *Times*, Rose, one
morning, with a lightening of the step-maternal bosom came upon the
following:

"Rare opportunity for Parents and Guardians.—A Lady of literary
attainments, socially unincumbered, and entertaining advanced ideas
as to the higher Culture and Destinies of her Sex, offers her society
and influence to any young Girl of good birth, for whom improvement
by Continental travel may be desired. Terms moderate, and paid
invariably in advance. References exchanged."

By the next post Mrs. O'Shea and the lady holding advanced ideas
were in communication. They interviewed each other; they exchanged opinions on the Destiny of the Sex; they exchanged references. After some battling the commercial part of the transaction
was brought to a satisfactory close, and Belinda, sullenly submissive
to anything that divided her from Rose, Brompton, and Uncle Robert,
made her next great step in life.

The name of her new preceptress (of whom more hereafter) was
Burke, Miss Lydia Burke; a name not unknown to fame, either in the
speech-making or book-making world. And under, or oftener without, this lady's care, Belinda's "culture" has been progressing up to
the present time; no material change occurring meanwhile at Brompton save Uncle Robert's death, which took place about three months
before the date at which this little history opens. Some smattering
of languages the girl, drifting hither and thither over Europe, has
picked up; some music and dancing of a vagrant kind; a good deal
of premature acquaintance with human nature: life, opened, I fear, at
somewhat tattered pages, for her class-book; neglect, not invariably
the worst educator, for her master.

A socially unincumbered lady, bent on correcting the mistakes made
by her sex during the past six thousand years, and with the Higher
Destinies of the future on her soul, could scarcely have time to waste
on the training of the one unimportant unit immediately beneath her
eyes. In few minds are broadness of vision and capacity for small
detail co-existent. The mind of Miss Lydia Burke was of the
visionary or far-embracing order: an order quite beyond the wretched
details of laundresses and darning-needles. Newton forgot his dinner-
hour: could a Miss Lydia Burke be expected to notice the holes . . .

But this brings me back exactly to the point at which a certain
pride in my poor little heroine forced me into retrospection—the
holes in Belinda's stockings.

## The Story of La Vallière.

BY THE AUTHOR OF "MIRABEAU."

---

FEW kings have experienced the felicity of being loved for themselves alone. Of the many exceptional blessings bestowed upon the *Grand Monarque* that was one of the rarest. Court love being usually a compound of vanity, avarice, and ambition.

Amidst the pomp and bustle, the brilliance and artificiality of the age of Louis the Fourteenth, the story of La Vallière comes upon us like some strain of soft pastoral music suddenly breathed among the drums and trumpets and clashing cymbals of a grand overture; as though while wandering among the stately magnificence, the artistically-planted groves, geometrically-cut trees, and exotic flower-beds of Versailles, we came unexpectedly upon some forgotten nook, unspoiled by art, where the grass grew unshaven, and where the sweet field-flowers revelled in wild freedom, and the luxuriant trees, ignorant of the pruning-knife, threw forth their arms with all the fantastic grace of untaught Nature.

Of the three victims of kingly love over which romance has cast its most roseate hues, Fair Rosamond, Jane Shore, and La Vallière, the latter is the purest, her story the most pathetic. Few among even the most rigid of moralists have cast a stone at her. Her youth, her simplicity, her all-absorbing love, her resistance, the almost impossibility of escape from the effects of her passion, her agony of remorse, the total absence of ambition and liking for display, and, above all, the long dreary years of austere penitence that closed her life, have gained for her the tears and sympathy of every gentle heart of all succeeding generations.

Louise-Françoise de la Baume le Blanc was the daughter of the Marquis de la Vallière, and was born at Tours in the year 1644. Her father died while she was yet an infant, and after a while her mother re-married with M. de St.-Rémy, comptroller of the household of Gaston Duc d'Orléans; and at Blois, the residence of that prince, Louise passed her girlhood.

It was in the year 1659 that she first beheld the King; he stopped at Blois for a few hours while on his way to claim the hand of the Infanta. Louis departed unconscious of her existence, but from that hour his image was graven upon her heart, never to be effaced until it was cold in death. But this love was unknown, unacknowledged to herself—it was dreamy, not passionate; she would sit for hours together recalling the tones of his voice, the lineaments of his face.

Ah! if she could but live for ever in his presence, to gaze upon him, to hear him speak, although no word to her, she could be happy. Such was the dream of fifteen.

Not long after this the Duc d'Orléans died; the establishment at Blois was broken up, and M. de St.-Rémy was deprived of his office. But soon afterwards, through the influence of Madame de Choisy, Louise gained admission as lady-in-waiting into the household of the Princess Henrietta, and took up her abode at Fontainebleau. It was impossible that her youth and prepossessing appearance should long escape the attentions of the libertine gallants of the court. The Count de Guiche made advances to her, but, too preoccupied with one image to admit the shadow of another, she quickly repelled them, and thus converted his love into enmity. In the meantime her eyes were frequently blessed with the passing vision of the idol of her dreams; but the idol was still unconscious of the presence of a worshipper.

The secret was revealed to him by a romantic incident during the marriage festivities of Madame. Among other magnificent entertainments given on the occasion was a splendid ballet in which the King appeared as Ceres.* He was then in his twenty-third year, with a face like Antinous and a figure like Apollo, the very beau-ideal of lusty manhood. The Greek dress displayed his noble form and handsome features to the finest advantage, and gazing upon this glorious vision Louise drank in new draughts of love. After the banquet she and two other ladies, one destined to be her rival, Athenaïs de Mortemar, the future Madame de Montespan, strolled into the forest through the soft, summer twilight, and sitting down beneath a large old tree began to converse of the events of the day. Their movements being observed by M. de Beringhen, he laughingly proposed to the King, who was standing near, to follow them and listen to their conversation, which would doubtless turn upon the merits of their favourite gallants. Entering fully into the spirit of the frolic the King eagerly assented, and after following the ladies at a safe distance until they were seated, the two gentlemen contrived to ensconce themselves behind the tree and hear the whole conversation that passed. M. de Beringhen was correct in his conjecture. Two of the ladies began an animated criticism upon the appearances of the different gentlemen who had prominently figured that day. The third, who was Louise, remained silent until she was appealed to. Her reply thrilled the heart of Louis with pleasure and gratified vanity. It was to the effect—that she wondered that any other should be noticed while the King was present. This reply was of course hailed with a shower of witticisms from her companions. Overwhelmed with confusion at having so openly expressed her thoughts, yet still unconscious that they deserved

* Louis the Fourteenth was in the habit of appearing in character and dancing in ballets until his thirty-sixth year.

the meaning imputed to them, she added that a crown could add nothing to the gifts which Nature had lavished upon him—it was rather a safeguard against the presumption of too ardent an admiration.

Eager to recognise the speaker, for it was now nearly dark, Louis made a movement forward and thus betrayed the presence of listeners. Greatly terrified the ladies sprang to their feet, and ran away so swiftly that they regained the company before their pursuers could overtake them.

The sarcasms and jests of her companions revealed to Louise the secret of her heart. In the solitude of her chamber she asked of herself the question: Are their imputations true? Is it then *love?* and her heart answered, "Yes." The revelation was terrible to her, for she was wholly pure. She prayed for strength to subdue her passion. She wept tears of shame lest her secret should be bruited abroad, and for two days, fearful of encountering the ridicule of such a discovery, she never quitted her room. But however long she might put off the evil hour it must come at last; her duties must compel her reappearance in public.

It so happened that at the very time when, after her seclusion, she first entered the apartments of her royal mistress, the King was there. As he passed down the room he addressed a few words of compliment to each lady. Louise was the last he approached. As with downcast eyes and trembling voice she made some brief reply to his gallantries, he started and fixed his eyes upon her. He recognised the voice. This then was the lady of the forest whose words had so thrilled his heart.

Every evening, from that time, he joined the circle of Madame Henrietta and never failed to hold some conversation, however brief, with Louise. This attention was quickly marked by the courtiers; but as he was suspected of a passion for the Princess herself it was thought to be only a mask worn the better to conceal other designs. And this interpretation Louis, for a time, preferred to humour. But as his love grew day by day he soon cast aside all disguise. One day there was a great hunt in the forest. While all were seated at a repast that had been hastily improvised beneath the trees, a terrible thunder-storm came on, and the rain descended in such torrents that every one, regardless of rank or etiquette, fled to the nearest shelter. Blinded by the rain, Louise unwittingly took refuge beneath the same tree as the King, and for two long hours, with the pouring rain pattering upon the leaves above and often dropping upon his bare head, the King held converse with her. The words were unheard, but her blushing cheek and his earnest manner spoke a language perfectly intelligible to the beholders.

In future, when the ladies of the court took their evening drive, Louis, as soon as he had paid his compliments to Madame, attached himself wholly to the carriage which contained Louise. Not content with these continual meetings they kept up a daily correspondence. There is a somewhat ludicrous anecdote told of this correspondence. The letters of the King were so beautifully written that Louise, who possessed but little talents and no brilliance of wit, despairing of being able to produce adequate replies, solicited the assistance of the Marquis de Dangeau, a gentleman remarkable for his accomplishments, to indite her letters. This brought about the discovery that he, the Marquis, actually performed the same office for his royal master, and was the real author of the epistles she had so much admired! The King enjoyed a good laugh over the *exposé*.

A still more marked and open proof of the King's favour was the presentation to her, in the presence of the Princess Henrietta, of a pair of magnificent bracelets that he had won in a court lottery. In the meantime the Queen was entirely unsuspicious. "That confidence was a sad misfortune for us all," writes La Vallière. "One tear from her would have saved me!"

When the nights came and she was alone with her thoughts, she trembled with fear as she looked back upon the events of each day and saw herself drawing nearer and nearer to a gulf of shame and infamy. With streaming eyes she prayed for deliverance from temptation, and vowed she would fly the danger ere it was too late. But with the morrow came bending over her that form and face which were to her as a god's, that entrancing voice breathing soft words of passion into her ear until her soul swooned with the ecstasy of her adoration. All resistance melted away; let death come—destruction —all, so that she might exist but that one hour to gaze and listen, her being absorbed in his. She had power to resist the fascination no more than the moth the flame that will devour it, the ship the whirlpool that will engulf it, the Indian the eye of the rattlesnake that will enfold him in its deadly coils. But no sin had stained her as yet.

Louise de la Vallière was now scarcely eighteen, fair complexion tinged with the bloom of the carnation, flaxen hair, blue eyes full of sweetness, features slightly marked with the smallpox, figure under the middle height, graceful but somewhat marred by a slight lameness. The Abbé de Choisy says in his Memoirs, " in childhood we have played together a hundred times," and he thus describes her : " She was not one of those perfect beauties that one often admires without loving; she was very loveable, and the words of La Fontaine, ' a grace more beautiful even than beauty's self.' seemed written for her. She had a beautiful complexion, fair hair, a sweet smile; her eyes were blue, with an expression so tender, and yet at the same time so modest, that it gained both our hearts and our esteem at the same moment. Her charm was inexpressible; her voice so melodious that while reading the verses of Racine they seemed purposely composed to suit its tones. Further, she had but little wit, but that she did not fail to cultivate continually by reading. No ambition, no interested views. More taken up with dreaming of him she loved than artfully studying to please him; totally absorbed in her passion, the only one of her life."

Referring to a later period than that at which we have at present arrived, he writes again: "Preferring honour to all things, and exposing herself more than once to death rather than allow her frailty to be suspected. Sweet tempered, liberal, retiring; never forgetting that she had erred, hoping always to return to the right path—a Christian feeling which has drawn upon her all the treasures of pity, and imparted a holy calm to a long life of austere penitence. From the time that she knew the King's love she had no wish to see her old friends, nor even hear of them, for her passion held the place of all."

Even the shield of the King's love did not protect her from the advances of one libertine—Fouquet, the celebrated Minister of Finance —who offered to place two hundred thousand livres at her disposal. "Were it twenty millions I would not stoop to such degradation," was her indignant reply. On hearing of this audacity Louis' rage knew no bounds.

Soon after this came the splendid fête at Vaux—a fête which, in costliness and magnificence, far surpassed those of Fontainebleau. The ground upon which the palace and gardens of Vaux stood formerly sufficed for three villages, which had been rased to make room for them. Their formation cost ten million livres. Fountains— then almost unknown, even in the King's grounds—cast their waters, brought from a distance of five leagues, into enormous basins of marble. Versailles was not yet rebuilt, and Fontainebleau was but a poor abode to this. The 'Fâcheux' of Molière was on this occasion represented for the first time. In the evening there was a ball and a grand display of fireworks. The fête cost the minister fifteen million francs. This monstrous ostentation filled the measure of the King's wrath, which had long been gathering against the minister, and but for the entreaties of Louise he would have arrested him there in his own dwelling; she saved the life of her insulter.

Fain would her royal lover have loaded her with jewels and costly gifts; but, unlike her successor, De Montespan, for these she had no liking, and persistently refused them. Fêtes of unexampled splendour were given in her honour. In all these the King took part. In one he led the procession, his dress and the housings of his horse blazing with jewels. After the pages, equerries, &c., came a gilded car eighteen feet high, fifteen wide, and twenty-four long, representing the chariot of the sun. This was followed by representations of the four ages of gold, silver, bronze, and iron, the signs of the zodiac, the seasons, and the hours. When night came the banqueting table was lit up by four thousand torches, and two hundred attendants, attired as dryads and wood nymphs, waited on the guests. Two persons, representing Pan and Diana, approached the royal circle on the summit of a moving mountain. A vast orchestra was erected as if by magic. Arcades lighted by five hundred chandeliers of green-and-silver surrounded the banqueting hall and theatre, and a gilt balustrade enclosed the whole exterior. The fête lasted seven days. During this time the first three acts of 'Tartuffe' were produced; but the play was prohibited as bearing too hardly upon the religious bodies.

La Vallière was now at the height of her favour; she had become the mistress of the King; but from that moment remorse never ceased to gnaw at her heart. At length came a terrible blow; Anne of Austria dismissed her from the court.* Overwhelmed with shame, she took refuge in her chamber and abandoned herself to despair. The King, finding her thus, questioned her as to the cause; but, fearful of creating a scene which could but add to her confusion, she would not tell him. Provoked by her silence, he left her in high displeasure. Utterly prostrated by this double blow, feeling herself abandoned by all, and tormented by remorse, who can describe her sufferings? But all could not conquer the anxiety of her love. Hour after hour through her sobs and groans she listened eagerly for the returning footsteps of her lover; but they came not. Midnight sounded, and still he returned not; and then came the awful thought that he had left her for ever. She sprang from the floor upon which she had been lying; she could no longer remain within those walls, and, delirious with despair, fled from the palace into the darkness and the silence of the night.

Early the next morning the King discovered her flight, and, half mad with grief, went forth himself in search of her. Certain information directed him to the convent of Chaillot, and there, lying insensible upon the cold stones of the courtyard, he found the fugitive. She had come to the gate while the nuns were at their devotions, and they had refused to admit her until they had finished. Prostrated by fatigue, she had swooned, and thus the King found her.

---

* There are several versions of the cause of her flight. One given by Madame La Fayette, an authority by no means unreliable, is to the effect, that the intrigue between the Princess Henrietta and the Count de Guiche had been revealed to La Vallière by Mademoiselle de Montalais with strict injunctions to secrecy. Now it had been agreed between herself and Louis that neither should have a secret from the other. The remembrance of this agreement weighed upon her mind, until the King, remarking her strangeness of manner, questioned her, she refused to tell him the cause. He left her in anger, did not return, and she fled to Chaillot.

Kneeling down beside her, he raised her in his arms, and his passionate kisses soon restored her to life. Clasped in his fond embrace, her head pillowed upon his breast, all was forgotten—remorse, shame, suffering—all, in the bliss of that reunion, in the joy of recovered love.

From that moment her empire over him was stronger than ever. Intrigues were set on foot to exasperate the Queen against her, but he thwarted them ere they could be put in action, or openly crushed them in their birth. He excused her from further attendance upon the Princess Henrietta, and obliged his mother, Anne of Austria—who had retired to the convent of the Val de Grâce—to receive her. Fain would La Vallière have forgone such triumphs, which she felt were truly only humiliations; but her lover's voice was law, and, devoted as he was to her, she dared not gainsay him.

In 1666 Anna Maria of Bourbon, afterwards Princess of Conti, was born. This was her second child; the first, a boy, had died at the age of ten months. Louis now created his mistress Duchess de la Vallière, and legitimatised the children she had borne or might bear. In 1667 she gave birth to Louis de Bourbon, created Count de Vermandois.

This child was educated by the wife of Colbert, and by that means La Vallière was brought into an intimacy with Madame de Montespan. The latter, united to a man she did not love, had already begun to throw out lures to attract the King. To advance this object she attached herself with much seeming ardour to Louise and her child, and always contrived to be with her during Louis' visit. La Vallière was neither witty, well-read, nor accomplished, Madame de Montespan was all these; La Vallière, ever a prey to remorse, often met her lover with tears; Madame de Montespan was ever sparkling with gaiety, and moreover was exceedingly beautiful. The King was not long in contact with such graces of mind and person without being moved to admiration; during his visits he often passed the whole time conversing with her; and the wily beauty lost no opening that might serve to advance her interest and undermine that of her rival. For this purpose she sought every opportunity of embittering the Queen against Louise, and her labours soon bore fruit.

The Spanish war was on, and La Vallière, in attendance upon the Queen, accompanied the King in the campaign. Goaded by Montespan the latter heaped such insults upon her rival, at one time causing every seat at the dinner table to be filled so that there should be no place for her, that she, La Vallière, determined to return to her children at Compiègne, and was already on her way when she was overtaken by a peremptory order from the King commanding her to return. Fearing, from the sternness of the mandate, that her enemies had been poisoning his mind with false tales, she was now more eager to return to him than ever she had been to leave. When she arrived

at Guise the army had departed. Without a moment's delay she
again started forward. Urging on the horses at a furious pace over a
ploughed field the carriage was overturned, and in the crash her arm
was broken. But, heedless of pain, and possessed only with the
thought of overtaking the King, she pushed on, and driving up to
the Queen's carriage she looked through the window. It was done
without thought, in the excitement of the moment, but no sooner done
than repented of. The King, whose love was chilling, received her
with an angry reproof, and turned his horse's head in another direction.
But soon repenting of his harshness he returned to her, and, upon
finding how severely she had been hurt, overwhelmed her with affectionate attentions. When they moved forward he insisted upon her
bearing the Queen company, and upon her being received in the
Queen's circle; once more the sycophants of the Court, who had deserted her when her influence seemed upon the wane, fawned and
flattered and crowded about her as before.

But day by day the King's infatuation for Madame de Montespan
increased, and La Vallière had soon convincing proofs that another
mistress had usurped her place in her lover's affections. The dis-
agreements of the royal favourites agitated the Court, and at last,
unable to endure the torturing sight of her rival's triumph, Louise
once more fled to the convent of Chaillot, and throwing herself at the
feet of the abbess poured forth her sad history. The abbess received
her kindly, and willingly vouchsafed to her the shelter of her peaceful
abode. But no peace came to the soul of the unhappy Louise. Not
the coldness and falsehood of her lover nor the anguish and remorse
of her own heart could as yet crush her love. No anguish was so
terrible as being absent from the sight of him whom she still adored
as ardently as when on that stormy day they stood together beneath
the tree in the forest of Fontainebleau. Would he come once more
and take her back as he did in the time gone by? Would she
again be aroused from some paroxysm of despair by the pressure of
his arms, the warmth of his kisses? Such thoughts ever mingled
with her tears, her remorse, and her prayers.

One day she heard the tramping of horses' feet in the court-yard.
Her heart leaped—her pale face flushed crimson. 'Twas he—'twas
the King come to take her back—he had not forgotten her! But she
was deceived—it was only Colbert, who bore a letter from Louis
requesting her to return. He had not forgotten her, but—" *the last
time he came himself!*" she murmured; and at that remembrance her
heart sank and its joy fainted. Yet the letter was loving, and although
she felt that the old passionate love which had betrayed her to remorse
and sin was a bliss she could never know again, still, even to live within
its shadow was to her a happiness which nought else on earth could
bestow. So she went with Colbert. But with a prophetic boding

of her coming fate, she said to the good abbess at parting, " Farewell for a time, but I shall soon return to end my days among you."

Her meeting with the King was an affecting one. The old love, although fast dying, blazed up for a moment with all its old fervour; and as he folded her in his arms he wept genuine tears of joy at their reunion. Madame de Montespan was warm in her gratulations, but she knew her own empire was secure, and that the King's ardour was but the evanescent excitement of the moment.

And so it proved. A little while, and ever increasing coldness and neglect smote her heart with the conviction that the old love was dead, and that this world had to her died with it. She would have retired to her estate at Vaujours, but this Louis would not permit; neither would he allow her to enter the convent of Chaillot; he could not as yet reconcile himself to her perpetual absence from the Court. But this clinging to the memories of the past daily grew weaker. The anguish of her mind brought on a dangerous illness, and for a time her recovery was despaired of. As she lay upon her sick bed she formed the resolution, that should God spare her life, she would devote the remainder of it to His service, and pass it in prayer and penitence for her sins. To this course she had long been counselled by Bossuet, who had latterly become her spiritual director, as well as by the Marquise de St.-Rémy, her mother, who had for some time been partly reconciled to her daughter, but who had ever regarded her connection with the King with profound horror. Louis came to her during her illness, and would fain have dissuaded her from her resolve; but, although she loved him as tenderly as ever, she had conquered the weakness of her heart with the knowledge that that love could never more bring aught but misery to her.

As soon as her strength would permit, she went to the Queen, and on her knees implored her pardon for the wrongs she had done her. That much-injured woman freely forgave her, and shed tears over their parting.* Her last meeting with the King was on the day that he departed for the Flemish campaign (1674). Mass was performed and prayers offered up for the success of his arms. All the Court was present; and when the holy service was over, Louise advanced from an obscure part of the chapel, where she had been offering up her fervent prayers for his success and safety, to speak the last words of earthly farewell to him who had been to her the life of this world. Her face was deadly pale, her limbs trembled so violently that she staggered, and her voice died away in her throat as she tried to speak

* Nothing can testify more eloquently to the natural goodness of La Vallière's disposition than the fact that the Queen never manifested any lasting resentment against her, but, when unbiassed by the malicious promptings of her enemies, treated her with uniform kindness and consideration.

the last bitter words that ever those lips would pronounce for him. But those lips, which had been once to him the rarest treasure of all his regal wealth, and upon whose accents he had once hung so fondly, had lost their charm. His voice was hard, it trembled with no emotion, there was no tenderness in its accents. Had he at that moment spoken one word whose tones would have recalled the love of the old times, it might have melted all her cold resolves; she might have fallen upon his neck, and been his slave again. Happily for her no such word was spoken. His farewell was cold and formal; perhaps he felt something of bitterness at the thought that she *could* leave him. For the last time she raised her swimming eyes to that adored face, and as he turned to leave her the gushing tears veiled him from her sight for ever.

The convent she chose was a Carmelite, the most austere of all the religious orders. Henceforth she was known as sister Louise de la Miséricorde. Madame de Sévigné, who visited her in 1680, thus writes of her: "She had in my eyes lost none of her youthful charms. She has the same eyes, with the same expression; neither hard diet nor lack of sleep has sunk nor dimmed them. The uncouth dress cannot mar her grace or mien. Her modesty is not greater than when she gave to the world a Princess de Conti, and yet it is enough, even for a Carmelite. In truth, this dress and the retreat bestow dignity upon her."

Her children, of whom three attained the age of maturity, and to whom from first to last Louis was devotedly attached, became great and powerful. After a seclusion of thirty-six years, Louise died peacefully at the age of sixty-six in the arms of her beloved daughter. Thus atoning by nearly two score years of penitence for those youthful sins which had resulted rather from the overweening sensibility of an ardent, poetic soul than from moral deformity of mind; sins which have bequeathed to posterity one of the saddest love-stories that fiction or history has recorded.

# Under the Cloak.

## By RHODA BROUGHTON.

If there be a thing in the world that my soul hateth it is a long night journey by rail. In the old coaching days I do not think that I should have minded it, passing swiftly through a summer night on the top of a speedy coach, with the star arch black-blue above one's head, the sweet smell of earth, and her numberless flowers and grasses, in one's nostrils, and the pleasant trot, trot, trot, trot, of the four strong horses in one's ears. But by railway!—in a little stuffy compartment, with nothing to amuse you if you keep awake; with a dim lamp hanging above you, tantalising you with the idea that you can read by its light, and when you try, satisfactorily proving to you that you cannot, and, if you sleep, breaking your neck, or at least stiffening it, by the brutal arrangement of the hard cushions. These thoughts pass sulkily and rebelliously through my head as I sit in my *salon* in the *Écu*, at Geneva, on the afternoon of the fine autumn day on which, in an evil hour, I have settled to take my place in the night train for Paris. I have put off going as long as I can.

I like Geneva, and am leaving some pleasant and congenial friends, but now go I must. My husband is to meet me at the station in Paris at six o'clock to-morrow morning. Six o'clock! what a barbarous hour at which to arrive! I am putting on my bonnet and cloak; I look at myself in the glass with an air of anticipative disgust. Yes, I look trim and spruce enough now—a not disagreeable object perhaps —with sleek hair, quick and alert eyes, and pink-tinted cheeks. Alas! at six o'clock to-morrow morning what a different tale there will be to tell! Dishevelled, dusty locks, half-open weary eyes, a disordered dress, and a green-coloured countenance.

I turn away with a pettish gesture, and reflecting that at least there is no wisdom in living my miseries twice over, I go downstairs, and get into the hired open carriage which awaits me. My maid and man follow with the luggage. I give stricter injunctions than ordinary to my maid never for one moment to lose her hold of the dressing-case which contains, as it happens, a great many more valuable jewels than people are wont to travel in foreign parts with, nor of a certain costly and beautiful Dresden china and gold Louis-Quatorze clock, which I am carrying home as a present to my people. We reach the station, and I straightway betake myself to the first-class *salle d'attente*, there to remain penned up till the officials undo the gates of purgatory and release us—an arrangement whose wisdom I have yet to learn. There are ten minutes to spare, and the *salle* is filling fuller and fuller every moment. Chiefly my countrymen, countrywomen, and country children, beginning to troop home to their partridges. I look curiously round at them, speculating as to which of them will be my companion or companions through the night.

There are no very unusual types: girls in sailor hats and blonde hair-fringes; strong-minded old maids in painstakingly ugly water-proofs; baldish fathers; fattish mothers; a German or two, with prominent pale eyes and spectacles. I have just decided on the companions I should prefer; a large young man, who belongs to nobody, and looks as if he spent most of his life in laughing—alas! he is not likely! he is sure to want to smoke!—and a handsome and prosperous-looking young couple. They are more likely, as very probably, in the man's case, the bride-love will overcome the cigar-love. The porter comes up. The key turns in the lock; the doors open. At first I am standing close to them, flattening my nose against the glass, and looking out on the pavement; but as the passengers become more numerous, I withdraw from my prominent position, anticipating a rush for carriages. I hate and dread exceedingly a crowd, and would much prefer at any time to miss my train rather than be squeezed and jostled by one. In consequence, my maid and I are almost the last people to emerge, and have the last and worst choice of seats. We run along the train looking in; the footman, my maid, and I. Full—full everywhere!

"*Dames seules?*" asks the guard.

"Certainly not! Neither '*Dames seules*' nor '*Fumeurs*;' but if it must be one or the other, certainly '*Fumeurs*.'"

I am growing nervous, when I see the footman, who is a little ahead of us, standing with an open carriage door in his hand, and signing to us to make haste. Ah! it is all right! it always comes right when one does not fuss oneself.

"Plenty of room here, 'm; only two gentlemen."

I put my foot on the high step and climb in. Rather uncivil of the two gentlemen!—neither of them offers to help me; but they are not looking this way, I suppose. "Mind the dressing-case!" I cry nervously, as I stretch out my hand to help the maid Watson up. The man pushes her from behind; in she comes—dressing-case, clock and all. Here we are for the night!

I am so busy and amused looking out of the window, seeing the different parties bidding their friends good-bye, and watching with indignation the barbaric and malicious manner in which the porters hurl the luckless luggage about, that we have steamed out of the station, and are fairly off for Paris, before I have the curiosity to glance at my fellow passengers. Well! when I do take a look at them, I do not make much of it. Watson and I occupy the two seats by one window, facing one another, our fellow-travellers have not taken the other two window seats; they occupy the middle ones, next us. They are both reading, behind newspapers. Well! we shall not get much amusement out of them. I give them up as a bad job. Ah! if I could have had my wish, and had the laughing young man, and the pretty young couple, for company, the night would not perhaps have seemed so long. However, I should have been mortified for them to have seen how *green* I looked when the dawn came; and, as to these *commis-voyageurs*, I do not care if I look as green as grass in their eyes. Thus, all no doubt is for the best; and at all events it is a good trite copy-book maxim to say so. So I forget all about them, fix my eyes on the landscape racing by, and fall into a variety of thoughts. "Will my husband really get up in time to come and meet me at the station to-morrow morning?" He does so cordially hate getting up. My only chance is his not having gone to bed at all. How will he be looking? I have not seen him for four months. Will he have succeeded in curbing his tendency to fat, during his Norway fishing? Probably not. Fishing, on the contrary, is rather a *fat-making* occupation; sluggish and sedentary. Shall we have a pleasant party at the house we are going to, for shooting? To whom in Paris shall I go for my gown? Worth? No, Worth is beyond me. There I leave the future, and go back into past enjoyments; excursions to Lansmere; trips down the lake to Chilton; a hundred and one pleasantnesses. The time slips by; the afternoon is drawing towards evening; a beginning of dusk is coming over the landscape.

I look round. Good heavens! what can those men find so interesting in the papers? I thought them hideously dull, when I looked over them this morning; and yet they are still persistently reading. What can they have got hold of? I cannot well see what the man beside me has; his *vis-à-vis* is buried in an English *Times*. Just as I am thinking about him he puts down his paper and I see his face. Nothing very remarkable; a long black beard, and a hat tilted somewhat low over his forehead. I turn away my eyes hastily, for fear of being caught inquisitively scanning; but still, out of their corners I see that he has taken a little bottle out of his travelling bag, has poured some of its contents into a glass, and is putting it to its lips. It appears as if—and, at the time it happens, I have no manner of doubt that he is drinking. Then I feel that he is addressing me. I look up and towards him; he is holding out the phial to me, and saying,

"May I take the liberty of offering madame some?"

"No thank you, monsieur!" I answer, shaking my head hastily and speaking rather abruptly. There is nothing that I dislike more than being offered strange eatables or drinkables in a train or a strange hymn book in church.

He smiles politely, and then adds,

"Perhaps the *other* lady might be persuaded to take a little?"

"No thank you, sir, I'm much obliged to you," replies Watson briskly, in almost as ungrateful a tone as mine.

Again he smiles, bows, and re-buries himself in his newspaper. The thread of my thoughts is broken, I feel an odd curiosity as to the nature of the contents of that bottle. Certainly it is not sherry or spirit of any kind, for it has diffused no odour through the carriage. All this time the man beside me has said and done nothing. I wish he would move or speak, or do something. I peep covertly at him. Well! at all events, he is well defended against the night chill. What a voluminous cloak he is wrapped in; how entirely it shrouds his figure!—trimmed with *fur* too! Why it might be January instead of September. I do not know why, but that cloak makes me feel rather uncomfortable. I wish they would both move to the window, instead of sitting next us. Bah! am *I* setting up to be a timid dove? I who rather pique myself on my bravery—on my indifference to tramps, bulls, ghosts? The clock has been deposited with the umbrellas, parasols, spare shawls, rugs, etc., in the netting above Watson's head. The dressing-case—a very large and heavy one—is sitting on her lap. I lean forward and say to her,

"That box must rest very heavily on your knee, and I want a footstool—I should be more comfortable if I had one—let me put my feet on it."

I have an idea that somehow my sapphires will be safer if I have them where I can always feel that they are *there*. We make the desired change in our arrangements. Yes, both my feet are on it.

The landscape outside is darkening quickly now; our dim lamp is beginning to assert its importance. Still the men read. I feel a sensation of irritation. What can they mean by it? It is utterly impossible that they can decipher the small print of the *Times* by this feeble shaky glimmer.

As I am so thinking, the one who had before spoken lays down his paper, folds it up and deposits it on the seat beside him. Then, drawing his little bottle out of his bag a second time, drinks, or seems to drink, from it. Then he again turns to me:

"Madame will pardon me; but if madame *could* be induced to try a little of this; it is a cordial of a most refreshing and invigorating description; and if she will have the amiability to allow me to say so, madame looks faint."

What *can* he mean by his urgency? *Is* it pure politeness? I wish it were not growing so dark. These thoughts run through my head as I hesitate for an instant what answer to make. Then an idea occurs to me, and I manufacture a civil smile and say, "Thank you very much, monsieur! I am a little faint, as you observe. I think I will avail myself of your obliging offer." So saying, I take the glass and touch it with my lips. I give you my word of honour that I do not think I did more; I did not mean to swallow a drop, but I suppose I must have done. He smiles with a gratified air.

"The other lady will now, perhaps, follow your example?"

By this time I am beginning to feel thoroughly uncomfortable; *why*, I should be puzzled to explain. What *is* this cordial that he is so eager to urge upon us? Though determined not to subject *myself* to its influence, I *must* see its effects upon another person. Rather brutal of me, perhaps; rather in the spirit of the anatomist, who, in the interest of science, tortures live dogs and cats; but I am telling you *facts*—not what I ought to have done, but what I *did*. I make a sign to Watson to drink some. She obeys, nothing loath. She has been working hard all day, packing and getting under way, and she is tired. There is no feigning about her! She has emptied the glass. Now to see what comes of it—what happens to my live dog! The bottle is replaced in the bag; still we are racing on, racing on, past the hills and fields and villages. How indistinct they are all growing! I turn back from the contemplation of the outside view to the inside one. Why, the woman is asleep already!—her chin buried in her chest, her mouth half open, looking exceedingly imbecile and very plain, as most people, when asleep out of bed, do look. A nice invigorating potion, indeed! I wish to heaven that I had gone *aux fumeurs*, or even with that cavalcade of nursery-maids and unwholesome-looking babies, *aux dames seules*, next door. At all events, I am not at all sleepy myself—that is a blessing. I shall see what happens. Yes, by-the-by, I must see what he meant to happen; I must affect to fall asleep too. I close my eyes, and gradually sinking my chin on my chest, try to droop my jaws and hang my cheeks, with a semblance of *boná fide* slumber. Apparently I succeed pretty well. After the lapse of some minutes I distinctly feel two hands very cautiously and carefully lifting and removing my feet from the dressing-box.

A cold chill creeps over me, and then the blood rushes to my head and ears. What am I to do? what am I to do? I have always thought the better of myself ever since for it; but, strange to say, I keep my presence of mind. Still affecting to sleep, I give a sort of kick, and instantly the hands are withdrawn and all is perfectly quiet again. I now feign to wake gradually, with a yawn and a stretch; and on moving about my feet a little, find that, despite my kick, they have been too clever for me, and have dexterously removed my box and substituted another. The way in which I make this pleasant discovery is, that whereas mine was perfectly flat at the top, on the surface of the object that is now beneath my feet there is some sort of excrescence—a handle of some sort or other. There is no denying it —brave I *may* be—I may laugh at people for running from bulls, for disliking to sleep in a room by themselves for fear of ghosts, for hurrying past tramps, but now I am most thoroughly frightened. I look cautiously, in a sideway manner, at the man beside me. How very still he is! Were they *his* hands, or the hands of the man opposite him? I take a fuller look than I have yet ventured to do, turning slightly round for the purpose. He is still reading, or at least still holding the paper, for the reading must be a farce. I look at his hands; they are in precisely the same position as they were when I affected to go to sleep, although the *pose* of the rest of his body is slightly altered. Suddenly I turn extremely cold, for it has dawned on me that they are not real hands—they are certainly false ones. Yes, though the carriage is shaking very much with our rapid motion, and the light is shaking too, yet there is no mistake. I look indeed more closely, so as to be quite sure. The one nearest me is ungloved, the other gloved. I look at the nearest one. Yes, it is of an opaque waxen whiteness. I can plainly see the rouge put under the finger-nails to represent the colouring of life. I try to give one glance at his face. The paper still partially hides it, and as he is leaning his head back against the cushion, where the light hardly penetrates, I am completely buffled in my efforts.

Great heavens! What is going to happen to me? what shall I do? how much of him is *real?* where are his *real* hands? what is going on under that awful cloak? The fur border touches me as I sit by him. I draw convulsively and shrinkingly away, and try to squeeze myself up as close as possible to the window. But alas! to what good? How absolutely and utterly powerless I am! How entirely at their mercy! And there is Watson still sleeping swinishly—breathing heavily, opposite me. Shall I try to wake her? But to what end? She being under the influence of that vile drug, my efforts will certainly be useless, and will probably arouse the man to employ violence against me. Sooner or later in the course of the night I suppose they are pretty sure to murder me, but I had rather that it should be later than sooner.

While I think these things, I am lying back quite still, for, as I philosophically reflect, not all the screaming in the world will help me: if I had twenty-lung power I could not drown the rush of an express train. Oh, if my dear boy were but here—my husband I mean—fat or lean, how thankful I should be to see him! Oh, that cloak, and those horrid waxy hands! Of course—I see it now!—they remained stuck out, while the man's red ones were fumbling about my feet. In the midst of my agony of fright a thought of Madame Tussaud flashes ludicrously across me. Then they begin to talk of me. It is plain that they are not taken in by my feint of sleep; they speak in a clear loud voice, evidently for my benefit. One of them begins by saying, "What a good-looking woman she is! Evidently in her *première jeunesse* too "—reader, I struck thirty last May—"and also there can be no doubt as to her being of exalted rank—a duchess probably."—(A dead duchess by morning, think I grimly.) They go on to say how odd it is that people in my class of life never travel with their own jewels, but always with paste ones, the real ones being meanwhile deposited at the banker's. My poor, poor sapphires! good-bye—a long good-bye to you. But indeed I will willingly compound for the loss of you and the rest of my ornaments—will go bare-necked, and bare-armed, or clad in Salviati beads for the rest of my life—so that I do but attain the next stopping place alive.

As I am so thinking one of the men looks, or I imagine that he looks, rather curiously towards me. In a paroxysm of fear lest they should read on my face the signs of the agony of terror I am enduring, I throw my pocket handkerchief—a very fine cambric one—over my face.

And now, oh reader! I am going to tell you something which I am sure you will not believe; I can hardly believe it myself; but, as I so lie, despite the tumult of my mind—despite the chilly terror which seems to be numbing my feelings—in the midst of it all a drowsiness keeps stealing over me. I am now convinced either that vile potion must have been of extraordinary strength, or that I, through the shaking of the carriage or the unsteadiness of my hand, carried more to my mouth and swallowed more—I did not *mean* to swallow any—than I intended, for—you will hardly credit it, but—I *fell asleep!*

\*     \*     \*     \*     \*     \*

When I awake—awake with a bewildered mixed sense of having been a long time asleep—of not knowing where I am—and of having some great dread and horror on my mind—awake and look round, the dawn is breaking. I shiver, with the chilly sensation that the coming of even a warm day brings, and look round, still half unconsciously, in a misty way. But what has happened? How empty the carriage is! The dressing-case is gone! the clock is gone! the man who sat nearly opposite me is gone! *Watson is gone!* But the man in the cloak and the wax hands still sits beside me; still the hands are holding the paper; still the fur is touching me. Good God! I am *tête-à-tête* with him! A feeling of the most appalling desolation and despair comes over me—vanquishes me utterly. I clasp my hands together frantically, and, still looking at the dim form beside me, groan out. " Well! I did not think that Watson would have forsaken me!" Instantly, a sort of movement and shiver runs through the figure; the newspaper drops from the hands, which, however, continue to be still held out in the same position, as if still grasping it; and behind the newspaper, I see, by the dim morning light and the dim lamp-gleams, that there is no real face, but a mask. A sort of choked sound is coming from behind the mask. Shivers of cold fear are running over me. Never to this day shall I know what gave me the despairing courage to do it, but before I know what I am doing, I find myself tearing at the cloak— tearing away the mask—tearing away the hands. It would be better to find *anything* underneath—Satan himself—a horrible dead body— anything, sooner than submit any longer to this hideous mystery. And I am rewarded. When the cloak lies at the bottom of the carriage— when the mask, and the false hands and false feet—there are false *feet* too—are also cast away, in different directions, what do you think I find underneath?

Watson! Yes: it appears that while I slept—I feel sure that they must have rubbed some more of the drug on my lips while I was un- conscious, or I never could have slept so heavily or so long—they dressed up Watson in the mask, feet, hands, and cloak; set the hat on her head, gagged her, and placed her beside me in the attitude occupied by the man. They had then, at the next station, got out, taking with them dressing-case and clock, and had made off in all security. When I arrive in Paris, you will not be surprised to hear that it does not once occur to me whether I am looking green or no.

And this is the true history of my night journey to Paris! You will be glad, I daresay, to hear that I ultimately recovered my sapphires, and a good many of my other ornaments. The police being promptly set on, the robbers were, after much trouble and time, at length secured; and it turned out that the man in the cloak was an ex-valet of my husband's, who was acquainted with my bad habit of travelling in company with my trinkets—a bad habit which I have since seen fit to abandon.

What I have written is literally true, though it did not happen to myself.

# Our Military Display of 1872.

"They who fight and die to-day,
Revive to-morrow, and blaze away!"

IT is told of a certain colonel of a dashing cavalry regiment once stationed at one of our large garrisons, that when desired by superior authority to instruct his officers on what they saw at field-days, his first pithy lecture was as follows: "Gentlemen, it is my duty to impress upon you the lessons to be learned from the field-days at this station. Now, field-days are of two kinds—positive and negative. A positive field-day is one at which everything you see is to be remembered and applied. A negative field-day is one at which everything you see should be forgotten as soon as possible, and for ever avoided in practice. Hitherto, gentlemen, the field-days at this station have been *negative*."

Thus ended the colonel's short but significant discourse.

Though we preface our remarks on the late manœuvres with this anecdote, it is not with the intention of applying its sentiment to them more than in part. There certainly was much in them to be avoided in future, but there was not a little also worthy of being remembered.

A good deal has been said and written of late on the utility of peace manœuvres, and, like all subjects of discussion, vehement advocates of opposing theories have ridden their favourite hobbies to death. The moderate view in this, as in most things, is the true one. It is absurd to regard the mimic field as teaching all the lessons of real war; it is equally untrue that it teaches none of these lessons.

As the result of careful observation of the English manœuvres of both 1871 and 1872, we have no hesitation in stating the broad principle that it is chiefly, we might almost say exclusively, in all that precedes the collision of the armies engaged, and not in the fighting part itself, that real and lasting instruction is gained.

In our army especially is this the case, for we are so utterly destitute of a permanent organization, that every opportunity of forming our troops into divisions and brigades must be of the highest importance. Our army, be it remembered, consists of scattered fragments sown broadcast over the United Kingdom, a few colonies, and India, without any fixed organisation or cohesion (except in India) beyond what is necessary for the transmission of letters—that is to say, a regiment is stationed at Winchester (let us suppose) this week, at Bristol or Liverpool the next, but its military status remains the same

—one of complete isolation. It simply reports through a different general when it moves. It is no part of any military organised body. These bodies (divisions or brigades) exist only at exceptionally large stations, such as Portsmouth, Dublin, the Curragh, and Aldershot, and it is only as the various corps happen to be quartered for a time at any one of them that officers and men have a chance of being associated for drill and manœuvre with other regiments, or with the other arms. Everything, therefore, which for a time counteracts the evil of this system of *disjecta membra* is a step in the right direction, and on this ground alone we hail the annual manœuvres as the omen of a coming amelioration of our military system.

Blumenthal is stated to have observed that "when the fighting begins, the instruction ceases;" and this, we think, represents the real state of the case. It is in the assembling, the organisation into divisions and brigades, the collection and distribution of transport, the marching and encamping, the working of the staff and supply departments; it is in all these that useful instruction and experience are gained, as.they are assuredly much needed. The authorities, however, seem to have drifted into the idea that any special information or experience to be derived from autumnal manœuvres is intended only for the generals in chief command, and perhaps a few favoured individuals about them. In no other way can we understand the marked absence of any attempt to make the manœuvres of the last or the present year instructive, and therefore interesting, to the junior ranks. Now if the country is to pay £100,000 for the manœuvres of 1872 (being at the rate of £25,000 for each of the four battles fought), it has a right to expect the best value for its money; but so far as the instruction of officers and men generally at the manœuvres of 1872 is concerned, we do not hesitate to affirm that the country has nothing to show for the expenditure. The regiments marched splendidly, and worked well— the infantry in particular. Four general actions were fought in five days (a marvellous triumph of energy as compared with real war!) but we should like to know what conception had any officer commanding a regiment—not to speak of his subordinates—of the part he was playing in the "horrid. game," or what opportunity he had, before or since, of gathering the slightest information on the subject ?

No arrangement seems to have been made or thought of for making the most, for all ranks, of the instruction to be gained. In fact, once the fighting began, even if there were the *desire* to communicate instruction (of which we can trace no evidence) there was no time for it. Generals returning late and weary from the "roar of battle," and "eager for the fray" next morning, had enough to think of in preparing for the coming strife, and endeavouring to save their reputation from the attacks of half-informed newspaper correspondents, without having also to provide instruction for officers and others. Just here we

should introduce a wholesome change.  Pitched battles should not be
of everyday occurrence.  They never are in real war.  Armies do not
fight "by the yard."  Quantity, we apprehend, is not the object.  We
cannot, of course, prolong the season of manœuvring unreasonably.
It would only increase the burdens of the taxpayer.  But, surely, it is
better to try less and do it well, and to teach every one the lessons to
be learned, than to have a series of *stand-up fights* under conditions
ill or hastily digested, and without giving time between them for im-
parting whatever instruction was to be derived from them.  There
should be at least one day's pause, as a rule, between the engagements.
The generals in chief command should regularly assemble the generals
and brigadiers serving under them, both before, to prepare for, and
afterwards to discuss, the features of each operation, and to point out
the mistakes made and the advantages gained, in connection with the
criticisms of the umpire-in-chief; the subordinate generals again
providing similarly for the information of those under them.

Instead of this, all that a colonel of a regiment or a captain of a
company under the present system knows of the campaign of 1872 is,
that he stood with his men, for an hour, more or less, here, and for
another hour there, in a wood or behind a ridge on Salisbury Plain,
without having then or since the faintest idea of the reason.

In these days of progress professional knowledge is demanded from
all ranks, not from generals and staff only.  The notion that military
bodies are mere unthinking machines, to be passively moved from
place to place, without the necessity of individual reflection or responsibility in any of their members, is an exploded thing of the past.
The teaching of recent wars points unmistakably to the necessity of
educating each individual man, soldier as well as officer, up to the
highest standard of excellence, in the duties of his sphere; and the
army that in all its separate parts (personal training and discipline as
well as organisation and administration) is best prepared will assuredly,
*cæteris paribus*, come out triumphant in the day of trial.

To get the greatest good from our autumn manœuvres we should
see to it that at all our large garrisons a uniform system obtains for
communicating individual instruction to officers and men.  Happily,
by the system of garrison instruction lately established, greater
facilities are now offered to zealous officers who are desirous of improving themselves, and a certain professional qualification is exacted
from all young officers in passing the obligatory examinations for
promotion.  But this is not enough.  Instruction should be made
more general among all ranks, especially in minor tactics, knowledge
of ground, cover, &c.  Besides the mechanical use of his weapon, the
soldier must be taught to appreciate the circumstances in which the
intelligent action of a few men working independently yet with combined effort may prove of vital consequence to the success or to the

saving of a force; and if this kind of teaching is necessary for the rank and file, much more is it necessary for the men who exercise command, from the lowest grade of non-commissioned officer upwards. Depend upon it, there is no greater mistake than to suppose that the officers and men of the British army do not take a great interest in their work when it is put before them in a way to call forth that interest. Our system has unfortunately been to put our men through certain exercises and combinations without ever teaching them the why and wherefore; but see the keen interest of officers and men when acting in opposing bodies, and judge how it may be executed and increased by a wise method of instruction. To ensure the greatest amount of teaching for all ranks, the garrison field days at our largest stations, as Aldershot, Portsmouth, Dublin, &c., should be announced at least a week beforehand. A "general idea" explaining the object of the operations should be published at the same time. The details affecting the intended positions and movements of the various brigades, regiments, companies, batteries, &c., should be thoroughly explained by brigadiers, colonels, captains, &c., to those under them. By this exhaustive system of instruction you will sharpen the interest, elevate the professional tone, and therefore greatly increase the efficiency, of the soldier. Instead of the ingrained aversion to " going to parade " as the one great affliction of the soldier's life, he will most probably look forward to the parade for the decision of the little problem explained during the week, and which he is to be one of the men to solve. Similarly the good points and mistakes should be commented on for the benefit of each class in regard to their own sphere of action.

Of the umpire system all that can be said in its favour is, that it is impossible to suggest any other. It is manifest, however, that any attempt to reduce the suddenly-changing circumstances of actual battle to a "rule of thumb" must be disappointing and not unfrequently absurd. To regulate the successes and defeats of opposing bodies of men by the addition or multiplication table may appear ridiculous; but in the absence of other means what else is to be done than counting heads, the position, the effect of artillery fire, and other circumstances of the opposing bodies being equal? Thus an incipient Wellington would, in an umpire's court, be defeated by a budding Napoleon by a majority of *one*. It should be explained to the general reader that as round shot and bullet do not attend peace manœuvres, and as no one in consequence suffers from that most disagreeable sensation so prevalent (as all honest persons will acknowledge) among men going into action, viz., a desire to be out of it, or to . run away at once if one only had the pluck, every one is equally brave, no skins are perforated, and naturally no one feels inclined to retire. But as he who brings a superior force against an inferior at the right time' and place *ought* to win, this theory is adopted as law in peace manœuvres, and the umpire acting at any *point* where two bodies come into collision always orders the inferior force to retire. This is simple enough with small bodies; but when the general fighting commences the umpire duty is a most trying one.   To determine relative advantages of position, the losses that in real warfare would be sustained in a few seconds under exposure to artillery fire, the length of time that villages and buildings supposed to have been put into a state of defence may be held when exposed to the fire of guns in position and the assault of infantry—all these are points which in war settle themselves, and for that reason are the more difficult to determine by theory or opinion.   The fact is, that the duty of the umpire is a most delicate one, for which but few men are qualified.   A man requires to have the largest experience, the coolest judgment, a far-seeing perception of circumstances, and a large amount of self-control, to avoid giving judgment hastily on appearances the value of which a little explanation from those concerned might greatly alter.   An umpire should be a man whose opinion carries with it a weight of its own ; not the ephemeral authority of a general order announcing his name, but the silent and more effective power of a personal reputation.

Not a few umpires, we fear, are influenced in their decisions by what they see around and close to them, without thinking how the same circumstances would appear from a different standpoint.   Suppose, for example, an umpire on the side of a defending army stands beside a battery of artillery, and, with the sound of gun after gun ringing in his ears, sees an enemy's line advancing to the attack.   If he be one of our hasty and impressionable umpires, he says, such or such a regiment is "annihilated," and after a few more rounds he sends to the regiment and orders it "out of action" for half an hour, or possibly for the day.   Now it is, no doubt, most uncomfortable for a regiment, even in line, to have a battery playing on it during its advance ; but this has often before been endured, and must be again, to gain a decisive point.   If we are not to have men killed in action, then all we can say is, we had better not fight.   The real point for the umpire to decide under the circumstances is with what amount of permanent loss the decisive point has been gained, if gained at all ; if not gained, real war should be imitated, and the regiment or force sent back under cover with a *defined permanent* loss of men for the day. It should not be allowed to advance again until reinforced to an extent to be stated clearly by the umpire, or until the position to be attacked be weakened, or otherwise affected from another direction.   In no circumstances can we see the reasoning on which a whole battalion is put "out of action" for *half an hour,* and then allowed to advance. Either all or a part were killed, and in either case the temporary inaction of the whole, to be followed by the advance again of all unscathed, seems an egregious blunder against common sense.

Another important defect in the system is that umpires never order generals, who expose themselves in the most suicidal manner, out of action, and their next in command to take their place. If they did, it would make the generals much more chary of going to the front. When, during the progress of an action, there are impossible operations attempted, and absurd situations attained, the umpire in chief's signal should be given, by bugle or otherwise, to stop the fight, and the errors made should be pointed out to all concerned. We, on the contrary, go at it "hammer and tongs," and no mistakes, if observed, are commented on till the end of the day, when it is too late to point effectively to the lessons to be taught by them. Stopping ridiculous movements in time may alter the whole character of the engagement. Not stopping them allows the development of circumstances which in real work would have been simply impossible. It should, in fact, never be forgotten that the one object in these manœuvres is *instruction*, and not merely to prove whether General Longnose is a superior tactician to General Squaretoes, however desirable that information in itself may be. If less were attempted (especially in our manœuvring infancy), and every movement were undertaken under a sense of being critically observed for the instruction of all, we should see less hurry-scurry and jostling of regiments under perplexing and contradictory orders, more thought of the conditions of real war exhibited, and the folds of ground oftener taken advantage of for sheltering the troops; but the fact is, when the "thud" of shell and "ping" of rifle bullet are unheard, we are all "brave to a fault."

If the duties of an umpire are difficult, and if, under the most favourable circumstances there must always be considerable dissimilarity between war and peace operations, how important it is that the instructions under which all are acting should be clear beyond the possibility of misconception. Moreover, once the "general idea" has been fixed on and communicated, it should never be altered. It is not fair on generals in command and others under them, when plans have been weighed and perhaps partly carried out, to order sudden changes in the conditions. It produces an uneasiness and uncertainty in the minds of men charged with responsibility to feel that at any moment all their arrangements may be upset. And this, we understand, is what did happen at the late manœuvres. We hear that instructions were changed and hours altered, with the natural result of misunderstanding and disappointment. This does not speak well for our military administration, for they surely had time enough to make up their minds about the operations and details. The question naturally suggests itself, if there is indecision when the game on both sides is in our hands, what is to happen in the sudden emergencies of war, when

unfortunately we have not the privilege of making the enemy's dis-
positions for him?

On the 31st of August there was promulgated the " general idea
of the operations," which described the march of the invading
(southern) army from Weymouth on London.   The defending
(northern) army was assembled at Pewsey.   In co-operation with it
were phantom forces, which were to hold Warminster, and also Salisbury and the strong position to the south of it, the force here being
6000 men.   Later orders stated the northern army held Salisbury and
Old Sarum, and had a "strong detachment" at Middle Woodford.
No subsequent alteration, so far as we can ascertain, was ever made in
these arrangements.   Now let us consider for a moment the last battle
—that of Amesbury—in the light of these orders.   Both armies, one
would think, must have gone out to battle without a doubt as to the
conditions.   Michel, commanding the invading army, advanced from
Winterbourne Stoke ; Walpole, commanding the northerns, took up a
position on the right bank of the Avon, and covering Amesbury from
the west.   He had the river on his back, but he was covering his communications and commanded the open country round Stonehenge,
across which Michel must advance if either attacking him directly in
front or threatening his right.   Instead of either, Michel very ably
worked round to Walpole's left, keeping his army admirably under
cover of the undulations which favoured the movement in that direction.   Nothing could surpass the carefulness with which the march of
these troops was conducted.   They were never exposed, and for a long
time were undetected by the scouts of the northern force ; but the
move, as one of strategy, was fatal to Michel's army.   He succeeded
in turning the enemy's left, and crossed the Avon above Middle
Woodford in reckless defiance of "the strong detachment," ghosts
though they were, which held this point, and utterly regardless of the
other 6000 phantoms of Old Sarum and Salisbury on his right,
whose bullets, of course, pierced no skins.   To do this he exposed his
own line of communications with the sea, the single thread on which
the lives of his army was hanging.   Walpole readily cut it, closed on
his rear, and shut him in.

His base thus lost, 6000 of the enemy on his right, an army
equal to his own on his left and rear (supposing even the Woodford strong detachment to have been swallowed), Michel's force must
have laid down their arms or perished.   Why did he, in the indulgence of the wild hope of getting between the defending army and
London, thus rush on death?   The answer is said to be, that he followed different instructions contained in certain " sealed orders " to the
commanders!   If they exist, and are in contravention of the circulated " general idea," we affirm there has been a most grave official
miscarriage.   It is no mitigation, but an aggravation of it, that it

occurred in peace manœuvres.  The germ of mismanagement in peace
would only bear the bitter fruit of disaster in war.

The nation, paying fourteen millions a year for its army, naturally
expects at least an absence of bungling in an arrangement requiring
brains and method not much higher than what may be reasonably
looked for in the regions of ordinary clerkdom.  We must say, the
weakness of our military administration in arranging the conditions of
manœuvre has been painfully prominent.

In the "manœuvres" of 1872 there was little "manœuvring," and
in tactics there was no dazzling instance of "heaven-born genius."
The one bold move was the rapid seizure of the line of the Wiley
River by Walpole's cavalry and horse artillery on the 4th of September.  Mr. Gleig, in *Fraser* for November, condemns this operation as
a mistake in itself, and as harassing to men and horses.  Now, under
the conditions laid down, both armies were approaching the river, the
invading (the southern) army had to cross it; and the rapid occupation of the fords and bridges by the northerners placed Michel's corps
at a very great disadvantage.  It seems strange, however, that the
commander of the northern cavalry did not also occupy the woods and
heights on the opposite side, until driven back on the infantry pickets
at the bridges.  When the northern army took up its position on the
6th of September, Walpole undertook (and by the instructions apparently could not help himself) to guard eight miles of river front with
some 9000 bayonets, 2000 sabres, and 42 guns.  His force was
wholly inadequate to do this (at least as it was tried to do it) and to
give battle too at the point of attack.  The brigades of the northern
army were scattered along this line, which was therefore too weak at
all points to meet the suddenly developed attack of the southern
army.  The latter effected the passage above Codford (Walpole's
right), which was attacked in force, and after a cannonade of short
duration was ordered by the umpires to be evacuated.

The same umpires would probably have ordered Wellington to fall
back on Brussels long before the Prussians came up, but, fortunately
for the great Duke, he had only French artillery, not umpires as well,
to contend with.  Well, Codford, under the combined deadly effect of
shot and umpire, was carried by the southerners; a terrible battle
raged with varying fortune at Codford Hill for three-quarters of an
hour; and when the bloodless engagement was stopped, reinforcements
were hurrying to Michel's support from his right (having crossed the
river lower down), and along the same route reinforcements were
pressing from Walpole's left in hot haste after them.  At first, as we
heard, the diluted decision of the umpires gave credit to both sides—
to Michel for the passage of the river, to Walpole for the defence of
Codford Heights; the final opinion being rather in favour of the
southern army; but in real war, who will say how it would have ended?

' The fact is, the line was altogether too extended. Walpole, we conceive (but it is much easier to judge after the event), should have held his infantry in hand by divisions, and depended on his cavalry for information. Had his cavalry, which had so opportunely seized the line of the Wiley, held the opposite ridges to the last, swept the country in small parties, and having once sighted the enemy never lost hold of him even at the risk of considerable loss, they would have done the special service for which we must in all future wars hold our cavalry responsible. Some of our cavalry leaders, however, are reluctant to let their regiments away from them; they cling to the hope of a cavalry charge; but they should remember that in these days no work they have to do is so important and none more honourable than that of efficient reconnaissance, that it is one requiring the highest order of military intelligence, and that on its right performance the safety of an army, and therefore the honour of a country, may depend.

Besides the battles of Amesbury and Codford there were two others, —those of Wishford and Wiley — but the less said about them the better. ' In the former the southern army was put out of court by the umpires for breach of the conditions in disregarding the imaginary bullets of a northern phantom army at Wilton, where the southerners crossed the river. The latter was a field day fight specially ordered, with a result akin to that of the traditional belligerent cats of Kilkenny, whose militia on this occasion had (strange enough) the opportunity of experiencing something of the historical *cata*strophe. There was a considerable expenditure of Her Majesty's powder, whole battalions swung gaily and defiantly across the Yasbury and Lamb Down slopes, while shot and shell (oh, if it had been!) ploughed up and smashed them. Everybody slaughtered everybody else, and when the horrid thirst for human blood was at length slaked, it was pleasant withal to see them—friend and foe—after mutual congratulations, march home to camp.

The drill and general tactical arrangements for attack and defence in those manœuvres were those which have long distinguished the fighting formations of the British army. Before next manœuvres, no doubt considerable modifications will have been introduced. The Duke of Cambridge has already sanctioned certain experimental changes in our drill, indicating a wise desire to accommodate our system to the new conditions of battle, altered as they have been by the increased ranges of rifled cannon and of the small arms of precision. It would not be suitable here, nor have we space, to enter into professional details; but with the daily increasing interest of the whole community in military matters, the country should watch with some anxiety the tendency of military agitation towards revolutionism. There are several military writers of the present day—many of them young, clever, enthusiastic students of the military art—who, because of the experience of the war of 1870–71, would Prussianize our whole army, just as many of the zealots of Crimean days would have Frenchified it. These young men would rudely tear up by the roots our historical military associations, telling us that as Wellington's genius taught him in his day the superiority of the line over the column, so would it now, if he were alive, inspire him to substitute "clouds" or "swarms" of skirmishers for the old British line; they say that our traditional steadiness and solidity (now old curiosities) must give way to looseness and extension, that every man, instead of clinging morally or physically to his neighbour, must go into action more or less "on his own hook;" battles are never again to be won nor defensive positions carried by the charge in line, but by flank movements with buzzing "swarms" of skirmishers unceasingly reinforced from the supports and crowding on the enemy until he is "stung to death;" there is no alternative, say they, between this and being swept off the face of the earth by the enemy's fire before you get at him. Never mind your companies and even your battalions being mixed up. It will all come right at the end. Of course you must keep your men under control; the rule must be absolute "order in apparent confusion."

Now, sudden revolutionary changes are as unwholesome for the body military, as for the body politic. Eager advocates of new ideas seem no wiser in these days than in those of old Juvenal, who said, "*Dum vitant stulti vitia in contraria currunt.*" The youngest tiro in arms sees that the tactics of the Great Duke's days are not applicable *in detail* to the present. We can no longer advance in a rigid line like a wall to within two hundred yards of the enemy, but we take exception to the revolutionary theories of the school of young military Radicalism that would on the experience of the Franco-Prussian campaign undo our whole English system of fighting in line, to which, it is not too much to say, our country chiefly owes the supremacy she can trace to her land battles. It suits the English national character (a grave element of consideration) if it does not suit the Prussians, and it remains yet to be proved, as we hold, whether the "swarm" system would suit us even if it suits the foreigner. A "cavalry officer," in a recent letter to the *Times*, sensibly pointed out that this swarm system had only been tried by an army uninterruptedly successful against an army demoralized almost from the beginning. It has yet to stand the test of a serious reverse. We should then be better able to appreciate it. All officers of experience under fire will tell you that even with British soldiers and the constant exercise of control over them it is difficult to maintain regularity in action. It is only that undefinable feeling that we are all hanging together in mutual reliance that keeps us going. The "independent swarming system," we suggest, might develop "individuality" so far that not a few would yield to their individual weakness in favour of a whole skin, and having once good cover would not so readily see the advantage of coming out of it.  If you could only be certain that the enemy would not stand when you got within a certain distance of him it would simplify the question ; but if he happens to stand, as British troops assuredly would, and your "swarm," notwithstanding the rein-forcements from supports, is checked and falls back, then your retire-ment may, with an unshaken enemy behind you, be converted into a disastrous rout.

The war of 1870–71, in which breechloaders were for the first time used on both sides, showed the superiority of the Prussian swarm over the Prussian column.  It does not necessarily establish the supe-riority of the Prussian swarm over the English line, accommodated as the latter must be to the changed conditions of battle.  Our line, instead of retaining the stiff rigidity of the iron bar, must attain the power of extension and flexibility of the elastic band, which, however stretched, never loses the tendency to spring back.  What we advocate is the line in its essence, with the advantage of a looser and more pliable formation, trained rapidity in opening it out, and, when neces-sary, moving in fractional parts over exposed ground.  For this a higher training must be imparted to officers and men in knowledge of ground, as well as in skirmishing and reinforcing skirmishers, observing that battalions should never be mixed, and companies of the same bat-talion as rarely as possible.  We advocate also two companies of picked shots in each battalion—intelligent, agile, and cool men, who would always skirmish in front of their own regiments.

The Duke of Cambridge having already introduced important modi-fications in our drill, will doubtless carry them through to the necessary point.  All the new formations are in the right direction.  There are, however, no instructions for opening out the line ; but these are sure to come, as well as special instructions about alternate bodies or fractions of the line dashing forward to secure cover.*  We cannot believe His Royal Highness will ever consent to the principle of the old English line being superseded by mobs of skirmishers.

In the late manœuvres every regiment had its own transport. Twenty men of each corps were beforehand instructed in the care of horses, and the required number of horses and carts were handed over to the various corps by the control department for the conveyance of their baggage.  This plan answered admirably for the regiments.  Of course, in a camp standing for days or weeks, such an amount of trans-

* An excellent pamphlet, "The British Line," by Colonel J. C. Gawler, explains clearly the principles of attack on the English system, modified to meet the circumstances of modern battle.  We strongly recommend it to the perusal of the professional reader.

port could not be allowed to remain idle and waiting for the next move ; and it has yet to be proved how far this regimental system would work when utilised for general army purposes. We do not see why it should not, but the manœuvres only demonstrated its great advantage to regiments.

A word about the new Control Department. The late manœuvres afforded no sufficient test of its efficiency for war. The supply of the troops was carried out by contracts made beforehand, and the officers had no opportunity of practising the active departmental duties they would have to perform on real service. The Control Department consists of all the old civil departments of the army—viz., commissariat, military store, purveyor, and barracks all rolled into one; the branches being still kept distinct, but all administered by one head, the local controller, instead of being, as before, independent, and reporting separately to the War Office. The theory is, that when a general marches his army, he gives his orders for the movement to his military staff (adjutant and quarter-master general), and to his controller, for the supply and transport required. The general is under the commander-in-chief, but the controller serves a different master. He is a War Office agent, and has to put the War Office drag on the general whenever he attempts to run out of the official groove of authorized expenditure. He (the controller), though a civilian, has become the general's staff officer for control services, with the privilege of reporting him to his War Office chief for the slightest departure from control rules. He communicates the general's decisions on control matters to generals of brigade and colonels of regiments, who do not like it; and he does not like it himself, for he feels he is forced to act as a staff officer without having the prestige or status of the latter. This is a grave error in administration. All the departments should be on the same footing, acting through the military staff on all questions not of absolute routine. The controller, we think, should be a *military* man of tried ability (more especially if he is to be an independent staff officer); and the military staff should itself have a " chief of the staff " —the single mouthpiece of the general, the one channel of communication to and from him.

On the whole, "our military display of 1872" was a great improvement on that of 1871. The manœuvres of 1873, we trust, will be a step still further in advance. What we want is—

1. A simple " general idea," early promulgated and communicated to every officer and soldier in the troops to be employed.

2. When the limits of operations are assigned, and the general idea is published, the general commanding on each side should arrange with his own controller (not the War Office for him) the formation of his depots of supply.

3. Non-interference from headquarters.

4. Very carefully-selected umpires, each one having experience of active service in the field.

5. The decision of the umpires to be published immediately after each fight, as well as the final remarks and decision of the umpire in chief, in more detail, at the end of the campaign.

6. An interval of a day, at least, between general actions, and a system of instruction on the past day's operations established for all . ranks.

# Roots.

I was standing in front of our little cottage in a state of perplexity. Twenty yards before me, caulking the bottom of his beloved sailing-boat, knelt my young philosophical friend, bare-throated, bare-armed, bare-footed, and coatless, as male creatures of all classes generally are in the summer in this barbarous, out-of-the-way little corner of the world.

"Charlie," cry I, in a most humble, entreating voice, "are you very busy?"

"Never am—never was—never shall be, in this world, I think," was his laconic answer.

"Dan Stringer's wife's got a baby," continue I, in the same tone.

"I don't quite see," replied he, with mock gravity, "what that has to do with my being busy;·nor why you should announce this extraordinary fact, as if you thought it a national calamity."

"Don't be silly," said I; "I mean that of course I must take her some things, and find what she wants, and so on. And it's such an awful walk over the hills, and through the forest, round to Dan's hut, especially if one has a horrid great bundle to carry."

"Hens," said he, provokingly seating himself on the bottom of his boat, and pointing at me solemnly with a roll of tow, "are more sensible than women on such occasions. When a hen lays an egg she sits on that egg, and does her duty by that egg, as a matter of course, unassisted by any of her female friends; but when a"——

"Oh, if you won't, I suppose I must manage as best I can," interrupted I, half angrily.

"Won't what?" replied he, trying to look astonished. "I'm not aware that you've asked me to do anything, yet. Now, to save time, allow me to say what you want to express. 'Dear Charlie, will you get out your skiff, and row me and my bundle of unnecessaries up to the creek at the head of the harbour as quick as you can (the distance is only five miles, and the thermometer only a hundred and ten in the shade), and then carry the bundle for me up to the cottage; and then, after I have satisfied my feminine love of cackling and fussing about, during which time you can amuse yourself by looking after the boat, row me back again by moonlight?' Cut along, and get the bundle—old gowns, mysterious linen, flannel, jelly, chickens, and the rest of it; and I'll have the boat out by the time you're ready."

"Oh, thank you so much," cried I, scuttling off; and behold me presently, my bundle having been already safely deposited in the boat, balancing myself on the top of a slippery rock, trying to get in. The first thing I did was nearly to topple forward into the sea; the next thing, naturally, was to topple backwards on to an oyster-bed—a most unpleasant thing to tumble on. Having regained the treacherous rock, I did manage, somehow, to find myself in the boat on top of my bundle; my young friend only 'commenting on my adventures with, "If you don't sit steady, we shall be spilt into the drink! Trim dish!"

In a minute, propelled by long, powerful strokes, we had rounded the rocky point which formed the corner of the little bay in which our house stood, and were in the long, narrow, main harbour, heading straight for our destination.

"*House*, indeed!" thought I, laughing to myself as I remembered the old country. "If some agent on a large English property saw that wooden dwelling, with only four rooms and a shed at the back, and no upstairs in it, and was told that it was a *house*, in which lived and were happy an ex-colonel of the line, his wife, and six children, he would have a fit."

Away we went, swiftly through the clear, calm water, the creaking of the straining rowlocks, and the swish and bubble of the water echoing amongst the steep, wooded cliffs on each side of us. There is nothing to me so pleasant as being rowed by an expert sculler in smooth water. The swish of the sculls, and the measured cadence with which they strike the water—the lifting, bubbling rush at the commencement of the stroke, and the long, steady shoot that follows— give a feeling, somehow, of strength and courage that makes rowing, above all things, the "poetry of motion."

No one who has not seen one of these inland harbours has a notion of their extraordinary romantic beauty. Imagine a long, narrow arm of the sea winding for four or five miles through sunlit, cloud-shadowed, forest-clad hills. On each side of you, as you pass each bold, rocky bluff, with weird-looking crags starting out of its very face, you open out some snug, fairy-like little bay, with, most likely, a little creek running into its head; with, perhaps, a little cottage on the bank—a tiny finger-mark of man on the glorious expanse of untamed nature. Far behind the cottage will run up into the hills a steep-sided, wooded gully, such as New Zealand alone can show, with all its glories of *kauri* pine and tree-fern; and as you gaze up the chasm, and away beyond it, you see

> "Far out, kindled by each other,
> Shining hills on hills arise;
> Close as brother leans to brother,
> When they press beneath the eyes
> Of some father praying blessings from the gifts of Paradise."

Oh, the charm of these little water-nooks! To slip on a hot, still, summer's day into their quiet shade, to let your boat glide under the overhanging branches of some majestic *ponuti kawa*, and there read, or more likely dream away, half the day. To lie there, thinking new thoughts and old, or painting in your mind visions of glorious scenes and noble deeds, till you begin to feel tearfully in love with all humanity; while the mullet, unconscious of your presence, plays joyfully upon the surface of the still water, while the little bell-bird sends forth his round, clear notes from the branches above your head; and the sarcastic *tui*, "the *nil admirari* man" amongst birds, parodies him with the most shameless Vandalism.

"Disgraceful idleness"—"A most mischievous and dangerous habit"—say some of my friends—all the more energetically, perhaps, because they can't understand the pleasure that is to be derived from it. Well, well! Though I honour the spirit that wrote

> "Be good, sweet maid, and let who will be clever;
>   Do noble things, not dream them all day long;
> Making past, present, and the vast forever
>   One grand sweet song."

I think that there are some spirits that would be utterly crushed and destroyed by the accumulated petty misèries of this life, if not occasionally refreshed by glimpses of some kind of heaven through the medium of dreamland. To some it would be simply spirit-death never to be allowed to dream of things beyond the petty common-places of life. Ay! and I am by no means sure that I envy those even-minded people who, in scenes like these, never feel the spell take possession of them, glorious in its beauty and its pleasure, almost terrible in its limitless immensity. For at these moments we are ever creeping to the very brink of the precipice, and vainly trying to peer into that vast, bottomless chasm—"the Unknowable." Is there nothing glorious in the hours when our existing selves and our commonplace life become shadowy, and the mysteries of our being and our future real living facts? In those moments, when

> "Each thought, as it forms and rises,
>   Is full of a solemn awe.
> Wildly it breaks and scatters
>   The germs of a thousand more.
> Onward and ever onward
>   The old thoughts lead to new,
> Waking and fading together,
>   The false lights and the true.
>
> "Truths unrevealed show dimly
>   And pass with a fitful gleam,
> The marks of the soul's great battles
>   Flit past like a misty dream.

Winding and changing quickly,
Clashing at times in strife,
Yet their bitterness all softened
By the spell of their Spirit-life."

\*  \*  \*  \*

" What a beautiful idea," remarked my young friend, slackening his stroke in order to talk, and gazing dreamily at a gorgeous bit of *kauri* forest at the top of the ridge, " the Maories have in their tradition of creation, of the Earth and the Sky in the first period of Great Darkness, when they were lying one on top of the other, being forced apart by the forest trees, until ' in these latter days Heaven remains far removed from his wife the Earth ; but the love of the wife is wafted up in sighs towards her husband. These are the mists which fly upwards from the mountain tops, and the tears of Heaven fall downward on his wife. Behold the dew-drops ! ' "\*

" I never could make head or tail of Maori mythology," said I. " In most of their traditions one seems forced to own that either their meaning is so terribly deep that one can't reach it, or else that they are simply silly stories."

" There are many things that make it difficult," replied he. " In the first place, I believe it is almost impossible to translate Maori meaning into English meaning (if you understand me.) Again, the traditions being merely orally transmitted from one priest to another, and the said priests having gradually lost sight of the meaning of many of the allegories, a stray word or expression has occasionally unconsciously been altered, until it becomes almost impossible to read the spirit of the original version. Again, later traditions have crept in, mixing themselves with the older ones, till the mass gets as hopelessly inconsistent as the book of Gen "——

" Stop ! " cried I. " If once you begin on that subject you will be a monomaniac for a week. Let's hear what you have got to say about the Maori one."

" Very well," replied he, smiling. " Listen. The Maori tradition of creation, like the Jewish one " (I groaned, but he took no notice)

---

\* This quotation is taken from an unpublished paper called ' The Maori Tradition of Creation,' written by the old Pakeha Maori, the talented author of ' Old New Zealand,' &c. It is a literal translation of the oral traditions of the *tobungas* (priests), communicated to him after goodness knows how many solemn vows, mystic initiations, and bargains with the Devil. He gave it to me with a solemn injunction to hold my tongue about it as long as I was in the country. Even now I dare not publish it, strongly tempted as I am to do so, by the romantic beauty of its allegories and their deep meaning, lest in a few months the neighbourhood of New Burlington Street should be startled by a select band of strapping young fellows calling at No. 8 to inquire the names, weights, and addresses of the editor and all the contributors. So I must content myself with the very baldest outline of the sacred mysteries.

"wisely does not profess to begin at the beginning of the world; in fact, neither of them are really an account of creation, but rather of development. Both the Jewish and the Maori tradition begin by stating the previous existence of the world, and strangely enough, neither attempt to account for its existence. The Jew says that at the time his history commences it was in a state of chaos, which always seems to me a disrespectful way of thinking about God's works; the Maori says it was in a state of uninhabitable darkness, or rather, in his mythical, poetical way, that the Heavens lay upon the bosom of the Earth, and this was the time of the Great Night. Then at last life* commenced, and the five children of the sun and earth resolved to separate them, all but the wind spirit, who was grieved by their cruelty. All tried, but only the forest god succeeded. 'Thus, by the destruction of their parents, they sought to make life increase and flourish; and in commemoration of these things are the traditionary sayings, The night! the night! The day! the day! The searching, the struggling for the light! the light!'† (Do you not think we may look on this as a most beautiful allegory of the struggles of nature towards organisation ?)

"But the storm spirit followed his father, Heaven, and resolved to make war on his brethen because they had separated his parents, and he attacked them with his children, the winds and the great rains. Tane Makuta, the forest god, went down like a reed before him. He would also have destroyed Ronga Matane and Kamia, the gods of tame and wild plants, but the Earth hid them in her bosom. Then his wrath was turned against Tangaroa, the ocean god, and he drove him away from the cliffs that he washed against. But the family of Tangaroa now divided: the swimming-fish taking to the sea, and Consternation, the great reptile, to the land. (The geological meaning of this allegory is too simple, I think, to need explanation.)

"Then the victorious storm god attacked the youngest of all his brothers, the mysterious Tu. (How shall I call him? Ohiu: Allfather; the war god, the god of destruction; *above all, 'the spirit of man.'*) But the warrior Tu stood upright and defied him. Then Tu resolved to make war against his brethren because they had not assisted him resolutely against the storm, and he set traps for the children of the forest god (birds), and soon they were hanging in the trees. 'He sought the children of Tangaroa, and found them swimming in the sea. He cuts the flax, he knots the net, he draws it in the water. Ha! the sons of Tangaroa are dying on the shore. And now he seeks his brethren, Ronga and Kamia, whom the Earth had concealed from the storm; but their hair appearing above the ground betrayed them. Now with the stone wedge he bursts the

* Not meaning human, nor even animal life, perhaps.
† 'The Maori Tradition of Creation.'

hardwood tree, and forms the pointed *ko*, the Maori spade. Now he weaves baskets, now he digs the earth. Ronga and Kamia lie drying in the sun. . . . . Then Tu sought prayers and incantations, by which to depress his brethren and reduce them to the condition of common food for himself. He had also incantations for the winds, to cause a calm; prayers for children, wealth, abundant crops, fair weather, and also for the souls of men. . . . . During the war with the storm the greater part of the earth was overwhelmed by the waters. . . . . The light now continued to increase, and as the light increased, so the life that had been hidden between heaven and earth increased; also Tu and his *elder* brethren, who had existed during the first great darkness, during the seeking and struggling, when old Earthquake reigned.' And so generation was added to generation down to the time of Mani-Potiki, who brought death into the world.

"Now this allegory seems simply to be a wild poetical account of the gradual fermentation of life in nature; then the destruction of the rank uninhabitable forests by floods and storms; also the first development of reptiles from fish; and lastly, the *gradual* victory of man over surrounding nature. If you don't want to go mad, examine into these traditions no further; for just as you think gleefully that you are beginning to understand what the scheme was, you will be met by some startling piece of extraneous information that utterly upsets and contradicts everything that has gone before. When you have despairingly choked and shut your eyes to this difficulty, and are imagining yourself, as you read on through the tradition, having a capital bit of swamp-shooting amongst the lively pterodactyls, you come across some such anachronism as

> " Fairshon had a son
> Who married Noah's daughter,
> And nearly spoiled ta Flood
> By drinking up ta water."

If this don't make you give it up in despair, the meaning of some name—Tu, for instance—will nearly finish you. At one moment you find it meaning apparently, life; at the next, intelligence; at the next, simply, man; at the next, the god of war, etc. This, combined with countless allegories, purposely mystified at first, accidentally mystified afterwards, until the original meaning has been lost, worse still, allegories altered to apply to later events—in short, an accumulated muddle of dates, words, and ideas—will bring you to the conclusion, that it is better to study Maori theology for the sake of its occasional poetical glimpses of grand truths than to try and reduce it to a consistent scheme. One can only think with a sigh, what a pity it is that such a many-meaninged no-meaninged muddle should be wasted on the nineteenth century, instead of being in vogue in the

Middle Ages, when it might have afforded endless work and interest to
countless theologians, besides supplying continual amusing spectacles,
in the shape of *autos da fe*, to their lighter-hearted fellows.

"But there are some peculiarities of the Maori religion which are
well worth noting, either caused by or causing some of the strangest
traits of the Maori character. You remember my saying the other
day that all religions were attempts to explain the origin, purpose, &c.,
of pain as comfortably to ourselves as possible. I confess the Maori
almost upsets my theory. With the exception of a careless mention
of Mani, the Maori Hercules, having brought human death into the
world by disobeying a demi-god, he treats this subject with stoical
indifference or Odin-like triumph. When the children of heaven and
earth are plotting how to separate their parents, what cries the man
spirit, Tu?—'Let us destroy them both!' The antagonism and
destruction that he describes as producing development, he takes with
a kind of triumphant stoicism, as a matter of course; he does not even
distress himself enough about the origin and purpose of pain to invent
a theory of a devil. He goes no further than to think that when a
man is sick he is possessed by an *atua*, or ghoul. He has no idea
of a good, *merciful* spirit above him, to supplicate in his hour of sorrow; no higher conception of prayer than *charming* a spirit by performing certain incantations correctly. The first converts to Christianity
retained this feeling (if not indeed the later ones), and before attacking their neighbours would repeat a Christian hymn word for word,
attributing their defeat, if they were thrashed, to some one having
left out a syllable accidentally. In short, their religion was extraordinarily godless, devilless, compassionless, stoical, and defiant.

"The missionaries, dear, simple souls, were delighted to find that
the old Maori creed was so extraordinarily like the old Jewish one;
never seeing that it was those very points, held in common by both,
that made the conversion of the Jews impossible."

"How can you call the religion of the Old Testament godless?"
asked I, astonished.

"I used a vague word for want of a better," replied he. "I meant
by 'godless,' a low, narrow, practical view of a Deity. What Jehovah
was to the Jews in the days of Moses and Joshua, Tu was to the
Maories. Jehovah was the God who confined his favour to the
Jewish tribe, Tu to the Maori one. All through the Old Testament
seems to run the same pæan: 'Is not our God stronger than those
of other nations?' Like Tu, he was a God of death and vengeance, with
still stronger personal animosities. Both seemed to have valued their
gods simply for their superior power. Elijah converted the Israelites
who had taken to Baal-worship by demonstrating the superior power
of Jehovah. The same feeling made the Maories rush eagerly at
Christianity on its first introduction, saying that ships, firearms, &c.

proved the superior power of the Christian God to their own. (When they found their mistake they dropped it as quickly as they had taken it up.)

"Their ways of *tapu*ing themselves before going to battle are literally identical, and both Jew and Maori priest accounted for defeat in exactly the same manner, i.e., the god being displeased because some one had broken the *tapu*. The story of Achan before Ai is Maori to the very letter. In short, if any one asked me for information concerning the old Maori religion I should say, ' Read your Old Testament literally, without looking out for types and prophecies, and you will catch both its rites and its spirit nearly exactly.' I have no doubt that Joshua and Te Waharoa, Gideon and Heke, spin each other many a grand old fighting yarn in the land of spirits; and that Samuel has found many a sympathetic friend on Agag questions among the stern old *tohungas* of the South Seas. So great was the similarity between the two religions that when the Old Testament was, by an unfortunate mistake, translated into Maori, it was greedily seized upon by the natives, to the utter ruin of the skin-deep Christianity that they professed.

" Like as they are in some ways to the old Jews, they differ on one or two points that make the chance of converting them to true Christianity still more hopeless; for they have a far less definite religious feeling, and a far more careless, stoical way of looking at both good and evil fortune. The glorious comforts of many of the Christian doctrines are looked on by the Maori with the greatest indifference."

"So you don't think," said I, "that they will ever become *real* Christians."

" There will be no time to make them so, I fancy, for in a hundred years or so they will have ceased to exist as a distinct race, and it is madness to suppose that they can be thoroughly altered in a generation or two. That is a fact that both many of the missionaries and many of those who abuse them often forget. They seem to think that two babies of different races born into the world are fitted with a couple of souls not necessarily very different in their tendencies until tampered with by people and circumstances. It is a most fatal mistake. As the Maori baby is brown and the other one pink, white, or mottled, so their little souls have on them the impress of the instincts, laws, prejudices, and so on, of a thousand ancestors. And consequently, in many cases, although you take the little savage away from evil communications, teach him to cut his Cannibalistic little teeth on civilised india-rubber, educate him with a view to the ministry, and dress him in the tight clothes and shining boots of the pale-face, it often happens that, on his arrival at the age of indiscretion, he bolts for the home of his fathers, and is next heard of eating the warm liver of some unfortunate colonist ! *You have not got to convert merely a single soul, but a mixture of thousands.* Hallo ! 'Ware mangroves !"

We had now reached the mangrove swamp that nearly always lies at the head of a New Zealand harbour, and were picking our way through it towards the mouth of the creek that emptied itself into their hideous forest. Oh, those mangroves! I never saw one that looked as if it possessed a decent conscience. Growing always in shallow stagnant water, filthy black mud, or rank grass, gnarled, twisted, stunted, and half bare of foliage, they seem like crowds of withered trodden-down old criminals, condemned to the punishment of everlasting life. I can't help it, if this seems fanciful; any one who has seen a mangrove swamp will know what I mean. A minute more brought us to the creek, and we glided onwards under the network of branches, till we were stopped by an enormous *kami* that had fallen right across it at the foot of the gully. So we landed, and, having made the boat fast, commenced scrambling upwards through the bush along the steep side of the ravine, sending stones and earth rolling down into the little creek, to the evident amusement of a jocose parrot, who followed and watched our progress with the greatest interest and amusement.

At last, hot and breathless, we emerged into an open glade, and came in view of a rude, comfortable-looking cottage. Out rushed two tawny little scamps at the sight of my young friend, stiffening however into sulky rigidity as my petticoated figure emerged from the bush, followed immediately by the stately form of Dan himself. Dan is rather a typical man in bush life. Standing six feet three inches on his bare feet, shaped like a Hercules, and always in perfect training, he could cut more lengths of timber in a day, swear harder at bullocks, was a better hand amongst pigs and wild cattle, a better fisherman, a better oar, and a better boat-sailer than any man on the island, except perhaps my young friend, who rivalled him in the three latter capacities. Between the two there was a strong friendship, differences of rank not making much of a gulf in these places between Dives and Lazarus, for the bush has a strange power of "bringing people together as wouldn't otherwise meet." He had come out to New Zealand as a sailor boy, had run his ship and joined a woodcutter's gang, and had finally located himself on our island, where he had taken to himself one of the daughters of the land for wife, who, after presenting him with half a dozen olive-skinned olive branches, had departed to the land of spirits. After a decent period of mourning, which I must say he bore most philosophically, he went up to Auckland, and to the great surprise of his friends returned in a week's time with a wife—a real white one—the interesting lady I had come to visit.

"Good-day to you," said Dan, raising his hat and speaking with that unconventional courtesy of manner that a wild solitary life (strange as it may seem) generally produces. "My wife will take your coming as very neighbourly, mam."

I hope I am not a snob, but I was thinking of the old country, and felt there was something very comic about this simple speech.

My young friend fell to chatting with Dan and chaffing the little half-castes, while I went in to see the lady of the house and be introduced to the new comer, whom I professed to be charmed with, like a humbug as I am; for it was a hideous little red thing, and I am not one of those women who admire all babies on principle. (I have since learnt to reconcile good manners with truth by always exclaiming, in an excited tone on such occasions, "What a baby!" which may be construed any way.) However, the mother evidently considered it "a thing of beauty and a joy for ever," and I thought it kind not to unsettle her mind by doubts.

Soon after I adjourned to the other room (there were only two), where I found my young friend sacrilegiously unpacking my bundle before the eyes of the grateful Dan. It was a comfortless looking apartment: the furniture consisted of a rough-hewn form, a rougher table, and a rickety chair; in one corner were a few axes, in another a gun, some fish spears, and a coil of rope; in a third a confused heap of blankets, which, I rightly conjectured, formed at night time the beds of the rising generation of Stringers. On the wooden walls were nailed some illustrations from the *London News*, and on one side a plank, supported by cords, formed a practical, if not ornamental, book-shelf. Obeying the impulse which always takes possession of me on entering a room for the first time, I ran my eye over its much-used, threadbare-looking contents. I am quite sure that no one who knows not wild life would guess what manner of books I saw. First came 'Paley's Evidences,' leaning as much away as it could from its neighbour, 'Paine's Rights of Man.' Between that and 'Midshipman Easy,' standing primly upright and regarding neither, was a 'Polite Letter-writer' of the year seventeen hundred and something, looking, in spite of its great age, far better preserved than its neighbours; on account, I suppose, of its cool, unexcitable temperament. Then came an odd volume or two of 'Macaulay,' 'Chambers' Information for the People,' 'Mills' Logic,' and a tattered backless 'Pilgrim's Progress.' Huddling close together in a corner I found 'The Vestiges of Creation' and Darwin's 'Descent of Man,' the constitution of the latter, in spite of its youth, evidently giving way from overwork.

It is not to be imagined, from this curious library, that our friend Dan was out of the way in his tastes for a man of his class. In many of the rough settlers' huts, in out of the way parts, you will find the same kind of solid literature. Whenever they come to my house to borrow books, as they often do, I always notice that they pick out the very stiffest reading (from our view of the tastes of uneducated men) they can lay hands on; on the principle, I suppose, that made the man prefer tough beefsteaks to tender ones, because they took so much longer to eat. And the amount both of thought-pegs and reflective power they will, aided by the solitude of their life, develop out of some really worthy book, is quite astounding to more civilised beings, who drive one book through their head after another until they wear a smooth hole, incapable of retaining permanently anything that passes through it. "You see," said one of these settlers to me (an old Scotchman)* "it's my opinion that there are some books that you can never derive full benefit from unless you spend almost as much time in reading them as the author did in writing; for how else are you to learn for yourself the different ramifications of thought that ended finally in the sentence you see before your eyes? It's but reading a fraction of the work to see but the sentences without the thoughts that shaped them; and not only do you thus learn to read the very mind of the author as he pored over his manuscript, but to strike out new thought-tracks for yourself, thus finding out the great secret of reading in order to think, instead of merely striving to cram an empty skull with a lot of ideas as disconnected as the words of a dictionary. Now," (so said this impertinent old person,) "you aristocrats, who have all the advantages of education that God, man and the Devil can give you, go gabbling through book after book, just like a man continuously taking one medicine on top of another, and never giving any of them time to take effect on his constitution. And what's the consequence? Why, after a whole lifetime of reading, you have nothing in your head but a vague jumble of other people's ideas, and seldom speak out a sentence worth listening to, because the poor creature don't know how it was born, not being developed by a systematic chain of thought, as it should be."

He was a rude, conceited, dogmatic old person, but I felt that there was a certain amount of truth in what he said, and understood better than before what it was that so often made these rough, wild, solitary settlers such charming companions.

I knew one man, inhabiting the wild Great Banier island, who had studied natural history to such purpose that even his little children knew the name and the family of every plant in the bush, with a correctness that was almost uncanny.

"Well, Dan," said I, sipping tea out of a tin mug, "I suppose we ought to congratulate you on this addition to your family?"

Dan's honest face clouded over,. and after a pause he apparently determined to relieve his mind, for he said, hesitatingly, "Well, you see, she never took any liking to my brats—which was my purpose in marrying her—and now she's got one of her own, I'm thinking it'll be worse."

"So you married for the sake of the children?"

"That's just where it was, mam, and a bl—I beg your pardon—a

---

* As I am trying to write the English language, my readers will be pleased to translate this speech into Scotch for themselves.

terrible mess I made of it. You see, for a year or two after my old woman died, we all worried along easy enough. I was a regular savage, and had no thought of eddicating beyond teaching Johnny and Tommy to split shingles. But then, you see, after a time he" (nodding towards my young friend) "crammed a lot of stuff into my head, and made me feel I wanted to teach them something, as it were. And then you see, my lass, Mary, what's now at school in Auckland, grew into a woman almost, and was as flighty as a hawk. So I made up my mind for a stiff bout, and began to try and teach 'em. Well, I made about the foolishest awkwardest job of it you ever see. Maybe it was I didn't know how to set about it, maybe I began too late with them, maybe both; but my teachings always ended the same way: Mary laughing at me, Tommy howling at one end of this old bench, and Johnny sobbing at the other. You had learnt 'em just to read and write at your school, so the ground seemed to be all ready cleared for sowing, one would think. Well, I tried 'em with every book you see on that shelf, but the little rascals never took the smallest interest in anything, barring the fights in the Old Testament and the 'Pilgrim's Progress.' And here I used to sit, wrastling with the long words, sometimes they mastering, sometimes I, till the sweat ran down my nose on to the paper, while they went to sleep or looked out of the window. I used to begin gently enough, but gradually get more and more riled at their pig-headed laziness, until it ended in my boxing their ears and going off with an axe to my work, with a face like a deformed potato. And then I used to chop and sweat, and sweat and chop like fury, until I got right again; for there's nothing raises a man's spirits like doing some work that he feels he *can* do.

"Things went on much the same, and I grew more and more desponding, until there came a day when no amount of sweating and chopping would bring me round. I had picked out a tree that would have raised any man's spirits, a good old tough, cross-grained *pohutikawa*, that might have turned the edge of a Harchangel's sword; but though I worked away till I could scarcely stand or see, it was no use. So I sat down, and bathed my head and arms in the sea and tried to think. I watched a little kingfisher * make five or six bad shots at the small fry, and almost grinned to think he was in the same lot as myself; but he nailed one the next shot, so I heaved a rock at him. And all the while, something kept whispering to me, 'It's no use, Dan; you've done your best, but nature made you for the purpose of chopping wood and not of eddicating brats. You'll never make any hand of it; not if you live till ninety. You stick to woodcutting.' So the long and short of it is, that by that night my mind was made up, and hearing that an emigrant ship had just arrived in Auckland, I took

* Kingfishers are the greatest duffers in piscatorial matters of all water-birds.

my passage in the *Sovereign of the Seas* cutter, and married the first decent-looking lass I came athwart of."

" Rather a rash way of doing things, that?" said my young friend, smiling.

" Lord bless you, sir," replied Dan, simply, " what was the use of a man like me trying to pick and choose? I'd be as like to get hold of the wrong sow last as first."

" How did you manage to win her affections so quickly, Dan? The receipt's worth knowing."

" Oh, that was simple enough," replied he. " The first night I arrived at the lodging-house, in Auckland, I found myself sitting next to a young woman at supper, who I soon found was one of the newly-arrived emigrants. I looked her over, and saw she was a round, strong, cheery-looking lass, with a laughing face, and thought she'd do. I didn't know how to go foolin' around her to find a soft place (as you would have done, sir, no offence to you), but just spoke a word or two with her, and when we came out into the passage give her a squeeze and a kiss. Says she, ' How dare you?' Says I, ' I wants to marry you, my dear.' ' Marry me!' cries she, laughing; ' why, I don't know you.' ' No more do I you, my dear,' says I, ' so that makes it all fair and equal.' She didn't know how to put a clapper on that, so she only laughed and said she couldn't think of it. ' Not think of it,' says I, artful like, ' not when you've come all these thousands of miles for the purpose?' ' What do you mean?' says she, staring. ' Come, now,' says I, ' don't tell me. I knows what's what. When a man immigrationises, it's to get work; when a woman immigrationises, it's to get married. You may as well do it at once.' Well, she giggled a bit, and we were spliced two days afterwards."

" Well? " said I, as he concluded.

" Well," said he, " it was a mistaken speculation as to the purpose intended. She never took to the brats, nor the brats to her. If they had been moody or ailin', she might ha' took to 'em, womanlike; but with such wild undependent little rascals, she never had no call."

Soon after this we started home. Night had come on, but the moon shone out brightly, and we scrambled down to the boat without any accident, and glided slowly down the little creek into the man-grove swamp. It was high tide, so that at times we were floating over the very tops of the trees. In shallower places the glasslike smoothness of the water, and the intense white light, caused a perfect reflection of their weird forms beneath them, making them look (as one could not distinguish the water-line) as if they had been dragged up from the soil and balanced on the tips of their roots on the bosom of the smooth sea. The stillness was almost oppressive, and it seemed as though the sound of the oars would have reached miles on miles. The cry of a " more pork " in a distant gully sounded close in our ears.

We crept along slowly and cautiously for fear of snags, the hideous mangroves stretching out their contorted limbs toward us, the harbour before us looking like a milky sheet, contrasting strangely with the black hills that surrounded it, until we gained open water once more and shot away towards home.

"There is no Arcadia," said my young friend, with a half laugh. "You rush to the wilderness to escape the evils connected with human life (and, as you think, civilisation), and there you find the same miseries, jealousies, heartburnings, and skeletons-in-the-closet generally, exactly the same. The same! the same! even to the woman's stays. Did you see Mrs. Stringer's hanging up behind the door? I hate stays.

"I came out into the wilderness," continued he, dreamily, "because I found myself utterly alone amongst men—with them, but not of them in any way. They all seemed to me to be incapable of judging anything from a broad, distant standpoint, to require a year or two's residence in another planet to teach them to look at their world and its affairs as a whole from outside. I felt myself painfully

> "'Like the poor ghost of some man lately dead,
> That's had but time the lesson to have read,
> That all his earthly faith was not correct,
> That God is not the leader of a sect,
> Is something different from a perfect man,—
> Then is sent back to shift as best it can,
> In its old world, and live among a race,
> Each damning each, and all assured of grace;
> Where every creed declares it's wholly right,
> And swears it has a patent for God's light.'

It is a very hard fate to be cursed with an eccentric way of thinking. Wherever I go, amongst Christians, Mohammedans, Buddhists, Hindoos, or cannibals, I am in the same position—an outcast from all sympathy. I flee into the bush, and, behold! both literally and metaphorically, I find stays!"

"Mrs. Stringer ought to have those stays preserved in the family archives after this," said I, laughing. "But don't despond, my dear boy, though I know your position is a hard one to bear. For you may be sure that a fair, liberal way of thinking has a good influence on those about you, though neither you nor they may be conscious of it:

> "'Good cheer, faint heart! Though all look dark,
> Though few men know, each leaves his mark.
> So each must struggle, straight and stark,
>     In this world's great fraternity.
> For every passing glimpse of thought,
> Fleeting, perhaps, and scarcely caught,
> Shows where some battle's being fought,
>     A landmark in Eternity."

And so we rowed home.

## A Hundred Years Ago.

PERUSING records that are a century old is something better than listening to a centenarian, even if his memory could go back so far. The records are as fresh as first impressions, and they bring before us men and things as they were, and not as after-historians supposed them to be.

The story which 1773 has left of itself is full of variety and of interest. Fashion fluttered the propriety of Scotland when the old Dowager Countess of Fife gave the first masquerade that ever took place in that country, at Duff House. In England, people and papers could talk or write of nothing so frequently as masquerades. " One hears so much of them," remarked that lively old lady, Mrs. Delany, " that I suppose the only method not to be tired of them is to frequent them." Old-fashioned loyalty in England was still more shocked when the Lord Mayor of London declined to go to St. Paul's on the 30th of January to profess himself sad and sorry at the martyrdom of Charles I. In the minds of certain religious people there was satisfaction felt at the course taken by the University of Oxford, which refused to modify the Thirty-nine Articles, as more liberal Cambridge had done. Indeed, such Liberalism as that of the latter, prepared ultra-serious people for awful consequences; and when they heard that Moelfammo, an extinct volcano in Flintshire, had resumed business, and was beginning to pelt the air again with red-hot stones, they naturally thought that the end of a wicked world was at hand. They took courage again when the Commons refused to dispense with subscription to the Thirty-nine Articles, by a vote of 159 to 64. But no sooner was joy descending on the one hand than terror advanced on the other. Quid-nuncs asked whither the world was driving, when the London livery proclaimed the reasonableness of annual parliaments. Common-sense people also were perplexed at the famous parliamentary resolution that Lord Clive had wrongfully taken to himself above a quarter of a million of money, and had rendered signal services to his country !

Again, a hundred years ago our ancestors were as glad to hear that Bruce had got safely back into Egypt from his attempt to reach the Nile sources, as we are to know that Livingstone is alive and well and is in search of those still undiscovered head-waters. A century ago, too, crowds of well-wishers bade God speed to the gallant Captain Phipps, as he sailed from the Nore on his way to that North-west

Passage which he did not find, and which, at the close of a hundred years, is as impracticable as ever. And, though history may or may not repeat itself, events of to-day at least remind us of those a hundred years old. The Protestant Emperor William, in politely squeezing the Jesuits out of his dominions, only modestly follows the example of Pope Clement XIV., who, in 1773, let loose a bull for the entire suppression of the order in every part of the world. Let us not forget too, that if orthodox ruffians burnt Priestley's house over his head, and would have smashed all power of thought out of that head itself, the Royal Society conferred on the great philosopher who was the brutally treated pioneer of modern science, the Copley Medal, for his admirable treatise on different kinds of air.

But there was a little incident of the year 1773, which has had more stupendous consequences than any other with which England has been connected. England, through some of her statesmen, asserted her right to tax her colonists, without asking their consent or allowing them to be represented in the home legislature. In illustration of such right and her determination to maintain it, England sent out certain ships with cargoes of tea, on which a small duty was imposed, to be paid by the colonists. The latter declined to have the wholesome herb at such terms, but England forced it upon them. Three ships, so freighted, entered Boston Harbour. They were boarded by a mob disguised as Mohawk Indians, who tossed the tea into the river and then quietly dispersed. A similar cargo was safely landed at New York, but it was under the guns of a convoying man-of-war. When landed it could not be disposed of, except by keeping it under lock-and-key, with a strong guard over it, to preserve it from the patriots who scorned the cups that cheer, if they were unduly taxed for the luxury. That was the little seed out of which has grown that Union whose President now is more absolute and despotic than poor George the Third ever was or cared to be; little seed, which is losing its first wholesomeness, and, if we may trust transatlantic papers, is grown to a baleful tree, corrupt to the core and corrupting all around it. Such at least is an American view—the view of good and patriotic Americans, who would fain work sound reform in this condition of things at the end of an eventful century, when John Bull is made to feel, by Geneva and San Juan, that he will never have any chance of having the best argument in an arbitration case, where he is opposed by a system which looks on sharpness as a virtue, and holds that nothing succeeds like success.

Let us get back from this subject to the English court of a century since. A new year's day at court was in the last century a gala day, which made London tradesmen rejoice. There were some extraordinary figures at that of 1773, at St. James's, but no one looked so much out of ordinary fashion as Lord Villiers. His coat was of pale

purple velvet turned up with lemon colour, "and embroidered all
over" (says Mrs. Delany) "with SSes of pearl as big as peas, and in
all the spaces little medallions in beaten gold—*real solid!*—in various
figures of Cupids *and the like!*"

The court troubles of the year were not insignificant; but the good
people below stairs had their share of them.  If the king continued to
be vexed at the marriages of his brothers Gloucester and Cumberland
with English ladies, the king's servants had sorrows of their own.
The newspapers stated that "the wages of his Majesty's servants were
miserably in arrear; that their families were consequently distressed,
and that there was great clamour for payment."  The court was never
more bitterly satirised than in some lines put in circulation (as Colley
Cibber's) soon after Lord Chesterfield's death, to whom they were
generally ascribed.  They were written before the decease of Frederick
Prince of Wales.  The laureate was made to say—

> "Colley Cibber, right or wrong,
>     Must celebrate this day,
> And tune once more his tuneless song
>     And strum the venal lay.
>
> Heav'n spread through all the family
>     That broad, illustrious glare,
> That shines so flat in every eye
>     And makes them all so stare!
>
> Heav'n send the Prince of royal race
>     A little coach and horse,
> A little meaning in his face,
>     And money in his purse.
>
> And, as I have a son like yours,
>     May he Parnassus rule.
> So shall the crown and laurel too
>     Descend from fool to fool."

Satire was indeed quite as rough in prose as it was sharp in song.
One of the boldest paragraphs ever penned by the paragraph writers
of the time appeared in the *Public Advertiser* in the summer of 1773.
A statue of the king had been erected in Berkeley Square.  The discovery was soon made that the king himself had paid for it.  Accordingly, the *Public Advertiser* audaciously informed him that he had
paid for his statue, because he well knew that none would ever be
spontaneously erected in his honour by posterity.  The *Advertiser*
further advised George the Third to build his own mausoleum for the
same reason.

And what were "the quality" about in 1773?  There was Lord
Hertford exclaiming, "By Jove!" because he objected to swearing.
Ladies were dancing "Cossack" dances, and gentlemen figured at balls
in black coats, red waistcoats, and red sashes, or quadrilled with
nymphs in white satin—themselves radiant in brown silk coat, with

cherry-coloured waistcoat and breeches. Beaux who could not dance took to cards, and the Duke of Northumberland lost two thousand pounds at quince before half a dancing night had come to an end. There was Sir John Dalrymple winning money more disastrously than the duke lost it. He was a man who inveighed against corruption, and who took bribes from brewers. Costume balls were in favour at court, Chesterfield was making jokes to the very door of his coffin; and he was not the only patron of the arts who bought a Claude Lorraine painted within the preceding half-year. The macaronies, having left off gaming — they had lost all their money — astonished the town by their new dresses and the size of their nosegays. Poor George the Third could not look admiringly at the beautiful Miss Linley at an oratorio, without being accused of ogling her. It was at one of the king's balls that Mrs. Hobart figured, " all gauze and spangles, like a spangle pudding." This was the expensive year when noblemen are said to have made romances instead of giving balls. The interiors of their mansions were transformed, walls were cast down, new rooms were built, the decorations were superb (three hundred pounds was the sum asked only for the loan of mirrors for a single night), and not only were the dancers in the most gorgeous of historical or fancy costumes, but the musicians wore scarlet robes, and looked like Venetian senators on the stage. It was at one of these balls that Harry Conway was so astonished at the agility of Mrs. Hobart's bulk that he said he was sure she must be hollow.

She would not have been more effeminate than some of our young legislators in the Commons, who, one night in May, "because the House was very hot, and the young members thought it would melt their rouge and wither their nosegays," as Walpole says, all of a sudden voted against their own previously formed opinions. India and Lord Clive were the subjects, and the letter-writer remarks that the Commons " being so fickle, Lord Clive has reason to hope that after they have voted his head off they will vote it on again the day after he has lost it."

When there were members in the Commons who rouged like pert girls or old women, and carried nosegays as huge as a lady mayoress's at a City ball, we are not surprised to hear of macaronies in Kensington Gardens. There they ran races on every Sunday evening, " to the high amusement and contempt of the mob," says Walpole. The mob had to look at the runners from outside the gardens. "They will be ambitious of being fashionable, and will run races too." Neither mob nor macaronies had the swiftness of foot or the lasting powers of some of the running footmen attached to noble houses. Dukes would run matches of their footmen from London to York, and a fellow has been known to die rather than that "his grace" who owned him should lose the match. Talking of "graces," an incident is told by Walpole of the cost of a bed for a night's sleep for a duchess, which may well excite a little wonder now. The king and court were at Portsmouth to review the fleet. The town held so many more visitors than it could accommodate that the richest of course secured the accommodation. "The Duchess of Northumberland gives forty guineas for a bed, and must take her chambermaid into it." Walpole, who is writing to the Countess of Ossory, adds : "I did not think she would pay so dear for *such* company." The people who were unable to pay ran recklessly into debt, and no more thought of the sufferings of those to whom they owed the money than that modern rascalry in clean linen, who compound with their creditors and scarcely think of paying their "composition." A great deal of nonsense has been talked about the virtues of Charles James Fox, who had none but such as may be found in easy temper and self-indulgence. He was now in debt to the tune of a hundred thousand pounds. But so once was Julius Cæsar, with whom Walpole satirically compared him. He let his securities, his bondsmen, pay the money which they had warranted would be forthcoming from him, "while he, as like Brutus as Cæsar, is indifferent about such paltry counters." When one sees the vulgar people who by some means or other, and generally by any means, accumulate fortunes the sum total of which would once have seemed fabulous, and when we see the fortunes of old aristocratic families squandered away among the villains of the most villainous "turf," there is nothing strange in what we read in a letter of a hundred years ago, namely: "What is England now ? A sink of Indian wealth ! filled by nabobs and emptied by macaronies ; a country over-run by horse-races." So London at the end of July now is not unlike to London of 1773 ; but we could not match the latter with such a street picture as the following: "There is scarce a soul in London but macaronies lolling out of windows at Almack's, like carpets to be dusted." With the more modern parts of material London Walpole was ill satisfied. *We* look upon Adam's work with some complacency, but Walpole exclaims, "What are the Adelphi buildings ? " and he replies, "Warehouses laced down the seams, like a soldier's trull in a regimental old coat ! " Mason could not bear the building brothers. "Was there ever such a brace," he asks, "of self-puffing Scotch coxcombs ? " The coxcombical vein was, nevertheless, rather the fashionable one. Fancy a nobleman's postillions in white jackets trimmed with muslin, and clean ones every other day ! In such guise were Lord Egmont's postillions to be seen.

The chronicle of fashion is dazzling with the record of the doings of the celebrated Mrs. Elizabeth Montagu. At her house in Hill Street, Berkeley Square, were held the assemblies which were scornfully called "blue-stocking" by those who were not invited, or who affected not to care for them if they *were*. Mrs. Delany, who certainly had a great regard for her who is now known as "a lady of the last century," has a sly hit at Mrs. Montagu in a letter of May, 1773. "If," she writes, "I had paper and time, I could entertain you with Mrs. Montagu's room of Cupidons, which was opened with an assembly for all the foreigners, the literati, and the macaronies of the present age. Many and sly are the observations how such a *genius*, at her age and so circumstanced, could think of painting the walls of her dressing-room with bowers of roses and jessamine, entirely inhabited by little Cupids in all their little wanton ways. It is astonishing, unless she looks upon herself as the wife of old Vulcan, and mother to all those little Loves!" This is a sister woman's testimony of a friend! The *genius* of Mrs. Montagu was of a higher class than that of dull but good Mrs. Delany. The *age* of the same lady was a little over fifty, when she might fittingly queen it, as she did, in her splendid mansion in Hill Street, the scene of the glories of her best days. The "circum-stances" and the "Vulcan" were allusions to her being the wife of a noble owner of collieries and a celebrated mathematician, who suffered from continued ill-health, and who considerately went to bed at *five* o'clock P.M. daily!

The great subject of the year, after all, was the duping of Charles Fox, by the impostor who called herself the Hon. Mrs. Grieve. She had been transported, and after her return had set up as "a sensible woman," giving advice to fools, "for a consideration." A silly Quaker brought her before Justice Fielding for having defrauded him. He had paid her money, for which she had undertaken to get him a place under government; but she had kept the money, and had not procured for him the coveted place. Her impudent defence was that the Quaker's immorality stood in the way of otherwise certain success. The Honourable lady's dupes believed in her, because they saw the style in which she lived, and often beheld her descend from her chariot and enter the houses of ministers and other great personages; but it came out that she only spoke to the porters or to other servants, who entertained her idle questions, for a gratuity, while Mrs. Grieve's carriage, and various dupes, waited for her in the street. When these dupes, however, saw Charles Fox's chariot at Mrs. Grieve's door, and that gentleman himself entering the house—not issuing therefrom till a considerable period had elapsed—they were confirmed in their credulity. But the clever hussey was deluding the popular tribune in the house, and keeping his chariot at her door, to further delude the idiots who were taken in by it. The patriot was in a rather common condition of patriots; he was over head and ears in debt. The lady had undertaken to procure for him the hand of a West Indian heiress, a Miss Phipps, with £80,000, a sum that might soften the hearts of his creditors for a while. The young lady (whom "the Hon." never saw) was described as a little capricious. She could not abide dark men, and the swart democratic leader powdered his eyebrows that he might look fairer in the eyes of the lady of his hopes. An interview between them was always on the point of happening, but was always being deferred. Miss Phipps was ill, was coy, was not i' the vein; finally she had the smallpox, which was as imaginary as the other grounds of excuse. Meanwhile Mrs. Grieve lent the impecunious legislator money, £300 or thereabouts. She was well paid, not by Fox, of course, but by the more vulgar dupes who came to false conclusions when they beheld his carriage, day after day, at the Hon. Mrs. Grieve's door. The late Lord Holland expressed his belief that the loan from Mrs. Grieve was a foolish and improbable story. "I have heard Fox say," Lord Holland remarks in the 'Memorials and Correspondence of Fox,' edited by Lord John (now Earl) Russell, " she never got or asked any money from him." She probably knew very well that Fox had none to lend. That he should have accepted any from such a woman is disgraceful enough: but there may be exaggeration in the matter.

Fox—it is due to him to note the fact here—had yet hardly begun seriously and earnestly his career as a public man. At the close of 1773 he was sowing his wild oats. He ended the year with the study of two widely different dramatic parts, which he was to act on a private stage. Those parts were Lothario, in 'The Fair Penitent,' and Sir Harry's servant, in 'High Life below Stairs.' The stage on which the two pieces were acted, by men scarcely inferior to Fox himself in rank and ability, was at Winterslow House, near Salisbury, the seat of the Hon. Stephen Fox. The night of representation closed the Christmas holidays of 1773-'4. It was Saturday, the 8th of January, 1774. Fox played the gallant gay Lothario brilliantly; the livery servant in the kitchen, aping his master's manners, was acted with abundant low humour, free from vulgarity. But, whether there was incautious management during the piece, or incautious revelry after it, the fine old house was burned to the ground before the morning. It was then that Fox turned more than before to public business; but without giving up any of his private enjoyments, except those he did not care for.

The duels of this year which gave rise to the most gossip were, first, that between Lord Bellamont and Lord Townshend, and next the one between Messrs. Temple and Whately. The two lords fought (after some shifting on Townshend's side) on a quarrel arising from a refusal of Lord Townshend, in Dublin, to receive Bellamont. The offended lord was badly shot in the stomach, and a wit (so called) penned this epigram on the luckier adversary:

> Says Bellmont to Townshend, "You turned on your heel,
>     And that gave your honour a check."
> " 'Tis my way," replied Townshend. "To the world I appeal
>     If I didn't the same at Quebec."

Townshend, at Quebec, had succeeded to the command after Monckton was wounded, and he declined to renew the conflict with De Bougainville. The duel between Temple and Whately arose out of extraordinary circumstances. There were in the British Foreign Office letters from English and also from American officials in the transatlantic colony, which advised coercion on the part of our government as the proper course to be pursued for the successful administration of that colony. Benjamin Franklin was then in England, and hearing of these letters, had a strong desire to procure them, in order to publish them in America, to the confusion of the writers. The papers were the property of the British Government, from whom it is hardly too much to say that they must have been stolen. At all events, an agent of Franklin's, named Hugh Williamson, is described as having got them for Franklin " by an ingenious device," which seems to be a very euphemistical phrase. The letters had been originally addressed to Whately, secretary to the Treasury, who, in 1773, was dead. The ingenious device by which they were abstracted was reported to have been made with the knowledge of Temple, who had been lieutenant-governor of New Hampshire. The excitement caused by their publication led to a duel between Temple and a brother of Whately, in whose hands the letters had never been, and poor Whately was dangerously wounded, to save the honour of the ex-lieutenant-governor. The publication of these letters was as unjustifiable as the ingenious device by which they were conveyed from their rightful owners. It caused as painful a sensation as one of the many painful incidents in the Geneva Arbitration affair, namely, when—it being a point of honour that neither party should publish a statement of their case till a judgment had been pronounced—the case made out by the United States counsel was to be bought, before the tribunal was opened, as easily as if it had been a " last dying speech and confession !"

In literature Andrew Stewart's promised 'Letters to Lord Mansfield' excited universal curiosity. In that work Stewart treated the chief justice as those Chinese executioners do their patients whose skin they politely and tenderly brush away with wire brushes till nothing is left of the victim but a skeleton. It was a luxury to Walpole to see a Scot dissect a Scot. "They know each other's sore places better than we do." The work, however, was not published. Referring to Macpherson's 'Ossian,' Walpole remarked, "The Scotch seem to be proving that they are really descended from the Irish." On the other hand, the 'Heroic Epistle to Sir William Chambers' was being relished by satirical minds, and men were attributing it to Anstey and Soame Jenyns, and to Temple, Luttrell and Horace Walpole, and pronouncing it wittier than the 'Dunciad,' and did not know that it was Mason's, and that it would not outlive Pope. Sir William

Chambers found consolation in the fact that the satire, instead of damaging the volume it condemned, increased the sale of the book by full three hundred volumes. Walpole, of course, knew from the first that Mason was the author; he worked hard in promoting its circulation, and gloried in its success. "Whenever I was asked," he writes, "have you read 'Sir John Dalrymple?' I replied. 'Have *you* read the 'Heroic Epistle?'" The *Elephant* and *Ass* have become constellations, and "*He has stolen the Earl of Denbigh's handkerchief*," is the proverb in fashion. It is something surprising to find, at a time when authors are supposed to have been ill paid, Dr. Hawkesworth receiving, for putting together the narrative of Mr. Banks's voyage, one thousand pounds in advance from the traveller, and six thousand from the publishers, Strahan & Co. It really seems incredible, but this is stated to have been the fact.

Then, the drama of 1773! There was Home's 'Alonzo,' which, said Walpole, "seems to be the story of David and Goliath, worse told than it would have been if Sternhold and Hopkins had put it to music!" But the town really awoke to a new sensation when Goldsmith's 'She Stoops to Conquer' was produced on the stage, beginning a course in which it runs as freshly now as ever. Yet the hyper-fine people of a hundred years ago thought it rather vulgar. This was as absurd as the then existing prejudice in France, that it was vulgar and altogether wrong for a nobleman to write a book, or rather, to publish one! There is nothing more curious than Walpole's drawing-room criticism of this exquisite and natural comedy. He calls it "the lowest of all farces." He condemns the execution of the subject, rather than the "very vulgar" subject itself. He could see in it neither moral nor edification. He allows that the situations are well managed, and make one laugh, in spite of the alleged grossness of the dialogue, the forced witticisms, and improbability of the whole plan and conduct. But, he adds, "what disgusts one most is, that though the characters are very low, and aim at low humour, not one of them says a sentence that is natural, or that marks any character at all. It is set up in opposition to sentimental comedy, and is as bad as the worst of them." Walpole's supercilious censure reminds one of the company and of the dancing bear, alluded to in the scene over which Tony Lumpkin presides at the village alehouse. "I loves to hear the squire" (Lumpkin) "sing," says one fellow, "bekase he never gives us anything that's low!" To which expression of good taste, an equally *nice* fellow responds: "Oh, damn anything that's low! I can't bear it!" Whereupon, the philosophical Mister Muggins very truly remarks: "The genteel thing is the genteel thing at any time, if so be that a gentleman bees in a concatenation accordingly." The humour culminates in the rejoinder of the bear-ward: "I like the maxim of it, Master Muggins. What though I'm obligated to dance a bear? A man may be a gentleman for all that. May this be my poison if my bear ever dances but to the very genteelest of tunes—'Water parted,' or the minuet in 'Ariadne'!" All this is low, in one sense, but it is far more full of humour than of vulgarity. The comedy of nature killed the sentimental comedies which, for the most part, were as good (or as bad) as sermons. They strutted or staggered with sentiments on stilts, and were duller than tables of, uninteresting statistics.

Garrick, who would have nothing to do with Goldsmith's comedy except giving it a prologue, was "in shadow" this year. He improved 'Hamlet,' by leaving out the gravediggers; and he swamped the theatre with the 'Portsmouth Review.' He went so far as to re-write 'The Fair Quaker of Deal,' to the tune of 'Portsmouth and King George for ever!' not to mention a preface, in which the Earl of Sandwich, by name, is preferred to Drake, Blake, and all the admirals that ever existed! If Walpole's criticisms are not always just, they are occasionally admirable for terseness and correctness alike. London, in 1773, was in raptures with the singing of Cecilia Davies. Walpole quaintly said that he did not love the perfection of what anybody can do, and he wished "she had less top to her voice and more bottom." How good too is his sketch of a male singer, who "sprains his mouth with smiling on himself!" But to return to Garrick, and an illustration of social manners a century ago, we must not omit to mention that, at a private party at Beauclerk's, Garrick played the "short-armed orator" with Goldsmith! The latter sat in Garrick's lap, concealing him, but with Garrick's arms advanced under Goldsmith's shoulders; the arms of the latter being held behind his back. Goldsmith then spoke a speech from 'Cato,' while Garrick's shortened arms supplied the action. The effect, of course, was ridiculous enough to excite laughter, as the action was often in absurd diversity from the utterance.

In the present newspaper record of births a man's wife is no longer called his "lady;" a hundred years ago there was plentiful variety of epithet. "The Princess of Mecklenburg-Strelitz, spouse to the Prince of that name, of a Princess," is one form. "Earl Tyrconnel's lady of a child," is another. "Wife" was seldom used. One birth is announced in the following words: "The Duchess of Chartres, at Paris, of a Prince who has the title of Duke of Valois." Duke of Valois? ay, and subsequently Duke of Chartres, Duke of Orléans, finally, Louis-Philippe, King of the French! whose sons are now astutely watching events in that unhappy France, which, for want of a patriot, or of an unselfish patriotic party, has not yet brought to a close the Revolution which was begun in 1789!

The chronicle of the marriages of the year seems to have been loosely kept, unless indeed parties announced themselves by being married twice over. There is, for example, a double chronicling of the marriage of the following personages: " July 31st. The Right Hon. the Lady Amelia D'Arcy, daughter of the Earl of Holdernesse, to the Marquis of Carmarthen, son of his Grace the Duke of Leeds." Lady Amelia having thus married my Lord in July, we find, four months later, my Lord marrying Lady Amelia. " Nov. 29th. The Marquis of Carmarthen to Lady Amelia D'Arcy, daughter of the Earl of Holdernesse." This union, with its double chronology, was one of several which was followed by great scandal, and dissolved under circumstances of great disgrace. But the utmost scandal and disgrace attended the breaking up of the married life of Lord and Lady Carmarthen. This dismal domestic romance is told in contemporary pamphlets with a dramatic completeness of detail which is absolutely startling. Those who are fond of such details may consult these liberal authorities: we will only add that the above Lady Amelia D'Arcy, Marchioness of Carmarthen, became the wife of Captain Byron; the daughter of that marriage was Augusta, now better known to us as Mrs. Leigh. Captain Byron's second wife was Miss Gordon of Gight, and the son of that marriage was the poet Byron. How the names of the half brother and half sister have been cruelly conjoined, there is here no necessity of narrating. Let us turn to smaller people. Thus, we read of a curious way of endowing a bride, in the following marriage announcement: " April 13th. Rev. Mr. Morgan, Rector of Alphamstow, York, to Miss Tindall, daughter of Mr. Tindall, late rector, who resigned in favour of his son-in-law." In the same month, we meet with a better known couple—" Mr. Sheridan, of the Temple, to the celebrated Miss Linley, of Bath."

The deaths of the year included, of course, men of very opposite qualities. The man of finest quality who went the inevitable way was he whom some call the *good*, and some the *great* Lord Lyttelton. When a man's designation rests on two such distinctions, we may take it for granted that he was not a common-place man. And yet how little remains of him in the public memory. His literary works are fossils; but, like fossils, they are not without considerable value. Good as he was, there are not a few people who jumble together his and his son's identity. The latter was unworthy of his sire. He was a disreputable person altogether.

Lord Chesterfield was another of the individuals of note, whose glass ran out during this year. He was always protesting that he cared nothing for death. Such persistence of protest generally arises from a feeling contrary to that which is made the subject of protest. This lord (as we have said) jested to the very door of his tomb. That must have reminded his friends during those Tyburn days, how convicts on their way up Holborn Hill to the gallows used to veil their terror by cutting jokes with the crowd. It was the very Chesterfield of highwaymen, who, going up the Hill in the fatal cart, and observing the mob to be hastening onwards, cried out, " It's no use your being in such a hurry; there'll be no fun till I get there!" This was the Chesterfield style, also its spirit. But behind it all was the feeling and conviction of Marmontel's philosopher, who having railed through a long holiday excursion, till he was thoroughly tired, was of opinion, as he tucked himself up in a feather-bed at night, that life and luxury were, after all, rather pretty things.

Chesterfield was, nevertheless, much more of a man than his fellow peer who crossed the Stygian ferry in the same year, namely, the Duke of Kingston. The duke had been one of the handsomest men of his time, and, like a good many handsome men, was a considerable fool. He allowed himself, at all events, to be made the fool, and to become the slave, of the famous Miss Chudleigh—as audacious as she was beautiful. The lady, whom the law took it into its head to look upon as *not* the duke's duchess—that is, not his wife—was resigned to her great loss by the feeling of her great gain. She was familiar with her lord's last will and testament, and went into hysterics to conceal her satisfaction. She saw his grace out of the world with infinite ceremony. To be sure, it was nothing else. The physicians whom she called together in consultation *consulted*, no doubt, and then whispered to their lady friends, while holding their delicate pulses, " Mere ceremony, upon my honour!" The widow kept the display of grief up to the last. When she brought the ducal corpse up from Bath to London, she rested often by the way. If she could have carried out her caprices, she would have had as many crosses to mark the ducal stations of death as were erected to commemorate the passing of Queen Eleanor. As this could not be, the widow took to screaming at every turn of the road, and at night was carried into her inn kicking her heels and screaming at the top of her voice.

Among the other deaths of the year 1773, the following are note-worthy. At Vienna, of a broken heart, from the miseries of his country, the brave Prince Poniatowski, brother to the King of Poland, and a general in the Austrian service, in which he had been greatly distinguished during the last war. The partition of Poland was then only a year old, and the echoes of the assertions of the lying czar, emperor, and king, that they never intended to lay a finger on that ancient kingdom, had hardly died out of the hearing of the astounded world. A name less known than Poniatowski may be cited for the singularity attached to it. " Hale Hartson, Esq., the author of the 'Countess of Salisbury' and other ingenious pieces—a young gentleman of fine parts, and who, though very young, had made the tour of Europe three times." An indication of what a fashionable quarter Soho, with its neighbourhood, was in 1773, is furnished by the following announcement: "Suddenly, at her house in Lisle Street, Leicester Fields, Lady Sophia Thomas, sister of the late Earl of Albemarle, and aunt of the present." Foreign ambassadors then dwelt in Lisle Street. Even dukes had their houses in the same district; and baronets lived and died in Red Lion Square and in Cornhill. Among those baronets an eccentric individual turned up now and then. In the obituary is the name of Sir Robert Price, of whom it is added that "he left his fortune to seven old bachelors in indigent circumstances." The death of one individual is very curtly recorded; all the virtues under heaven would have been assigned to her, had she not belonged to a vanquished party. In that case she would have been a high and mighty princess; as it was, we only read, "Lately, Lady Annabella Stuart, a relation of the late royal family, aged ninety-one years, at St.-Omer." A few of us are better acquainted with the poet, John Cunningham, whose decease is thus quaintly chronicled: "At Newcastle, the ingenious Mr. John Cunningham. A man little known, but that will be always much admired for his plaintive, tender, and natural pastoral poetry." Some of the departed personages seem to have held strange appointments. Thus we find Alexander, Earl of Galloway, described as "one of the lords of police;" and Willes, Bishop of Bath and Wells, who died in Hill Street when Mrs. Montague and her blue-stockings were in their greatest brilliancy, is described as "joint Decypherer (with his son, Edward Willes, Esq.) to the king." We believe that the duty of decypherer consisted in reading letters that were opened, on suspicion, in their passage through the post-office. Occasionally a little page of family history is opened to us in a few words, as, for instance, in the account of Sir Robert Ladbroke, a rich City knight, whose name is attached to streets, roads, groves, and terraces in Notting Hill. After narrating his disposal of his wealth among his children and charities, the chronicler states that "To his son George, who sailed a short time since to the West Indies, he has bequeathed three guineas a week during life, to be paid only to his own receipt." One would like to know if this all but disinherited young fellow took heart of grace, and, after all, made his way creditably in the world. Such sons often succeed in life better than their brothers. Look around you *now*. See the sons born to inherit the colossal fortune which their father has built up. What brainless asses the most of them become! Had they been born to little instead of to over-much, their wits would perhaps have been equal to their wants, and they would have been as good men as their fathers.

It was a son of misfortune, who, on a July night of 1773, entered the *King's Head* at Enfield, weary, hungry, penniless, and wearing the garb of a clergyman. He was taken in, poor guest as he was, and in the hospitable inn he died within a few days. It was then discovered that he was the Rev. Samuel Bickley. In his pockets were found three manuscript sermons, and an extraordinary petition to the Archbishop of Canterbury, dated the previous February. The prayer of the petition was to this effect: "Your petitioner, therefore most humbly prays, that if an audience from your Grace should be deemed too great a favour, you will at least grant him some relief, though it be only a temporary one, in our deplorable necessity and distress; and," said the petitioner with a simplicity or an impudence which may have accounted for his condition, "let your Grace's charity cover the multitude of his sins." He then continues, "There never yet was any one in England doomed to starve; but I am nearly, if not altogether so; denied to exercise the sacred functions wherein I was educated, driven from the doors of the rich laymen to the clergy for relief; by the clergy, denied; so that I may justly take up the speech of the Gospel Prodigal, and say: 'How many hired servants of my father have bread enough and to spare, while I perish with hunger!'" Here was, possibly, an heir of great expectations, who, scholar as he was, had come to grief, while, only a little while before him, there died a fortunate impostor, as appears from this record: "Mr. Colvill, in Old Street, aged 83. He was much resorted to as a fortune-teller, by which he acquired upwards of £4000;" at the same time, a man in London was quintupling that sum by the invention and sale of peppermint lozenges.

Let us look into the newspapers for January 1773, that our readers may compare the events of that month with the present January, a hundred years later. We find the laureate Whitehead's official New Year Ode sung at court to Boyce's music, while king, queen, courtiers and guests yawned at the vocal dullness, and were glad when it was all over. We enter a church and listen to a clergyman preaching a sermon; on the following day we see the reverend gentleman drilling with other recruits belonging to a regiment of the Guards, into which he had enlisted. The vice of gambling was ruining hundreds in London, the suburbs of which were infested by highwaymen, who made a very pretty living of it—staking only their lives. We go to the then fashionable noon-day walk in the Temple Gardens, and encounter an eccentric promenader who is thus described: "He wore an old black waistcoat which was quite threadbare, breeches of the same colour and complexion; a black stocking on one leg, a whitish one on the other; a little hat with a large gold button and loop, and a tail, or rather club, as thick as a lusty man's arm, powdered almost an inch thick, and under the club a quantity of hair, resembling a horse's tail. In this dress he walked and mixed with the company there for a considerable time, and occasioned no little diversion." The style of head-decoration then patronised by the ladies was quite as nasty and offensive as that which they adopt at the present time. It was ridiculed in the popular pantomime 'Harlequin Sorcerer.' Columbine was to be seen in her dressing room attended by her lover, a macaroni, and a hairdresser. On her head was a very high tower of hair, to get at which was impossible for the *friseur* till Harlequin's wand caused a ladder to rise, on the top rung of which the *coiffeur* was raised to the top surface of Columbine's chignon; having dressed which they all set off for the Pantheon. While pantomime was thus triumphant at Covent Garden there were something like cavalry battles close to London; that is to say, engagements between mounted smugglers and troops of Scots Greys. The village of Tooting in this month was a scene of a fight, in which both parties shot or cut down antagonists with as much alacrity as if they were foreign invaders, where blood, and a good deal of it, was lavishly spilt. Sussex was a favourite battle-field; a vast quantity of tea and brandy, and other contraband, was drunk in Middlesex and neighbouring counties where there was sympathy for smugglers, who set their lives on a venture and enabled people to purchase articles duty free.

At this time the union of Ireland with the other portions of the British kingdom was being actively agitated. The project was that each of the thirty-two Irish counties should send one representative to the British Parliament. Forty-eight Irish Peers were to be transferred to the English Upper House. One very remarkable feature in the supposed government project was, that Ireland should retain the shadow of a parliament, to be called " The Great Council of the Nation." The Great Council was to consist of members sent by the Irish boroughs, each borough to send one representative, "their power not to apply further than the interior policy of the kingdom." The courts of law were to remain undisturbed. It will be remembered that something like the above council is now asked for by those who advocate Home Rule; but as some of those advocates only wish to have the council as the means to a further end, the Irish professional patriot now, as ever, stands in the way to the real improvement and the permanent prosperity of that part of the kingdom.

In many other respects the incidents of to-day are like the echoes of events a hundred years old. We find human nature much the same, but a trifle coarser in expression. The struggle to live, then as now, took the guise of the struggle of a beaten army, retreating over a narrow and dangerous bridge, where each thought only of himself, and the stronger trampled down the weaker or pushed him over into the raging flood. With all this, blessed charity was not altogether wanting. Then, as in the present day, charity appeared on the track of the struggle, and helped many a fainting heart to achieve a success, the idea of which they had given up in despair.

# Stage-Coaches.

In a former article we gave a rapid sketch of the various changes that have occurred at different times in the modes of conveyances in England, but we made no mention there of stage and mail coaches, and as the history of these vehicles form a very important chapter in the annals of antiquated travelling, we shall now proceed to discuss it.

Stage-coaches were not introduced into England until the middle of the seventeenth century, but previously to this time carriers conveyed persons as well as packages from place to place. Stow refers to long waggons (afterwards called caravans) for passengers and commodities about the year 1564, and Fynes Moryson tells us that "these carryers have long covered waggons, in which they carry passengers from city to city; but this kind of journeying is so tedious, by reason they must take waggon very early, and come very late to their innes, as none but women and people of inferior condition or strangers (as Flemmings with their wives and servants) use to travell in this sort." These waggons were not much injured by the introduction of coaches, and they continued in use for many years into the last century. They travelled particularly slowly, by reason that they seldom if ever changed horses, and if not stuck in the mud they managed to creep over ten or fifteen miles in a long summer day. Sometimes, when the journey was a long one, a quicker pace was attained, and all will remember the eventful journey of Roderick Random from Scotland to London in the stage-waggon, which took eleven or twelve days to do the distance in. Samuel Sorbière, the historiographer of Louis XIV., when he commenced his travels over England in 1663, chose to travel by waggon, and thus describes that conveyance, but he does not tell us how long a time the journey occupied: "That I might not take post or be obliged to make use of the stage-coach, I went from Dover to London in a waggon. It was drawn by six horses, one before another, and drove by a waggoner who walked by the side of it: he was clothed in black, and appointed in all things like another St. George; he had a brave mounteero on his head, and was a merry fellow, fancy'd he made a figure, and seemed mightily pleased with himself." Perhaps the earliest instance of a regular service of stage-coaches is to be found in Scotland. Henry Anderson, an inhabitant of Stralsund, Pomerania, offered, in 1610, to bring from that country to Scotland coaches and waggons, with horses to draw and servants to attend them, if he was secured in the exclusive privilege of keeping them. His offer was accepted, and a royal patent was granted to him conferring the privilege for fifteen years of keeping coaches to run between Edinburgh and Leith. About fourteen or fifteen years after this stage-coaches had become tolerably common in England. In Sir William Dugdale's Diary, under the date 1659, the Coventry coach is referred to; and in 1661 Ant. Wood mentions the Oxford coach, which took two days to reach London. A few years afterwards (1669) a flying coach was started to travel from Oxford to London in thirteen successive hours, but in the winter time it was discontinued, and the old coach took its accustomed time of two days to perform the journey. As late as the year 1742 the Oxford stage left London at 7 A.M., reached Uxbridge at midday, arrived at High Wycombe at 5 P.M., and rested there for the night. On the morrow it proceeded on its journey to Oxford. In 1662 there were only six stage-coaches on all the roads of the country; and in the following year a certain Mr. Edward Parker made a journey in one, which he notices in a letter to his father, printed in the 'Archæologia:' "To his honoured father Edward Parker, esquire, at Browsholme, these: Leave this letter w^{th} ye Post Master, at Preston, in Lankashire, to bee sent as above directed. Honoured Father,—My dutie premised, &c., I got to London on Saturday last; my journey was noe ways pleasant, being forced to ride in the boote all the waye; y^e company y^t came up w^{th} mee were persons of greate quality, as knights and ladyes. My journey's expense was 30s. This traval has so indisposed mee, y^t I am resolved never to ride up again in the coatch . . . ."

In the opening scene of Sir Robert Howard's play of the 'Committee,' which was written soon after the Restoration, a stage-coachman and certain persons who have travelled by his coach are introduced. One of these (Mrs. Day) says, "I have rode formerly behind Mr. Busie, but, in truth, I cannot now endure to travel but in a coach; my own was at present in disorder, and so I was fain to shift in this; but I warrant you if his honour Mr. Day, chairman of the Honourable Committee of Sequestrations, should know that his wife rode in a stage-coach, he would make the house too hot for some."

In 1662 there was an Aylesbury coach, and in the following year one to St. Alban's. In 1677 we find references to a Chester coach, in 1679 to a Birmingham coach, and in 1680 to a Bedford coach. About this time stage-coaches were placed on most of the principal roads of the kingdom, but they only ran during the summer time. In 1672 they seem to have become pretty general, for in that year a writer, named John Cresset, inveighed against the "multitude" of stage-coaches and caravans, and suggested that all or most of them should be suppressed. This person tried to prove that they were mischievous to the public, destructive to trade, and prejudicial to land. As they destroyed the breed of good horses, hindered the breed of watermen, and tempted the gentry to come too often to London, he proposed that the coaches should at least be limited to one for every shire-town in England, to go once a week backwards and forwards.

The old stage-coach was a very clumsy machine, partly because improvements in construction had not then been made, but also partly because the bad state of the roads necessitated a strong and heavy vehicle. In 1682 a journey from Nottingham in a stage-coach occupied four whole days; and the reasons for this slowness were that the conveyance could not travel fast on account of its weight, nor far because the travellers could not bear the dreadful jolting for any length of time. Mr. Parker, to whom we just now referred, mentions the boot as the part of the coach in which he travelled so uncomfortably. This boot was a projection on each side of the coach, where the passengers sat with their backs to the carriage. Taylor, the water-poet, in his diatribe against coaches, says that "it weares two bootes and no spurs, sometimes having two paire of legs in one boote, and oftentimes (against nature) most preposterously it makes faire ladies weare the boote; and if you note, they are carried backe to backe, like people surpriz'd by pyrats." In course of time these projections were abolished, and the coach then consisted of three parts—viz., the body, the boot (on the top of which the coachman sat). and the basket at the back.

In 1678 Provost Campbell established a coach to run from Glasgow to Edinburgh, "drawn by sax able horses, to leave Edinboro' ilk Monday morning, and return again (God willing) ilk Saturday night." There could not then have been much intercourse between these two cities if such an infrequent communication was sufficient for the wants of the time. In the *London Gazette* for August 17–20, 1696, we find the following advertisement: "Cirencester stage-coach goeth out every Monday and Wednesday and Friday from the *Bell Savage Inn* upon Ludgate Hill to the *King's Head Inn*, Cirencester, in Gloucestershire, or any part of that road, in two days, and returns from thence on the same days from London." That is only forty-five miles in a day; and a few years after, in 1706, the York coach only did its fifty miles in a day. "All that are desirous to pass from London to York, or from York to London, or any other place on that road, let them repair to the *Black Swann* in Holbourne, in London, and to the *Black Swann* in Coney Street, in York. At both places they may be received in a stage-coach every Monday, Wednesday, and Friday, which performs the whole journey in four days (if God permits), and sets forth at five in the morning, and returns from York to Stamford in two days, and from Stamford, by Huntingdon, to London in two days more, and the like stages on their return, allowing each passenger fourteen pounds' weight, and all above threepence a pound." The foregoing notices are explicit as to the time of departure, but there is a charming indefiniteness in the announcement, which must have been very encouraging to the intending passengers, put forth by John

Dale in May, 1734, that a coach would set out from Edinburgh "for London *towards the end of each week*, to be performed in nine days, or three days sooner than any coach that travels that road." This speed does not seem to have been kept up, for twenty years later we find the following notice of a new coach: "The Edinburgh stage-coach, for the better accommodation of passengers, will be altered to a new genteel two-end glass machine, hung on steel springs, exceedingly light, and easy to go to London in ten days in summer, and twelve in winter." In the same year as this last (1754) a company of merchants in Manchester started a new vehicle called the "flying-coach," to run at the speed of five miles an hour, which they appear to have thought very great, for they open their prospectus thus: "However incredible it may appear, this coach will actually (barring accidents) arrive in London in four days and a half after leaving Manchester." In another three years a Liverpool flying-coach was started to do the journey to London in three days. About this time the journey to Dover was rather more expeditiously accomplished, for M. Grosley, in his 'Tour to London,' tells us that he travelled from Dover in a flying-machine in one day at a cost of one guinea. On this occasion that place was so crowded that the police law, by which public carriages were forbidden to travel on Sunday, was dispensed with. A flying-machine on steel springs, from Sheffield to London, was set up in 1760. This coach took three days on its journey, and slept the first night at the *Black Man's Head Inn*, Nottingham, the second at the *Angel*, Northampton, and arrived at the *Swan with Two Necks*, Lad Lane, on the evening of the third day. The old stage-coaches continued to travel slowly until the mail-coaches had become general; and Mr. Pryme, in his 'Autobiographical Recollections,' tells us of a man who was in the habit of walking from Bury St. Edmunds to Newmarket, and was frequently given a lift on the coach as it passed him. On one occasion, however, when offered a seat, he answered: "No, thank you;' I'm in a hurry to-day." Mr. Pryme travelled with his uncle from Nottingham to Hull by a coach which took two days to perform this journey of twenty-two miles, and saw two men, who spoke to the coachman as he left Newark, arrive on foot at the halfway-house between that place and Lincoln (a distance of sixteen miles) just as they drove out of it after baiting the horses. As late as the year 1800 the Shrewsbury and Chester "Highflyer" took about twelve hours to do the forty miles between those two cities. Part of this time was occupied by the dinner at Wrexham, over which about two hours were spent. The coachman was never in any hurry, and he would look in at the door of the coffee-room, and mildly inform his fares that all was ready to start, but would add: "Don't let me disturb you, gentlemen, if you wish for another bottle."

Slowness of locomotion, however, was not the only annoyance with which coach-travellers had to put up. Very frequently the stage-coaches were stopped by highwaymen, even in the immediate vicinity of London, and an amusing account of one of these adventures is given in the 'Percy Anecdotes.' The passengers in a certain coach, on its way to London, began to talk about robbers. One gentleman, expressing much anxiety lest he should lose ten guineas, was advised by a lady who sat next to him to take it from his pocket, and slip it into his boot, which he did immediately. It was not long before the coach was stopped by a highwayman, who, riding up to the window on the lady's side, demanded her money. She declared that she had none, but if he would examine the gentleman's boot he would there find ten guineas. The gentleman submitted patiently; but when the robber departed he loaded his female travelling companion with abuse, declaring her to be in confederacy with the highwayman. She confessed that appearances were against her, but said that if the company would sup with her the following evening in town she would explain a conduct which appeared so mysterious. After some debate, they all accepted her invitation, and the next evening they were ushered into a magnificent room, where an elegant supper was prepared. When this was over, she produced a pocket-book, and, addressing herself to the gentleman who had been robbed, said: "In this book, sir, are bank-notes to the amount of a thousand pounds. I thought it better for you to lose ten guineas than me this valuable property, which I had with me last night. As you have been the means of my saving it, I entreat your acceptance of this bank-bill of one hundred pounds."

It was the custom in Scotland for the male travellers in a stage-coach to treat the ladies to breakfast and dinner on the road; but this custom was discontinued after the first mail-coaches from London to Edinburgh and Glasgow were established. Southey describes, in his 'Espriella's Letters,' a journey from London to Oxford in a stage-coach, and tells us that, when one woman only was in the company, all the other passengers paid her reckoning at the inns, and divided the cost among themselves. Such a custom as this shows us as much as anything what a gulf there is between the present system of travelling and that of the past generation.

Before passing on to notice the revolution made in stage-coach organization by the establishment of the very perfect system of mail-coaches, we may stop to say a few words about a small public carriage with two horses, made to accommodate three inside passengers, which ran from place to place, and was called a Diligence—a name usually contracted to Dilly. Two of the passengers sat with their faces towards the horses, and the third sat in an opposite seat, partly inserted into a recess in the carriage, but projecting a little outwards. Canning's well-known lines in the 'Anti-Jacobin'—

"So down thy vale, romantic Ashbourne, glides
The Derby Dilly with its three insides,"

s 2

refer to this conveyance. When O'Connell adopted the quotation, and applied it to the late Earl of Derby, he changed the number three to six, and thus, while making it more applicable to the nobleman in question, he destroyed the accuracy of the original description. Although these Dillies were much lighter than the stage-coaches, they do not appear to have travelled at any great speed; for we find that one in the last century left London at nine in the morning, dined at Bagshot, had tea and supper at Farnham, started on again the next morning, arrived at Winchester in time for dinner, and ended the second day's journey at Southampton.

Perhaps nothing brings home to us more thoroughly the change that has taken place in our habits of locomotion than the difficulties that formerly existed in the way of passing from one part of London to another. In the memory of not very old men it was necessary for them to book their places overnight if they wished to journey from Chelsea to Islington; and in the last century it was not an unusual thing for the Chelsea stage to be stopped by highwaymen in the King's Road. With all these difficulties some persons appear to have enjoyed coach travelling in and about London. This feeling rose to infatuation in one Samuel Crisp, who died in 1784 at his house in Macclesfield Street, Soho, for he adopted the habit of making a purposeless journey daily by the stage-coach to Greenwich, and returning immediately. This practice he kept up for fourteen years, and, as an equivalent for his fare, he paid the proprietor of the coach 27l. a year.

A new era in travelling may be dated from the year 1784, when Mr. John Palmer introduced mail-coaches. Previously to that time the whole postal communication of the country was in the hands of the post-boy, of whom Cowper sings:

> "He comes, the herald of a noisy world,
> With spattered boots, strapped waist and frozen locks.
> News from all nations lumbering at his back.
> True to his charge, the close-packed load behind,
> Yet careless what he brings,—his one concern
> Is to conduct it to the destined inn,
> And, having dropped th' expectant bag, pass on.
> He whistles as he goes, light-hearted wretch,
> Cold and yet cheerful; messenger of grief
> Perhaps to thousands, and of joy to some;
> To him indifferent, whether grief or joy."

We find that, in 1635, a post was established between Edinburgh and London, running day and night, going there and back in six days.

This, however, was a very exceptional speed, and the post soon became notorious as the slowest mode of conveyance in the country. The post-boy ought to have ridden at the rate of five miles an hour, but he frequently dawdled on the road, and was sometimes stopped by highwaymen, so that his pace seldom exceeded four miles an hour. In the year 1757 the boy who carried the Portsmouth mail dismounted at a public-house in Hammersmith and called for some beer, when certain thieves made use of the opportunity afforded them, of running away with the mail-bags. After a time robbers discontinued the practice of stopping the post-boys, because they found out that the public had ceased to send anything of value by such an unsafe mode of conveyance. Naturally, as the want of a better communication was felt, a system so incorrigibly slow became impracticable; but in the middle of the last century the correspondence appears to have been so small that this imperfect medium was found to be sufficient. In 1745 the letter-bag from London is said to have once arrived in Edinburgh with only one letter, for the British Linen Company; and about the same time the Edinburgh mail reached London with but one letter, for Sir William Pulteney, the banker. In course of time the stage-coaches improved, but the post-boys remained as dilatory as ever, and when tradesmen were anxious to have a letter carried with speed and safety, they made it up into a parcel and sent it by coach, although, in consequence, they paid a much higher rate than the postage would have come to.

John Palmer, to whose foresight and genius of organisation the almost perfect system of English mail-coaches was due, was originally a brewer, but at the time when he developed his great scheme he was manager of the Bath and Bristol Theatre. De Quincey refers to his achievements in a very amusing manner. " Some twenty or more years before I matriculated at Oxford, Mr. Palmer, at that time M.P. for Bath, had accomplished two things very hard to do on our little planet, the Earth, however cheap they may be held by eccentric people in comets; he had invented mail-coaches and he had married the daughter of a duke. He was, therefore, just twice as great a man as Galileo, who did certainly invent (or, which is the same thing, discover) the satellites of Jupiter, those very next things extant to mail-coaches in the two capital pretensions of speed and keeping time; but, on the other hand, who did *not* marry the daughter of a duke." The lady here referred to was Lady Madeline Gordon, daughter of the Duke of Richmond. When Palmer had matured his scheme, by which the Post office was to make use of a system of fast coaches, he confided it to Lord Camden, who recommended it to Pitt, then Prime Minister and Chancellor of the Exchequer, and the consequence was that Palmer was directed to send in a report. As might be expected, the Post-office officials strenuously opposed the plan, and one of them stated his opinion that there was no reason why the post should be the swiftest conveyance in England. In spite, however, of all objections, Palmer was appointed Controller-General of the Post-office, with a salary of £1500 a year, and a commission of two and a half per cent.

on any excess of the revenue of the office over £240,000, the sum at which it stood when he was appointed. The result of the change was seen when the Secretary of the Post-office issued the following order on the 24th of July, 1784:—"His Majesty's Postmasters-General, being inclined to make an experiment for the more expeditious conveyance of letters by stage-coaches, machines, &c., have been pleased to order that a trial shall be made upon the road between London and Bristol, to commence at each place on Monday, the 2nd of August next." This date was not adhered to, but the first mail-coaches were started on the 8th of August. The benefits of the new system were soon appreciated by the public, and the municipalities of the largest towns in the kingdom vied with each other in their applications for coaches to be allowed to run through their towns. The Liverpool merchants were the first to apply, but York followed in October, 1784, with an application for a mail-coach to pass through its city to the North.

Soon after the introduction of the new coaches a copper medal, called "The Mail-coach Halfpenny," was struck, which is thus described by Mr. Lewins in his entertaining work, entitled 'Her Majesty's Mails:' underneath the representation of a coach-and-four and its team of horses at full speed are the words, "To Trade expedition and to Property protection;" on the reverse, "To J. Palmer, Esq. This is inscribed as a token of gratitude for benefits received from the establishment of mail-coaches."

Although the public thoroughly appreciated the boon they had received, the Post-office officials still continued to fret under the management of Mr. Palmer, so that after much dissension that gentleman was forced to resign, but his plans were adhered to, and the Post-office was not allowed to return to its old system. Palmer obtained on his resignation a pension of £3000 a year, but this he did not consider sufficient reward for his labours, and he therefore memorialised the Government for further compensation. During the discussions in Parliament on his case he was eulogised by several members; and Sheridan said that "No man in this country, or any other, could have performed such an undertaking but that very individual—John Palmer." This benefactor, however, never received any grant himself; but in 1813, after twenty years' struggle, his son, General Palmer, obtained £50,000 from Parliament. If ever a Parliamentary grant was deserved this one was, for, through the impetus given to trade by the improvements in travelling and the rapid system of letter despatch, the revenue of the Post-office was raised, in thirty years, from £240,000 to one million and a half sterling!

When the roads were improved the speed of the coaches was increased, and the light stage-coach began to emulate the mail in its rapid flight through the country. All this emulation so thoroughly awakened the public spirit that travelling was enormously developed, and the necessity for a cheaper mode of conveyance made itself felt. In consequence, the long coach holding twelve, fourteen, and even sixteen passengers was introduced. This conveyance was something like an omnibus, but if we are to believe the writers who describe it, it was infinitely superior as an instrument of torture to its more modern imitation. Southey, in his 'Letters of Espriella,' says: "The atmosphere was neither fresher nor more fragrant than that of a prison; to see anything was impossible, as the little windows behind us were on a level with our heads." De Quincey, in his 'Confessions of an Opium Eater,' throws a little more darkness into the shading of the picture, thus: "As ventilation was little regarded in those days, the very existence of an atmosphere being ignored, it followed that the horrors of Governor Holwell's black cage at Calcutta were every night repeated in smaller proportions upon every great English road." In order that we may know what this disagreeable conveyance was like, Southey describes it: "We are now in the track of the stage-coaches; one passed us this morning, shaped like a trunk with a rounded lid placed topsyturvy. The passengers sit sideways; it carries sixteen persons withinside, and as many on the roof as can find room; yet this unmerciful weight, with the proportionate luggage of each person, is dragged by four horses at the rate of a league and a half within the hour. The skill with which the driver guides them with long reins, and directs these huge machines round corners, where they go with increased velocity, and through the sharp turns of the inn gateways, is truly surprising."

The mail-coach system was brought to such wonderful perfection that elements of error were hardly ever allowed. While travelling long distances at great speed the coach's punctuality was a thing to swear by. De Quincey tells us, "One case was familiar to mail-coach travellers, where two mails in opposite directions, north and south, starting at the same minute from points six hundred miles apart, met almost constantly at a particular bridge which bisected the total distance." It is evident from what we read that this perfection deeply moved the feeling of the country, and was keenly enjoyed. It was so total a change from all that had gone before that most travellers appreciated this "glory of motion," and felt that they themselves were conquerors. De Quincey says, "For my own feeling, this Post-office service spoke as by some mighty orchestra, where a thousand instruments, all disregarding each other, and so far in danger of discord, yet all obedient as slaves to the supreme bâton of some great leader, terminate in a perfection of harmony like that of heart, brain, and lungs in a healthy animal organisation." There were some, however, who prophesied sad disasters when the coaches attained a speed of ten miles an hour, and it was whispered that passengers had died of apoplexy from the rapidity of the motion. The usual speed attained by the mail-coaches was about ten or eleven miles an hour, including stoppages; and when we take into account the inequality of ground travelled over in a long journey, we shall find that they must have flown over some part of the way at a prodigious rate. The Manchester mail did its 187 miles in 19 hours, the Liverpool mail did its 203 miles in 20 hours 50 minutes, the Devonport mail its 227 miles in 20 hours, the Holyhead mail its 261 miles in 26 hours 55 minutes; but the most remarkable instance of sustained speed was the Edinburgh mail, which travelled over its 400 miles in 40 hours. Some of the light coaches almost rivalled the swiftness of the mails: thus the "Herald," Exeter day coach, did its 171 miles in 20 hours; and the Shrewsbury and Manchester coaches journeyed from London to their respective destinations in a single day. On all these roads little time was wasted in stoppages, and the changing of horses was a very rapid proceeding. Everything was ready prepared, and what had often, under the old system, taken half an hour to perform, now occupied barely three minutes. To obtain this speed no expense was spared, and the outlay on a single coach was enormous. The horses required were at the rate of one to every mile; thus, as it is 154 miles to Shrewsbury from London, 150 horses were required for the "Wonder" coach. By this ample supply the horses were kept in good condition, for though the work they performed was hard, it occupied but a short time. The horses were fine animals, and they rested for twenty-three hours out of the twenty-four, besides remaining quiet every fourth day. They were well treated, and fed with as much as they could eat, for each horse's stomach was alone the measure of his corn. The coaches were built so as to combine great strength with great lightness. The mails were especially light, as they carried no luggage on the roof, and they were frequently called "paper carts" by rival coachmen. Early in the present century the Post-office authorities thought it desirable that all the mail-coaches should be built and furnished on one plan. Mr. John Vidler contracted for the building and repairing of these patent coaches; but he was paid by the mail contractors, as the only amount paid by the Post-office was that of £2200 a year for cleaning, oiling, and greasing them. All the mail-coaches were under the superintendence of the Postmaster-General, and various stringent rules relating to them were made by that distinguished officer; thus, four outside passengers only were allowed— one on the box, and three behind—and no passenger, on any pretence, was permitted to sit beside the guard. The guard, as the representative of the executive, wore the royal livery, and his responsibilities were great and his duties often hazardous. In consequence, it was considered necessary to supply him with firearms, and it was believed that, if any one was allowed to sit next to him, a highwayman might take advantage of the position, and under the disguise of an honest man overpower the guard and rob the bags. When Palmer proposed this scheme of arming the guard, one of the Post-office officials objected to it on the ground that if desperate men had determined on robbery, it was better to submit, for resistance would only lead to murder. The mail-coach guards were a most respectable body of men, and they were much trusted by the public. There is ample evidence to prove that they were deserving of the trust reposed in them; and Mr. Lewins gives an interesting anecdote which illustrates this in one instance, and many more of a similar character might be cited. "A mail-coach having travelled during a driving snow-storm as far as it could advance, the guard, as the custom was in such cases, took the bags with him on horseback for some miles farther; then the horse, sinking deeper at every step, was sent back to the coach, while he, essaying to carry the bags on foot, was found with them round his neck next morning quite dead." The coachman did not wear a scarlet coat by right, as did the guard, but it was given to him by way of distinction after long (or, if not long, trying and special) service.

Soon after the introduction of mail-coaches an Act was passed, declaring that all carriages and stage-coaches employed to carry His Majesty's mails should henceforth be exempt from the payment of toll both on post and cross-roads. In consequence of this Act, inn-keepers, who were the principal owners of stage-coaches, bargained for the carriage of mails frequently at merely nominal prices, in order to obtain the privilege of running their coaches free of toll. The turnpike-keepers naturally looked upon the mails and all connected with them as moving in a sphere beyond their control. At the approach of the mail-coach turnpike gates flew open, and all around was deference and obedience to the omnipotent will of the driver. The feeling of importance thus engendered communicated itself to the passengers, and they felt themselves, in consequence, to be formed of a superior clay. Even here, however, there was a divided opinion, for the inside passengers considered that they were porcelain, while the outsiders were merely delf. De Quincey makes some amusing remarks on this feeling, and tells us that for some time the insides would not sit at the same table with the outsides; and if the latter were so presuming as to push into the coffee-room, the waiter would beckon and entice them into the kitchen. At last the outside passengers rebelled, and, after a great struggle, obtained recognition.

Mr. Palmer suggested that all the coaches from the different roads should leave the General Post-office, then situated in Lombard Street, at the same time in the evening, and this starting of the mails thus became one of the numerous sights of London. Every night, from eight o'clock to fifteen or twenty minutes later, Lombard Street was crowded with sightseers gathered together to witness the procession and departure of the coaches which filled the street in double file.

In the last year of mail-coaches the number which left London every night was twenty-seven.

But if the nightly departure was a sight worth seeing, what words can express the excitement exhibited on those nights, during the time of the great war, when the country learned that it had gained some grand victory. On those occasions the coaches, horses, and men were all decorated with laurels and flowers, with oak-leaves and ribbons, so that wherever they passed the glad news might be made apparent to all, and be quickly circulated through the land. Victories followed each other so rapidly that all were in a state of expectation, and the mail-coach was known to be the national and authorized medium of communication, by which the first news of any great event was published to the world. De Quincey says, "The mail-coach it was that distributed over the face of the land, like the opening of apocalyptic veils, the heart-shaking news of Trafalgar, of Salamanca, of Vittoria, of Waterloo;" and under the influence of the fervour of his subject, he expresses the feeling that "five years of life it was worth paying down for the privilege of an outside place on a mail-coach when carrying down the tidings of any such event." To prove his words, he then gives a magnificent description of the start from London under these circumstances, a part of which we shall now quote: "Liberated from the embarrassments of the city, and issuing into the broad uncrowded avenues of the northern suburbs, we soon begin to enter upon our natural pace of ten miles an hour. In the broad light of the summer evening, the sun, perhaps, only just at the point of setting, we are seen from every storey of every house. Heads of every age crowd to the windows—young and old understand the language of our victorious symbols—and rolling volleys of sympathising cheers run along us, behind us, and before us. The beggar, rearing himself against the wall, forgets his lameness—real or assumed—thinks not of his whining trade, but stands erect, with bold exulting smiles, as we pass him. The victory has healed him, and says, Be thou whole! Women and children, from garrets alike and cellars, through infinite London, look down or look up with loving eyes upon our gay ribbons and martial laurels; sometimes kiss their hands; sometimes hang out, as signals of affection, pocket-handkerchiefs, aprons, dusters, anything that, by catching the summer breezes, will express an aërial jubilation."

Another fine sight which Londoners enjoyed was the annual procession of mail-coaches which took place on the king's birthday. The route was from Milbank to Lombard Street. About noon the postmen, guards and coachmen, with their friends, dined at Milbank, and at five o'clock the gay procession set out. All the horses had new harness and the guards and postmen new scarlet coats. The cavalcade was headed by the general post letter-carriers on horseback; then followed the coaches filled with the wives, children, friends, and relations of the guards and coachmen, and the rear was brought up by the post-boys. Bells rang out, and all was gaiety and joy till the arrival at the Post-office, when the coaches were prepared for their departure to the country at the regular hour. All this is now as if it had never been; roads that once were filled with conveyances are now deserted, and inns that once exhibited signs of the most vigorous life, echo in their vacant rooms to the footsteps of the solitary travellers who successively visit them. The giant Railway has gradually swallowed up and annihilated all other modes of conveyance. The five-and-twenty coaches that ran daily to Brighton in 1832 are now superseded by the seventeen trains that now leave London each day for that place. Who, however, will not agree that there was more enjoyment to be obtained by riding on the " Red Rover," which flew along the road in five hours, than by travelling in the third-class train which creeps over the same distance in two hours and a half? Those who prefer the " Red Rover " will sympathise with the old gentlemen who are never tired of telling of the glories of the antiquated stage-coach. They can remember the time when Sir Charles Bamfylde, Sir John Rogers, Colonel Prouse, and Sir Lawrence Palk were the pride of the Devonshire road, when the Hon. Thomas Kenyon, Sir Henry Painell, and Mr. Maddox were looked up to as demi-gods by all the coachmen on the Holyhead road, and when Sir Henry Peyton, Lord Clonnell, Sir Thomas Mostyn, Mr. Annesley, and Mr. Harrison gave a high tone to the frequenters of the Oxford road.

All these names are now forgotten, but they were powers in their day. The fashionable Brighton road was an especial favourite among aristocratic coachmen. The Brighton day-mail was driven by the Hon. Frederick Jerningham, son of Lord Stafford, and the " Age " by Sir Vincent Cotton. At another time the " Age " was driven and horsed by Mr. Stevenson, a Cambridge graduate, who was an ex-quisite of the first order. At a certain change of horses on the road a silver sandwich-box was handed to the passengers by his servant, who had instructions to offer a glass of sherry to such as were inclined to accept of such hospitality. The " Age " was renowned far and wide, and a crowd collected every day to see it start.

We cannot be surprised that many of those who remember the stage-coaches in their time of prosperity occasionally regret their fall. We may also remember that the appreciation of fast travelling is really felt more thoroughly in a coach than it is in a railway carriage. There was more excitement on the coach, and the perfect system of organisa-tion was more perceptible to the passenger. Of course the advantages of the railway system are so great that the two cannot for one moment be compared; but still, while appreciating all the blessings of railway travelling, we may be allowed to give a " lingering look behind " upon the past glories of the old mail-coach.

# The Wooing O't.

## A NOVEL.

### CHAPTER XVIII.

THE weeks which ensued, while Maggie waited for the season prescribed by Mr. Dunsford as most suited for her advertisement, were about the most unpleasant, though not the saddest of her young and troubled life. Nothing of after years ever equalled the agony and desolation which fell upon her when her mother died. Nor did any bitterness enter her soul so deeply as the insults and tyrannies she sustained from her aunt; but this early autumn of her third year's emancipation was tormented by a perpetual struggle in heart and mind—a constant maintaining of the lines within which reason, sorely beset by the overwhelming forces of imagination, memory, taste, and tenderness, had entrenched herself—and, indeed, it pleases me to think how gallantly and true to her higher instincts my modest little heroine carried herself all through the silent strife, without one word of sympathy or help. Nothing but the honest woman-pride to keep her from sinking into despondency, sentimentalism, or bad health! Simply the instinctive consciousness that she must not, in a matter such as this, give more than she received. And although it may militate against her character as a heroine, and prove her too reasonable to be interesting, I must be veracious, and, moreover, avow my conviction that such a struggle is certain of success, and brings after it strength and peace. Maggie began to experience this before many months were over; but I must not anticipate, and only set this down for the encouragement of young ladies whose affections have wandered to objects who do not want them. The sweetest, the most modest girl, may find herself on the verge of, or in, such a predicament; but to a true womanly woman such a wound carries its own cure.

One thing comforted Maggie: it was John's assurance, as they finished those mutton pies, that they were to be like brother and sister. She smiled at her own conceit as she remembered the horror and alarm with which she received his first advances to a renewal of their old and familiar acquaintance. "I must not be so silly as to imagine every one who is kind must be in love with me," she said to herself; "I am sure I can be very fond of John if he will be just like a brother." But even as a brother she could not feel towards him as she wished to do. He was so rough and untidy; he used the authority which success and experience had given so ruthlessly—albeit for the general good; he was so unsparing of his father's weakness, of his sisters' follies, and far, far too sympathetic with Mrs. Grey, in her business-like hardness—though he frequently administered a moral squeeze to her also, just to show her she must not presume. Then the terribly ugly aspect of the house was another unconfessed worry to Maggie, who loved prettiness and neatness. With Mrs. Berry all minor matters were in her own hands, and their rooms were always gracefully arranged and scrupulously clean.

However, John's intense energy left no one too much time to think. He was always at work himself, and making others work. "Here Mag!" he cried one morning, a few weeks after their visit to Mr. Dunsford's office; "I wish you and Bell—all of you—would set to work and make an inventory of every stick in the house. Begin right away at the top, and call those rat-holes attics, d'ye mind?"

"What in the world do you want that for, John?" asked Bell, as discontentedly as she dared.

"I want it done, and that ought to be enough for you," returned John, helping himself a second time to the bacon and poached eggs, served especially for him, and which he failed not to appropriate. "But Mag, you know, if we arrange about this business for the governor at Ditton Market, we'll have an auction of everything here, and an inventory all ready will be a save and a gain both; so see about it, like a good girl."

"I will," said Maggie, readily.

"And do you really think you will be able to manage this matter?" asked Mr. Grey.

"Yes, I will; the more I inquire into it the better it seems. But mark you, I'll have to borrow some of the money, so you must make it pay, by jingo! or I'll be coming back to know the reason why—there, Dick, there's a bit of bacon I can't manage."

Dick was not proud—and accepted it.

"And I say, governor, you and I had better run down look at the place; it will be the right thing, and rouse you up a bit. I expect the country will freshen you wonderful."

"Indeed, I was always partial to the country, John, and your conduct gives me new life and energy."

"I hope so," returned the son; "I am sure you want both."

"If you had found them a little sooner," grumbled Mrs. Grey, "we might have had a flourishing business here, and there's no place like London, after all."

"Oh, stop that!" cried John, rising. "Nagging never raised a man's spirit yet. I wish I could find a straightforward, pushing young man with a trifle of ready rhino, for a partner in the concern. Dick here isn't old enough to be of much use."

"How do you know," said Dick. "I can roll pills like any-thing."

"We'll have my father up for manslaughter, if you go rolling your pills down people's throats," returned the family benefactor.

"Then you are not going to Paris?"

"I have other fish to fry—other employment for my capital," said John; "besides"—as he left the room—"it was Maggie, here, I wanted to see, and she has saved me the journey. Now, gals, don't you forget the inventory!"

True to his intention, John carried his father away to the new Eldorado a few days after.

"Much good *he* will do there," grumbled Mrs. Grey to her daughters. "Now, if I had gone there would have been some sense in it. I could see with half an eye whether the place would answer or not; but of course John knows best!"

The eagle eye of John being removed, the Demoiselles Grey left the task of the inventory to Maggie's unassisted efforts. She accordingly progressed all the better; while her cousins divided their time between making up smart autumn garments, and exhibiting the same in the park and elsewhere.

The captivating Fred Banks, too, appeared, to comfort Mrs. Grey with sympathy—anent the absent Tom—and consoling prophecies respecting the certainty of his coming out first-rate—"a regular top-sawyer," or, as Dick rudely paraphrased it, "a top sawbones."

Jemima was consequently in a state of beatitude, and both young ladies, who had always been tolerant of their cousin, now regarded her with positive liking, so kindly and useful did they find her in lending patterns, in cutting out and fitting in. And then Mrs. Grey had been tempted to have the old piano tuned, because Maggie promised to help Bell with her practising. So when Uncle Grey and John returned, which they did in a state of much contentment, Maggie was able to relieve the tedium of the evening by singing and playing simple melodies, which delighted the chemist's soul, and even had charms to soothe John's savage breast.

Thus Maggie multiplied occupation to herself, and the weeks flew over; still Mrs. Berry made no sign.

By her aunt's advice, Maggie went nearly every morning to a neighbouring news-agent, where she read the advertisement sheet of the *Times* diligently, and even answered two or three, but with no result; the only answer she received being from a pious lady, who wished to give a happy home to some evangelical young person, who would in return undertake the education of nine young souls, ranging from twelve to three years of age.

John growled and laughed at this—while he rather annoyed Maggie the same evening by suddenly kissing her when saying good-night. Even had she time she would hardly have liked to refuse. Yet it was singularly unpleasant to her; so much so that she took herself to task for over-fastidiousness, ingratitude, and a dozen other errors of nature, before she could dismiss it from her mind.

However, there was not now much time for thought, for having completed all his arrangements with the fast son and heir of the late chemist at Ditton Market, who longed to finger the cash for the excellent bargain he was bestowing on the incoming tenant, John, to use his own expression, turned all hands to clear the decks. The inventory was found complete. Mother and the girls were set to pack up their belongings; and John himself, with Maggie's help, set diligently to work to make up the "governor's" books, and gather together what he could of the small amounts due.

Then the auction was organised—confusion and discomfort had almost reached their culminating point; poor Maggie—nervous at the idea of leaving London and the chances of employment behind her, yet shrunk from intruding her affairs on any one in such a supreme moment, especially as she had no plan to offer—was therefore infinitely relieved when one evening, after cogitating in his father's armchair for some time in silence, John suddenly spake.

"I have been thinking it won't do for you all to leave this on Wednesday. I can't see after everything when the auction is over; and I'll be deuced uncomfortable in a lodging all by myself. I tell you what you'll do"—to his stepmother; "leave Mag and Bell behind! Mag's a capital clerk—first-rate, and no mistake—and Bell—well, we'll make some use of her—at any rate, one room will do for the two gals, and it will be the same cost."

"Oh, John," put in Jemima, "can't you let *me* stay?"

"No! I won't, miss, replied her brother; "you are no use at all! But that's the plan, m'am." No question asked as to the inclinations of the individuals destined to carry out cousin John's immutable decrees.

"I shall be glad to stay, on account of my putting in my advertisement," said Maggie; "and I shall also be glad to be of any use."

"Use! Why you are the most useful little brick I ever met," said John, enthusiastically. "I say, governor, she would give her skin for you; though I don't think she cares much for any of the rest of us. Now then, gals, you start to-morrow morning and find a lodging for us—nice tidy rooms, five and twenty shillings a week, not a rap more. And if you look sharp and keep me right down comfortable, I'll be whipt if I don't take you to the theatre now and then—but you must earn it!"

"Agreed," said Maggie, laughing. "We will be diligent, and you must be reasonable."

"So I am—always reasonable, you monkey!" retorted John, pinching her ear with a familiarity she could not resent. And with a huge yawn he marched away to bed.

It was altogether like a hurried dream—uncle and aunt Grey being uprooted and transplanted; Maggie could scarcely imagine London without them. However, the dream was fulfilled, and one fine morning, about two months after her parting from Mrs. Berry, she found herself in charge of Cousin John's luggage, her own, and Bell, in a tolerably neat lodging in one of the small streets that lead from the Edgeware Road. It will, probably, further militate against our little heroine's character, as a heroine, if it is stated that she rather enjoyed being mistress and manager. She was too thorough a woman not to enjoy household work. To obtain the nicest and freshest goods at the most moderate price—to bestow a look of comfort and prettiness on the rooms which her little party occupied—to save some trifle in essentials to expend on ornament, these were her ambitions; and although Bell considered her a fidget, and John was only half alive to the results of her exertions, the success was its own reward.

"I wish," she thought, "I might be housekeeper to John. I might civilise him a little, and be tolerably useful; but of course, it would not be proper."

For habit works wonders, and though John was still very dreadful in many ways, the keenness of her first impression had worn off; especially as she felt that, however familiar, even to disrespect, he might be, her opinions always had a certain weight with him. What most revolted her was his irrepressible purse-pride—his obtrusive consciousness of success. Still she was very thankful he had kept her in London, and as soon as the business connected with the auction was over she would write her advertisement and set to work for herself.

The first day at her disposal, she set forth to ascertain from Mr. Dunsford if he had heard from Mrs. Berry, as she had firmly believed that lady would have written to her before this; and she feared her poor friend's evil days had begun, even sooner than she had anticipated.

On this occasion, however, Maggie determined to dispense with Cousin John's escort, and therefore permitted him to depart without mentioning her intentions. Breakfast had been to his liking, and he lit the short pipe he persisted in smoking, in great good humour.

"Now, girls, I must say I think you have done capital, so far, and not asked for much money either. Have tea half an hour earlier, and I'll take you to the Princess's. We can walk there and back too; and I say, Bell, you are in great luck, for I daresay you've done precious little towards the general good."

"Yes, indeed she has;" cried Maggie, vexed that John should mortify his sister. "Our work and success is a joint-stock concern, only, we hope, unlimited."

"You are a brick, Maggie! I always said so, and now I wouldn't mind giving you a kiss in token of my brotherly approbation."

"No, thank you. Not when you are smoking, certainly"—in a displeased tone.

"Of all the stand-off little devils I ever met, Mag, you are the stand-offest! Here, Bell! brush my hat, will you?"

As Maggie communed with herself—for this can be accomplished amid the rattle of an omnibus as well as in the stillness of one's own chamber—she felt how ardently she longed to escape from her present surroundings. "If," she thought, "I could find some nice old lady in delicate health, who would grow fond of me, and confide her early griefs and trials to me, how delightful it would be! Or two or three sweet little girls, somewhere in the country, with a charming sensible mamma!" so ran her reveries; for with all her practicality in action Maggie was an imaginative romantic little goose in many ways; and the prospect of having some one to lavish affection upon was too delightful to be put out of sight altogether. "I wonder," began her brain afresh, "if Mr. Trafford remembered to mention me to Lady Torchester. I think he would remember a promise; but I am glad she never wrote; I do not want to have anything more to do with great people. Yet, oh! how glad I should be to see Lord Torchester! What a nice, honest, kind creature he was! How could I have ever thought him like Cousin John? He was so modest and simple. What *would* John be were he as great a personage as Lord Torchester? But then everything would be different. How rough and presumptuous *he* is! Had I been a princess Mr. Trafford could not have been more deferential to me; but he is unlike every one else, and I must not think of him."

"Lady for St. Paul's Churchyard," said the conductor, and Maggie got out.

Mr. Dunsford was in, and received her at once this time. He had heard from Mrs. Berry, or Madame de Bragance, and a very unsatis-factory letter she had written. She stiffly announced her marriage, and directed Mr. Dunsford to sell out a thousand pounds India Railway Stock, as M. de Bragance had a better investment for it; and moreover, ordered that all stocks standing in her name should be changed into that of de Bragance. She had written from Florence, and on Mr. Dunsford writing to remonstrate with her, she had replied by a sharp and decided dismissal. She further directed that his account should be sent in, and all her papers, &c., handed over to another solicitor, named in her. letter, &c. Mr. Dunsford was even now engaged in the operation, and so cross under the infliction, that poor Maggie dared not fulfil her intention of asking him if it was now time to advertise; so she soon retreated, much mortified to find that Madame de Bragance had not even mentioned her name.

As she walked along, sad enough, she was startled by a strong grasp laid upon her shoulder; turning, she looked into Cousin John's eyes.

"Why, what the deuce are you scheming after, Madame Mag?" cried he, drawing her hand through his arm and squeezing it close to his side. "You never told me a word of your intending to visit the City. Where have you been?"

"To Mr. Dunsford's," returned Maggie, considerably annoyed at this encounter. "I did not tell you, because I knew it would only waste your time to come with me.".

"Look here," said John. "I have cleared off my morning's work, and I'll just go straight back with you. We'll take a Piccadilly bus, get out at Hyde Park Corner, and have a walk in the park. We'll be as jolly as sand-boys; come along;" and John's face, so far as it was visible through the red hair that encumbered it, shone with glee.

It was a clear bright day, crisp with the first faint frostiness that sometimes tinges the days of September, and yet, though considerably liable to skyey influences, Maggie could not raise her spirits. The feeling of her own helplessness and isolation pressed heavily upon her, and John's jovial patronage and cousinly familiarity humiliated her unreasonably.

The park was empty, of course; a rare equestrian or two dotted the row, and decided John as to the direction they should take.

"Come along, Mag, we will have a look at the horses. I used to stick on pretty well myself, at the Cape, and I know a good horse when I see one, *I* can tell you. I took to riding quite natural. Do you think you would have pluck enough to mount a horse, Maggie?"

"Yes, of course I should, if it was quiet," said Maggie, her thoughts flying back to the last proposition respecting horse exercise that had been made to her.

John talked on of his own exploits, and how he had ridden to this station and the other kraal. He laughed at some of the stout old 'buffers' who were pounding along for exercise conscientiously on powerful cobs, bearing strong resemblance to their riders. At last, he exclaimed, 'There, that fellow sticks on capital.'

The man he remarked had already caught Maggie's attention. He was mounted on a large handsome chestnut, which appeared possessed of the bad temper with which chestnuts are generally credited. But the fiery animal had met his master. In vain he plunged, and reared, and bolted, his rider sat unmoved; and finally horse and horseman disappeared at a gallop.

Although the rider's back had been to them, there was something familiar to Maggie's eye in his figure and carriage, nay, even in the back of his hat; for, let sceptics scoff if they will, there *is* individuality even in the back of a·man's hat.

"I fancy he has learnt to ride in some of the colonies," said John.

" I am sure he has not," returned Maggie, somewhat aggressively.

" Why, I would like to know ? "

" Oh, I cannot tell ; only he is so well dressed, and looks like a gentleman."

" Do you know, Mag, though you keep it to yourself, I begin to think you are a conceited monkey ? Why shouldn't gentlemen go to the colonies—and come out of them too ? "

" Of course they may. I know nothing about it."

" What has vexed you ? I think you are a trifle cantankerous."

" I don't intend to be so. Perhaps I am a little put out, because Mrs. Berry never mentioned me in her letter, not once ; and it *is* sad to be forgotten."

" Pooh ! " replied John. " Don't you fret about that old cat ; there are better people left to care for you. Where is she ? "

Maggie told him all she had learned from Mr. Dunsford, as they strolled slowly along ; and John made uncomplimentary comments, and Maggie still felt and seemed dull.

" Come," said John, at last, " you are in the dolefuls ; here, take my arm, and we'll cut away home, for you have made those lodgings uncommon like home. You take my arm—you must," and Maggie's reluctant little hand was drawn through his arm once more. " It's rather cool here ; you can't think how delightful it is just now at the Cape, mild, and bright, and——stop ! here is the chestnut again—quiet enough now."

It *was* the chestnut, pacing soberly along, and followed by a smart groom on a brown horse, older and graver than that which bore his master. As the chestnut approached, his rider guided him across to where the cousins stood. Maggie felt for an instant as if giddy and in the dark, as she recognised Geoffrey Trafford. He dismounted quickly and threw the rein to his servant, then, raising his hat, stood before her and took the hand she hesitatingly held out.

" I had no idea you were in town, Miss Grey," said the dear, well-known voice, so clear, refined, and yet commanding, with its indescribable, high-bred ring. " When did you arrive?"

"Oh ! about two months ago," said Maggie, gathering up her forces, and making a grand successful effort for composure and self-control. " Mrs. Berry left Paris about ten days after you did."

" Indeed, and are you still with her ?"

" No," a smile and shake of the head, " she is married."

" To that card-playing fellow, de Bragance ? "

" Yes."

" Ah ! poor woman, what a 'finale ! And where are you ? " looking keenly into her soft eyes, his own softening as he looked.

" I am with my uncle, that is, with my cousins."

" Ah ! " a sharp inquisitive glance at her companion.

T 2

"This is my cousin John, of whom you have heard me speak," said Maggie observing it, and colouring vividly, though becomingly.

"Indeed," said Trafford, raising his hat as though presented to a prince. Cousin John instinctively touched his, intending to raise it, but stopping short produced an ungraceful effect.

"I have then to congratulate you on his return," continued Trafford gravely.

"Yes, Mag and I are fast friends," said John, patronisingly, and with agonising familiarity, quite elated, or rather confirmed in his estimate of his own importance by this mention of him by Maggie. "Were you ever at the Cape, sir? You stuck to that beast of yours as if you had learned to ride in the colonies."

"I was there for a few months once," replied Trafford courteously, "but I always thought England the best school for riding," and while he spoke to John, he looked at his companion—looked earnestly and interrogatively. She felt utterly and unspeakably miserable. To see Trafford, tall, slight, distinguished, in his admirably fitting and perfect morning dress, worn so easily; his careless grace of manner, that bearing as though the cream of life had always been his. And then to look at John, tall too, but lumbering and heavy, with the ends of his blue tie flying loose, and the brown patches of his trousers distractingly visible! His rough untutored red hair, and profuse beard, his great red hands innocent of gloves, his bumptious air, his appalling low crowned hat! The contrast was too dreadful; and then, when he said, with an unmistakable air of proprietorship, "Take my arm, Mag," she felt she must obey, that she would not, could not, seem to slight him then, though he was deepening "full many a fathom" the great gulf already fixed between her and such as Trafford. "Do not let me keep you standing," said that gentleman, "I will turn with you, if you will allow me," beckoning to his groom to follow; and so Maggie walked on as if in a dream, her hand held tightly against John's ribs, and Trafford at the other side of her. "Do you stay long in town, Miss Grey?"

"I do not know, I am rather unsettled at present."

"Good God!" thought Trafford, "going to marry this ourang-outang. What creatures women are!" But he only said, "I fancy London does not suit you so well as Paris; you are not looking so bright as I remember you, at the ball for instance." This bit of irrepressible malice was intended for "Cousin John."

Maggie gathered spirit enough to look up at him with something of her old smile, saying "Ball dress and looks you know are not to be worn every day. But you look very much better than when last I saw you."

"I have been away on the moors, which suits me, and have just come up from Mount Trafford, where I have been staying with

Torchester. By the way, why did you never answer Lady Torchester's letter ?"

"Lady Torchester's letter! I never received one, never!"

"That's a nuisance. I know my aunt wrote to you, and I rather fancied you must have left Paris, as she received no reply; but were your letters not forwarded ?"

"My letters—no, indeed. I never thought of giving any directions about them. I never had any except from my cousins, and I was going to see them."

"I was vexed, however, that you and Lady Torchester did not become acquainted. Will you write to her now and say you never had her letter ?"

"Oh no! I couldn't," said Maggie, shrinking from such an undertaking, and mournfully but proudly determined to renounce all intercourse with people so far out of her reach.

"As you like," said Trafford coldly, considering this embarrassed refusal another infallible token of her engagement to the "ourang."

"And who may Lady Torchester be ?" asked John, with an air of authority. "I never heard of her before."

"She is Mr. Trafford's aunt, and he was good enough to think she might be of some use to me," said Maggie with great steadiness, but breaking off suddenly.

"Oh! I see," said John. "Fact is, sir," to Trafford, "this is such an independent piece of goods, she can't rest in her uncle's house, where she is like a daughter. But I think she'll find the best sort of independence in the colonies, eh!" and he winked knowingly at Trafford, the aristocratic, fastidious Trafford, as if they thoroughly understood each other. Maggie's misery and confusion were crowned by perceiving this triumphant indication; but she was too overwhelmed to utter a word. It speaks highly for the moral restraints of civilised life that Trafford, instead of then and there pouncing on Cousin John, tearing Maggie from him, and carrying her off bodily on the fiery chestnut, only smiled rather grimly, and said, "At all events, life is freer everywhere than in England;" but it was more than he could endure. Maggie too, who at first sight he thought looking pale and sad, had, between annoyance and embarrassment, gained a brilliant colour; she was evidently quite content, and it was all infernally disgusting; so with an imperious gesture he called up his groom, and bowing somewhat haughtily, he said to Maggie, "I must say good morning, Miss Grey. Torchester will be pleased to hear of you. He and I start the day after to-morrow for St. Petersburg, with very vague ulterior intentions; I must not therefore venture to say *au revoir*."

"Good-bye, then," said Maggie, simply, not offering her hand, as he seemed inclined to be satisfied with his own lofty salutation; but there was a sadness in her voice that made him hesitate a moment and long to say good-bye kindly; it was scarce a moment, and he mounted his horse, raised his hat once more, and then rode rapidly away—rapidly and more rapidly still, while his groom wondered where the "dickens" his master was going. Away up the Edgeware Road, threading in and out through vans and carriages and obstructive omnibuses — past Kilburn, and away into the open country, raging against himself for the idiotic weakness which permitted this brown-haired simple girl so to entwine herself with his heart, or his fancy, or his passions, or whatever was the source of the maddening irritation he felt, against her and himself, and that brute, her cousin, and the world in general, with its absurd bondage of social distinction. What an unpardonable little traitor she was, to think of such desecration as to give her sweet dainty self to this ourang! What undiscriminating dolls women are! Yet what was it all to him? What right had he to expect anything from her? Even if she was his, and all difficulties surmounted by his resolution to gratify an overwhelming whim, would he not feel that it had cost him too dear? This very cousin, how would he like to have him at dinner? Trafford was too well and safely placed to care with whom he was *seen* in public; it was from personal intercourse he shrank; and the very sincerity and loyalty he loved in Maggie would make her cling to everyone who had ever been kind to her. But could she, with her innate good taste, her quick sympathies, her graceful, instinctive appreciation of everything that was noble and beautiful in art, could she absolutely take this clown 'for better, for worse'? Oh! it was too degrading! "And," Trafford thought, "I fancied I had nearly cured myself of this folly. Well, she will finish the cure now. I can never again think of a girl who could be content with such a fate. Yet, poor lonely child! the world is a hard place for her to battle through; and after all, it is not unnatural that she should give herself where she finds help and shelter—something more real than the sympathy and appreciation which, nevertheless, left her to Mrs. Berry's vagaries and her aunt's brutality. That Cousin John does not look like a brute, rugged as he is. There's an honest and not unkindly expression in the dog's eye; so I suppose it's all for the best, and there's an end of it." Arriving at this satisfactory conclusion, he drove the spurs into his horse's sides, and gave him another breather for a mile or so; and then, pulling up, remarked calmly to his groom, "I think I tamed the chestnut tolerably, Rogers?"

"Yes, sir, I think you have," returned the man, somewhat breathless from following after.

"Whereabouts are we?"

"Somewhere near the *Welsh Harp*, sir."

Meantime, Cousin John and Maggie had quickened their pace as Trafford rode away. "Why, that's no end of a swell, and no mistake! Where did you meet him, Mag?" asked John.

"Oh! in Paris, with Mrs. Berry," replied Maggie, listening to her own voice as if somebody else was speaking, and appalled at the black desolation that seemed to settle down upon her heart, as Trafford's cold look of disdain remained fixed upon her vision.

"How did she come across him? Now, why didn't she set her cap at him, instead of that beggarly Frenchman?"

"Because—because—even she never thought of such a thing. It was so utterly out of the question."

"Then what was he after? You? Ay! you are a little trump. So you told him you had a cousin John, away seeking his fortune, that you kept a corner of your heart for? Quite right, Mag! nothing like being honest and open."

"I wish you wouldn't talk, John, I have a headache. I never told Mr. Trafford anything of the kind. I said you had been very good to me when I was almost a child—and—oh! I don't know what."

"Well, there, I'll not bother you. You'll tell me all about it by-and-by. Come along, we'll have a cup of tea and be off to the theatre. There's the 'Overland Route,' a capital play, and that will put you all to rights." So spake John, giving himself credit for both prudence and magnanimity while he reflected: "I'm not so sure I can afford a wife this year; but at any rate I see it's all safe here, so I'll not bother Mag till we can go straight away to church."

Everything was cloudy and unreal to Maggie that wretched night. She was utterly humiliated in her own eyes, to think that she should have been so shaken and upset by meeting that proud, haughty Mr. Trafford. How different from what he was in Paris! No, she would not write to Lady Torchester; she would have no more to do with the Traffords. And John, how detestable John had made himself! How conceited, how patronising! Come what might, she would advertise to morrow, and take the first thing that offered; even a happy home with an evangelical lady, nine small children, and no salary.

The visit to the theatre was a great relief; Maggie was carried away from self by the scenery and the fun. She laughed and she cried, and was altogether so charming in the sort of recklessness with which she snatched the little bit of enjoyment that obliterated for a while the sharp pain of memory, that John found it rather hard to stick to his own programme.

Supper was finished, and John's feelings did not prevent him from doing ample justice to it. Maggie and Bell had said good-night, and begun to ascend the stairs to their loftily placed dormitory, when John was heard calling authoritatively, "Mag! come back I say! I want you."

"What is it?" she asked, returning, while Bell continued to ascend.

"Are you going off without saying good-night, after our nice long walk to-day?"

" But I have. I have said good-night this moment."

"I want a better good-night than that!" and he threw his arms round her; but she repulsed him with a vehemence and passion that astonished him.

"I will not and cannot kiss you," she cried. "If I want to kiss you I will do it of my own accord; but if you dare to kiss me against my will, you shall repent it bitterly," and bursting into an agony of tears, she ran hastily out of the room.

"Phew!" whistled John, throwing himself into the only arm-chair. "Now what was all that for? She can't really object to kiss me. What humbugs these girls are!"

## CHAPTER XIX.

MAGGIE felt a little uneasy at meeting John after this ebullition, though she considered it quite justifiable; but he entrenched himself in an air of business and preoccupation, intending, he told himself, to let her come to her senses. So he departed in peace after breakfast, and it was not till evening that Maggie found time to plan out her advertisement, which she was quite resolved should not be delayed another day.

Tea was over. John was apparently absorbed in the City article of the *Times*—for the day of penny papers had only begun to dawn—and Bell was yawning over some needlework, when Maggie placed her writing things on the table very quietly, and, as she thought, unobserved. She was soon absorbed in the difficulties of her task, and grew absolutely nervous over it. What would she not have given for a few words of counsel with dear kind Uncle Gray?

" What are you about now, Mag?" asked Cousin John, so suddenly that she started.

"Trying to write an advertisement," she answered promptly, and laughing rather nervously. John stood up, stirred the fire, and then continued standing on the hearth-rug magisterially.

"Now, ain't you a foolish positive girl, to be bothering about an advertisement and wasting your money, when you've the governor's house to put up in till better times? I'm really vexed with you."

"And why?" urged Maggie gently. "You know I have no right to impose myself on Uncle Gray when I can earn anything for myself; and as to the better times, why should I not work while waiting for them as well as idle? I can accept fortune wherever it finds me."

John rumpled his hair and seemed to think profoundly as he played with his watch-chain. "Well," said he at last, "there is some truth in that; so advertise away in God's name—only, if you change your mind, remember my father's house is nearly as much mine as his, and if I say you shall be welcome there, you shall. Now what have you written?"

"Law, Maggie! what have you put?" cried Bell, laying down her work.

"I am very stupid about it," said Maggie, blushing, "Will this do?—'As companion to an elderly lady, or governess to young children. A young lady who can speak and read French and teach music. A moderate salary.'"

"Bosh!" growled John. "You would be just as likely to get an immoderate salary, if you asked it, and be a deuced deal more thought of into the bargain. And why don't you say you are a smart accountant?—it's altogether a washy concern—put a little more 'go' into it, can't you?"

"It is very hard to know how to put it. I wish my uncle was here."

"Well, I flatter myself I can advise you as well, if not better than the poor governor, only you like him better—eh, Mag?"

"I do," replied Maggie ruthlessly, "of course I do."

"Well, you are an ungrateful little toad!" cried John energetically, "and I'll be hanged if I take any more trouble about you. Didn't I stand to you stouter by long chalks than ever the governor did? He might cry over you in private, but he'd never prevent the missus from wiping her shoes on you. Wasn't I going over to Paris just to see you? and didn't I keep you in town because I saw you were breaking your heart about leaving? Don't I do all I can for you every way? And yet if a fellow asks for a kiss, you fly at him as if he was dirt under your feet! What is it you don't like in me? Just speak out."

"I am not ungrateful," said Maggie, frightened at this rough outbreak, and trying hard to keep back her tears, conscious that she did not feel towards John quite as she ought. "I am fond of you, and you see I *did* think of you and speak of you when you were away" (dexterously recalling Trafford's soothing remarks); "but what I don't like in you is, that you think so much of yourself, and make little of your father, who is so simple and high-minded, and"——

"And pray why shouldn't I think well of myself?" interrupted John, still angry, but mollified. "Haven't I got on where another would have starved? Haven't I worked hard and lived hard? And now am I spending the fruits of my work on myself? Do I act as if I didn't care for my father? I show what I feel, without pretending to think that because he is my father he must be a wiseacre. He *is* a good fellow, but he is a d——d sight too soft to be of much use. But nothing will please *you* that isn't a gentleman, a swell, like what we saw yesterday. I didn't think you would let such nonsense turn you against an old friend, ay! and a true friend."

Maggie's heart beat fast. She knew there was truth in all John said, and she also felt that there was truth in her objections to him, only she could not express her meaning, and if she did, it would do no

good. Moreover, like a true woman, she was intimidated by the force
and vigour of a man's anger. So, wisely declining the contest, she
exclaimed, "You are angry and unreasonable, and I will go away."
She was hastily putting her writing things together, and shaken as
she had been by the event of yesterday and a somewhat sleepless
night, she could *not* keep back the tears. They dropped visibly on her
portfolio.

"I'll be hanged if you go like this!" cried John, interposing himself between her and the door. "You have riled me till I spoke
rough, and now I'll not let you go till we are friends. I am sorry
I vexed you, Mag—come, will you say as much?"

But Maggie couldn't say anything. She sat down and covered
her face with her hands, while she struggled to resist a hysterical fit
of weeping. John was somewhat puzzled at this utter break-down,
and attributed it to her sorrow at having angered him. He little
knew its complicated causes. There were the remains of yesterday's
agitation; there was the painful feeling of having vexed her true
friend—the shame of knowing she would at that moment like to banish
him for ever from her sight; there was the unspeakable dread that he
had penetrated her secret weakness and folly; and, lastly, that awful
sensation of being misunderstood and alone, which must madden if it
lasts.

"Don't take on so, Mag! I say, Mag, I am ever so sorry I spoke
hard."

"And I am sorry I vexed you—that you misunderstood me," said
Maggie at last in a trembling voice. "Some day you will know me
better. And now I am tired and stupid; I will go to bed."

"Well, we are friends again," said John earnestly, holding out his
hand.

"Oh, yes, I hope always."

"Now, then, I will not offer to take a kiss, but give me one of your
own accord, as you said last night."

"I will, Cousin John," said Maggie with sad humility, and so stood
up on tiptoe and gave him a little refrigerated kiss.

But John was no nice observer. He had got what he wanted, and
giving his fair cousin an elephantine pat on the shoulder, told her to
go to bed, sleep sound, and be as right as a trivet in the morning.

The morning, however, brought with it a mighty change. The
post, in addition to John's letters, had one for "Miss Grey," which
Bell claimed and opened, but soon renounced: "It must be for you,
Maggie." And it was. As Maggie turned over the paper a slip of
newspaper fell out. She picked it up, and then with sparkling eyes
cried, "Listen to this, John!"

"'Miss Dunsford's compliments to Miss Grey, and begs to forward
her the enclosed advertisement cut from this morning's *Times*. No time

should be lost in applying, and Miss D. hopes it may prove suitable.' The advertisement is from yesterday's paper. 'Female amanuensis or secretary wanted by a lady of literary pursuits. Clear handwriting and a thorough knowledge of English required; also a person sufficiently well-bred to associate with her employer. Good references expected. A comfortable home and liberal salary will be given.'"

"There's a go, by Jupiter!" cried John. "Let's have a look," and he caught the slip of newspaper out of Maggie's hand. "'Apply personally, between twelve and one o'clock to-morrow and Thursday, at No. 63, Hamilton Terrace, St. John's Wood.' That's to-day. You go in and win, Mag; I'll not interfere."

"But," said Maggie between hope and fear, "I am afraid I am not clever enough for such a great lady as this must be, and I am sure I have not a thorough knowledge of English; but I will certainly try."

"Who can it be?" wondered Bell. "Perhaps Mrs. S. C. Hall—or the authoress of 'Emilia Wyndham.'"

"How delightful that would be!" cried Maggie.

"I wonder what they consider a liberal salary?" said John. "Thirty pounds a year?"

"And so it would be—very liberal," replied Maggie. "Seven pounds ten a quarter—nearly as much as I got for a whole year from Mrs. Berry."

"She was a frightful screw," remarked John. "Now mind, Maggie, you do not close with anything till you consult me."

"I will not, indeed," cried Maggie, eager to be friends again, especially as she began to hope there might be a way to escape.

It was with the utmost doubt and diffidence that Maggie arrayed herself in her very best garments for this tremendous undertaking. She dared not hope for success, and she dared not contemplate failure; her fortunes seemed at a low ebb; and she revolved the advertisement over and over in her mind during her long lonely walk to Hamilton Terrace.

On arriving there she found it was a lady's school, evidently of high pretensions. She was ushered into an uncarpeted room looking into the garden, where, to her dismay, she found already assembled ten other applicants; some of whom were writing at a table, whereon a goodly display of writing materials were set forth.

"Will you please to write down your name and address, and references, and anything else you like," said the servant; "I will come back in a few minutes, and take in the papers to Miss Colby." And gathering up some papers already written, she departed.

Maggie glanced at her rivals. There were a couple of neat fresh-looking girls, but the majority were severe, elderly, iron-grey females, not at all refined or prepossessing in appearance, "though, no doubt," thought Maggie, "miracles of ability in all matters connected with pens, ink, and paper." She sat down, however, and tried hard to write as prettily and clearly as possible, her short statement. The result was that she thought she had never written so badly. It was finished long before the servant returned, and when she did she summoned one of the grisly females to an interview.

Hours seemed to have elapsed, and two or three more ladies were called away, before the smart servant came back once more, and looking uncertainly round, said " Miss Grey."

Maggie rose at once and followed her, trembling.

In what seemed to Maggie a gorgeous drawing-room, overflowing with Berlin woolwork, vases of wax flowers and richly-gilt albums, and hung round with hazy water-colour and pencil sketches, sat the arbiter of her fortunes, enthroned in state. She was a small, stout woman, with wide-awake spectacles, a broad eager-looking face, an elaborate cap of fine lace, and a substantial brown silk dress; a small table beside her was heaped with letters and papers.

" Well," she said querulously, but not uncivilly, " I am sure I hope you will suit, for I am nearly worn out. A—Miss Grey, I see you only left the lady you mention here because she married. I suppose this Mr. Dunsford will vouch for this?"

" He will. He has permitted me to apply to him because Mrs. Berry, I mean Madame de Bragance, is moving about on the Continent. I scarcely know where to apply to her."

After a few more queries as to her antecedents, Miss Colby plunged into a description of the splendour of the appointment of which she had the disposal. " The work would be entirely literary," she said; " accounts, and that sort of thing, would not be in the least required. The lady is young, nobly-born, and very wealthy; a most charming person—a former pupil of my own—of high literary and artistic taste, and indeed genius, but she finds it difficult to keep up society and—study, writing, and all that. She therefore requires a tolerably well-educated young person to copy compositions, to follow up ideas, and be generally useful with the pen. Do you think yourself equal to undertake this?"

" I am afraid to say much," replied Maggie, colouring; " but I am diligent, very glad to be useful, and though I think I can write tolerable English, a lady such as you describe could only want me to copy, not to originate."

" Still a proper knowledge is essential; but you probably have it. Now I will keep your address, and let you go, for I have a number more people to see. I will write to you in any case in a few days—oh! I forgot to mention the salary is sixty pounds a year. You would have (in the country) your own sitting-room, but I fancy you would not live with the family. Good morning."

And Maggie was dismissed.

As she walked back she tried hard to dismiss all hope from her heart. It was altogether such a golden chance, she feared it could not be for her. Some all-accomplished mistress of the English tongue would appear to-morrow, and be chosen forthwith. Maggie only hoped Miss Colby would remember her promise and write, to put her out of pain.

"Well, Mag," cried John, as he sat down to tea that evening, "what luck? Got the place?"

"No!" said Maggie, shaking her head, "only not quite rejected."

"Come, tell us all about it," said John.

And Maggie did.

"Hum!" said the family mentor, when she ceased. "I don't think much of it. This rich young lady will be marrying, as your widow did, and then you will be adrift again."

"Still I will gladly take it if I have the chance."

"I suppose you will; and when another marriage knocks you on the head you will be obliged to marry, in self-defence, yourself, eh, Mag?"

"Sufficient to the day is the evil thereof," said Maggie, laughing.

\* \* \* \* \* \*

Four days went over, and still no communication reached our young waiter on Providence.

"Had I not better give it up, and put in my own advertisement?" she asked earnestly of Cousin John.

"No! hang it, no! Wait a day or two longer before you throw away any money on it. Look here, I am going to run down to Ditton Market to-night, just to see what the governor's doing. I'll be back late to-morrow. Wait till I come back, and then we will see what's to be done."

"Very well, John."

"And just see my things put in the bag, like a good girl. I say! you've been as good as gold ever since I gave you that blowing-up the other night. Ah! 'A woman, a spaniel, and a walnut-tree, the more you lick them '—eh, Mag?"

"You are a heretic and a Turk! Remember I have never withdrawn my accusations against you."

"Pooh! if you can say no worse than that—I am not a sentimental chap—I don't care."

The day John left, was diversified by a stiff breeze with Bell. The agreeable Fred Banks called, and offered to take her and Maggie to a promenade concert. Maggie declined, and Bell was deeply indignant, and spoke some sharp and insulting words, which she afterwards tried rather abjectly to recall, having the fear of John before her eyes.

Tuesday morning was dull and raw; and though the absent John had made himself peculiarly obnoxious of late, Maggie confessed to herself that he was preferable to Bell alone and in the sulks. But all reflection and meditation were put to flight, by the receipt at the twelve o'clock delivery of a note for " Miss M. Grey."

Miss Colby presented her compliments, and requested Miss Grey, if still disengaged, to call as soon as possible after the receipt of this.

" Dear, dear! you have got the place, I am certain. What luck, Maggie!" cried Bell.

" I really begin to hope it," said Maggie, preparing for her expedition, and feeling "all of a tremble," as sensitive ladies term it.

On this occasion, our heroine indulged in an omnibus to a point near Hamilton Terrace, and found the redoubtable Miss Colby attired in out-door dress, evidently waiting for her.

" I am so glad you have come at last, for there is a good deal to arrange, and I must go out. Your reference to Mr. Dunsford is satisfactory, and Miss Grantham has decided to try you for three months, at all events. She wants you down as soon as possible. Can you go on Thursday?"

" Where?" asked Maggie, quite dazed with the rapidity of Miss Colby's conclusions and communications.

." Why, to Grantham. They will be there till after Christmas. It is in Limeshire, near Castleford—a beautiful country."

" This is Tuesday. Do you not think the lady might allow me till Saturday? I have a few preparations to make, and it would be a great accommodation if I could stay till Saturday."

" I really am afraid to take upon me to say," and Miss Colby looked puzzled and vexed. " She says," taking up a note with an elaborate monogram, and covered with large straight writing, " she says, ' send this young lady down to me at once. I am standing still in every sense : nothing to do and no one to see.' "

" Still," urged Maggie, a little appalled at the seeming magnitude of the work which awaited her, " I should like to stay till Saturday, if Miss—Grantham, I think you said?—will permit."

" I tell you what; I'll telegraph and beg her to telegraph back to you direct. That will show a proper attention to her wishes. Then if she says you must go on Thursday, you must. We will drive to the telegraph-office, and then you can return home. I have to go out to pay calls to-day."

" But," said Maggie, feeling her heart beat at the tremendous importance of her new mistress, " will you not be so kind as to give me some idea of my duties—my work?"

" I have not an idea myself. I only know what Miss Grantham wrote. You will soon find out. Miss Grantham is most kind and generous—a little peculiar—and if you make yourself useful and obliging it may be a great hit for you. The carriage, I suppose," to the smart servant who opened the door at that moment. " Come then, Miss Grey. Oh, I forgot, Miss Grantham desired me to pay your travelling expenses. It is a long journey, and you *must* go first class. So I daresay, with cabs and that, it will cost nearly three pounds. There are three sovereigns, and full directions in this envelope. Come now, we will drive to the telegraph-office."

Maggie returned to Bell, morally breathless, and was subjected to a severe cross-examination—what she said, and what Maggie said, and what Miss Grantham's note looked like, et cetera, et cetera; and then, with the full consciousness that she had quantities to do, Maggie sat down on the horse-hair sofa in their little sitting-room, and began to dream of the new future opening before her. How tenderly she remembered poor Mrs. Berry, fanciful and selfish and provoking as she was! She never could have the same feeling of equality and "at-homeishness" with this great high and mighty Miss Grantham. Her life in Germany and Paris, dear, delightful Paris—ah! all that must be forgotten!

But she roused herself at last, and set diligently to work to turn out and arrange her belongings.

Time flew on, and as she settled herself to work, after a late tea, a sharp knock at the front door was followed by the entrance of the servant, with a mysterious yellow envelope. "Oh, the telegram!" exclaimed Maggie. "It is short enough: 'Saturday will do; come down by the 2 P.M. train.' I am so glad I need not hurry away on Thursday."

"And what in the world shall I do all alone here with John?" asked Bell in some dismay.

"Oh, just do your best! He is not so hard after all."

"You don't know what he was till you came."

The object of Bell's terrors, true to his appointment, returned to a late supper that night. The weather was raw and cold, so Maggie took care to have a nice bright fire, with a kettle singing beside it, an appetising little repast, and all things in readiness for the formidable John.

"Well, girls, how have you got on without me? By George, this is nice and comfortable! I declare it's worth while to go away to find such cosiness when you come back," cried John, when he had got off his overcoat and muffler. He was in high good humour; all things looked promising at the new Dorado. "You can't think how the governor's come out—quite sharpened up. I believe we'll make a man of business of him at last. He says he'll be very glad of your help, Mag, with the books—and, eh?"——

For Maggie murmured, "Oh, John!"

"She's going away to this grand literary lady on Saturday," cried Bell.

"Gone and engaged yourself while I was away!" shouted John, indignant.

"But I thought we agreed I had better take the chance, if I got it?"

"Yes, but to go absolutely and fix it, without consulting any one, was coming it rather strong. And how about references?"

"Oh, they are quite satisfied with Mr. Dunsford's, I know!"

"But you—have you had no reference?"

"*I?* I never dreamed of such a thing."

"Well, you ought," replied John sternly. "How do you know this Miss Grantham may not be an impostor? How do you know you are not going into some disreputable place?"

"Oh, John! you would never think of such a thing if you had heard Miss Colby speak. She says this lady is nobly born, and wealthy, and "——

"She might *say* anything. It's our business to prove it. I will see Dunsford about it to-morrow."

"I am sure it is all right," cried Maggie, dreading that the chance of independence and escape might be wrenched from her; for Cousin John did not seem at all willing to let her go.

"Well, I'll *make* sure, I can tell you," said John, significantly.

\* \* \* \* \* \*

And he did; but all his researches proved satisfactory. There was a residence called Grantham, near Castleford. It did belong to a lady of the same name, a personage of importance, who had livings in her gift and a small borough on her estates. So John had nothing for it but to give up his cousin, of whom he longed to make a petted slave, and let her escape into the higher atmosphere of personal liberty.

# TEMPLE BAR.

### FEBRUARY 1873.

## The New Magdalen.

### By WILKIE COLLINS.

### Chapter XVI.

#### THEY MEET AGAIN.

ABSORBED in herself, Mercy failed to notice the opening door or to hear the murmur of voices in the conservatory.

The one terrible necessity which had been present to her mind at intervals for a week past, was confronting her at that moment. She owed to Grace Roseberry the tardy justice of owning the truth. The longer her confession was delayed, the more cruelly she was injuring the woman whom she had robbed of her identity—the friendless woman who had neither witnesses nor papers to produce, who was powerless to right her own wrong. Keenly as she felt this, Mercy failed nevertheless to conquer the horror that shook her when she thought of the impending avowal. Day followed day, and still she shrank from the unendurable ordeal of confession—as she was shrinking from it now!

Was it fear for herself that closed her lips?

She trembled—as any human being in her place must have trembled —at the bare idea of finding herself thrown back again on the world, which had no place in it and no hope in it for *her*. But she could have overcome that terror—she could have resigned herself to that doom.

No! it was not the fear of the confession itself, or the fear of the consequences which must follow it, that still held her silent. The horror that daunted her was the horror of owning to Horace and to Lady Janet that she had cheated them out of their love.

Every day, Lady Janet was kinder and kinder. Every day, Horace was fonder and fonder of her. How could she confess to Lady Janet? how could she own to Horace, that she had imposed upon him? " I can't do it. They are so good to me—I can't do it !" In that hopeless way it had ended during the seven days that had gone by. In that hopeless way it ended again now.

The murmur of the two voices at the further end of the conservatory ceased. The billiard-room door opened again slowly, by an inch at a time.

Mercy still kept her place, unconscious of the events that were passing round her. Sinking under the hard stress laid on it, her mind had drifted little by little into a new train of thought. For the first time, she found the courage to question the future in a new way. Supposing her confession to have been made, or supposing the woman whom she had personated to have discovered the means of exposing the fraud, what advantage, she now asked herself, would Miss Roseberry derive from Mercy Merrick's disgrace?

Could Lady Janet transfer to the woman who was really her relative by marriage the affection which she had given to the woman who had pretended to be her relative? No! All the right in the world would not put the true Grace into the false Grace's vacant place. The qualities by which Mercy had won Lady Janet's love were the qualities which were Mercy's own. Lady Janet could do rigid justice —but hers was not the heart to give itself to a stranger (and to give itself unreservedly) a second time. Grace Roseberry would be formally acknowledged—and there it would end.

Was there hope in this new view?

Yes! There was the false hope of making the inevitable atonement by some other means than by the confession of the fraud.

What had Grace Roseberry actually lost by the wrong done to her? She had lost the salary of Lady Janet's "companion and reader." Say that she wanted money, Mercy had her savings from the generous allowance made to her by Lady Janet; Mercy could offer money. Or say that she wanted employment, Mercy's interest with Lady Janet could offer employment, could offer anything Grace might ask for, if she would only come to terms.

Invigorated by the new hope, Mercy rose excitedly, weary of inaction in the empty room. She, who but a few minutes since, had shuddered at the thought of their meeting again, was now eager to devise a means of finding her way privately to an interview with Grace. It should be done without loss of time—on that very day, if possible; by the next day at latest. She looked round her mechanically, pondering how to reach the end in view. Her eyes rested by chance on the door of the billiard-room.

Was it fancy? or did she really see the door first open a little—then suddenly and softly close again?

Was it fancy? or did she really hear, at the same moment, a sound behind her as of persons speaking in the conservatory?

She paused; and, looking back in that direction, listened intently. The sound—if she had really heard it—was no longer audible. She advanced towards the billiard-room, to set her first doubt at rest. She stretched out her hand to open the door—when the voices (recognisable now as the voices of two men) caught her ear once more.

This time, she was able to distinguish the words that were spoken.

"Any further orders, sir?" inquired one of the men.

"Nothing more," replied the other.

Mercy started, and faintly flushed, as the second voice answered the first. She stood irresolute close to the billiard-room, hesitating what to do next.

After an interval, the second voice made itself heard again, advancing nearer to the dining-room; "Are you there, aunt?" it asked, cautiously. There was a moment's pause. Then the voice spoke for the third time, sounding louder and nearer. "Are you there?" it reiterated, "I have something to tell you." Mercy summoned her resolution, and answered, "Lady Janet is not here." She turned, as she spoke, towards the conservatory door, and confronted on the threshold Julian Gray.

They looked at one another without exchanging a word on either side. The situation—for widely different reasons—was equally embarrassing to both of them.

There—as Julian saw *her*—was the woman forbidden to him, the woman whom he loved.

There—as Mercy saw *him*—was the man whom she dreaded; the man whose actions (as she interpreted them) proved that he suspected her.

On the surface of it, the incidents which had marked their first meeting were now exactly repeated, with the one difference, that the impulse to withdraw, this time, appeared to be on the man's side, and not on the woman's. It was Mercy who spoke first.

"Did you expect to find Lady Janet here?" she asked, constrainedly.

He answered, on his part, more constrainedly still.

"It doesn't matter," he said. "Another time will do."

He drew back as he made the reply. She advanced desperately, with the deliberate intention of detaining him by speaking again.

The attempt which he had made to withdraw, the constraint in his manner when he had answered, had instantly confirmed her in the false conviction that he, and he alone, had guessed the truth! If she was right—if he had secretly made discoveries abroad which placed her entirely at his mercy—the attempt to induce Grace to consent to a compromise with her, would be manifestly useless. Her first and foremost interest now, was to find out how she really stood in the estimation of Julian Gray. In a terror of suspense, that turned her cold from head to foot, she stopped him on his way out, and spoke to him with the piteous counterfeit of a smile.

"Lady Janet is receiving some visitors," she said. "If you will wait here, she will be back directly."

The effort of hiding her agitation from him had brought a passing colour into her cheeks. Worn and wasted as she was, the spell of her beauty was strong enough to hold him against his own will. All he had to tell Lady Janet was that he had met one of the gardeners in the conservatory, and had cautioned him as well as the lodge-keeper. It would have been easy to write this, and to send the note to his aunt on quitting the house. For the sake of his own peace of mind, for the sake of his duty to Horace, he was doubly bound to make the first polite excuse that occurred to him, and to leave her as he had found her, alone in the room. He made the attempt, and hesitated. Despising himself for doing it, he allowed himself to look at her. Their eyes met. Julian stepped into the dining-room.

"If I am not in the way," he said, confusedly, "I will wait, as you kindly propose."

She noticed his embarassment; she saw that he was strongly restraining himself from looking at her again. Her own eyes dropped to the ground as she made the discovery. Her speech failed her; her heart throbbed faster and faster.

"If I look at him again" (was the thought in *her* mind) "I shall fall at his feet and tell him all that I have done!"

"If I look at her again" (was the thought in *his* mind) "I shall fall at her feet and own that I am in love with her!"

With downcast eyes he placed a chair for her. With downcast eyes she bowed to him and took it. A dead silence followed. Never was any human misunderstanding more intricately complete than the misunderstanding which had now established itself between those two.

Mercy's work-basket was near her. She took it, and gained time for composing herself by pretending to arrange the coloured wools. He stood behind her chair, looking at the graceful turn of her head, looking at the rich masses of her hair. He reviled himself as the weakest of men, as the falsest of friends, for still remaining near her —and yet he remained.

The silence continued. The billiard-room door opened again noiselessly. The face of the listening woman appeared stealthily behind it.

At the same moment Mercy roused herself and spoke: "Won't you sit down?" she said, softly; still not looking round at him; still busy with her basket of wools.

He turned to get a chair—turned so quickly that he saw the billiard-room door move, as Grace Roseberry closed it again.

"Is there any one in that room ?" he asked, addressing Mercy.

"I don't know," she answered. "I thought I saw the door open and shut again a little while ago."

He advanced at once to look into the room. As he did so, Mercy dropped one of her balls of wool. He stopped to pick it up for her—then threw open the door and looked into the billiard-room. It was empty.

Had some person been listening, and had that person retreated in time to escape discovery? The open door of the smoking-room showed that room also to be empty. A third door was open—the door of the side-hall, leading into the grounds. Julian closed and locked it, and returned to the dining-room.

"I can only suppose," he said to Mercy, "that the billiard-room door was not properly shut, and that the draught of air from the hall must have moved it."

She accepted the explanation in silence. He was, to all appearance, not quite satisfied with it himself. For a moment or two he looked about him uneasily. Then the old fascination fastened its hold on him again. Once more he looked at the graceful turn of her head, at the rich masses of her hair. The courage to put the critical question to him, now that she had lured him into remaining in the room, was still a courage that failed her. She remained as busy as ever with her work—too busy to look at him ; too busy to speak to him. The silence became unendurable. He broke it by making a commonplace inquiry after her health.

"I am well enough to be ashamed of the anxiety I have caused and the trouble I have given," she answered. "To-day I have got downstairs for the first time. I am trying to do a little work." She looked into the basket. The various specimens of wool in it were partly in balls and partly in loose skeins. The skeins were mixed and tangled. "Here is sad confusion !" she exclaimed, timidly, with a faint smile. "How am I to set it right again ?"

"Let me help you," said Julian.

"You !"

"Why not ?" he asked, with a momentary return of the quaint humour which she remembered so well. "You forget that I am a curate. Curates are privileged to make themselves useful to young ladies. Let me try."

He took a stool at her feet, and set himself to unravel one of the tangled skeins. In a minute the wool was stretched on his hands, and the loose end was ready for Mercy to wind. There was something in the trivial action, and in the homely attention that it implied, which in some degree quieted her fear of him. She began to roll the wool off his hands into a ball. Thus occupied, she said the daring words which were to lead him little by little into betraying his suspicions, if he did indeed suspect the truth.

## CHAPTER XVII.

### THE GUARDIAN ANGEL.

"You were here when I fainted, were you not?" Mercy began. "You must think me a sad coward, even for a woman."

He shook his head. "I am far from thinking that," he replied. "No courage could have sustained the shock which fell on you. I don't wonder that you fainted. I don't wonder that you have been ill."

She paused in rolling up the ball of wool. What did those words of unexpected sympathy mean? Was he laying a trap for her? Urged by that serious doubt, she questioned him more boldly.

"Horace tells me you have been abroad," she said. "Did you enjoy your holiday?"

"It was no holiday. I went abroad because I thought it right to make certain inquiries"—— He stopped there, unwilling to return to a subject that was painful to her.

Her voice sank, her fingers trembled round the ball of wool—but she managed to go on.

"Did you arrive at any results?" she asked.

"At no results worth mentioning."

The caution of that reply renewed her worst suspicions of him. In sheer despair, she spoke out plainly.

"I want to know your opinion "—— she began.

"Gently!" said Julian. "You are entangling the wool again."

"I want to know your opinion of the person who so terribly frightened me. Do you think her "——

"Do I think her—what?"

"Do you think her an adventuress?"

(As she said those words the branches of a shrub in the conservatory were noiselessly parted by a hand in a black glove. The face of Grace Roseberry appeared dimly behind the leaves. Undiscovered, she had escaped from the billiard-room, and had stolen her way into the conservatory as the safer hiding place of the two. Behind the shrub she could see as well as listen. Behind the shrub she waited, as patiently as ever.)

"I take a more merciful view," Julian answered. "I believe she is acting under a delusion. I don't blame her: I pity her."

"You pity her?" As Mercy repeated the words, she tore off Julian's hands the last few lengths of wool left, and threw the imperfectly-wound skein back into the basket. "Does that mean," she resumed abruptly, "that you believe her?"

Julian rose from his seat, and looked at Mercy in astonishment.

"Good heavens, Miss Roseberry! what put such an idea as that into your head?"

"I am little better than a stranger to you," she rejoined, with an effort to assume a jesting tone. "You met that person before you met with me. It is not so very far from pitying her to believing her. How could I feel sure that you might not suspect me?"

"Suspect *you!*" he exclaimed. "You don't know how you distress, how you shock me. Suspect *you!* The bare idea of it never entered my mind. The man doesn't live who trusts you more implicitly, who believes in you more devotedly, than I do."

His eyes, his voice, his manner, all told her that those words came from the heart. She contrasted his generous confidence in her (the confidence of which she was unworthy) with her ungracious distrust of him. Not only had she wronged Grace Roseberry—she had wronged Julian Gray. Could she deceive *him* as she had deceived the others? Could she meanly accept that implicit trust, that devoted belief? Never had she felt the base submissions which her own imposture condemned her to undergo with a loathing of them so overwhelming as the loathing that she felt now. In horror of herself, she turned her head aside in silence, and shrank from meeting his eye. He noticed the movement, placing his own interpretation on it. Advancing closer, he asked anxiously if he had offended her?

"You don't know how your confidence touches me," she said, without looking up. "You little think how keenly I feel your kindness."

She checked herself abruptly. Her fine tact warned her that she was speaking too warmly—that the expression of her gratitude might strike him as being strangly exaggerated. She handed him her work-basket, before he could speak again.

"Will you put it away for me?" she asked in her quieter tones. "I don't feel able to work just now."

His back was turned on her for a moment, while he placed the basket on a side table. In that moment, her mind advanced at a bound from present to future. Accident might one day put the true Grace in possession of the proofs that she needed, and might reveal the false Grace to him in the identity that was her own. What would he think of her then? Could she make him tell her, without betraying herself? She determined to try.

"Children are notoriously insatiable if you once answer their questions, and women are nearly as bad," she said, when Julian returned to her. "Will your patience hold out if I go back for the third time to the person whom we have been speaking of?"

"Try me," he answered, with a smile.

"Suppose you had *not* taken your merciful view of her?"

"Yes?"

"Suppose you believed that she was wickedly bent on deceiving others for a purpose of her own—would you not shrink from such a woman in horror and disgust?"

"God forbid that I should shrink from any human creature!" he answered earnestly. "Who among us has a right to do that?"

She hardly dared trust herself to believe him. "You would still pity her?" she persisted, "and still feel for her?"

",With all my heart."

"Oh, how good you are!"

He held up his hand in warning. The tones of his voice deepened; the lustre of his eyes brightened. She had stirred in the depths of that great heart the faith in which the man lived—the steady principle which guided his modest and noble life.

"No!" he cried. "Don't say that! Say that I try to love my neighbour as myself. Who but a Pharisee can believe he is better than another? The best among us to-day may, but for the mercy of God, be the worst among us to-morrow. The true Christian virtue is the virtue which never despairs of a fellow-creature. The true Christian faith believes in Man as well as in God. Frail and fallen as we are, we can rise on the wings of repentance from earth to heaven. Humanity is sacred. Humanity has its immortal destiny. Who shall dare say to man or woman, 'There is no hope in you'? Who shall dare say the work is all vile, when that work bears on it the stamp of the Creator's hand?"

He turned away for a moment, struggling with the emotion which she had roused in him.

Her eyes, as they followed him, lighted with a momentary enthusiasm—then sank wearily in the vain regret which comes too late. Ah! if he could have been her friend and her adviser on the fatal day when she first turned her steps towards Mablethorpe House! She sighed bitterly as the hopeless aspiration wrung her heart. He heard the sigh; and, turning again, looked at her with a new interest in his face.

"Miss Roseberry," he said.

She was still absorbed in the bitter memories of the past: she failed to hear him.

"Miss Roseberry," he repeated, approaching her.

She looked up at him with a start.

"May I venture to ask you something?" he said gently.

She shrank at the question.

"Don't suppose I am speaking out of mere curiosity," he went on. "And pray don't answer me, unless you can answer without betraying any confidence which may have been placed in you."

"Confidence!" she repeated. "What confidence do you mean?"

"It has just struck me that you might have felt more than a common interest in the questions which you put to me a moment since," he answered. "Were you by any chance speaking of some unhappy woman—not the person who frightened you, of course—but of some other woman whom you know?"

Her head sank slowly on her bosom. He had plainly no suspicion that she had been speaking of herself: his tone and manner both answered for it that his belief in her was as strong as ever. Still those last words made her tremble; she could not trust herself to reply to them.

He accepted the bending of her head as a reply.

"Are you interested in her?" he asked next.

She faintly answered this time. "Yes."

"Have you encouraged her?"

"I have not dared to encourage her."

His face lit up suddenly with enthusiasm. "Go to her," •he said, "and let me go with you and help you!"

The answer came faintly and mournfully. "She has sunk too low for that!"

He interrupted her with a gesture of impatience.

"What has she done?" he asked.

"She has deceived—basely deceived—innocent people who trusted her. She has wronged—cruelly wronged—another woman."

For the first time, Julian seated himself at her side. The interest that was now roused in him was an interest above reproach. He could speak to Mercy without restraint; he could look at Mercy with a pure heart.

"You judge her very harshly," he said. "Do *you* know how she may have been tried and tempted?"

There was no answer.

"Tell me," he went on, "is the person whom she has injured still living?"

"Yes."

"If the person is still living, she may atone for the wrong. The time may come when this sinner, too, may win our pardon and deserve our respect."

"Could *you* respect her?" Mercy asked sadly. "Can such a mind as yours understand what she has gone through?"

A smile, kind and momentary, brightened his attentive face.

"You forget my melancholy experience," he answered. "Young as I am, I have seen more than most men of women who have sinned and suffered. Even after the little that you have told me, I think I can put myself in her place. I can well understand, for instance that she may have been tempted beyond human resistance. Am I right?"

"You are right."

"She may have had nobody near at the time to advise her, to warn her, to save her. Is that true?"

"It is true."

"Tempted and friendless, self-abandoned to the evil impulse of the moment, this woman may have committed herself headlong to the act which she now vainly repents. She may long to make atonement, and may not know how to begin. All her energies may be crushed under the despair and horror of herself, out of which the truest repentance grows. Is such a woman as this all wicked, all vile? I deny it! She may have a noble nature; and she may show it nobly yet. Give her the opportunity she needs—and our poor fallen fellow-creature may take her place again among the best of us; honoured, blameless, happy once more!"

Mercy's eyes, resting eagerly on him while he was speaking, dropped again despondingly when he had done.

"There is no such future as that," she answered, "for the woman whom I am thinking of. She has lost her opportunity. She has done with hope."

Julian gravely considered with himself for a moment.

"Let us understand each other," he said. "She has committed an act of deception to the injury of another woman. Was that what you told me?"

"Yes."

"And she has gained something to her own advantage by the act?"

"Yes."

"Is she threatened with discovery?"

"She is safe from discovery—for the present, at least."

"Safe as long as she closes her lips?"

"As long as she closes her lips."

"There is her opportunity!" cried Julian. "Her future is before her. She has *not* done with hope!"

With clasped hands, in breathless suspense, Mercy looked at that inspiriting face, and listened to those golden words.

"Explain yourself," she said. "Tell her, through me, what she must do."

"Let her own the truth," answered Julian, "without the base fear of discovery to drive her to it. Let her do justice to the woman whom she has wronged, while that woman is still powerless to expose her. Let her sacrifice everything that she has gained by the fraud to the sacred duty of atonement. If she can do that—for conscience' sake and for pity's sake—to her own prejudice, to her own shame, to her own loss—then her repentance has nobly revealed the noble nature that is in her; then she is a woman to be trusted, respected, beloved! If I saw the Pharisees and Fanatics of this lower earth passing her by in contempt, I would hold out my hand to her before them all. I would say to her in her solitude and her affliction, 'Rise, poor wounded heart! Beautiful, purified soul, God's angels rejoice over you! Take your place among the noblest of God's creatures!'"

In those last sentences, he unconsciously repeated the language in which he had spoken, years since, to his congregation in the Chapel of the Refuge. With tenfold power and tenfold persuasion, they now found their way again to Mercy's heart. Softly, suddenly, mysteriously, a change passed over her. Her troubled face grew beautifully still. The shifting light of terror and suspense vanished from her grand grey eyes, and left in them the steady inner glow of a high and pure resolve.

There was a moment of silence between them. They both had need of silence. Julian was the first to speak again.

" Have I satisfied you that her opportunity is still before her? " he asked. " Do you feel, as I feel, that she has *not* done with hope? "

" You have satisfied me that the world holds no truer friend to her than you," Mercy answered gently and gratefully. " She shall prove herself worthy of your generous confidence in her. She shall show you yet, that you have not spoken in vain."

Still inevitably failing to understand her, he led the way to the door.

" Don't waste the precious time," he said. " Don't leave her cruelly to herself. If you can't go to her, let me go as your messenger, in your place."

She stopped him by a gesture. He took a step back into the room, and paused; observing with surprise that she made no attempt to move from the chair that she occupied.

" Stay here," she said to him in suddenly-altered tones.

" Pardon me," he rejoined, " I don't understand you."

" You will understand me directly. Give me a little time."

He still lingered near the door, with his eyes fixed inquiringly on her. A man of a lower nature than his, or a man believing in Mercy less devotedly than he believed, would now have felt his first suspicion of her. Julian was as far as ever from suspecting her, even yet.

" Do you wish to be alone? " he asked considerately. " Shall I leave you for awhile and return again? "

She looked up with a start of terror. " Leave me? " she repeated, and suddenly checked herself on the point of saying more. Nearly half the length of the room divided them from each other. The words which she was longing to say were words that would never pass her lips, unless she could see some encouragement in his face. " No! " she cried out to him on a sudden, in her sore need, " don't leave me! Come back to me! "

He obeyed her in silence. In silence, on her side, she pointed to the chair near her. He took it. She looked at him, and checked herself again; resolute to make her terrible confession, yet still hesitating how to begin. Her woman's instinct whispered to her, " Find courage in his touch! " She said to him, simply and artlessly said to him, " Give me encouragement. Give me strength. Let me take your hand." He neither answered nor moved. His mind seemed to have become suddenly preoccupied; his eyes rested on her vacantly; He was on the brink of discovering her secret; in another instant he would have found his way to the truth. In that instant, innocently as his sister might have taken it, she took his hand. The soft clasp of her fingers, clinging round his, roused his senses, fired his passion for her, swept out of his mind the pure aspirations which had filled it but the moment before, paralysed his perception when it was just penetrating the mystery of her disturbed manner and her strange words. All the man in him trembled under the rapture of her touch. But the thought of Horace was still present to him: his hand lay passive in hers; his eyes looked uneasily away from her.

She innocently strengthened her clasp of his hand. She innocently said to him, "Don't look away from me. Your eyes give me courage."

His hand returned the pressure of hers. He tasted to the full the delicious joy of looking at her. She had broken down his last reserves of self-control. The thought of Horace, the sense of honour, became obscured in him. In a moment more he might have said the words which he would have deplored for the rest of his life, if she had not stopped him by speaking first. "I have more to say to you," she resumed abruptly; feeling the animating resolution to lay her heart bare before him at last; "more, far more, than I have said yet. Generous, merciful friend, let me say it *here!*"

She attempted to throw herself on her knees at his feet. He sprang from his seat and checked her, holding her with both his hands, raising her as he rose himself. In the words which had just escaped her, in the startling action which had accompanied them, the truth burst on him. The guilty woman she had spoken of was herself!

While she was almost in his arms, while her bosom was just touching his, before a word more had passed his lips or hers, the library door opened.

Lady Janet Roy entered the room.

## CHAPTER XVIII.

### THE SEARCH IN THE GROUNDS.

GRACE ROSEBERRY, still listening in the conservatory, saw the door open, and recognised the mistress of the house. She softly drew back and placed herself in safer hiding, beyond the range of view from the dining-room.

Lady Janet advanced no further than the threshold. She stood there and looked at her nephew and her adopted daughter in stern silence.

Mercy dropped into the chair at her side. Julian kept his place by her. His mind was still stunned by the discovery that had burst on it; his eyes still rested on her in a mute terror of inquiry. He was as completely absorbed in the one act of looking at her as if they had been still alone together in the room.

Lady Janet was the first of the three who spoke. She addressed herself to her nephew.

"You were right, Mr. Julian Gray," she said, with her bitterest emphasis of tone and manner. "You ought to have found nobody in this room on your return but *me*. I detain you no longer. You are free to leave my house."

Julian looked round at his aunt. She was pointing to the door. In the excited state of his sensibilities at that moment, the action stung him to the quick. He answered without his customary consideration for his aunt's age and his aunt's position towards him:

"You apparently forget, Lady Janet, that you are not speaking to one of your footmen," he said. "There are serious reasons (of which you know nothing) for my remaining in your house a little longer. You may rely upon my trespassing on your hospitality as short a time as possible."

He turned again to Mercy as he said those words, and surprised her timidly looking up at him. In the instant when their eyes met, the tumult of emotions struggling in him became suddenly stilled. Sorrow for her—compassionating sorrow—rose in the new calm and filled his heart. Now, and now only, he could read in the wasted and noble face how she had suffered. The pity which he had felt for the unnamed woman grew to a tenfold pity for *her*. The faith which he had professed—honestly professed—in the better nature of the unnamed woman strengthened into a tenfold faith in *her*. He addressed himself again to his aunt in a gentler tone. "This lady," he resumed, "has something to say to me in private which she has not said yet. That is my reason and my apology for not immediately leaving the house."

Still under the impression of what she had seen on entering the room, Lady Janet looked at him in angry amazement. Was Julian actually ignoring Horace Holmcroft's claims, in the presence of Horace Holmcroft's betrothed wife? She appealed to her adopted daughter. "Grace!" she exclaimed, "have you heard him? Have you nothing to say? Must I remind you"——

She stopped. For the first time in Lady Janet's experience of her young companion, she found herself speaking to ears that were deaf to her. Mercy was incapable of listening. Julian's eyes had told her that Julian understood her at last!

Lady Janet turned to her nephew once more, and addressed him in the hardest words that she had ever spoken to her sister's son:

"If you have any sense of decency," she said—"I say nothing of a

sense of honour—you will leave this house, and your acquaintance
with that lady will end here. Spare me your protests and excuses;
I can place but one interpretation on what I saw when I opened that
door."

"You entirely misunderstand what you saw when you opened that
door," Julian answered quietly.

"Perhaps I misunderstand the confession which you made to me,
not an hour ago?" retorted Lady Janet.

Julian cast a look of alarm at Mercy. "Don't speak of it!" he
said, in a whisper. "She might hear you."

"Do you mean to say she does'nt know you are in love with her?"

"Thank God, she has not the faintest suspicion of it!"

There was no mistaking the earnestness with which he made that
reply. It proved his innocence as nothing else could have proved
it. Lady Janet drew back a step—utterly bewildered; completely at
a loss what to say or what to do next.

The silence that followed was broken by a knock at the library
door. The man-servant—with news, and bad news, legibly written in
his disturbed face and manner—entered the room.

In the nervous irritability of the moment, Lady Janet resented the
servant's appearance as a positive offence on the part of the harmless
man. "Who sent for you?" she asked sharply. "What do you mean
by interrupting us?"

The servant made his excuses in an oddly bewildered manner.

"I beg your ladyship's pardon. I wished to take the liberty—I
wanted to speak to Mr. Julian Gray."

"What is it?" asked Julian.

The man looked uneasily at Lady Janet, hesitated, and glanced at
the door, as if he wished himself well out of the room again.

"I hardly know if I can tell you, sir, before her ladyship," he
answered.

Lady Janet instantly penetrated the secret of her servant's hesitation.

"I know what has happened," she said; "that abominable woman
has found her way here again. Am I right?"

The man's eyes helplessly consulted Julian.

"Yes? or no?" cried Lady Janet, imperatively.

"Yes, my lady."

Julian at once assumed the duty of asking the necessary questions.

"Where is she?" he began.

"Somewhere in the grounds, as we suppose, sir."

"Did *you* see her?"

"No, sir."

"Who saw her?"

"The lodge-keeper's wife."

This looked serious. The lodge-keeper's wife had been present while Julian had given his instructions to her husband. She was not likely to have mistaken the identity of the person whom she had discovered.

"How long since?" Julian asked next.

"Not very long, sir."

"Be more particular. *How* long?"

"I did'nt hear, sir."

"Did the lodge-keeper's wife speak to the person when she saw her?"

"No, sir: she did'nt get the chance, as I understand it. She is a stout woman, if you remember. The other was too quick for her—discovered her, sir; and (as the saying is) gave her the slip."

"In what part of the grounds did this happen?"

The servant pointed in the direction of the side hall. "In that part, sir. Either in the Dutch garden or the shrubbery. I am not sure which."

It was plain, by this time, that the man's information was too imperfect to be practically of any use. Julian asked if the lodge-keeper's wife was in the house.

"No, sir. Her husband has gone out to search the grounds in her place, and she is minding the gate. They sent their boy with the message. From what I can make out from the lad, they would be thankful if they could get a word more of advice from you, sir."

Julian reflected for a moment.

So far as he could estimate them, the probabilities were, that the stranger from Mannheim had already made her way into the house; that she had been listening in the billiard-room; that she had found time enough to escape him on his approaching to open the door; and that she was now (in the servant's phrase) "somewhere in the grounds," after eluding the pursuit of the lodge-keeper's wife.

The matter was serious. Any mistake in dealing with it might lead to very painful results.

If Julian had correctly anticipated the nature of the confession which Mercy had been on the point of addressing to him, the person whom he had been the means of introducing into the house, was—what she had vainly asserted herself to be—no other than the true Grace Roseberry.

Taking this for granted, it was of the utmost importance that he should speak to Grace privately, before she committed herself to any rashly-renewed assertion of her claims, and before she could gain access to Lady Janet's adopted daughter. The landlady at her lodgings had already warned him that the object which she held steadily in view was to find her way to "Miss Roseberry," when Lady Janet was not present to take her part, and when no gentlemen were at hand to protect her. "Only let me meet her face to face" (she had said), "and I will make her confess herself the impostor that she is!" As matters now stood, it was impossible to estimate too seriously the mischief which might ensue from such a meeting as this. Everything now depended on Julian's skilful management of an exasperated woman; and nobody, at that moment, knew where the woman was.

In this position of affairs, as Julian understood it, there seemed to be no other alternative than to make his inquiries instantly at the lodge, and then to direct the search in person.

He looked towards Mercy's chair as he arrived at this resolution. It was at a cruel sacrifice of his own anxieties and his own wishes that he deferred continuing the conversation with her, from the critical point at which Lady Janet's appearance had interrupted it.

Mercy had risen while he had been questioning the servant. The attention which she had failed to accord to what had passed between his aunt and himself, she had given to the imperfect statement which he had extracted from the man. Her face plainly showed that she had listened as eagerly as Lady Janet had listened; with this remarkable difference between them, that Lady Janet looked frightened, and that Lady Janet's companion showed no signs of alarm. She appeared to be interested; perhaps anxious—nothing more.

Julian spoke a parting word to his aunt.

"Pray compose yourself," he said. "I have little doubt, when I can learn the particulars, that we shall easily find this person in the grounds. There is no reason to be uneasy. I am going to superintend the search myself. I will return to you as soon as possible."

Lady Janet listened absently. There was a certain expression in her eyes which suggested to Julian that her mind was busy with some project of its own. He stopped as he passed Mercy, on his way out by the billiard-room door. It cost him a hard effort to control the contending emotions which the mere act of looking at her now awakened in him. His heart beat fast, his voice sank low, as he spoke to her:

"You shall see me again," he said. "I never was more in earnest in promising you my truest help and sympathy than I am now."

She understood him. Her bosom heaved painfully; her eyes fell to the ground—she made no reply. The tears rose in Julian's eyes as he looked at her. He hurriedly left the room.

When he turned to close the billiard-room door, he heard Lady Janet say, "I will be with you again in a moment, Grace; don't go away."

Interpreting these words as meaning that his aunt had some business of her own to attend to in the library, he shut the door.

He had just advanced into the smoking-room beyond, when he thought he heard the door opened again. He turned round. Lady Janet had followed him.

"Do you wish to speak to me ?" he asked.

"I want something of you," Lady Janet answered, "before you go."

"What is it ?"

"Your card."

"My card ?"

"You have just told me not to be uneasy," said the old lady. "I am uneasy, for all that. I don't feel as sure as you do that this woman really is in the grounds. She may be lurking somewhere in the house, and she may appear when your back is turned. Remember what you told me."

Julian understood the allusion. He made no reply.

"The people at the police-station close by," pursued Lady Janet, "have instructions to send an experienced man, in plain clothes, to any address indicated on your card the moment they receive it. That is what you told me. For Grace's protection, I want your card before you leave us."

It was impossible for Julian to mention the reasons which now forbade him to make use of his own precautions—in the very face of the emergency which they had been especially intended to meet. How could he declare the true Grace Roseberry to be mad ? How could he give the true Grace Roseberry into custody ? On the other hand, he had personally pledged himself (when the circumstances appeared to require it) to place the means of legal protection from insult and annoyance at his aunt's disposal. And now, there stood Lady Janet, unaccustomed to have her wishes disregarded by anybody, with her hand extended, waiting for the card !

What was to be done? The one way out of the difficulty appeared to be to submit for the moment. If he succeeded in discovering the missing woman, he could easily take care that she should be subjected to no needless indignity. If she contrived to slip into the house in his absence, he could provide against that contingency by sending a second card privately to the police-station, forbidding the officer to stir in the affair until he had received further orders. Julian made one stipulation only, before he handed his card to his aunt.

"You will not use this, I am sure, without positive and pressing necessity," he said. "But I must make one condition. Promise me to keep my plan for communicating with the police a strict secret"——

"A strict secret from Grace?" interposed Lady Janet. (Julian bowed.) "Do you suppose I want to frighten her? Do you think I have not had anxiety enough about her already? Of course I shall keep it a secret from Grace !"

Reassured on this point, Julian hastened out into the grounds. As soon as his back was turned, Lady Janet lifted the gold pencil-case which hung at her watch-chain, and wrote on her nephew's card (for the information of the officer in plain clothes): "*You are wanted at*

*Mablethorpe House.*" This done, she put the card into the old-fashioned pocket of her dress, and returned to the dining-room.

Grace was waiting, in obedience to the instructions which she had received.

For the first moment or two, not a word was spoken on either side. Now that she was alone with her adopted daughter, a certain coldness and hardness began to show itself in Lady Janet's manner. The discovery that she had made, on opening the drawing-room door, still hung on her mind. Julian had certainly convinced her that she had misinterpreted what she had seen; but he had convinced her against her will. She had found Mercy deeply agitated; suspiciously silent. Julian might be innocent (she admitted)—there was no accounting for the vagaries of men. But the case of Mercy was altogether different. Women did not find themselves in the arms of men without knowing what they were about. Acquitting Julian, Lady Janet declined to acquit Mercy. "There is some secret understanding between them," thought the old lady, "and she's to blame; the women always are!"

Mercy still waited to be spoken to; pale and quiet, silent and submissive. Lady Janet—in a highly uncertain state of temper—was obliged to begin.

"My dear!" she called out sharply.

"Yes, Lady Janet."

"How much longer are you going to sit there, with your mouth shut up and your eyes on the carpet? Have you no opinion to offer on this alarming state of things? You heard what the man said to Julian—I saw you listening. Are you horribly frightened?"

"No, Lady Janet."

"Not even nervous?"

"No, Lady Janet."

"Ha! I should hardly have given you credit for so much courage after my experience of you a week ago. I congratulate you on your recovery. Do you hear? I congratulate you on your recovery."

"Thank you, Lady Janet."

"I am not so composed as you are. We were an excitable set in *my* youth—and I hav'n't got the better of it yet. I feel nervous. Do you hear? I feel nervous."

"I am sorry, Lady Janet."

"You are very good. Do you know what I am going to do?"

"No, Lady Janet."

"I am going to summon the household. When I say the household, I mean the men; the women are no use. I am afraid I fail to attract your attention?"

"You have my best attention, Lady Janet."

" You are very good again.  I said the women were of no use."

" Yes, Lady Janet ?"

" I mean to place a man-servant on guard at every entrance to the house.  I am going to do it at once.  Will you come with me ?"

" Can I be of any use if I go with your ladyship ?"

" You can't be of the slightest use.  I give the orders in this house—not you.  I had quite another motive in asking you to come with me.  I am more considerate of you than you seem to think—I don't like leaving you here by yourself.  Do you understand ?"

" I am much obliged to your ladyship.  I don't mind being left here by myself."

" You don't mind ?  I never heard of such heroism in my life—out of a novel !  Suppose that crazy wretch should find her way in here ?"

" She would not frighten me this time, as she frightened me before."

" Not too fast, my young lady !  Suppose —— Good Heavens! now I think of it, there is the conservatory.  Suppose she should be hidden in there ?  Julian is searching the grounds.  Who is to search the conservatory ?"

" With your ladyship's permission, I will search the conservatory.",

" You ! ! !"

" With your ladyship's permission."

" I can hardly believe my own ears !  Well, ' Live and learn' is an old proverb.  I thought I knew your character.  This is a change !"

" You forget, Lady Janet (if I may venture to say so), that the circumstances are changed.  She took me by surprise on the last occasion ; I am prepared for her now."

" Do you really feel as coolly as you speak ?"

" Yes, Lady Janet."

" Have your own way, then.  I shall do one thing, however, in case of your having over-estimated your own courage.  I shall place one of the men in the library.  You will only have to ring for him, if anything happens.  He will give the alarm—and I shall act accordingly.  I have my plan," said her ladyship, comfortably conscious of the card in her pocket.  " Don't look as if you wanted to know what it is.  I have no intention of saying anything about it—except that it will do.  Once more, and for the last time—do you stay here ? or do you go with me ?"

" I stay here."

She respectfully opened the library door for Lady Janet's departure as she made that reply.  Throughout the interview she had been carefully and coldly deferential ; she had not once lifted her eyes to Lady Janet's face.  The conviction in her that a few hours more would, in all probability, see her dismissed from the house, had of necessity fettered every word that she spoke—had morally separated her already from the injured mistress whose love she had won in disguise. Utterly incapable of attributing the change in her young companion to the true motive, Lady Janet left the room to summon her domestic garrison, thoroughly puzzled, and (as a necessary consequence of that condition) thoroughly displeased.

Still holding the library door in her hand, Mercy stood watching with a heavy heart the progress of her benefactress down the length of the room, on the way to the front hall beyond. She had honestly loved and respected the warm-hearted, quick-tempered old lady. A sharp pang of pain wrung her, as she thought of the time when even the chance utterance of her name would become an unpardonable offence in Lady Janet's house.

But there was no shrinking in her now from the ordeal of the confession. She was not only anxious, she was impatient for Julian's return. Before she slept that night, Julian's confidence in her should be a confidence that she had deserved.

"Let her own the truth, without the base fear of discovery to drive her to it. Let her do justice to the woman whom she has wronged, while that woman is still powerless to expose her. Let her sacrifice everything that she has gained by the fraud to the sacred duty of atonement. If she can do that, then her repentance has nobly revealed the noble nature that is in her; then, she is a woman to be trusted, respected, beloved." Those words were as vividly present to her, as if she still heard them falling from his lips. Those other words which had followed them, rang as grandly as ever in her ears: "Rise, poor wounded heart! Beautiful, purified soul, God's angels rejoice over you! Take your place among the noblest of God's creatures!" Did the woman live who could hear Julian Gray say that, and who could hesitate, at any sacrifice, at any loss, to justify his belief in her? "Oh!" she thought longingly, while her eyes followed Lady Janet to the end of the library, "if your worst fears could only be realised! If I could only see Grace Roseberry in this room, how fearlessly I could meet her now!"

She closed the library door, while Lady Janet opened the other door which led into the hall.

As she turned and looked back into the dining-room, a cry of astonishment escaped her.

There—as if in answer to the aspiration which was still in her mind; there, established in triumph, on the chair that she had just left—sat Grace Roseberry, in sinister silence, waiting for her.

## Chapter XIX.

### THE EVIL GENIUS.

RECOVERING from the first overpowering sensation of surprise, Mercy rapidly advanced, eager to say her first penitent words. Grace stopped her by a warning gesture of the hand. "No nearer to me," she said, with a look of contemptuous command. "Stay where you are."

Mercy paused. Grace's reception had startled her. She instinctively took the chair nearest to her to support herself. Grace raised a warning hand for the second time, and issued another command:

"I forbid you to be seated in my presence. You have no right to be in this house at all. Remember, if you please, who you are, and who I am."

The tone in which those words were spoken was an insult in itself. Mercy suddenly lifted her head; the angry answer was on her lips. She checked it, and submitted in silence. "I will be worthy of Julian Gray's confidence in me," she thought, as she stood patiently by the chair. "I will bear anything from the woman whom I have wronged."

In silence the two faced each other; alone together, for the first time since they had met in the French cottage. The contrast between them was strange to see. Grace Roseberry, seated in her chair, little and lean, with her dull white complexion, with her hard threatening face, with her shrunken figure clad in its plain and poor black garments, looked like a being of a lower sphere, compared with Mercy Merrick, standing erect in her rich silken dress; her tall, shapely figure towering over the little creature before her; her grand head bent in graceful submission; gentle, patient, beautiful; a woman whom it was a privilege to look at and a distinction to admire. If a stranger had been told that those two had played their parts in a romance of real life—that one of them was really connected by the ties of relationship with Lady Janet Roy, and that the other had successfully attempted to personate her—he would inevitably, if it had been left to him to guess which was which, have picked out Grace as the counterfeit and Mercy as the true woman.

Grace broke the silence. She had waited to open her lips until she had eyed her conquered victim all over, with disdainfully minute attention, from head to foot.

"Stand there, I like to look at you," she said, speaking with a spiteful relish of her own cruel words. "It's no use fainting this time. You have not got Lady Janet Roy to bring you to. There are no gentlemen here to-day to pity you and pick you up. Mercy Merrick, I have got you at last. Thank God, my turn has come! You can't escape me now!"

All the littleness of heart and mind which had first shown itself in Grace at the meeting in the cottage, when Mercy told the sad story of her life, now revealed itself once more. The woman who, in those past times, had felt no impulse to take a suffering and a penitent fellow-creature by the hand, was the same woman who could feel no pity, who could spare no insolence of triumph, now. Mercy's sweet voice answered her patiently, in low pleading tones.

"I have not avoided you," she said. "I would have gone to you of my own accord, if I had known that you were here. It is my heart-felt wish to own that I have sinned against you, and to make all the atonement that I can. I am too anxious to deserve your forgiveness to have any fear of seeing you."

Conciliatory as the reply was, it was spoken with a simple and modest dignity of manner which roused Grace Roseberry to fury.

"How dare you speak to me as if you were my equal?" she burst out. "You stand there, and answer me, as if you had your right and your place in this house. You audacious woman! _I_ have my right and my place here—and what am I obliged to do? I am obliged to hang about in the grounds, and fly from the sight of the servants, and hide like a thief, and wait like a beggar; and all for what? For the chance of having a word with _you._ Yes! you, madam! with the air of the Refuge and the dirt of the streets on you!"

Mercy's head sank lower; her hand trembled as it held by the back of the chair.

It was hard to bear the reiterated insults heaped on her, but Julian's influence still made itself felt. She answered as patiently as ever:

"If it is your pleasure to use hard words to me," she said, "I have no right to resent them."

"You have no right to anything!" Grace retorted. "You have no right to the gown on your back. Look at Yourself, and look at Me!" Her eyes travelled with a tigerish stare over Mercy's costly silk dress. "Who gave you that dress? who gave you those jewels? I know! Lady Janet gave them to Grace Roseberry. Are _you_ Grace Roseberry? That dress is mine. Take off your bracelets and your brooch. They were meant for me."

"You may soon have them, Miss Roseberry. They will not be in my possession many hours longer."

"What do you mean?"

"However badly you may use me, it is my duty to undo the harm that I have done. I am bound to do you justice—I am determined to confess the truth."

Grace smiled scornfully.

"You confess!" she said. "Do you think I am fool enough to believe that? You are one shameful brazen lie from head to foot! Are _you_ the woman to give up your silks and your jewels, and your position in this house, and to go back to the Refuge of your own accord? Not you—not you!"

A first faint flush of colour showed itself, stealing slowly over Mercy's face; but she still held resolutely by the good influence which Julian had left behind him. She could still say to herself, "Anything rather than disappoint Julian Gray!" Sustained by the courage which *he* had called to life in her, she submitted to her martyrdom as bravely as ever. But there was an ominous change in her now: she could only submit in silence; she could no longer trust herself to answer.

The mute endurance in her face additionally exasperated Grace Roseberry.

"*You* won't confess," she went on. "You have had a week to confess in, and you have not done it yet. No, no! you are of the sort that cheat and lie to the last. I am glad of it; I shall have the joy of exposing you myself before the whole house. I shall be the blessed means of casting you back on the streets. Oh! it will be almost worth all I have gone through, to see you with a policeman's hand on your arm, and the mob pointing at you and mocking you on your way to gaol!"

This time the sting struck deep; the outrage was beyond endurance. Mercy gave the woman who had again and again deliberately insulted her a first warning.

"Miss Roseberry," she said, "I have borne without a murmur the bitterest words you could say to me. Spare me any more insults. Indeed, indeed, I am eager to restore you to your just rights. With my whole heart I say it to you—I am resolved to confess everything!"

She spoke with trembling earnestness of tone. Grace listened with a hard smile of incredulity and a hard look of contempt.

"You are not far from the bell," she said; "ring it."

Mercy looked at her in speechless surprise.

"You are a perfect picture of repentance—you are dying to own the truth," pursued the other satirically. "Own it before everybody, and own it at once. Call in Lady Janet—call in Mr. Gray and Mr. Holmcroft—call in the servants. Go down on your knees and acknowledge yourself an impostor before them all. Then I will believe you—not before."

"Don't, don't turn me against you!" cried Mercy entreatingly.

"What do I care whether you are against me or not?"

"Don't—for your own sake don't go on provoking me much longer!"

"For my own sake? You insolent creature! Do you mean to threaten me?"

With a last desperate effort, her heart beating faster and faster, the

blood burning hotter and hotter in her cheeks, Mercy still controlled
herself.

"Have some compassion on me!" she pleaded. "Badly as I have
behaved to you, I am still a woman like yourself. I can't face the
shame of acknowledging what I have done before the whole house.
Lady Janet treats me like a daughter; Mr. Holmcroft has engaged
himself to marry me. I can't tell Lady Janet and Mr. Holmcroft to
their faces that I have cheated them out of their love. But they
shall know it for all that. I can, and will, before I rest to-night, tell
the whole truth to Mr. Julian Gray."

Grace burst out laughing. "Aha!" she exclaimed, with a cynical
outburst of gaiety. "Now we have come to it at last!"

"Take care!" said Mercy. "Take care!"

"Mr. Julian Gray! I was behind the billiard-room door—I saw
you coax Mr. Julian Gray to come in. Confession loses all its
horrors, and becomes quite a luxury, with Mr. Julian Gray!"

"No more, Miss Roseberry! no more! For God's sake, don't put
me beside myself! You have tortured me enough already."

"You haven't been on the streets for nothing. You are a woman
with resources; you know the value of having two strings to your bow.
If Mr. Holmcroft fails you, you have got Mr. Julian Gray. Ah! you
sicken me. I'll see that Mr. Holmcroft's eyes are opened; he shall
know what a woman he might have married, but for Me"——

She checked herself; the next refinement of insult remained suspended on her lips.

The woman whom she had outraged suddenly advanced on her. Her
eyes, staring helplessly upward, saw Mercy Merrick's face, white with
the terrible anger which drives the blood back on the heart, bending
threateningly over her.

"'You will see that Mr. Holmcroft's eyes are opened,'" Mercy
slowly repeated; "'he shall know what a woman he might have
married, but for you!'"

She paused, and followed those words by a question which struck a
creeping terror through Grace Roseberry, from the hair of her head
to the soles of her feet:

"Who are you?"

The suppressed fury of look and tone which accompanied that
question told, as no violence could have told it, that the limits of
of Mercy's endurance had been found at last. In the guardian angel's
absence the evil genius had done it's evil work. The better nature
which Julian Gray had brought to life sank, poisoned by the vile venom
of a woman's spiteful tongue. An easy and a terrible means of avenging
the outrages heaped on her was within Mercy's reach, if she chose to
take it. In the frenzy of her indignation she never hesitated—she
took it.

"Who are you?" she asked for the second time.

Grace roused herself and attempted to speak. Mercy stopped her with a scornful gesture of her hand.

"I remember!" she went on, with the same fiercely suppressed rage. "You are the madwoman from the German hospital who came here a week ago. I am not afraid of you this time. Sit down and rest yourself, Mercy Merrick."

Deliberately giving her that name to her face, Mercy turned from her and took the chair which Grace had forbidden her to occupy when the interview began.

Grace started to her feet.

"What does this mean?" she asked.

"It means," answered Mercy contemptuously, "that I recall every word I said to you just now. It means that I am resolved to keep my place in this house."

"Are you out of your senses?"

"You are not far from the bell. Ring it. Do what you asked *me* to do. Call in the whole household, and ask them which of us is mad —you or I?"

"Mercy Merrick! you shall repent this to the last hour of your life!"

Mercy rose again, and fixed her flashing eyes on the woman who still defied her.

"I have had enough of you!" she said. "Leave the house while you *can* leave it. Stay here, and I will send for Lady Janet Roy."

"You can't send for her! You daren't send for her!"

"I can and I dare. You have not a shadow of a proof against me. I have got the papers; I am in possession of the place; I have established myself in Lady Janet's confidence. I mean to deserve your opinion of me—I will keep my dresses and my jewels, and my position in the house. I deny that I have done wrong. Society has used me cruelly; I owe nothing to Society. I have a right to take any advantage of it if I can. I deny that I have injured you. How was I to know that you would come to life again? Have I degraded your name and your character? I have done honour to both. I have won everybody's liking and everybody's respect. Do you think Lady Janet would have loved you as she loves me? Not she! I tell you to your face, I have filled the false position more creditably than you could have filled the true one, and I mean to keep it. I won't give up your name; I won't restore your character! Do your worst, I defy you!"

She poured out those reckless words in one headlong flow which defied interruption. There was no answering her until she was too breathless to say more. Grace seized her opportunity the moment it was within her reach.

"You defy me?" she returned resolutely. "You won't defy me long. I have written to Canada. My friends will speak for me."

"What of it, if they do? Your friends are strangers here. I am Lady Janet's adopted daughter. Do you think she will believe your friends? She will believe me. She will burn their letters, if they write. She will forbid the house to them if they come. I shall be Mrs. Horace Holmcroft in a week's time. Who can shake *my* position? Who can injure Me?"

"Wait a little. You forget the matron at the Refuge."

"Find her, if you can. I never told you her name. I never told you where the Refuge was."

"I will advertise your name, and find the matron in that way."

"Advertise in every newspaper in London. Do you think I gave a stranger like you the name I really bore in the Refuge? I gave you the name I assumed when I left England. No such person as Mercy Merrick is known to the matron. No such person is known to Mr. Holmcroft. He saw me at the French cottage while you were senseless on the bed. I had my grey cloak on; neither he nor any of them saw me in my nurse's dress. Inquiries have been made about me on the Continent—and (I happen to know from the person who made them) with no result. I am safe in your place; I am known by your name. I am Grace Roseberry; and you are Mercy Merrick. Disprove it if you can!"

Summing up the unassailable security of her false position in those closing words, Mercy pointed significantly to the billiard-room door.

"You were hiding there, by your own confession," she said. "You know your way out by that door. Will you leave the room?"

"I won't stir a step!"

Mercy walked to a side-table, and struck the bell placed on it.

At the same moment, the billiard-room door opened. Julian Gray appeared—returning from his unsuccessful search in the grounds.

He had barely crossed the threshold before the library-door was thrown open next by the servant posted in the room. The man drew back respectfully, and gave admission to Lady Janet Roy. She was followed by Horace Holmcroft with his mother's wedding-present to Mercy in his hand.

# 'Fifine at the Fair,' and Robert Browning.

IF we do not agree with one of Mr. Browning's critics that his readers must pass through five stages of misunderstanding before even attaining a distinct consciousness that he is not to be understood at all, we admit that they have at least a three-fold difficulty to contend with : the difficulty attendant on all abstract operations of thought, the difficulty of performing them through the medium of another person, and the special difficulty infused into them by the complexity of the author's mind. Mr. Browning is a living expression of all the problems of life ; an embodiment of its conflicting elements and tendencies; and though they are in some measure harmonised in the unity of his strong self-consciousness, they too often give to his special utterances an uncertain and contradictory character. We feel this in all his philosophical poems, and most of all in the one now before us; for it combines the intellectual subtleties to which the subject so fully lends itself, with an indistinctness of moral purpose all the more perplexing because the whole work presents itself as a confession of faith, and because we are clearly intended to believe that that faith is Mr. Browning's own.

'Fifine at the Fair' is a serio-fantastic discussion on the nature of sexual love and its relation to all other modes of æsthetic life, and turns mainly on the question whether such love best fulfils itself in constancy or in change, in devotion to one object, or in the appreciation of many. Mr. Browning says everything that can be said on either side, and neutralizes each argument in its turn; he mingles sophistry with truth, self-satire with satire, and leads us finally to conclude that he neither judges nor sees any ground for judgment; that he holds the mirror to life with the indifference of life itself, and that we must seek him, not in the preference for any one aspect of existence, but in his equal sympathy with all.

The form he has chosen is that of a monologue, which opens with a vivid comment on the sights of a village fair, and passes into a half dreamy development of the thoughts suggested by them. It is spoken by a supposed Don Juan to an imaginary Elvire, whose probable remarks he answers or anticipates, thus giving all the animation of dialogue to the undisturbed flow of his own ideas. Elvire is discernible throughout the poem, but under a form so vague that she seems scarcely more than a phantom conscience, or a haunting idea of stability and truth. She forms the strongest contrast to the third personage in the drama, the gipsy rope-dancer, Fifine, whose vivid humanity identifies itself with all that is fleeting and equivocal in life.  Fifine is the poetry of the flesh ; Elvire the purer life of the soul.  This double tendency of existence, the amphibious nature of human desires and strivings, is symbolised in a prologue, in which the author represents himself as floating out into the sea one sunny morning, dreaming of a disembodied existence, but still pleasantly conscious of life in the flesh.  A strange butterfly *creature, as dear as new*, hovers in the air above him, and as he watches the *sun-suffused* wings, they appear to him as a type of the complete ethereal freedom which the human mind can only imagine and the human body only mimic.  He asks himself whether this be not a soul early escaped from its mortal sheath, to whom his fancied liberty conveys a pitying sense of the earthly trammels from which she has herself escaped—and concludes with these lines :

> "Does she look, pity, wonder
>     At one who mimics flight,
> Swims—heaven above, sea under,
>     Yet always earth in sight ? "

The scene opens amidst the bustle of Pornic fair :—

> " O trip and skip, Elvire ! Link arm in arm with me !
>     Like husband and like wife, together let us see ✦
> The tumbling-troop arrayed, the strollers on their stage,
>     Drawn up and under arms, and ready to engage."

But Elvire is soon to be forgotten.  Fifine has arrived at the fair.  A red pennon waves high above her booth, flinging out its scarlet length towards the ocean ; towards

> " The home far and away, the distance where lives joy."

A sudden restlessness possesses Don Juan's mind ; he is seized with a wild desire for lawless liberty and the mysterious pleasures of a wandering life.  He speculates curiously on the nature of that life in which men seem the richer for all they lose, the lighter in heart for destitution and disgrace, and concludes with the emphatic question :

> " What compensating joy, unknown and infinite,
>     Turns lawlessness to law, makes destitution—wealth,
>     Vice—virtue, and disease of soul and body—health ? "

Elvire is distressed at this sudden perversion of her husband's mind ; she warns and protests by look and gesture, and finally by a burst of words, but her warnings are in vain.  Don Juan has seen Fifine vaulting through the air, with every vein and muscle of her fairy form bare to the public gaze.  He has seen the beauties of her face :

> "The Greek-nymph nose, and—oh, my Hebrew pair
> Of eye and eye—o'erarched by velvet of the mole—
> That swim as in a sea, that dip and rise and roll,
> Spilling the light around! While either ear is cut
> Thin as a dusk-leaved rose carved from a cocoa-nut."

He owns himself conquered. He knows that in her girlish beauty and her boyish impudence she is but a *sexless sprite, mischievous* perhaps, and *mean :*

> "Yet free and flower-like too, with loveliness for law,
> And self-sustainment made morality."

And he condemns her as little for the evil she may do as if she were a poisonous flower by whose fatal sweetness the idle insect is enticed and destroyed. He discusses Fifine at length; her merits and demerits, her actual degradation and her possible redeeming motives —alternately denies and justifies the semi-passion with which she has inspired him—declares that he has no undue regard for the beauties of the flesh; it is the *inward grace which allures him through the outward sign.* Even Fifine may have her portion of that inward grace. There is no grain of sand of the millions heaped upon the beach but may once have been the first to flash back the light of the rising sun. There is no man or woman of our mass whose life may not emit at its own time its own self-vindicating ray. Finding, however, no refuge in these vague generalities against the facts of her position, he plunges into a novel line of argument. He makes a virtue of her vices; and imputes it to her as a merit, that being pledged to an ignominious life she does not shrink from its ignominy. He passes in review some of the real and ideal types of higher womanhood, the ancient Helen and Cleopatra, the mediæval saint, his own Elvire; each secure in her special claim on the homage or esteem of men—in imperial beauty or attested holiness, or the dignity of married love—and declares by implication, if not in direct words, that, ignoble as is Fifine in comparison with such as these, she possesses, in her frank surrender of all social regard, a grace which they have not. We can only quote a few lines from the eloquent harangue which is partly spoken by Fifine herself, but they contain the pith of her defence :

> "Be it enough, there's truth i' the pleading, which comports
> With no word spoken out in cottages or courts:
> Since all I plead is 'Pay for just the sight you see,
> And give no credit to another charm in me.'"

⌈It is impossible to read these opening pages without being carried away by the distinctive emotion with which every line of them is saturated, and which combines with an originality of idea scarcely attained in any subsequent part of the poem. ⌉There is something half-ingenuous in the sleight of thought with which the hero tries to adjust his new emotions to his acknowledged position; defines, vindicates or denies the temporary fascination in which the fever of the flesh is perhaps really tempered by a curious and pitying interest. His self-entanglement is so manifest, that it can entangle no one; but the final defence of Fifine has a mischievous cogency which strikes at the very root of life. We all know that the best human happiness is bound up in those permanent affections from which the sense of responsibility can never be divorced, but we know also how a restless pleasure-loving, danger-seeking nature recoils from such a sense; we know, too, that there may arise in every mind a temporary rebellion against the banking system of society, in which the most slender income of enjoyment implies the tying up of the capital of a life; a temporary reaction towards the hand-to-mouth simplicity of an intercourse in which if little is given, little also is required, in which there is no devotion, but also no jealousy; no possibility of sympathy, but no tedious striving after it; no promise made in the dark, and no noonday revelation of the difficulties of fulfilment. When Elvire weeps and upbraids, compares what has been with what is, contrasts her unfailing love with her husband's failing appreciation of it, there is a charm in the voice of Fifine saying: "Take from me the pleasure of the moment, and give me what it is worth to you." In Mr. Browning's opinion, there is virtue in the very profligacy of such an attitude, because there is perfect frankness in it, and frankness, in Mr. Browning's eyes, covers almost every sin. Whenever he is disposed for a crusade against social virtues he takes his stand on the hypocrisy which they engender. He considers that every relation which presupposes the highest level of feeling, leads to the concealment of whatever falls below it; and he thinks an understanding which is distinctly based on the selfishness of the persons concerned in it may easily be more moral in its results, if not in its nature. This represents one mood of his mind. But from another, he evolves a very animated, if not a very logical defence of the opposite view of the question. The defence proceeds from Elvire, who feels bruised all over as would any other wife, and answers as most other wives would do; she does not directly meet her husband's arguments, but she overflows in a passionate, pathetic, and at the same time satirical protest against a state of mind in which she sees nothing but indifference to what is lawfully his own, and a morbid craving for everything that has the charm of novelty and the excitement of theft. She concludes with the lines,

> "Give you the sun to keep, forthwith must fancy range:
> A goodly lamp, no doubt,—yet might you catch her hair,
> And capture, as she frisks, the fen-fire dancing there!
> What do I say? at least a meteor's half in heaven;

Provided filth but shine, my husband hankers even
After putridity that's phosphorescent, cribs
The rustic's tallow-rush, makes spoil of urchin's squibs;
In short prefers to me—chaste, temperate, serene—
What sputters green and blue, the fizgig called Fifine!"

Don Juan answers these accusations by reminding his wife of a certain picture of Raphael's which decorates their home; of his long desire for it, and the suspense he endured before the purchase was secured to him. How he spent the first week of possession in palpitating delight, a fortnight in Paradise, a month in challenging the congratulations of his friends. This year he saunters past without looking at it, and even occasionally turns his back upon his Raphael to busy himself in some new picture-book of Doré's. But let his possession of it be once more threatened, let a cry of fire break out, and he will scatter Doré to the winds, though its portfolios were million-paged, and rescue his *precious piece* or perish with it. A happy illustration, containing the best comfort which the imperfectness of human relations concedes to the race of Elvires. Elvire is pacified, and her husband's tenderness is once more at its height. He has already told her that this and that being good, her beauty is to him the best of all, and, in order to prove this, he completes her portrait already sketched in his imaginary procession of women. ⌈This whole description, beginning with the line

"How ravishingly pure you stand in pale constraint,"

is an effusion of such tender and majestic poetry that we can scarcely imagine it surpassed.⌉ But reaction with our poet is inevitable and sudden. Elvire's husband addresses her a little longer in the same strain, declaring that her face *fits into just the cleft of the heart of him, makes right and whole once more all that was half itself without her*—then suddenly asks himself where in the world are all the beauties of that face? Her mirror does not reflect them; where are they else but *in the sense and soul of him, the judge of art?* On this novel position he erects his theory of love, or rather his theory of the creative action of the soul, which he recognises equally in love, in art, and in religion; love being the fundamental impulse from which its other modes are evolved. Love is to him both yearning and possession, both desire and fulfilment. It is a creative intuition, which restores the imperfect to perfection, the incomplete to completeness, life's broken utterances to their divine significance. Such creative intuition is art. Art is the evidence of all possible existence, but as distinct from things themselves as flame from fuel. Every perception of beauty is thus due to such an intimate co-operation of the mind with its objects, that it is difficult to retrace such effects to their external cause, though the emotion remain ours for ever. The idea is thus strikingly expressed :

> . . . "Once the verse-book laid on shelf,
> The picture turned to wall, the music fled from ear,
> Each beauty, born of each, grows clearer and more clear,
> Mine henceforth, ever mine!"

### 42.

> . . . But if I would retrace
> Effect, in Art, to cause—corroborate, erase
> What's right or wrong i' the lines, test fancy in my brain
> By fact which gave it birth ?  I re-peruse in vain
> The verse, I fail to find that vision of delight
> I' the Razzi's lost profile, eye-edge so exquisite.
> And, music: what ?  that burst of pillared cloud by day,
> And pillared fire by night, was product, must we say,
> Of modulating just, by enharmonic change,
> The augmented sixth resolved,—from out the straighter range
> Of D sharp minor,—leap of disimprisoned thrall,—
> Into thy light and life, D major natural ?

The same idea is presented, though under a different aspect, in the history of a statue which Don Juan has completed from so slight an indication of the sculptor's design, that the dawning life was still *death for the world.* He has bought the block of marble, mere *magnitude man-shaped, as snow might be,* and so brooded over it in the divining sympathy of art with art, that he has brought to gradual birth the intended form of a goddess.  Eidothee, whom no eye shall ever see, but who lives in the soul's domain, emerges *ravishingly* from the Master's fancy evoked by a kindred soul, *and he achieves the work in silence and by night, daring to justify the lines plain to his soul.*

The yearning for completeness through something other than one-self, which is the essence of love and the vital principle of art, is also the foundation of religious beliefs.  Religion is but a transformation of the primitive instincts of human love.

> . . . "Each soul lives, longs, and works
> For itself, by itself, because a lode star lurks,
> Another than itself,—in whatsoe'er the niche
> Of mistiest heaven it hide, whoe'er the Glumdalclich
> May grasp the Gulliver; or it, or he, or she—
> The osutos e broteios eper Kekramane,—
> (For fun's sake, where the phrase has fastened, leave it fixed!
> So soft it says—God, man, or both together mixed!)
> This guessed at through the flesh, by parts which prove the whole.
> This constitutes the soul discernible by soul
> —— Elvire by me!"

This treatment of the religious emotions places us in a dilemma, because it impresses on them a purely subjective character ; whereas we have every reason to believe they correspond to a transcendent reality in Mr. Browning's mind. The belief in such a reality

permeates more or less every part of the poem; it is distinctly stated
in page 156:

> "The individual soul works through the shows of sense
> (Which ever proving false, still promise to be true),
> Up to an outer soul as individual too."

Elvire does not concern herself with the logical consistency of
these arguments, but she loses patience at so much discoursing on
sympathies of the soul, which in her opinion tend to nothing but the
gratification of every desire of the flesh, and she descants on her
husband's self-deception or hypocrisy in many animated words. We
cannot help regarding her remonstrance as in some measure a
spontaneous confession, on Mr. Browning's part, of the equivocal
nature of his doctrines, for their language has been hitherto far
more mystical than material, their sensualism rather suggested than
expressed. Elvire is, however, fully justified by the sequel. It is
part of her complaint against her husband that whilst he parades a
universal love of mankind, his practical interest lies only in women,
and he defends himself by defining at some length, and with singular
force of illustration, the distinctive characteristics of the two sexes.
Women gravitate towards men in frank acceptance and frank
surrender of their mutual being; jealousy and self-seeking mutilate
every relation of man with man: woman is the rillet which rushes
headlong from the pleasant places of its birth, to pour life and
substance into the sea; man is but the jelly-fish which inflates
itself at its expense. Woman's fullest life is love. *The strong, true
product of a man* is only evolved in hate. He must be stung into
fertility as was the vine of old, when the browsing goat nibbled away
its promise of flower and tendril, and gained the indignant wine from
their arrested growth.

Don Juan does not intend to prove that all women are intrinsically
good. There are Fifines as well as Elvires. But he vindicates the
Fifines of society as teaching a lesson of self-defence which no true
woman or permanent love can afford. Life is one long trial of self-
conscious strength. Such strength is not discovered in the steady
voyage, but in the fitful trip, not in guiding the steady bark whose
perfect structure co-operates with wind and tide, but in straining mind
and energy to navigate some rotten craft in safety. Elvire is the
good ship. Fifine the rakish craft. Elvire is honesty's self.
Fifine is wily as a squirrel. Elvire is too safe a companion to teach
the true lesson of life; why should she grudge Fifine the credit of that
experience of deceit and danger, which restores her husband to her
a stronger and wiser man? The less noble relations of life are thus
a mental gymnastic, in which *by practice with the false, one gains the
true.* They are the constant struggle to breathe the purer element,
whilst surrounded by one more gross (an ingenious inversion of

the idea which such situations usually suggest). They are paralleled in the condition of a swimmer, who learns, by constant practice, to rise or sink so completely at his pleasure that he acquires with every skilfully drawn breath a greater delight in air, but also a greater confidence in water. In this confidence lies his safety; any direct attempt to free his head and shoulders from the waves, submerges them the more completely; but a mere side movement of the hands, a mere grasping at the water, which he knows cannot be grasped, sends his face above it. He is saved by the very attempt to *treat liquidity as stuff*.

We have here one of the most prominent ideas of our poet's philo-sophy; the value of error as an indirect presentation of truth; as an expression of the onward groping of our minds which constitutes for us its only direct evidence, and perhaps its only absolute form. Mr. Browning's peculiar conception of the nature and relations of truth and falsehood pursues us throughout the poem under a Protean variety of aspect, which makes his meaning very difficult to grasp, whilst it impresses us with a sense of the vital significance which it possesses for his own mind. It is strange that a person so strongly convinced of the existence of a transcendent source of truth, should apparently regard it as never to be realised in life except as an atti-tude of the mind, or at best as a shifting balance between thought and things; but we have already seen this duality of conception under-lying his religious beliefs. He is more true to his objective point of view in his treatment of the idea of falsehood, which he represents as something more actual than truth, or at least anterior to it; as the necessary negation through which truth springs into life, as the re-fracting medium by which it is rendered visible. This attitude of mind relates itself in some indefinable manner to the keen sense of anomaly which gives so great a pungency to Mr. Browning's appreci-ation of life, and which inspires the last words of his defence of Fifine. We are told that she and all her tribe have a crowning charm—the charm of falseness avowed. We too are actors, but they only warn you that they are that and nothing else; they only *frankly simulate;* and Don Juan loves the dramatic pleasure of a lie which does not deceive, the delusion of the senses which leaves the judgment free to perceive it. We take it for granted that this impression of Bohemian life and character includes the more intimate experiences already indicated; though the instances given in this particular passage only present the Gipsy in his quality of strolling player, in which he aims at neither more nor less deception than dramatic artists of a higher kind.

From the midst of this mental juggling breaks forth almost a cry of longing for that rest to the soul which is denied to us in the fleeting appearances of life. Husband and wife are wandering homewards by the sea-shore. Night is fast overtaking them. In the creeping twilight, the plains expand into the significance of sea, whilst the sea itself fades murmuring out of sight:

> "All false, all fleeting too! and nowhere things abide,
> And everywhere we strain that things should stay,—the one
> Truth, that ourselves are true!"

So far 'Fifine at the Fair' is an apology for liberty of life; above all for discursiveness in love, which, in whatever form it assumes, is something gained to the soul; but we now pass from the individual to the general, from the changes of human life and feeling to their counterpart in the history of the world. The thought of actors and acting has recalled Don Juan to the subject whence he started, and he comments on the dreaming habit which has prompted so much digression, and which he thinks peculiar to *prose-folk* as opposed to poets. Poets possess the proper outlet for their poetic fancies, and can thus maintain the mental soundness that keeps *thoughts apart from facts*, the actual from what only might be. We should have thought the dream constituted the poet as much as the written poem, or only in a lesser degree; but we will not dispute Mr. Browning's judgment in this matter. Don Juan goes on to relate how this wandering mood has possessed him since the beginning of the day; how his morning idleness was burdened with *intrusive fancies* and *memories old and new*, that came crowding in from all the corners of the earth; and how he sought relief in music, the *recording* language of all complex emotion. He plays Schumann's 'Carnival,' and as he plays, remarks the new clothing of each familiar theme; and life spreads out before him as a banquet of successive ages, at which there is one viand dressed in an ever-changing sauce; at which each generation rejects the flavouring of the age which came before it, and old perfection strikes flat upon the palate till it has received a novel pungency. He sees that this is true in art as it is in life, and in music more than any other art,

> . . . . . . "Since change is there
> The law, and not the lapse: the precious means the rare,
> And not the absolute in all good, save surprise."

And contemplation finally passes into sleep, and sleeping he dreams himself in Venice. He is overlooking St. Mark's Square from some neighbouring pinnacle. At his feet is a crowd of men and women, each so masked as to simulate some face of bird or beast, or some incarnate desire or passion, or some excessive form of human ugliness or infirmity. He descends amongst them, and these monstrosities gradually disappear from sight. Distance had magnified into actual deformity, such mere deviations from the perfect human type as are forced upon it by the varying struggle of life. The mask of evil was but the surface hardening of each individual nature, no more to be confounded with the softer life within, than is the natural crystal casing of the Druidical divining dew-drop with the drop itself. We do not understand the meaning of this allegory which separates the individual soul from the collective life it contributes to create, and amounts to a denial of all actual moral evil, not easily reconciled with Mr. Browning's general beliefs. But the dream soon passes into another phase. Don Juan still thinks he gazes on the buildings of St. Mark's Square, and yet a subtle change is gliding over them: they stir, and tremble, and are still again; transformed into the likeness of something new, yet older and more familiar. It is not Venice, but the world; no carnival, but the life-long masquerade of humanity. Here, too, nothing abides. Temples towering aloft in all the apparent fixity of fate, struggle vainly against the creeping change. Inward corruption first obscures their marble glories, then quenches them in the darkness of that utter dissolution from which new life will arise. Not only temples and their worship, but the halls of science and philosophy, and all the minor structures that cluster at their base, live their day, and are gone. Each parades, in its special manner, its long promise and its short fulfilment.

A fantastic alternation of sentiment and satire runs through this part of the poem. In dealing with what he believes to be the higher forms of mental life, Mr. Browning represents this constant change in all the poetry of transformation; but in hunting it through the successive dogmatisms of history and minor morals, and even science and art, he draws a picture of mere upstart pretensions and absurd defeat. He is especially severe on the vicissitudes of science, which he typifies in the periodical rise and fall of a last new absolutely certain theory of the conversion of tadpoles into frogs. In this universal wreck of human strivings, he claims for Poetry the lion's share of spoils. Each other art has trumpeted her own achievements. Here is the poet's work to prove what he can do.

He has shown that change is *stability itself*. Persistence under another name. This is the lesson Don Juan has learnt from his phantasmagoric dream. He has seen life constantly transformed, but never destroyed. Each death was a new birth; each new delusion a fresh effort of truth. Beyond every deception and change there is something that does not deceive or pass away. The long experience of mutation forces on us the belief in permanence as its underlying condition and lasting result.

A final transformation is at hand. Some silent impulse compels edifice into edifice; the *multiform* into the *definite*; the restless life into a *blank severity of death and peace*.

What form does the gigantic unity assume? It is that of a Druid monument which religion has levelled with the ground, because simple-hearted superstition still honoured it with the profane rites of a once conscious worship. A thing of primitive, world-wide, mystico-material significance. Ignorance feels the meaning of the gaunt colossus, but learning fails to decipher it.

> . . . . . . "Magnificently massed
> Indeed, those mammoth-stones, piled by the Protoplast
> Temple-wise in my dream! beyond compare with fanes,
> Which, solid-looking late, had left no least remains
> I' the bald and blank, now sole usurper of the plains
> Of heaven, diversified and beautiful before.
> And yet simplicity appeared to speak no more
> Nor less to me than spoke the compound. At the core,
> One and no other word, as in the crust of late,
> Whispered, which, audible through the transition-state,
> Was no loud utterance in even the ultimate
> Disposure. For as some imperial chord subsists,
> Steadily underlies the accidental mists
> Of music springing thence, that run their mazy race
> Around, and sink, absorbed, back to the triad base —
> So, out of that one word, each variant rose and fell
> And left the same, 'All 's change, but permanence as well.'"

By a natural transition, Don Juan returns to his own experiences, carrying with him the newly acquired conviction, that, as permanence is the highest law of life, self-controlling constancy must be its highest freedom, and therefore its best happiness. And he bemoans his mistakes and follies in the tone of one who at least desires to be convinced of them. He need not have thus surrendered, unless he chose to do so. He might have argued that in his case, as in that of humanity at large, true permanence lay in the continued possibility of feeling, and not in the persistence of any one of its modes. But the closing pages of ' Fifine ' give stronger reasons for constancy than the fact that in nature nothing dies; and we quote one passage from Don Juan's final confession, as expressing the strongest argument in its favour which pure philosophy can afford:

> . . . . "His problem posed aright
> Was—' From the given point evolve the infinite !'
> Not—' Spend thyself in space, endeavouring to joint
> Together, and so make infinite, point and point.'"

He recognises inconstancy as a waste of life. But the end is not yet come. Elvire and her husband have reached the door of home. Her paleness strikes him with a sudden terror. He entreats her not to vanish from the repenting sinner, to give him the hand that shall satisfy him she is still present in the flesh. We may suppose that the hand is regained, and the husband reassured. He proposes to draw a picture of their future life and the conjugal happiness to which he has once more surrendered himself, and satirises it so unmercifully by the description that the ensuing catastrophe becomes a matter of course. He habitually walks with one hand open behind him. It suddenly appears that somebody has profited by the opportunity and slipped a letter under the glove. Some mistake has arisen out of the very large gift with which he owns to having relieved the pleading emptiness of Fifine's tambourine.

> " Oh, threaten no farewell! five minutes shall suffice
> To clear the matter up. I go, and in a trice
> Return; five minutes past, expect me! If in vain—
> Why, slip from flesh and blood, and play the ghost again."

We may conclude that the worst has happened, for we find our hero, in the Epilogue entitled 'The Householder,' expiating his vagaries in lonely respectability, when the wife, whose love was stronger than death, suddenly reappears and carries off the subdued if not converted sinner to his final conjugal rest. They wind?up by composing their joint epitaph, of which the last line, suggested by Elvire's ghost, is perhaps a true summary of Mr. Browning's belief : *Love is all and Death is naught.*

[If this singular tissue of truth and sophistry has any practical tendency, it is that of a satire upon marriage, or at least on domestic life ; and so far it were better that it had not been written.] The self-ridicule of the hero's final escapade adds considerably to the dramatic effect of the poem, and is perhaps a necessary result of the serio-comic spirit in which it was conceived, but it leaves an impression none the less unpleasant for the slight relation it probably bears to any definite purpose of the author's mind. The race of Elvires perhaps need a lesson : they are sometimes short-sighted and intolerant, and disposed to exact a maximum of fidelity in return for a minimum of charms ; but they have some virtues and many sorrows, and [we wish Mr. Browning had given to the attractions of his typical wife, just the added degree of pungency or of sweetness that would have ensured her husband's devotion at least for four-and-twenty hours longer. In his more direct advocacy of free love, he almost disarms criticism ; for he treats the subject with a large simplicity which places it outside morality, if not beyond it ; while the frankly pagan worship which he dedicates to material beauty is leavened by all the mystic idealism of a semi-Christian belief.] The half-religious language of Don Juan's amorous effusions has, at least, a relative truth to Mr. Browning's mind. If it were otherwise, 'Fifine at the Fair' would be more easy to understand, and also less worth the understanding.

[We must not, however, consider it as the mere discussion of one question of social morality, or even one aspect of the emotional life. It is, from the author's point of view, an epitome of human existence. The wide range of feeling and reflection that is evoked by the slight incidents of the poem redeems its doubtful tendency and often cynical tone, and converts what would otherwise be a mere satire upon life into a semi-serious but poetic study of it.⌉ Mr. Browning's theories contain nothing that is intrinsically new. They relate to subjects upon which too much has been said and too little can be discovered; but they possess a novelty which is peculiarly their own—the novelty of a poetic conception of philosophic truth. ⌈He is not a systematic philosophic reasoner; but his powerful intuitions anticipate the results of the most abstract, and also the most opposite processes of thought. His genius is purely metaphysical; but in his unflinching generalisation of the elemental facts of existence, and in his clear perception of all that is subjective in our moral and æsthetic life, he joins issue with the most positive thinkers of our day. His philosophy is too hybrid to be accepted by any purely reasoning mind. No such mind could have produced it. But the contradictions of philosophy must resolve themselves in the highest poetic synthesis of life, and the poetic truthfulness of Mr. Browning's genius, its accordance with the nature he strives to reproduce, is attested by its ardent vitality and continuous productive power.⌉ Herein lies the excuse, not only for his subjective intricacies and conflicting currents of thought, but for the poetic form in which he chooses to cast them. To use the language of a modern French philosopher,⌈he thinks in images and not in formulæ,⌉and the language of imagery is his by right, however he may use or abuse it, however it may limp or break down under the weight of meaning it is compelled to carry. ⌈That his poetry is occasionally tortured into something less than prose, is a fact which his warmest friends cannot deny; but those who assert that his poetry is always prose cannot have read the smallest half of what he has written.⌉ In his argumentative passages,⌈his verse often grates upon the ear;⌉in his most tender moods it does not always caress it; but it adapts itself with vigorous elasticity to every modulation of feeling, and no poet has echoed more truly the entire range of human emotions⌉ from the *fine faint fugitive first of all* to their loudest utterances in the harmonies or the discords of life.

⌈Some of Mr. Browning's readers have seen in him more than a poet and a thinker. They have invested him with the character of moralist. We do not think such a term could be justly applied to him at any period of his literary career. He is a moral writer in so far that he strives to promote a true knowledge of life. He teaches morality as life itself teaches it, by allowing the right to plead its own cause; but he does not always distinctly advocate the right.⌉ He is an ardent champion of truth; but truth means for him the uncompromising self-assertion of vice as well as of virtue. He is warm in his denunciation of injustice; but his justice as often identifies him with the pleader as with the judge. ⌈'Fifine at the Fair' will certainly remain one of his most interesting works; it is perhaps that in which the greatest wealth of imagery is combined with the greatest depth of thought; but it is surely also his least moral; not by reason of the tendencies we have already discussed; not because it sacrifices Elvire to Fifine, or asserts the natural law by which we oscillate between both; but because all its argument is carried on from an egoistic point of view, such as Mr. Browning does not habitually assume. His hero investigates all things with exclusive reference to his individual good; his theory of love is one of absolute sympathy; but his theory of life takes no account of any pains or pleasures but his own. Self is the central idea of Mr. Browning's philosophy, as the love which tends to the completion of self is in the present work the central idea of his æsthetics. But no one has a deeper reverence for the love which annihilates self; few perhaps are so capable of feeling it, and if he had chanced to write in another mood he might have advocated such self-annihilation as the crowning glory of the individual life. His instincts are absolutely religious. His imagination treasures the idea of each separate human spirit in all its transcendent mysteriousness. He hates the scientific mode of thought which merges the individual in the group, and reduces the action of the mind to the operation of general laws. Even whilst he asserts the development of the most complex emotions from the simplest instincts of life, he refuses to admit the usual premisses or the usual conclusions of such a belief. He accepts all the conditions of an abstract morality; it is only through the wilfulness of creative genius that he can identify himself with a nature which recognises no morality but expediency in the selfish sense of the word. His Don Juan approaches to a certain phase of the German spirit in his estimation of the uses of life. There is something Goetheësque in his idea of the just subservience of its successive experiences to the development of every truly self-conscious mind; but his egotism is even less ingenuous than that of Goethe, because he is the outcome of a later civilization, and is stimulated to a still keener consciousness of self by the greater power and more frequent opportunity of anomalous and complex sensation.

As we have already observed, these considerations lie outside the special charm and special merit of Mr. Browning's works. We only desire to prove that though he teaches many things in his own way, he teaches none with the direct aim and in the direct manner of a moralist. The attempt to prove him what he is not, can only confuse the perception of what he is; and to modify even in the sense of improvement an originality so marked as his, would be to destroy its psychological value and even its educative force. Mr. Browning does not think for us; he only stirs us into thinking for ourselves. In every mood of the heart or mind, we may turn to him for sympathy, but he will not help us to organise what we think or what we feel. Let us not expect this, and he will not disappoint us.

Soon after the publication of the first chapter of 'Roots' the editor received the following letter:

" ' ROOTS.'

" DEAR SIR,—Lo! the audacity of a poor remote little country mouse, who will officiously nibble the meshes which seem to have entrapped one great literary lion!

" The publication of 'Roots' in ·your November number, has this month in its season propagated a species of bulb, which can only be a 'root of bitterness.'

" My dear sir, you know not what you do in admitting such to your pages; but since sanitary laws ought to be the more rigidly enforced upon and by those who are not alive to the risk of neglecting them, in the name of all that is sacred, confine the pages of TEMPLE BAR to secular things, and let Religion and Irreligion fight their duel on another field. The safety-valve may swing upon a loose hinge, but all editorial weight should press upon the trap, which emits nothing but noxious vapour. Forget which is which; and as our mental and intellectual purveyor, you are answerable for furnishing diseased meat to our craving millions.

" True—the skipper of the 'brave little cutter leaping furiously at the waves,' may be a lovable private character—but if, in his contempt for *arrière pensée,* he will pitch overboard his quadrant (prayer), his compass (the Bible), his anchor (faith), his telescope (hope), his log-book (conscience), his ensigns (profession), and all the conventional paraphernalia which tend to make him a 'machine-made' sailor, he is responsible for the lives, not only of all those who sail with him, but of all lookers-on who, trusting their lives to the security of their impulses, are content to toss themselves in exciting uncertainty on the billows of fancy.

" It was Wisdom who said, ' It must needs be that offences come, but *woe* to him through whom they come.'

" Would you ventilate *these* views, even though you may disown them?—and pardon, dear sir, the suggestions of

AN OBSCURE WELL-WISHER."

This letter commands a certain amount of respect, for two reasons:

in the first place, it expresses an opinion that would be felt equally by a large proportion of men of all countries in the world, of every religion that exists in it, on a mode of speculation such as is ventilated in 'Roots.' In the second place, it is not disfigured by the malignant dullness and reasonless assertion that usually accompany a justification of not thinking.

I must begin by saying, with all due deference to my anonymous friend, that the last part of his letter is hardly to the point, being a mere repetition (I hope he won't be shocked) of the whole spirit of the first chapter of 'Roots.' The one thing I tried to paint most conspicuously was my young friend's intense appreciation of the utility to mankind of the dogmas he thoroughly disbelieved in, and the impossibility at present of men's discarding them without harm. It seems a truism, at first sight, to say that a thing not perfect may do enormous good, even through its imperfections, but it is a truism not yet acknowledged as a truth in the world of religious thought. Who ever knew a missionary who thoroughly appreciated the good that was daily being worked by the religion he was trying to supplant?

Now, my young friend's strongest characteristic was this power of liberal perception, springing from a firm belief in the omnipotence and omniscience of the unknown Creator, which taught him to look for a use and a purpose in everything.

The most enthusiastic priest could scarcely believe more firmly in the practical service performed by what the "obscure well-wisher" calls, in metaphorical language, quadrants, compasses, anchors, telescopes, log-books, &c.; but he would say that their practical utility was quite apart from the question of their being perfect Divine truth.

His stand-point was something of this kind: "I do not believe in the infallible Divine truth of either Christianity, Judaism, Mohammedanism, Buddhism, Hindooism or Parseeism, or any other theory concerning unknowable things that now exists; I should not deem myself justified in claiming Divine authority for any creed, however beautiful, *having no prior knowledge of God to enable me to decide what His truth is;* but I can see the good all these contradictory religious beliefs have done and are doing; I can understand the good influence they supply and the voids they fill in men's minds; so I learn naturally to look on these as God's means to effect the improvement of humanity. When I call them 'virtue-making machines' I am testifying to their worth. And when I see that the very quality I consider most wrong in them—i.e., their conceited assumption that they possess infallible truth, their utter ignoring of the great fact that religion is to an enormous extent an accident of birth—is the one that gives them their greatest power for good, I come to the simple conclusion that it is neither wise nor possible to improve them off the face of the earth. Of course they will die or change, as other religions have done before them, as soon as they become unsuitable and unnecessary to men's minds—but not before. I hold that a destruction of all these creeds from outside men's minds would do great harm. I say to my bugbear, 'the conceited certainty of ignorance,' or dogma, 'I see the good you are doing. Go on in peace; but be not aggressive, for if your zeal takes the shape of persecution in any way I will knock you down, and laugh at you, and show the world what an unjustifiable sham you are. You will be put on the shelf and forgotten some day, but the time is not yet come. You are a pleasant wanton, and flatter men so delicately that they cannot bear to leave you, though conscience tells them it is time for their minds to go to work.' I will go no further at present than to try, by showing the grounds on which scepticism stands, and differs from religious assertions, to clear away some of the barrowfulls of mud that are daily heaped upon it by ignorance and prejudice."

This is a short sketch of his way of regarding all the religions of the world, watching the causes, uses, and effects of their different dogmas with an impartiality and a comprehensiveness that gave one the idea that he was taking a bird's-eye view of humanity with a telescope from a different planet—a way of judging that made him terribly alone among men; for even the small school that agreed with his criticisms on religious subjects could not as a rule keep their eyes open to the good that these condemned doctrines worked every day; they could not quite understand how he could demonstrate that some dogma was a groundless offspring of human conceit and want of faith, and yet believe, as strongly as any who held it, the work it did in the path of human improvement. He would say, "Here is such and such a dogma—absurd, because it lays down the law positively on questions beyond human knowledge; and often leading to both blasphemy and cruelty when carried to the full length of its meaning; and yet it fills such a want in the human mind, and has such a strong practical power to influence men for good, that in spite of its absurdities and crimes it is better that men should believe in it as they are at present." But the members of his little band of comrades, unconsciously imitating the narrow-mindedness of the fanatical priests they hated so bitterly, would reply in effect, 'It is untrue, therefore it must be destroyed. You yourself own that it leads to great evils, both of thought and action, and truth in any case must be acknowledged before utility.' And he would reply (Jesuitically, they used to say),

> " Think not I'm one of those
> Who calmly claim omniscience, and suppose
> That God Almighty scarcely knows the worth
> Of this or that existing on the earth,

And cry, 'False creeds I cannot bear to see,
Because I'm sure that God agrees with me.'
I feel but sure of one thing, which is this :
*God's* truth is not quite what *I* think it is." *

I myself thought him, not Jesuitical, but larger-minded than the rest of that little band of earnest thinkers that I loved so well (though he was by no means the cleverest), and appreciated the liberality which could utterly separate the question of the absolute truth of an opinion with its utility to that ever-changing, ever-growing phenomenon of nature—man.

The root, perhaps, of his freethinking lay in the fact that he simply could not judge of a corner of the world as if it was the whole—could not cut off a portion of the world's history and leave the rest half out of sight. The opinion so commonly held by men of *all* religions, that one portion of mankind have actually a patent for God's truth, while all the rest are groping about in a state of carnal darkness, was to him an absurdity rendered evident by the fact that men of *every* religion considered themselves the patentees ; and he could not look on any stage of religious belief as utterly final, because of his firm conviction of the improvement of humanity.

He disagreed, he would laughingly say, with most of his sceptical comrades on a mere matter of dates. Both they and he were of opinion that a time would come when modes of thought would become far more unanimous, by all men pulling off (metaphorically speaking) the clothes of superstition and false claims to knowledge, and treading the earth with minds naked ; but he differed from them by believing most firmly that the time for such a transformation had not come, that it would do harm—in fact, that an attempt to steal their mental breeches unawares would probably be impracticable, and if practicable, excessively mischievous.

Well, the way I laboured to demonstrate the two-sided phase of my young friend's mind on religious questions—the way I prosed to inculcate his belief in the superior power for good on men, as they are, of the lowest form of religion over the highest form of scepticism, in the plainest English, was simply piteous. The thought of the platitudes, repetitions, and simplifications on this subject that I had inflicted on the public quite sickened me for some days. But, lo! in the letter of an "obscure well-wisher," and all the comments, friendly and hostile, that I have heard on the subject, the moral and intent of the conversation have been entirely omitted. I begin to sympathise

* This quotation has been introduced once before in 'Roots,' but I think that a truth so generally forgotten—not only by the adherents of all religions, but also by their free-thinking opponents—will stand a little repetition, and should be familiarised to men's minds by what my young friend would call the "Poll-parrot system."

with the feelings of the unfortunate gentleman who cut his throat after trying vainly for an hour and a half to convince a deaf old lady that he thought it was a fine day. The fact is, that the general heterodoxy of the tone of thought stuck so fast in people's throats that they were unable to swallow any of the conclusions at all.

With regard to the first part of the letter, my young friend would have said, "Its spirit is that breathed in the glorious old nursery ballad—

"'Tis the voice of the sluggard! I heard him complain,
You have waked me too soon, I must slumber again.'

It is nothing, in fact, more than the usual defence of not thinking on such subjects.

"There is the usual cry of 'Do confine your pages to secular subjects;' as if the commonest thing on the earth was not part of the same great mystery—as if religion should or could be something suspended in mid-air like a balloon; the usual implication that such questions are all comfortably settled, in defiance of the fact that all mankind are perpetually changing and differing about them; the usual not very flattering admission, that when such things are stirred up by the pole of honest investigation, they emit odours which require the compression of the religious nose; in short, the astounding assumption that this subject, which I venture to think by far the most important in life, is the only one on earth which is not to be honoured with the test of earnest impartial examination.

"The 'let-it-alone' theory does not, in my opinion, treat religion with very real respect. The conclusions it leads to from its premises, that religious theories are not to be impartially and strictly examined, are something of this kind: 'You are born into a world full of opposing religious theories. You are to lay hold of the one nearest to you and swallow it whole. Of course, if you chance to be born in England you will be Christian, if in Turkey, Mohammedan, if in the Marquesas, Cannibal, and so on. You are not to examine into your creed with human reason or common sense, if Providence has given you any—that is sinful. You must shut your eyes to the fact that there are millions entirely disagreeing with your belief, and yet as positive that they are right as you are. *You may pass judgment on their convictions as much as you like.* You may call them names—you may pity them, if you feel inclined. Yes, you should pity them certainly, because of their bad luck in not being born in the only country where the true faith exists. It was not the fault of that missionary that you eat the other day: it was only his bad luck in being born in the wrong part of the world, that prevented him from seeing the blessings of an enlightened Cannibalism.'

"Fancy some scientific man taking the non-investigation line about his theories. 'So you want to know the grounds of my assertions, do you? I am right, and that is enough. Lots of people utterly disagree with me, do they? So much the worse for them, that's all I can say. Don't go bringing your 'diseased meat,' of investigation here, sir. I am right, and—and—you! you are a conceited fool!'

"'But,' the obscure well-wisher and many of his way of thinking will perhaps say, 'the cases are not parallel; because we declare that religion is not a thing on which to exercise our human judgment.' To which I reply, that in making such a declaration they were using their human judgment in a most unmistakable manner.

"The fact is, that you cannot entirely shift the responsibility of what you believe or disbelieve on to the shoulders of any church or creed. Whatever religious opinions you may hold, if you trace back the reasons why you believe them honestly to the end, you must find your human judgment and opinion at the bottom of them.

"The pious Romanist or Mohammedan who says, 'I know such and such a doctrine is true, because it is in such and such a book; and I know the book is true because my religion says so; *and I know (or am sure, or believe,) that my religion is the only true one,*' exercises his human judgment to a wider extent than the sceptic who says, 'I do not think that my powers of judgment give me a right to lay down the law positively on matters upon which I see all the world disagreeing.'

"It is an acknowledgment of this truth that turns men, generally bitterly against their inclinations, into sceptics; so when religious folks revile them with 'conceit' and a too great reliance on the powers of human judgment, they naturally return the accusation with interest—and so the pot and kettle call each other black.

"An acknowledgment of this fact, that the root (however far back it may lie) of what a man believes or disbelieves is grounded on personal judgment and opinion, would go far to produce the toleration that I and many others desire to see; but I do not suppose that religions will open their eyes to it if they can help it, for it would place the opinions they worship on a lower, though a truer pedestal."

Now these are the sort of comments that my young friend would probably have made on the letter of the "obscure well-wisher." I myself am unable to see all the method of thought that he supposes is implied in it. It seems to me that all the "obscure well-wisher" meant by his rather abusive language was, that such kind of writing is noxious (whether true or false), because it may do harm to some minds by weakening the strength of the religion that has hitherto had power to keep them virtuous—a question that my young friend (as I have shown) regarded as nearly an open one, in his cool moments. What was the final conclusion that he came to, on the probable balance of the good *versus* the evil likely to be produced by the non-concealment of free thought, will be related in the next and last chapter of 'Roots.'

Yet I do not think that I have erred in putting these not strictly pertinent comments into his mouth, for he knew, poor fellow! from bitter experience, the kind of religious thought which called free honest thought by such names as "diseased meat" and "noxious vapours," and would at once suspect it, whether it lay behind these expressions or not, and, in his indignant vindication of his own style of thinking, would forget his usual impartiality for the moment. He did not possess a perfect temper, poor boy! Under his peculiar mental circumstances it would have been strange if he did.

Let us get out of this bitter atmosphere for a while, and refresh ourselves with a sniff of the sea-breeze.

Our little bay is looking brighter, greener, wilder than ever. The white flashes on the open water in the distance promise a quick passage to Auckland for the little cutter that lies twenty yards from the shore, getting ready for sea. Dan Stringer, a fine young half-caste without a surname, called Jack, and my young friend, are loading her, by means of a dingey and a punt, with firewood; while the sailors, with equal speed and energy, stow the cargo as fast as it comes on board. On a rock close to them sits Dan's half-caste daughter Mary, about to return to the custody of friends in town, for whom, in spite of my selfish delight at getting rid of her, I cannot help feeling a sincere pity. For she had already begun to sow discord in our little paradise. Jack already has fallen desperately in love with her, and wears a Cain-like expression of face whenever she speaks to any one but himself; while she, though too thorough a flirt to discard his attentions entirely, cares for him a little less than her father's kangaroo dog. One glance, as she sits there, at the tall womanly figure, and the dark, dare-devil, irregular beauty of her face, directing (as I fancy) occasional flashes of fascinating softness towards my young friend, would convince the most superficial observer that she ought not to be allowed to go anywhere without being decorated with a warning red flag.

Doctor Watts once made a proverb about idleness, with which all my readers are doubtless familiar. It was exemplified in this case by my young friend taking it into his head that it was his business—the young prig—to devote himself to this young lady's education. Now, the process of a young gentleman of twenty-one educating a young lady of eighteen is in my opinion not unlike that of warming a heap of loose gunpowder with a lighted match.

Educationally speaking, the experiment was a decided success. She, ordinarily utterly wild and intractable, proved a most willing and obedient pupil. She would pore over the same book with him for hour after hour, without showing a sign of weariness; she would go long

walks with him and listen to and remember and believe every word
that he spoke; in short, he taught her more in a week than she had
learnt in four years of school; but still I had very strong misgivings,
which every mother of a family will understand, as to whether the end,
taken as a whole, would quite justify all these proceedings.

It strikes me as something ghastly that I should be able already to
write so lightly of all this. Well! well! Time and a busy life combined will soon blunt the most painful remembrance; but if I could
only have guessed——stop: I am getting on too fast. Let us enjoy
our little glimpse of sunshine before the black clouds murder it.

With my hat dangling from my fingers, I stroll lazily towards the
rock where "the firebrand" is sitting. Ordinarily reserved and silent,
in spite of her wild mischief, she is more so than ever now, and answers
all my platitudes with mechanical monosyllables, whilst the tearless
black eyes have a look about them that I have never seen before.
"Humph!" think I to myself with an indignant sniff; "here's a pretty
mess that reckless young gentleman has been making in his character
of male schoolmistress! Thank goodness the silly girl is going out of
the place." Women, even while making common cause against their
common enemy, men, contrive to think very cruelly of each other.

Meanwhile, our conversation having died a natural death, I stroll
nearer to where the work is going on. There is a general atmosphere
of energy, perspiration, and, it must be owned, occasional forcible language. The little punt, with timber piled high above her gunwale, is
shoved off for the last time, Jack the half-caste standing on top of the
heap, and paddling cautiously towards the cutter. He inclines his
weight in the least degree to one side, and the overladen little craft
turns slowly and solemnly over, spilling Jack and all his cargo into six
feet of water. Whereon, both from his unsanctified lips and those of
Dan, came a chorus of exclamations so horribly expressive that I was
forced to stop my ears for very shame.

"I shouldn't think you found this society altogether improving,"
cried I indignantly to my young friend, who was standing close to me
at the moment.

"It's not pleasant language to listen to, certainly," replied he with
a cool grin, "but it is only language—neither more nor less than
their way of expressing 'What a bore.' Dan and Jack are good men
and true; shall I discard them because they speak a foreign tongue?"

"You are incorrigible in the matter of excuses," cried I, marching
with scornful dignity out of earshot, while he went back to help to
collect the floating timber.

At last the work was finished and the cutter ready for sea. My
young friend (rather unnecessarily I thought) carried Mary into the
dingey and seated her on board, at which poor Jack looked as black as
thunder. The dingey came back, the anchor was weighed, the sails

loosed, and amidst a multitude of good-byes, and a parting chorus of chaff between Dan and the sailors, the little vessel rounded Farewell Point and was lost to view, and as the end of the main-boom disappeared behind the rocky cliff I found myself unconsciously heaving a sigh of relief. With a civil "Good day " Dan shouldered his axe and trudged stoutly homeward, like one who had done his duty as a woodcutter and a father, while poor Jack sauntered off with a listless air that told pretty plainly what he was thinking of. My young friend laid himself out to dry in the sun, as if colds and rheumatism were as yet uninvented.

"I'm glad she's gone," said I significantly, nodding seawards.

"Poor little black cat, why?" inquired he, with dutiful unconsciousness.

"Can't you, or *won't* you see, that you were making poor Jack more crazy with jealousy every day?" asked I sharply.

"The sooner poor Jack gets accustomed to that the better," answered he, rather pityingly, "for if I don't make him jealous you may be sure half a dozen other people will. Why, I believe that girl did flirt with her godfather when she was in long clothes, and will flirt with the clergyman who administers to her the last consolations of religion."

"Well," said I forcibly, "If she comes down here again she will bring mischief with her."

"That's as certain as the sunrise," replied he with a lazy laugh. And here I stopped short. If I could only have foreseen, but it is too late to think of that now. The fact was that, honourable and trustworthy as I knew my young friend to be, I could not hide from myself that to tell him that I knew the girl loved him already would be to break one of the most decided and sacred laws of that very contradictory and elastic catalogue—the feminine code of honour. "She won't marry Jack," added he, after a pause, during which he had been reflecting, taking shots at a bit of wood floating in the water; "and if she did she would make his life miserable by her vanity and wilfulness. What a strange mixture of comedy and tragedy some women are! They will break their hearts and their necks too to get the rubbishing apple that hangs out of their reach, and kick aside contemptuously the far finer one that lies at their feet."

"Don't be priggish," interrupted I. "I am no admirer of the shallow claptrap of young cynics. Their half-true platitudes are made neither wise nor witty by being feebly malicious."

"I really think," continued he, smiling and taking no notice of my caustic admonitions, "that the Persian legend of the creation of woman must be the right one after all. Would you like to hear it?"

"I can see by your face," said I resignedly, "that it is something impudent and silly, but as time and experience only can teach you greater wisdom and humility you may as well go on." He took no more notice of me than if he had been deaf. The fact was, that I was a great deal too fond of the boy to snub him properly, and like most spoilt children, he was quite aware of the fact.

"To begin with," said he, "I have several reasons for believing that the story of the Garden of Eden was taken, during the Babylonish captivity, with many other things, from the Magians, and adopted by the Jews. By the way, what an interesting study it would be to trace the influence of their grand old monotheism* (for it was originally a real Monotheism, until that stumbling-block, 'the origin of evil,' tripped them up, like all the rest of the world,) on Judaism, and through that on Christianity and Mohammedanism!"

"Oh, that theology!" cried I, despairingly; "whatever we talk about seems to lead back to that eternal subject."

"So it should," replied he rebelliously. "As all theology takes its root in man's impressions and theories on all that he sees around him, it is more or less indissolubly connected with everything, and "——

Here I stopped my ears, and he, consequently, his tongue.

"Let us to the legend, then," said he. "Whether it is one held to be absolutely authentic by the modern Parsees, who are the sole remnant of the once widespread faith, I know not, but it differs from the Jewish one in one very important particular, as you shall hear.

"Ormuzd (the Good Deity) had placed Adam in the Garden of Eden, giving him full power and authority over everything in it, except the tree of knowledge and the tree of life. But after a while he thought that it was not good for man to be alone, and he determined to create woman. So he threw Adam into a deep trance under a tree in the garden, and took a rib from his side, wherewith to make woman. And Ormuzd stood there, turning the rib over in his hands, like one not quite sure of the wisdom of what he was doing; and the more he thought about it the more he determined to take time to consider. So at last, he laid the rib down by Adam's side, and calling an angel to come and watch it, went for a walk in the garden. Now whether this angel was tired from flying on errands or from fighting the followers of Ahriman, or whether the weather was hot and drowsy, the legend saith not; it merely states that the angel went fast asleep at his post.

---

* The deity of Zoroaster was too far off, too intangible, to suit or have hold on the minds of men, so his disciples, like all the rest of the world, dragged him down to the level of their comprehension, by making him a perfect idealised man-spirit, and invented a devil, to account for pain and evil. And so this Monotheism died out of the world, as all *real* ones have as yet done.

"Now, as luck would have it, the great Father of Apes came sauntering by, brimful of curiosity, as usual; and he examined Adam, and he examined the angel, and finally he examined the rib, till at last, having fully satisfied himself that it couldn't possibly belong to him or be any business of his, or be of any possible use to him, he determined (this is monkey-reasoning) to appropriate it. This done, he proceeded to climb the tree under which the sleepers were lying, to have a more deliberate examination of his newly-acquired treasure. But in so doing, he knocked a bit of bark on to the angel's nose; this woke him, and seeing the rib gone and the monkey above his head, he realised what had happened and flew up the tree in pursuit. But the monkey gained the topmost boughs, while the angel's wings became entangled in the branches, so that the most he could do was to seize the end of the monkey's tail and pull lustily. But the monkey held on like grim death, and refused to drop the bone, while, to the angel's horror, he heard Ormuzd walking slowly towards the tree. He gave one desperate tug, and away he went crashing to the bottom of the tree, with the monkey's tail in his hands. With great presence of mind, he laid the tail down by Adam's side exactly where the rib had been. Absently and pensively Ormuzd walked up, and without further scrutiny transformed the tail into a woman.

"This exquisite legend accounts for several things. In the first place it tells us how apes came to have no tails. Secondly, it gives us the key to Eve's fatal curiosity. Thirdly, it explains why women are—ahem!—women."

"It amuses me," remarked I scornfully, "to watch you playing at being a misogynist, or a 'gynothrope,' as Mayne Reid delightfully calls it in one of his books. I have always noticed that small-minded men, who are peculiarly enslaved by admiration and respect for women, take a mean bombastic delight in proclaiming their contempt for them as loudly as possible."

"Be pacified," cried he, laughing. "Has not the great Darwin shown that very likely men, as well as women, are descended from the same hairy parent? And upon my word," added he, "a study of the *jeunesse dorée* of the present day has almost led me to believe he is right.

"The 'prodigal son' of the nineteenth century is a strange animal truly. Like an animal, he is negatively bad more than positively. His only business is the pleasure of the moment. He is scarcely wicked, because his moral nature is so blunted that he really never thinks what is wrong and what right, except in the matter of violating some 'honour among thieves' kind of law which he and those like him have made sacred. His soul is drugged till it is well nigh dead. He is generally a simple believer in the religion he has been brought up in, because thinking is not in his line; but as for realising his religion and trying to act up to it, that is not in his line either. He is *the* most exasperating specimen of humanity to all earnest people of whatever opinions, excepting his brother 'the respectable worldling' —a type to be met in all nations and classes. His law (by no means a bad one, mark you,) is that of conventional respectability. The religious faculties of his mind are quite as fast asleep as those of his sinful brother, and he looks on all who are not as stupefied as himself as more or less crazy. If you told him he was an infidel, he would be honestly astonished and indignant. Yet, as far as not realising and not caring about what he professes to believe, he is an infidel to the backbone. Like Gallio, he cares for none of these things. He may be an amiable worldling or an unamiable one, but a godless animal worldling he is, not only not seeking, but not feeling the want of, mental inquiry and realisation in religion.

" These two brothers, so unlike in their outward life, so like as regards thought and religion, are, as I said, the most intolerable bugbears to earnest men of all sorts. The preacher thunders at them from the pulpit; the freethinker shoots bitter words at them from his study; but still, smiling like South Sea Islanders under the influence of *kava*, the worthless, selfish, profligate, godless prodigal, and his equally godless, thoughtless, respectable brother, float calmly down the river of life, continually run into by the barks of their living-souled fellow-creatures, yet, like the elastic surf-boats of Madras, never the least feeling the effects of a collision.

" Well, believing as I do that everything in the world has a purpose, whether we can see it or not, I cannot call them unmitigated evils. I fancy, moreover, that I can see the good worked by that sluggishness and shallowness of mind that priests and sceptics alike detest so bitterly. For they act as a drag and a safeguard upon humanity, doing good to their kind by sheer indifference. Suppose all these people cleared out of the world, and the earnest people left to themselves. The whole lot of them would be carrying out their opinions to their logical or illogical consequences, till, either metaphorically or literally, they hung each other in every market-place. Whereas as things are now, when a tendency of such a kind is displayed, these great, lazy, apparently worthless giants rouse themselves yawningly, saying, with a kind of sluggish common-sense: 'Now listen. I don't know which of you people are right and which wrong, and what's more, I don't care. But this kind of row isn't the right thing, and I want to sleep comfortably; so, if you are not quiet, I'll gag the lot of you.'

" And this animal indifference of theirs does good too in a nearly opposite direction; for it stimulates earnestness even while it checks its possible consequences. A great vice produces almost invariably an opposing virtue. The impurity of a nation produces a Puritan reaction, and so on."

"So," said I sarcastically, "let us inscribe on the tombstone of every horrible criminal :

> "'Stranger! here lies one
> Who
> (Whether you be Saint or Sinner)
> Has done as much as you
> In his own peculiar Fashion
> Towards the Improvement of Humanity,'"

"And how do you know," replied he, "that the life and example of every criminal do not teach a good lesson to humanity? The ascetic purity of early Christianity was greatly aided by the filthy licentiousness around it. Great drunkenness and its consequences produce a fanatical Temperance party. In fact, the presence of sin stimulates virtue."

"When I was a little girl they used to teach me that evil communications corrupted good manners," said I.

"I never denied," cried he impatiently, "that what we call sin spreads sin, but merely stated that at the same time it stimulates virtue. When a man comes in contact with some crime one of two things usually happens: either he is seduced by it, or he is horrified by it, his love of virtue being thereby stimulated. Why, it is a mere truism to say that men are deterred from sin by seeing its consequences."

"Well," retorted I provokingly, misunderstanding his drift, "it is a comfort to think that it is so easy to improve the world that one can do it by sinning comfortably. Why don't you give us the benefit of your help by committing a murder or two?"

But he heeded me not, for rising to his feet, and gazing wildly over the crisp blue sea at the many-coloured hills beyond, he was following the path of his thoughts:

"In all that glorious landscape there is not one particle of matter, animate or inanimate, that is not apparently at war with another, destroying or being destroyed—that is not really changing or being changed. Death is creating life and life death at every moment, in every place; for though apparently employed in mutual annihilation, their strife is but the striking of an awful but harmonious chord. What seems destruction is but fresh creation. So too with good and evil—Ormuzd and Ahriman.

"Their seemingly destructive antagonism is the key to their ceaseless existence. Every deadly blow that they strike generates fresh force. Can it be that even Ormuzd should utterly conquer Ahriman, and bring the promised Millennium? We cannot imagine it, for Evil being utterly destroyed, Good would become a nonentity, and life would not be life, or the world the world. Yet we know not. Somewhere adown the dim vista of eternity it *may* come to pass that the

two powers, wrestling closer and closer in their creative struggle, may
at last become one, and thus pass into non-existence, the life of each
having been dependent on that of the other.  But we cannot imagine
it.  For to render it possible, change and antagonism in the world,
which seem now to be the mainspring of its existence, must have
ceased.  We cannot conceive it paralysed at the halting point of perfection.  And while change through antagonism is the mainspring of
its existence, what we call pain and misery must in some form or
another remain.  *Our* path seems to me plain : to trust the purpose
of it all blindly to the Almighty Power, and to suffer and be brave."

And as he stood there with his hair fluttering in the breeze, and a
rigid, painful earnestness expressed in his attitude, his hands, his eyes,
and every line of his face, a sense of awe stole over me, for it seemed
for the moment as though I were looking upon the embodied type of all
the truth-loving sorrowing men that have existed through all ages,
who have been driven almost to madness by a knowledge of their
ignorance, by a sense of the insoluble mystery of everything around
them.

I broke the spell, saying quietly, " There is death in the pot.  The
only hope you hold out as legitimate is so utterly vague that the moral
of all you have said seems plainly to be, ' Let us eat and drink, for to-
morrow we die.' "

" To me," replied he, " the moral seems to be, ' Let us strive to develop in ourselves a complete trust in God, a great unselfish love for
our fellow-creatures, and a manly courage, until the very miseries of
our life seem to us means of improvement.' "

I shook my head.  "A very ingenious and almost miraculously
orthodox conclusion for your wild speculations to lead to ; but it seems
to me that if mankind were persuaded that the drones and criminals
were as necessary to the improvement of mankind as the earnest and
virtuous they would tend towards idleness and crime themselves,
crying, ' *Sessa!* Let the world slide.' "

My young friend paused awhile, and I flattered myself that he was
posed ; but after performing a *post-mortem* examination on a dead crab
he replied, " I am not quite sure of that.  I said that the drones and
the criminals were as necessary as the earnest and virtuous in the
work ; firstly, because they act as a drag upon the extremes which
earnest people are always apt to run into ; and secondly, because, by the
law of repulsion and antagonism which I afterwards wandered away
upon, they irritated and strengthened earnestness and virtue.  I don't
think that an acknowledgment of this fact need make a man either a
drone or a criminal.

" Take an analogy in politics.  We will suppose a man to be a conscientious Liberal.  Yet, unless he is a mere fanatic, he will own that
an opposition on the whole is a good thing, because it is a safeguard

against over-hasty legislation, checking sudden and often faulty impulses and principles. To carry out the analogy, he would very likely own further, that by the very fact of its being an opposition it did good in another way, by sharpening the wits and the energy of the side he believed right. He does not become any the less a conscientious and earnest Liberal because he owns this fact."

I really don't know how to answer this, so take refuge in satire. "It seems to me," said I, "that your theory of the use of evil is much like the Spanish one of the use of beggars. When a Spaniard sees a beggar, which he does every ten yards he walks, he gives him a small coin, with the philosophical reflection that it is a great mercy that beggars exist, because if they didn't neither he nor any one else would have the means of getting to Heaven."

"It seems to me," replied this impudent young person, mimicking my voice and manner, "that your method of dealing with a point under discussion is much like a sight I once saw of a poor half-paralysed wretch trying to eat his dinner. He made so many bad shots at his mouth with his fork that he finally gave it up in despair, and left off hungry. Let us get up on Farewell Point and see if the cutter is still in sight."

And we clambered up, and lay down in the long grass to regain our breath. The breeze had died away, and the little cutter, not two miles off, was rocking lazily on the swell.

However unartistic it may seem, I must honestly confess that this slight circumstance did not fill me with any vague mysterious presentiments. Nor do I, like some people I have met, have my presentiments *afterwards*. But as my eyes wandered lazily from the little cutter to the thoughtful face of my young friend, I rejoiced secretly over the departure of "the firebrand," and wondered vaguely what would happen if she came back again.

"What are you thinking about?" asked I, suddenly and sharply.

"I was thinking," replied he, scrutinising my face with a mischievous twinkle in his eyes, "how dreadfully sea-sick that unfortunate girl must be at this moment. And what, pray, were *you* thinking of?"

"I was thinking," said I, "that—that you looked as if you thoroughly believed in your pet proverb: 'Idleness with contentment is great gain.'"

# A Vagabond Heroine.

## By MRS. EDWARDES,

### AUTHOR OF 'ARCHIE LOVELL,' 'OUGHT WE TO VISIT HER?' &c.

---

## CHAPTER II.

### AMBROSIAL CASH.

IT is but too obvious that they are a haphazard unlawful pair. Belinda darns not, neither does she sew. Her clothes go uncounted to the washerwoman and return, or do not return, as they list; by natural processes of selection, such as are of tougher fibre than their fellows survive and come together in the end, irrespective of any primitive differences in colour or design. Of these stockings that she now wears, one being grey the other brown, both ragged, it would indeed be hard to conjecture the original stock; nor is their incongruous effect lessened by a well-worn pair of the sandals of the country—*espargottes*, in Basque parlance, linen slippers, roughly embroidered in scarlet, and bound high above the instep by worsted braid. Her frock is of rusty black, texture indescribable; her hat of unbleached coarse straw, so battered out of shape that one must see it on a human head to recognise it as a hat at all. And she wears her hair in plaits, tight hideous plaits, tied together at the ends according to the fashion of the Spanish peasants, by a piece of frayed-out, once green ribbon.

Nothing lovely, nothing artistic, even, about her. Yet 'tis a picture that a stranger of discriminative eye could scarce pass unnoticed—this poor little girl, with her tattered frock and illicit stockings and sunburnt high-bred face, audaciously gay one minute as any Paris gamin's, sad the next as that of a woman who already has tasted the fruit of knowledge and found it bitter.

Spain or Clapham? Raising herself lazily from the sward—such mixture of dust and lifeless stalk as here in the south we dignify by the name of sward—Belinda, after several more yawns, draws forth from her ragged pocket a letter, written on sea-green English notepaper, that must certainly have cost the sender double postage, and in a characterless little boarding-school ladies' hand.

"'MY DEAREST BELINDA:'

("Dearest!—for her to call me 'dearest,' when papa himself used to think 'my dear little girl' sufficient! But Rose must be a hypocrite, even in writing.)

"'You will be surprised, and *I hope pleased*, to hear that I am

coming all the way to the south of France to see you. I am sure
when I look at St. Jean de Luz on the map it quite takes my breath
away. I have always had a horror of the Bay of Biscay, and can
never sleep in the train, as most people do ; and then I am such a
coward about strange beds ! But of course Spencer will be with me ;
and as there have been several cases of smallpox close at hand, and I
am so frightened about it, Doctor Pickney says the wisest thing I can
do is to pack up my boxes and run. I have been vaccinated three
times, and, although the doctors say not, I think it always *took a
little*. I do hope there is no smallpox about in the south. If you
have not been vaccinated already, you might get it done as a precaution before I arrive. I trust, dear, you will find me looking pretty
well. I am in mourning still, but of course slight, for poor Uncle
Robert has been dead three months—indeed, the milliners scold me
for wearing it any longer. But I consult feeling, not fashion, in such
things ; and what can be more becoming than pale lavender silk
richly trimmed, or a white sultane polonaise edged with black velvet
and a *deep* fringe ? I wish I knew whether hats or bonnets were best
style in foreign watering-places. I have written to the *Queen* to ask,
but I am afraid I shall not get the answer before I start. Nothing
is seen in London but those large flat crowns, which never suited me,
and the Dolly Vardens have got so dreadfully common. Really, as I
often say to Spencer, dress is one long trial. Were it not for those I
love, I would—but this is a subject on which I dare not trust myself
to speak. My dearest Belinda, I shall have news to tell you when we
meet of the most deeply interesting nature, affecting the future *of us
both*. I am glad you have made acquaintance with Augustus Jones.
He is a prime favourite of mine—indeed, he *will* make me correspond
with him—young men are so foolish—and as I tell them all, an old
woman like me! What you say about his ' vulgarity ' is simply ridiculous. How can it matter whether his father sold patent stoves or
not? Has a young man money?—not, How was his money made?—
is the question the world ask. I only hope he will be still at St. Jean
de Luz when I arrive, which may be almost as soon as this letter.
Present my compliments to our excellent friend, Miss Burke, and
believe me,

" Your own affectionate mamma,<br>" ROSE.

" P.S.—Augustus Jones has a villa at Clapham, *elegantly* furnished,
everything in the first style. I have often dined there in his
father's time with poor dear Uncle Robert. Augustus will be an excellent parti, I can assure you, Belinda, for *any* girl who may be
fortunate enough to win him."

Belinda crushes the letter together contemptuously, flings it up-twice or thrice, ball fashion, into the air, then thrusts it away, still in its crumpled state, out of sight, and lapses back into castle-building.

"Spain or Clapham?" Just as she has for the third time asked herself this fateful question, an Englishman, in full afternoon Hyde Park dress, emerges from the Hotel d'Isabella, about fifty yards distant from the little Place or square where the girl is sitting, and espying her, approaches.

The new comer is young, florid, not distinctly ill-looking as far as features go, but most distinctly vulgar. The way he wears his hat, his jewelry, his neck-tie—everything about the man, in short, jars on your taste, you know not wherefore. And then he is mosquito-bitten; and mosquito-bites are not wont to improve the expression of the features, or to confer, even on worthier men than Mr. Jones, an air of distinction.

"A villa at Clapham, elegantly furnished—an excellent parti for *any* girl who may be lucky enough to win him," thinks Belinda, as the hero of her air-built romance draws near. "What a pity Rose does not appropriate so much good fortune herself! I must see about making the match up as soon as I get them together."

And with this she laughs aloud, not as young ladies who have learnt to do all things prettily laugh, still less as the British school-girl giggles. Shrill, rather, and impish, laughter savouring of malice, not mirth, is the laughter of Belinda O'Shea. Mr. Jones's face, a spot of warm colour at all seasons, has grown to the hue of a well-ripened tomato by the time he reaches her.

"Good afternoon, Miss Belinda. Upon my word you have found out the only bit of shade in the place. Glad to see you find your own thoughts so amusing." Augustus attempts the drawl of the high-bred swell, as he has seen that personage depicted on the stage. Not with very marked success.

Belinda pushes her ragged hat a little further back from her forehead, stretches out her shabby, sandalled feet in the dust, then, glancing up at Mr. Jones, much as one small boy glances at another with whom he is inclined to quarrel, but whose strength he measures, begins to whistle.

"I thought yesterday you told me you meant to give up that—that slightly unfeminine accomplishment of yours," he remarks, after a minute.

"And I," retorts the girl, "thought you promised never again to make use of that shocking 'Miss Belinda.' If you had pluck enough to say 'Belinda' outright, I could bear it; but as you have not, and as you seem to think it necessary to call me something, do say 'Miss O'Shea.' You have no idea how *caddish* 'Miss Belinda' sounds."

The tomato hue extends itself over poor Mr. Jones's very ears and neck. "Oh! For the future, then, it's to be 'Belinda' between us, is it? Only too happy, on my side, I am sure. But I must ask one thing back." He has taken a place beside her, after carefully selecting a comparatively clean patch of turf on which to deposit his Hyde Park splendour—"I must ask one thing back—that you always call me Augustus."

She looks at him through and through with her fearless child's eyes.

"'Augustus,' I hope you have brought me some macaroons. Augustus. Augustus, try not to kick Costa when you think I am not looking. No, I could not. If I saw you every day till I died, and if I lived to be a hundred years old, I could never call you 'Augustus.' I might do it once"—she corrects herself—"half a dozen times, even, if you bribed me handsomely; but from my heart, never!"

"In other cases you don't appear to feel much shyness about doing so," remarks Mr. Jones, cuttingly. "It seems to me that you call half the English and American fellows in the place by their Christian names."

"Ah! they are only boys," says Belinda, with a smile brimful of unconscious coquetry. "You would not have me 'mister' my chums —the fellows I play paume with, would you?"

"I would have you not play paume, as you call it, at all," replies the young man, in a tone of deliberate, half-tender patronage. "I like a dash of chic as well as any man" (I am afraid poor Augustus pronounces it chick), "but it must be chic of the right kind, bong tong, and all that sort of thing. Now, what—what should we think in England of a girl who would be seen playing fives as you do, and in such company?"

Belinda shoots a sharp glance at him from under her long lashes. I forgot to mention that the child has long lashes, black as night, too, and overshadowing iron-grey eyes.

"Not play paume, not dance the bolero, not whistle, not take moonlight walks with Costa! What *would* you have me do, I should like to know, Mr. Jones?"

A London beauty of a couple of seasons' standing could not have brought an elder son more neatly and more innocently to the point. Mr. Jones examines the opera dancer who reposes in silver on the end of his cane, the huge cameo ring that he wears upon his little finger, then he delivers himself of his sentiments thus: "I should like, Miss Belinda—Belinda—I beg your pardon, Miss O'Shea"—for the life of him he cannot get to the familiar Christian name, as she sits there in her ragged frock, in her palpable out-crying poverty, and with her little high-bred face held aloft, and her dark eyes mutely dissecting him and his speech to atoms—"I should like to see you the model in all respects of your mamma. My beau idéal—I mean," says Augustus, suddenly recalling recent French lessons, and struggles with French genders, "my belle idéal, of everything most to be desired in an English lady is Mrs. O'Shea."

"Belle idéal! Why can you never let a word alone when by extraordinary accident you have got it right?" cries Belinda, cruelly. "Who ever heard of a belle idéal? Ah! and so my stepmamma is your beau idéal of everything to be desired in an English lady, and you would advise me to take her as a model in all respects? Thanks. Now I know exactly what courses to avoid and imitate. No more paume."

"Paume is the last game I should think an English lady of tong would be seen playing," says Mr. Augustus Jones, oracularly, and giving a contemptuous glance towards the schistera which lies at the girl's side. A schistera, I should explain, is the spoon-shaped basket or hand-shield with which paume is played in the Basque Provinces. "I am quite sure Mrs. O'Shea would think as I do about such a game."

"But then you must remember *I* love it passionately," cries Belinda—"passionately—to distraction! What do I care about being lady-like? If you could play yourself, you would not be such a muff as to talk about 'tong.' Ah! the moment," cries the child, clasping her graceful dark hands—"the moment of moments, when you are twenty all!—the ball with the enemy—you see it spinning through the air—you know that the game is to be made off your own schistera— you strike, you . . but of course," breaking off, with mild pity of her hearer's ignorance "of course it's no use talking paume to people who don't understand paume. Well, then comes the bolero. Surely you would allow me one now and then, Mr. Jones, just between the lights, you know, and under shadow of the trees?"

"I don't mind the bolero, or fandango, or any other of the native cancans, provided they are danced by the right people," answers Mr. Jones, with his drawl. "Quite the reverse. When one of these Basque peasant wenches has gone through her barbarous gesticulations, and brings me her tin cup for payment, I put my sous into it with all the pleasure in life."

Belinda's eyes flash daggers at him. "I cannot imagine your giving a sou to any one on any occasion with pleasure," she exclaims with spiteful emphasis. "And you speak as you do because you know no better! You don't understand the peasants or their dances. You measure everything by your own Clapham tastes, sir! However, we will not argufy." The reader is asked to pardon this and other linguistic peculiarities on the part of Belinda. "I have my ideas, you yours, and no doubt Rose will back you up in them when she is here. You did not know, by-the-by, that my mamma was coming to St. Jean de Luz, did you, Mr. Jones?"

Mr. Jones hesitates. Talleyrand's advice as to not following one's first impulse for fear it should be a good one, is, although I daresay he never heard of Talleyrand, a first principle with this excellent young man. Prudence, distrust, disbelief in impulse of all kinds, rather than special genius for the development of kitchen grates, raised Mr. Jones, senior, inch by inch, from a shake-down beneath the counter to a Clapham villa and liveries. Prudence, distrust, disbelief in impulse, are qualities born and nurtured in the very life-blood of the son.

"Rose corresponds with you, I know," cries Belinda, scanning his face. "Don't be ashamed of your little weaknesses, Mr. Jones. 'Young men are so foolish,' as Rose says. I can see you know, just as well as I do, that my stepmamma is coming to St. Jean de Luz."

"Well, yes, I know that Mrs. O'Shea is coming here, certainly," says Augustus, deliberation having shown him, perhaps, that to tell the truth can, for once, cost nothing. "Indeed I had a few lines from her, written from Paris, by to-day's post. I have her letter in my pocket," where, however, he has the discretion to let it rest. "As far as I can make out, we shall have the pleasure of seeing Mrs. O'Shea and Captain Temple arrive this evening."

Up rushes the crimson in a flood over Belinda's face. "Captain Temple! I don't know what you mean by Captain Temple!" she exclaims, suspecting what he means only too well, and colouring with hot shame over her own suspicions. "Rose is coming here alone, with her maid, of course."

"Oh, of course!" repeats Augustus, with the slow affected drawl that irritates Belinda to such desperation. "I don't for a moment mean that Mrs. O'Shea, under these or any other circumstances, would act otherwise than with the most lady-like propriety. Still, when one considers everything, Miss Belinda, there is no great wonder in Captain Temple *happening* to travel in the south of France, and in this particular district of the south of France, just at the time when Mrs. O'Shea and her maid *happen* to travel here too!"

His smile, his tone, a sudden scorching remembrance of certain lachrymose allusions in more than one of Rose's recent letters, bring Belinda from suspicion to certainty.

"If I thought—if I could believe such a thing!" she exclaims, then stops short: both sunburnt fists tight clenched, her lips set together like a small fury's.

"If you could believe that two people who loved each other in their youth—I conclude you have heard the romantic story before this?—if you could believe that two people who were in love with each other some dozen or more years ago were fated to marry and be happy at last, what then?" asks Augustus. "Mrs. O'Shea's second marriage would not interfere with your life much, as far as I can see."

"If Rose marries again, I swear never to speak to her or to her husband while I live," cries Belinda tempestuously. "I will not believe such disgraceful news until she tells it me with her own lips, and I have not the very smallest curiosity in the matter. Is he dark or fair?—good heavens, are you dumb, Mr. Jones? What kind of man, I ask you, is this miserable Captain Temple?"

"Roger Temple is fair—yellow, rather; all these Indian fellows are alike—shuts his eyes at you as he speaks—deuced nasty trick for a man to shut his eyes at you as he speaks. I met him once or twice dining at your mamma's before I left town, and we had not two words to say to each other. I don't care for your haw haw Dundreary army men," says Augustus. "Too much of the shop about them for my taste."

"Too much of *what* for your taste?" asks Belinda with profound disdain. Ah! was not the only human being she ever loved of this same Dundreary army genius as Captain Temple?

"Too much of the shop—their shop. Too much patronage of other fellows whose line doesn't happen to be in ramrods and pipe-clay like their own."

"And I," says the girl, stoutly, "love soldiers; and if ever I marry anybody it shall be a soldier. How different you and I are in everything—difference of the blood, I suppose! We O'Sheas are a fighting family. Two great-uncles of mine fell side by side across the hills there, at Badajoz," she indicates by a nod of her head the distant ridge of Spanish Pyrenees. "And my papa was a soldier; and though it happened he never came in for foreign service, he did a great many brave acts, I can tell you, during the different riots and electioneerings in Ireland. Most likely you have no connection with the army, Mr. Jones?"

"None, excepting a maternal uncle, who was an army tailor," Mr. Jones might answer, if he had a mind to speak the truth. He waives the question adroitly enough, however, by returning to the matter in hand. "Well then, as you are so fond of the fighting profession, Miss O'Shea, you will have an additional reason for loving your new papa."

Belinda snatches up the schistera which lies at her side, and for a moment affairs look threatening. Not much more provocation, evidently, would it need to fire the warlike blood of the O'Sheas that runs in her veins.

"I—I was going to ask you to come down to Harrambour's," says Mr. Jones, springing up hastily to his feet. "Don't be angry with me, Belinda!" He can call her Belinda, at the safe distance that separates them now. "And let us make all our differences up over some macaroons."

Every man, says the cynic, has his price. Belinda's price, as a very short acquaintance has taught Mr. Jones, is macaroons. Sweetstuff, generally, may be said to be Belinda's price in the present scraggy, unfledged stage of her moral life. Angel hair—*cabello de angel*—frozen apricots, chocolate creams, every varied confection, half French half Spanish, with which the shops of St. Jean de Luz abound, are dear to her. But, above all, she adores macaroons; the speciality of the place, as history shows, even back to the days when the great Napoleon and the English Duke successively lodged here. And then she is so absolutely penniless! The miserable pittance which comes to her quarterly, after Miss Burke has swallowed the lion's share of her small income—the quarterly pittance, I say, which is vouchsafed to her for dress, postage, pocket-money, confectionery, goes so piteously soon, leaves her so absolutely insolvent when it is gone!

A child of seventeen without a sou in the world for macaroons, and an Augustus Jones, his pockets lined with British bank-notes, ready to buy them for her: does it require a very profound knowledge of human nature to foresee how things are likely to end?—unless indeed some other actor, offering something sweeter than macaroons, chance to cross the stage of Belinda's little life-drama.

She hesitates, relents, and a minute later they have quitted the Place, and are making their way down the principal street of the town towards the macaroon shop. St. Jean de Luz is taking its wonted afternoon siesta at this hour. The balconies are deserted; the very churches, filled morning and evening to overflowing with fans, prayer-books, and flirtations, are empty. A bullock-dray or two are to be seen in the market-place, the bullocks in their brown-holland blouses, patiently blinking, with bullock philosophy, at existence, the drivers asleep within the wine shops. A team of close-shorn Spanish mules stand, viciously whisking at the flies with their rat tails, in the shade; the muleteer, his face prone to mother earth, reposes beside them. Other living forms are there none, save an occasional half-broiled Murray-guided Briton, and five or six ghostly cur dogs—the cur dogs in St. Jean de Luz *never* sleep. It being low water, the river mouth and harbour are sending forth "liberal smells of all the sun-burnt south." The distant mountain-sides are absolutely painful to the eye in their shadeless ochre yellow. Heat, as of a very rain of fire, quivering, piercing, intolerable, is everywhere.

And Mr. Jones does not bear heat gracefully. By the time they reach the macaroon shop Mr. Jones is in a state of evaporation made visible, and anathematises the climate, pavement, scenery, people—all in the very ugliest Cockney vernacular, and with the ugliest Cockney ignorance.

"He is horribly, horribly vulgar!" thinks Belinda, as she bites her macaroons and glances from beneath her eyelashes at the dewy, blistered, mosquito-scarred face of her companion. "If macaroons were only attainable through any other means!"

Which they are not. And the macaroons are super-excellent, fresh made this morning; and after the macaroons come a vanilla ice and a chocolate cream—and more macaroons. And then—of so generous a temper is Augustus this afternoon—then they adjourn from the shop to the refreshing shade of the awning outside, and Belinda is told to call for whatever cooling drink she chooses, while Mr. Jones (who holds the firmest English belief as to alcohol and a thermometer at a hundred and ten in the shade going well together) orders himself —oh, in what execrable French!—a brandy-and-seltzer, and prepares to smoke a cigar at her side.

A bizarre love-making, it may be said, in which the lady's favour is to be won by lollipops. But any one who keeps his eyes open must know that what we call the bizarre differences of life are on the surface—merest accidental diversity of local colouring; human nature being much the same whatever dress she wears, whatever quarter of the globe she inhabits. If Augustus Jones were courting some full-grown London Belinda, his offerings would have to be of bracelets, certainly; bracelets—opera tickets, bouquets, as the case might be, instead of sweetstuff. And who, I should like to know, would consider *that* bizarre?

Mr. Jones smokes his cigar, Belinda sips her iced orangeade, Spanish fashion, through a barquilo, beside him, and so a drowsy hour glides away. Then the sun dips westward behind the toppling old scarlet-roofed, many-storeyed houses that form the seaboard of St. Jean de Luz, and comparative coolness begins to make itself felt in the streets. Little by little shutters open; sleepy faces peep out on balconies; the bullock drivers come lazily forth from the wine shops; the muleteer rises as far as his elbow, rubs his handsome eyes, swears a little at the mules, crosses himself, and folds a cigarrito. The world is awakening.

"And I must be off," says Belinda, jumping up as the clocks of the town strike five. "We are all in for a match of paume as soon as the sun is off the upper Place."

"We? and who are 'we'?" asks Mr. Jones with a tender smile. The brandy-and-seltzer has softened him; but unfortunately tender smiles lose half their effect when they are associated with mosquito-bites.

"Oh, the usual set. Jack Alston and Tom and me against the two Washingtons and Maurice la Ferté. Which side will you back? You must not judge by what you saw last night; Jack Alston and I can beat the lot, when we play our best."

"I should like to bet that you will let Mr. Jack Alston and his friends play their match without you." And now Augustus rises, now the mosquito-bitten face is affectionately, horribly near Belinda's. "I should like to think you care just enough for me, Miss O'Shea, to give all these fellows up for once, if I ask you."

His tone is more earnest than Belinda has ever heard it yet, and she wavers, or appears to waver. The remembrance of macaroons that are past, the hope of macaroons that are to come; vanity grati-fied by a full-grown man, an Augustus Jones though he be, taking so deep an interest in her affairs;—all these considerations, and perhaps something a little deeper than these, sway the girl, and she wavers; casts down her eyelashes, plays irresolutely with the strings of her schistera.

"You will promise me to play no more at that confounded game, either this evening or any other evening?" whispers Augustus, with growing emphasis.

Another moment, and Belinda will certainly have committed herself—heaven knows to what compromising renunciations! But even as the words rise to her lips an unexpected ally, against Mr. Jones, and on the side of paume playing, bolero dancing, and all the other sweet unlawful pleasures of her vagabond life, appears on the scene.

"Costa, why, Costa, old boy! where have you been all day? Down, sir, down. When will you learn that Mr. Jones does not value your attentions?"

Costa is a grand-looking old Spanish hound, not altogether of purest breed, perhaps, but a noble brute, despite the blot upon his scutcheon, possessing much of his nation's grave dignity of demeanour, and a face brimful of fine dog-intellect and feeling. You may see such a head as Costa's beside the knee of more than one of Velasquez' portraits.

His acquaintance with Belinda came about haphazard—as everything seems to come about in the girl's haphazard life.

Some Madrid hidalgo, to whom the poor brute belonged, happening to be called away to Paris towards the close of last summer's bathing season, the dog, with true Spanish indifference, was left upon the streets of St. Jean de Luz to starve. For a time he kept body and soul—what poor dog-soul was in him—together, as best he might; his lean carcase daily becoming leaner, kicks and blows from housewives who found him unlawfully prowling about their doorsteps more frequent. At last a bone or two came through the skin; the creature's strength was gone—just enough left to drag himself painfully along the gutters, and look up with wistful hungry supplication in the faces of the passers-by.

And so Belinda found him: Belinda, as it chanced, flush of money, her quarter's pittance newly paid, and on her road at that moment to the macaroon shop, with all the lightness of spirit a full purse begets.

"What, Costa, my friend!" She knew the dog and his name well; had admired him often in his palmier days, striding majestically along at the hidalgo his master's heels. "Costa, my old friend, have you come to this? Has that *brute* left you alone here to starve?"

She forgot the macaroons; she took Costa round to the butcher's market, and she gave him to eat; would have had him home and sheltered him, but for Miss Burke's stern opposition. It would better befit Belinda's immortal soul to take thought of the regeneration of humanity than be occupied with the life or death of a miserable cur dog. A knock on the head and a plunge into the Nivelle were the greatest mercy in such a case. Miss Burke, for her part, would not mind hiring some man or boy to perform the deed, and——

"At your peril you get Costa murdered!" cried Belinda, with tragical mutinous eyes. "Deny him shelter, if you like. He must lodge as the beggars lodge, at least till winter comes, and I will feed him. What do I care for humanity? I love the dog! And as for you . . . hire an assassin, make yourself accomplice in a murder, madam, at your peril!"

Thus doubly saving Costa's life, of such slender value as the poor life was!

And the creature repaid her with that absolute, blind, unstinted gratitude, that is one of the cardinal dog virtues—shall we say an exclusive dog virtue? Without a word of explanation he understood the delicacy of the relations between himself and Miss Burke, yet, for Belinda's sake, never betrayed his knowledge otherwise than by a stealthy, ghastly roll of the eye or grin of the upper lip in that lady's presence. Of a morning he would sit, demure of demeanour as a bishop, outside the gateway of Miss Burke's lodging, waiting for the light step of his little benefactress, but shifting his quarters instantly, and with an air of the most Pharisaic innocence, if Miss Burke chanced to appear instead of Belinda. At night he would guard the girl faithfully to the door of her home, but never, no, not even if Belinda in play invited him thereto, would cross the threshold. If it were possible for the quality of self-respect to exist in a dog's heart, one would say this gaunt, forsaken, Spanish hound possessed it.

Self-respect, gratitude, love! I seem to be making a tolerably long list of Costa's virtues; but he had vices enough to counterbalance them. Society generally looked upon him as an abandoned thievish reprobate, and with good reason. Society always has good reason for its condemnatory verdicts. How could it be otherwise? How could Costa, supperless, houseless, live the decent Philistine life that had been so easy to him in the well-fed days of the hidalgo, his master?

As long as Belinda's funds lasted he ate meat; when these failed he had such crusts and scraps as the girl could save from her own meals and carry away, unseen by Miss Burke, in her pocket. But scraps and crusts were not enough for Costa's sustenance. He must be dishonest or die; and (some Christians have felt the same) he preferred being dishonest.

In his youth he had been trained as a sporting dog, and, in all the pride of untempted virtue, had held by the code of honour of his peers, the arbitrary code which brands the slaughter of a barn-door fowl with indelible disgrace. But with other times, other manners. If nobility oblige, how much more so does an empty stomach! Some lingering scruples, some remnants of the old finer sentiment, Costa had to get over; at first would only scare his victims, next pursue them, but not kill. At last, one autumn twilight—hunger sharp, Belinda, I regret to say, witness of the crime—he murdered a fat old hen asleep upon her roost, devoured, enjoyed her to her very feathers, and murdered conscience with the act.

The downward path lay smooth enough before Costa now. No man, it is remarked, becomes so finished a scamp as your scamp who was a gentleman once. The rule is not without its parallel as regards the demoralisation of dogs. Where an ordinary cur would have committed his highway thefts or murders in a gross sort of bungling way, certain of instant detection, Costa, aided by a hundred remembrances of his old greenwood craft, got through the work like an artist. He became "suspect," as you may imagine. Not a housewife within a couple of miles of St. Jean de Luz, but knew him by sight or by reputation. And still he lived. These southern people combine with the most absolute callousness as to animal suffering a curious superstition as to taking animal life. They will see a starving dog die, inch by inch, rather than knock him on the head ; will bury an obnoxious cat alive, not drown her. Costa lived—a disreputable, idle, lawless existence enough—but with fidelity, love, gratitude to the little girl who had saved him, ever strengthening.

So different of its kind is the deterioration of dog nature to that of man.

When Belinda was out late at night, as too often happened, Costa, with the strength and will to pull down half a dozen Carlists at a time, would keep sentry by her side; when she was playing paume amongst her not too gentle comrades, would sit, winking his eyes with an air of dignified superiority in the shade, not interesting himself in the frivolous details of the game, but ready at any time, should dispute arise, to put himself forward as judge and executor of the law on Belinda's side. He knew when the child was glad or sorry, rich or poor. He knew her enemies, knew her friends ; and from the first moment of meeting till the present one had cast ugly looks at the calves of Augustus Jones's legs.

"Try not to be frightened, Mr. Jones," says Belinda, glancing maliciously at the expression of her admirer's face. "Perhaps he won't bite, if you keep very quiet. Dogs know so well when people are afraid of them ! Have you come for macaroons, my old Costa, eh ? You have, have you ? Mr. Jones, Costa says he has come for macaroons." It may be observed that Belinda has not a grain of false pride on the score of begging alms for her friends. "Costa has come for macaroons, and I have not a single sou left in the world."

She stoops down, and with one arm bent fondly round the old dog's neck, looks up, with the prettiest beseeching air imaginable, at

Augustus Jones.  But Jones buttons up his pockets.  He is not altogether a miser, as different sections of the London world have practically learnt; will spend money freely enough on riding horses, bracelets, opera-stalls, churches that need showy windows, philanthropic effort that publishes printed lists; on his vices, his virtues, *his* anything.  But macaroons for a dog!  This absolute waste, this simple flinging of money, for the sake of flinging it, into the sea, Mr. Jones cannot stand.  Looking upon the folly as a speculative investment, means to a possible end, 'twere different.  " You desire to marry yourself, as you consider, well," could some voice whisper to him ; " the ambition of your heart has been ever to wed your gold to aristocratic blood, and despairing of better chances you would fain win this out-at-elbows little Arab, the grand-daughter of the great Earl of Liskeard, for your wife.  Humour her whims, even this present babyish one, if you would hope to succeed."  Could Mr. Jones realise this as truth, the macaroons were Costa's.  But he does not realise it.  He is devoid alike of sympathy and of tact; qualities, both of them, springing from imagination, not reason ; and goes no further than his own light illumines the path.  He detests all dogs, detests Costa in particular, with the bitterest of hatred, that which springs from fear.  And, as I have said, Mr. Jones buttons up his pockets.

" Macaroons for Costa !" repeats Belinda, stretching out to him a little suppliant sunburnt palm.  "Not like them ?  You should see whether he likes them !  Try the experiment.  Why, when Maria José was here we gave him two francs' worth all at once, and he ate them up before you could say Jack Robinson."

"Did he indeed ?" says Augustus, looking disgusted, whether at the allusion to a rival or at the vulgarity of Belinda's speech, who shall say ?  " Then the only thing I can remark is, I am sorry Mr. Maria José had not better sense than to waste his money on such absurdity."

Quitting her hold on Costa, Belinda starts to her feet, and stands, upright and determined, before Augustus; her small child's face flaming red as any pomegranate flower.  " Mr. Jones," she exclaims, " if I asked you to give Costa two francs' worth of macaroons at this moment, do you mean to tell me you would not do it?"

" I should prefer giving the money to the first worthy object of commiseration who happened to pass along the street," Mr. Jones answers, didactically.

" Will you give Costa one franc's worth of macaroons, now, this instant ?"

" I—I never heard of feeding a dog on macaroons.  I think it a deuced ridiculous waste of money," stutters Jones, without offering to put his hand into his pocket.  " I can be as liberal as most people, Miss Belinda, on the right occasion, but if I *have* a predilection, and a very strong one too, it's against seeing good money wasted."

Belinda looks at him, from his mosquito-bitten forehead down to the tips of his Bond Street boots; looks at him, with those clear eyes of hers, not only up and down bodily, but morally, through and through.

" Oh! I understand. I know now why Costa hated you from the first. Dogs are not such Fools. If you *have* a predilection, you say 'tis against seeing good money wasted. If I *have* a predilection and a very strong one too, 'tis for wasting it. Money—bah! what is money? So many dirty bits of silver, stamped with this head or that, and good just for the quantity of sweetstuff it will bring you. To spend, to waste, to scatter money to the winds, is one of my predilections; paume playing, bolero dancing—liberty, sweet liberty!—are the others! And I am no more likely to change in my opinions than you are in yours. Good-bye, Mr. Jones."

She turns on her heel, and swinging her schistera to and fro, in a way to shock Mr. Jones's nicest susceptibilities, walks off; Costa, his head well erect, as though he felt himself master of the situation, at her side.

CHAPTER III.

LIGHT WEDDED, LIGHT WIDOWED.

ST. JEAN DE LUZ is awakening from its afternoon siesta. By the time that the Paris train arrives, an hour later, every nook, every corner of the quaint little Basque town is full of life and colour. Castilian nurses, in the gay scarlet bodices and silver buttons of their order, are airing olive-faced babies in the Place; watersellers, with their sing-song "*Agua! quien quieri agua?*" throng the streets; men smoking their final cigarrito before dinner, are to be seen under the awnings of the different cafés. The younger women are ogling from behind their fans, the old ones resuming their eternal tresillo on the balconies. Smoking, flirting, and card-playing, in short—the three great occupations of Spanish life—going on actively. And St. Jean de Luz, at the height of its brief bathing season, is as completely Spanish as any town in the Peninsula, the natives vanishing like mice into cellars and attics the moment good Spanish dollars can be got in exchange for their first and second floors.

As six o'clock strikes a carriage draws up, with the extra flourishing of whips indicative of new arrivals to be fleeced, before the Grande Hotel Isabella. Waiters, chambermaids, mine host himself, all come out, salaaming, to secure their prey, and forth steps an elegant fool of the very first water—English, and of the sex whose helplessness is its charm—upon the pavement. A clothes-artist might know that this fair being is dressed in what the craft have agreed to call "slight mourning." To the unprofessional eye, her attire, a cunningly blent mixture of white and lilac, is suggestive of no other grief than the despairing envy of every woman who may chance to behold it, and the absolute collapse and annihilation of man.

"*Mes baggages—où est mes baggages?*" sighs a voice, in that curious language known as French in suburban boarding-schools, but unintelligible south of the Channel. "*Dix baggages, tout adressé,* and a piece of blue ribbon on each. *Dix*—ten—oh! *would* anybody make them understand? *Dix*"—holding up ten helpless, lavender-gloved fingers. "Really, Spencer, I think you might try to be of some little use."

At this appeal, another elegant fool—but of second water; a cheap copy of the first; flimsy glacé silk instead of richest cord—steps languidly forth from the carriage. She too is admirably helpless, and she too speaks a tongue incomprehensible out of England—the polyglot smatter of advertising Abigails who "talk three languages with ease, and are willing to undertake any duties, not menial, while on the Continent."

They address themselves to the host, to the waiters, to the coachman. Nobody understands them; they understand nobody.

"If I had only bespoken Belinda!" sighs the lady piteously. "If you had had the slightest consideration, Spencer, you might have reminded me to telegraph to Miss O'Shea."

The words have scarcely left her lips when a knot of little lads, English and French, shoulder their way along the street—lads from about eleven to fourteen, sunburnt, dare-devil looking young Arabs enough, bare-footed most of them, and with schisteras in hand. At the word "Belinda," the foremost of the gang turns, and nudges the boy who comes next. They all stop, they all stare; one of them gives a low meaning whistle across his shoulder, and in another second or two Belinda appears upon the scene, her battered hat more battered than when we saw her first two hours ago, the flush of heat and victory on her brow, her espadrilles so kicked to pieces that how they keep upon her feet at all is miraculous.—Belinda, like her associates, schistera in hand, with Costa, who has been rolling in the dust, and has a more disreputable look than usual, at her heels. She passes along, whistling, forgetful of Mr. Jones and their quarrel, of Rose's letter and threatened arrival—forgetful of everything except the game of paume she has just played and won—when suddenly our elegant fool number one looks full into the girl's face, and, electrified, recognises her.

"What, Belinda?—can that be you?"

"What, Rose?—arrived already?"

"How dirty she is!" (mentally).

"How painted she is!" (all but aloud).

And then the ladies kiss, hugely to the entertainment of Belinda's comrades, who have certainly never before beheld Miss O'Shea engaged in any of these feminine amenities.

"You—you have grown, I think," says Rose, scrutinising, with horror-stricken eyes, the girl's ragged, dust-stained clothes, and remembering, with all the shame of which her small soul is capable, that the lady's-maid scrutinises them also. "And you are sunburnt—you are very sunburnt, Belinda."

"I should say I was, just! If you had been playing paume under such a sun as this you would be sunburnt too. But where is your maid? You don't mean to say you have travelled all the way from Brompton to St. Jean de Luz alone?"

Rose on this gives a side glance at her gorgeous Abigail, and whispers in Belinda's ear: "That is my maid, my dear, and the most helpless, the most unbearable creature in the world; still, as I had her from Lady Harriet Howes—and a particular favour her ladyship made of it—I don't like to change. It's an immense thing" (plaintively) "for one's maid to have lived in a *good style* of place, you know."

"I know!" repeats Belinda, with her mocking, gamin laugh. "Yes, I am just the fellow to know about fine ladies and their maids, am I not? But do you mean to say, Rose, that you and that magnificently dressed young woman have travelled from one end of France to the other without getting run away with?"

"I—I have not been altogether without an escort," responds the widow, and blushes.

Belinda thinks she must have been wrong about the paint, not knowing that there are women who blush and paint too.

"I was fortunate enough in Paris to come across a very old and dear friend, who took me about a little, and then, somehow or another, I met with him again at Bordeaux. Curious coincidence, was it not?" laying her plump hand with girlish playfulness upon Belinda's slender arm. "But I have more curious things still to tell you when we are alone. *Mes baggages.*" This to the dignified Basque coachman, who, with the air of a prince, his cap on his head, stands waiting to be paid. "Belinda, will you make that savage comprehend that I want my luggage? I'm sure," says Rose, "my French must be better than most people's, for I had the prize two halfs following at Miss Ingram's. Poor mamma cried, I had worked myself to such a shadow. But the French speak with such an extraordinary accent there's really no understanding them. Ten large boxes, tell him, each with a blue ribbon, and—oh, the awful dog! Some one take the awful dog away!" Costa has been critically examining the new comers, mistress and maid, and conveys his poor opinion of them to Belinda by a short gruff bark. "I thought all the dogs in France had to be muzzled by law. Spencer—Spencer! Get between me and that *monster!*"

It is long before Rose can be made to believe that her precious boxes will be brought from the station, like all other people's boxes, on the hotel omnibus. Then, when rooms have to be selected for her, arise new troubles. She must have a bed-room communicating with a drawing-room (and the drawing-room must have a balcony *covered* with flowers), a bed-room near some one else's, in case of fire; a bed-room not too near some one else's in case of his talking in his sleep; and Spencer must be on the same floor; and is there any way of ascertaining who slept in the rooms last? Will Belinda request the people of the house to swear that there has been no one here with smallpox this summer?

"Swear? Why a Basque will swear anything you ask him," cries the girl mischievously. "Of course people with smallpox have slept here this summer, as they have at every hotel in the place. What does it matter, Rose? You will be so mosquito-bitten, like our friend Augustus, by to-morrow morning, that you won't recognise yourself in the glass. A touch of smallpox, more or less, cannot matter."

With which scanty consolation Rose, the tears rising in her foolish frightened eyes, has to be contented.

"If I only knew where all these dreadful doors lead to," she sighs, looking round her with pretty timidity as soon as Mrs. Spencer, her nose well in the air, has retired to inspect her own apartment. "But I have heard such stories of what goes on in foreign hotels—it was all in the papers, once, 'Judas doors,' I think they called them, and indeed the way Frenchmen stare at one in the street is enough. I declare nothing would ever tempt me to go out on the Continent alone."

She languishes away to a mirror, and taking off her veil begins to dust her delicate rose-and-white face with her cambric handkerchief. I use the word "dust" intentionally. Belinda, under the same circumstances, would rub her sun-tanned skin as vigorously as a housemaid rubs mahogany. But women of fashion have complexions, not skins. Rose treats hers fearfully, tenderly; as you will see a connoisseur treat the surface of some fine enamel, or other piece of perishable art; not, it may be, without reason.

"I have grown quite an old woman, have I not?" She puts a smile on the corners of her lips, then turns and presents her face for the girl's admiration. "I daresay you would hardly have known me if you had met me, without warning, in the street? Now tell me the honest truth, dear; I hate flattery."

Rose, at this present time of her mortal life, has approached, as near as it is possible for a good-looking woman ever to do, to her fortieth year. But, if there be truth in that delightful French adage, that a woman is the age she looks, we may call her nine-and-twenty: of course I mean, after her art-labours are over for the day.

"Few sorrows hath she of her own," this comely silver-tongued bewitching widow, and no sorrows of others could by any possibility make her grieve. So she is without wrinkles. The lines in which strong love, strong grief, strong feelings of any kind grave their story on human faces are all absent from hers. Round cheeks, breaking into dimples, like a baby's, when she smiles; wide-open eyes, of that unchanging yellow-hazel that often accompanies flaxen lashes and eyebrows; the most charming, most insignificant little nose you ever saw, and a mouth, not altogether good-tempered by nature, perhaps, but trained to every artificial "sweetness" of smile and word—such is Rose. Her hair, that once was palest hempen, is now as auriferous a copper as Bond Street chemistry can make it, and a marvel of luxuriance—such exquisite plaits and tresses, such sly-nestling unexpected little ringlets! (Has Belinda forgotten the old dinnerless days when her tired fingers had to crimp and plait and curl in the shabby London lodgings?) Her figure is plump, would be over plump, but for the corset-maker's torturing aid, and Rose's heroic resolve *never* to own a waist of more than twenty-two inches. Her complexion, fair naturally, improved by art, is—well, a complexion, not a skin. Need I say more?

Belinda examines her with eyes that would pierce all the enamel, all the rice-powder, in the world. "We none of us get younger, Rose; you no more than other people. But you look well in health. I am surprised to see you out of mourning," she adds, giving a cold glance at her stepmother's white and lilac finery. "Has your uncle Robert been dead six, or eight weeks? I do not remember, exactly."

"Eight weeks! Oh Belinda, dear, how thoughtless, you are!" Rose, to do her justice, feels far more amiably disposed towards Belinda than Belinda feels towards Rose. Life flows at its smoothest just at present with Cornelius O'Shea's widow. Dear Uncle Robert opportunely removed to a better world; his will all that could be desired by surviving relatives; good looks within the reach of one's own industry still, and a lover, handsome, young, well-born, to crown all. How can Rose feel anything but amiable, especially now that she sees how unfortunately plain this poor little alien stepdaughter of hers has grown up? "Uncle Robert has been dead more than three months, and I am only just in second mourning. The milliners tell me it's ridiculously deep, and indeed I remember seeing Lady Harriet wear scarlet less than six weeks after old Miss Howe's death, but I— I know *what* a friend I have lost! Of course I could not enter upon these delicate subjects in a letter, Belinda, but Uncle Robert has left me everything, unconditionally. Money, house, plate—everything. I only hope I may be guided"—says Rose, turning up her eyes, "guided to make a right use of what is intrusted to me."

Colder and harder grows the expression of Belinda's face. Can the girl forget by whose absence, whose death, Rose's good fortune was purchased?

"Oh, you are very lucky, Rose, very! But somehow I cannot find words just now to wish you joy. What are your future plans? Are you going to live in that big house at Brompton all alone?"

Mrs. O'Shea's eyes sink to the ground. " I—I have many things to talk to you about, Belinda, as I hinted in my letter. But when I have told all my little story I am sure you will *feel for me* in my position. The romance of two young lives!" murmurs Rose, modestly apologetic. "Love sacrificed to duty — a heart slowly breaking during a dozen years! Belinda, my dear girl, you have heard . . . you must have heard of Roger Temple?"

But not by a word or look will Belinda assist the widow's bashfulness, or help her forward in her confession.

"I believe that I have heard of such a person, somewhere," she answers, in a tone of the most freezing indifference. "Your friend Mr. Jones mentioned him, I think, Rose. But I pay so little attention to anything Mr. Jones says."

"Belinda, when we were both young—the day will come, I hope, child, when you will sympathise more with the trials and temptations of others—when we were both young, Roger Temple and I first met. And he cared for me."

Dead silence: the widow confused, and stroking down the folds of her silk dress with her white fingers; Belinda's slip of a figure standing upright beside the window, her arms folded, her lips and eyes about as "sympathetic" as though they had been carved in granite.

"He cared for me—too much for his own peace—but duty stood between us, and we parted." Of this the reader shall know more than by Rose's hazy utterances. "We parted. Fate was hard upon us both. And now . . . Belinda, must I say more?"

"Say everything, please, if you want me to understand you."

"Roger Temple has asked me to be his wife at last, and I "——

"And you are going to be married again!" interrupts Belinda, cruelly. "For the Third time! Then all I can remark is, you are very fond of being married, Rose."

A heartless, unwomanly speech enough; but Belinda, like many other raw girls of her age, is absolutely heartless in matters of love; and at this moment passionate unreasoning jealousy against the rival of her dead father is sending the blood to her brain too quickly for her to be very nice in the choice of words.

"I'm sure I don't know how you can be so unfeeling," says Rose, almost crying. "But you were always the same. Even when you were little you had no more sensibility than a stone. And Roger always expresses himself so beautifully about you, and the Temples are such a good family, and everything—and then to say that I—*I* of all women living—am fond of being married! I do hope, Belinda, whatever your own opinions may be, you will not express yourself in this most heartless and indelicate manner before Captain Temple."

"Captain Temple!" repeats Belinda, all innocence. "Why, when am I ever likely to see Captain Temple?"

"You will see him here, in St. Jean de Luz, to-day."

"Captain Temple in St. Jean de Luz! You mean to tell me, Rose, that you *and a young man* are travelling about the world together?"

And Belinda, the first and last time in her life such hypocrisy can be recorded of her, puts on an air of outraged virtue edifying to behold.

"Roger met me in Paris and again in Bordeaux," says poor Rose, blushing through her rouge with vexation. "Roger was the old friend I told you of. And there was always Spencer . . . and we have taken care never to stop at the same hotel even. He has gone now to look at a lodging in quite another part of the town. If you knew, Belinda, if you only knew what a soul of honour Roger Temple has, you would not talk so lightly!"

"Ah, but you must remember I know nothing at all about him," retorts the girl, "and my education does not dispose me to take any man's honour on trust. Never mind, Rose," she goes on, with an assumption of pitying complaisance. "I am shocked, I own, but I will keep what I think to myself. I will not say a word, even to Burke."

"And you will behave with feeling, with consideration, to Roger Temple for my sake?"

Before the girl can answer, a man's step sounds in the corridor, a knock comes at the door.

"*Entrez*," cries out Belinda, in her clear young voice.

"My things!" sighs the widow, all in a tremor, her heart reverting to the possessions which lie nearer to it even than her lover—her bandboxes.

And the door opens.

"Roger! You have found your way already, then?" Rose exclaims, with rather a forced little laugh, and retreating hastily from the light that falls unbecomingly full upon her through the open window. "Belinda, dearest, my very old acquaintance, Captain Temple. Now mind," with infantine candour, "I shall never forgive either of you if you don't fall in love with each other *at once*. I have been like that always—Miss Ingram used to say I was quite absurd. Whoever I am fond of must be fond of all my friends."

But long before Rose has ceased twittering her small falsities, Belinda's eyes and Roger Temple's have met—met and spoken the truth.

"In life as on railways," a master-hand has written "at certain points, whether you know it or not, there is but an inch, this way or that, into what train you are shunted."

Into what train has Belinda's passionate heart been shunted, all unknowing, at this moment?

## The Baron in England.

WHEN Louis de Rouvroi, Duc de Saint-Simon, was yet a very young fellow, he was appointed one of the pages, or officers of about the same dignity, to Louis the Fourteenth. One day, the Grand Monarch, as he was absurdly called, encountered the young gentleman of his household in the Gallery of Glasses, at Versailles. The king honoured the page by entering into conversation with him; but it was not for the sake of the honour.

"De Rouvroi," said his majesty, "do you take notes of what passes here?"

"No, sire!"

"Write no letters of description?"

"None, sire."

"Do you keep a diary?"

"I can assure your majesty that I never dreamed of doing such a thing."

"Good!" rejoined the sovereign. "We are well pleased with you;" and the great king passed on, with a smile.

The young gentleman looked after him, also with a smile. That evening, in his own room, he addressed himself to a great work. A blank-paged writing-book was before him, and pen and ink. The smile was probably still on his face, as he remembered the questions of his royal master. "Not a bad idea, that of the king's; I had never thought of keeping a diary of court life; but I will begin, at once, doing so!" Some sentiment that might be thus interpreted, in all likelihood, possessed him. On that night, at all events, he dipped his pen into the ink, and wrote the first words of that marvellous work which is known to us under the title of 'Mémoires de Saint-Simon.'

For many years after the death, in 1755, of Saint-Simon, who has made live again the family and court of Louis the Fourteenth and that of the Regent Duke of Orleans, the huge manuscript (in which every one was depicted like those figures in art books, which show us the skeleton of the man side by side with the same man in full dress,) was sealed up. It somehow came into the possession of Louis the Fifteenth, who allowed no one to read it but himself, and *he* revelled in the details of scandal and in the truthful lights thrown into dark places. The Duc de Choiseul, his minister, would not be baulked. He procured a false key, read the manuscript at leisure, and copied the parts with which he was best pleased. Gradually, detached portions got into print, but nothing like a satisfactory edition of the Memoirs appeared till 1830.

The first *complete* edition, founded on the original manuscript, was not published till 1856–7. It is in twenty volumes, edited by M. Chéruel, and is such a history of the times (regarding France) as nowhere else exists. We may add that there is nothing like it in other countries, etching and photographing so mercilessly accurately the scenes and the men who moved in them. The acid of the work proves the metal of the men, and under its application seemingly golden idols become mere copper captains. Saint-Simon is not more reserved with regard to the ladies. Under a peculiar lime-light of his own, we see clear into the most secret recesses, and gaze with amazement on scenes where

> Round and round the ghosts of beauties glide,
> Viewing the places where their honour died.

We are reminded of these things by the appearance of another court revelation—the 'Memoirs of Baron Stockmar.' With astounding recklessness, the late Baron's son has published details, not offensive indeed in any scandalous sense, but details that should have been covered under the sacred veil of silence. It is said that these revelations have not a little irritated personages who may dread what else may yet be said of them. The want of taste is as great as the want of common respect for personal feelings. When we read that Stockmar was at the bedside of the dying Princess Charlotte, when we are allowed to see her agony, to witness her struggles, to hear her cries, and when we are told that she screamed to "Stocky" to help her, we are simply shocked. We find, in later days, Stockmar resident in Queen Victoria's palace, as a sort of counsellor to herself and husband, and we are a little surprised; but when it is added that the Baron was allowed to wear trowsers at the royal dinner parties, as his thin shanks would have looked ridiculous in breeches, we can hardly keep from laughter.

This Baron Stockmar, whose name was utterly unknown to most of the present generation till his memoirs came before them, was originally of the middle class. Born in 1787, at Coburg, of a father who was a very good scholar and a gentleman, and of a mother whose sententious humour is illustrated in her stereotyped observation, "Heaven takes care that the cows' tails shall not grow too long," this elder son of a family of two boys and two girls manifested very early his far-seeing spirit. Once, at the family table, looking at the plates and dishes, the boy seriously remarked, "Some day, I must have all this of silver." To which his mother quietly replied, "If you can manage to get it, pray do." Stockmar lost no opportunity to accomplish the end in view. He began life as a medical man; he was with the German army all through its disastrous war with the French, and he never

despaired of that future of his country which has now commenced
with the establishment of a German empire under a Protestant Cæsar.
In the course of his medical career (every way honourable to him) he
became known to Prince Leopold, who showed how he valued the man
by attaching him to his personal service as body physician. When
Stockmar came first to England, in March 1816, he landed at Dover,
and to avoid travelling too late at night, on account of highwaymen,
he only proceeded as far as Rochester. The next day he entered London,
and soon began his professional office. After the death of the Princess
Charlotte the widowed Leopold induced Stockmar to promise never to
leave him. The bond of union, however, was broken when Leopold
became King of the Belgians. Stockmar, who had ceased to be his
physician, but who was secretary, keeper of the privy purse, and
comptroller of the household, soon withdrew. The Belgians would
not have tolerated, however they might have respected, a foreigner
holding any political offices. Stockmar resigned his less important
duties, but he probably saw where his future field began to display
itself.

Already married himself (in 1821)—he settled his cousin-wife at
Coburg, and visited her at long intervals—he was soon engaged in
marriage negotiations of great personages. One would almost suppose
that without him Prince Albert would not have married the Queen,
nor been in anything else so successful a personage as he proved to
be. In the new royal household the Baron (he had been ennobled by
a Saxon patent) acted as secretary, confidential adviser, friend, and so
on. Yes, "so on" is the proper phrase, for we are told that "he considered it to be his duty, in the interest of the Queen and that of the
crown, as such, to resist the ministers when he perceived that the
latter were acting too much from mere party motives." If this be
true, and Stockmar is described as keeping the Queen in this or that
attitude, it exceeds in impudence the act of the king of Prussia when
he telegraphed to London to stay the execution of the murderer
Müller. It is only matched by the alleged assertion that this private
secretary presumed to advise the ministry to enter into confidential
negotiations with the heads of the opposition on the subject of Prince
Albert's regency under a certain possible contingency. It is utterly
incredible. If true, there was then some ground for giving Stockmar
that Mephistophelian character which he was delighted to see applied
to him. The private secretary's influence at court is further illustrated in the following incident. "A rich Englishman—an author
and member of Parliament—called upon him one day, and promised
to give him £10,000 if he would further his petition to the Queen
for a peerage. Stockmar replied, 'I will now go into the next room,
in order to give you time. If upon my return I shall find you here
I shall have you turned out by the servants.' There is no English-

man who will believe in a story so utterly absurd. Stockmar, if he ever told it, must have been under a delusion. He was often at least simple-minded. " The Princess Royal," says the son, " honoured him as a second father;" and adds naïvely, ," he had the very highest possible opinion of her." The father further remarks of the Princess, who saw in him a second sire, " I hold her to be exceptionally gifted, to be in many things almost inspired." The example given of the young Princess's inspiration is not very lively. Prince Albert's secretary, Prätorius, was not a handsome man. One day the little Princess was reading the Bible to her mother. She came upon the passage, " God created man in his own image, in the image of God created He him;" upon which, we are told, " the child, gifted with an early sense of beauty, exclaimed, ' But, mamma, surely not Dr. Prätorius!'" We fancy that Stockmar had little appreciation of what is really humorous, though he was himself an " original." He thought the Belgian Count de Mérode was an original too, with this sample in support of the thought: Mérode was irritated by our fogs—as if Belgium had none! *"Partout le brouillard.' Je découpe mon beefsteak, sort le brouillard."*

The Baron's reason for retiring from the office he held under the Queen and Prince is very characteristic: " They have passed the point at which leading is required." They probably resisted it, for Stockmar complains (1857) that he could no longer give advice " with freshness and force," nor produce, as of old, " right impressions." Accordingly, in 1857 the Baron retired. In 1858 we meet him at Berlin, whither he had repaired to offer, unasked, his counsel as to future political action. Nobody was gratified by his appearance, however patriotic might be his intentions. He was looked upon, by those who could make no allowance for his patriotism, as the Peter of the German proverb, who scattered his parsley into everybody's soup. Count K——, who had seen a friend walking with a stranger over the bridge at Potsdam, asked him with whom he was walking? " Stockmar," replied the friend. " Ah!" exclaimed Count K——, " why did you not pitch him into the river ?"

Stockmar, in March 1863, writing to King Leopold on his severe illness, rendered a testimony unfavourable to the art which he had once practised. " The King," he writes, to Leopold, " complains of medicine. I can write no apology for the art, because I have learned to know the exact limits of its power. In the majority of cases physicians do not know what they ought to know, and in very few cases are they able to do what the sick man requires. Hence recourse to deception, or even lying. It is only for the prevention of disease that a good and great physician can be of real use." There never was more nonsense put in so few words ; but be this as it may, apoplexy put the Baron von Stockmar beyond the aid of the greatest physician in July, 1863. The old man sleeps beneath a splendid

vault in Coburg, erected in honour of the sleeper "by his friends in
the reigning families of Belgium, Coburg, England, and Prussia."
If those families supposed that there slept with the old man all the
confidential passages connected with them, they were grievously mistaken. The Baron's son remarks, at the end of the biographical
sketch, "He *was* content to remain always half hidden before the
eyes of posterity. Faithful to his spirit, this book also lifts the veil
but a little." But who will guarantee that the veil will not be lifted
higher? Let us hope that one day it may be, but not till the families
enumerated above have no living heroes in the stories, when they may
listen unwincingly to the Baron's queer tales of their ancestors and
may feel their withers unwrung. Does the Baron's son suppose that
the ill-fated Princess Charlotte thought his father would blab to the
world her remark, made to him in unsuspecting confidence, "My
mother was bad, but she would not have become as bad as she was
if my father had not been infinitely worse?"

Stockmar etches, both gracefully and vigorously, the personages at
court, whom he seems to inspect as if they were purposely called up
for exhibition. Queen Charlotte is done in a single stroke: "Small and
crooked, with a true mulatto face." All her sons, except the Regent,
are described as talkative; the Duke of Sussex, however, is left out of
account altogether. The Duke of Clarence is said to be the one who
most resembled his small and crooked mother. The stout Regent is
credited with fine figure and distinguished manners, great appetite,
devotion to drinking, and "a brown scratch wig, not particularly
becoming." He spoke French fairly, as did the stouter Duke of York,
whose accent, however, was bad. Many men yet remember the handsome but unintelligent face, the huge body, thin legs, the bald head,
and the too upright carriage, which gave him the air of being about to
fall backwards. His wife, a Prussian princess, with restless lips and
blinking eyes, was a good-humoured, loud-talking, loud-laughing lady,
who took her husband's infidelities with patience and kept his accounts
honestly, and with a vain hope of getting him out of debt. Stockmar
draws her at full length. "As soon as she entered the room she
looked round for the banker, Greenwood, who immediately came up to
her with the confidentially familiar manner which the wealthy go-
between assumes towards grand people in embarrassed circumstances.
At dinner the Duchess related how her royal father had forced her, as a
girl, to learn to shoot, as he had observed she had a great aversion to
it. At a grand *chasse* she had always fired with closed eyes, because
she could not bear to see the sufferings of the wounded animals.
When the huntsman told her that in this way she ran the risk of
causing the game more suffering through her uncertain aim, she went
to the King and asked him if he would excuse her from all sport in
future, if she shot a stag dead. The King promised to grant her

request if she could kill two deer, one after the other, without missing, which she did." Stockmar says the Duke of Clarence was the least good looking of the brothers; but he describes the tall, strong, Duke of Cumberland, "with a hideous face; can't see two inches before him; one eye turned quite out of its place." Clarence again is "as talkative as the rest," while the Duke of Kent (who as much resembled his father as Clarence did his mother), "is the quietest of all the dukes." In one page he is described as being as bald as a man can be; but this was only on the crown of his head. In another we are told that the Duke "dyed his hair," and, what is quite as bad, or indeed much worse, that he also died over head and ears in debt. We wish we could add that the creditors had since been paid. The youngest brother, Cambridge, like the eldest, wore a dandy blonde wig, and talked German, French, and English, with a rapidity which rendered him almost unintelligible. Of the cousin of these princes, the son of the Duke of Gloucester (brother of George the Third) and his wife, Lady Waldegrave, Stockmar "signalises" him, as if he were making out a passport: " Prominent, meaningless eyes, a very unpleasant face, with an animal expression; large and stout, but with weak, helpless legs. He wears a neckcloth thicker than his head." All this is true, but this duke was a thoroughly honest man. He loved his wife, Mary, youngest daughter of George the Third, with an almost romantic love, although they married late in life; and, oh ye unpaid creditors of some of the other free-and-easy dukes! when Gloucester died he owed no man a farthing.

The late Duke of Wellington is still too well remembered to need reproducing. "At table he sat next the Princess" (Charlotte). "He ate and drank moderately, and laughed at times most heartily, and whispered many things to the Princess's ear which made her blush and laugh." The Marquis of Anglesea is done to the life, and we learn that just before Waterloo he was sitting for his full-length portrait. It was finished except one leg, when Lord Anglesea, who was about to join the army, said to the artist, "You had better finish the leg now, I might not bring it back with me." He lost that very leg. Stockmar saw in handsome Castlereagh, who spoke English almost as ill as he did French, "a thoughtless indifference," which some people mistook for statesmanship of a high order. The visit of the Grand Duke Nicholas (afterwards the Czar) to Claremont, added another portrait to Stockmar's collection. " He ate, for his age, very moderately, and drank nothing but water. When Countess Lieven played after dinner on the piano he kissed her hand, which struck the English ladies present as peculiar but decidedly desirable. Mrs. Campbell could not cease praising him ... 'he is devilish handsome!' ... When it was time for bed a leathern sack was filled in the stable with hay for the Grand Duke by his servants, on which he always sleeps.' Our English friends thought this affected."

We wish we could congratulate the editor of Stockmar's book, Professor Max Müller, on having taken the trouble to correct the most absurd of the Baron's errors. The grossest is under date of the year 1817. Speaking of the prevailing distress and discontent, Stockmar says that " there was little to cheer the people in the sight of the blind and insane king," as if poor George the Third was exhibited to the public like the mad patients in old Bedlam. It would have been some proof of good taste if half the chapter containing details of the confinement of the Princess Charlotte had been omitted. To say that the details are painful is to use a very mild term. The chapter, however, throws light on the character of Stockmar. He never loses an opportunity of praising himself. His reiterated assertions of his modesty are unerring proofs of a vain man. "I never allowed myself," he writes in 1818, "to be blinded by vanity, but always kept in view the danger that must necessarily accrue to me if I arrogantly and imprudently pushed myself into a place in which a foreigner could never expect to reap honour, but possibly plenty of blame." Here is a correct portrait of the painter, painted by himself. Stockmar had vanity, but he was too clever to be blinded by it. He pushed himself, but he did not arrogantly or imprudently push himself into anything. He declined, as a physician, to have any part whatever at the confinement of the Princess Charlotte; "but," says the prudent and modest Baron, "as after the course of the first three months of the period, I, as a daily observer, thought I could detect errors in the treatment, I gave the Prince a long lecture, and entreated him to make my observations known to the physicians of the Princess." He is not arrogant; he only lectures his princely master at length! He will have nothing to do with the physicians in attendance, as their colleague, but he tells the Prince that they are wrong in their practice. Stockmar, so modest, will incur no responsibility; and Stockmar, so prudent, made the Prince Leopold the mouthpiece of his censure! The Rose of England, as she was so fondly called by the people, lay withered and dead; "but," writes our Baron, after the catastrophe, "all blame was averted from the man who had abstained from hunting after honour and emolument. . . . Every one would be now rejoicing over my interference, which could never have availed anything." And the not at all arrogant Baron complacently winds up his remarks by oracularly exclaiming, " It is impossible to resist the conviction that the Princess was sacrificed to professional theories,"—and he washes his hands of the whole affair.

It is a pity, seeing the mentor-like influence which Stockmar exercised over the greatest personages, he was unable to keep his pupil, or friend, or master, Prince Leopold, out of debt. When the Prince, by the grace, favour, and council of the Baron, was helped to the throne of Belgium, he was £83,000 in debt; £16,000 of which—

debts of the Duchess of Kent—he 'had taken on himself. England had settled on the Prince an annuity of £50,000 a year. A man, having such an income, and not choosing to measure his expenses by it, subjects himself to be called by a very ugly name. When the Prince became a foreign king, he gave up the annuity which he could not have retained, with or without honour, for no English government would have paid such an income to the sovereign of a foreign state. After all, England had to pay Leopold's debts out of the annuity thus surrendered, and various other items, including a pension to Stockmar himself, besides the expenses of keeping up the Prince's estates in England; so that the English treasury did not profit by the matter to a greater extent than £20,000 a year. In all this the only dishonourable part was the indebtedness of Leopold; for it is dishonourable for a man with a competent income to keep a poor creditor waiting for his due. One such creditor makes many, and there is a chain of misery that finds its origin in the selfish and guilty recklessness and indifference of men—princes, peers, or commoners—who live beyond their means.

Of the Baron's two great works, the moulding and making of Prince Leopold and of Prince Albert, it is not easy to say of which he is the prouder. If he lets a shadow in upon his portraits it is unconsciously. So, when we hear of King Leopold, in 1838, talking over with his nephew, Prince Albert, the subject of a marriage with Princess Victoria, Stockmar quotes a passage from a letter he received from Leopold, describing the conversation. The passage certainly is one to excite surprise. "He" (Prince Albert) "considers that troubles are inseparable from all human positions, and that therefore, if one must be subject to plagues and annoyances, it is better to be so for some great and worthy object than for trifles and miseries." The Belgian King calls this, looking at the question, by the Prince, "from its most elevated and honourable point of view." To us it seems "worldly." The philosophy of it is that of Skimpole, Mantalini, Micawber, Turvydrop, Pecksniff, all in one; and we are disposed to believe that the King must have misunderstood his nephew.

The proposal to endow Prince Albert with £50,000 a year was met by a query from blunt Joseph Hume, as to what a young German lad would do with such a sum in his pocket. On the motion of the ultra-Tory, Colonel Sibthorpe, the sum was reduced to £30,000. Stockmar was leaving the palace after the news of this result, and he met Lord Melbourne entering. The former was shocked at the result brought about by the Tories, but Melbourne frankly told him that the Prince need not be angry with the Tories alone. It was done, he said, "by the Tories, the Radicals, and a great many of our own people." With Melbourne and other ministers, Stockmar seems to have exercised a sort of back-stairs influence, not to be disguised by any fine name put upon it. What is far more astounding is that he seems to have exercised what he himself calls an "ascendant" over the English press. When the question of the regency (in case of the demise of the Queen) was about to be brought forward, Stockmar feared that the friends of the Duke of Sussex might be troublesome. What he wrote to the "Fourth Estate" we cannot make out, but he ends a note on the matter with these remarkable words: "The short but very friendly article in to-day's *Times* proves that I still have some ascendant over the obstinate nature of my old friend Barnes" (the then editor).

The regency affair was settled, and Prince Albert, should the contemplated contingency arise, was to be at the head of it. Meanwhile, Stockmar was employed in drawing up a memorandum for the education of the Princess Royal and the Prince of Wales. In that document is the following passage: "Down to the present day, England honours the memory of George the Third, because he cultivated the domestic virtues. History is already taking the liberty of questioning his services as a sovereign, but praises without exception his private life. But George the Third either did not properly understand his duties as a father or he neglected them. Three of his sons, George the Fourth, the Duke of York and William the Fourth, were all brought up in England; the Dukes of Kent, Cumberland, Sussex, and Cambridge, for the most part abroad. The faults committed by George the Fourth, the Duke of York, and William the Fourth, already belong to history. Unfortunately, they were of the most marked kind, and we can only explain them by supposing either that the persons charged with their education were incapable of inculcating principles of truth and morality in their youth, or that they culpably neglected to do so, or, lastly, that they were not properly supported in the fulfilment of this duty by the royal parents."

We are told that when the last surviving of the fifteen children of George the Third, the Duchess of Gloucester, used in her old days to tell stories of her early family times and the family doings she used to end her stories with the remark, "The fact is, there were too many of us." Stockmar thinks that the conduct of the princes lowered the national respect for monarchy; and that George the Fourth was saved from exclusion from the throne by the strength of the constitution. Of William the Fourth the Baron's judgment is, that he was "for no part of his life either a moral or a wise man," and he wonders that the King became popular, and "obtained at the end of his reign the flattering sobriquet of 'the good old sailor king.'" William, certainly, was never as wise as Leopold, but the "sailor king" in his mature years never manifested such principles, or exhibited such practices, as made many Belgians say, "As a king, he suits us; we cannot complain. But, as man, do you see? that's his affair, and does not regard us."

But let us return to England. The royal household there was not in such confusion during the reign of William the Fourth as it was at a preceding period. There were no four o'clock in the morning suppers or breakfasts given at Carlton House by certain officials below stairs to actors and actresses; but the disorganisation which existed was a result of the old free-and-easy time. In the early days there were men in the King's service who seriously thought that the most reckless hospitality was in accordance with the place and its master. The lord chamberlain, lord steward, and the master of the household, had jurisdiction within the palace, but where their limits began or ended they could not tell. Stockmar was employed to examine into the matter. He found that the outside of the palace was under the Woods and Forests. The inside obeyed the lord chamberlain, to a certain extent. My lord could order his Majesty's windows to be cleaned on the inside, but, says the Baron, "the degree of light to be admitted into the palace depends proportionably on the well-timed and good understanding between the lord chamberlain's office, and that of the Woods and Forests." So housekeeper and maids were ruled by the chamberlain, while the livery servants were placed under the control of the master of the horse, and the rest of the servants obeyed the lord steward." "The last official," so wrote the Baron, "for example, finds the fuel and lays the fire, and the Lord Chamberlain lights it." Stockmar was one day sent by her Majesty to Sir Frederick Watson, the master of the household, to complain that the dining-room was always cold. Sir Frederick gravely answered, "You see, properly speaking, it is not our fault. The lord steward lays the fire only, and the lord chamberlain lights it." In like manner the lord chamberlain found the lamps, but the Lord Steward trimmed and lit them. It cannot be said that the routine of the circumlocution office has yet ceased. We might describe in Stockmar's own words the means by which small wants in the palace are still satisfied, or dissatisfied. He tells us that if a pane of glass or a cupboard door in the scullery wanted mending, the chief cook had to draw up and sign the requisition, which was countersigned by the clerk of the kitchen, who took it for further signature to the master of the horse, who sent it to the lord chamberlain for his authorization; from whose office it went before the clerk of the works, under the office of Woods and Forests, by which office the broken pane of glass or the cupboard-door was mended in the course of time—perhaps! Even now a visitor, let us say to that quiet and mysterious office, the Board of Green Cloth, may by chance find his foot entangled in an old mat. The mat is rarely trodden, the office doors do not give frequent access to that mat, and above the door might be fittingly inscribed, *Janua amat limen.* But to get that mat repaired, and to obtain official authority to procure a new one, would require a time, during which a fellow's hair might become thinned and turned grey. So careful are we now of the public money, that if in the Houses of Parliament a new lock and key should be required for any of the doors, application must be made for the former at one seat of power, but permission to have a key must be officially sought for at another.

It is not many months ago that some palings were required for official fencing in Ireland. The wood might have been bought therefor next to nothing, but the rails were bought in England, and a ship was chartered to carry them to Dublin quay.

As the great officers who were supposed to have control in the palace were seldom there, and were not represented by deputy, there was practically no control at all. Servants did very much as they liked, and yet it is with wonder that we read how illustrious visitors have been negligently received, left to find their own apartments, and, on issuing from them, to wander helplessly about the corridors in search of the dining-room. Stockmar remarks that when the boy Jones was discovered, at one o'clock in the morning, under a sofa in the room adjoining her Majesty's bed-room, nobody was responsible. The lord steward was not to blame, as he had no control over the pages near the Queen's person. The lord chamberlain was not blamable, because the porters were not within his department. But Jones got in when porters should have detected him; and if the pages had had their eyes open the rascal would never have reached one of her Majesty's sofas.

Stockmar suggested reforms which were, for the most part, adopted, and these, with others additional, were carried out by Prince Albert with unexampled strictness, not to say rigour. Waste and extravagance and disorder were stopped. Order reigned within the imperial palaces, but there came with it a system which savoured of meanness. We have heard of a wealthy tradesman who, having been paid his account at the proper office in one of the royal palaces, expressed a desire, just for once in his life, to taste the Queen's ale. No objection was made, but as, on lifting the glass to his lips, he was told that the liquor would be duly booked, with his name, as the recipient of it, he straightway set the glass down and left it untasted. This story has a parallel in that of the gentleman abroad who, out of respect for the memory of the Duke of Kent, from whom he had received some essential service, sent to the Queen a cask of rare wine. Presents are generally declined now by sovereigns, but it is said that this wine was not only received and acknowledged, but that the sender was required to pay the import duties. If this be really true, the demand was certainly an act of official impertinence.

Stockmar, who formed and reformed princes, saw and foretold the fate of nations, and comprehensively embraced everything, from political constitutions to rules and regulations for royal kitchens, saw through and through all the English notabilities with whom he came in contact. Peel thought the Baron by far too free, and, to show how correct was that thought, Stockmar says: "One day I had brought him to talk of an important political event in which he had himself been concerned. He was just about to make some uninteresting disclosures; only the last word of the secret was wanting, when he paused. To help him I exclaimed, 'Well, don't gulp it down.' This disconcerted him; he made an odd face and broke off." Stockmar never suspected that Peel was amusing himself with the Baron's inquisitiveness, disappointing it just as the German gentleman thought the secret was about to be divulged. How does the Baron avenge himself? By agreeing to the verdict of Peel's enemies, that he was "the most successful type of political mediocrity." We are bound to say Stockmar adds, "that ninety-nine hundredths of the higher political affairs can be properly and successfully conducted by such ministers only as possess Peel's mediocrity." One highflying genius may bring political affairs to a particularly happy issue, but also he may bring them, Stockmar thinks, to something quite the reverse.

We see a particularly highflying genius when we behold the Baron seated at the side of Louis Napoleon. It was after 1840, when the dynasty of Louis Philippe seemed perfectly safe, Louis Napoleon remarked that the dynasty was not safe at all, and that Louis Philippe would be unable to maintain himself. Stockmar asked, "And what then?" The Prince replied with confidence, "Then it will be my turn." This showed, Stockmar thinks, "a firm faith in his own star," adding, "It is no more than human, if the star will not rise quickly enough, to help it on a little."

Years ago Victor Hugo—who has written hymns in praise of Henry the Fifth, and has been of every shade in politics by turns, from ultra-legitimist, when he saw a miraculous child in the little Duc de Bordeaux, to ultra-republican, at which he remains, at least for the present —advocated an alliance between Germany and France, in order that Germany, with her arm stretched on one side, might smite the Moscovite, and France, with her sword pointing in another direction, might give a mortal thrust to dear old England. Stockmar, at the period of the Crimean war, had another idea, namely, a union of Prussia, Austria, and the Western Powers, in order to destroy the preponderating influence of Russia and to keep France back from excesses. Prussia, however, is a power with which no other nation would form an alliance without much forethought. Prussia was never yet faithful to a friend or generous to a foe. Of France, allowing all her merits, Stockmar has little to say that is not disparaging. He evidently as much believed in her civilisation as he did in that of the Fiji Islanders. In a mass, he looked on them as children imperiously demanding the moon, crying because it could not be had, whipt for the crying, and then sulkily acknowledging the justice of the whipping, yet swearing to have revenge for it.

Altogether the impression which this book leaves of Stockmar's character is not so satisfactory as the son seems to think it. If the Baron was not as much detested by the people of England as royal favourites and palace factotums generally are by the people among or over whom they move, the reason is, that Stockmar was not only discreet, but he was not a man who hungered and thirsted after ostentatious honours, and he was an honest man. Nevertheless, he was so near the throne and so busy about and about it as to cause his presence and his acts to be questioned. A less discreet man would have come to grief; but Stockmar was a busybody affecting to have nothing particular to do with anybody. Yet, in his own mind, he certainly thought that he, the ex-Coburg doctor, pulled the strings that moved the foremost puppets of the world. In his mind he was the better self, first of Leopold, next of Prince Albert; these were Stockmar-manufactured, according to Stockmar's idea. Repudiating all influence, he never seems to have missed an opportunity of exercising it when he could get a prime minister or a secretary of state by the button. His hints or his advice must have often appeared amusingly impertinent to some of our ministers; but what could be done in the way of snubbing a man who was authorized to come to the royal dinner-table in trousers when breeches were the only wear, and who might retire after dinner whenever he chose, without observing the etiquette which keeps men imprisoned till the sovereign's self has withdrawn. We strongly suspect that Stockmar was rather a bore, except to the princely personages whom he loved to serve and who loved him for his service. It is very certain that to him a court was the only true Elysium; to be with princes was to the twice-patented Baron a far more exquisite delight than any delight he could find in home. A man who marries, and yet who voluntarily dwells far away from the home in which he plants his wife, and who spends his years with princes, and performs moments of penance in flying visits, few and far between, to the wife who never accompanied him abroad, and to the children who could hardly have known their father with children's intimacy, may have been an excellent, honest, trustworthy servant of princes, but he does not come up to our idea of a man who accomplishes his duty within the circle where are marked the not unimportant duties of a parent and a citizen.

# The Turquoise Ring.

## A ROMANCE OF NEUFCHATEL.[1]

### By JOHN SHEEHAN.

#### I.

By Bethune's banks, in days of courtoisie,
　There lived a young and gallant chevalier;
Save lance and charger brave no wealth had he,
　But served, like gentle knight, his mistress dear.
　　　To her he cried,
　　　One morn in pride,
"Brave news! Once more our barons bold uprear
'Gainst England's power their glorious banners fair!

#### II.

"Dear France's right may God for aye maintain,
　And bless the knight who combats for his king!
Whilst thou, my lady love, shalt still retain
　In pledge of my fond faith this turquoise ring,
　　　Its azure blue
　　　Shall keep its hue
With Hubert's life; but should its brightness wane,[2]
Weep for thine own true knight in battle slain."

[1] More celebrated in modern times for its delicious *bondons*, or cream cheeses, than its knightly romances. It is situated near the head waters of the Bethune, in the valley of which, at Arques, Henry the Fourth won one of his most gallant and important victories. Almost under the old castle walls it was that he took a fortified position, and drew up his devoted little army of not more than four thousand strong to meet the shock of the Leaguers, amounting to thirty-six thousand, led on by the Duc de Mayenne. Just before this battle the Béarnais prince uttered the noble sentiment, in answer to a superior officer of the League, his prisoner at the time, who had asked him rather contemptuously, where were his forces to encounter such an overwhelming host as was arrayed against him? "You do not see all," said the king, "for you do not count God and the Right, which are on my side."

[2] It is still believed by many that this Persian mineral, first introduced to Europe by the Crusaders, changes colour and fades considerably with the serious illness of its wearer.

### III.

Some gentle tears the lady shed, as o'er
  The knight's cuirass her snow-white scarf she tied;
And on her flushing cheeks the tints she bore
  Of love's fond grief and woman's nobler pride.
        Then bending low
        To saddle bow,
He kissed her brow, and vowed his cry should be
"Sweet Lady Claire, for honour, love, and thee!"

### IV.

As down the forest glade at early dawn
  Her parting knight pricks on his gallant steed,
His weeping dame still watches from the lawn,
  As fading form and footfalls faint recede,
        Till pennon light
        And plume snow-white
No longer waving on the morning air,
She looks to Heaven and breathes her fondest prayer.

### V.

Three years the Eastern ring shone pure and bright.
  Three years for honour, love, and lady fair,
Sir Hubert fought, till tidings came at night—
  Sad tidings from the battle field—to Claire.
        She knew too well
        What page could tell.
"The ring! the fatal ring!" she fainting cried;
Beheld the azure's fading hue, and died.

# Kill or Cure.

A STORY OF THE AMERICAN CIVIL WAR. ¦

———

"THE Major is a capital fellow, Doctor," I said, as we sauntered out to smoke our cigars in the garden, after an early dinner; "but he ought to be more merciful to us wretched bachelors. What with his charming wife and that exemplary baby, he makes it difficult to respect the tenth commandment."

"You admire Mrs. Layton?"

"Admire her! If she were not Charlie's wife, I should fall head over ears in love with her. I have seen fairer faces, but for dear, pretty, delicate womanly ways, I never met her equal."

"You couldn't understand a man's thirsting for her blood?"

"Good gracious! A wretch who could touch one of her golden hairs roughly deserves to be crucified."

"And yet for many days she was in deadly peril of her life."

"For her fortune?"

"She had none."

"Don't tell me, Doctor, that an innocent creature like that could give any one cause for revenge."

"No; I won't tell you anything of the sort."

"I think I see. Some one was madly in love with her?"

"If you were to guess till this day out you would not find the cause," said my friend. "Let us sit down here, and I will explain. It's no secret; I wonder the Major has not told you."

"Down here" was on a rustic seat that the Major's pretty wife had made at the end of his garden, close to where a little rill, soon to be lost in the blue Hudson, tinkled its way through his grounds.

"During the war," began the Doctor, "I served in the army, in the same regiment with an old schoolmate. He was as fine a soldier as ever drew sword. Hale, hearty, and sound in mind and body; eager to see service—and he saw plenty. I thought that he bore a charmed life, till one day he was carried into the hospital tent in a bad way. A ball had entered his shoulder, glanced on the clavicle (what you call the collar-bone), and had gone—*somewhere*. That was all we could tell, for there was no other orifice; but whether it had passed up or down, or taken some erratic course round about, such as balls will take, we knew not, and no probing could find out. Well, he recovered, went North to regain his strength, and for nearly three years I lost

sight of him. When the war was over, and I had begun to practise as
a civilian in New York, I met him again. But how changed! He was
a living skeleton, and I saw in a moment that he had become habi-
tuated to opium. Do you know what that means? No? Well, throw
a bucket of water into a piano, and then light a fire under it, and its
strings will not be more out of tune than an opium-smoker's nerves
are out of order. He asked me if he might call on me at my office,
and of course I assented; but it was days before he came, and when he
did arrive I knew that he had been preparing himself for a fight with
himself. Some foolish patients come prepared to hide the truth, some
to magnify their ills. It is part of our business, in serious cases, to
examine a man's mind before we ask about his body, and hardened as
a surgeon must be, I confess that the condition of my poor friend
frightened me. There was an expression in his eye that I had never
seen in any sane being; and what made this worse was the calm
business-like manner in which he spoke. He told me that soon after
he had (apparently) recovered from his wound, he began to suffer from
pains in his head, which increased in severity till they became so
agonising that he had recourse to opiates to alleviate them. 'But I
have not come to consult you about this,' he said, 'this I can bear—
*must* bear. Would to God that they were always tearing me! The
worst is when they are not.'

"'They leave you very weak?' I suggested.

"'They leave me,' he replied, quite calmly, '*with a burning, all but
unconquerable, desire to take human life.*'

"I am not generally a nervous man, but I started, and looked round
me for some weapon of defence. 'Don't be afraid,' he continued, with
a sad smile, 'the fit is not on me now. I should not have come if it
had been. I have been nearly starved once or twice, not daring to leave
my room. I *can* conquer my madness now; the question is, how long
I can continue to do so. I feel that it is growing upon me. I feel my
power of resistance becoming weaker and weaker—the craving for
blood getting stronger and stronger. I am like a man who has slipped
over a precipice, and feels the earth and shrubs to which he clings,
slowly, slowly, surely, surely, giving way with him. I have brought
wretched curs out of the street, and killed them in my frenzy, in the
hope to exhaust it on them. It is no use. I must have *human* life.'

"'Any human life?' I inquired, 'or some one in particular?'

"'Why do you ask this, Doctor?' he cried, getting suddenly excited.

"'No matter; go on.'

"'Sometimes,' he resumed, 'it seems that *any* life would do; and
sometimes——Doctor, four days before I saw you I met, upon a
New Jersey ferry boat, a young girl. So pretty, so refined and nice!
I followed her to her home—the devil, that has taken possession of
me, led me. She went in, and soon came out again into her little

garden, and tended her flowers—poor child! Doctor, if I had had a pistol with me I should have shot her. You may smile; but some day soon I shall take a pistol on purpose, and shoot her.'

"It was clearly no use arguing with him. The best way with such people is to admit their facts and try to work round them.

"'Then,' said I, 'the only thing you can do is to submit to the restriction of an asylum, till this feeling has passed.'

"'It will not pass. If I were to go to a madhouse I should sham sane. Sooner or later their vigilance over me would be relaxed. Then I should murder my keeper, and go straight for that innocent girl.'

"'Then leave the country.'

"'Well, that would save her; but, Doctor, one life is as dear to its holder as another. If I don't kill her, I shall kill some one else.'

"'My dear fellow,' I replied, in as light a tone as I could assume, 'these fancies are curable. Put yourself under skilled medical treatment. You are all to bits, physically. Get sound in body, and you'll get all right in your mind.'

"'On the contrary, I am all to bits, as you say, mentally, and my body suffers through my mind. Medical treatment! I have consulted every practitioner of note here and in Europe. Some think I'm fooling them, some look wise, and talk as you do about 'treatment.' All have failed. Doctors are no use to me.'

"'Then may I ask why you have come here?'

"'To ask your advice as a friend,' he answered, drawing his chair nearer to me; 'and,' lowering his voice, 'to ask you one question as a friend and a God-fearing man, and to which I pray you to give me a plain *yes* or *no*.'

"'Go on.'

"'Feeling as I feel, shall I be justified before God in taking my own life? Will it be deadly sin for me to do for myself what I would do to a mad dog?'

"I repeat his words almost as he spoke them. I cannot give you the faintest idea of the solemn deliberation with which he put this awful question. For some moments I could not say a word. Then I started up and told him that I would not answer him *yes* or *no*—that it was not fair to ask me to take such a responsibility. Then he rose too, and said that he must resolve it for himself, and I saw plainly which way it would go. 'Give me till to-morrow to think it out,' I said, detaining him.

"'To-morrow may be too late,' he replied. 'The fit may come upon me to-night for all I know.'

"'Come home with me; I'm not afraid. You won't hurt me,' I said.

"'I would try very hard not to do so—but—I know myself. I cannot trust myself. Don't you trust me.'

"'I *will* trust you; but I'll do more. You are not armed, I suppose?'

"'No,' he replied with a shudder, 'not now.'

"'I'll take care that you shall not be, and I'll carry my Derringer in my pocket. On the first indication of homicidal mania I give you my word I'll shoot—and I shoot straight.' I said this to satisfy him, poor fellow! In his weak state I could have laid him down like a child. It did satisfy him, and we went home together. I led him to talk of our old soldiering days, and gradually got him back to his wound. I made him describe the first sensations of pain in his head, and repeat all that his different medical advisers had said. I happened to have a strong preparation of hasheesh by me. I gave him a dose, and whilst under its influence I carefully examined his head. Now the head, you must know, does not fatten or waste away in proportion to other parts of the body. Still his had become mere skin and bone; and this state, perhaps, gave me an advantage over others who had made the same examination. At last I felt, or thought I felt, a faint twitching—a sort of abnormal pulsation—about two inches above the left ear. It might be merely nervous, *but it might be caused by the ball.*

"I then set my mind to work, and thought the whole case over steadily. In the first place was that impulse to take human life, of which my poor friend had spoken, *really* uncontrollable? For example, suppose that one day he did take a pistol '*on purpose,*' and go to that young lady's garden—would he shoot her? To suppose that the insane mind never changes its purpose, or turns from the fell completion of its purpose, is to say in other words that the insane mind is stronger than the sane mind. If a man with a freshly broken leg were to tell you he was going to run a foot-race you would not believe him, because your common sense revolts against the idea of his running with a leg disabled. But if one with his *brain* disabled declares that he is going to do something dependent upon the action of his mind common sense does not always argue so well.

"In the second place, did my poor friend, with his impaired means of judgment, *believe* that the impulse was uncontrollable? Because if he did the end would be the same, so far as he was concerned. He would sacrifice his own life to protect that of others, though they were in no actual danger.

"In the third place, might not this story of the impulse be a mere pretence to excuse the commission of suicide? Now there are no forms of madness more obscure in their origin, more difficult to detect, more persistent, and more fatal than suicidal mania; and as there have been numerous cases in which persons who have destroyed themselves have carefully prepared evidence tending to show that their death was accidental, why should there not be one in which the fatal act was to be (so far as possible) justified?

"In the fourth place, granting that there was either real homicidal mania or fancied homicidal mania tending to suicidal, or simply the latter—was there a possibility of cure?

"As the three first questions rested for their solution on one set of facts, and the deductions to be drawn therefrom, I considered them together. A victim of suicidal mania rarely if ever speaks of suicide. When a man says he is going to drown himself you may generally direct him to the cars which will take him to the river side with the fullest conviction that he will not breakfast with the crabs. If, in an exceptional case, suicide is mentioned, it will either be treated lightly, as an act that is not a crime, or the patient will be very earnest in his assurances that he would never commit it. Remembering my poor friend's manner, I noticed that he spoke of taking his own life with much more emotion than he evinced when he told me of the impulse to shed the blood of others. His words, "*I must have human life—if I had had a pistol with me I should have shot her—some day soon I shall take a pistol on purpose and shoot her—I should murder my keeper and go straight for that innocent girl,*" were spoken as calmly as though he said, "I owe five dollars—I must go and pay them," and at the same time with a tone of deep commiseration for the predestined victims. They were to die for no fault of their own, but they were doomed to death—if he lived. When, on the other hand, he spoke of saving their lives at the sacrifice of his own, his manner changed. No one afflicted with suicidal mania ever treated self-destruction with the horror, the consciousness of its wickedness, and the religious doubts as to its being pardonable under any circumstances, with which he considered it. He had never once spoken of murder as a crime.

"After a long and careful consideration I came to the following conclusions:

"He is not labouring under suicidal mania.

"His impulse is real, and will have fatal results.

"Confinement in an asylum would have no curative effect.

"Then I took down my books bearing upon the anatomy of the human head.

\* \* \* \*

"The next morning I addressed him thus:

"'Before I answer you as to whether you would be justified before God, under the impulse you have told me of, in taking your own life to save that of another, you must answer me several questions.'

"'Go on,' he said.

"'When you consulted those doctors did you tell them all that you have told me?'

"'No. I did not dare. I said that I had horrible thoughts and cravings, but without entering into details as to what they were.

Once I went so far as to say I feared I was becoming dangerous, and the fool smiled.'

"'Good. Did they ever speak of searching for that ball?'

"'Yes, they said it might be the cause of my sufferings, supposing it had lodged near the brain, but that no one would take the responsibility of searching for it—so to speak—in the dark.'

"'They were right—the operation might kill you, and the ball be not found after all.'

"He looked up, and the dull dejected look that had become habitual passed from his face.

"'And even if it were found,' I went on, 'its extraction might cause your death all the same.'

"He laid his hand on my arm, and tried to speak, but he could not.

"'Still it would give you a chance—just a chance of more than life.' His grasp tightened. I could feel his heart beating. 'And submitting to such an operation—almost hopeless though it be—would not be *quite* suicide.'

"He fell on his knees and sobbed like a child. 'You'll do it?' he cried, 'God Almighty bless you! You'll do it?'·

*　　*　　*　　*　　*　　*

"Well," said my friend, lighting a fresh cigar, "to make my story short, I did it, with the assistance of a young surgeon whose nerve I could trust. We found that miserable piece of lead near where I had suspected it to be. It was just a case of touch and go. Had my knife wavered twice the breadth of its own edge—had the assistant been unsteady with the forceps—it would have been fatal. I don't want to appear vain of my success, so I'll say no more than this—*he recovered.*"

"And has'nt killed anybody?"

"No, and doesn't want to."

"By Jove! I wouldn't be too sure of that. And so the girl he wanted to murder married the Major?"·

"She did."

"Then if I were her husband I'd take precious good care that your interesting patient didn't come into the same State with her."

"My dear fellow if you were her husband you'd do exactly as her husband does."

"Does he know?"

"None better."

"And doesn't care?"

"Not a bit."

"Then he's a brute!"

"You'd better tell him so—here he comes."

"Does *she* know?"

"She does."

" And she's not afraid ?"

" No."

" One other question. Does your interesting patient still live in this country ?"

" He does."

" In what State ?"

" This State."

" Near here ?"

" Very near."

" Then, with all possible deference for our friend the Major, I think he is very foolish. Were I in his place I should say, ' My good sir, I admit that the ball from which you suffered so long cannot get back into your brains, but I am by no means sure that the *ideas* it engendered may not return. At any rate your presence near my wife is likely to make her nervous, and I appeal to you as a gentleman to locate yourself in some other part of the country. If you do so I shall have the highest respect for you ; if you do not, and ever have the misfortune to pass within a mile of my house, the interior of your skull will become more intimately acquainted than ever with lead in the usual form.' "

" Very neatly put," said the Doctor, " but our friend does not think of committing suicide now."

" Mercy, Doctor !" I cried, " you don't mean to say that the man who wanted to murder the Major's wife is—is——"

" The Major himself. Yes, sir."

## Autumn Days in Stockholm.

FIFTY or sixty years ago it was not the habit of those belonging to the middle class of society to leave their homes every year for a certain time in search of novelty and change of air; a visit to some accessible watering-place in their own country once in two or three years was all that could be attempted. Now that so many facilities are offered for travelling, so many cheap arrangements can be made for trips abroad, the only difficulty is to find some spot unspoilt by the too frequent visits of tourists, unchanged by the introduction of foreign habits and manners. Switzerland, the Rhine, Belgium, Holland, and many parts of France, are well known and visited yearly; but Sweden and Norway, though beginning to be resorted to by English and Americans, still present much that is fresh and attractive to those who love whatever is true, simple, and unhackneyed.

So seldom does anything realise our expectations, that my dreams were not of a golden hue as I steamed from London to Gottenburg. In fact there was not much to make them agreeable; three days and nights of gales, with thunder and lightning, a pitching and rolling vessel, and everybody ill around me, only suggested that the sight of land of any kind would be delightful. The people on board had come from all parts of the world: Norwegians and Swedes were returning to their country; there were passengers from California, others from New York; a young girl from the Empire City particularly amused me. She was travelling with her brother all over the world as fast as possible, and was then going to Stockholm on her way to St. Petersburg. She was sharp in appearance and sharp in everything she did; nothing escaped her observation; and she kept her eye-glass pertinaciously fixed in one eye, peering closely at everybody and everything. I could not help laughing when, on looking at her during the night, I saw that she had still the glass in her eye, though she was fast asleep.

That anybody could rest was quite astonishing, for we were in a heavy storm from the time we were fairly out at sea at midnight one Friday till the following Monday morning at ten o'clock, when we neared the shores of Sweden. Two whole nights the captain had been obliged to remain on deck, feeling rather anxious about our safety, and had said that this passage was not one to have been undertaken by ladies except in case of urgent necessity. How glad, therefore, we were to be told that Gottenburg could be seen will be readily imagined after all we had endured ; yet the weather was too bad to allow us to go on deck, and we were actually in the harbour before we could get a glimpse of the city.   The first thing which would strike a stranger are the bridges and the quays, which are fine, and give the idea that the city is much larger than it is in reality ; there is, however, nothing to detain the traveller beyond a day or two, the churches and public buildings not being particularly interesting.   Some pretty gardens, in which a band plays every evening, are worth visiting, as well as the place of a Mr. Dickson, of a Scotch family, whose fortune is derived from timber which his grandfather cut down in Norway and Sweden, and sold some years ago.   The house is built in the Italian style, the grounds are tastefully laid out, the surrounding scenery very pretty and English, and the drive thither exceedingly pleasant.

Through the kindness of a Swedish acquaintance, I was put in the way of securing my berth in the canal boat from Gottenburg to Stockholm, which is the most inexpensive as well as the most interesting mode of travelling.   The journey takes about three nights and two days ; but as the steamer, like all the Swedish vessels I have been in, is beautifully clean and nicely fitted up, there is no great hardship in being so long on board.   The night we started I went to my cabin about ten o'clock ; though the beginning of August, it was still light ; but the scenery, we were informed, would be very flat for some hours. At six the next morning coffee and rusks awaited us on deck ; and we were told that if we wished to breakfast before setting out for the falls of Tröllhätten we must make haste.   The vessel puts to shore at any special place of interest, and the passengers have plenty of time to explore if they choose.   The waterfalls of Tröllhätten are certainly very beautiful, but those who have seen the finest in Switzerland and in Wales will not, I think, remark anything grander in them.   The winding path, however, by which we walked to them was lovely, and we came back in great spirits from the exercise and the enjoyment of the fresh morning, and found a second breakfast ready for us, to which we did ample justice.

Till in the course of the day we entered the lake Wener, about one hundred and fifty English miles in length, there was nothing interesting for the eye to rest on.   Wenersborg, which heads it, is very picturesque, on account of its carved wooden houses—like Swiss houses, which are everywhere to be seen in Sweden.   Here, and all the way to Stockholm, there is no scenery that can be called fine, no mountains, no lofty trees, but all is soft, green, and smiling ; firs and weeping birches clothe the banks, and small islands start up everywhere to add to the beauty of the landscape and occasionally to ruffle the lake.   The next day we stopped at an interesting place called Wadstena, where there is an old castle and the remains of a nunnery, founded by St. Brita ; several royal personages became sisters of the order, and among them Queen Margaretha, the Semiramis of the North.

After quitting Wadstena, we rested only a few minutes occasionally at two or three small villages, charmingly nestled in the banks of the canal. The bright red-painted wooden cottages stood out in pleasant relief against the fresh green foliage, and formed quite a picture. Here the peasants came to the side of the vessel, with little baskets of fruit temptingly piled up, and with bags containing rings of something between biscuit and bread, which I observed were much liked by the Swedes, and were bought by most of the passengers. At length Sunday morning arrived, and we were informed that in less than an hour we should arrive at our destination. It may be guessed with what a throb of eager expectation we hurried on deck that we might not lose the first glimpse of the beautiful city.

I do not know how Stockholm would strike people who have seen Venice; to me it was altogether new and fascinating. Gardens everywhere sloping down to the edge of the water and filled with people, tiny steamers plying hither and thither, close at hand, not to speak of larger vessels which go to greater distances, naturally give to the whole scene a very animated aspect. From the approach to Stockholm by the river its full grandeur is seen. The principal points of interest are the city proper and the royal palace; the intersecting water fills up the whole picture. From the Baltic, it appears, if possible, to greater advantage; and a fine view of it may be obtained from the garden of the Mosebacke, which is situated on one of the loftiest hills of the Södermalm.

The public buildings are not numerous, but they are so placed as to be seen to the greatest advantage, and from this circumstance add greatly to the imposing effect of the city. The old palace, the National Museum, the Riddarhüset, where formerly the nobility held their sittings during the diets, and the Riddarholms Kyrkan, which may be called the Westminster Abbey of Stockholm, are among the most interesting. The vaults of this old church are lighted up once a week, and the tombs uncovered, when it ought to be visited; a few *ore** are then paid, but all other days it may be entered gratis.

Though the principal inhabitants leave Stockholm during the hottest months of summer, enough remain to make the gardens lively in the evening. The Djurgården, one of the prettiest, which has the best band, and this season, in addition, a Hungarian band of celebrated performers, is generally well filled, and to a new comer presents a very spirited scene. Waiters thread their way amidst endless marble tables, bearing aloft trays with coffee and ices, granite ice especially, and liqueurs and Swedish punch, through throngs of visitors. The people, who have been called the French of the North, do not gesticulate as in France, but a murmur of voices accompanies the music,

---

* An *ore* is less than a farthing.

and the language, which is almost as soft as the Italian, makes this pleasant. Gentlemen walk in and out among the groups of ladies, seeking for those they especially desire to notice, and having found them, take off their hats with a graceful sweep which hitherto I have only seen accomplished by Swedish gentlemen. As far as living out of doors, the Swedes, though inhabitants of a cold climate, resemble the southern nations, and spend very little time at home; indeed, our idea of home, from my observation, and from what I was told, is much more understood by the Danes than the Swedes, and domestic virtues are less cultivated by the latter than the former.

After the first week, which I passed in one of the principal hotels, I found it would be more agreeable to board in a Swedish family; I should in this way have society, and see the Swedes in their own homes. In the Brunkeberg's Torg I was received by a very amiable and intelligent lady, a widow, who, to increase her income, had always a few people with her. Her arrangements were very good, but the diet was certainly a trial, as, under the happiest circumstances, the cooking is so different from either English or French cooking, so bad, I must really say, that it requires a great deal of fortitude and a certain amount of health to endure it. The bread is nearly all flavoured with aniseed, that is, all the softer kind of bread; there is a rye bread, however, of which they eat a great deal, which is thin, full of holes, and hard as sailor's biscuit; this they consider good for the teeth; perhaps it is; at any rate, good teeth are required to bite it. I noticed a great many soups; for without soup no Swede would imagine he had dined, and in families who live moderately, very little in the way of substantial food comes afterwards. There were sweet fruit soups, curds-and-whey soup sweetened, many white soups with vegetables prettily cut up, and some gravy soups, that seemed as if they ought to be nice; but they were spoilt for an English palate by the introduction of some uncongenial flavour; dumplings, for example, which we think good in broth, they perfume with peach-water, or some kind of scent, and put into gravy soup.

The habits at table, even of people of good birth and education, strike an English person oddly. The great rapidity of eating, the perpetual approach of the knife to the mouth, the fork held up in the air, and the elbows thrust out, are scarcely reconcilable to our ideas of civilisation. I must in justice say, however, that I noticed many persons very particular in this respect. At supper, nobody attempts to sit down, but each person takes a fork and a piece of bread, and plunges his fork into half a dozen dishes, taking a little piece from each and putting it on the same piece of bread; meat, fish, sweets, and cheese, seemed alike acceptable. I was told by one of my English acquaintances that a Swede had said to him, " that the correct behaviour of English people at table fidgeted him to death."

But all those with whom I came in contact were so unaffected, so unselfish in their kindness to me, that though at first I could not speak a word of their language, I soon felt at home with them, for I saw that everybody wished to be good to me. They do not seem to care for rank and riches, but to like people for their personal qualities.

I found them generally clever and very accomplished; good musicians, for only those play who are likely to play well; good artists, and really thoroughly educated; many speak two or three languages very correctly. Simple things, I observed, appear to amuse them. It was rather chilly one evening before I left, and two or three young men in the house lighted the stove and invested some money in almonds, molasses, &c., for making hardbake. Then, with some young girls, they busily set to work to chop almonds and prepare the sweetmeat, all the time singing merry songs and telling anecdotes. They explained to me that they frequently passed many hours in this way in the long winter evenings, as well as in dancing, music, and singing. With some friends I went to one of the many pretty places just outside Stockholm, to keep a "name's day"; it took us nearly an hour, going by the little steamer, and on reaching the rustic bridge we had a pleasant walk of almost a mile through a forest of thickly planted, though not lofty, trees; and when we emerged from this, we came in sight of a little colony of two or three wooden houses, one of which was occupied by the lady whose name's day we were going to celebrate. We found her with her friends, and her husband and children, sitting on the lawn before the house; a table was covered with fruit, with light wines and Swedish punch; the men were smoking, the women chatting, and the little children dancing and running from one to the other. Each of the gentlemen who came to visit the lady presented her with a bouquet, and we were taken into the house to see how many she had received; two tables were quite covered with them. As it grew dark, her husband brought out pretty coloured Chinese lanterns and lighted up the interior of the house, the front, and the shrubbery which backed the lawn. What a magic scene this little spot appeared to us in the distance as we wended our way home through the forest, our host accompanying us, and carrying a Chinese lantern, till we came into the open space by the water side, when the moon and stars lighted us to the little bridge, whence the last steamboat left. To catch this boat we had been obliged to leave all the merry people behind to partake of the grand supper. Coming in sight of Stockholm was another Fairyland for us; myriads of lights sparkled on the face of the water, the beautiful buildings stood out in bold relief from the brightness of the summer lightning, which illuminated everything around, and music and ringing voices echoed from the gardens and filled the air.

In many persons' experience of life all that is joyous, brightest, and promising, is nearly allied to that which is deeply tragic and pathetic. In one of the most frequented promenades, I spent part of almost every day; in the evening it was a blaze of light with coloured lamps; the most brilliant overtures, the most fascinating waltzes, were performed; in the midst of this gay scene, day after day, hour after hour, for the last six years, has walked up and down a poor woman, whose history is known only by the few, and who is passed by altogether unnoticed by the multitude. Still good-looking and attractive, not much more than thirty, dressed with scrupulous care and coquetry, she paces up and down incessantly: her unearthly pallor and vague look draw the attention of the sympathetic, and those who feel for all suffering are painfully impressed as they see her continually stop the passers-by, gentlemen particularly. She talks at first excitedly, and then with utter inconsequence. This poor demented creature six years ago was beautiful and happy, like many of those around her, on the point of marriage—nay, the wedding-day was not only fixed, but had arrived; but no bridegroom was forthcoming. From that day to this no tidings have ever been received of him, and she wanders forth listlessly, hour after hour, striving to find in each new face some likeness to her old old love. She is allowed to walk about unmolested, and is generally treated with respect and sympathy. Another poor afflicted woman visits some of these promenades. She, however, belongs to a lower class of society; she, too, is allowed to go freely where she likes. Her fancy is to bedizen herself with old tattered ball dresses, and to decorate her hair with flowers, while at the same time she carries a large basket filled with the rudest kitchen utensils. I did not hear her history; but she occurred to my recollection when mentioning the other poor woman.

A lively and totally different picture is to be seen in the Skeppsbron. There merchants are hurrying to and fro, and large vessels are being laden for the north of Sweden (Norrland) and St. Petersburg—a three days' journey by sea, with stoppages, from Stockholm. Opposite the Skeppsbron is Skeppsholmen, one of the pretty islands forming part of Stockholm, and in the warm weather furnishing shady seats and walks. On this side is the National Museum, in which is a fine collection of pictures, especially of the Dutch and Swedish schools. In the same building is a curious apartment containing old armour and the wedding dresses and costumes of former kings, queens, and favourites; all this can be seen gratis, except on one or two days of the week, when only a few *ore* are paid. Of course, at Stockholm, as in all great cities, there are museums for various kinds of collections: for natural history, for minerals, for coins, &c., but these are mentioned in the guide books. I did not wish to occupy my time entirely in visiting public buildings, but rather to note the habits of the people, and such social traits as might come in my way during so short a stay.

One morning I went to call on a Swedish acquaintance and found her doctor with her. He was merely paying a complimentary visit, as his services were not required. I learned that an arrangement is made with the medical man; a small sum of £5 or £6 a year contents him, and for that he attends the whole family, however often they may happen to be ill. The difficulty seems to be to get hold of him quickly enough in an urgent case; for if he has gone on his rounds he finishes every visit before he goes to the new patient. A lady with whose relatives I was slightly acquainted had a husband who had always very delicate health, and upon one occasion, when they were staying with her, he was seized with a sharp attack connected with a heart complaint. They urged her to send at once for the doctor, but she only used some simple remedies, because she said she had just dismissed her usual medical attendant, and had made no fresh arrangement with any body else, so that she could not ask any one to come to her assistance. A poor lady while I was there lost a child from water on the brain, and she sat by it for hours in the most terrible anxiety, waiting the doctor's time for coming. To people accustomed to command prompt advice in illness, Stockholm, or, indeed, Sweden, would not seem to be a desirable place to be attacked in.

In my walks I occasionally observed some very refined-looking ladies in white aprons, those worn by English parlour-maids; they had also large white collars, with bands down the front of the dress, turning into a sash round the waist, and tying in a bow behind. These were worn over black dresses, and intended for mourning; generally six or eight months, according to the relationship is the time for wearing mourning in Sweden, but crape is not used. A very pretty mark of attention to a parting guest is the custom of presenting bouquets; but however inconvenient they may be to carry they must not on any account be left behind; it would give great offence. The Swedes are not a rich people; but they have a thousand ways of doing little kindnesses and paying civility, which are agreeably felt by those living among them. They have also many simple pleasures for the unsophisticated; the number of little clean steamboats, going daily for a few *ore* or a rix-dollar (1s. 1½d.) to charming spots not far from Stockholm, enable most people to make frequent and pleasant excursions; and there are so many beautiful palaces, containing fine pictures, curious china, and other interesting things, that during the warm months these boats are thronged, especially on Sunday, when the fares are considerably reduced. Ulriksdal, Drottningholm, and Gripsholm, have daily visitors. Independently of the beautiful rooms to be seen in these palaces, it is most enjoyable and heart-filling to find yourself in the midst of the lovely, soft, lakelike scenery which surrounds them. Towards the end of September, when the leaves are beginning to change rapidly previous to falling, the little islands in the river and in the lakes which it forms seem as if decorated with nosegays, so bright and vivid in hue is the decaying foliage, and in such regular clusters does the alteration of colour take place.   The lime tree has the most beautiful shades of pink and rose colour in its varying leaves.   There are other trees which from the palest yellow deepen into the richest golden shade.   Nowhere except in Sweden do I remember to have seen such charming effects from this cause.

A pleasant trip I must mention can be made to Upsala by the steamboat, which starts at eight o'clock in the morning from Stockholm, and the scenery is interesting nearly all the way.   Though the boat does not reach Upsala till half-past two o'clock, there is quite time to see the city and return at night by train to Stockholm—a distance of nearly fifty miles.   The air of Upsala is considered more invigorating than that of Stockholm, and the walks around it are beautiful and various.   When the Cathedral and the University have been visited, it is worth while to mount a winding path by the side of the governor's residence—a very old castle—and on reaching the top of the hill to sit down and breathe the fresh heath-scented breeze. From this spot three mounds can be seen, the three burial-places of Thor, Odin, and Frey; if the walk of two or three miles were taken to reach them, no further object would be obtained.   At Upsala, there are the usual pretty gardens and cafés, also good bands, which play every evening, while the students, known by their white caps, lounge about and smoke, or sit and sip liqueurs and punch.

Among the many delightful recollections I have carried away from Sweden are those connected with a visit to Wisby, in Gottland, one of the Hanse Towns, once of great importance, and the birthplace of pure Gothic architecture.   The bands of stonemasons who started from Wisby in olden time, and travelled through the different countries of Europe (journeymen—the origin of our word for superior workmen), led to the gradual formation, no doubt, of that body of men known as Freemasons.   Wisby is now silent as the grave, and many of its streets are grass-grown.   The still beautiful ruins of seven or eight churches give it a very picturesque appearance.   Though there are altogether eighteen or nineteen ruins, most of them are only fragments of pillars and arches, and in the pretty gardens and walks at Wisby it is sad, though poetical, to find what must once have been so exquisite in design defaced and moss-grown.   The larger ruins are yet in a sufficient state of preservation to make a visit to them exceedingly interesting; many of the delicate rose windows are quite perfect, and the long majestic aisles are still standing.   An arch or two of the otherwise roofless St. Catherine trembles in the air, and stray branches and creepers have twined themselves round some of the pillars, adding to the beauty of the scene.   The gentleman at whose house

I remained while at Wisby, and by whom I was most hospitably entertained, was a direct descendant of one of the old sea-kings. His own residence was part of some ruined cloisters, and the bedroom which I occupied had the vaulted roof of a church. Most persons, he told me, feared to sleep in it because it was said to be haunted; perhaps I was too heartily tired for a ghost to make any impression on me, but I was certainly undisturbed by one. My host had a genuine love of these wonderful ruins in his old home, and his cultivated mind and tastes made him a guide of no common order. With this gentleman and another of his guests I went to the pretty Botanical Gardens, so well situated that they command a magnificent view of the sea. Fruits and flowers will grow in Wisby out of doors which will not thrive or ripen in Stockholm, and the air is soft and balmy and recommended for the consumptive.

Close by these gardens is the Maiden's Tower, celebrated in one of Emilie Carlen's charming tales. Here a poor maiden was walled up some centuries ago for having betrayed her country to the Danes, in consequence of her great love for the Danish king. That women should punish their own sex for such delinquency would not appear surprising, but it is scarcely to be reconciled with the merciful treatment which men might be expected to show women under such trying circumstances.

The only drawback to an expedition to Wisby is the rough passage. The sea is perfectly wild, and no doubt the Vikings of old revelled in it, but in these civilised times the voyage cannot be considered at all pleasant. In winter the boats do not go this route, but start from a small place considerably south of Stockholm, when the passage occupies only four hours. The captains on the vessels are generally gentlemen by birth and education, and have frequently served in the English navy. The sea phrases employed by the Swedish sailors are all English, and the men are very like our own Jack Tars—a frank, handsome, fine race. Sixteen hours in a gale of wind brought me back, knocked up, but safe, to Stockholm, where I resolved to rest a few weeks before starting on my journey homewards by a different route, which I settled.

My first day's journey after I quitted Stockholm took me to Jönköpping, beautifully situated between two lakes, the Munk and the Wettern; here was a good hotel, and, as usual, pretty gardens and promenades. The next day I reached Malmö, and the boat started on the following for Copenhagen, the passage only lasting an hour. Here, of course, everybody stays to see Thorwaldsen's Museum, if for nothing else, and is richly rewarded. This splendid museum does as much credit to the nation as it does to the lofty genius whose colossal productions it encloses, together with precious works of art, gifts, and collections made by the mighty sculptor himself. I, alas! had only one afternoon to spare for it; I was rapidly making my way home, and one day must be devoted to the Exposition; for who could be in Copenhagen without seeing it? Then there was Tivoli to be visited, where every sort of amusement goes forward daily and nightly for a small sum, something like sixpence.

I went on board the steamer at night for Kiel, and after a very stormy passage I found myself travelling by rail to Hamburg. This wonderful city, which seems at every turn to speak of riches and to be peopled by Jews, was quite worth halting in. The next day brought me to Hanover and Cologne, whence I returned, through Malines and Ostend, to London.

# America and her Literature.

## By JOHN C. DENT.

IT is a generally received opinion in this country—not only among
the public at large, but also among men of letters—that America
has, strictly speaking, no distinctive literature of her own. The
doctrine has been propounded so frequently, and in such an endless
variety of shapes, that—although, like most other doctrines, it has
not met with universal acceptation—the subject has become as musty
as Hamlet's proverb. But the truth, in this instance, can hardly be
told too often; and it must be confessed that up to a comparatively
recent period, the opinion in question has been pretty fully justified
and borne out by the actual state of the case. A national *character*
—and that not of an altogether enviable kind—America certainly
has long since acquired: but the development of a distinctively
national literature seems to have been a matter requiring time for
its consummation, even with so fast and enterprising a race of beings
as our brethren on the other side of the Atlantic are universally
acknowledged to be. The writings of Prescott and Motley in history,
Emerson in speculative philosophy, Theodore Parker in rationalistic
theology, Holmes and Lowell in discursive essay, Whipple in literary
criticism, Longfellow, Poe and Bryant in poetry, and Irving and
Hawthorne in the lighter walk of fiction, are an honour to literature,
and will lose nothing by comparison with the best works of their
respective classes, either in England or elsewhere. The works of
these, and many other authors not so well known to English readers,
are works of which Americans are justly proud. But, so much being
conceded, the undeniable and oft-repeated fact still remains, that the
best efforts of those writers have no claim to be regarded as distinctively
American productions. They do not smack of the soil. They are not
redolent of the wild western breeze. They do not photograph for us
the mighty river, the lone ranch, and the boundless prairie. Nine-
tenths of them might have been written by Englishmen, and the other
tenth might just as well, both as regards the writers and the public,
never have been written at all.

We do not wish to be misapprehended in this matter. It is not
that the works alluded to are deficient in point of originality. Some
of them are conspicuous for an originality to which a mass of their
English compeers can lay no claim. Edgar Poe wrote strikingly
original poetry, and no poetry breathes forth the true, the divine Erōs,

more eloquently than his. But anything less suggestive of America can scarcely be imagined. His 'poetic fire sprang, not from his contemplation of the scenery and characteristics of Young America, but from the inherent melancholy of his unhappy temperament, intensified by a defective and injudicious system of education, and a morbid contemplation of the abstruse and mystic lore of Old Europe. His career, too, was one of almost unparalleled misery and degradation, and could not fail to leave its impress upon his literary efforts. As one of his critics has observed, he was himself that

"unhappy master, whom unmerciful disaster
Followed fast and followed faster, till his songs one burden bore."

Longfellow's 'Evangeline' has an exquisitely picturesque passage here and there—witness his description of the cuckoo warbling from the thicket—but the poem as a whole is deficient in force, owing in a great measure to the ponderous impracticable hexameter in which it is dressed. 'Hiawatha' is deficient both in music and in force. Holmes's lyrics are genial, fanciful, unequalled in their way; but they are precisely such as two or- three of his English contemporaries might have written had they been clever enough. Cooper's novels, at the first cursory glance, seem to be American: but in no sense of the word can they be termed photographs, and as a whole they are inartistic. The 'Biglow Papers' are not inartistic: such a term, indeed, would sound like a paradox if applied to anything from the pen of Mr. Lowell. The humour is fine, and 'Birdofredum,' is irresistibly funny. We are introduced to the quaint provincialisms of the Down-Easter in such a manner as to afford conclusive proof that the author has made the dialect a study: but no one is better aware than Mr. Lowell that the book is nothing more than a slashing and powerful political squib. In short, search as carefully as you will among all the many emanations from the American press previous to the last few years, with a view to discovering among them a production which is exclusively American, in spirit and tone, and your quest will prove as hopeless as was that of the blind Ethiopian who, with an extinguished candle, in a dark cellar, hunted for a black cat that was not there.

No persons are more conscious of the truth of the foregoing statements than American authors themselves. Cooper, Lowell, Emerson, and a host of others, have admitted and deplored the fact, in terms indeed so little stinted as to have more than once brought down upon their heads a storm of acrimony and ill-feeling from some of their less liberal-minded and more thin-skinned compatriots. We emember to have seen in a prominent New York periodical a review of 'A Fable for Critics,' wherein the reviewer savagely quoted and enlarged upon the expressive old Scotch proverb which says, "It is an ill bird that fouls its ain nest;" and this notwithstanding that Mr. Lowell states, both on the title-page and in the preface to his book, that he sits, for the nonce, in the tub of Diogenes. Americans are not more fond of having their shortcomings thrown in their teeth than their neighbours, even when the assailant is one of themselves.

It is a fact well known to every one who is at all familiar with their characteristics that the Americans are a nation of readers. Although we have no published statistics at our elbow to guide us in arriving at such a conclusion, we presume it is not too much to say that a greater number of books are sold in the United States than in any other nation on the face of the earth. A vast majority of the books so sold are reprints of the works of English authors. One mammoth publishing house in the city of New York makes a point of reprinting every novel—or, at any rate, every novel worthy of the name—that issues from the London press; and this in addition to an immense number of more solid works in history, philosophy, and general literature. The inevitable inference to be drawn is that these innumerable volumes would not be thus periodically poured forth unless they found a remunerative sale: and a further legitimate inference is that the Americans have been too busily occupied in reading foreign literature to permit them to devote sufficient time and attention to the production of a literature of their own.

Nearly a hundred years have elapsed since the citizens of the American States first became an independent nation. Since that time they have been actively employed in commercial speculation, in the acquisition of new territory, in opening up and bringing under cultivation an expanse of country so vast as almost to justify their characteristic boast that Uncle Sam has ample room in his capacious bosom for all creation: and lastly, they have passed through an internecine struggle compared with which the struggles of old-world nations seem petty and insignificant. It is, therefore, scarcely to be wondered at that the development of the peculiar intellectual genius of the Great West should have remained almost entirely in abeyance. But our own magnificent literature was not the growth of a day, nor of a century. We never did anything in the way of letters until we were thrown upon our own resources. Our connection with the continent of Europe was—fortunately for us—dissevered by the over-reaching cupidity and short-sightedness of a race of tyrants, and we were left to our own insular devices. The result has been the formation and development of a language which will be spoken, and a literature which will be read and admired in the dim vista of futurity. London Bridge and St. Paul's may be destroyed, and may become antiquated relics of a past civilisation: but the English language and literature are as imperishable as language and literature themselves.

The United States are now luxuriating in the enjoyment of great, and to all appearance permanent, peace and prosperity. The great events of the last few years have stirred the minds of the people to their innermost depths. The acquisition of the almighty dollar is no longer the exclusive, nor even the primary object of every man, woman, and child in the Republic. Their intellectual seed is beginning to germinate, and the first upshoots already give out unmistakable indications of a prolific harvest. The labourers are neither few nor indolent, and are constantly on the increase.

We would by no means be understood as asserting that any very great progress has been made in the establishment of a purely American literature, even yet; but we think we are justified in saying that there has been a commencement. The poems of Walt Whitman, and in an inferior degree the poems and sketches of Mark Twain, Joaquin Miller, and Bret Harte, according to the best judgment we are able to form, furnish abundant evidence to the careful reader that a time has arrived when our trans-Atlantic friends are about to cast off their literary allegiance, and when an adherence to English precedents, both as respects turn of thought and method of expression, is beginning to be at a discount among the rising literary names of the Great Republic. And, so far from feeling aggrieved at this manly self-assertion on their part, it surely behoves us to commend their laudable ambition, and to give them due credit for their patriotic spirit. It must, moreover, be borne in mind that whatever is a gain to American literature will be a gain to us. We both speak and write the same language. The mother-tongue taught in the schools and academies of the one, is precisely the same mother-tongue taught in the colleges and universities of the other. As Mr. Trollope observes, in the entertaining and discriminative work in which he has embodied the convictions resulting from his six months' sojourn in the West: "An American separates himself from England in politics, and perhaps in affection, but he cannot separate himself from England in mental culture." This is as true as it is well expressed: and if, as we believe will be the case, America shall ere long succeed in building up an independent literary reputation for herself, we in England cannot fail to reap a benefit therefrom. And this is no more than just. She has had the benefit of our five centuries of experience, and if there is a probability of our shortly being placed in a position to make reprisals, let us bid them "God speed" in their labours, and be unfeignedly thankful.

Of the four writers to whom allusion has been made in the preceding paragraph, Mr. Whitman is incomparably the most original. It is to him that the more discerning among his countrymen are especially looking for something great; and, judging from such of the products of his genius as have already reached us, we believe that they will not look in vain. If such unquestionable promise do not ere long result in an equally unquestionable fulfilment, there will be an end of arguing what a man *may* do from what he has already done. In an eloquent and manly letter to a friend, he confesses to an ambition to give something to the literature of his native land which shall be exclusively its own, " with neither foreign spirit, imagery, nor form, but adapted to our case, grown out of our associations, boldly portraying the West, strengthening and intensifying the national soul, and finding the entire fountains of its birth and growth in our own country."

Our estimate of his writings will probably appear to some of our readers to be extravagantly high. Even in his native land some of the best and noblest of his effusions have been ridiculed as doggerel, and by more than one writer of eminence he has been pronounced to be a lunatic without lucid intervals. One anonymous writer, who seems to have a very inadequate regard for the amenities of literature, has published his opinion that when Walt Whitman puts pen to paper he must be either drunk or mad. Another, also anonymous, pronounces him to be more absurd than Artemus Ward, without any self-consciousness of his buffoonery.

But, as has already been intimated, there are others of his countrymen who give a different account of the poet and his writings, and who do not hesitate to declare that a poetical luminary of the first magnitude is beginning to be visible in the western horizon. We have no room to spare for quotations; but if we had we have no doubt that such quotations would meet with equally opposite verdicts from the readers of this magazine.

It is no easy matter for one who has been educated in the Byronic or Tennysonian schools of poetry to do justice to the writings of such an author as Mr. Whitman. It will be remembered that a good many years ago, when the nineteenth century was yet in its teens, a light-whiskered, commonplace-looking man wandered among " untrodden ways " among the green hills and valleys, and on the margins of the sunny lakes of his native Cumberland ; and from thence sent forth, from time to time, a succession of volumes of poetry which rendered him the butt and laughing-stock of the reviewers; amongst whom the most uncompromising assailant was Francis Jeffrey, a critic who was recognised as the most competent judge of poetry of his day. Byron hurled anathemas at him from his Italian retreat, and pronounced him an idiotic driveller, alike devoid of rhyme and reason. Time, however, makes all things even. William Wordsworth was conscious of being endowed with a lofty and original genius : he knew that his day must come, and could afford to wait. Long before his death his claims were recognised by both his critics and the public, and he became the chief professor of an original school of poetry, to which his native lakes have given a name. The brain that conceived, the hand that penned those ballads, have long since mouldered away beneath the turf of Grasmere churchyard; but the ballads themselves still remain to us.   They have found an echo in the hearts of little children, and they have stirred the enthusiasm of the ripe scholar. We have heard them lisped by infant lips many leagues beyond the Rocky Mountains, and we have seen them made the subject of eloquent and appreciative essays by one of the soundest critics of this genera- tion.   Shades of Byron and Jeffrey!   Where be your gibes now?— Your flashes of ungenerous merriment, which used to set your readers in a roar?

It is within the bounds of probability that Walt Whitman will be compelled to pass through quite as fiery an ordeal in America as erewhile fell to the lot of Wordsworth in England; but, if so, we here beg to record our sincere conviction that the ultimate result in his case will be the same as was that in the case of Wordsworth.   There is, indeed, a great deal in common between the two.   The same passionate susceptibility of feeling, the same depth of philosophic meditation, the same homeliness of expression, the same disregard for, and contempt of, classic precedents, are perceptible in each.   Each has a poetic standard peculiar to himself, and each acts up to that standard.   Wordsworth, at the outset of his career, proposed to himself a definite object; and, unmindful of the sneers of the world, he pursued that object until it was fully attained.   Whitman has proposed to himself an object equally definite; and, unless we are egregiously mistaken in the man, he will attain it.

We do not think it probable that he will ever be popular in this country during his lifetime—unless, indeed, his days should happily be lengthened out beyond the allotted term prescribed by the Psalmist as the duration of human life.   He is now upwards of fifty years of age, and has not yet succeeded in penetrating to the hearts of a majority even of his own countrymen.   Yet he has deserved well at their hands, independently of his literary attainments.   He has not only written the strains, but has lived the life, of a true poet. While the dire conflict was raging between North and South, he did good service at the bedsides of the sick, the wounded, and the dying. By those (and their name is Legion) who witnessed or experienced his noble and self-sacrificing devotion to poor suffering humanity during those long and weary months, his name will ever be held in grateful remembrance.   Many a disabled Federal soldier now living is indebted for his life to the untiring exertions of the " good, grey poet."   Of many a last word and message was his breast made the repository. His life has afforded the best assurance he could possibly have given of the depth of his conviction that—

> " To have a great poetic heart
> Is more than all poetic fame."

Poetic fame, however, will be his; though it may be posthumous. He is the very incarnation of American democracy: fresh, hopeful, and above all things self-reliant. Nothing like an adequate conception of the man and his powers can be formed without a close and searching perusal of his works; but the reader who will employ such means will find something to reward him for his trouble.

As this paper is devoted to a brief exposition of the present tendency of American literature in general, and not to an elaborate inquiry into the merits of the poetry of Mr. Whitman in particular, we do not propose to enter upon any minute examination of his works. The English reader who wishes to know more of him, and to judge for himself as to the accuracy of the preceding estimate, may consult the English edition of some of his poems edited by Mr. Rossetti: but he will not even then have an opportunity of seeing the poet at his best, as the editor has omitted from his collection the author's masterpiece, which has not yet been reprinted in this country. It contains, indeed, many passages which would scarcely prove acceptable to the fastidious tastes of English readers.

Joaquin Miller, while possessing some points of resemblance to Walt Whitman, is by no means devoid of originality. He is almost equally unconventional, but is by no means so *strong*. With all his uncouth bombast, his dramatic power is such as to stamp him as a writer of no ordinary powers. His wild life among the Sierras has developed in him a vivid power of description which is peculiarly his own. Defective in elegance and finish, his poetry has the ring of the true metal. We are glad to perceive that, acting upon the judicious hint of a Westminster reviewer, he is biding his time, and not publishing quite so profusely as formerly.

Mr. Miller's coming over here to publish his poems was a mistake, and has done more to retard his recognition as a poetical genius among his fellow-countrymen than most persons are aware of. And then, that apostrophe at Niagara was a very ill-judged proceeding on his part, and displayed a self-conceit utterly unworthy of one who aspires—as every true poet must aspire—to be a teacher. His parade of his conjugal relations, moreover, in which the only end he could possibly have had in view must have been to attain notoriety, richly deserves all the condemnatory epithets that have been bestowed upon it.

Mark Twain is a personage of a very different stripe. His great defect is that he is *too thin:* but perhaps no writer in the language is more uniformly droll. The digestive organs of the man who can go over many pages of Mark's publications without being called upon to exercise his risible faculties must surely require immediate looking after. His humour, too, is always *good* humour, and is never cynical. It is thoroughly American. No foreigner is capable of duly appre-

-ciating his quaint and characteristic sayings: though we fancy his works would necessarily evoke laughter if they were translated into Chaldee. And this power of constraining the reader to grin in spite of himself is not the result of false spelling and barbarous grammar, -as in the instances of Josh Billings and Artemus Ward. It is quite independent of any such adventitious aids. He often uses slang -expressions, because it is impossible to depict Western character without resorting to such means; but his slang is never disgusting, and rarely offensive. His 'Jumping Frogs' and 'Overland Sketches' introduce a class of persons and nomenclature unknown in polished -circles, but the dullest reader cannot fail to perceive that the author is *among* them but not *of* them. He, even more than Mr. Miller, seems to be reposing under the shade of his laurels just at present: and he is right—his latest contributions to the 'Galaxy' displayed a very perceptible falling off. He needed rest; and as his literary ventures have made him pecuniarily independent of the world, he is taking what he needed. All things considered, we believe that when the history of American literature comes to be written, the name of Samuel Langhorne Clemens will be mentioned among its founders.

Bret Harte is, and deserves to be, well known in this country. In respect of mere finish, he is far in advance of any of the other three writers whose works we have been considering. He is an artist, and an artist who wields a graphic pencil. For many months his sketches and poems furnished the cream of the 'Overland Monthly.'

Like Whitman, Miller, and Clemens, he is a purely American production. He has a host of imitators, but not one of them is fit to be mentioned in the same breath with him. In his vivid, soul-stirring pictures of Californian life, the miner, the ranchman, and the bully of twenty years since, live and move again, in all their wild semi-savagery. He possesses and imparts a consciousness of the grotesque peculiarities of the dwellers in that singular region, for which we will look in vain in the pages of any other writer who has attempted to depict mining life and its incidents in the far West. His experience has been principally limited to the quarter from whence he has derived the material for his effusions, but his sympathies are universal, and are by no means restricted within such narrow limits. Whether he describes the ruffianly digger, the desperate gambler, or the fallen woman, the description is pervaded by a delicacy and chasteness, which, when the nature of the theme is taken into consideration, appear little less than miraculous. He treats of vulgar, wicked, ferocious people; but he himself is never vulgar, wicked, or ferocious. The wretched denizens of Red Dog and Poker Flat are photographed for us with all their hideous crimes perceptible in every lineament; yet an undercurrent of tenderness runs through the descriptions from first to last. The author everywhere preaches a doctrine of broad humanitarianism; and it is quite evident that the theory that the imaginings of man's heart are only evil and that continually, if accepted by him at all, is accepted with very many reservations. At all events he makes a reservation in favour of the hearts of such of mankind as are commonly supposed to afford the least justification for such an exception. A part of this is doubtless due to sentimentality; but it is a kind of sentimentality much less repulsive than that of those who run into the opposite extreme, and will not admit the possibility of anything good coming out of the Nazareth of poverty, ignorance, and degradation.

His canvas is narrow, but he suggests far more than he expresses. Several of his short sketches might without difficulty be expanded into a three-volume novel. The little story entitled ' Tennessee's Partner ' —notwithstanding the extraordinary conclusion at which the writer arrives in the last sentence—is of exceptionally great merit. There is a weird suggestiveness about the trial scene, where the " pardner " stands mopping his brow with his handkerchief, and " disremembers any sich weather before on the bar," that alone proclaims the author to be something very far removed from the ordinary tale-teller: and we do not envy the intellectual adjustments of the man or woman who can read * the account of ' How Santa Claus came to Sampson's Bar,' without experiencing a huskiness in the throat and a dimness in the eyes.

We have not included Mr. Leland in our category of writers who are laying the foundations of a distinctively national literature in America, because, though he is nothing if not American, his Americanism, like that of the ' Biglow Papers,' is restricted in its application, and can hardly, with strict propriety, be called national. He is, however, a quaint humourist, a trenchant satirist, and no contemptible social philosopher. His hero, Hans Breitmann, is a moving, breathing, lager-imbibing impersonation of those oddly-mingled qualities which go to make up the Teutonic Pennsylvanian—a compound of Fluellen, Hudibras, Dugald Dalgetty and Sir John Falstaff. The doughty Hans argues and philosophises in clever, witty couplets, many of which have already passed into proverbs in the United States.

Other writers there are, of less note, who are putting their shoulders to the literary wheel in America. Colonel John Hay, the author of ' Little Breeches,' has attracted some attention, both in his own country and in England; but he charges his works with too much irreverence, and writes too recklessly, to have much permanent influence in helping on the popular movement. Dan de Quille is the last candidate for public favour to whom we shall refer.

The periodical literature of America affords unquestionable evidence

* In the ' Atlantic Monthly.' The story has not yet been reprinted.

of the learning, acuteness, and breadth of thought of the writers who
furnish it.   The 'North American Review' will compare favourably
with the best of our quarterlies; while the 'Atlantic Monthly' is
quite up to the mark of any magazine of its class in the world.
'Appleton's,' 'Scribner's,' 'Putnam's,' 'Harper's,' and 'The Galaxy'
in the eastern States, and the 'Overland Monthly' in California, are all ably-conducted periodicals, and are all more or less
known here.   In legal, medical, and scientific magazines, the
Americans are more than respectable.   Our quarterlies, and 'Blackwood,' as is well known, are regularly reprinted at New York at a very
low price; and they have a circulation in America many times greater
than in England.

Before concluding, we have a few words to say about American
journalism, and we regret that those words cannot be complimentary.
The standard of American journalism—more especially of New York
journalism—is low: not only far below our own, but below that of any
other country in the world.   With two, or at the most three, honourable exceptions, the leading American newspapers are a reproach to
the enterprise and intelligence of the nation.   The paper which enjoys
the largest favour of all is perhaps the least creditable.   Every one
buys it, every one reads it, but every one holds it in contempt.   Its
editorial articles are not only slovenly in respect of style, but crammed
with scurrilities and misrepresentations.   Its primary object, and
indeed the primary object of American papers in general, is to create
a sensation; and to this end truth, justice, and integrity itself are
alike sacrificed.   In matters political it is absolutely at the disposal of
the highest bidder; and, if public report is to be relied upon, the
biddings have sometimes been very high.   This principle of management—or, rather, this absence of all principle in management—has
met with its just reward; for the paper in question has less political
influence to-day than almost any other journal throughout the United
States.

Our remarks upon this particular paper will, in a minor degree,
apply to the great mass of American journalism.   And yet there are
many members of the newspaper press of America who are by no
means deficient in journalistic ability; and who, apart from their
editorial capacities, are thoroughly honourable and high-minded gentlemen—gentlemen who have an accurate knowledge of what a properly
conducted journal should be.   They seem, however, generally speaking, to feel themselves constrained to sail with the popular current
and to await the benignant influences of time.   But gentlemen of
their intellectual calibre should be in advance of their time, and should
aspire to lead popular feeling, instead of being content to follow in its
wake.   It is gratifying to know that a change for the better is taking
place, but it must be confessed that the change is very gradual.

One word as to another class of periodicals, and we shall have done. A considerable amount of license is accorded to sporting journals, all the world over. We do not expect *Bell's Life* to deal with so elevated a class of subjects as a quarterly review; nor do we expect that the matters treated of will be handled as delicately in the columns of such a journal as in the pages of a young lady's magazine. But there *is* a point at which forbearance ceases to be a virtue. Some of the sporting periodicals of America are a shame and a disgrace, not to civilisation only, but to humanity itself; and make one think, for the moment, that the 'Voyage to the Houynhymns' is hardly so exaggerated and distorted a mockery after all. If anything like a correct estimate of transatlantic morals were to be drawn from the news items and advertisements in these vile repositories of wickedness, it would hardly be matter of surprise if the catastrophes of Sodom and Gomorrah were to be repeated in New York, Boston, and Philadelphia.

# The Wooing O't.

## A NOVEL.

---

### CHAPTER XX.

NEVERTHELESS, when it came to saying good-bye, and she was absolutely in the train, Maggie felt a little sad. Yet the regret was more for the impossibility of loving John as she should like to do than for parting with him.

"I am deuced sorry you are going, Mag. However, you won't be out of reach; we can get you back. Now, mind you write to me direct. I won't be plagued with second-hand letters, and I will run down and see you as soon as I make my way a little clearer. God bless you!"

As he left the door of the carriage, a gentleman with a large black leather bag jumped in. He was considerably out of breath, but wore a complacent expression, having evidently just succeeded in catching the train, and proceeded to change his hat for a travelling-cap, to arrange his railway rug, to unfold his papers, and evidently prepare himself for a long journey. He was a large fair man, about forty-five or fifty, with a broad, honest, open face, and whiskers of the peculiar tinge known as pepper and salt. Maggie observed him idly, for she had omitted to provide herself with book or paper; so sat watching the country as it flew past them, scarce able to believe that she was once more afloat and free.

Her fellow-traveller's newspaper lasted him for nearly forty miles; then he unlocked the bag, and drew forth a long blue paper, with a parchment angle and a green tie through it, which opened into a large folio, or rather many folios; into this he plunged, and was absorbed for another half hour, till Maggie, finding herself grow chill, endeavoured to draw up the window at her side.

"Allow me," said her companion, laying down his document and coming to her assistance. "The evenings grow cold now. Would you like to look at the *Times?*"

"I should, very much, thank you."

The voluminous sheet helped Maggie over many a mile. At Bletchly a lady and two little girls got in. Maggie soon made friends with the children, and as the shades of evening closed, her other travelling companions entered into conversation and chatted pleasantly enough. Maggie gathered that the gentleman was, like herself, going to Castleford. She was glad to think she should not be alone; company keeps up the spirits wonderfully. At C—— the lady and her children left them, and the gentleman asked Maggie if he could get her anything; he was going to have a biscuit and a glass of sherry himself. Maggie declined.

"Quite a frosty evening," he said, as he seated himself in the carriage. "Afraid we'll have a sharp, early winter. Going much further?"

"To Castleford."

"Indeed! We will not be there till 8.40, and I have some way to drive after." So saying he settled himself to sleep, and Maggie endeavoured to follow his example. However, she could but doze uneasily, waking every now and then with a start, to feel half frightened at the rocking of the carriage (it was an express train) and the weird effect of the dimly-seen hedges and half-luminous smoke, as they flew past; growing very weary and rather sad, as the length of the journey impressed her with the idea that she was indeed going far away, into great unknown solitudes, wherein were dangers innumerable.

At last she was at her journey's end.

As she stepped out of the warm and well-lit carriage into the darkness of a bleak country station, the platform being raised high above the natural level of the country, Maggie could not control the trembling dread that seized her, partly the effect of exhaustion. As far as she could see into the gloom all looked open, drear, and bare. How was she to get on to her destination? The question was soon solved. A porter ran up with a lantern, exclaiming, "Carriage here from Grantham for a lady and gentleman," and set to work to extricate her luggage.

"We are still to be fellow-travellers," said the man with the bag courteously. "I suppose you have got your belongings?"

"Yes, thank you."

"Then follow me down these steps; mind, it is rather dark at the bottom. Oh, here we are."

A smart brougham, the coachman in mourning, and a large, spirited horse, stood at the foot of the steps.

The driver touched his hat, and assisted the porter to put up Maggie's two boxes. "If there's any more we'll send over in the morning for it."

"That's all," said the porter.

Maggie was handed in most politely by her companion and they drove off rapidly, she feeling quite comforted not to be alone.

"Charming person, Miss Grantham," said the stranger, who was evidently a little curious as to his companion, "and a charming place."

"I have never seen either. I am going to be Miss Grantham's secretary or amanuensis, and was engaged by a lady in London."

"Oh, ah!" as though half amused. "Well, I dare say she will be inundated with letters for some time. You will be pleased with the country. There is much to interest you in Grantham itself; very old place—lots of relics and family pictures—rather dull in the winter; but I fancy Miss Grantham will keep the ball going. Five minutes to nine, I protest!—we were behind time a little. I shall not be sorry to have dinner, or something; and you, why you must be fainting! It is nearly five miles from the station to the house, but we will do it in twenty minutes more."

Maggie was conscious of a short cessation of the rapid motion, of a shout of "Gate!" and passing an open cottage door, from out of which came the ruddy glow as of a bright fire, and then rolling on over an exceptionally smooth road, while the rushing groaning sound of the wind, which had risen with nightfall, suggested the idea of thick trees, after what seemed an immense time since they passed the lodge, Maggie's companion exclaimed, "There—there's the house!"

She looked, and there on the left, apparently over them, stood a large vague pile, four or five windows of which were brightly illuminated. It passed out of sight, and the carriage turned to the left and went up a short steep ascent. The next moment they stopped opposite a wide open door, which showed a large, brilliantly-lighted hall. Two men-servants in black, with all the trappings of liveried woe, came out as they drew up; and one magnificent personage, the depth of whose mourning was only enlivened by a prominent shirt frill, stood in dignified readiness in the doorway. To Maggie's unsophisticated eyes he looked duke at least. She ascended the steps, longing in her heart to take fast hold of her new acquaintance's arm.

"Call Mrs. Hands," said the ducal functionary. "Miss Grantham will see you at once, sir," he added respectfully to Maggie's companion.

"And this young lady?" said the gentleman kindly, seeing our little heroine look pale and miserable.

"Mrs. Hands will be here, sir, immediately to attend to Miss Grey," and bowing, he motioned the new arrival forward. "Good evening," then, said he to Maggie, and as he spoke a tall, stout, solid, elderly woman in black, with grey ribbons in her cap and a white apron—a woman of authoritative air, and somewhat old-fashioned servant-like appearance—came into the hall.

"Carry up the luggage at once," said she to one of the gentlemen of the shoulder-knot. "Come with me, ma'am, you must be cold and tired."

The hall was large, nearly square, and very lofty. It was lit by long narrow windows right and left of, and also above, the entrance, warmly draped with rich crimson stuff. Opposite the door two broad flights of steps, with balustrades of the same dark polished wood with which the hall was panelled, formed an arch over another door leading into the interior of the house. The ceiling was richly carved and gilt in the Louis Quatorze style, and the floor tesselated with black, white, and grey marble; pathways of crimson carpets led across it in various directions, groups of hot-house ferns filled the angles; a large carved-oak table, loaded with plaids, and fur rugs, and riding-whips, stood in the centre; numerous portraits hung upon the walls.

Maggie took all this in at a glance. The tremendous grandeur, the jump she seemed to have made into another world, all seemed to oppress her, as she followed her conductress up the stair and along a passage and down a few steps past a projecting window; and then they stopped at a door and entered a charming room of moderate size, with a mossy green carpet, pink and white chintz curtains, mirrors, a sofa, easy-chairs, ottoman, writing table, a cottage piano, a bright fire in a pretty tiled fireplace, and a tempting tea-table set forth beside it; the lamp lit —everything that could be desired, even some flowers. Maggie could not help uttering an exclamation of delight.

"This used to be Miss Colby's room," said Mrs. Hands; "and," throwing open a door beside the fire-place, "there is your bedroom"— another smaller but equally dainty apartment, full of every comfort and elegance.

"I will make the tea while you take off your things," said the grave Mrs. Hands, and retired.

"Surely," thought Maggie, with much gratitude, "my lines have fallen in a pleasant place. I trust this is not too fair a beginning."

"You have had a long journey," said Mrs. Hands, as she poured out the tea, and pressed cold ham and hot cutlet on her charge.

"I have been nearly eight hours travelling."

"Yes, it is a weary journey from London. I seldom take it now. Would you not like some wine instead of tea?"

"Oh no! thank you. Nothing is so refreshing as a cup of tea."

"Miss Grantham desired me to say she was sorry she could not see you to-night, but hopes to make your acquaintance to-morrow."

"Very well," said Maggie, glad to secure a quiet night before encountering the formidable Miss Grantham.

"She's busy with the lawyer to-night. That was the lawyer as came down with you."

"Oh indeed!" After a little more talk—in which Mrs. Hands informed Maggie that she had been "our young lady's nurse," and now had the charge of her wardrobe and the French lady's maid, who was a regular handful—Mrs. Hands rang. A neatly-dressed, fresh, country-looking girl answered the bell. "Take away the things, Jane;" then, as she went out, added, "she's a grand-niece of mine, and is to answer your bell and attend these rooms. When do you wish to be called in the morning?"

"Oh! at seven—eight—whatever time every one else gets up."

"At eight, then. And look here," opening the door; "you see that door opposite there, next the big window? That's my room. And now can I do anything more for you?"

"No. I am very much obliged to you."

"Good night, ma'am; and I hope you will sleep well."

\* \* \* \* \* \*

Maggie did sleep well. There is something undoubtedly consoling in material comfort: a sense of security and elevation, when our surroundings are refined and pleasant to the eye, when food and drink are placed before us without effort on our own part, and we are free to believe that we can afford to leave our lower wants to the care and attention of lower creatures, while we develope our higher and nobler selves, independent of thought for what we shall eat or drink, or what we shall put on. Which, I hope, proves the necessity of an upper and an under crust to society, for ever and ever.

It seemed to Maggie that she had not long closed her eyes, when she woke again, and it was daylight. She felt wonderfully refreshed, and almost equal to the impending interview with Miss Grantham.

After a few minutes' dreamy thought she rose, anxious to view her new abode. The window of her bed-room looked into a paved yard, in which was an old-fashioned stone fountain, all mossed with age, and sheltered by a walnut-tree, the leaves of which were falling fast. It seemed to appertain to some of the offices, for a buxom kitchen or scullery maid, in a tucked-up dress and pattens, clattered across it while Maggie looked.

Her toilet completed, she proceeded to inspect her sitting-room. The window there looked over a wide undulating park, sloping away from the house till it sank between two wooded hills, and gave a distant view of some green uplands with patches of brown ploughed land, all crowned by a far away blue line of mountain.

This fair scene was but dimly visible through sheets of drifting rain, blown hither by a strong shifting wind. The aspect of things without sent Maggie with a keen sense of comfort to the glowing ruddy fire—a delightful combination of coal and wood.

"Am I not very late?" she asked, as the neat little maid brought in her breakfast, seeing that the pretty clock on the mantelpiece pointed to ten.

"You were asleep 'm when I first knocked, and Mrs. Hands said I was not to disturb you."

It was curious to eat her breakfast alone, Maggie thought, but not unpleasant for once. She was utterly ignorant of the habits and customs of the life into which she was suddenly plunged, and everything attracted her attention. The snowy white of the delicate table linen, a luxury in itself; the beautiful polish of the slender old-fashioned silver; the queer little square tea-pot, its tracery faint, its ivory handle yellow from age. The lovely china, with the exquisite colours of its butterflies and honeysuckle standing out on a clear, transparent, white ground. How delightful it all was! How suggestive of centuries of wealth, accumulated elegance, practised refinement. "What a different world from mine!" thought Maggie. "This is Lord Torchester's world. How could he ever think of me?" And though even in thought she would not name him, Lord Torchester was but the equivalent for another. "I wonder, if I get used to this, shall I be loth to leave it? Not if I am left alone much. Loneliness is so depressing. Yes; this is very, very delightful! but I would give it all for the dear old parlour behind the shop at Altringham. *That* was Paradise to me. How my sweetest mother would have been charmed with this china!" And Maggie mused on dreamily enjoying the unwonted freedom and luxury of an easy-chair all to herself. After her breakfast had been removed the respectable Mrs. Hands made her appearance.

"Miss Grantham hopes you have rested well, and wishes to know if you would like to go to church—the carriage will be at the door in twenty minutes."

"Oh! no thank you; I did not think of going; it is so wet and I have not my things unpacked."

Still no chance of seeing Miss Grantham. So Maggie read the Morning Prayers and Lessons, as she used to her mother on extra wet Sundays, and then she unpacked her rather scanty array of goods and settled them in the ample drawers and wardrobes, which, even after she had laid by her last ribbon, seemed an uninhabited desert.

"Now," she thought, with virtuous resolution, "I shall write to John and to Aunt Grey—both." So she set forth her writing materials and began. But she had scarce finished the first page when a knock at the door arrested her progress.

"Come in," said Maggie, laying down her pen, and only expecting Mrs. Hands or Jane.

The door opened, and Miss Grantham entered. Maggie felt it must be the fair châtelaine. Yet she entered gently, with a smooth gliding step, her long rich black silk and crape dress trailing behind, and with the sweetest smile, Maggie thought, she had ever seen, held out a hand, so fair and taper, and loaded with jewels, that Maggie felt half inclined to kiss it, as if the owner were a queen.

"I have to apologise, Miss Grey, for this tardy welcome," she said, in a rich, carefully modulated, but rather deep voice. "I have been a victim to my lawyer, who travelled down with you—a most respectable diligent person, but just a little tiresome—and even now I have only a few minutes to myself—but sit down." And Miss Grantham drew a chair at the opposite side of the fire to where Maggie sat. "I hope you are rested and comfortable, and that Hands has taken care of you?"

"She has, indeed," said Maggie, gazing, with sincerest admiration in her clear frank eyes, at her new mistress. "My room is delightful, and so is this one."

Miss Grantham smiled again very pleasantly; she was quite alive to the impression she had made upon her new secretary, who enjoyed a thorough good look at the splendid picture opposite to her.

A tall woman, whose outlines, though she was only just of age, had in them a rich full grace; a snowy throat; the faintest suspicion of a double chin; the jaw somewhat heavy; the lips full and crimson, parting to show spotless rows of pearly teeth. Large light blue eyes shone out steadily, fearlessly, from under a white brow and masses of golden fair hair, which were evidently too much for the skill even of a skilled lady's maid. The soft, creamy-white skin, the peachy bloom of the cheek, made up a splendid specimen of Saxon beauty; and as she leant back in her chair there was an indefinable, haughty, careless grace in every attitude and motion.

"I shall not be free until Tuesday morning, when we shall set to work. I suppose Miss Colby told you what I wanted?"

"Not very clearly—and I sincerely hope I shall be equal to my task."

"Oh! I am sure you will," said Miss Grantham, kindly. "Dear old Colby sent me a specimen of your writing—it is very nice; the rest I shall supply. You have been on the Continent, that is an advantage. Did you not like it?"

"Very, very much," said Maggie, with a sigh. "You have been there, of course?"

"A little; only a few months altogether. Poor grandpapa hated it, and I could not often get away. Pray, if not too impertinent a question, how old are you, Miss Grey."

"I was twenty in August last," replied Maggie, blushing under Miss Grantham's cool searching gaze.

"Indeed!"—another soft sweet smile. "I should not have thought you so much. Now, tell me—how old would you take me to be? Speak frankly."

"Oh! I cannot think," said our heroine, too deeply interested in her subject to be conventional. "You look as if you had ruled for many years. And yet your cheek is so fair and smooth, your mouth so soft, your expression so tender—altogether you must be quite young, perhaps not older than myself. Forgive me," added Maggie, checking herself, and colouring deeply, "I speak too freely."

"Not at all; you speak *en artiste*, and show no mean powers of observation. I came of age last June, so I am not much your senior. Come, I see we shall accomplish a great deal of work together. Intelligence and legible writing—what a treasure Miss Colby has found for me!"

Another knock at the door. Maggie looked at Miss Grantham, who did not seem to notice it.

"It is your room," said the heiress courteously, in reply to the look.

"Come in," cried Maggie.

Enter the ducal butler, who with profound respect observed, "Luncheon waits."

"I am coming," said Miss Grantham, without turning her head. "I am afraid"—addressing Maggie—"I shall not be able to see you again to-day or to-morrow; but you read—you like reading? I will send you some papers and magazines—and ring for whatever you want. If to-morrow is fine, Lady Dormer will take you out to drive. Adieu for the present." And Miss Grantham swept away, evidently well-pleased with her new acquisition, while Maggie remained standing where Miss Grantham had left her, penetrated with a sudden enthusiasm for this lovely, gracious, queen-like patroness, whose grandeur was yet so genial that, modest as was Maggie's estimate of herself, she felt no dread, no diffidence; rather all personal feelings were swallowed up in complete admiration; all the suppressed romance, of which our lonely little waif had enough and to spare, sprang into light, and fastened upon this delightful subject.

"She is like a princess for whom kings might do battle!" said Maggie to herself; "and so sweet and kind! How wonderfully fortunate I am! How grateful I ought to be to God for directing me here! I do hope I shall please her—but I must, for I shall understand her."

So Maggie finished her letter to John in a most rapturous tone, and then she thought of the contrast between that right trusty cousin and the high-born dame who had just left her. "I wonder," speculated Maggie, "if John would feel any awe of Miss Grantham! I daresay he would lay down the law to her as if she was like any one else—he has no imagination;" but she might have added—a right manful and independent spirit.

Miss Grantham, true to her promises, sent Maggie a pile of weekly papers and publications; and between reading, writing, and reverie, Sunday passed over very well.

Monday was again wet, and dragged a little heavily, though Maggie had her needlework, and tried to be busy.

After her early dinner, Mrs. Hands came in. "Lady Dormer's compliments; she would be happy to see you, if you would like to pay her a visit."

"Yes, I should," said Maggie, a little puzzled. "Please tell me who is Lady Dormer."

"Oh! she is our young lady's aunt, and always lives with her, by way of taking care of her; and a very nice, harmless lady she is—not like Miss Grantham, you know."

"No, no! no one is like her," cried Maggie, with a genuine enthusiasm that won the old nurse's heart; "she is so lovely and so kind. But am I dressed enough to go and see Lady Dormer?"

"Ay! you are as neat as a new pin; she will be quite pleased with you."

Maggie accordingly followed Mrs. Hands to the staircase, where she was committed to the guidance of a tall footman, who conducted her across the hall and down a passage, and then, throwing open a door, announced "Miss Grey," in what Maggie considered a terrific manner.

By the side of a large fire, in a luxurious easy-chair, a work-table and a large basket of bright coloured wools beside her, sat a decidedly elderly lady, very stout, with a broad, placid, and rather unmeaning face. She was dressed, like every one else, in deep mourning; and as the room was furnished with a somewhat dingy green, the eye was not a little relieved by a mass of crimson wool which lay in her lap, and on which she was operating with a huge wooden crochet needle.

"Put a chair here" were her first words, addressed to the footman. She made an effort to rise, but failed, as Maggie came forward with a slight courtesy. "Very glad to see you—pray sit down. Shocking weather—winter all at once. If it had been fine, I should have taken you out with me. My niece said it would have been very nice—she is quite worn out, poor dear! with that tiresome lawyer."

"It must be very tiresome," echoed Maggie, rather at a loss what to say. Lady Dormer's voice was pleasant for the first sentence or two, and then it grew wearisome from its unvarying tone.

"Do you like the country?" after a pause.

"Yes, very much; this must be a beautiful place in fine weather."

"Oh, very nice, indeed; so quiet. I sleep much better here than in London. But I sleep very badly at night; very badly, indeed."

"That is very trying," said Maggie, seeing she paused for a reply.

"Yes! isn't it. I am often glad to get a little sleep in the day-time. Do you like crochet, Miss Grey?"

"I do not know much about it; but I can do the stitch."

"It is very pretty and useful. I am doing a shawl for Hands—she feels the cold a good deal. I offered to do one for Miss Grantham; but she says it would make an old woman of her, and that I had better make it for Hands. It is a pity these patterns are so complicated; I can scarcely make this one out. My niece often helps me; but she is too busy to-day. Miss Grantham really seems to understand everything."

"If I could assist you," said Maggie, shyly, "I would be very pleased."

"I am sure you are very good," replied Lady Dormer, brightening. "You see where this shell comes—the pattern ought to stand out, and it won't."

"Let me see," said Maggie, taking the bright, warm mass from her ladyship's fingers, and gazing with intent eyes upon a magical receipt, where words and figures were jumbled in the most cabalistic fashion. An interval of intense application ensued, and then for more than a mortal hour did Maggie gently instruct the dullest of pupils in the mysteries of chain 6, miss 3, 9 chain, 1 plain, &c.

"I am sure I am greatly obliged to you," said Lady Dormer at last; "I shall go on all right now. If to-morrow is fine, and Miss Grantham does not want you, I shall take you out to drive after luncheon." And Maggie felt she was dismissed.

"What a wonderful household," she thought as she regained her own quarters without guidance. "I have seen three men-servants, two women-servants, and an aunt, and heard of an indefinite multitude of other retainers; and all seem to hang on the will of a girl not much older than myself. One need be born in the purple to sustain such a weight!"

Mindful that Miss Grantham had said she would be free on Tuesday, Maggie rose early, and had finished breakfast long before the expected announcement reached her—"Mademoiselle Grantham vous demande, mademoiselle;" for it was a little dark-eyed French girl, in a poetic cap, that brought the message.

Maggie replied in the same language, pleased to speak it again; and the *femme de chambre* was delighted.

Miss Grantham was in her dressing-room, a charming but old-fashioned apartment, adorned with rose-brocaded silk panels, white and rose curtains, couches, and footstools, while the chairs in green velvet were a pleasant contrast.

She was at breakfast, in a long *peignoir* of white cashmere embroidered with an elaborate pattern in black silk.

"I am an escaped bird this morning," said Miss Grantham, laughing, as Maggie entered, "though just the least bit of an invalid. I have a slight cold, and am indulging in a solitary breakfast. Have you breakfasted?"

"Some time ago."

"Well, sit down. I have one or two letters here you might answer for me; but in the meantime—Some more coffee, Cécile," interrupting herself—"I must tell you that the work in which I particularly want your assistance is a novel. I sketched it out and began it a long time ago, but met with so many interruptions that I have not got beyond the third chapter. Now I cannot go much into society or do anything for the next six months; so I thought if I could give a couple of hours daily to it, with your help in copying and carrying out my ideas, I might get it done by February or March, before I go up to town to be presented. It would be charming to hear every one wondering 'who the author of so-and-so can be.' By the way, I cannot think of a title, and yet I have the whole plot sketched out; perhaps you will be able to give me an idea—and if you only have as much genius for literature as Aunt Dormer says you have for crochet, you will indeed be a treasure-trove."

" Literature and crochet are widely different."

" *Allons, nous verrons*—Eh! Cécile. No, nothing more, thank you. Come, Miss Grey"—rising and leading the way through a door nearly opposite to that by which Maggie had entered—" this is my study."

It was a handsome room, three sides filled with book-shelves, the other occupied by two windows draped in rich red brown velvet, with busts between. The mantelpiece was enlivened by a clock and vases in old Dresden china. A leather-covered writing-table was loaded with appliances for writing; and jardinières, in every position, lightened the chamber with colour and perfume.

"Oh! what a quantity of books," cried Maggie, delighted.

"You love reading, then," said Miss Grantham. "Well, you may come here and read whenever you like; only, when I am in a very solitary mood, I shall tell you to run away to your own room with the book of your choice. Now here are these two epistles: one is from the Society of Female Artists—they want me to be an honorary member; the other from the Emancipated Missionaries for the Conversion of the Zooloo Tribes, who want me to subscribe. I shall be proud to be enrolled amongst the former, and send them a cheque to help their funds. Tell the others I am a thorough Churchwoman, and would prefer their leaving the unfortunate Africans to their *original* fetish. I shall finish dressing while you write. You will find everything you want on that table."

It was a tremendous task, for Maggie had no idea how to set about it. However, she read over the first letter carefully, and framed her reply upon it. Before she had quite concluded Miss Grantham returned.

"Let me see," she said, taking the paper from her hand. "You write for me, not for my signature—well, perhaps it is better. That will do. I see you have left a blank after the word 'cheque': fill in ' fifty pounds.' Now as to the other—oh, never mind, I will not answer it; it is not worth attending to. Now I must show you what I have done," opening a large portfolio and taking out numerous loose sheets. "Here is my novel. I will read you a little and then tell you the plot." Miss Grantham leaned back in her chair, reading rapidly and somewhat monotonously:

"It was a dull rainy morning, and the purlieus of St. Paul's were darker than ever, when the head waiter at the *Crown and Anchor*, in Paternoster Row, coming into the bar, which was lit with gas, said to the blooming young lady who presided over the bottles and preserves, ' This is a rum go.'

"'What?' asked the barmaid.

"'Why, the baby, to be sure. The old lady what came here last night with the baby went out this morning to buy a heasy pair of boots, and has never come back, and the child's screaming in No. 11, and no one knows what to do with it.'

"'Poor little soul!' cried the barmaid, the maternal instincts of whose feminine heart had defied years of chaff, of sordid routine, and even the indurating effect of doubtful money, to stifle. 'A ha'p'orth o' milk boiled down with a rusk will comfort it. P'raps the woman will turn up in an hour or two.'

"'Not she,' returned the head waiter; 'she has bolted.'" And so on for nearly an hour, detailing how the buxom barmaid took the deserted infant and formed a profound attachment to it, feeling convinced, from its lovely form and delicate garments, that it was the child of noble parents.

"There, I am really quite tired," said Miss Grantham, pausing suddenly. "Now, what do you think of that?"

"It is very interesting. I wonder how it could all come into your head," said Maggie, dimly conscious that she had heard something like it before, yet really surprised that so great a lady should begin her narrative at so low a stage of life.

"Well, you see, I want to describe a heroine whose native nobility will come out under the most adverse circumstances. She is really of very high race. Her father and mother have been privately married, and the father has been killed—oh, somewhere—and then the mother, who must be a bad, ambitious woman, wants to marry a Russian prince, and so wishes to suppress this baby, and gives it, with a large sum of money, to a cruel, avaricious old nurse, who determines to keep the money and get rid of the child. Of course all sorts of adventures can be introduced. She must go on the stage—I mean the baby—and fascinate her own cousin, besides quantities of other men—and, oh, I have such a charming hero!" and, quite animated with her subject, Miss Grantham turned over the pages to find the description of the hero.

"But," said Maggie, sincerely interested, "I wish you could make the father bad and the mother good. A bad mother is so horribly unnatural."

"Do you think so?" said Miss Grantham, pausing in her search. "Well, there are plenty of bad mothers in novels, and it is so easy to kill a man. He goes into all sorts of dangers, a soldier especially. Besides, a baby isn't such a drawback to a man as to a woman. You are quite right to give me your candid opinion, but I think I must keep my wicked mother. I cannot find the passage I want, but we shall come to it as we go on. Now, suppose you copy out what I have read. It is horribly written and full of mistakes, but you can make it right. You must call my attention to any alterations that suggest themselves. I want you to be perfectly candid."

"I will be, indeed. I only wish I was more experienced and learned to be of more use to you."

"You would only interfere with my originality if you were," said Miss Grantham. "Do you understand about the inverted commas, and paragraphs? Leave plenty of room, and only write on one side of the paper." So saying, she placed ruled paper, a forest of pens, and a huge inkstand, beside her secretary. "I shall go and see Aunt Dormer and hear if she has letters, and then I shall come back and answer my own."

Maggie set very diligently to work, and had produced three fair legible sheets, with all proper paragraphs, marks, and signs, before her employer returned. Her training with poor Uncle Grey stood her in good stead, though she did not like to confess to herself that it was less tiresome to copy his papers than the conversations of Miss Grantham's characters. True, there was much of Uncle Grey's lucubrations which she could not understand, but then there were bits she did, and those interested her intensely.

"What a quantity you have done! how nice and clear!" cried Miss Grantham, peeping over her shoulder. "You must have done this sort of thing before."

"I used to copy papers for my uncle."

"Was he a literary man?"

"No, he was scientific, rather; he is a chemist."

"Indeed! I should like to understand chemistry above all things. In short, I should like to know everything; but one hasn't time. Have you made any alterations?"

"Oh, no. I would not do so unless I pointed them out to you. I have left a blank for 'Paternoster Row': I fancy somehow there are no hotels there, only booksellers."

"Well, perhaps not; we can easily find another." Then Miss Grantham sat down to her own special writing-table—a marvel of convenience and taste—and wrote for a few minutes, then talked for a while, and wrote again, and then exclaimed, "It is almost luncheon-time. We have done quite a hard morning's work, and I feel as if I had quite earned my luncheon; while you must be almost faint with starvation. You breakfasted an hour before me. Come down with me; I shall not leave you in solitary confinement any longer. Lady Dormer will be charmed to see you at luncheon."

I fancy Maggie would have enjoyed her dinner more alone. Nevertheless it was an experience that amused her.

Miss Grantham did not use the great dining-room when there was no company at the Hall. Still the smaller one seemed magnificent to Maggie. The display of the table—the plate, the fruit, the flowers—

all appeared too grand for common use. It was appalling, too, to be waited on by a powdered epauletted gentleman, to have the ducal butler, who did not even seem a duke in disguise but a duke evident and unmistakable, inquiring confidentially if she preferred sherry or hock.

It all seemed natural and common enough to Miss Grantham. She was a little fastidious, and spoke rather sharply about a salmi of partridges which did not please her.

"Wheeler" (to the butler), "this is not at all right. Pray tell Pécheron that he must not grow careless because we are alone. If he does not care to please me, why he had better leave."

"Yes 'm," said the noble functionary, with profound attention.

"Take it away. You cannot eat that, Miss Grey."

"It is not so bad," remarked Lady Dormer, contentedly.

"Bad! Why is it not good?" said the heiress.

And then there was silence, and Lady Dormer observed that "Poor dear Lord Brockhurst was ordered away to Algiers."

"Indeed," cried Miss Grantham. "Is Lady Brockhurst going with him?"

"I don't know. Miss Ashton mentions it."

"I fancy she will not. It would be such banishment for her."

"What do the Longmores say about coming here?" asked Lady Dormer—and so on about people and things quite unknown to Maggie. Just before they rose from table Miss Grantham said to her aunt, "Oh! I am going to take Miss Grey out with me, she can go with you another day, if you don't mind."

"Very well," said Lady Dormer, placidly.

"I shall be ready in about half an hour, and show you something of the country. I drive at a better pace than Aunt Dormer. You would like to come?"

"Yes, very much; but ought I not to stay in and write?"

"Oh! you need not be so very indefatigable! we shall grow stupid if we have no recreation."

When Maggie descended with her bonnet on she found a beautiful pony carriage with a pair of perfect little white ponies, sleek and rampant with spirits, standing at the door. A tiny groom, in spotless buckskins, exquisitely fitting top-boots and livery, standing at their heads. While Mr. Wheeler looked on critically and approvingly from the doorstep.

Miss Grantham issued from the morning-room a moment after looking superb in a crape and bugle bonnet. The butler and two footmen assisted each other in the tremendous task of handing the ladies in and arranging a tiger-skin rug, and then Miss Grantham took the reins, shoulder-knot No. 1 called out "all right" to the tiny groom, who stepped aside, and the white ponies darted away at a speed that half frightened Maggie.

"They are very fresh this morning," said Miss Grantham, " but you need not be alarmed, I am a capital whip."

It was a fine calm autumnal day after the previous storm and rain, and deeply Maggie enjoyed the beautiful woodland scenery through which their road lay—wide rolling uplands, wooded dells, open park-like spaces dotted with deer, deep lanes, their broken rocky banks clothed with a wealth of many-tinted leaves. The smell of the pine trees, the rush of rivulets swelled by the late rains, the delicious, cool, clear air. What a paradise it all seemed to poor Maggie. What a delightful change it created in the current of her thoughts.

Miss Grantham seemed to enjoy her enjoyment. "Yes, it is a lovely country. I am very fond of it, but it is fearfully dull; and now poor Lord Brockhurst is obliged to go away the county will be a desert, Southam shut up and Grantham shut up, for it would not be decent to fill the house for three or four months. I suppose Lime-shire will not have had so dull a winter for many years. I am very vexed about the Brockhursts. Lady Brockhurst is my greatest ally— the most fascinating woman—knows everything and everyone—has been everywhere. I always was flattered by her notice—she is older a good deal than I am, and is very exclusive—abhors commonplace; but she always liked *me*."

Maggie speculated on who and what this lady could possibly be, whose notice could flatter so great a personage as her companion.

Miss Grantham talked on and enlightened her secretary as to her views on various subjects—her intended doings in London, and pos-sible travels in foreign countries. She seemed to Maggie as if she was somewhat intoxicated with a sense of freedom and power, though too well bred to show it in any offensive manner, but that she could scarce make up her mind which path of pleasure to choose among the many that offered.

On approaching the Hall, which they did not, until dusk, the diligent secretary said, "I suppose I can go into your study and write this evening. It is really a pity to waste too much time."

"You will overtake me too soon," said Miss Grantham, smiling. "But you can do so, certainly, if you like."

"The rector is with her ladyship," said the butler, as they alighted.

So Miss Grantham, with a pleasant nod of dismissal, went towards the drawing-room, and Maggie mounted to her own quarters.

The next morning brought her a letter from Cousin John, who wrote in a rather surly tone. He warned her that all was not gold that glittered, that the finery which she described would only make her more conceited than ever, and when she was sent adrift, as she would be one day, she would be glad to fall back on plain honest people who knew their own minds.

"Poor dear John," thought Maggie, who was always fonder of

him at a distance, "how'cross he was when he wrote. But in one thing he is right, my tenure of office is very uncertain, and always will be, I am afraid, so I must make the most of the present."

## CHAPTER XXI.

THE stream of life settles very quickly into new channels. In a week Maggie had become accustomed to the routine of Grantham, though she found steady application under Miss Grantham's auspices quite impossible. Some new and urgent occupation for her pen was found nearly every day: a catalogue on an improved plan was designed for the library; a descriptive list of the family portraits, with anecdotes and sketches of the periods to which they belonged was eagerly begun, and Maggie was excessively sorry to be withdrawn from it, to arrange and decipher the rough drafts of a poem in blank verse which Miss Grantham had commenced on 'Simon de Montfort.'

What a lavish waste of time it all seemed to our little Maggie, trained in such a different school; however, she told herself she had no right to complain. She found time for some steady reading, and an unlimited supply of standard authors in the library. Finally, she steadily grew in favour with Miss Grantham, who made her the constant companion of her drives and walks.

Sometimes her kind but whimsical mistress was amused to hear the reminiscences of her simple life, and was evidently charmed and touched by Maggie's description of her mother and her home. She seemed flattered by Maggie's timid offer to show her her greatest treasure—her mother's picture. "It is a sweet face," said Miss Grantham, after looking at it earnestly, "and looks like a gentlewoman. You are like her a good deal. What was her name?"

"Everard," said Maggie, more than ever drawn to her fascinating patroness.

"A good name," remarked Miss Grantham, thoughtfully. "Do you know anything of your mother's people?"

"Nothing whatever. I do not think she did."

"My dear Miss Grey! I shall write a story about you some day. I am sure you are, or will be, the centre of a romance."

So October fled away; and Miss Grantham, in spite of her varied employments, began to be intolerably bored.

Maggie was quite grieved to see a restless dissatisfied expression saddening her countenance, but was ignorant how to dispel it. Indeed, from time to time, she caught glimpses of a vacuum in her admired friend's life, or heart, or fancy, which neither rank, riches, conscious beauty, or intellectual occupation seemed to fill.

One day Miss Grantham had gone out, after luncheon, with Lady Dormer, and Maggie had taken advantage of their absence to play over some of her old lessons with poor M. Duval. She was so employed when Miss Grantham, returning sooner than she expected, entered unperceived, and listened for a few minutes without speaking. "You really have a very nice touch, Miss Grey," she said, to Maggie's confusion. "You ought to practise every day. Do you think you could play my accompaniments? I cannot bear to sing and play both."

"I am afraid I could not do well enough—but I should be so delighted if I could!"

"We will try at once," cried Miss Grantham, throwing aside her bonnet. "Come to my study, my music is there; you may find something you know."

After turning over the voluminous store, Maggie found a pretty little *chansonette*, over which she had toiled wearily with Mrs. Berry, striving with indifferent success to make that lady sing in tune.

"I think I might manage this."

"Begin, then; though I have not sung it for months."

Miss Grantham's voice was of rare quality, clear and rich. It had been most carefully cultivated; while nature had bestowed upon her a real genius for music. All her other pursuits were mere whims. Music—dramatic music—was her true vocation. Maggie was soon too much entranced to think of her own possible failure, and acquitted herself very creditably.

"How deliciously you sing! How is it I have not heard you before?" she cried, turning to Miss Grantham, her eyes moist with genuine delight. "It is like a peep into another life to hear you! I wonder you are not singing all day.",

"I have been out of humour with many things lately, music among them; and then, imagine singing to Lady Dormer! Now that I find you are musical, it will be quite different. You really can be of the greatest use to me as an accompanyist; but you must practise and get up all my songs. Let me see what else you can play." And so the whole afternoon went pleasantly over; and after dinner Miss Grey was requested to join Miss Grantham and Lady Dormer in the green drawing-room, to play for the latter's admiration; and her ladyship did admire to the best of her ability, and then fall asleep.

"You must look over all my music, and get up the songs I have put down here," said Miss Grantham, "while I am away; for I was going to tell you to-day, only the music put it out of my head, that Aunt Dormer and I are going over to Oatlands, the Longmores' place, for a week or ten days, and I shall probably go on to London for a day or two. I have not been there since grandpapa died, and I want various changes before we go up for the season, if I go; so you will have plenty of time to practise and write and read. I hope you will not feel very lonely. You must drive every day if you like, and work my ponies a little."

"And when do you go?" asked Maggie, somewhat dismayed at the idea of being left all alone in that huge house.

"The day after to-morrow. You are to be sure and ask for everything you want; and all my music and books are heartily at your service. You will have Nurse, too, to take care of you, so pray do not look melancholy."

"Oh! no. I shall miss you dreadfully—you have been so wonderfully good to me—but of course I can never hope to see so much of you again, when the first days of your mourning are over."

Miss Grantham smiled graciously. "I am not sure I would not rather have you with me, provided we had a few additions, than go to the Longmores. They are cousins of mine, some of the immense family tribe; old Mrs. Longmore was grandpapa's sister. They are very good-natured, commonplace people. They think me—oh! I don't know what they think of me; they are such old Tories, and I am, you know, extremely Liberal; but for all that, they are most palpably anxious to marry me to the son and heir, Grantham Longmore. Such a well-bred, unobjectionable muff! Imagine *me* marrying the quiet respectable representative of a quiet respectable country family!"

"If you do not like him, that is the best reason against such a marriage," said Maggie, gravely; deeply interested, for it was the first approach to the usually attractive topic of matrimony which Miss Grantham had made. "But you have everything in the world already, what more could any one give you—except the devotion of a character worthy of you?"

"Yes! I should like rank," said the heiress thoughtfully. "I don't mean to marry a man of rank, but to have it myself. It is such a shame that the barony of Grantham did not descend in the female line. I should then be the twenty-first possessor of the title! but I am determined to get it. As to a possible husband, I do not care if he be rich or poor, titled or untitled, but he *must* be well born, well bred, well educated; with pluck, ability, and force of character; high-minded enough not to care for my possessions or my position; and with warm blood enough in his veins to love me passionately for my own sake. I don't care for his being handsome, but he must be tall and *distingué*, and a good deal older than myself."

"Ah!" said Maggie; "where will you find all that?"

"It can be found," said Miss Grantham, with a far-away look in her large blue eyes, and a slight tender smile on her lips.

"She thinks she has found her hero," said Maggie to herself. "Perhaps such chivalrous compounds are to be more easily found among her class than mine. God grant her happiness, at all events." But she said nothing, only touched a few chords absently.

After a variety of directions respecting the sixth chapter of the novel, for which Miss Grantham only left notes to be amplified by her secretary, the heiress, with her aunt, her French maid, and the illustrious Wheeler to escort them as far as Castleford, departed.

Maggie did not feel quite so desolate as she anticipated. In her own bright little sitting-room, she did not realise the immensity and emptiness of the house, and she had plenty to do. Most earnestly she practised all the songs indicated by her kind, genial employer, and worked, not less willingly, yet certainly less *con amore*, at her literary labours.

Each morning she received a polite message from the butler to know if she would drive that afternoon, and as regularly she sent a polite reply, stating she would not. To have that exquisite little carriage with its spicy ponies and saucy groom paraded on her account would have been about as severe an infliction as she could well have been condemned to!

Busy, however—and pleasantly busy as she kept—she could not through all these solitary hours help sometimes remembering the previous occasion on which she had been left alone by Mrs. Berry! She certainly enjoyed *that* interval considerably more—but then it was all a piece of folly which she must forget—a weakness of which she ought to be and was ashamed. Surely such an unsubstantial vision would not haunt her for ever!

After mature reflection, she asked the respectable Mrs. Hands to walk with her sometimes, as she did not like to go far alone; and that worthy female was much pleased. During their peregrinations the good nurse told many family matters to " my young lady's secretary," matters, not secrets—for a word derogatory to that sacred house would never cross her lips. She also showed Maggie the old lord's part of the house—with the old family pictures which had been saved when the castle which used to stand on the site of the present house, was burned. Then Miss Grantham wrote twice—first from Oatlands, giving an amusing and rather sarcastic description of the party there assembled; and next from London, evidently written under depression of spirits.

Altogether, nearly six weeks had gone by, and still the mistress of the mansion had not returned.

At last, on a Monday afternoon, Mrs. Hands came into Maggie's room as she was rejoicing in having conquered ' *Robert le Diable*.' (I mean the music of that work.)

" I'm glad to tell you, Miss Grey, Mrs. Deane, the housekeeper, has just had a telegram. Miss Grantham and my lady will be back tomorrow—and they are bringing company—for we are to have the east bedroom and the blue room ready—they will come by the 2.0 express."

"Then you have no idea who Miss Grantham is bringing with her?"

" I suppose it's Miss Longmore and her brother; she could not very well have regular company."

Maggie felt quite exhilarated at the prospect of having Miss Grantham at home once more. She was proud to think how well she had prepared her tasks.

A long, lonely, but agreeable ramble in the park helped the day well over, and about half-past eight the noise of the arrival penetrated even to Maggie's sanctum. Had Miss Grantham and her aunt been unaccompanied by any guests, Maggie would have ventured down to greet them, but as they were not alone she did not like to intrude.

She half hoped Miss Grantham would look in for a moment or send for her, but no message came.

"Miss Grantham has arrived, then?" she said to her little attendant when she brought in her supper.

"Yes 'm—they are at dinner now. Miss Grantham and Lady Dormer have brought two gentlemen with them; but I don't know their names."

After waiting up considerably past her usual hour, Maggie went to bed just a shade disappointed.

Next morning she had just finished breakfast, when Miss Grantham came in dressed and evidently on her way downstairs. She looked handsomer than ever—there was the radiance as of a great joy in her face.

" We were so late last night I thought there would be no use in looking for you when I came up," she said, kissing Maggie lightly on the brow. "But I am very glad to see you again, and very glad to come back. Though I shall be rather engaged for a few days. I must see what you have been doing, however ; so let me find you in the study after breakfast. You must come down to luncheon to-day—I want to know what you think of my guests. Do you know, I think Grantham must agree with you. You look so much better than when you came down."

" And London must agree with you," said Maggie, gazing at her with sincerest admiration. " You are looking several shades more bright and beautiful than when you left ! "

"Do you really think so," said Miss Grantham earnestly ; and looking deliberately into the chimney-glass. " But there is the bell, good-bye for the present."

About an hour after Maggie settled herself to re-arrange and touch up the sheets she had prepared during her fair patroness's absence. They looked very nice and clear, she thought, and then she wished Miss Grantham would come, but she didn't; and, tired of waiting unemployed, Maggie rose to take down a book. Some old volumes of Blackwood into which she was fond of dipping, occupied a corner of the bookshelf near one of the windows, and she paused as she did so to look out on the scene below.

Miss Grantham's apartments and her own occupied the second floor of one wing, which stood on a sort of terrace or sudden acclivity ; and the study windows looked down on a mass of trees, which clothed its side, and then away over a magnificent prospect of undulating park and distant blue hills. She had never enjoyed the view so much before. 'Tis true the leaves were gone, but the innumerable branchlets sparkled with the lightest frost—and the bright cold blue of the sky seemed an atmosphere wherein healthy energy and cheerful self-help must flourish. She stood awhile, drinking in all this beauty in an unusually pleasant frame of mind, when she was disturbed by the opening of the door at the further end of the room, while Miss Grantham's voice said, "We shall find her here." That lady entered, saying, "I have brought a stern and incorruptible critic to inspect our work, Miss Grey." A tall, thin, dark man followed her leisurely—could Maggie believe her eyes!—Yes! it was Mr. Trafford!

Mr. Trafford, a little less embrowned and healthy-looking than when Maggie met him in the Park; but as grave, almost stern, as he always looked when neither speaking nor smiling.

Maggie stood quite still—too astonished to think—but Trafford came forward at once with complete composure, and taking the hand she mechanically held out, said, "Very glad to see you, Miss Grey! Had no idea I should find you at Grantham!"

"How!—What!—is it possible you know Geoffrey, Mr. Trafford? Where on earth did you meet each other! Why did you not tell me you knew him, Miss Grey?" cried the heiress infinitely surprised.

"I never thought of it," returned Maggie in all sincerity. "I never imagined you knew Mr. Trafford."

"I had the pleasure of meeting Miss Grey at the house of the renowned Mrs. Berry—where Torchester introduced me!"

"And did you know Torchester too?" asked Miss Grantham, still astonished.

"Oh, yes," replied Maggie, growing more collected,—"that is, I used to see them both at Mrs. Berry's."

"And you so often talked of that Mrs. Berry! It is curious you should never have mentioned Mr. Trafford or Lord Torchester."

"Shows the small impression either made upon you," said Trafford, laughing. "To think of you two ladies having been shut up here for —how long? six weeks—together, and having, no doubt, discussed all the male creatures of your acquaintance, without once remembering that Torchester or myself existed! It is really a lesson in humility!"

"Of which you are much in need," returned Miss Grantham. "Well! I expect Torchester, and, I think, the Countess, next week—so you can renew your acquaintance, Miss Grey." Looking sharply, though good-humouredly at her, and Maggie was infinitely annoyed to feel herself blush. "You know," continued Miss Grantham, "Torchester and I are cousins, second or first, once removed—which is it, Geoff?"

"Cannot tell! I only know that you are my first cousin one

degree nearer," said Trafford smiling ; and Maggie was foolish enough to fancy he was watching her, as she sat opposite to Miss Grantham and himself.

"Nonsense! You are no relation of mine, you know ; only I am good enough to consider you "——

"A right trusty and entirely beloved cousin," put in Trafford coolly.

"You may confer what titles you like on yourself. Pray remember they are not ratified," replied Miss Grantham gaily.

"A cousin is a very charming relation, is it not so, Miss Grey?" said Trafford mischievously, as Maggie thought, bringing the quick blushes to her cheek, which caught Miss Grantham's attention, as he intended them to do.

"Is Miss Grey especially aware of its charm?" she asked.

"I suppose it is no treachery to say that I saw you one morning in the Park just before I went to St. Petersburg, holding close converse with a certain Cousin John, who was rather a hero in your eyes."

"Not at all," said Maggie, stoutly, and nettled by what she considered his somewhat heartless chaff. "Cousin John is my best and truest friend."

"Well caught," cried Miss Grantham. "You see," to Maggie, "how misplaced your confidence has been. You must not let this untrustworthy kinsman of mine into any more of your secrets."

"And now tell me," said Trafford, looking round, "what are the plots which you hatch in this very enviable retreat. You have made wonderful improvements, I must say, in the old schoolroom."

"I have taken it into my head to write," said Miss Grantham with a slight hesitation that struck Maggie as a wonderful admission of Trafford's influence.

"To write," repeated that gentleman. "Not letters, for I am told it is almost impossible to get a reply from you."

"A decided calumny. No! I have sketched out the plot of a story, and with Miss Grey's help I am writing it *in extenso.* You must look at it, Geoff."

"Certainly; but I am no fit judge. I seldom read novels. Sometimes I am caught by a delightful fragment in a magazine, and blaze up into the fiercest interest, bestow maledictions on the delay which the intervening month creates, but am burnt out by the time it expires, and so lose the thread. What's your style, foreign or domestic?"

"Oh, domestic ; I know very little beyond England."

"And not much of that, eh, Marguerite des Marguerites?"

"I am not quite so ignorant and uncultivated as you fancy."

"*Belle cousine!* you misinterpret me ; and what about your heroine, dark or fair?"

"Oh, fair!" cried Maggie, "and such a charming creature."

"I am glad she is fair," said Trafford, gravely. "I have come to the conclusion that fair women have much more *diablerie* than dark ones, and a woman without *diablerie*, what my Persian friends call *nemik*, or salt, is not *worth* her salt."

The cloud that had for a moment rested on Miss Grantham's brow was gone, and she was again radiant. "Shall I read you a chapter or two, Geoff?" she said.

"No, thank you," decidedly. "I should be incapable of that strict and impartial criticism which I intend to bestow upon your lucubrations were I to submit to such a corrupting influence. No, let me have the composition in the stern solitude of my own room; there, with the help óf a mild cheroot "——

"Certainly not," cried Miss Grantham. "What, smoke over the pages Miss Grey has written so beautifully!"

"Very well, if you will take the consequences of depriving me of the soothing weed."

"What will you do then?" asked the hostess. "There are guns and preserves; both sadly neglected, I fear."

"Well, I'll have a try," said Trafford, rising. "Fortunately I have brought my own gun—a neglected breech-loader is much more formidable than neglected preserves." And Trafford left the room, followed by Miss Grantham.

"We lunch at two, Geoff," said the beautiful *châtelaine*, as she stood in the hall to see him put on his shot-belt; "you must try and be back in time."

"*Sans faute*," said Trafford, buttoning his shooting-jacket. "And after? Do you never ride, now? Might we not have a canter somewhere?"

"It is nearly two months since I was on horseback; but I will see what is available. Wheeler, tell Andrews I want him. It is so dull to ride alone. With you for a cavalier it is quite different. By-the-by, Geoff, it is very odd you never noticed Miss Grey's name—and I have talked so much of her."

"Yes, as the most admirable secretary in the world; but I am not sure you mentioned her name, or if you did, I did not notice it, or supposed there was more than one Miss Grey in the world."

"I suppose you did, for I have *often* mentioned her name."

"Very likely," with much indifference, as he examined his gun, "so good-bye till luncheon." And Trafford raised his hat to his cousin and descended the steps.

Miss Grantham looked after him, and stood in deep thought by the large table in the hall, till roused by the approach of the head groom, with whom she held counsel.

"It is the most curious *contretemps*, your meeting Geoff Trafford," said Miss Grantham, again seating herself before the fire in her study, "and having known him and Torchester; do tell me all about it."

"There is very little to tell. Some French friends of Mrs. Berry's brought Lord Torchester to one of her receptions (she received every Wednesday), and then he came very often; and when Mr. Trafford came to Paris, Lord Torchester brought him."

"And used *he* to go often?" asked Miss Grantham curiously.

"Yes, rather often, not so often as his cousin."

"What could have induced Geoffrey to go often to such a person as you describe this Mrs. Berry to be? You know he is a little eccentric, but in his way exceedingly fastidious. Was she handsome, this madame—what is her name now?"

"De Bragance. She was rather good-looking. But oh, Mr. Trafford would not look at her," cried Maggie, unguardedly, and immediately longed to retract her words, for Miss Grantham looked up steadily at her, and said sharply,

"Whom did he look at? What in the world took him there?"

"I really scarcely know; but, you see, the men Mrs. Berry knew were, I imagine, gamblers. And I always thought Mr. Trafford came to take care of Lord Torchester and keep him out of mischief," returned poor Maggie, instinctively fencing off these agonising queries, yet striving hard to tell the truth.

"Ah!" said Miss Grantham, "that is very likely, and accounts for Lady Torchester sounding Geoff's praises so much when he returned from Paris." Then she remained silent for a while, her great blue eyes gazing into the fire.

"And what do you think of Mr. Trafford?" she asked, abruptly. "Do you think him handsome?"

"No, not handsome; nice-looking."

"My dear Miss Grey, what a description of Geoff Trafford! Nice! Why, he looks like Brian de Bois-Guilbert, or Ernest Maltravers. Well, but he is agreeable—clever."

"Oh, yes, very; but I saw more of Lord Torchester."

"Torchester! Oh, he is a great, shy, stupid booby."

"There is more in him than you think," cried Maggie, thankful to lead Miss Grantham away from the topic that so evidently interested her. "And he was so good to me, that I shall always remember him with pleasure. You know," she went on, rapidly, "my position with Mrs. Berry was very undefined, and she was so different from you; kind in her way, but considered me as a sort of servant, and sometimes treated me like one. When she saw Lord Torchester's kindness and consideration for me—why, I rose considerably in her estimation."

"I suppose Torchester has the instincts of a gentleman," said Miss Grantham; "and perhaps more *savoir-faire* than we give him credit for," laughing gaily. "You may as well make a clean breast of it, for I shall find out everything from that traitor Geoff. It was too bad, his betrayal of your *tendresse* for your cousin John."

"I have no *tendresse* for him," said Maggie, carelessly. "He is a good friend—that is all."

"It is quite amusing. I cannot help picturing Geoff Trafford at Mrs. Berry's. What used he to do there?"

"Oh—he talked—and he listened to the music—and he played cards—like every one else."

"What a dreadful place for you, poor child, amongst a set of gamblers! Really, with your experience, you ought to supply some thrilling chapters to my book. But, come, I am going to ride, after luncheon, with Mr. Trafford, and I want to try on my habit and hat. I had a new mourning turn-out from town, but I have never put them on."

A delightful hour ensued. The hat was all that could be desired; but the habit required what Cécile termed *une nuance* of alteration, and she devoted herself to it at once.

"Lady Torchester and papa were first cousins," said Miss Grantham, strolling back with the secretary to her apartments. "My name, you know, was Wallscourt. Mamma was poor Lord Grantham's only child. I imagine he was not pleased at her marrying papa, who was only a captain in the Guards; but so handsome and charming. I was very fond of papa; but I do not remember my mother. While papa lived I used to be a great deal with Lady Torchester at Mount Trafford, and very doleful it was, except when Geoffrey was there. Tor and I used to long for him to come. You know Geoff is the son of the late earl's only brother; so he is not really any relation of mine."

"Yes," said Maggie. "And when your father died?"

"Oh, then grandpapa would hardly let me out of his sight; in short, I was rather sacrificed to his whims. And here, too, Geoffrey and Torchester were quite at home. So they are like brothers to me; all the pleasure I have ever known is connected with them. When grandpapa died, I was obliged to take his name. He directed it in his will. So I am Margaret Grantham Wallscourt Grantham. Of course I drop the first Grantham; it sounds ridiculous, like Clara Vere de Vere. But I must not neglect poor Mr. Bolton. He came down with us yesterday. He is the family lawyer—quite an institution. Not the man you travelled with; a different class of person altogether. He was ill with the gout then, and could not come. So, adieu till luncheon time."

And Maggie was left alone with her thoughts, which began to be a little more distinct after the shock and surprise she had received.

To be actually under the same roof with Trafford! To see him, and hear his voice every day, or nearly every day. Oh! be it folly—or madness—or want of dignity—or what it might, it was a blest gleam of joy that seemed to lift up the curtains of her soul.

And then, with the distance between them more visible and clearly defined than ever, she would surely learn to regard him as a kind, pleasant friend. But she must be very careful never to let him, or any one else, suspect that she gave him a thought—that she was such an unguarded, immodest girl—so she called herself—as to care so very, very much for one who was simply kind to her. For all these dreams and fancies respecting his looks and tones, which had nearly overturned her reason in Paris with a mingled terror and delight that she could never, never forget—they were but dreams; he thought only of her as an honest little bread-winner, whom he would like to help.

"And I, why should I not be true myself, and accept him as a kind patron, respecting him too much to suppose for an instant he would think of me in any way that he would be ashamed to avow?"

Maggie felt quite strengthened by these profound reflections; and so, feeling quite sure of her own prudence and common sense, she might surely permit herself to be happy. Miss Grantham was so kind; and Grantham was such a delightful place. It was altogether such a charming episode in her life, that she was naturally inclined to enjoy it to the full.

She therefore brushed her hair, and arranged her simple black silk dress—her best, alas!—and she felt obliged to wear it every day, in compliment to the mourning of the household; and otherwise prepared herself for the delightful, though awful, ordeal of luncheon.

# TEMPLE BAR.

MARCH 1873.

## The New Magdalen.

### By WILKIE COLLINS.

### CHAPTER XX.

#### THE POLICEMAN IN PLAIN CLOTHES.

JULIAN looked round the room, and stopped at the door which he had just opened.

His eyes rested—first on Mercy, next on Grace.

The disturbed faces of both the women told him but too plainly that the disaster which he had dreaded had actually happened. They had met without any third person to interfere between them. To what extremities the hostile interview might have led, it was impossible for him to guess. In his aunt's presence, he could only wait his opportunity of speaking to Mercy, and be ready to interpose if anything was ignorantly done which might give just cause of offence to Grace.

Lady Janet's course of action, on entering the dining-room, was in perfect harmony with Lady Janet's character.

Instantly discovering the intruder, she looked sharply at Mercy. "What did I tell you?" she asked. "Are you frightened? No! not in the least frightened! Wonderful!" She turned to the servant. "Wait in the library; I may want you again." She looked at Julian. "Leave it all to me; I can manage it." She made a sign to Horace: "Stay where you are, and hold your tongue." Having now said all that was necessary to every one else, she advanced to the part of the room in which Grace was standing, with lowering brows and firmly-shut lips, defiant of everybody.

"I have no desire to offend you, or to act harshly towards you," her ladyship began, very quietly. "I only suggest that our visits

to my house cannot possibly lead to any satisfactory result. I hope
you will not oblige me to say any harder words than these—I hope
you will understand that I wish you to withdraw."

The order of dismissal could hardly have been issued with more
humane consideration for the supposed mental infirmity of the person
to whom it was addressed. Grace instantly resisted it in the plainest
possible terms.

"In justice to my father's memory, and in justice to myself," she
answered, "I insist on a hearing. I refuse to withdraw." She
deliberately took a chair and seated herself in the presence of the
mistress of the house.

Lady Janet waited a moment—steadily controlling her temper. In
the interval of silence, Julian seized the opportunity of remonstrating
with Grace.

"Is this what you promised me?" he asked gently. "You gave
me your word that you would not return to Mablethorpe House."

Before he could say more, Lady Janet had got her temper under
command. She began her answer to Grace by pointing with a
peremptory forefinger to the library door.

"If you have not made up your mind to take my advice by the
time I have walked back to that door," she said, "I will put it out of
your power to set me at defiance. I am used to be obeyed, and I will
be obeyed. You force me to use hard words. I warn' you, before it
is too late. Go."

She returned slowly towards the library. Julian attempted to interfere with another word of remonstrance. His aunt stopped him by a
gesture which said plainly, "I insist on acting for myself." He
looked next at Mercy. Would she remain passive? Yes. She never
lifted her head; she never moved from the place in which she was
standing apart from the rest. Horace himself tried to attract her
attention, and tried in vain.

Arrived at the library door, Lady Janet looked over her shoulder
at the little immovable black figure in the chair.

"Will you go?" she asked, for the last time.

Grace started up angrily from her seat, and fixed her viperish eyes
on Mercy.

"I won't be turned out of your ladyship's house, in the presence of
that impostor," she said. "I may yield to force—but I will yield to
nothing else. I insist on my right to the place that she has stolen
from me. It's no use scolding me," she added, turning doggedly to
Julian. "As long as that woman is here under my name, I can't
and won't keep away from the house. I warn her, in your presence,
that I have written to my friends in Canada! I dare her before you
all to deny that she is the outcast and adventuress, Mercy Merrick!"

The challenge forced Mercy to take part in the proceedings, in her own defence. She had pledged herself to meet and defy Grace Rose-berry on her own ground. She attempted to speak—Horace stopped her.

"You degrade yourself if you answer her," he said. "Take my arm, and let us leave the room."

"Yes! Take her out!" cried Grace. "She may well be ashamed to face an honest woman. It's her place to leave the room—not mine!"

Mercy drew her hand out of Horace's arm. "I decline to leave the room," she said, quietly.

Horace still tried to persuade her to withdraw. "I can't bear to hear you insulted," he rejoined. "The woman offends me, though I know she is not responsible for what she says."

"Nobody's endurance will be tried much longer," said Lady Janet. She glanced at Julian, and, taking from her pocket the card which he had given to her, opened the library door.

"Go to the police station," she said to the servant in an undertone, "and give that card to the inspector on duty. Tell him there is not a moment to lose."

"Stop!" said Julian, before his aunt could close the door again.

"Stop?" repeated Lady Janet, sharply. "I have given the man his orders. What do you mean?"

"Before you send the card, I wish to say a word in private to this lady," replied Julian, indicating Grace. "When that is done," he continued, approaching Mercy, and pointedly addressing himself to her, "I shall have a request to make—I shall ask you to give me an opportunity of speaking to you without interruption."

His tone pointed the allusion. Mercy shrank from looking at him. The signs of painful agitation began to show themselves in her shift-ing colour and her uneasy silence. Roused by Julian's significantly distant reference to what had passed between them, her better impulses were struggling already to recover their influence over her. She might, at that critical moment, have yielded to the promptings of her own nobler nature—she might have risen superior to the galling remembrance of the insults that had been heaped upon her—if Grace's malice had not seen in her hesitation a means of referring offensively once again to her interview with Julian Gray.

"Pray don't think twice about trusting him alone with me," she said, with a sardonic affectation of politeness. "*I* am not interested in making a conquest of Mr. Julian Gray."

The jealous distrust in Horace (already awakened by Julian's request) now attempted to assert itself openly. Before he could speak, Mercy's indignation had dictated Mercy's answer.

"I am much obliged to you, Mr. Gray," she said, addressing Julian (but still not raising her eyes to his). "I have nothing more to say. There is no need for me to trouble you again."

In those rash words she recalled the confession to which she stood pledged. In those rash words she committed herself to keeping the position that she had usurped, in the face of the woman whom she had deprived of it!

Horace was silenced, but not satisfied. He saw Julian's eyes fixed in sad and searching attention on Mercy's face, while she was speaking. He heard Julian sigh to himself when she had done. He observed Julian—after a moment's serious consideration, and a moment's glance backward at the stranger in the poor black clothes—lift his head with the air of a man who had taken a sudden resolution.

"Bring me that card directly," he said to the servant. His tone announced that he was not to be trifled with. The man obeyed.

Without answering Lady Janet—who still peremptorily insisted on her right to act for herself—Julian took the pencil from his pocketbook, and added his signature to the writing already inscribed on the card. When he had handed it back to the servant he made his apologies to his aunt.

"Pardon me for venturing to interfere," he said. "There is a serious reason for what I have done, which I will explain to you at a fitter time. In the meanwhile, I offer no further obstruction to the course which you propose taking. On the contrary, I have just assisted you in gaining the end that you have in view."

As he said that, he held up the pencil with which he had signed his name.

Lady Janet, naturally perplexed, and (with some reason perhaps) offended as well, made no answer. She waved her hand to the servant, and sent him away with the card.

There was silence in the room. The eyes of all the persons present turned more or less anxiously on Julian. Mercy was vaguely surprised and alarmed. Horace, like Lady Janet, felt offended, without clearly knowing why. Even Grace Roseberry herself was subdued by her own presentiment of some coming interference for which she was completely unprepared. Julian's words and actions, from the moment when he had written on the card, were involved in a mystery to which not one of the persons round him held the clue.

The motive which had animated his conduct may, nevertheless, be described in two words: Julian still held to his faith in the inbred nobility of Mercy's nature.

He had inferred, with little difficulty, from the language which Grace had used towards Mercy in his presence, that the injured woman must have taken pitiless advantage of her position at the interview which he had interrupted. Instead of appealing to Mercy's sympathies and Mercy's sense of right—instead of accepting the expression of her sincere contrition, and encouraging her to make the completest and the speediest atonement—Grace had evidently outraged and insulted her. As a necessary result, her endurance had given way—under her own sense of intolerable severity and intolerable wrong.

The remedy for the mischief thus done was (as Julian had first seen it) to speak privately with Grace—to soothe her by owning that his opinion of the justice of her claims had undergone a change in her favour—and then to persuade her, in her own interests, to let him carry to Mercy such expressions of apology and regret as might lead to a friendly understanding between them.

With those motives, he had made his request to be permitted to speak separately to the one and the other. The scene that had followed, the new insult offered by Grace, and the answer which it had wrung from Mercy, had convinced him that no such interference as he had contemplated would have the slightest prospect of success.

The one remedy now left to try was the desperate remedy of letting things take their course, and trusting implicitly to Mercy's better nature for the result.

Let her see the police officer in plain clothes enter the room. Let her understand clearly what the result of his interference would be. Let her confront the alternative of consigning Grace Roseberry to a madhouse, or of confessing the truth—and what would happen? If Julian's confidence in her was a confidence soundly placed, she would nobly pardon the outrages that had been heaped upon her, and she would do justice to the woman whom she had wronged.

If, on the other hand, his belief in her was nothing better than the blind belief of an infatuated man—if she faced the alternative, and persisted in asserting her assumed identity, what then?

Julian's faith in Mercy refused to let that darker side of the question find a place in his thoughts. It rested entirely with him to bring the officer into the house. He had prevented Lady Janet from making any mischievous use of his card, by sending to the police-station, and warning them to attend to no message which they might receive unless the card produced bore his signature. Knowing the responsibility that he was taking on himself—knowing that Mercy had made no confession to him to which it was possible to appeal—he had signed his name without an instant's hesitation: and there he stood now, looking at the woman whose better nature he was determined to vindicate, the only calm person in the room.

Horace's jealousy saw something suspiciously suggestive of a private understanding in Julian's earnest attention and in Mercy's downcast face. Having no excuse for open interference, he made an effort to part them.

" You spoke just now," he said to Julian, " of wishing to say a word in private to that person." (He pointed to Grace). "Shall we retire, or will you take her into the library?"

"I refuse to have anything to say to him," Grace burst out, before Julian could answer. "I happen to know that he is the last person to do me justice. *He* has been effectually hoodwinked. If I speak to anybody privately, it ought to be to you. *You* have the greatest interest of any of them in finding out the truth."

"What do you mean?"

"Do you want to marry an outcast from the streets?"

Horace took one step forward towards her. There was a look in his face which plainly betrayed that he was capable of turning her out of the house with his own hands. Lady Janet stopped him.

"You were right in suggesting just now that Grace had better leave the room," she said. "Let us all three go. Julian will remain here, and give the man his directions when he arrives. Come."

No. By a strange contradiction, it was Horace himself who now interfered to prevent Mercy from leaving the room. In the heat of his indignation, he lost all sense of his own dignity; he descended to the level of a woman whose intellect he believed to be deranged. To the surprise of every one present, he stepped back, and took from the table a jewel-case which he had placed there when he came into the room. It was the wedding present from his mother which he had brought to his betrothed wife. His outraged self-esteem seized the opportunity of vindicating Mercy by a public bestowal of the gift.

"Wait!" he called out sternly. "That wretch shall have her answer. She has sense enough to see, and sense enough to hear. Let her see and hear!"

He opened the jewel-case, and took from it a magnificent pearl necklace in an antique setting.

"Grace," he said, with his highest distinction of manner, "my mother sends you her love, and her congratulations on our approaching marriage. She begs you to accept, as part of your bridal dress, these pearls. She was married in them herself. They have been in our family for centuries. As one of the family, honoured and beloved, my mother offers them to my wife."

He lifted the necklace to clasp it round Mercy's neck.

Julian watched her in breathless suspense. Would she sustain the ordeal through which Horace had innocently condemned her to pass?

Yes! In the insolent presence of Grace Roseberry, what was there now that she could *not* sustain? Her pride was in arms. Her lovely eyes lighted up as only a woman's eyes *can* light up when they see jewelry. Her grand head bent gracefully to receive the necklace. Her face warmed into colour; her beauty rallied its charms. Her triumph over Grace Roseberry was complete! Julian's head sank.

For one sad moment he secretly asked himself the question: "Have I been mistaken in her?"

Horace arrayed her in the pearls.

"Your husband puts these pearls on your neck, love," he said proudly, and paused to look at her. "Now," he added, with a contemptuous backward glance at Grace, "we may go into the library. She has seen, and she has heard."

He believed that he had silenced her. He had simply furnished her sharp tongue with a new sting.

"*You* will hear, and *you* will see, when my proofs come from Canada," she retorted. "You will hear that your wife has stolen my name and my character! You will see your wife dismissed from this house!"

Mercy turned on her with an uncontrollable outburst of passion.

"You are mad!" she cried.

Lady Janet caught the electric infection of anger in the air of the room. She too turned on Grace. She too said it:

"You are mad!"

Horace followed Lady Janet. *He* was beside himself. *He* fixed his pitiless eyes on Grace, and echoed the contagious words:

"You are mad!"

She was silenced, she was daunted at last. The treble accusation revealed to her, for the first time, the frightful suspicion to which she had exposed herself. She shrank back, with a low cry of horror, and struck against a chair. She would have fallen if Julian had not sprung forward and caught her.

Lady Janet led the way into the library. She opened the door —started—and suddenly stepped aside, so as to leave the entrance free.

A man appeared in the open doorway.

He was not a gentleman; he was not a workman; he was not a servant. He was vilely dressed, in glossy black broadcloth. His frock coat hung on him instead of fitting him. His waistcoat was too short and too tight over the chest. His trousers were a pair of shapeless black bags. His gloves were too large for him. His highly-polished boots creaked detestably whenever he moved. He had odiously watchful eyes—eyes that looked skilled in peeping through keyholes. His large ears, set forward like the ears of a monkey, pleaded guilty to meanly listening behind other people's doors. His manner was quietly confidential, when he spoke; impenetrably self-possessed, when he was silent. A lurking air of secret-service enveloped the fellow, like an atmosphere of his own, from head to foot. He looked all round the magnificent room, without betraying either surprise or admiration. He closely investigated every person in it with one glance of his cunningly-watchful eyes. Making his bow to Lady Janet, he silently showed her, as his introduction, the card that had summoned him. And then he stood at ease, self-revealed in his own sinister identity—a police officer in plain clothes.

Nobody spoke to him. Everybody shrank inwardly, as if a reptile had crawled into the room.

He looked backwards and forwards, perfectly unembarrassed, between Julian and Horace.

"Is Mr. Julian Gray here?" he asked.

Julian led Grace to a seat. Her eyes were fixed on the man. She trembled—she whispered, "Who is he?" Julian spoke to the police officer without answering her.

"Wait there," he said, pointing to a chair in the most distant corner of the room. "I will speak to you directly."

The man advanced to the chair, marching to the discord of his creaking boots. He privately valued the carpet, at so much a yard, as he walked over it. He privately valued the chair, at so much the dozen, as he sat down on it. He was quite at his ease: it was no matter to him, whether he waited and did nothing, or whether he pried into the private character of every one in the room, as long as he was paid for it.

Even Lady Janet's resolution to act for herself was not proof against the appearance of the policeman in plain clothes. She left it to her nephew to take the lead. Julian glanced at Mercy before he stirred further in the matter. He knew that the end rested now, not with him, but with her.

She felt his eye on her, while her own eyes were looking at the man. She turned her head—hesitated—and suddenly approached Julian. Like Grace Roseberry, she was trembling. Like Grace Roseberry, she whispered, "Who is he?"

Julian told her plainly who he was.

"Why is he here?"

"Can't you guess?"

"No."

Horace left Lady Janet, and joined Mercy and Julian—impatient of the private colloquy between them.

"Am I in the way?" he inquired.

Julian drew back a little, understanding Horace perfectly. He looked round at Grace. Nearly the whole length of the spacious room divided them from the place in which she was sitting. She had never moved since he had placed her in a chair. The direst of all terrors was in possession of her—terror of the unknown. There was no fear of her interfering; and no fear of her hearing what they said, so long as they were careful to speak in guarded tones. Julian set the example by lowering his voice.

"Ask Horace why the police officer is here," he said to Mercy.

She put the question directly. "Why is he here?"

Horace looked across the room at Grace, and answered, "He is here to relieve us of that woman."

"Do you mean that he will take her away?"

"Yes."

"Where will he take her to?"

"To the police station."

Mercy started, and looked at Julian. He was still watching the slightest changes in her face. She looked back again at Horace.

"To the police station!" she repeated. "What for?"

"How can you ask the question?" said Horace irritably. "To be placed under restraint, of course."

"Do you mean prison?"

"I mean an asylum."

Again Mercy turned to Julian. There was horror now, as well as surprise, in her face. "Oh!" she said to him, "Horace is surely wrong? It can't be?"

Julian left it to Horace to answer. Every faculty in him seemed to be still absorbed in watching Mercy's face. She was compelled to address herself to Horace once more.

"What sort of asylum?" she asked. "You don't surely mean a madhouse?"

"I do," he rejoined. "The workhouse first, perhaps—and then the madhouse. What is there to surprise you in that? You yourself told her to her face she was mad. Good heavens! how pale you are! What is the matter?"

She turned to Julian for the third time. The terrible alternative that was offered to her had showed itself at last, without reserve or disguise. Restore the identity that you have stolen, or shut her up in a madhouse—it rests with you to choose! In that form the situation shaped itself in her mind. She chose on the instant. Before she opened her lips, the higher nature in her spoke to Julian, in her eyes. The steady inner light that he had seen in them once already shone in them again, brighter and purer than before. The conscience that he had fortified, the soul that he had saved, looked at him, and said, Doubt us no more!

"Send that man out of the house."

Those were her first words. She spoke (pointing to the police officer) in clear, ringing, resolute tones, audible in the remotest corner of the room.

Julian's hand stole unobserved to hers, and told her, in its momentary pressure, to count on his brotherly sympathy and help. All the other persons in the room looked at her in speechless surprise. Grace rose from her chair. Even the man in plain clothes started to his feet. Lady Janet (hurriedly joining Horace, and fully sharing his

perplexity and alarm,) took Mercy impulsively by the arm, and shook
it, as if to rouse her to a sense of what she was doing. Mercy held
firm; Mercy resolutely repeated what she had said : "Send that man
out of the house."

Lady Janet lost all patience with her. "What has come to you?"
she asked sternly. "Do you know what you are saying? The man
is here in your interest, as well as in mine; the man is here to spare
you, as well as me, further annoyance and insult. And you insist—
insist, in my presence—on his being sent away! What does it
mean?"

"You shall know what it means, Lady Janet, in half an hour.
I don't insist—I only reiterate my entreaty. Let the man be sent
away!"

Julian stepped aside (with his aunt's eyes angrily following him)
and spoke to the police officer. "Go back to the station," he said,
"and wait there till you hear from me."

The meanly-vigilant eyes of the man in plain clothes travelled side-
long from Julian to Mercy, and valued her beauty as they had valued
the carpet and the chairs. "The old story," he thought. "The
nice-looking woman is always at the bottom of it; and, sooner or
later, the nice-looking woman has her way." He marched back across
the room, to the discord of his own creaking boots; bowed, with a
villainous smile which put the worst construction upon everything; and
vanished through the library door.

Lady Janet's high breeding restrained her from saying anything
until the police officer was out of hearing. Then, and not till then,
she appealed to Julian.

"I presume you are in the secret of this?" she said. "I suppose
you have some reason for setting my authority at defiance in my own
house?"

"I have never yet failed to respect your ladyship," Julian answered.
"Before long you will know that I am not failing in respect towards
you now."

Lady Janet looked across the room. Grace was listening eagerly,
conscious that events had taken some mysterious turn in her favour
within the last minute.

"Is it part of your new arrangement of my affairs," her ladyship
continued, "that this person is to remain in the house?"

The terror that had daunted Grace had not lost all hold of her yet.
She left it to Julian to reply. Before he could speak, Mercy crossed
the room and whispered to her, "Give me time to confess it in
writing. I can't own it before them—with this round my neck."
She pointed to the necklace. Grace cast a threatening glance at her,
and suddenly looked away again in silence.

Mercy answered Lady Janet's question. "I beg your ladyship to permit her to remain until the half hour is over," she said.  " My request will have explained itself by that time."

Lady Janet raised no further obstacles.  Something in Mercy's face, or in Mercy's tone, seemed to have silenced her, as it had silenced Grace.  Horace was the next who spoke.  In tones of suppressed rage and suspicion, he addressed himself to Mercy, standing fronting him by Julian's side.

" Am I included," he asked, " in the arrangement which engages you to explain your extraordinary conduct in half an hour ?"

*His* hand had placed his mother's wedding-present round Mercy's neck.  A sharp pang wrung her as she looked at Horace, and saw how deeply she had already distressed and offended him.  The tears rose in her eyes ; she humbly and faintly answered him.

" If you please," was all she could say, before the cruel swelling at her heart rose and silenced her.

Horace's sense of injury refused to be soothed by such simple submission as this.

" I dislike mysteries and innuendoes," he went on harshly.  " In my family circle we are accustomed to meet each other frankly.  Why am I to wait half an hour for an explanation which might be given now ? What am I to wait for ?"

Lady Janet recovered herself as Horace spoke.

ι  " I entirely agree with you," she said.  " I ask too, what are we to wait for ?"

Even Julian's self-possession failed him when his aunt repeated that cruelly plain question.  How would Mercy answer it ?  Would her courage still hold out ?

" You have asked me what you are to wait for," she said to Horace, uietl and firmly.  " Wait to hear something more of Mercy Merrick."

q Lady Janet listened with a look of weary disgust.

" Don't return to *that* !" she said.  " We know enough about Mercy Merrick already."

" Pardon me—your ladyship does *not* know.  I am the only person who can inform you."

" You ?"

She bent her head respectfully.

" I have begged you, Lady Janet, to give me half an hour," she went on.  " In half an hour I solemnly engage myself to produce Mercy Merrick in this room.  Lady Janet Roy, Mr. Horace Holmcroft, you are to wait for that."

Steadily pledging herself in those terms to make her confession, she unclasped the pearls from her neck, put them away in their case, and placed it in Horace's hand.  " Keep it," she said, with a momentary faltering in her voice, " until we meet again."

Horace took the case in silence ; he looked and acted like a man.

whose mind was paralysed by surprise. His hand moved mechanically. His eyes followed Mercy with a vacant questioning look. Lady Janet seemed, in her different way, to share the strange oppression that had fallen on him. A vague sense of dread and distress hung like a cloud over her mind. At that memorable moment she felt her age, she looked her age, as she had never felt it or looked it yet.

"Have I your ladyship's leave," said Mercy, respectfully, "to go to my room?"

Lady Janet mutely granted the request. Mercy's last look, before she went out, was a look at Grace. "Are you satisfied now?" the grand grey eyes seemed to say mournfully. Grace turned her head aside, with a quick petulant action. Even her narrow nature opened for a moment unwillingly, and let pity in a little way, in spite of itself.

Mercy's parting words recommended Grace to Julian's care:

"You will see that she is allowed a room to wait in? You will warn her yourself when the half hour has expired?"

Julian opened the library door for her.

"Well done! Nobly done!" he whispered. "All my sympathy is with you—all my help is yours."

Her eyes looked at him, and thanked him, through her gathering tears. His own eyes were dimmed. She passed quietly down the room, and was lost to him before he had shut the door again.

## CHAPTER XXI.

### THE FOOTSTEP IN THE CORRIDOR.

MERCY was alone.

She had secured one half-hour of retirement in her own room; designing to devote that interval to the writing of her confession in the form of a letter addressed to Julian Gray.

No recent change in her position had, as yet, mitigated her horror of acknowledging to Horace and to Lady Janet that she had won her way to their hearts in disguise. Through Julian only could she say the words which were to establish Grace Roseberry in her right position in the house.

How was her confession to be addressed to him? In writing? or by word of mouth?

After all that had happened, from the time when Lady Janet's appearance had interrupted them, she would have felt relief rather than embarrassment in personally opening her heart to the man who had so delicately understood her, who had so faithfully befriended her in her sorest need. But the repeated betrayals of Horace's jealous suspicion of Julian warned her that she would only be surrounding herself with new difficulties, and be placing Julian in a position of painful embarrassment, if she admitted him to a private interview while Horace was in the house.

The one course left to take was the course that she had adopted. Determining to address the narrative of the Fraud to Julian in the form of a letter, she arranged to add, at the close, certain instructions, pointing out to him the line of conduct which she wished him to pursue.

These instructions contemplated the communication of her letter to Lady Janet and to Horace, in the library, while Mercy—self-confessed as the missing woman whom she had pledged herself to produce— awaited in the adjoining room whatever sentence it pleased them to pronounce on her. Her resolution not to screen herself behind Julian from any consequences which might follow the confession, had taken root in her mind from the moment when Horace had harshly asked her (and when Lady Janet had joined him in asking) why she delayed her explanation, and what she was keeping them waiting for. Out of the very pain which those questions inflicted, the idea of waiting her sentence in her own person, in one room, while her letter to Julian was speaking for her in another, had sprung to life. " Let them break my heart if they like," she had thought to herself in the self-abasement of that bitter moment; "it will be no more than I have deserved."

She locked her door and opened her writing-desk. Knowing what she had to do, she tried to collect herself and do it.

The effort was in vain. Those persons who study writing as an art are probably the only persons who can measure the vast distance which separates a conception as it exists in the mind from the reduction of that conception to form and shape in words. The heavy stress of agitation that had been laid on Mercy for hours together, had utterly unfitted her for the delicate and difficult process of arranging the events of a narrative in their due sequence and their due proportion towards each other. Again and again she tried to begin her letter, and again and again she was baffled by the same hopeless confusion of ideas. She gave up the struggle in despair.

A sense of sinking at her heart, a weight of hysterical oppression on her bosom, warned her not to leave herself unoccupied, a prey to morbid self-investigation and imaginary alarms.

She turned instinctively, for a temporary employment of some kind, to the consideration of her own future. Here there were no intricacies or entanglements. The prospect began and ended with her return to the Refuge, if the matron would receive her. She did no injustice to Julian Gray; that great heart would feel for her, that kind hand would be held out to her, she knew. But what would happen if she thoughtlessly accepted all that his sympathy might offer ? Scandal would point to her beauty and to his youth, and would place its own vile interpretation on the purest friendship that could exist between them. And *he* would be the sufferer, for *he* had a character—a clergyman's character—to lose. No! for his sake, out of gratitude to *him*, the farewell to Mablethorpe House must be also the farewell to Julian Gray.

The precious minutes were passing. She resolved to write to the matron, and ask if she might hope to be forgiven and employed at the Refuge again. Occupation over the letter that was easy to write might have its fortifying effect on her mind, and might pave the way for resuming the letter that was hard to write. She waited a moment at the window, thinking of the past life to which she was soon to return, before she took up the pen again.

Her window looked eastward. The dusky glare of lighted London met her as her eyes rested on the sky. It seemed to beckon her back to the horror of the cruel streets—to point her way mockingly to the bridges over the black river—to lure her to the top of the parapet, and the dreadful leap into God's arms, or into annihilation—who knew which?

She turned, shuddering, from the window. "Will it end in that way," she asked herself, "if the matron says No?"

She began her letter.

"DEAR MADAM,—So long a time has passed since you heard from me, that I almost shrink from writing to you. I am afraid you have already given me up in your own mind as a hard-hearted, ungrateful woman.

"I have been leading a false life; I have not been fit to write to you before to-day. Now, when I am doing what I can to atone to those whom I have injured, now, when I repent with my whole heart, may I ask leave to return to the friend who has borne with me and helped me through many miserable years? Oh, madam, do not cast me off! I have no one to turn to but you.

"Will you let me own everything to you? Will you forgive me when you know what I have done? Will you take me back into the Refuge, if you have any employment for me by which I may earn my shelter and my bread?

"Before the night comes I must leave the house from which I am now writing. I have nowhere to go to. The little money, the few valuable possessions I have, must be left behind me: they have been obtained under false pretences; they are not mine. No more forlorn creature than I am lives at this moment. You are a Christian woman. Not for my sake—for Christ's sake, pity me and take me back.

"I am a good nurse, as you know, and I am a quick worker with my needle. In one way or the other, can you not find occupation for me?

"I could also teach, in a very unpretending way. But that is useless. Who would trust their children to a woman without a character? There is no hope for me in this direction. And yet I am so fond of children! I think I could be—not happy again, perhaps, but content with my lot, if I could be associated with them in some way. Are there not charitable societies which are trying to help and protect destitute children wandering about the streets? I think of my own wretched childhood—and oh! I should so like to be employed in saving other children from ending as I have ended. I could work, for such an object as that, from morning to night, and never feel weary. All my heart would be in it; and I should have this advantage over happy and prosperous women—I should have. nothing else to think of. Surely, they might trust me with the poor little starving wanderers of the streets—if you said a word for me? If I am asking too much, please forgive me. I am so wretched, madam—so lonely and so weary of my life.

"There is only one thing more. My time here is very short. Will you please reply to this letter (to say yes or no) by telegram?

" The name by which you know me is not the name by which I have been known here. I must beg you to address the telegram to ' The Reverend Julian Gray, Mablethorpe House, Kensington.' He is here, and he will show it to me. No words of mine can describe what I owe to him. He has never despaired of me—he has saved me from myself. God bless and reward the kindest, truest, best man I have ever known!

" I have no more to say, except to ask you to excuse this long letter, and to believe me your grateful servant,          ———"

She signed and enclosed the letter, and wrote the address. Then, for the first time, an obstacle which she ought to have seen before showed itself, standing straight in her way.

There was no time to forward her letter in the ordinary manner by post. It must be taken to its destination by a private messenger. Lady Janet's servants had hitherto been, one and all, at her disposal. Could she presume to employ them on her own affairs, when she might be dismissed from the house, a disgraced woman, in half an hour's time? Of the two alternatives, it seemed better to take her chance, and present herself at the Refuge, without asking leave first.

While she was still considering the question, she was startled by a knock at her door. On opening it, she admitted Lady Janet's maid with a morsel of folded note paper in her hand.

" From my lady, miss," said the woman, giving her the note. " There is no answer."

Mercy stopped her, as she was about to leave the room. The appearance of the maid suggested an inquiry to her. She asked if any of the servants were likely to be going into town that afternoon?

" Yes, miss. One of the grooms is going on horseback, with a
message to her ladyship's coachmaker."

The Refuge was close by the coachmaker's place of business. Under
the circumstances, Mercy was emboldened to make use of the man. It
was a pardonable liberty to employ his services now.

" Will you kindly give the groom that letter for me?" she said.
" It will not take him out of his way. He has only to deliver it—
nothing more."

The woman willingly complied with the request. Left once more
by herself, Mercy looked at the little note which had been placed in
her hands.

It was the first time that her benefactress had employed this formal
method of communicating with her when they were both in the
house. What did such a departure from established habits mean? Had
she received her notice of dismissal? Had Lady Janet's quick intelligence found its way already to a suspicion of the truth? Mercy's
nerves were unstrung. She trembled pitiably as she opened the
folded note.

It began without a form of address, and it ended without a
signature. Thus it ran:

" I must request you to delay for a little while the explanation
which you have promised me. At my age, painful surprises are very
trying things. I must have time to compose myself, before I can
hear what you have to say. You shall not be kept waiting longer
than I can help.- In the meanwhile, everything will go on as usual.
My nephew Julian, and Horace Holmcroft, and the lady whom I
found in the dining-room, will, by my desire, remain in the house
until I am able to meet them, and to meet you, again."

There the note ended. To what conclusion did it point?

Had Lady Janet really guessed the truth? or had she only sur-
mised that her adopted daughter was connected in some discreditable
manner with the mystery of " Mercy Merrick"? The line in which
she referred to the intruder in the dining-room as "the lady," showed
very remarkably that her opinions had undergone a change in that
quarter. But was the phrase enough of itself to justify the inference
that she had actually anticipated the nature of Mercy's confession? It
was not easy to decide that doubt at the moment—and it proved to be
equally difficult to throw any light on it at an after-time. To the end
of her life, Lady Janet resolutely refused to communicate to any one
the conclusions which she might have privately formed, the griefs
which she might have secretly stifled, on that memorable day.

Amid much, however, which was beset with uncertainty, one thing
at least was clear. The time at Mercy's disposal in her own room, had
been indefinitely prolonged by Mercy's benefactress. Hours might
pass before the disclosure to which she stood committed would be

expected from her. In those hours she might surely compose her mind sufficiently to be able to write her letter of confession to Julian Gray.

Once more she placed the sheet of paper before her. Resting her head on her hand as she sat at the table, she tried to trace her way through the labyrinth of the past, beginning with the day when she had met Grace Roseberry in the French cottage, and ending with the day which had brought them face to face, for the second time, in the dining-room at Mablethorpe House.

The chain of events began to unroll itself in her mind clearly, link by link.

She remarked, as she pursued the retrospect, how strangely Chance or Fate had paved the way for the act of personation, in the first place.

If they had met under ordinary circumstances, neither Mercy nor Grace would have trusted each other with the confidences which had been exchanged between them. As the event had happened, they had come together, under those extraordinary circumstances of common trial and common peril, in a strange country, which would especially predispose two women of the same nation to open their hearts to each other. In no other way could Mercy have obtained at a first interview that fatal knowledge of Grace's position and Grace's affairs which had placed temptation before her, as the necessary consequence that followed the bursting of the German shell.

Advancing from this point, through the succeeding series of events which had so naturally, and yet so strangely, favoured the perpetration of the fraud, Mercy reached the later period when Grace had followed her to England. Here again, she remarked, in the second place, how Chance, or Fate, had once more paved the way for that second meeting which had confronted them with one another at Mablethorpe House.

She had, as she well remembered, attended at a certain assembly (convened by a charitable society) in the character of Lady Janet's representative, at Lady Janet's own request. For that reason, she had been absent from the house when Grace had entered it. If her return had been delayed by a few minutes only, Julian would have had time to take Grace out of the room; and the terrible meeting which had stretched Mercy senseless on the floor would never have taken place. As the event had happened, the period of her absence had been fatally shortened, by what appeared at the time to be the commonest possible occurrence. The persons assembled at the society's rooms had disagreed so seriously on the business which had brought them together, as to render it necessary to take the ordinary course of adjourning the proceedings to a future day. And Chance, or Fate, had so timed that adjournment as to bring Mercy back into the dining-room exactly at

the moment when Grace Roseberry insisted on being confronted with
the woman who had taken her place.

She had never yet seen the circumstances in this sinister light. She
was alone in her room, at a crisis in her life. She was worn and
weakened by emotions which had shaken her to the soul.

Little by little, she felt the enervating influences let loose on her, in
her lonely position, by her new train of thought. Little by little, her
heart began to sink under the stealthy chill of superstitious dread.
Vaguely horrible presentiments throbbed in her with her pulses,
flowed through her with her blood. Mystic oppressions of hidden
disaster hovered over her in the atmosphere of the room. The
cheerful candlelight turned traitor to her and grew dim. Supernatural murmurs trembled round the house in the moaning of the
winter wind. She was afraid to look behind her. On a sudden, she
felt her own cold hands covering her face, without knowing when she
had lifted them to it, or why.

Still helpless under the horror that held her, she suddenly heard
footsteps—a man's footsteps—in the corridor outside. At other times
the sound would have startled her: now, it broke the spell. The
footsteps suggested life, companionship, human interposition — no
matter of what sort. She mechanically took up her pen; she found
herself beginning to remember her letter to Julian Gray.

At the same moment the footsteps stopped outside her door. The
man knocked.

She still felt shaken. She was hardly mistress of herself yet. A
faint cry of alarm escaped her at the sound of the knock. Before it
could be repeated she had rallied her courage, and had opened the
door.

The man in the corridor was Horace Holmcroft.

His ruddy complexion had turned pale. His hair (of which he was
especially careful at other times) was in disorder. The superficial
polish of his manner was gone; the undisguised man, sullen, distrust-
ful, irritated to the last degree of endurance, showed through. He
looked at her with a watchfully-suspicious eye; he spoke to her without preface or apology, in a coldly angry voice:

"Are you aware," he asked, "of what is going on downstairs?"

"I have not left my room," she answered. "I know that Lady
Janet has deferred the explanation which I had promised to give her,
and I know no more."

"Has nobody told you what Lady Janet did after you left us? Has
nobody told you that she politely placed her own boudoir at the disposal of the very woman whom she had ordered half an hour before to
leave the house? Do you really not know that Mr. Julian Gray has
himself conducted this suddenly-honoured guest to her place of retire-
ment? and that I am left alone in the midst of these changes, con-

tradictions and mysteries—the only person who is kept out in the dark?"

"It is surely needless to ask me these questions," said Mercy, gently. "Who could possibly have told me what was going on below stairs before you knocked at my door?"

He looked at her with an ironical affectation of surprise.

"You are strangely forgetful to-day," he said. "Surely your friend Mr. Julian Gray might have told you? I am astonished to hear that he has not had his private interview yet."

"I don't understand you, Horace."

"I don't want you to understand me," he retorted irritably. "The proper person to understand me is Julian Gray. I look to *him* to account to me for the confidential relations which seem to have been established between you behind my back. He has avoided me thus far, but I shall find my way to him yet."

His manner threatened more than his words expressed. In Mercy's nervous condition at the moment, it suggested to her that he might attempt to fasten a quarrel on Julian Gray.

"You are entirely mistaken," she said warmly. "You are ungratefully doubting your best 'and truest friend. I say nothing of myself. You will soon discover why I patiently submit to suspicions which other women would resent as an insult."

"Let me discover it at once. Now! Without wasting a moment more!"

There had hitherto been some little distance between them. Mercy had listened, waiting on the threshold of her door; Horace had spoken standing against the opposite wall of the corridor. When he said his last words, he suddenly stepped forward, and (with something imperative in the gesture) laid his hand on her arm. The strong grasp of it almost hurt her. She struggled to release herself.

"Let me go!" she said. "What do you mean?"

He dropped her arm as suddenly as he had taken it.

"You shall know what I mean," he replied. "A woman who has grossly outraged and insulted you—whose only excuse is that she is mad—is detained in the house at your desire, I might almost say at your command, when the police-officer is waiting to take her away. I have a right to know what this means. I am engaged to marry you. If you won't trust other people, you are bound to explain yourself to Me. I refuse to wait for Lady Janet's convenience. I insist (if you force me to say so)—I insist on knowing the real nature of your connection with this affair. You have obliged me to follow you here; it is my only opportunity of speaking to you. You avoid me; you shut yourself up from me in your own room. I am not your husband yet —I have no right to follow you in. But there are other rooms open to us. The library is at our disposal, and I will take care that we are not interrupted. I am now going there, and I have a last question to ask. You are to be my wife in a week's time: will you take me into your confidence or not?"

To hesitate was, in this case, literally to be lost. Mercy's sense of justice told her that Horace had claimed no more than his due. She answered instantly.

"I will follow you to the library, Horace, in five minutes."

Her prompt and frank compliance with his wishes surprised and touched him. He took her hand.

She had endured all that his angry sense of injury could say. His gratitude wounded her to the quick. The bitterest moment she had felt yet was the moment in which he raised her hand to his lips, and murmured tenderly, "My own true Grace!" She could only sign to him to leave her, and hurry back into her own room.

Her first feeling, when she found herself alone again, was wonder —wonder that it should never have occurred to her, until he had himself suggested it, that her betrothed husband had the foremost right to her confession. Her horror at owning to either of them that she had cheated them out of their love, had hitherto placed Horace and Lady Janet on the same level. She now saw for the first time, that there was no comparison between the claims which they respectively had on her. She owed an allegiance to Horace, to which Lady Janet could assert no right. Cost her what it might to avow the truth to him with her own lips, the cruel sacrifice must be made.

Without a moment's hesitation, she put away her writing materials. It amazed her that she should ever have thought of using Julian Gray as an interpreter between the man to whom she was betrothed and herself. Julian's sympathy (she thought) must have made a strong impression on her indeed, to blind her to a duty which was beyond all compromise, which admitted of no dispute!

She had asked for five minutes of delay before she followed Horace. It was too long a time.

Her one chance of finding courage to crush him with the dreadful revelation of who she really was, of what she had really done, was to plunge headlong into the disclosure without giving herself time to think. The shame of it would overpower her if she gave herself time to think.

She turned to the door, to follow him at once.

Even at that trying moment, the most ineradicable of all a woman's instincts—the instinct of personal self-respect—brought her to a pause. She had passed through more than one terrible trial since she had dressed to go downstairs. Remembering this, she stopped mechanically, retraced her steps, and looked at herself in the glass.

There was no motive of vanity in what she now did. The action was as unconscious as if she had buttoned an unfastened glove, or shaken out a crumpled dress. Not the faintest idea crossed her mind of looking to see if her beauty might still plead for her, and of trying to set it off at its best.

A momentary smile, the most weary, the most hopeless that ever saddened a woman's face, appeared in the reflection which her mirror gave her back. "Haggard, ghastly, old before my time!" she said to herself. "Well! better so. He will feel it less—he will not regret me."

With that thought she went downstairs to meet him in the library.

# The Late Lord Lytton.

A NATION without a visible and conspicuous Pantheon or Campo Santo, where the dust of all its most illustrious dead may repose, in memory of their heroic works or deeds, and in enduring encouragement to those who come afterwards to aspire to a like life and a like immortality upon earth, stamps itself as devoid equally of gratitude and intelligence; and there is scarcely a modern nation, when we have made exception of Italy, to which such a reproach may not in great measure be addressed. England is perhaps more open to reproof on this head than any other civilised country; though we have to thank rather our imperfect state organisation, with which we appear to be so placidly contented, than any special or inherent disregard of individual greatness, or any sordid unwillingness to pay it honour. Still, be the cause what it may, want of intelligence or want of due thankfulness must be charged with the shortcoming; since were we, as a people, very keenly alive not only to the debt we owe to those who have exalted our fame as a community by the lustre of their achievements, but to the duty we owe to ourselves and our posterity of perpetually inciting each fresh generation to a spirited emulation of the past, we should contrive to constitute some recognised body whose function it should be to see that no man went unhonoured, or too little honoured, to his grave, who had deserved well of his country.

We need not dwell upon the sepulchral *olla podrida* which goes by the high-sounding name of Westminster Abbey, nor do we think there can be much call to insist that it is monstrous to allow any one single individual to decide whether a person is deserving of being interred within its ancient walls. Dean Stanley is a man of large parts and generous ideas, and would be much more likely to err on the side of toleration than of exclusiveness. But, as we shall see directly, even the leaning to liberality's side may be serious misfortune, whilst when the leaning is the other way, as it was in the case of Milton and of Byron, an outrage is committed, with every legal adjunct, upon the common sense and propriety of the community. What we wish really to call attention to, is the levity with which monuments to deceased persons are both admitted and excluded; and though, doubtless, we fancy that, unlike our predecessors, we are exercising a most judicious discrimination, few thoughtful persons can doubt that we are only perpetuating that hap-hazard collocation of incongruous celebrities which we find so exceedingly ludicrous in the tombs and inscriptions

of older date which still litter the Abbey. For how are we more
likely to avoid the mistakes, over which we make so merry, than our
forefathers who committed them? It seems to us that we are considerably more likely to be wrong in our hasty verdicts upon merit,
even than they were. It was not so easy to be a successful impostor
by power of talk, by power of swagger or chicanery, or by well
organised and unblushingly purchased advertisement, in the olden
times, as it is now.

A man in the stern genuine old days had really to do something
which very few people could do, in order to get himself recognised as a
person of importance. In these times, a man may with much facility
succeed in seeming to do things he does not do at all, but gets done
for him, or still more in doing that which almost anybody could do,
but whose apparent importance consists in its being extensively talked
about, and so manage to *afficher* himself as what, in the detestable
parlance of the day, is called a Man of the Time. We have a huge
dictionary of Men of the Time—all alive; impudent creatures, for the
most part, who have let slip no opportunity of posting their names on
every bare bit of hoarding, aware that notoriety is sure to bring them
much money, and may possibly bring them some distinction, or that
imitation of it which amply satisfies them. A man has been very
popular in his generation, very useful to it, has led it—even if astray;
has flattered, pampered, humbugged it. He dies. And lo! up to
Heaven goes the cry, "Let us bury him in Westminster Abbey."
Thither is he carried, there interred; and a hundred and fifty years
later, the curious admirers of departed greatness ask in a hesitating
whisper, "Who was he?"

What, then, is our conclusion? It is, firstly, that any nation which
respects itself, and which has a keen sense and appreciation of its
national existence, as something distinct from a mere congeries of
shifting living atoms all covered by a convenient generic name, would
take care to have a National Pantheon or shrine of National Gods;
and secondly, that whilst there should exist a competent and duly-
appointed tribunal to decide who should be admitted to that exalted
and enduring Walhalla, it should be in no hurry to arrive at a conclusion. A term should be named, before the expiration of which no
man's claim should be considered to be made good; and it would probably not be safe to make that term less than a hundred years. In
the lapse of a century, feet of clay get pulverised and fronts of brass
are detected. The highly-popular author has long since made his last
journey to the butterman, and he is buried, not in Westminster Abbey,
but in the British Museum. The much-applauded politician has ceased
to figure in any but family histories; and the distinguished man of
science is forgotten even as a rash empiricist, which he was amply
demonstrated to be two generations back. Posterity is wonderfully

dispassionate, and separates the sheep from the goats with an almost divine instinct. It has a fine faculty of oblivion for things and folks there is no necessity to remember ; and it is only by remitting contemporaneous verdicts to its revision, that a National Pantheon can be rescued from becoming a mere lumber-room—a painful exhibition of ill-assorted specimens of fame.

The late Lord Lytton has been buried in Westminster Abbey ; and before attempting to inquire how far he would have been deserving of such an honour, had the conditions of the case allowed it to be an honour at all, which we have seen they do not, we have availed ourselves of the opportunity afforded by the event to say what we believe many people feel, and what, in any case, we are of opinion much needed saying. We must not, however, be any longer delayed from entering upon our more special task, which is that of paying a grateful, but we trust dispassionate, tribute to the great writer who has so recently passed away. We may say at once that we believe he could well have afforded to wait a hundred years for admission to a National Walhalla, for that, at the expiration of that period, it would have been ungrudgingly conceded to him. It is, of course, of the very essence of the argument on which we have been insisting, that we may be utterly wrong; and it must be understood that we pretend to do no more than offer our own contribution to the present general estimate of his merits, which is necessarily not the final one. We do not in the least overlook or forget our fallibility, and we are quite sure that, if posterity contradicts our conclusion, posterity will be right and we shall be wrong. Meanwhile, we can only write with such light as is afforded us by the times in which we live—conscious only of one thing at least, that we are influenced in our opinion neither by the misleading enthusiasm or rancour of a clique, nor by the collective voice of a generous, but always too impetuous, crowd.

We are much assisted in the effort to arrive at a conclusion as to whether, in the late Lord Lytton's writings, there resides the important quality of permanence, by the fact that he was before the public incessantly for forty years, and that, far from his popularity as a writer ever flagging, waning, or oscillating, it steadily and surely increased. We should exhaust all the space at our disposal if we were to attempt to enumerate the writers who, during that long interval of time, won for themselves a passing celebrity, almost equal at the moment to that of Lord Lytton, to be utterly forgotten in a year or two, and to be headed in turns by fresh writers whose success was equally sudden and equally ephemeral. Lord Lytton maintained his popularity to the last, and maintained it equally by his earlier works and by his later ones. Moreover, his popularity was the broadest and deepest of that of any writer of his time. We do not wish to imply that that one consider-

ation is of itself enough to give him a higher place than any of his
rivals; but it is an important element in any comparative estimate we
may seek to make. And we fancy we are correct in saying, that
whilst there are many people who do not, and cannot, read Dickens,
Thackeray, and George Eliot, all who read the works of those great
writers read Lytton's works also. He is read by all classes—the rich,
the poor, the learned, the unlearned, the scientific, the shallow—and
all alike find something in him to satisfy them. *Omne tulit punctum.*
And it should never be forgotten, any more than it can too often be
repeated, that the really greatest writers are *not* caviare to the multitude. Shakespeare and Byron are out and away the two most popular
writers in the English language—meaning by popular at once loved
of the people and of the highest and best intellects; and it is impossible to conceive the Greek, no matter what his rank in life, and if
ancient Greek were still a living language, who would not revel in a
perusal of the Iliad; or a Roman, under similar conditions, to whom
Virgil would not afford endless delectation.

True genius is a universal conqueror; or if any exception is to be
made to its conquests, we must look for it in that small and important
class called pedants, but who unfortunately are too prominent and too
often heard in our own day. These are the persons who affect what
they call culture, and who can tolerate no compositions but what have
a fine university aroma. These are they who prefer a Clough—who
is he? many of our readers will exclaim, but it really is not worth
while to stop and tell them—to a Scott; and who periodically air
their superiority by informing us what inferior creatures we must
have been not to perceive that Dickens had no pathos and a very
limited and provincial humour. To this race of pedants Bulwer's
popularity was in itself an offence, since they cannot endure to share
admiration of anybody or anything with the vulgar. Accordingly,
though they read such books as 'Night and Morning,' and 'My
Novel,' since they could not resist doing so, they affect to regard
them as good for sempstresses, and comfort themselves generally
in matters of literature in much the same way as those contemporaneous critics who preferred Ben Jonson to Shakespeare. It is quite
certain they would have done the same. They are, however, as we
have said, a small and unimportant class, and, save for the fact that
they happen to be able to express their opinions in what are called
critical journals, it would not have been necessary to refer to them at
all. This trifling exception made, it may be said that Bulwer's works
have found their way into the homes of all classes and ranks of the
community, and have done so for forty years without intermission,
being more popular at this moment than they ever were before. The
fact, we repeat, is not conclusive as to the permanence of the interest
which his works will excite; but it raises a strong and forcible pre-

sumption to that effect. Nor, when we are urging this point, should we forget that it is applicable to his plays as much as to any other class of his works; and the acting drama is perhaps the one department of literary composition in which taste changes most rapidly, and in which one favourite succeeds another with most frequency.

We have no wish, however, to overlook the fact that there are persons whose opinion is entitled to consideration, and who are rather disposed to hold that the utmost which can be attributed to the late Lord Lytton is what is called universal cleverness, by which it is intended to deny him the quality of genius. Were this view correct, it would doubtless go far to upset our calculation that, a hundred years hence, he would be deemed deserving of a place in the society of the Immortals. We are aware that, by dint of great good fortune in subject, joined to exquisite skill and care in execution, one or two men have survived, and probably will for ever survive, in some short but well-known composition, to whom genius might and would probably have to be denied. But Lord Lytton clearly does not come in any such category. For, though he wrote with care and finish, there is no one work of his for whose acceptance by Fame he was content to rely upon the mere subject and perfection of style. He puts too much of himself into all his works for that. Bulwer must be judged by all his works taken together, or not at all; since there is no one of them of which it may be said that, if it stood alone, it would even in quality give us an adequate conception of his powers. We must think of him not only not as the writer of this particular novel, but not as merely the writer of novels solely; and the observation might be repeated at each mention of a new class of compositions to the production of which he dedicated himself. It is not an easy thing to bear in mind at one and the same time all his novels, many and various as they are, all his plays, all his essays, all his poems, all his speeches, all his translations. Yet, short of this, there is no chance of doing him justice.

We cannot but think that versatility so amazing as that of this deceased writer in itself constitutes genius. There is, perhaps, no worse reproach to address to a man than to say that he is Jack of all trades and master of none. But Lord Lytton ventured upon every known species of literary composition, and was unquestionably master of all. The success he achieved in any one of them would, of itself, have won for him very considerable distinction. Had he been only a playwright—had he never written anything but 'Richelieu,' the 'Lady of Lyons,' 'Money,' and 'Not so Bad as We Seem,' it can hardly be doubted that the British Stage would not willingly have let his memory die. We might name a fair number of dramatists who have done not as much for the Theatre as Lord Lytton, and absolutely nothing for any other department of literature, but whose works and fame are still alive, and are likely to remain so for no inconsiderable time. Let us keep this fact well in mind, as we pass on to reflect how much Bulwer has done in other walks, cognate, and sometimes superior. The Essay is one of the most charming, the most popular, and the most difficult forms of human composition; and though the men who have attempted it are numerous almost as the sands of the sea, the men who have written essays of enduring delight may be counted on the fingers of one's hands. The qualities requisite for success in this particular species of composition are at once various and rare. In the first place, knowledge of the world, and of the world both in its domestic and its social aspects, is indispensable; and with this knowledge there must be combined two faculties seldom found in unison—warm sympathy and keen discernment, or, in other words, the critical spirit and a due amount of generous enthusiasm. Nor can any one hope to write essays which will commend themselves in the long run to the approval of mankind, unless he conjoin with the masculine characteristics thus briefly indicated the milder and more feminine gifts of tact and delicacy of touch. An essayist, as we have seen, must be strong; but there must be gentleness in his strength. The strength must be quiet strength; subdued, not in reality, but only in outward seeming. To the muscular power of the lion the essayist should unite the lithe and graceful agility of the panther. Forbidden to venture upon what is ordinarily known as action in composition, he has to contrive to inspire each individual sentence with a subtle movement of its own. Style, therefore, is of cardinal importance in an essayist. Without being oratorical, he must be eloquent; without being epigrammatic, he must be pointed and incisive; and whilst imagination proper is not supposed to glitter in his page, he must let his fancy sport, though not too unrestrainedly, through sentences which have to be linked to each other by a sort of suppressed but still efficient reasoning. Furthermore, the exquisite quality of humour must glint amongst even his most solid and stately passages; and just as he is on the point of arousing the reader's scorn or indignation, he must distract him with the suggestion of a tear, or win him from the verge of solemnity by suddenly leading him into the region of charitable smiles. In fact, a perfect essayist must be an accomplished gentleman and comprehensive-minded man of the world.

It was because Bulwer brought all these talents to his desk that his essays are of such remarkable merit and possess so conspicuous a charm. He knew so much; he was so serious; he was so playful; he was so lofty in his own view of life, yet so forgiving of those who could not ascend to such exalted heights; he had so powerful yet so supple an intellect, and was so consummate a master of all those sudden yet appropriate turns which give vitality to writing, and which are nowhere more needed than in the Essay. And, last of all, he had such a care and such a reverence for style. His danger lay in being too ornate, and even to the last he was often betrayed into excessive ornamentation; but, if we except this one defect—and whilst it is almost the least objectionable defect from which a great author can suffer, Bulwer exhibited it to but a limited extent—we may say that his essays are faultless. And in this age of slipshod or affected and extravagant writers, how precious is this quality of clear, lucid, straightforward, gentlemanly composition! We cannot better illustrate our meaning than by quoting one of Joubert's passages on style, already made familiar to many English readers by Mr. Matthew Arnold's paper on that penetrating critic. "It is," says Joubert, "by means of the familiar use of words that style takes hold of the reader and gets possession of him. It is by means of these that great thoughts get currency and pass for true metal, like gold and silver which have had a recognised stamp put upon them. They beget confidence in the man who, in order to make his thoughts more clearly perceived, uses them; for people perceive that such an employment of the language of common human life betokens a man who knows that life and its concerns, and who keeps himself in contact with them. Besides, these words make a style frank and easy. They show that an author has long made the thought or the feeling expressed his mental food; that he has assimilated them and familiarized them, that the most common expressions suffice him in order to express ideas which have become everyday ideas to him by the length of time they have been in his mind. And lastly, what one says in such words looks more true; for, of all the words in use, none are so clear as those which we call common words; and clearness is so eminently one of the characteristics of truth, that often it passes for truth itself. . . . Be profound," he continues, "with clear terms, and not with obscure terms. What is difficult will at last become easy; but as one goes deep into things one must still keep a charm, and one must carry into those dark depths of thought, into which speculation has only recently penetrated, the pure and antique clearness of centuries less learned than ours, but with more light in them."

Golden words! words which every modern writer ought to have by rote, to guard him against the danger of being seduced by that atrocious jargon—that monstrous mixture of obscurity of thought and affectation of expression—which we see employed all around us, and which a gang of semi-illiterate charlatans are trying to pass off for originality. But Bulwer needed no such reminder; he was "profound with clear terms," and therefore, in the eyes of our noisiest critics, he was not profound at all. His essays are always and easily intelligible; therefore, in the opinion of such judges, they are not worth reading, for there can be nothing in them. Being one of those lovers of light who, again in the language of Joubert, "when they have an idea to put forth, brood long ever it first, and wait patiently till it shines," Bulwer is considered by these persons obviously

inferior to those misty writers who are imagined by them to be gods
because their heads are enveloped in cloud. His clearness, brightness, power of shining, are regarded by them as defects, a demonstra-
tion of the commonness of his ideas. Until the world has been rid
once more of all such shallow and pernicious judgments, literary
criticism, however much it may lead the indolent crowd, can only be
viewed by the serious with a feeling something bitterer than contempt,
on account of the mischief which it incessantly works.

Regarded, then, only as an essayist—as the writer of the 'Cax-
tonia,' 'The Student,' and 'England and the English,' Lord Lytton
would have to be assigned a prominent and distinguished place in the
ranks of dead men of letters. But we have to remember that we
were compelled to make the same observation of him, viewed only as a
dramatist. What, then, would have to be our verdict if we regarded
him as essayist and dramatist both, though yet as nothing more?

At that point, however, as every one knows, it is impossible to stop.
Lord Lytton aspired to be a poet, not only in so far as he was a
dramatist and the writer of such plays as 'Richelieu,' but as a poet,
epic, lyrical, didactic, and satirical. We are not sure that his fame
would not have stood higher, at the present moment at least, even
than it does, if he had rigidly abstained from this particular attempt to
widen the field of his literary labours and conquests and thus to extend
the area of his reputation. He is a dramatist, an essayist, an orator,
a novelist, of the first class. He is certainly not a poet of the first
class, and in the higher walks of poetry it must be confessed that he
has failed. Here is his one only failure, but undoubtedly it is a serious
one, and it at present clouds the estimate men form of him. To succeed
in the highest walks of poetry—to succeed as Shakespeare, Milton, and
Byron have succeeded, or even to succeed as Burns, Jonson, Goldsmith, Scott, and Mr. Tennyson have succeeded—is a mighty matter
—is, in fact, to do the greatest thing that can be done in literature.
The best prose comes nowhere near the poetry that is not even the
best. One of the 'Idylls of the King'—or, at least, one of the good
ones—is more highly esteemed than all Macaulay's history and essays
put together, and the 'Deserted Village' is a more precious possession than even Gibbon's 'Decline and Fall.' To be able to produce
great, or even all but great poetry, is considered to argue the possession
of a divine gift, whilst the very best and highest prose is under the
patronage of a purely earthly muse. Lord Lytton's 'King Arthur'
is an ambitious bid for immortality on the score of its being a great
poem; and we can scarcely doubt that the demand will be refused by
posterity as sternly as it has been refused by the noble author's
contemporaries. It is just *not* poetry.

How was this? And can the conclusion be avoided that Bulwer
had not—as one organ of critical opinion, which carries more weight

with the mass of readers than, we must frankly state, it does with us, has roundly asserted he had not—the *mens divinior* of which we have spoken?  It certainly cannot be avoided if we are prepared to affirm that, as far as literary composition is concerned, the *mens divinior* can be attributed to no writers save poets.  Nor should we be disposed to quarrel with those who maintained that this jealous limitation of the phrase involved not only a convenient, but a just distinction.  But what then?  Suppose that Bulwer did not possess the *mens divinior*, is that as much as to say—what the organ we have referred to does in effect assume—that the *mens divinior* and genius are convertible terms, and that, therefore, Bulwer had no genius, but only universal cleverness?  The writer who fails in poetry is no more without genius, to say the least of it, than the writer who has never attempted to succeed; since we never assume in any one the *mens divinior*, and are, indeed, exceedingly exacting and scrutinising when the proofs of it are distinctly offered to us.  Yet such are the prevailing confusions in most people's minds, that we feel sure Lord Lytton stands lower in the estimation of hundreds of people for having written ' King Arthur' than he would have done had he written everything else now known as his, but not written ' King Arthur.'  The conclusion, however, is the absurdest imaginable, and never could be reached by any one whose ideas were not in a hopeless jumble.  Lord Lytton, though in our opinion he has certainly not made good his claim to be regarded specifically as a poet by the production of ' King Arthur,' is unquestionably a greater writer by reason of having produced it than he would have been had he not produced it.  It is not poetry, but it is wonderfully good and in many places picturesque verse, rich in illustration, not devoid of fancy, and testifying to rare powers of language; and instead of detracting from the general merit of all his other works, it necessarily adds something to it.

To be reasonable therefore, even if we regard ' King Arthur' as an absolute failure, we must affirm one of two things—either that no prose writer has genius, or that this one particular failure of Bulwer's does not in the very faintest degree prejudge or affect the question whether he, as a prose writer, possesses it.  That point we will consider directly; but before doing so, we must not fail to point out that, in speaking of ' King Arthur' as though it were the only poetical composition of Lord Lytton's, we have been treating his claims to be regarded as a poet most inadequately, and did so for the moment only because ' King Arthur' is his single absolute failure even in verse, and because we wished to clear away and remove the prejudice which, owing to confusion of thought, attaches to the fact that it is a failure. But how about ' The New Timon,' ' Saint Stephen's,' ' The Lost Tales of Miletus,' and numerous short stories in verse, songs, ballads, and lyrics?  These are by no means failures.  We again concede that none of them manifest that *mens divinior* which we have agreed to restrict to those who show themselves unmistakably, specifically, and distinguishably as poets, as against writers of verse and all prose writers. But it must be remembered that in the bulk of these compositions the distinct poetic faculty, as distinguished from the poetic craft or talent, is not indispensable. A man may be a very considerable satirist in verse, and even write a tolerable didactic or political poem, and yet fall short of being a poet. What we mean may be seen by the fact that many persons—though, it is true, they are not persons of much consequence—have gone so far as to doubt if Pope was a poet; and no doubt passages may be produced from that great writer, which, magnificent as satire, do not attempt even to display the poetic qualities which Pope amply manifests elsewhere. But had Pope been only a satirist and not a poet, he would still have been a great writer, just as, had Byron died after the publication of 'English Bards and Scotch Reviewers,' he would have survived in the annals of English literature, though his position would have been very different from what it is now that he is remembered as the author of 'Manfred,' 'Cain,' and 'Childe Harold.' To put the matter plainly and succinctly, had Bulwer written nothing but 'The New Timon,' 'Saint Stephen's,' and 'The Lost Tales of Miletus,' he would still have had a claim—and the claim would have been conceded—to be long remembered as a distinguished and brilliant English man of letters of the nineteenth century.

Once more, however—it is not only as the writer of those works, as a verse-writer of rare skill and power, that we know him; but as the writer of those works, plus a number of dramas which are likely to keep the stage for an indefinite length of time, plus again a number of essays, whose subjects, treatment, and style will procure for them as long a life as is conceded to one of the most popular forms of human composition. Of how many people can a similar summing-up of work done be predicated? Of how many authors can it be said that their dramas will endure? Of how many, that posterity will embalm their essays? Of how many, that future ages will read their verse with curiosity and pleasure? And that is not the whole question. The real question is, how many authors are there who, singly, have written dramas, essays, and verse, all of which will, for generations to come, be granted an honourable place in the great muster-roll of standard productions? Bulwer has done this, and, as we shall see, considerably more. But even had we to stop here, should we not be forced to feel that we were dealing with a literary name of, at least, all but the highest order?

But we have not yet touched upon the works which, more than all the rest, have conduced to his fame, upon which his chief popularity has been built, into which he has thrown the largest and best part of himself, his knowledge of man and the world, his imagination, his love of beauty, his worship of virtue, his wit, his humour, his playfulness, his enormous, and, as far as Englishmen are concerned, unequalled constructive literary power. And before doing so, it would be to wrong him, were we to leave out of the account those other compositions, many in number, and various in character, which come under no head to which we have as yet alluded, and cannot be classed with the one great category we have yet to mention.

Bulwer, besides being a great essayist, a famous and efficient dramatist, a writer of didactic and satirical poems which will hold their place among English classics as long as the taste for that admirable style of composition endures, was the author likewise of such books as 'England and the English,' 'The Pilgrims of the Rhine,' 'The Coming Race,' 'Translations from Schiller,' 'Translations from Horace,' to say nothing of his brilliant volumes on Athénian history. And this is to say nothing of his speeches, which will bear comparison, when read, with any delivered in our time, and will probably be affirmed by discerning judges to bear the palm away from them all. Who has translated Schiller as well as Lord Lytton? Whose translations of Horace equal his? And all these works are, as it were, his trifles—the mere ornamentation and garnishing of his more ambitious productions. They are light skirmishers, only testifying to the presence of a solid and powerful army of labour and thought behind. But they would of themselves have made the reputation of most other authors. Let us ask ourselves for a moment how many Englishmen there have been in this century whose literary position is greater than it would have been had he been the author merely of the books we have enumerated in this one paragraph—the mere leavings, as it were, of Bulwer's industry and renown. Of no one is it so true as of him that he has constantly eclipsed himself. He seems to have laboured to make us forget one portion of his works by the yet greater brilliancy and fascination of another. We cannot grasp even the idea of so much mental activity all at once. It is this which makes it so difficult to do him justice. As it is, we feel that the reader will almost already have forgotten a considerable portion of the list of triumphs we have been enumerating, though we have as yet named only the smaller half of his successes.

We must hasten to approach them; or even the most liberal allowance of space would find us still lagging behind our subject. Whatever may be the estimate formed of Bulwer by individual or class preferences, by the world at large he is thought of, principally if not exclusively, not as a dramatist, not as an orator, not as an essayist, not as a translator, not as a satirist or writer of brilliant verse, but as a novelist—a novelist of boundless fertility, of infinite resource, of stirring interest, of ever-varying style, a master of prose pathos, prose sentiment, prose humour, a story-teller never wearisome, always pleasing, often delightfully exciting, sometimes lifting one to heights of mental exaltation all but equalling the flights of the poet. Had Bulwer genius as a novelist? To most readers the question will seem absurd; and their answer, their swift, semi-indignant answer, will be, "Why, of course he had. Or if he had not, what novelist has?" Let us make haste to say that we need no convincing on such a point. But there are those who have affirmed, or at least hinted, the contrary; and it is therefore necessary to set them right in a matter on which there never could be any contention, but for those flimsy reasons which people are in the habit of hastily allowing to form the basis of opinions which they wear with all the air of solid conviction.

To state the grounds upon which the quality of genius is denied to Bulwer, is to expose it. He has written, it is said, a great number of novels, interesting, elegant, ingenious, various, and full of motion ; but he has not added to the stock of characters which have become part and parcel of the mental life of the nation. He has not enriched our store of thought by a Falstaff, a Weller, a Becky Sharp, a Mrs. Poyser. To begin with, has he not ? We should have imagined that Uncle Jack was some such personage; and if Englishmen were capable of taking genuine interest in anybody but Englishmen, perhaps Doctor Riccabocca would have served that end for them. A dispute about contested facts, however, is generally a lengthy, a tiresome, and an inconclusive one; and though we by no means concede the fact thus alleged to be such, we will content ourselves with arguing as though it were one. But since when, we should like to ask, has it begun to be true that the one sole test of genius in a writer is the capacity for so limning a character that all the lines and colouring, all the light and shade, all the outside and inside of him, should seem to be as thoroughly well known to you, as though you had lived with him, walked arm in arm with him, confessed him, cross-questioned, and made his will for him. It is a talent, no doubt, to do this; but whether it is a talent of a high order, depends. We can quite conceive a person without a spark of genius doing it, though it is certain that it has been done in some instances by writers of incontestable genius. But has it never occurred to the people who air this theory that, though criticism is by no means a discovery of the nineteenth century, but, on the contrary, nineteenth-century criticism is an opprobrium to it, this particular theory has indeed been hatched very recently indeed? Furthermore, has it ever struck them that this immense admiration of theirs for character-painting, which constitutes the theory, springs rather from a modern and now greatly prevailing curiosity about people's characters, than from any intrinsic value or superiority in the art of painting characters ? It is a trick of mankind to glorify and apotheosise its prevalent conceit. Once on a time the world had a passion for sonnets; and in the opinion of such a world the greatest of mankind were sonneteers. Then a passion for epic poems raged, and if every line could begin with the same letter the preceding one ended with, all the better; and in a community so disposed the sterling man of genius was he who could pile up twenty-four books of high-sounding metre, which has long been silent, and will for ever remain so. Later on, masques were the mania of courts and multitudes; and the writers of masques were assured of an immortality, the term of which has already ended. So are we constituted for the most part. Our tastes are final judges, from which we allow no court of appeal. Men have played just the same conceited trick with their religion, indeed with their God, compounding even the latter of the attributes which happened to be in fashion at the moment; and we all know that to the nineteenth century the notion of any God but a Scientific God is a grovelling superstition. Such are the conclusions infallibly reached by people who live exclusively in their own times, the breath of whose nostrils are its vanities, who can think only its thoughts, and who grow windy on its extravagances. But those who "look before and after," who do not forget that there were many centuries and many modes of thought before the nineteenth century and its modes, and that there will succeed many other centuries and many other modes of thought, smile at such shallow assumptions, and refuse to be infected by this puerile provincialism.

The foregoing reflections will enable any one to judge for himself how very insecure must any conclusion be, formed in this age, which attributes genius in a supereminent degree, much more in an exclusive degree, to those novel writers whose chief distinction is what is called the realistic rendering of character. At most, people should content themselves with saying that the doing so is what interests them most, what they like best, and what gives them the greatest amount of satisfaction. Nobody will quarrel with them for their taste, or dissent from them when they add that character-painting, when it attains such perfection as it reaches sometimes in the hands of George Eliot, is a proof of very high genius indeed. It is only when they rashly assert that the absence of it in a novelist leaves no room for genius, that a sane and sober critic parts company with them, and classes them with the ephemeral partisans who make their personal tastes the groundwork of their literary verdicts.

Much might be written on this subject, and, we will venture to add, much that might be instructive to Englishmen, if they would condescend to read it. This weighing of great writers in our little domestic, class, or clique balances, is the curse of English criticism. Take up some priggish organ of opinion, supposed to be written by gentlemen for gentlemen, and you will there read that it is impossible to read Dickens with any pleasure, because he never describes a gentleman. His stories are all stories of low life, or of low middle-class life, for which no cultivated human being can much care. Take up some sentimental Radical organ, and you will find much the same remarks set down to the account of Bulwer. His heroes are nearly all fine gentlemen, and his heroines nearly all fine ladies. There is an aristocratic flavour about his books which is intolerable. Then turn to some goody-goody exponent of taste, and you will find that Thackeray is a mass of unendurable cynicism, that he is acquainted only with the bad and base side of human nature, and that he is too narrow a writer to win the sympathies of mankind. All of which only means that these various critics have various personal tastes. That is not criticism at all. Criticism must begin by looking at a man's work from precisely the same point of view that he himself looked at it when he conceived and executed it; and if the man's conception was a good one, and the execution worthy of the conception, then the man's work must be praised, whether the critic, personally, happens to like it or not. True, the task of the critic ends not here. He may stop at that point if he chooses, and if he carefully does so no one has a right to blame him. But if he wishes to exercise his function to its full extent, then begins the work of comparison—the work of comparing the production thus accepted and praised with other productions of a similar or of a different character. But the second process is not indispensable, and should on no account be attempted till the first process is completed. Otherwise, the first process will be injured and prejudiced by the very comparisons which constitute the value of the second.

We do not purpose to inquire here, for the requisite space would fail us, though the inquiry would be both interesting and legitimate, whether Bulwer, Dickens, Thackeray, or George Eliot, as novelists, gives proof of the highest genius. We must content ourselves with saying that, merely as a novelist, Bulwer in our opinion shows greater genius than Thackeray, and certainly as much as George Eliot; whilst though he exhibits considerably less than Dickens, it would be a question for consideration whether the greater versatility of Bulwer as a writer, looked at altogether and through the sum total of his works, would not compel us to place him nearer to Dickens in respect of genius than a mere comparison of their respective novels would permit of. We say we must content ourselves with stating the result of the comparison we have made in our mind, and suppressing the process, for which we have no room. But the other and first part of the critic's task we must not pretermit. We must consider Bulwer's works, standing by themselves, without comparison with those of other people—looking at them, as we said, from his own point of view, both of conception and execution. They must be divided into four classes: the domestic, e.g. 'The Caxtons;' the romantic, e.g. 'Night and Morning;' the historical, e.g. 'The Last Days of Pompeii;' and the strictly imaginative, e.g. 'Zanoni.' Now it is idle, not to say childish, to complain that a novel professedly historical is not domestic, or that one obviously intended to be imaginative is not historical. The only proper question to be asked is—Is this novel a good and efficient one of the sort to which it professes to belong? We entertain no doubt whatever that this question, applied to any and every one of Bulwer's novels, must be answered in the affirmative. For any historical, rómantic, or imaginative novel produced by any other hand, we can produce an historical, romantic, or imaginative novel by Bulwer of equal merit; and we are strongly inclined, when thinking of 'The Caxtons,' to make the same assertion as regards domestic novels. But where, we must ask, is the other novelist who can show us four works so excellent, yet at the same time so dissimilar as 'Zanoni,' 'My Novel,' 'The Caxtons,' and 'The Last of the Saxon Kings'? It is not only the number, it is not only the excellence, nor yet is it the number and the excellence; it is the number, excellence, and variety together of Bulwer's novels which make up his claim to the great position we are obliged to concede him. To try everything, and to succeed in everything—surely this is genius, and genius of a very high order. Johnson thought that genius was universal ability accidentally forced in a particular direction. What would he have thought of Bulwer, whose universal ability actually found an outlet through every channel? We shall not pretend to define genius. But we will say that we never heard of a definition of genius under which Bulwer would not be included, and should much like to hear one that excluded him, which did not violate everybody's notion of what genius is.

It follows from what we have already said that, in the opinion of most people now living, the best novels of Bulwer, and those most likely to endure, are his domestic novels; and this view has already found expression in a thoughtful critique of his romances. But the opinion arises only from the fact that domestic novels are at present the fashion, if not the rage. Far be it from us to decry them! We admire them vastly. But our admiration, or anybody's admiration, has very little to do with the matter. What are the works the world least willingly lets die? They are not the domestic works, not the works which delight this generation or that generation. They are the imaginative works, which delight for ever, or the historical works, because they blend what really did happen on the great stage of the world with the imagination, fancy, and narrative power of the author, that have a like faculty of endurance. The more that works of imagination have to do with their own time, unless it be with the *public* aspects, or in other words, with the history of their time, the earlier are they doomed to be forgotten. No age willingly thinks this, but posterity invariably demonstrates it.

We must bring our observations to a close. But before doing so, one more remark must be made. Bulwer has been much criticised for his ideality—realism having in art acquired the ascendant during the last twenty years. Hear a great French critic. "Fiction has no. business to exist unless it is more beautiful than reality. Certainly the monstrosities of fiction may be found in the bookseller's shops; you buy them for a certain number of francs, and you talk of them for a certain number of days; but they have no place in literature. because in literature the one aim of art is the beautiful." We do not mean to say that this passage does not require qualifying, or at least explaining; but it is as close an approximation to the truth as can be stated in so small a compass. Substantially it is true, and must serve here as our defence for Bulwer's almost invariable habit of making fiction "more beautiful than reality." It was Bulwer's generous, high-souled instinct, to try to make everything beautiful, because he had essentially the spirit and the hand of an artist. He beautified life, he beautified men and women, he beautified nature; in a word he laboured to exalt, and if you will, to exaggerate the celestial in us. He worked greatly, and he worked unflaggingly. He died working. He has left behind him a mountain of literary energy, and a name which can never perish as long as men are able to recognise their best benefactors.

## A Dream.

In the cathedral of Eternity—
Wherein high Time holds his imperial reign,
And stars, like mystic torches, burn for ever—
The Queen of Night lay down, to rise no more;
The hum of men was hushed by some cold thought,
They knew not what; the winds rustled and moaned
For sleep in every corner; Night's breath grew thick,
And dark-browed Fancy leapt from wall to wall.
Then aged Time grew listless on his throne;
The mighty sea's innumerable waves
Were heard no longer pacing down the sands.
Then from the wide wastes, from the windows seen,
A fearful step was hurrying—then Death came,
Closing the doors of Life, one after one,
And all Eternity was hushed and still.

KYRIE ELSARDON.

# The City of Lilies.

Twenty years is a short time in the life of a European city: a very short time in the life of so venerable a mother of civilisation as Firenze la bella. And yet within that space of twenty years what changes and chances have befallen the fair old Tuscan capital! These changes, this rapid growth, are the best proof of the vigorous vitality of Florence. She is still a living, breathing organism; no fossil monument of past greatness. She buds and blossoms, loses old leaves and puts forth new, like a deep-rooted plant as she is, sucking food from the century-rich Italian soil, and being healthily nourished by all influences of the universal air and sun.

Twenty years! In twenty years Florence has seen herself twice discrowned of her supremacy as a capital—which supremacy had dated from her earliest records. After the flight of the last grand duke of Tuscany, Leopoldo, of the house of Hapsburg-Lorraine—a feeble figure to close the historic procession of Florentine rulers, yet unstained with the crime and cruelty which smirch most of his predecessors—Tuscany fell into her place as a province of the new Italian kingdom, Florence became merely the chief town of that province, and Turin was nominally the metropolis of Italy. Nominally, I say, because the social influence of Turin never rivalled, never even approached, that of the more central cities of the peninsula. Then came a time when the advancing tide of patriotism and brotherhood swept away more and more of the cunning barriers reared to keep asunder by artifice those whom God and nature had joined together, and the capital of Italy was declared to be Florence. Lastly, as we all know, great Rome has burst her secular shackles, and the soul-stirring words, "Roma, capitale d'Italia," are no longer the faint echo of a mighty past, but the expression of a living present.

And for the City of Lilies herself, how have these changes affected her? Certes they have not passed over her without leaving traces of their passage. And yet in almost all the characteristics which give Florence a peculiar charm, indefinable, but distinctly recognised, she is the same as ever. Nature has bestowed on her a dower whereof she cannot be despoiled; has spread a carpet of fertile fields at her feet, has reared a noble circle of protecting hills around her, and has stretched above her turret-crowned head the royal canopy of an Italian sky. And then the storied memories that throng her streets and palaces! Dante says that the light of the sun makes itself into wine when mingled with the juice of the grape:

> "Vedi il raggio del sol che si fa vino,
> Giunto all' umor che dalla vite cola."

So it has often seemed to me that Florence has been steeped in the light of great minds, which has penetrated the very stones of her streets, until even the ignorant and indifferent are impressed by her with a vague wonder and admiration, and the cultured intellect is aware of a subtle sense of sympathy beyond the mere pleasure in her outward beauty.

Life in the City of Lilies is a smoother business than in any other place with which I am acquainted. You float along with the stream in a soft, lazy, lotos-eating fashion, which has its own perils for the voyager no less than stormy waters have. These perils, however, are chiefly for the young, whose souls cannot be too full of the conviction that—

> "Life is real, life is earnest,
> And the grave is not its goal."

In the sunset hour of our days I know no sweeter spot whence to look back upon the dewy morn and burning noontide of life's pilgrimage.

The lotos-eating has perhaps diminished of late years. Experienced elders will tell you so, at least. Is it that the lotos loses its flavour to the palate of middle life? Thackeray, in one of his delightful ballads, avers, on the contrary, that you must "wait till you come to forty year" before you can appreciate the true worth of many sublunary pleasures. Or is it, perhaps, that the lotos has grown dearer, and is not so easily come by? The truth probably is, that the very circumstances which make in favour of the prosperity of the native population, militate against unlimited lotos-eating on the part of foreign visitors. Energy and enterprise have travelled southward, from rugged Piedmont and from beyond the Alps, into our City of Flowers. Competition and commerce have once more opened their keen eyes in the whilom capital of European finance. Since the days of that eminent banker Filippo Strozzi, the creditor of popes and kings, Florence has nodded through many a sleepy century of comparative stagnation: She is awake now, and her native intelligence will be found equal to most business occasions.

But let not the reader conceive to himself this Italian city as rivaling even our second-rate great towns in the rapidity and activity of their transactions. It is far otherwise. Everything in this world is comparative, and when I speak of business and competition in Florence, I mean something of a far rounder, smoother, more leisurely kind than is suggested to an English ear by those angular words. True, there are fine French-looking shops now in the Via Tornabuoni; shops with plate-glass windows, and gilding, and velvet. Even the excellent and old-established British pharmacy has conformed to the tone of the times so far as to extend its frontage upon the street, and to adorn its windows with large coloured bottles, bright of hue in the gaslight of a winter evening.

The Via Tornabuoni, with its immediate surroundings, the Piazza Santa Trinità, Piazza San Gaetano, &c., is the Florentine version of Regent Street, Pall Mall, and Piccadilly, all in one, with the Mansion House added. There are jewellers' shops whose rich and tasteful wares may vie with any similar display in Europe; there are mercers with a tempting show of silks and laces and other feminine elegancies; there is Doney's Café, as well known to tourists in Italy as Florian's historic establishment on the Piazza di San Marco at Venice; there is *the* Club to stand for all Pall Mall, the grand and ancient Palazzo Strozzi, sternly regarding these modern fopperies from out the jealous windows in its massive walls of hewn stone, and the fine, somewhat modernized Palazzo Corsi. Huge monuments these, of a concentration of family wealth and power, beside which the most splendid mansion in Piccadilly or Park Lane would show slight and small. There is Vieusseux's library and reading-room; and lastly the battlemented walls of the venerable Palazzo del Municipio, the official seat of the syndic and civic powers of Florence, tower up near the bridge of the Holy Trinity, looking southward on to the Arno and the olive-clad slopes beyond, and having its western front and its great entrance on the Piazza Santa Trinità, which is indeed but a continuation of the line of the Via Tornabuoni.

Doubtless in the grand-ducal days, before the revolution of '59, there was less plate glass, less gilding, a milder blaze of jewelry, a smaller and less bustling crowd upon the pavement; and moreover, among all the foreign passers-by there were very few in those days who were not acquainted with the rest, at least by sight. Perhaps one of the best proofs of the progress of Florence towards a metropolitan character, is the fact that it is now possible for an English or American family to pass the whole winter there unknown and unseen by many of their fellow-countrymen. Formerly this was scarcely practicable. Sooner or later everybody met everybody else, if not at one house then at another. Probably things in this respect will go back in some measure to their old conditions in consequence of the removal of the capital to Rome and the exodus from Florence of the diplomatic body, together with the ministries, the houses of legislature, and the government civil servants. The class of visitors attracted to settle in Florence by the presence of these bodies will probably in large numbers follow them to Rome. Florence, however, will never entirely relapse into her former state. Like the Eternal City, and in a more hopeful sense than the poet's "*non è più com' era prima*,"

But leave the tourist-haunted central point near the bridge of Santa Trinità, and come into the remoter streets and places of the town, and you will see how the ancient, picturesque, intensely Tuscan sights and sounds predominate over such surface influences as the fluctuation of foreign colonies and the coming or going of ministers plenipotentiary. It is these fundamental characteristics which give its peculiar attraction to a residence in Florence. The daily routine of life presents itself in a series of dramatic pictures, framed by the historic architecture of such matchless buildings as the Palazzo Vecchio, the Bargello, the Loggia de' Lanzi, the cathedral, and the crowd of grim, massive old fortress-homes, wherein the mediæval citizens of Florence dwelt in patriarchal state, and which they defended to the death against turbulent outbursts of white or black factions, Guelph or Ghibelline. The stranger in Florence has sometimes the odd sensation of looking on at the spectacle of life from a private box. It is as though the whole city were a theatre, got up for the amusement and delectation of the *forestieri.* There is often a sense of unreality about it all, especially to the new-comer. He is received by very courteous officials, and ushered into his box; a bouquet is placed on the velvet ledge; he is furnished with a bill of the performance, and when he wants to go away his carriage is called for him with much bowing and vociferation. They really are extremely amusing and interesting, those lively folks on the stage; and then what a *scenario!* What sky painting, and architectural effects! But one scarcely conceives of them as eating and drinking, marrying and dying—doing, being, and suffering, in dread earnest. Of course the effect produced varies with the nature of the visitor. Some get their spirit borne aloft by the poetry of the performance and surroundings; others merely criticise the toilets of their fellow-spectators, and find the *corps dramatique* very much over-rated.

These transalpine people pass so much of their existence and perform so much of their business in the open air that an observer who should haunt the Piazza della Signoria thoughout one entire day would probably see something of all classes of citizens, from cabinet ministers downward, and witness many phases of city life. The Piazza della Signoria is the very heart of Florence. Here is the Palazzo Vecchio, with its noble and singular tower rising boldly above the roofs of the town; here is the beautiful Loggia de' Lanzi, sheltering its wealth of sculptured forms. On this wide, irregular, paved piazza Savonarola preached and perished. Here, within the twenty years we are considering, stood the long low building used in the grand-ducal days as the post-office, and known as the Tetto de' Pisani, because it was chiefly built by the Pisan prisoners taken in one of the numerous wars waged between the rival republics of Florence and Pisa. The Tetto de' Pisani has disappeared to make way for a very fine building, the upper portion of which is occupied by the well-known Banca Fenzi. The architect of the new building has accomplished the exceedingly difficult task of rearing a structure which, in its style and proportions, does no discredit to the mighty neighbours around it. Those who have seen mediæval Italian architecture will comprehend that to say this, is to say that the artist has achieved a feat of no mean order.

The Piazza della Signoria, in short, was from the earliest times the centre of popular movement, and is still a focus of social, civic, and political life. Let us take a peep at it on a Friday morning. Friday is the day on which the peasants and farmers of the surrounding districts meet in Florence to settle their business, and their place of rendezvous is the Piazza della Signoria. Here bargains are struck, agreements entered into; *fattori* (farm-bailiffs) pay and are paid from voluminous greasy leather pocket-books or undressed calf-skin pouches, full of still greasier tattered and filthy bank-notes. A goodly, broad-shouldered, sun-browned breed of men, these Tuscan rustics; very different from the meagre, pallid, half-fed looking race of towns-people among whom they come on Fridays and *festa* days. The line of demarcation between town and country is a very distinct and easily recognised one in Florence. The pure-bred Florentine looks down upon the *contadino* (peasant) from as lofty a height of self-sufficiency as that from which any boulevard-nurtured Parisian might regard a Berrichon clod-hopper; nor is the *contadino* backward in returning this disdain. Town and country intermarry very rarely, and the *contadino* has quite as much pride in his large-limbed powerful family of strapping sons and daughters, as the city shopkeeper can feel in the acuteness and nimble wit of his own sharp-faced, quick-eyed, somewhat unwholesome-looking brood. Formerly, when Florence was still surrounded by her high walls, the contrast between the urban and rural populations was so sudden and immediate as to be startling. Now, however, the change is more gradual, the real rustics being approached by degrees of boulevard and straggling suburb.

But meanwhile here stand the solid sturdy *contadini* on the great piazza this Friday morning—a difficult mass of humanity to manipulate or remodel; amenable only to the supreme touch of time; slow to change, stubborn to resist; good-humoured, observant, prejudiced, and suspicious to the very marrow of their bones. One characteristic they share with all the agricultural populations whom it has been given to me to observe—namely, a bovine aversion to moving, or to using any of their muscles more than necessity demands. An exception, indeed, must be made for the muscles which move the tongue and jaw. Here their humanity victoriously asserts itself over the dumb lower creatures. Hodge and Dick are usually as slow and heavy of speech as of foot, but Nanni and Gigi will discourse you throughout a long summer's day—fluent, tautological, and proverbial talk—in very choice Italian. There they stand, peasant and *fattore*, small proprietor and rural money-lender, blocking up the king's highway with their massive Dutch-built figures. Your Casentino farmer is apt to be a very portly personage; the citizens seem very poor frail creatures beside him.

The stream of talk flows on in a full murmur, occasionally rising to a pitch of wild excitement in voice and accent, although except the rapidly gesticulating right hand thrown upward and the quick dark eye, no part of the speaker seems stirred in sympathy. Many gods, chiefly Pagan, are appealed to in the course of every bargain, to corroborate assertions or confound counter-assertions; but the superfluous caloric is safely discharged in words. The brutal practicality of a punch on the head is never resorted to; and after listening for a minute or two to a duel of tongues which, it appears to you, must end in manslaughter at the very least, you are relieved and surprised to find that the quarrel is totally appeased by a concession of three *centesimi*, and that the parties are better friends than before.

Here are faces and forms and attitudes which tell how truly the old Tuscan artists reproduced the real beings whom they saw around them. You have Ghirlandajos, Fra Bartolommeos, Lippo Lippis, Andrea del Sartos, by the score. Very few of the peasants are ugly; none, broadly speaking, are awkward. Their gestures are what we are apt to term theatrical—that is to say, they are *intended* to be effective. And there is, undoubtedly, a dramatic instinct in these people which enables them, without taking thought about the matter, to assume *poses* which a painter might copy line for line. Many persons will say that the reason why Southern nations are usually so graceful is their "unconsciousness," and that our insular reserved pride is the fruitful cause of clumsy movements and unpleasing bearing. My observation, on the contrary, would lead me to believe that an Italian is always "conscious," more or less, but that his consciousness by no means embarrasses him as it would an Englishman. I have seen a muddy carter in the street put on a new manner and gait on perceiving that he was observed; but he changed his bearing decidedly for the better. He *liked* to be looked at. That "to attract attention" is a bugbear to the average Englishman is a fact entirely incomprehensible to an Italian. Why should he not attract attention? He has no misgiving that he will not be found to repay any amount of attention. And then one must do the Tuscans the justice to say that they are excellent spectators as well as performers. Their sympathy with the mood of the moment is so quick and subtle that each man is sure of having his *points* taken and his effects understood.

In a curious way too, even in these days of decadence, there lingers among the *basso popolo* a sense and perception of artistic things.    It is like the echo of an almost extinct religion—a dim recognition of the great dethroned idol, Artistic Beauty, which once counted its priests and worshippers by the thousand throughout the length and breadth of little Tuscany.    For example, a common stone-mason, a mere day-labourer, was once employed to assist in placing a large marble vase in a villa garden near Florence, and in discussing the comparative advantages of one or two sites proposed, exclaimed in a tone of conviction, "*Bisogna contentare l'occhio!*"—"The eye must be satisfied." He did not base his recommendation of one spot rather than another on any utilitarian grounds, as an English workman might have done. He did not say "Here the soil is firmer for our foundation," or "The drainage of the water which overflows from the vase will be better from this spot than another."    No; "*Bisogna contentare l'occhio!*"    Beauty was recognised as a desirable and even necessary thing in the placing of an artistic object.

Again, the exterior of this same villa had to be coloured.    The men employed to do it were mere white-washers, or yellow or brown-washers, as the case might be, without the least pretention to be skilled artisans; but they offered their suggestions to the master of the house in just the same way as the stone-mason.    The question to be decided was, the precise tone among various shades of fawn colour which would look best.    One man preferred a very pale wash, pretty enough in itself; but his comrade pointed out to him with considerable eloquence that the house was entirely isolated, was visible from a great number of points in the neighbourhood, and must be viewed against a background of greyish olive trees or sombre ilex.    "From a distance," said he, "that wash would look white against the dark green of the grove. No, no; we want a little warmer tone of colour."    And he was right, and his suggestion was attended to.

Do the artificers employed to paint the outside of gentlemen's villas at Clapham or Richmond look upon their calling in the same spirit? If so, it is to be feared that their eyes are most pitiably afflicted sometimes in the performance of their daily task.

All the world knows that many of the great Tuscan artists sprang from the artisan class.    Indeed in the days of the *Quattrocentisti*, the glorious men of the fifteenth century, the line of demarcation between artist and artisan was by no means a hard and fast one.    The great stone quarries around Florence, at Fiesole, Settignano, and so forth, have been nurseries for sculptors.    Men who handled the coarser stone-cutting tools understandingly—and, let me say, lovingly, for there is no art without love—came to conceive hidden shapes within the massive rugged blocks, and learned to release those imprisoned forms already visible to the eye of imagination, and reveal them, by means of the sculptor's finer chisel, to the gaze of men.

Quite recently, in the quarries of Settignano there worked a man who might have rivalled great names, had the Fates spared him to live longer, or thrown him, whilst he lived, into better hands. Visitors to the monastery of San Marco, in Florence, will remember the striking terra-cotta bust of Savonarola to be seen there. In addition to the merits of force and life-like expression in the face, which are obvious to every one, the connoisseurs find in this bust a singular reproduction of the characteristic handling of mediæval artists. The spirit of the old Tuscan workmen, their realistic fidelity to fact and nature, their unsophisticated sincerity of style, are here presented to us in this work of Bastianini. The man was poor, untaught, unknown; but he had within him a spark of the undoubted Promethean fire which once upon a time blazed up in Tuscany high enough to be a beacon to all the world of Art.

The story of the way in which Bastianini's singular talent first became recognised is well known in Florence. It is also well known in Paris, but to a very much smaller and more select circle. It is briefly this:

Giovanni Bastianini began life as a poor workman. His father had been a mere day-labourer, employed in the stone quarries of Settignano. Our Bastianini dressed like a working-man to the end of his days, although he was a man of singularly good and even cultured manners;—a combination perhaps less rare in Florence than in any other place in the world. But, following the artistic impulse within him, he became a sculptor and had a studio in Florence. He was qualified however in a formal document, by one who knew him well, as "*lo scultore* Giovanni Bastianini *da Fiesole*." (How the epithet reminds one of those spiritual ancestors of his, the Mino da Fiesole, Benedetto da Maiano, Desiderio da Settignano—all cradled like himself among the Tuscan quarries!) Bastianini made busts and figures in terra-cotta. He imitated the only models with which his peculiar talent seems to have been in sympathy, namely, the works of Tuscan sculptors of the fifteenth century. These were his school. But he made no Chinese copies. He worked liked those men because he felt as they felt and saw as they saw. So marvellously, however, did he reproduce their touch and manner, as to win for himself the whimsical honour of being denied to be the author of his own work.

One Freppa, a well-known Florentine dealer in antiquities, towards the end of the year 1863 *ordered* of Bastianini a bust representing Girolamo Benivieni, a famous Tuscan man of letters, who flourished at the end of the fifteenth and beginning of the sixteenth centuries. Having discovered a chance likeness to an *authentic* engraved portrait of Benivieni existing in the national collection, in the person of an old man named Giuseppe Buonaiuti, employed in the government tobacco manufactory, Bastianini used the old workman as a model, and produced a most admirable portrait bust of him in terra-cotta. For this bust Bastianini was paid by Signor Freppa the small sum of three hundred and fifty francs; and as the poor artist afterwards alleged in his own defence, the extreme modicity of the price he obtained exonerates him from all suspicion of wilful imposture in the matter. Imposture, however, there was. Two Parisian dealers saw the bust in Freppa's shop, bought it of him for seven hundred francs (an advance, truly, on the author's price, but still obviously far too small a sum to be asked for a genuine piece of fifteenth century work,) and finally sold it in a great auction at Paris as an undoubted original portrait of Girolamo Benivieni by some contemporary master hand, to the Count de Nieuwerkerke, intendant of the imperial museums of France, for thirteen thousand six hundred francs, and by him it was placed in the collection of the Musée du Louvre, among the masterpieces of the Renaissance period.

So far the affair is not of an unprecedented nature, although the case is a strong one. Dealers have been what the Yankees euphuisti-cally call "smart," and connoisseurs have been deceived before now. But the singular point remains to be told. In the bargain between Freppa and his Parisian customers there was this proviso: that should the bust realise more than a certain sum when disposed of at the great auction a certain proportion of the surplus should be paid over to Signor Freppa. The "certain proportion" was not. forth-coming, despite the very large sum which the bust fetched; Signor Freppa began to talk rather loudly of his wrongs, and in short, the whole transaction became public. The authorities who presided over the Musée du Louvre were informed that they had made a mistake; that the so-called portrait of Benivieni was in reality no antique masterpiece, but the work of a Florentine sculptor and the faithful likeness of an old workman in the Florentine tobacco factory; the imitation of the style of an ancient master was so close, the execution so marvellously forcible and clever, that the best judges might be excused for having been deceived. Whereupon the authorities in question—acknowledged their error, and vented a good deal of natural indignation on the Parisian dealers, Messieurs Nolivos and Rivet, who had taken them in? By no means. Why, that would have been to confess themselves fallible! *Que diable!* Their course was a much more energetic one. They simply denounced Freppa *and Bastianini* as wretched impostors, who, in order to profit by the extraordinary price obtained for the Benivieni bust, had set on foot a " Florentine intrigue," wherein (it should seem) a vast number of persons conspired to foist a lie on the public of Paris in general and the directors of the Louvre in particular.

The witnesses to the fact of Bastianini being the real author of the bust were in truth as numerous and unanimous as a chorus at the opera. Documents, duly signed and legally attested in presence of the then chief magistrates of Florence, setting forth that Giovanni Bastianini had been *seen* to make the portrait of Benevieni, are extant, and may be consulted by any who choose to search them out. Most of them have been published in a little work in French, by Dr. Foresi of Florence, called 'La Tour de Babel.' There is the testimony of the firm from whom Bastianini bought the clay for his model, and in whose factory the bust was baked when finished. There is a paper signed by eight and twenty workmen of the tobacco manufactory, testifying to the fact that the Benivieni bust was really a portrait of their comrade Giuseppe Buonaiuti, and they had all distinctly recognised his lineaments in it. There are certificates from painters, sculptors, merchants, dealers, agents of exchange, and others, well known in Florence, to the same effect, and solemnly attesting, in some cases that they had seen Giovanni Bastianini at work with his model before him. Lastly there was a statement of Freppa, couched in no doubtful terms, and the indignant asseveration of the artist himself that he had really done his own work. But all would not do. The Parisian authorities scouted the idea that they could under any circumstances have made a mistake, and the Parisian press followed suit. Article after article was printed in the leading journals of Paris, denouncing " the well-known impostor and forger Bastianini " with all that vituperative eloquence in which our neighbours so highly excel. Some went so far as to deny Bastianini's existence altogether. Like Betsy Prig, when driven to bay, they " didn't believe there was no such a person." Still the bust of Girolamo Benivieni remained as a tangible fact. *Somebody* had modelled it, that was clear; and one journalist, in the enthusiam of his art-erudition, very nearly decided on Benedetto da Maiano (who flourished between 1442 and 1498) as the author of the bust, but finally is indulgent enough to allow his readers to choose among a group of "anonymous scholars of Verrocchio"; and adds in an inspired tone, that the work so resembles a drawing of the painter Lorenzo di Credi as to make one fancy that that great artist " was behind the chair of the unknown modeller of the Benivieni, encouraging him by his words, and perhaps adding example to precept." (!) Of course in the face of such flights as these fact and common sense stood but a poor chance of prevailing. It is now generally acknowledged (except in the Musée du Louvre, which seems, like the Vatican, to have promulgated the dogma of its own infallibility,) that Bastianini was as much the author of the portrait of Benivieni as of the bust of Savonarola which is exhibited at San Marco. Both are remarkable works of a peculiar genius, and both testify to the lineal artistic descent of Giovanni Bastianini *da Fiesole* from those great ones whom I have pointed out as his spiritual ancestors.

Poor Bastianini died at the age of thirty-five, and I have given here the outline of his story because it illustrates what has been said above of the subtle way in which the power and the worship of art still linger amidst the true Tuscan *popolo.*

We all remember Steele's fine compliment to a lady, that to know her was a liberal education: almost it may be said of fair Florence that to know *her* is an artistic education. Pass between the arcades of the Uffizi, and look from side to side at the statues of great Tuscans, which bear dumb witness, in their marble niches, to her vanished glories. The list of mighty ones is amazing in its extent and variety. With pen, pencil, and chisel, they have created for us whole realms of beauty, and like their countrymen, the marvellous Genoese, have bequeathed to mankind the knowledge of new and wonderful worlds, none the less precious because we do not find them on the map.

Turn we now from the noise of the city, from the clatter of horses' hoofs over the flat stone pavements, from the loud discordant cries of itinerant vendors, from the clatter of loungers before the café doors and the shrill whoopings of the ubiquitous street-boy, whose leading characteristics are, I am ready to lay a good wager, essentially the same in every big town, "from China to Peru"—turn we from all this, and let us mount the hill to hoar Etruscan Fiesole. The ascent is a long and somewhat fatiguing one to limbs of flesh and blood, despite the goodness of the new road thither; but we are cumbered with no such weight to carry. We journey in the spirit, and shall be aloft ere sunset.

We will approach the hill of Fiesole from the rear, so that the grand view thence—Arnowards—may burst upon us at once in its entirety: See those Cyclopean walls slowly slowly crumbling to decay, yet owing more of their ruin to the hand of man than to the touch of time! They were built by that mysterious Etruscan people, to whose dim antiquity our mediæval records are things of yesterday. The ivy and clematis overgrow the mighty blocks of stone, and nestle in their mortarless crevices. The meadow running steeply down the slope beyond is green with springing wheat, and spangled with dainty wild flowers of all hues that the sun shines upon. A remembered verse flits swiftly into one's brain and sings there. It seems to be written in bright characters upon the meadow:

> " And Phœbus 'gins arise
> His steeds to water at those springs
> On chaliced flowers that lies."

Surely here be those chaliced flowers! And yonder trickles the silver stream, meet to slake the thirst of the god's fiery coursers. But Phœbus has nearly run his race. The west is glowing. Let us gain

the piazza—the great, irregular, open place of Fiesole, where stand
her Palazzo del Commune and ancient Duomo.  If we enter the
church, there is yet light enough to see Mino da Fiesole's two exquisite works—the tomb of Bishop Salutati, surmounted by his bust,
and the lovely Madonna, in the bas-relief over the altar in the same
chapel.  What a celestial grace and beauty in this group!  The Madonna seems to have drunk in pure goodness, as a flower drinks dew,
and to be steeped in it.  Higher rises the rosy flush upon the sombre
wall.  Come! whilst yet the level rays illuminate the landscape;
step forth and look, leaning on yon low parapet wall, upon the wide
Val d'Arno!

O heavens! how beautiful it is!  Far as the eye can see, the poet-
praised river winds along beneath us.  Through fields where stands
the hoary olive, knee-deep in wheat, and where the blossoming vine
hangs its perfumed wreaths from branch to branch, or hides the bare
stem which supports it in a pyramid of luxuriant foliage; past margins vivid with the rank Tuscan grass, where cream-coloured oxen
bow their patient necks beneath the yoke, and drag home the creaking
wain, heavy with fresh-cut hay; past the feet of swelling hills, velvety
with rich groves of ilex, or girdled with grey olives, and crowned
with the memorial cypress black and still against the evening sky;
past solid stone-built farm-house and homestead; past reaches fringed
with tall reeds, or edged with a dreary waste of brown alluvial mud
which the fierce mountain torrents have dragged down from the
treeless Apennine—past these and many another scene, old Arno
flows into the heart of the City of Lilies.  There she lies, far beneath
us—Firenze la bella—the central glory even of this lovely scene!
Close at our feet the sloping terrace gardens break away steeply.  Rose,
and oleander, and camellia, and magnolia, and a thousand more familiar
plants—either in leaf or flower or blossom—are heaped together with
a soul-satisfying lavishness, and lead the eye down, by soft degrees of
beauty, to where the spires and turrets of Florence seem to prick the
crystal sky.  Supreme in reposeful majesty, the great dome of the
cathedral shows its giant curves above all compeers.  There is a sense
of "peace, good-will toward men," in those perfect lines; and close
at hand rises, straight and slender, Giotto's bell-tower—beautiful as
an expiring soul.  A more eager and earthly ambition is expressed by
the wondrous tower of the Palazzo Vecchio, flinging itself into the air
from the battlemented walls of the building, and throwing out, midway
in its height, a daring buttress to support a further flight, as though
one vaulting tower had leaped upon another's shoulders!  There are
Santa Croce, with its dazzling marble front; Santa Maria Novella;
the dome of the Medicean chapel of San Lorenzo; the square, lofty
mass of Or San Michele; the ancient tower of the Bargello, and
(besides a multitude more towers and churches) the singularly

picturesque city gateways, with their massive archways and time-embrowned stonework.  Across the river, the old gate of San Niccolo is one of the most striking of these monuments of a time when Florence was girt with walls as with a girdle.  Behind it rises the hill of San Miniato, with its beautiful basilica, and the cypress-shadowed Franciscan church of San Salvatore del Monte.  There is not a foot of Arno's banks, as the river flows through Florence, which is not rich in storied memories; the attempt to enumerate even a few of the most interesting would bewilder us; let us only look and be thankful.  See how the Ponte Vecchio—the old jeweller's bridge—shows quaint and old-world above the stream.  Beneath its arches the water—for the most part turbid and dull enough—has caught a ruby tint from the sinking sun.  From this distance all the city, save those loftier structures we have noticed, seems melting in a golden haze.  There is a press of red roofs, like a thronging crowd on a holiday, jostling each other, around the great centres, such as the Piazza del Duomo and della Signoria.  There swings a bridge, like a thread, from shore to shore, and yonder is the fresh green line of the Cascine woods, running westward.  All around—upon the plain, the lower slopes, and even the higher eminences—are strewn fair villas and palaces, showing like white pebbles dropped among the gardens of the Val d'Arno.  Away—away the silent stream flows westward towards Pisa, and the sun is sinking, sinking that way too.  There is a glory as of molten gold in the heavens, and splashes of dazzling brightness gild one long horizontal line of cloud above the sun.  Little fleecy cloudlets fleck the opposite sky, and are tinged with a divine rose colour.

Close before us little sparks begin to flit to and fro under the dark bowering shrubs; these are the fire-flies, showing their pulsing lamps. Hark!  From the thicket, amongst that tangle of roses and evergreens, comes the sound of the first nightingale, beginning her even-song with that low, chinking, silver sound I love; and all at once the blaze of glory is gone from the sky, and Hesperus comes forth and quivers alone above the City of Lilies!

# A Vagabond Heroine.

## By MRS. EDWARDES,

### AUTHOR OF 'ARCHIE LOVELL,' 'OUGHT WE TO VISIT HER?' &c.

---

## CHAPTER IV.

### WHAT MEN CALL LOVE.

ROSE spoke of the romance of two young lives, of love sacrificed to duty, of a heart slowly breaking during a dozen years. This we may set down as the poetic form of the story about herself and Roger. Now let us have it in the prose.

And in the first place I would remark, that if Roger Temple's heart has been breaking during the length of time Rose imagines, either it must have been an extraordinarily tough heart when first the process was set up, or the process itself is one that slightly affects a man's outward strength and health. He is a well-knit, handsome-looking fellow; a little sallow, perhaps, like most men whose digestions have been too long tried by climate and curry, and with a touch of Indian listlessness in his English honest blue eyes. But as to heart-break—wasting in despair—moral dyspepsia of any kind!—ask his brother officers, the comrades who know him best, what man in the regiment they would consider the most absolutely free from all such disorders, and ten to one the answer will be, "Roger Temple." A first-rate shot, a bold rider, a capital fellow at the bivouac or mess-table—these are the things you will hear respecting Roger among men. And as regards softer matters? Oh, well, flirtation and young ladies are not very much in old Roger's line. If marriage is fated to overtake him, if the best fellow on earth is fated to be spoilt, it will have to be done by a *coup de main*. Roger might not have the heart to say no to a very pretty woman, if she asked him outright to marry her; but he would certainly never have energy to undertake the preliminaries of courtship himself.

Thus the coarse indiscriminative voice of his fellow-men. How account for the discrepancy?

You remember Holmes's fancy as to the three distinct personalities to be found in every man? First, the man himself, the real veritable Thomas. Second, Thomas's ideal Thomas. Third, the ideal Thomas of Thomas's friends. To these I would add, the ideal Thomas of Thomas's mistress; a man in love, judged with a woman's power of judging, from a woman's stand-point, being a human being as totally strange to the poor fellow's male friends and acquaintance as to his own consciousness.

The story, in the prose form, is simply this. Rose, married in her girlhood to an elderly London lawyer (with whom, as an absolute nonentity, the conventional husband of a charming wife, this little history has no concern,)—Rose, early married, and launched into a narrow circle of dull professional respectability, was, at six and twenty, as really fresh and ingenuous a young person as ever breathed. Neither perruquier nor Bond Street chemist needed then. Her flaxen hair, smoothly braided according to the fashion of the day, adorned her youthful face. Her complexion, innocent of cosmetics, was, in spite of some few freckles, like a just opened dog rose. Same order of intellect, same depth of heart as now; no knowledge of the world, save of her own little Pharisaical Bloomsbury Square world; small scope for vanity, less for sentiment. So Roger Temple met and loved her.

The Indian Mutiny was just over at that time, and Roger, a fair-faced boy of nineteen, had come back, wounded, after his first dark taste of soldier's work, to England. He made Rose Shelmadeane's acquaintance at an East London dinner-party, to which a family lawyer of the Temples, or other unimportant agent, had led him; made her acquaintance, sat opposite to her at table, and, not knowing, till dessert at least, that she was the crown and blessing of another man's life already, conceived for her as wild a passion as ever foolish lad conceived for still more foolish woman since the world began.

The London season was at its height; even Rose's humdrum life enlivened by an unwonted share of parties, theatre-going, drives in the park, visits to the Zoological—country cousins, who must be amused, staying in the house. Roger saw her, dogged her, worshipped her, everywhere. One of the country cousins being female and unmarried, it might be assumed that Mr. Temple's attentions were honourably matrimonial. Mr. Temple being well-born, young, handsome, of good expectations, was it not a manifest duty to afford him encouragement?

Thus Rose, with small platitudes, stifled her small conscience for a fortnight or so. Then the end came; the end to the prologue, not the play.

Watching the hippopotamus together one July Sunday afternoon at the Zoological, the country cousins, the nonentity of a husband, all but within earshot, young Master Roger made a fool of himself; in stammering passionate whispers told Mrs. Shelmadeane a secret which Mrs. Shelmadeane had been calmly aware of for some time past, but which it was shocking—oh, unendurably shocking!—even to think of, the moment the confession happened to find its way into words.

She walked away from him, her fair young matron face ablaze, and, with the air of a new Cornelia, laid her hand upon her husband's arm. Three evenings later, Rose—twenty-six, remember, Roger nineteen—

was waltzing with him at a ball, to which duty bade her chaperon her country cousins, at the Hanover Square Rooms.

Mr. Temple had been wicked—so wicked that it really took one's breath away to think of it—in daring to regard her, an honoured wife, save with feelings of iciest respect and esteem. But then Rose, gentle soul, felt constrained to pity the poor misguided fellow—to lead him, if it might be, into better ways. And that Bloomsbury Square life and husband of hers, illumined by present experience, were so hideously monotonous; and the homage of a man, handsome, young, distinguished, like Roger, was so honey-sweet to vanity. And then think how the papers had spoken of Mr. Temple's bravery in India; think of all the horrid Sepoys he must have killed; his arm still in that interesting black sling! What could Ro-e do but accord the lad the friendship for which he pleaded, and agree to forget that fatal, erring, not altogether charmless moment, when they watched the hippopotamus together at the Zoo?

A better woman, or a worse one, a woman inspired by imagination or guided by experience, might have been terrified at such a position. Good, passionless, unimaginative, self-saturated Rose, the first little cold shock of the plunge over, felt no terror at all. What she did feel strongest, I think, (when one can disinter it, sufficiently for analysis, from the mass of small vanities, triumphs before partnerless country cousins, et cetera, in which it was embedded,) was—gratified sense of power.

"Scratch a slave's skin, you find a tyrant underneath." Rose, like some other millions of her sisters, had been a slave from her birth, first as a girl then as a wife—I speak of moral servitude, of course. All at once she found herself in the position of a ruler; and she used her new prerogative as human beings who are not to power born are apt to use it.

The young fellow gave up for her his time, his friends, his pleasures; gave up for her his life; and received in return—what? Sermons; a soiled white glove or two; and enough half-dead flowers—he has some of these in his possession still—to fill a respectable herbarium.

By degrees the story got known, not in Rose's starched Bloomsbury Square circle, but among Roger Temple's bachelor friends, most of whom, indeed, contrived to gain a glimpse of Mrs. Shelmadeane. Heavens! what a common-place dowdy little mortal poor Roger's divinity was pronounced to be by men not, like himself, under the glamour of passion! Pretty, if you will; the kind of red-and-white stupid beauty you will meet a dozen times a day in any provincial town; but nothing, positively nothing, more. And Roger of all others, with his fastidious tastes, his high-flown boyish ideal of feminine grace and refinement, to have lost his senses about this little Bloomsbury Square prude! Roger, to whom half the best houses in town stood open, upon whom good and handsome and well-born women by the score would have smiled, had he so chosen!

The infatuation lasted out the London season. Then old Shelmadeane carried his wife off to Margate, tardily suspicious, perhaps, as to the kind of sacrifice she was making to duty; and Roger's leave of absence came to an end. He was angry, bitter, sick of heart; his divinity, during their last interview, having sermonised and sympathised, and altogether tortured him beyond measure; determined to return to India without seeing her again, determined to despise, to forget her. He determined all this; likelier than not, would have carried it into execution to the letter—at nineteen so much is possible to the human heart—had Mrs. Shelmadeane been willing. But Mrs. Shelmadeane was very far indeed from willing.

She was (I make the statement advisedly, unconditionally, so as not to have to go over the same ground again), both now and hereafter, one of the most rigidly virtuous women, as far as conduct goes, that ever breathed. She was not, certainly at that early period of her life, in any ordinary sense of the word, a coquette. But she loved her new taste of power with all the faculties for loving nature had bestowed upon her; and for no consideration, short of saving her soul from actual transgression, would have given her slave back his freedom. He must look forward to nothing; not even to the day when he might legitimately claim her hand. She would feel herself—oh, dear! the guiltiest of creatures if she could encourage anybody to look forward with hope to anybody else's death. What is such hope, Rosie would say, piously shaking her blonde head, but another kind of murder? Mr. Temple must look forward to nothing in the future, must ask for nothing in the present; must always remember, please, that she was married to a man whose *moral worth* she respected, always speak and act as if Mr. Shelmadeane were present. But whether he remained in England, or whether he went back to India, Roger Temple must not regain his freedom.

She wrapped up her feelings, even to her own soul, in the very prettiest tinsel-paper of all hypocrisy's store. To let that poor boy depart in his present frame of mind would be to let him depart desperate. He might even go and marry some Dreadful Creature, in revenge, as men with blighted affections have been known to do, and she would have the burthen on her conscience. Who should say what effect a perfect reconciliation, a few solemn sisterly words at parting, might have upon all the poor young fellow's future career?

And she wrote to him, a sweet little plaintive kind of note, in her school-girl hand, with her school-girl phrases—that, also, Roger Temple keeps still!

Accidentally Mr. Shelmadeane had heard in the City that Mr. Roger Temple was going back to India at once. Surely he did not

mean to start without bidding his sincerest friends and well-wishers
adieu? They had gone to Margate for change, and Margate was
rather dull, Rosie confesséd ingenuously; but Mr. Shelmadeane, on
the whole, complained less of his gout, so she must be grateful. And
they dined at six. And Mr. Shelmadeane was always at home, except
on Mondays and Tuesdays. When would Mr. Temple come?

Neither on a Monday nor a Tuesday, as some older men, versed in
the world's ways, might, after the receipt of such a note, have ventured upon doing. For no personal gratification would young Roger
have abused the angelic, child-like simplicity of the woman he loved.
Honourably, Quixotically, on a day when he was certain of finding the
husband at home, he went down to Margate; and for the last time
held Mrs. Shelmadeane's white hand in his.

What a parting scene it was to him! Dinner first—with the old
lawyer prosing politics and grumbling over the dressing of his turbot,
his wife with her girlish innocent face smiling nuptial smiles at him
across the table. Then the dessert—torture of tortures—when Rosie
insisted upon leaving her husband and "his" friend alone. Finally,
the half hour's stroll on the beach, "just to smoke *one last* cigar
with poor Mr. Shelmadeane," said Rosie, a tremor, discernible to Roger
if to no one else, in her soft voice. For about three minutes out of
this half hour—divinest, cruellest moments Roger's young life had
experienced—chance willed that they should be alone; and in these
their farewells were spoken—a madness of farewells, among the Margate
bathing-machines. And then old Shelmadeane pounced down upon
them: "A quarter to nine, sir. Unless you mean to miss your train,
you must be off." And for a dozen shifting fateful years they saw
each other's faces no more.

Long letters passed betwen them, with or without Mr. Shelmadeane's
knowledge—I refrain from speaking with certainty on this point; but
letters, certainly, that Mr. Shelmadeane, or any one else in the world,
might have read with safety. Rosie, indeed, half thought, at times,
that her victim repressed all allusion to his tortures too successfully.
Every mail, every second mail, at first; then once in three or four
months; then twice a year. So the correspondence attending
Roger's ill-starred passion was carried on. At last Mr. Shelmadeane
died.

And Roger Temple, of course, flew to England to put in first claim
for the possession of his beloved one's hand? No; Roger Temple
did nothing of the kind. He was away up the country, pig-sticking,
when the letter containing the news of Rosie's widowhood reached
him, after some delay. And he loved sport passionately; and the
two or three men who formed the party happened to be his closest
friends. And must not weeds be worn a decent time before they are
replaced by wedding favours? Considering Rosie's fine propriety of

sentiment, her highly-strung shrinking nature, could a man dare
. . . . Well, 'twas a curious little imbroglio altogether, highly
illustrative of human weakness in the matter of attainable and unat-
tainable desires. But our business at present being rather with
the chronicling of fact than the dissection of feeling or motive, I
proceed.

Roger neither rushed to England nor wrote any letter designed to
compromise his Rosie's newly-gained liberty. It must be remembered
that he had now been wasting in despair during a good many years;
also that men get into the habit of everything, even hopeless passion,
and, against their better reason, may feel disturbed by having to
abandon a settled mode of thought. Like the proverbial Frenchman
who exclaims, when, after a lifetime's separation, he is about to be
lawfully united to the woman he loves, " But what shall I do with my
evenings?" Roger Temple, on old Shelmadeane's death, might have
been tempted to ask himself, " But what shall I do with my despair?"

"The greatest charm of a married woman," says a spiteful
dramatist, " is invariably—her husband."

When Roger's foolish lips first stammered their secret in the Zoological Gardens or trembled out their mad farewells upon the Margate
beach it would have been hard to convince him that Mrs. Shelmadeane's
greatest charm was Mr. Shelmadeane. But time sharpens many an
epigram that seems pointless to us in our youth.

He wrote the widow as exquisitely delicate a letter of condolence
as was ever penned; putting himself, and his own selfish hopes and
fears, utterly away in the background; dwelling wholly on her and
on her loss. He spoke tenderly, but with vagueness, of the long years
of their separation; he spoke with greater vagueness still of the day
of their possible reunion. Of marriage, of anything that could by
possibility be construed into a hint of marriage, he spoke not a
word.

An ordinarily intelligent woman, before she had read such a letter
to the end, would have known that her lover's love for her was over.
Rose, guided by the irrefragable logic of folly, deduced from it only a
new proof of her slave's devotion.

"There is one, far distant, who adores me, but who is too high-
souled, too generous, to think of anything but my grief!" she would
say to Major O'Shea, who obtained an introduction to the pretty
widow, and indeed set steadily to work love-making, before her crape
was six weeks old. " Ah, Major O'Shea, if you had only the con-
scientiousness, the noble, forbearing, unselfish nature of that poor
fellow in India!"

And then Cornelius would respond to the effect of his heart being
stronger than his reason, of his impetuous feelings (he was nearer
fifty than forty at the time, and had been in love after one fashion or

another since he wore jackets) his impetuous feelings hurrying him beyond the cold bounds of conventional decorum. And the widow would sigh and blush and wipe a tear or two, and call him a sad, sad man, as she yielded her hand to be kissed. And the upshot of it all was, that the next news Roger Temple got of Rose Shelmadeane was a flowery announcement in the *Times* of her infidelity to him—by special license, an archdeacon and three or four of the lesser clergy assisting, at St. George's, Hanover Square.

Singular perversity of men's nature! The news of this marriage cost him not only the most poignant jealousy; but a revival of his love in all its first fresh ardour. The existence of a husband, of any husband, seemed really some necessary mysterious condition of Roger Temple's passion. You should have seen the letter of good wishes that he wrote the bride; bitterest veiled reproach discernible through every courteous phrase, every pleasant little congratulatory message to Major O'Shea! Rosie cried herself almost plain for the day after receiving it, hid it jealously from Cornelius; to whose philosophic mind the whole matter, you may be sure, would have been one of profoundest indifference; and wrote Roger a pleading self-extenuating reply by return of mail with three violets—ah, did Captain Temple remember the bunches of violets he used to bring her during the *happy days* of their friendship in Bloomsbury Square?—enclosed.

And Captain Temple, Rose has had his own word for it since, kissed violets and letter both, and set up the writer on the old pedestal in his imagination—I was very nearly writing his heart—that she had ever held.

As Roger himself stands, hat in hand, all this time, awaiting Belinda's reception of him, we will have done in as few words as possible with retrospect of the love story. Some slight insight into Rose's domestic grievances, as Mrs. O'Shea, the reader has had already; we need not further enlarge upon them. Cornelius spent her money, neglected her, went to America, where his fate awaited him. And Rose, on her Uncle Robert's death, found herself once more free —free, and with a handsome little income, villa at Brompton, plate, linen and accessories at her own disposal.

And then it was that she and her old lover looked again upon each other's faces. Roger had returned to England unexpected by his friends, his long leave having been given him some months earlier than he anticipated; and on a certain May night, Rose at that moment believing him to be thousands of miles away in India, knocked at the door of the Brompton villa and inquired, in a voice whose accents he vainly strove to command, if Mrs. O'Shea was at home.

It was late for a visit of ceremony, between ten and eleven o'clock, and the starched looking butler of occasion who answered his knock informed him pompously that "Mrs. O'Shea was at home, but not visible to strangers. Mrs. O'Shea had had company to dinner, and "——

"Mrs. O'Shea will see me," interrupted Roger. "You need not even announce me. I am expected."

And in another minute he found himself among the wax-lights and guests and brand-new gilding and upholstery of Rose's drawing-room.

He slipped in, unannounced, as he desired, and looked round the assemblage in vain for Rose. Seven or eight women, of quasi-fashion, bare-shouldered, jewelled, flower-bedecked, were present. He looked among them in vain for the modest face and smoothly-braided blonde head of Rose Shelmadeane.

At last a fluffy-haired, brilliantly complexioned—alas, that I must write it !—middle-aged lady, came forward to him and bowed : a lady extremely overdrest or undrest, as you like to term it. "I am not aware that I have the honour "—she began, looking at him strangely.

And then he knew her voice.

Poor Rose, if she could have seen into her quondam lover's heart just at that moment !

He watched her during the next hour or so, with feelings about equally balanced of disappointment and blank surprise.

Every woman's good looks must decline after the lapse of the twelve best years of her maturity, and Rose's had really, in the common acceptation of the phrase, "worn well." But it was not any fading due to age ; it was not Time's natural footprints on cheek or brow that shocked him thus : it was the absolute startling *transformation* of her whole personality !

Soberest, most dove-like of young matrons at twenty-six, Rose, a dozen years later, had developed into the very friskiest of mature syrens, all her girlish promise of silliness ripened into a bounteous harvest of meridional folly. The lint-white smooth-braided locks were copper-gold now, frizzled high in wondrous monstrous pyramids above her head, with outlying curls and puffs and chignons that defy description. The faint rose-bloom complexion had become definite pearl and carmine, the pale eyebrows grown dark ; the eyes, not wholly innocent of belladonna, were a little fixed and hard ; the decorous half-high dress of the old Bloomsbury Square days was replaced by—well, by the drapery of a Greek statue.

Roger, who had lived so long away from London, did not know that this is the received way in which the modern English matron of re-pute "grows old gracefully," and, as I said, gazed at poor Rose's full-blown charms with a sensation curiously blent of amazement and repulsion—a sensation, let me add, of which he was himself heartily ashamed.

This lasted till the departure of Rose's guests left them alone ;

then, hearing more of the old, sweet, appealing voice—no meretricious change had affected that—and his eyes, it may be, growing accustomed to the outward plastering of his ruined idol, Roger's heart got softer.

He had not really dined, Mrs. O'Shea discovered—had arrived in London late that afternoon, and forgetful of bodily sustenance, had rushed away to call on her at once. So a little supper was organised, accompanied by a bottle of Uncle Robert's best champagne. And then this man and woman, who had played at love so long, began looking into each other's eyes, to talk of all that they had suffered (in imagination or reality) since they parted; and the cruel intervening years faded away. They were whispering beside the hippopotamus; they were murmuring farewells upon the Margate beach again; and by-and-by Rose's hand, youthful and white still, found its way into Captain Temple's. It trembled; he pressed it to reassure her. Rose, with a sigh, made a feint of moving away, and then, for the first time in their lives, their lips met—and Roger's fate was sealed.

The wax lights had burnt low by now, and Rose kept her face well in shadow—nay, hid it bashfully out of sight on her lover's breast. And when he kissed her beautiful golden hair it never occurred to him to think from what dead head it might have been sheared; and when at last she lifted up her face to falter out softest promises of life-long truth, he did not even see the deposit of rice-powder it had left upon his waistcoat.

Who loves cavils not; and Roger Temple, or Roger's Temple's imagination, loved, during this hour's intoxication, at least.

What he thought and felt next morning, when he had to review his position and Mrs. O'Shea's complexion by daylight, none but Roger Temple ever knew.

He was not, it must be borne in mind, a ladies' man, had associated little with women during the later years of his life, had studied them less; and his reverence for the whole sex was extreme, based rather on ideal foundations, indeed, than on fact. If sometimes the sense of his mistake galled him, if sometimes he felt the shame inseparable from the position of a lover who loves not, you may be sure that Rose and the world never found it out. Rosie loved him! What matters some disparity of years if a woman's affections be young? When the fruit after which a man has longed for years drops between his lips at last, has he a right to complain because time has somewhat over-mellowed its flavour?

So Roger would fain argue himself into good conceit with his bargain—so reconcile his heart to the attainment of its fondest desires.

And still, at times, his spirit is heavy laden; still, through rouge and bismuth and pearl-powder, old age *will* peer out at him from the face of his betrothed, and turn his heart cold.

"You really grow more and more foolish every day you live, my dear Roger!" Rose will remark, prettily conscious of her own charms, as she meets his gaze. "What can it be, I wonder, that makes you look at me as you do?"

"The years of our separation, my love," is invariably Roger's answer. "I have to make up now, remember, for the dozen years during which I never saw your face."

And Rose, promptly satisfied by any appeal to vanity, asks no more.

## CHAPTER V.

### COMPLIMENTS, NOT CARESSES.

BELINDA'S eyes have met Roger's, and, in spite of all her foregone jealous resolves, the girl finds it hard to steal herself against Rose's future husband. Never in her whole vagabond loveless life has such honest human sunshine shone on her as shines now in Roger Temple's smile.

"I don't know about falling in love, but I am sure Belinda and I mean to be friends, Rosie," he says, advancing. "Do we not, my dear?"

And before Belinda can find time to put herself on guard Captain Temple's bronzed moustache has touched her cheek. It is the kind of salutation that could scarce, by the very iciest prude, be stigmatised as a kiss, and yet it bears a sufficiently marked family resemblance to one to be unpleasant exceedingly, in Rose's sight.

"I—I—really, Roger, Belinda looks so ridiculously younger than she is!"

"Not a bit," cries Roger; and now he rests his hand kindly on the little girl's shoulder. "Belinda is fifteen years old—you told me, did you not, that she was fifteen? Well, and she looks it. Don't mind Rosie, Belinda. Rosie turns rusty at the thought of having a grown-up daughter."

"I shall be seventeen the week after next," says Belinda, holding up her chin. "I don't know what people mean by taking me for a child. I have certainly seen enough of the world and its wickedness to make me *feel* old," she adds, with the accustomed hard little rebellious ring in her voice.

"Belinda will look different—I trust Belinda will look totally different when she is properly dressed," says the widow, glancing down at her own elegantly flowing draperies. "I must really have a serious talk with Miss Burke about these short skirts."

"Ah! but Miss Burke is not here to be talked with, Rosie," cries Belinda, bent, it would seem, on disclosing every obnoxious truth she can hit upon. "My natural guide and protector has been away in

Spain a week or more, collecting facts for her book, and I am knocking about alone, as you see me—me and my dog Costa."

"Alone!" stammers Rose, shocked not so much at the fact itself as at having the fact exposed before Roger. " You don't mean actually alone, my dear ?"

"Well, no; I have my chums, of course—the fellows who were with me in the street when you arrived. Now, Rose," she goes on pitilessly, " tell the truth. Were you, or were you not, ashamed when you first saw me ?"

"I—I was surprised, Belinda," says Rose, in her sweetest little feminine treble. " It is not usual in England, you know, to see a girl of seventeen wearing her dress above her ankles; and then those fearful —what must I call them, Belinda ? What do they call those fearful door-mat things you have on your feet ?"

"They call those fearful things alpargetas in Spanish, espadrilles in French," answers Belinda, coolly holding out a ragged sandalled foot for inspection. " If you played paume on the hot sand for hours together as I do, you would be glad to wear espadrilles, Rose; yes, or to go bare-foot altogether, as I do oftener than not."

A blush of burning shame rises over the widow's face. She has made a good deal of small capital, one way or another, out of Belinda's high birth, to Roger, who is somewhat unduly sensitive about his future wife's connections generally. The Earl of Liskeard's grand-daughter—so like all the Vansittart family—without being regularly pretty—a great air of breeding, of distinction, about our poor little Belinda, et cetera. And now to find her—what?—ragged, dirty, with the speech and manner (this is Rose's verdict, not mine,) of a charity-school child, and mentioning, actually mentioning before a gentleman, the indelicate word "bare-foot."

"Our dear Belinda wants a year or two of sound English training," she remarks, in a tone that to Roger sounds dove-like, but that Belinda remembers and interprets only too well. " That is the worst of Continental education. One has to sacrifice so many good solid English qualities for accomplishments. Still, in these days a girl *must* be accomplished. A couple of years in a select English boarding-school will, I have no doubt, render Belinda all that our fondest wishes could desire."

Belinda, on the conclusion of this little tirade, looks hard into her stepmother's eyes for a moment or two; then, shouldering her schistera, she moves across to the door.

"I must be off, Rosie," turning and bestowing a nod full of caustic meaning on the lovers. " And unless you want me to join some gang of wandering Gipsy players, as I have often thought of doing, you had better not talk about boarding-schools any more. My accomplishments, Captain Temple!" looking with an air of mock modesty at Roger. " Rose talks of my accomplishments, for which the 'good solid English qualities' have been sacrificed. I will tell you what they are, and you shall say which I am best suited for—a booth in a Basque fair or a select English boarding-school. Paume playing—'tis the same game, Mr. Jones tells me, as your English fives; paume," checking off each "accomplishment" on her dark slim fingers as she proceeds; "bolero dancing; a tolerable acquaintance with slang in four languages "——

"Belinda!"

"Oh, let me finish the list, Rose! ˗ Let me make the best of myself that I can in Captain Temple's eyes. Bolero dancing, slang, paume—of each a little. Knowledge, learnt practically, of how to keep myself and my dog, on twenty sous a day board wages; and a taste for bull-fights so strong—oh, so strong!"—this with unaffected enthusiasm—"that I would sooner go without meat for a fortnight and church for a year, than miss the chance of going to one. For further particulars, apply to Mr. Augustus Jones."

And so exit Belinda, whistling—yes, Rose, whistling!—keep from fainting if you can—as she goes.

"A quaint little original, our future daughter," says Roger, whose eyes have certainly opened wider during the conclusion of Belinda's tirade; "but a good-hearted child, I'll be bound. You must not be too hard on her, Rose."

"I hard!" sighs the widow, looking at him reproachfully. "When was I ever hard on any one? If you knew, Roger—but of course men never understand these things—the trial that poor girl has always been! I can assure you, I look upon Belinda as a Chastise-ment, sent to me for some wise purpose by Providence."

She seats herself on a sofa, discreetly away in the half-light, and with an air of resignation takes out her pocket-handkerchief. "I have made sacrifices no real mother would have made for her—can I ever forget the *devoted blind* attachment of her dear papa for me?—sending her away, Heaven knows at what expense, to the Con-tinent, and always writing that she should have the best of masters and everything; and now this is the result! How painfully plain she is!"

"Plain? No, Rosie, anything but plain. Belinda is just at that awkward age when one does not know what to make of girls, and her dress is not quite like other eo le's, is it? But she has magnificent eyes and a pretty hand "——p p

"A pretty hand! Belinda's hands pretty! Why, they are enor-mous—six and three-quarters at least, two sizes bigger than mine; and as brown! But you think every one you see lovely, Roger," says Rose, pettishly. "I declare one might just as well be ugly oneself. I have never heard you speak of any woman yet that you could not find something to admire in her "——

"And all because of you, my dearest!" cries Captain Temple, with warmth. "When a man admires one woman supremely, can you not imagine that every other woman—yes, even the plainest—must possess something fair in his sight, for her sake?"

He comes across to her, stoops, and rests his hand on his betrothed's fair head. It is a favourite action of Roger's, and one that Rose would be exceedingly well pleased to see him abandon. Who can tell what horrible trick postiche or plait may not play one in some unguarded moment of more than common tenderness?

"Oh, Roger, how can you?" She shifts a little uneasily from his touch. "Really, you get sillier and sillier every day." It is a fixed idea of the widow's that Roger Temple's feelings for her are precisely of the same irrepressible and rapturous nature as they were when he was a boy of nineteen; a happy fixed idea, lightening Roger's courtship more than he wots of. "Lucky, I am sure, that Belinda is gone. Do you know, I was so afraid you would say or do something *embarrassing* before her. How do I look, Roger, dear? Tired and hideous, don't I? Now, I insist upon you telling me the truth."

"How do I look, Roger, dear?" is the burden ever of their love scenes. Compliments, not caresses, are what Rose's heart of hearts yearns for; and Roger, after the past few weeks' apprenticeship, finds it no very difficult task to frame them. To have to pay compliments to the same woman during six or eight hours of every consecutive day would, in most cases, be a tolerably severe strain on a man's imaginative faculty. Rose, who is absolutely without imagination herself, requires the exercise of none in others. A parrot gets no more wearied with its own eternal "Pretty Poll," than does poor Rosie of the eternal pointless stereotyped commonplaces of flattery.

"You look charming, Rose. I never saw you look better. Your eyes are as bright "—— Roger does not find a simile come readily to his hand, but Rose is content to take his good intentions on trust. "And your dress—all these lavender frills, and this white lace! Rosie, how is it that you always manage to wear prettier dresses than any other woman in the world?"

He must have asked her the same question, on a moderate calculation, about two hundred times since they were first engaged. At this moment he knows how often he has asked it, and the precise flutter of denial and little bewitching foolish laugh with which Rosie will respond. And he sighs; if he had courage to relieve his soul in the way nature prompted, would yawn. Terrible point in a love affair when we have learnt to disguise a yawn under a sigh! Terrible point in a love affair when we have learnt to disguise anything!

"I shall be quite unhappy about my dresses if they do not arrive soon," Rose goes on presently. "Ten large cases, you remember "—does not Roger remember those awful ten cases well—in Paris, Bordeaux, everywhere?—"and a bit of blue ribbon on each. There can be no mistake, if the railway people are honest—but abroad one never knows. I'm sure nothing would have been easier than for Belinda to run back to the station; still, she did not offer, and in my delicate position, as a stepmother, I have never required the slightest attention from the poor girl. Oh, Roger"—Rose's hand is in her lover's now and he is beside her on the sofa—"if I dared, how much I should like to tell you a secret—something we are all concerned in!"

Roger's natural reply is, what should prevent her telling it? Ought there to be any secret, present or to come, between persons whose lives, like theirs, are to be spent in one long delightful confidence?

"Well, then—I'm a very naughty girl, I know," Rose avows, kittenishly, "and I daresay you will scold me sadly; but I've been matchmaking. It is not quite by accident that Mr. Augustus Jones is in St. Jean de Luz."

"Accident or no accident, the fact is a deuced unpleasant one," remarks Captain Temple. "How or why Mr. Jones came here is Mr. Jones's own concern; but the bore of having to encounter him! I really did hope, Rose, that we had seen the last of that atrocious man when we left London."

"You are prejudiced against him, sir. I'm afraid you don't like poor Augustus because he was a little too attentive to me."

"Rose!"

"Oh, come, Roger, I know what your ruling passion is, and always has been. The green-eyed monster, sir"——

"Rosie, I swear"——

"Well, we cannot help these things, my dear. I am ridiculously without jealousy myself. Poor Major O'Shea often said he wished he could see me a little *more* jealous, but I can make every allowance for it in others. I ought, I am sure," adds Rose, with a reminiscent sigh, "I ought to be able to bear all the jealous suspiciousness of men's natures after the experience I have had."

There is silence for a minute, and any one watching Roger Temple's face attentively might discover there a good deal the look of a man who is trying to repress his weariness under the perpetual exacting babble of a child. "I don't think you judge of me quite correctly, Rose," he remarks, after a time. "Who ever judges another correctly? Who can read but by his own light? We were talking of Mr. Jones, were we not? Ah, yes. And you think me jealous of Jones? So be it, my dear. Poor little Rosie!" He bends forward and salutes the widow's cheek tenderly, I may almost say fearfully. Roger is better acquainted with feminine weakness, as regards rice powder especially, than he was on that first fatal night at Brompton. "And now what about this grand secret of yours? You have been matchmaking, have you? I hope you don't mean to marry our little daughter Belinda to Mr. Augustus Jones?"

"He would be an extremely nice husband for her, from a worldly point of view," says Rose, turning over and over the diamond—a gift of Roger's—that rests on her plump third finger; "and as to education, old Mr. Jones was sensible of his own deficiencies, and had his son coached up by the most expensive tutors. Any one hearing Augustus talk would say that he was quite well educated enough, for a moneyed man."

"And presentable enough, refined enough?—the sort of husband a girl could not only love, but be proud of? Well, Rosie, manage it as you choose. If you like Mr. Jones, and if Belinda likes Mr. Jones, you may be sure I shall not forbid the banns."

"Ah! there is the difficulty. Belinda does not like Mr. Jones. Belinda and I have never liked the same thing or person yet." Poor Rosie! If the mantle of prophecy could but fall upon her shoulders at this moment! "But you could help me so much, dear, if you would—and you will, I know"—upraising her eyes coaxingly to her lover's. "You will help me in my plans for Belinda's happiness? It was all through me, Roger—don't be cross with me if I confess the truth—it was all through me that Mr. Jones came to St. Jean de Luz."

"Through you that Mr. Jones came to St. Jean de Luz! And why should I be cross with you, you little goose?"

Rosie talks like a girl of sixteen: Roger treats her like a girl of sixteen; yet is sensible, mournfully sensible ever, of the grotesqueness of so doing.

"You see, I knew that Augustus was anxious to marry. I suspected—feared," says Rose, with modest grace, "that his hopes *in some directions* might have been just a little blighted; and the thought struck me—as he was going abroad and had asked me to plan his tour for him—the thought struck me to bring him and Belinda together. What he wants is, connection; what she wants is, money"——

"But Belinda is a child still," interrupts Roger Temple. "You are building all these castles in the air, dear kind little soul that you are, Rosie, for her good; but the thing is ridiculous. Belinda's home must be with us for the next three or four years; ample time then to begin matchmaking. How could a child of her age possibly decide?" goes on honest Roger. "How could an innocent-hearted child of Belinda's age decide whether she ought or ought not to sell herself for the carriage-horses and diamonds of a snob like Jones?"

"Roger, my dear," answers Rosie, in her sweetest, most angelic tones—whenever she is annoyed, Mrs. O'Shea's angelic proclivities become more marked—"excuse me if I tell you that all those romantic ideas about 'selling oneself' are out of date. Belinda never was a child. Belinda has not one youthful sentiment belonging to her; and as to innocence, poor thing! you heard what she said about bull-fights. Do you think," says the widow, "*I* could go to a bull-fight without fainting? Those fine interesting looking fellows in such danger, and the horrid bulls goring everybody! I'm sure to see a picture, to read a description of one, is sickening enough."

"A matter of custom and nerve, Rosie. I have known some Englishwomen capable of worse cruelty than being present at a bull-fight."

"And the very best thing for the girl's safety and our peace of mind will be to get her respectably settled as quickly as possible. My own opinion of Belinda—I would say so to no one but you, Roger— is, that she is without heart; and a woman without heart "——

But the generalisation is opportunely cut short by the arrival of the boxes and blue ribbons. In her joy over her recovered finery Rosie forgets all other human considerations; and her lover, with orders only to smoke one cigar and to be back at the post of duty in an hour at latest, recovers a breathing space of liberty.

2 κ 2

# Edward Wortley Montagu.

## By Dr. DORAN, F.S.A.

LADY MARY PIERREPONT, when she wrote to Mr. Wortley touching the death of his sister, said she had lost what she loved most, and could thenceforth only love those who were nearest and dearest to her departed friend. Out of this hint, it may be, came the marriage of Lady Mary and Mr. Wortley. It seemed a disinterested match on both sides, but it was not fruitful in happiness. Of this union were born a son and daughter; the mother reserved all her love for the latter.

The son was born in May, 1713. Within two months from that date Lady Mary had left her firstborn to mercenary, but perhaps efficient and kindly care. In July she wrote to her husband, "I heard from your little boy yesterday, who is in good health." In that phrase, so cold in its unmotherly temper, may perhaps be found the cause why that "little boy" became so wayward, and why he developed into a man so wilful and so irreclaimable. In 1717 the boy was taken by his parents to Constantinople, where Mr. Wortley acted, for a few months, as English representative. On the return from this embassy, Lady Mary tarried for a while at Belgrade. At that time the smallpox was a deadly scourge in England. In Turkey it was less mortal. The infidel Turk anticipated and modified the disease by inoculation. Lady Mary had the courage to submit her child to the novel system of "engrafting," as it was called. In a letter written at Belgrade in March 1718 she says: "The boy was engrafted last Tuesday, and is at this time singing and playing, very impatient for his supper. I pray God my next may give as good an account of him." For society at large the step which Lady Mary took was most beneficial; but few mothers, however courageous, would have had the heart, in a foreign land too, to suffer such an experiment to be made on an only son, not yet five years of age. She had, however, full confidence in the efficacy of the proceeding: and she remarked that she would have imparted the matter to the doctors generally, only that they were too selfish to sanction a course which would diminish their incomes!

In the following year commenced the daring escapades of this young gentleman. In 1719 he became a Westminster Scholar. Within six months he was missing from the school, and his friends had such knowledge of his tastes that they searched for him in the lowest purlieus of London. They sought for this mere child in vain; till after some time a Mr. Forster and a servant of Mr. Wortley, being in the neighbourhood of Blackwall, heard a boy crying " Fish !"  The voice was familiar, the boy, on being seen, was recognised, and his master, a fisherman, to whom the child—so it is said—had bound himself to help to sell the fish which they had caught together, parted from him with a regret that was felt on both sides.  The truant was reinstated at school, if not at home, but in a brief time the bird was flown and left no trace behind him.  A year or two, perhaps more, had elapsed when the Quaker captain of a ship trading to Oporto, and the British consul in that city, were looking at a young fellow driving some laden asses from the vineyards through the city gates.  The captain saw in the lad a sailor who had come on board in the Thames, and run away from his ship on its arrival at Oporto.  He had gone up country and found employment, although he was ignorant of the language.  The consul knew him in his real personality, and the adventurous hero was shipped for home, where he was kept not so strictly as if the keepers would be sorry at his again escaping.  Edward Wortley took a convenient opportunity to do so, and when he was next recognised he was acting diligently, as he had always done, this time as a common sailor in the Mediterranean.  There was the making of a hero in this resolute boy, if he had only been allowed to follow his inclinations.  On the contrary, he was exiled to the West Indies, with Forster to attend him as teacher and guardian.  They spent several years there ; and the boy, who preferred to battle with and for life, to spending it in ease and luxury, had nothing to do but study the classics, which he did, as he did most things, with energy and a certain success.  How he failed, or neglected to leave Forster in the lurch, is not explained.  Neither do we know anything of his actual life after his return to England, for many years.  Had he been left at sea, Edward Wortley would probably have distinguished himself.  As it was he abused life, but only as other " young sparks " did in England ; and he filled up the measure of his offences by marrying a handsome honest laundress, older than himself, of whom he got tired in a few weeks.  A small annuity reconciled her to living comfortably by herself.  After this, all is dark, and we cannot come again upon the trail but by the help of Lady Mary's letters.

There are few references made to her son by Lady Mary, except in letters to her husband when she was living abroad, ranging from 1741 to 1752.  In a letter from Genoa, in 1741, she regrets having to bring before her husband " so disagreeable a subject as our son."  The son was then anxious to procure a dissolution of his marriage with the laundress, but the laundress was a decent woman, living a blameless life, and she could defy Parliament to pass an Act annulling her marriage, even if the father had been willing to help the son to such purpose, which he was not.  The mother was unmotherly severe on the son. "Time," she writes, "has no effect, and it's impossible to convince him of his true situation." The son. then passed by an assumed name. The name being mentioned to Lady Mary by a stranger, with reference to the responsibility of the bearer of it, she replied, "the person was, to my knowledge, not worth a groat, which was all I thought proper to say on the subject."

In 1742 this "fool of quality" was now wandering, now tarrying, on the Continent, under the name of M. de Durand. In the June of that year his mother encountered him, and passed two days with him at Valence, an ancient city on the Rhone. In various letters to her husband, she speaks of "our son" as altered almost beyond recognition, with beauty gone, a look of age not warranted by his years, and, though submissive, with an increase of the old wildness in his eyes that shocked her, as it suggested some fatal termination. He had grown fat, but was still genteel and agreeably polite. She was charmed with his fluently-expressed French, but she noted a general volubility, yet without enthusiasm, of speech, which inconsiderate people took for wit ; and a weakness of understanding and of purpose, exposing him to be led by more resolute spirits. "With his head," she says, "I believe it is possible to make him a monk one day and a Turk three days after." Flattering and insinuating, he caught the favour of strangers, "but," says the not too-indulgent lady, "he began to talk to me in the usual silly cant I have so often heard from him, which I shortened by telling him I desired not to be troubled with it ; and that the only thing that could give me hopes of good conduct was regularity and truth." She credited him with "a super-ficial universal knowledge," as the result of what he had seen. His acquaintance with modern languages was undoubted, but she did not believe that he knew Arabic and Hebrew. He promised to proceed to Flanders, and there wait his father's orders ; adding, that he would keep secret the interview with his mother ; but M. de Durand, " rode straight to Montélimart, where he told at the Assembly that he came into this country purely on my orders . . . talking much of my kind-ness to him, and insinuating that he had another name, much more considerable than that he appeared with."

Edward Wortley was in England in the early part of the above year. In the latter part he went to Holland, where he resided, a sort of prisoner at large, by desire of his father, who allowed him a small income on condition of submission to the paternal will. "I hear," wrote Lady Mary, "he avoided coming near the sharpers, and is grown a good manager of his money. I incline to think he will, for the future, avoid thieves and other persons of good credit." When persons of really "good credit" spoke well of him, as Lord Carteret did, the mother rather doubted than accepted the testimony. " When-ever," she wrote to her husband, "he kept much company, it would be right to get him confined, to prevent his going to the pillory or the gallows;" and she described his excuses for his conduct as "those of murderers and robbers!" Young Wortley was desirous of joining the army in Flanders; his mother doubted his sincerity, and insisted that he should go as a volunteer. If his father bought him a commission, she was sure it would be "pawned or sold in a twelvemonth." Whether as volunteer or commissioned officer, he did serve in Flanders. No news to grieve a parent's heart came thence; upon which circumstance Lady Mary wrote to her husband in 1744: "I think it is an ill sign you have had no letters from Sir John Cope concerning him. I have no doubt he would be glad to commend his conduct if there were any room for it;" and she was inclined to blame the father for over-indulgence to his son. She had no sympathy even for the amiable weaknesses of the latter; and yet she was so sentimentally affected by the tragedy of ' George Barnwell,' the rascal hero of which murders his real uncle in order to gratify the rapacity of a harlot, that she said, whoever could read the story or see the play without crying, deserved to be hanged.

Edward Wortley's countrymen did not think so ill of Lady Mary's son; for in 1747 the electors of Huntingdonshire returned him, with Mr. Coulson Fellowes, member for the county. He was a silent but highly respectable member. In the year 1748 Mr. Wortley, the father, wrote to his wife some pleasant news he had heard of their son. The mother coldly replied, " I should be extremely pleased if I could depend on Lord Sandwich's account of our son. As I am wholly unacquainted with him I cannot judge how far he may be either deceived or interested." This singular mother cultivated her antipathies rather than her sympathies. The father seems to have considered his paternal duty was discharged by, wisely perhaps, keeping his son on a small allowance. The son lived as if he had already his inheritance in hand, and for a year or two he found society in London quite to his mind.

Among the ladies who figured on the Mall by day, who drew crowds around them at Vauxhall by night, and who were never out of the ' Scandalous Chronicle' of the period, was " the Pollard Ashe," as she was called. This miniature beauty was in some measure a mysterious individual. She was the daughter of a high personage, it was said, and such affinity was all she had to boast of in the way of family. In the June of 1750, Walpole thus wrote of her to George Montagu:

"I had a card from Lady Caroline Petersham, to go with her to Vauxhall. I went accordingly to her house, and found her and the little Ashe . . . they had just finished their last layer of red, and looked as handsome as crimson could make them. *. . . We issued into the Mall to assemble our company, which was all the town. . . . . We mustered the

Duke of Kingston, Lord March" (the old Second Duke of Queensbury of later years)," Mr. Whitehead, a pretty Miss Beauclerc, and a very foolish Miss Sparro. . . . We got into the best order we could, and marched to our barge, with a boat of French horns attending and little Ashe singing. We paraded some time up the river, and at last debarked at Vauxhall. . . . A Mrs. Lloyd, seeing the two girls following Lady Petersham and Miss Ashe, said aloud, 'Poor girls! I am sorry to see them in such bad company!' Miss Sparre, who desired nothing so much as the fun of seeing a duel—a thing which, though she is fifteen, she has never been so lucky to see—took due pains to make Lord March resent this . . . but he laughed her out of this charming frolic.   Here we picked up Lord Granby . . . very drunk. . . . . He would fain have made love to Miss Beauclerc, who is very modest; and did not know what to do at all with his whispers or his hands.   He then addressed himself to the Sparre, who was very well disposed to receive both. . . . At last, we assembled in our booth, Lady Caroline in our front, with the vizor of her hat erect, and looking gloriously jolly and handsome. . . . We turned some chicken into a china dish, which Lady Caroline stewed over a lamp, with three pats of butter and a flagon of water, stirring, and rattling, and laughing, and were every minute expecting to have the dish fly about our ears. . . . The whole air of our party was sufficient to take up the whole attention of the garden. . . . It was three o'clock before we got home."

Very early in the year 1751 our hero made love to Miss Ashe, and at the same time appeared in public as the first "macaroni" of the day, but with science and philosophy enough to render him worthy of being taken into brotherhood by the Royal Society.   On the 9th of February, 1751, Walpole writes:

" Our greatest miracle is Lady Mary Wortley's son, whose adventures have made so much noise; his parts are not proportionate, but his expense is incredible.   His father scarce allows him anything, yet he plays, dresses, diamonds himself, even to distinct shoe-buckles for a frock, and has more snuff-boxes than would suffice a Chinese idol with a hundred noses.   But the most curious part of his dress, which he has brought from Paris, is an iron wig; you literally would not know it from hair; I believe it is on this account that the Royal Society have just chosen him of their body."

His father, however, made no complaint of his son in his letters to his wife.   The anxious mother invariably concluded that when nothing was said there was something to be dreaded.   Accordingly, in a letter to her husband, dated May 1751, Lady Mary writes:

(24th May, 1751.)  " I can no longer resist the desire I have to know what is become of my son.   I have long suppressed it, from a belief that, if there was anything good to be told, you would not fail to give me the pleasure of hearing it.   I find it now grows so much upon me, that whatever I am to know, I think it would be easier for me to support than the anxiety I suffer from my doubts.   I beg to be informed, and prepare myself for the worst with all the philosophy I have."

Her son was not in such a desperate condition as his mother supposed.   The new Fellow of the Royal Society was simply making love to " the Pollard Ashe." In the summer of this year, 1751, Vaux-hall and the Mall missed her; but the world knew very well whither she had wended, and with whom. In September 1751 Mrs. Elizabeth Montagu wrote to her husband : " Young Wortley is gone to France with Miss Ashe. He is certainly a gentleman of infinite vivacity; but methinks he might as well have deferred this exploit till the death of his father." Walpole wrote to Mann that " Wortley, who, you know, has been a perfect Gil Blas, is thought to have added the famous Miss Ashe to the number of his wives."

While London was busy with the story of the elopement of Miss Ashe with Edward Wortley Montagu, and this rather airy couple were on their amorous way to Paris, there was a young Mr. Roberts, not yet quite twenty-one years of age, sojourning at the *Hôtel d'Orléans* in that city, with a Miss Rose for a companion, Miss Rose's sister for a friend, and various servants to wait on all three. Roberts lived like a *milor*, and he gave out that he was about to make the grand tour to Italy and back. Montagu's quarters were at the *Hôtel de Saxe*. Roberts was a stranger to him, but Montagu not only called upon the wealthy traveller, on the 23rd of September, but sent him an invita-tion to dinner. The company consisted of Roberts, Lord Southwell, Mr. Taafe, M.P., and Montagu, who was also a member of the House of Commons. After coffee the party adjourned to Montagu's room. Taafe produced dice and proposed play. Roberts declined, on the ground of being without money ; but this and other pleas were overruled, and, " flustered with wine," which he said he had been made to drink, he sat down to tempt fortune. Fortune used this gambler ill; when he rose to return to his hotel he had lost 870 louis d'ors—400 to Taafe, 350 to Southwell, and 120 to Montagu. Taafe speedily demanded the amount he had won, and not finding it forthcoming, the British legislator, with Lord Southwell, broke into his room about midnight, and under dreadful threats, made with swords drawn, com-pelled him to give drafts for the entire sum. The crafty Roberts, however, however, drew upon bankers with whom he had no effects; and, probably that he might be out of reach of arrest till he could give an explanation, he hurriedly set off for Lyons.

The bird had just flown when the three more fortunate gamblers, their drafts having been dishonoured, forcibly entered Roberts's rooms and rifled them of everything valuable—a large sum in gold and silver, a very valuable assortment of jewelry and precious stones, and the two Miss Roses. There was 40,000 livres' worth in all, not in-cluding the sisters. One of these ladies consented with alacrity to accompany Mr. Taafe, with his other booty, to his quarters at the *Hôtel de Pérou.* The sister went thither also, for society's sake, and after a three days' sojourn Taafe kissed their hands and sent them to England under the guardianship of another gentleman.

Perfect tranquillity prevailed among those who remained in Paris, but on Sunday night, the 25th of October, just before one o'clock, as Montagu was stepping into bed with, as he says, "that security that ought to attend innocence," a commissary of police, backed by an armed force, entered his room, and, despite all protest, carried him off to the Châtelet. Before they locked him up for the night, the gaolers would scarcely utter a word save a rough one, and he could not get even a cup of water. The night was cold, and a small bit of candle enabled him the better to see the horrors of his cell. "The walls were scrawled over," he says in the memoir he published, "with the vows and prayers of the vilest malefactors before they went to the axe or the gibbet." Under one of the inscriptions were these words: "These verses were written by the priest who was hanged and burned, in the year 1717, for stealing a chalice of the Holy Sacrament."

On the 2nd of November the charge made by Roberts—namely, that Montagu's party had made him half drunk, the better to cheat him at dice, and had subsequently plundered his rooms—was made known to him. "I answered," he says, "in a manner that ought to have cleared my own innocence, and to have covered my antagonist with confusion." But he was remanded to prison. Some amelioration of his condition was permitted and he was allowed to be visited. Consequently it was the fashion to go and look at him, but the solaces of his friends could not compensate for the cruel wit, jeers, and sarcasms cast at him by curious strangers. Influential persons interested themselves in this notorious case. The English ambassador interfered with effect. The king, on being moved, replied that he could not meddle in a private case; but a king can do many things without appearing to meddle. The charge was again looked into, and the method of examination may be seen in the result. The sentence of the court, delivered on the 25th of January, 1752, was to the effect that the accused be discharged; that Roberts be compelled to confess the accusation to be false, also to pay 20,000 livres damages to Montagu and Taafe; and pay all the costs of suit on both sides, including the expense of publishing the judgment. '

As soon as Montagu was free, he published a memoir, explanatory and defensive. It was not so much a denial as an evasion. It was made up of assertions that he had "never deviated from the sentiments and conduct of a man of honour"; that regard ought to be had to "the probability of the charges, the rank of the accused, and the character of the prosecutor;" that he was of "distinguished condition," and that his accuser was infamous in character and inconsistent in his evidence; that Lord Albemarle, the English ambassador, had told him that he was as convinced of his innocence as he was of his own. Montagu protested that the whole thing was a conspiracy "against his Honour and Person," at the head of which was the so-called

Roberts, whom he had discovered to be a fraudulent bankrupt Jew,. Payba by name, who had fled from England to avoid the gallows. Montagu acknowledged that he had invited this "infamous bankrupt" to dinner, but that, instead of winning 120 louis d'ors of him, he had formerly lent that sum to the Jew, who had " trumped up this story in order to evade payment." He had made the first call on the *soi-disant* Mr. Roberts, taking him for a man of fashion, and it was the custom for the last comer to make such calls in his neighbourhood, and not to wait to be called upon; and the visit having been returned the invitation to dinner naturally followed. As to playing after dinner, Montagu does not deny it; but he says that the imputation of playing with loaded dice filled him with horror. The conclusion of the so-named defence is that, as the judgment of the court was so completely in favour of Montagu and Taafe, the innocence of those two gentlemen was perfectly established.

Before we see if this was exactly the case, let us see what was thought of the affair in England. The public press barely alluded to the scandal, and were not at all grieved at the locking up of a couple of British senators in a French prison. Private individuals noticed the scandal in their letters.

In October 1751 Mrs. Montagu wrote to Gilbert West some details of the gambling affair and its consequences. She described the offence of Montagu and Taafe as " playing with a Jew at Pharaoh, with too much *finesse*."

"*Finesse*," she adds, " is a pretty improvement in modern life and modern language. It is something people may do without being hanged, and speak of without being challenged. It is a point just beyond fair skill and just short of downright knavery; but as the medium is ever hard to hit, the very professors of finesse do sometimes deviate into paths that lead to prisons and the galleys, and such is the case of those unhappy heroes. The Speaker of the House of Commons will be grieved to see two illustrious senators chained at the ignoble oar. The King of France has. been applied to, but says he does not interpose in private matters. So how it will go with them no one can tell. In the meantime, poor Miss Ashe weeps like the forsaken Ariadne on a foreign shore."

The conduct of Edward Wortley in England was noticed by his. father, in a letter to Lady Mary, who, replying to it in a letter from Louveres (November 10, 1751,) when the Paris scandal was known, says : " I will not make any reflections on the conduct of the person you mention; 'tis a subject too melancholy to us both. I am of opinion. that tallying at bassette is a certain revenue (even without cheating) to those who can get constant punters and are able to submit to the drudgery of it; but I never knew any one pursue it long and preserve a tolerable reputation." Therewith, the mother dismissed further notice of her wayward son, to talk of an old woman at the baths of Louveres, who in her hundredth year had recovered sight, teeth,.

and hair, and who had died ten years later, not of age, but of tumbling
down a stone staircase; something like the apocryphal Countess of
Desmond—

"Who lived to the age of a hundred and ten.
And died of a fall from a cherry-tree then."

Even after the son had escaped the galleys, the mother made no
reference to the circumstance in a letter to her daughter, the Countess
of Bute (February 1752), but was full of 'Peregrine Pickle' and of
the rather lively sayings and doings of Lady Vane.

As the maternal susceptibilities were not much ruffled, the sympathy
of the public was not to be expected. We learn more from Walpole
than from Lady Mary. In November 1751 Walpole, writing to
Mann, remarks that all the letters from Paris were very "cautious of
relating the circumstances." He styles Montagu and Taafe as the
"two *gentlemen* who were pharaoh-bankers to Madame de Mirepoix"
in England, and "who had travelled to France to exercise the same
profession." Walpole adds that they had "been released on excessive
bail, are still to be tried, and may be sent to the galleys or dismissed
home, where they will be reduced to keep the best company; for,"
says Walpole, "I suppose nobody else will converse with them." The
letter-writer describes Montagu as having been a "perfect Gil Blas,"
and as having added "the famous Miss Ashe to the number of his
wives." Walpole says of Taafe, "He is an Irishman, who changed
his religion to fight a duel, as you know in Ireland a Catholic may
not wear a sword." But as Taafe was M.P. for Arundel when Catholics
could not sit in Parliament, it is quite as probable that Taafe changed,
or professed to change, his religion—if he had any religion—that he
might become a borough member. "He is," writes Walpole, "a
gamester, usurer, adventurer, and of late has divided his attentions
between the Duke of Newcastle and Madame de Pompadour; travelling
with turtles and pineapples in post-chaises to the latter, flying back to
the former for Lewes races and smuggling burgundy at the same
time." The Speaker was railing at gaming and White's apropos to
these two prisoners. Lord Coke, to whom the conversation was addressed, replied: "Sir, all I can say is, that they are both members of
the House of Commons, and neither of them of White's."

While "society" was discussing this matter, Miss Ashe reappeared
in England and reassumed her former distinguished position. In
December 1751 the town witnessed the happy reconciliation of Miss
Ashe with the gay Lady Petersham, who had been offended at the
indiscretion of the younger nymph. Lady Petersham's principles
were very elastic; she pardoned the Pollard Ashe on her own assurances that she was "as good as married" to Mr. Wortley Montagu,
who, according to Lord Chesterfield, seemed "so puzzled between the

*châtelet* in France and his wife in England, that it is not yet known in favour of which he will determine."

Soon after Lord Chesterfield's flying comment on the Ariadne who had really abandoned her Theseus, " society " received her to its arms as readily as Lady Petersham. The example of both was followed by one individual. A certain naval officer, named Falconer, made an honest woman of the Pollard Ashe ; and with this marriage ends our interest in one of the many " wives " of the English Gil Blas.

If some surprise was raised by the judgment given in favour of Montagu and Taafe, none need exist at present. The two gentlemen who were such useful friends at the pharaoh tables of Madame de Mirepoix, the French ambassadress in England, and one of whom supplied Madame de Pompadour, the French king's mistress, with turtle and pineapples, could dispense with the good offices of Louis the Fifteenth, or perhaps obtained them through the mistress and the ambassadress. But Abraham Payba, *alias* James Roberts, possessed as influential friends as Taafe and Montagu. Payba appealed against the judgment, his appeal was successful, and the two English members of Parliament stood very much in danger of the galleys. In their turn, however, they appealed against the legality of quashing the judgment given in their favour. The question came once or twice before the courts, and then it ceased to be argued. It would seem as if powerful friends on both sides had interfered. Each party could claim a decision in his favour and could boast of honour being saved, but the public feeling was that they were all rogues alike.

After the lapse of a few years, Wortley Montagu came into the possession of a fixed income after the death of his father in 1755. He had sold a reversion of £800 a year. His father now left him an annuity of £1000. The disgrace of the Paris adventure was not altogether forgotten, but Taafe was in favour at Versailles (by what lucky chance nobody could tell), and Montagu, after a few years of pleasure, took to better ways than of old. There seems to have come over the half-outcast a determination to show the better side of his nature and his ability. In 1759 he published his ' Reflections on the Rise and Fall of the Ancient Republics ; adapted to the present State of Great Britain.' In this work—an able and spirited review of the republics of Greece, Rome, and Carthage—the author probably stated his own idea of religion in the words, "To search out and adore the Creator in all his works is our primary duty, and claims the first place in every rational mind." Two years subsequent to the publication of this most creditable work, certain Cornish men thought that Edward Wortley would be their most fitting representative. In 1761 he was elected member for the borough of Bossiney. But he was weary of England and the legislature, and he resolved to leave both for ever.

Before Mr. Montagu left England "for good" in 1762 he made
necessary preparations for at least a long residence abroad. Among
those preparations, the most curious may be said to be indicated in
the following copy of a bill of articles purchased at an optician's.
Moses's gross of green spectacles sinks into insignificance by the side
of the assortment of spectacles, reading-glasses, pocket telescopes, &c.,
with which Mr. Montagu provided himself to meet the exigencies of
foreign travel. The bill is now in the possession of Lord Wharncliffe, as are some of the articles enumerated. I am greatly indebted
to his lordship for a sight of both, and to the prompt courtesy of his
permission to copy and reproduce this very singular bill.

"EDWD. WORTLEY MONTAGU, Esq.              *Dr.* to G. ADAMS.

| 1761 | | £ | s. | d. |
|---|---|---|---|---|
| Dec. 23 | Six Ellis's Microscopes at £2 in the Box marked A. | 12 | 1 | 0 |
| — | 12 Reading Glasses, in horn boxes, at 4s. each, in the Box marked B. | 2 | 8 | 0 |
| — | 24 Reading Glasses, Ruff Shell and Silver, at 18/s. in the Box C. | 22 | 16 | 0 ? |
| — | The large Reading glass in Ruff Shell and Silver, in the Box C. | 2 | 2 | 0 |
| — | 12 Concave glasses in Ruff Shell and Silver, at 9/s. in the Box C. | 5 | 8 | 0 |
| — | A Silver case inlaid with pearl, | 2 | 2 | 0 |
| | With a pair of Silver Temple Spectacles, in the Box C. | 0 | 13 | 0 |
| — | 12 Pockett Tellescopes, Nurse Cases, 4 glasses mounted in Brass, at 16/s., in the Box D | 9 | 12 | 0 |
| — | 24 Dozen of Concaves in horn boxes at 18/s. per Doz³., in the Box E | 21 | 12 | 0 |
| — | 10 Doz³ of Steel Temple Spectacles, at 2/s. each, in the Box F | 12 | 0 | 0 |
| — | 10 Doz³ of paper cases to D° at 4/s. per Doz., in the Box G | 2 | 0 | 0 |
| — | 6 pair of the Best Steel Temple Spectacles, in Black Fish Cases, at 7/s., in the Box H | 2 | 2 | 0 |
| — | 6 pair D° in Nurse Cases, at $\frac{1}{1\frac{3}{3}}$=20/s., in the Box H | 6 | 0 | 0 |
| — | Six pair of Silver Temple Spectacles in best Nurse Cases, at $1\frac{3}{13}$=29/s., in the Box marked H | 8 | 16 | 0 |
| — | Six pair Steel Temple Spec., at 2/s. | 0 | 12 | 0 |
| — | Six paper cases to D°, Box H | 0 | 2 | 0 |
| — | 12 Camp Tellescopes at 16/s., in the Box marked K | 9 | 12 | 0 |
| — | 6 Two foot Achromatic Tellescopes, at £2., in the Box L | 12 | 0 | 0 |
| — | 12 Ring Dials, at 10/6, in the Box M | 6 | 6 | 0 |
| — | 2 12-inch Reflecting Tellescopes | 9 | 9 | 0 |
| — | Six metallic Cones with Six Setts of Deformed pictures, at £2 2 0, in the Box N | 12 | 12 | 0 |
| — | Six pair of goglars, Box | 1 | 10 | 0 |
| — | 12 Reading glasses in Mahogany frames with handles, in the Box marked , at 14/s. | 8 | 8 | 0 |

| 1761. | | £ | s. | d. |
|---|---|---|---|---|
| Dec. 23 | 12 Leather purses to D° . . . . . . | 0 | 4 | 0 |
| — | 6 Treble Magnifiers in Ruff Shell and Silver, at | | | |
| | 25/s., in the Box marked H . . . . . | 7 | 10 | 0 |
| — | 24 Black Skin prospects, at 1/6 . . . . | 1 | 16 | 0 |
| — | 24 D°, at 2/s . . . . . | 2 | 8 | 0 |
| — | Two thermometers to Boiling Water . . . | 3 | 0 | 0 |
| — | Two Brass Box Steering Compasses with Muscovy | | | |
| | Tale Cards, 11 Inch . . . . . . | 1 | 10 | 0 |
| — | One D° 10 Inches . . . . . . . | 0 | 13 | 6 |
| | | 187 | 1 | 6 |
| — | 14 Small Deal Boxes . . . . . . | 0 | 12 | 0 |
| — | 2 Strong Packing Cases . . . . . . | 0 | 14 | 0 |
| | | 188 | 7 | 6 |

"Dec. 30, 1761. Rec⁴ of Edw⁴ Wortley Montagu, Esq., the full contents of this Bill and all Demands.

J. GEO. ADAMS & Co."

The bill being duly discharged, Edward Wortley took, as it proved, a final farewell of England. But his friends there soon heard of his whereabout. He proved that he was not a mere ignorant traveller, by addressing to the Earl of Macclesfield two letters on an ancient bust at Turin, the quality of which is warranted by the fact that they were thought of sufficient importance to be read before the Royal Society. Wortley Montagu was in a fair way to be a votary of science, but he might have said with Southwell,

"Tho' Wisdom woo me to the saint,
    Yet Sense would win me to the shrine."

He had some reason, perhaps, to feel careless and embittered, for in this year, 1762, his mother died, showing her cruel contempt for him by leaving him a guinea, which he gave to Mr. Davison, a friend and companion in his wayfaring. It was from his mother, said Mrs. Piozzi, that the "learned" and accomplished Edward Wortley Montagu inherited all his "tastes and talents for sensual delights."

In the same year, 1762, the English consul at Alexandria was a Scandinavian, a native either of Denmark or Sweden, named Feroe. His wife was a beautiful young woman, born at Leghorn in 1741. Her father (sometimes said to be an innkeeper) was English, or of English descent. His name was Dormer, the name of a family that had once given a duchess to one of the Italian states, and that has given a line of barons to the English peerage since the year 1615 to the present day. The mother of the lady in question was an Italian; her maiden name was Maria Sciale. There were several children of this marriage, but we have only to notice the beautiful Caroline

Dormer, who married Consul Feroe, of Alexandria. This Caroline is said to have been as much distinguished for her virtue as for her beauty. The Dormer family record (in Lord Wharncliffe's possession), in which this double distinction is chronicled, perhaps "doth protest too much" with respect to the virtue, as that quality would now be understood; but of this the reader may judge for himself.

The consul and his wife were happily settled at Alexandria, when Wortley Montagu was sojourning in that city. Her beauty, as the Scripture phrase expresses it, took his mind prisoner. The object he had in view—that of carrying her off from her husband—seemed un-attainable; but Montagu did not allow himself to be deterred by difficulties, and he found a way to surmount them. It was the way of a very unscrupulous man, but he had few scruples in compassing any end. He appeared as the friend of the family. He made no advances to the lady, but he manifested great interest in the welfare of her husband. Egypt was too dull a place for a man of such abilities. Montagu succeeded in inducing Feroe to leave it for a while on some pretended mission to Europe, which was to prove very lucrative to the poor consul, who took men and things for what they seemed to be. After Feroe's departure there came news of his sudden illness. A little additional time elapsed, and then came intelligence of his death. The decease of the consul in Holland was officially attested, and in 1763 Montagu presented the mournful document to the beautiful young widow. After she had made herself mistress of its contents, and saw herself left alone in a strange land, he took pity on her exquisite grief, made love to her at once, and proposed a remedy for her loneliness by her taking him for husband. The fair young widow was not hard to woo. She did not indeed yield at once. She suggested some becoming objections. She, a Roman Catholic, had erred, she thought, in marrying Mr. Feroe, who was a Protestant. She could not bring herself to repeat the error, but she intimated that she might be won if her handsome lover would turn from his heretical ways and become a true son of the true church. As nothing more than this trifle stood as an obstacle to his success, Montagu re-solved to become Roman Catholic. Perhaps he reflected long enough on the matter to persuade himself that he had a true call to that church. At all events, he professed to be somewhat divinely driven. He repaired to Jerusalem, and made his profession at the fountain-head of Christianity. In October 1764 Montagu presented himself in the Holy City to Father Paul, prefect of the missions in Egypt and Cyprus. The traveller said that he had come to Jerusalem rather out of curiosity than devotion, but that the hand of God had fallen upon him. From his youth up, he stated (truly enough) that he had been the dupe of the devil. He made the statement with manifestations of grief, especially as he had obstinately resisted the impulses of the Holy Spirit, for which he now expressed penitence and humbly sought pardon. Father Paul gave heed to the repentant sinner's statement, and finding him cleansed from all heretical depravity, freed him from all pains and penalties decreed by the church against heretics, gave him plenary absolution, and received him into communion with Rome. Father Paul thought much of his convert, whom he styles, in the official certificate of Montagu's conversion, "Dominus Comes de Montagu" (as every Englishman abroad in those days used to be called "mi lord,") and the good father bids all the faithful to refrain from snubbing the convert, but on the contrary, to rejoice and be merry over him, as they would be over the unexpected finding of a treasure. A copy of the original document, which still sparkles with the silver dust showered over the finely written Italian letters, was printed in *Notes and Queries*, 4th of January, 1873.

There is no reason to doubt that soon after this act was accomplished Mr. Wortley Montagu and Madame Feroe *née* Dormer, were duly married. Their conjugal felicity, however, was slightly disturbed by the reappearance of the consul Feroe, who very naturally expressed the greatest surprise at the household arrangements which had taken place in his absence and he laid claim to his beautiful wife. The Catholic lady was persuaded that her first marriage with the Protestant consul was null and void, the validity of such a union not being recognised by her church. At the same time she looked with some doubt, or she affected so to look, on the contract with her second husband. Appeal was made to the law tribunals of Tuscany, and pending the appeal, the wife of two husbands retired to a religious house at Antoura, in Syria. Montagu solaced himself with travel: he possibly knew that Italian judges were tardy in coming to conclusions. Whither he wended is quite easy to tell, for in 1765 Mr. Montagu was encountered at Venice. Mr. Sharp, in his Letters from Italy, has one dated Venice, September 1765, in which he gives the following account:

"One of the most curious sights we saw among these curiosities, was the famous Mr. Montagu, who was performing quarantine at the Lazaretto. All the English made a point of paying him their compliments in that place, and he seemed not a little pleased with their attention. It may be supposed that visitors are not suffered to approach the person of any who is performing quarantine. They are divided by a passage of about seven or eight feet wide. Mr. Montagu was just arrived from the East; he had travelled through the Holy Land, Egypt, Armenia, &c., with the Old and New Testaments in his hands for his direction, which, he told us, had proved unerring guides. He had particularly taken the road of the Israelites through the Wilderness, and had observed that part of the Red Sea which they had passed through. He had visited Mount Sinai, and flattered himself he had been on the very part of the rock where Moses spake face to face with God Almighty. His beard reached down to his breast, being of two years and a half growth; and the dress of his head was Armenian. He was in the most enthusiastic raptures with Arabia and the Arabs. Like theirs, his bed was the ground, his food rice, his beverage, water, his luxury, a pipe and coffee. His purpose was to return once more among that virtuous people, whose morals and hospitality, he said, were such, that were you to drop your cloak in the highway, you would find it there six months afterwards, an Arab being too honest a man to pick up what he knows belongs to another; and, were you to offer money for the provision you meet with, he would ask you, with concern, why you had so mean an opinion of his benevolence, to suppose him capable of accepting a gratification. 'Therefore, money,' said he, 'in that country, is of very little use, as it is only necessary for the purchase of garments, which, in so warm a climate, are very few and of very little value.' He distinguishes, however, between the wild and the civilized Arab, and proposes to publish an account of all that I have written."

In 1765, Wortley Montague (while sojourning at Pisa), wrote his well-known account of his journey to ' The Written Mountains ' in the East. It is a clever and modest record ; his conclusion being that the rock inscriptions were undecipherable, and probably would not, if interpreted, be worth the outlay of means. This account was read before the Royal Society. In March 1766 he was still at Pisa, whence he wrote to M. Varsy, a merchant from Marseilles, established at Rosetta, and married to a sister of Mrs. Feroe, or Mrs. Montagu, as the Tuscan judges might decide. The letter in French (now, with others quoted below, in Lord Wharncliffe's possession,) contains the following personal matter :

. . . " On my way back I shall go through Alexandria and Rosetta to see you, and also to see whether I cannot establish myself at Rosetta rather than in Syria. As my father-in-law sets out for Syria next week, I shall not be obliged to take the shortest road; my wife will be at ease, and I shall have at least time to assure you how charmed I shall be to find opportunities of testifying to you my gratitude, and of renewing our old and dear friendship—a friendship which wil_ always be dear to me, and with which I shall never cease to be, &c. &c.        DE MONTAIGU."

I have before me the original ' dispensation,' to enable him to neglect keeping Lent in the usual abstinent way. That he should take the trouble to procure such a power would seem to be warrant for a sincerity for which we can hardly credit him. It is dated ' 6 March, 1767,' and he is styled ' Excellentissimus Dominus Eduardus de Comitibus Montagu.' Meanwhile the question of the marriage was still undecided. The ecclesiastical and civil judges were perhaps not long in forming, but they were very slow in delivering judgment. Mrs. Montagu, however, or ' the Countess,' as she was sometimes called, seems to have formed a judgment of her own ; or, at all events, to have accepted that of her second husband. They lived together at Smyrna, where for two years both applied themselves to the study of

Turkish, in which language, as in others of the East, Montagu became a proficient scholar. On New Year's day, 1769, he addressed a joyous letter to his brother-in-law Varsy. The Tuscan and the Roman tribunals had at length pronounced on the great question. The rich and orthodox second husband was declared to be the legal possessor of the lady, and her previous marriage with the poor heretical consul was decreed to be no marriage at all.

"You cannot imagine," thus runs the letter, "the great joy I feel at being able to tell you that Mr. Feroe has the final decree of the Court of the Nuncio at Florence. Accordingly, as Madame is already here" (Smyrna), "we reckon on being as soon as possible at Rosetta. But prudence requires that we should first write to you to beg you to find us a suitable house. That in which we were before would be good enough, but I think and fear that the consul may have it. Without the servants, there are myself, my wife, and her father" (*monsieur son père*). "We live more in the Turkish fashion than ever. Accordingly, the women's apartments must be comfortable and convenient for the *salamlike* (*sic*), and there must be a chamber for my father-in-law. You know what is necessary. The quarter in which we live must be free from disturbance, from plague, and from robbers. Have the kindness to inform me if the country is tranquil, and if you believe that there is no danger from the government; for here no end of stories is being circulated. Write by the first ship. Be convinced of the constant friendship with which I am, my very dear friend, entirely yours,                                                                    DE MONTAIGU."

There seems to have been some obstruction to impede the desired settlement in Egypt. In a letter, dated 'Antoura' (Syria), 'January, 1771,' there is the following passage :

"Many accidents have prevented me from following my design and my inclination for Rosetta; and indeed it seems more prudent to wait till the government (in Egypt) is authorized (*affirmé*) by the consent of the Ottoman Porte, before we establish ourselves in Egypt. However, here I am nearer to you, and I shall not fail to follow my first plan as soon as circumstances will allow. Madame thanks you for your *souvenir*, and sends many compliments. Keep yourself well, continue to love me, and be assured of the constant and perfect friendship of your very humble servant,                                                              CHEV. DE MONTAIGU."

It may be mentioned by the way, that Wortley Montagu reckoned among his friends men not at all likely to entertain respect for worthless individuals. "My learned friend, the Bishop of Ossory," is a phrase which bears one of these indications. It was written at Cairo. Meanwhile, here is another characteristic note from Cyprus. The writer speaks of his wife, as if the laundress of old no longer existed.

"À M. JOSEPH VARSY, négociant français, à Rosette.
                                        "Chipre, 24 juin, 1771.
"MONSIEUR,—Enfin, mon très-cher ami, je touche au moment de vous embrasser. Cette lettre vous sera envoyé d'Alexandrie par ma femme,

qui va à Rosette avec M. son père et Mademoiselle sa sœur.    Je vous
supplie de leur procurer ou une maison commode ou un appartement suf-
fisant dans l'oquel (?), où ils attendront jusqu'a ce que je leur écrive du Caïre,
où je vais par voie de Damiette.

" Chev. De Montaigu."

In July, he writes thus from Damietta :

" À M. Joseph Varsy, négociant français, à Rosette.

" Damiette, 14 juillet, 1771.

" Me voici, mon très-chèr ami, arrivée proche de vous; aussi je me flatte
que dans peu j'aurai l'honneur de vous embrasser.  Ma femme doit être
arrivée à Alexandrie, et elle m'attendra à Rosette.  Ayez la bonté de lui
faire avoir un appartement, ou deux, s'il le faut, et de l'assister en ce dont
elle aura besoin pour la maison.  Je crois être assez assuré de votre amitié
pour être persuadé que vous ne me refuserez pas cette service.  Je vous
écrirai du Caïre le moment que j'arriverai.  En attendant soyez assuré que
je serai toujours comme vous m'avez toujours connu.

" Votre très-humble serviteur et véritable ami,

" Chev. De Montaigu."

Five days later, he acknowledges, from Alexandria, the arrival of a
box of pipes, from Constantinople.  Soon after, the Egyptian home
was established.  It was on a thoroughly Eastern footing, and the two
chief inmates seem to have devoted themselves to the study of Eastern
languages and literature.  But in August 1772 the home seems to
have been abandoned by Montagu.  There was a report that he had
embraced Mohammedanism, in order to visit Mecca in safety, and that
his wife having refused to follow his example, or to recognise a negro
boy who was with him as his heir, he separated from her.  The following note shows that he was again roaming, but also that he was
careful for his wife's comforts and on friendly terms with her family.

(À Varsy.)

" Alexandrette, août 4, 1772.

" Nous voici, mon très-cher ami, après un heureux navigation de trois
jours, arrivé à Alexandrette.  C'est un village précisément comme Tor.
Nous y avons trouvé des chevaux et un domestique de M. Belleville. Ainsi,
nous partons ce soir pour Aleppe, sans attendre l'escorte.  Les gens que l'on
dit obsèdent le chemin ne sont que cinq ou six; et nous sommes trois,
bien armés, sans compter M. Belleville, ainsi nous n'avons rien à craindre.
Il n'y a pas de peste, ni rien de semblable. , Le Pacha est à Aleppe et non à
Damas; assez loin de votre maison.  Je vous prie d'avoir toutes les
attentions que vous pouvez pour ma femme.  Mes complimens à ce que
vous avez de plus chèr.  M. Raymond vous enverra . . . une pellisse neuve;
il vous en dira aussi le prix; si ma femme le trouve belle et le prix honnête
elle le prendra, et M. Raymond vous le passera avec compte; si non, vous
en disposerez selon les ordres de M. R.  Adieu.  Je monte à cheval.

Similar notes tell of his progress, of certain inconveniences from
being too long in the saddle, exposed to the sun ; and in the autumn,
of his approaching return home.  In September, he writes to Varsy :

" I am well persuaded of the care you take of our house, and I beg you to hurry on the workmen, and that everything be done absolutely in accordance with my wife's inclinations. Let the men put up the paper as she orders it, but let no one touch my room below, unless he can paint it perfectly in the Arab fashion."

After expressing surprise that Mohammed Kiaja, a supposed friend, is intriguing against him, and stating that if his return to Rosetta should create any difficulties or perils, it would be better to have them smoothed away while he is at a distance, he writes :

" . . . J'ai dépensé ici 800 piastres; il est vrai que je les ai dépensé en des choses qui valent plus chez nous, et quand les dames auront pris ce que les accommode, nous ferons faire de l'argent du reste; mais en attendant cela vous incommode; il faut en ce cas-là prendre de l'argent à intérêt pour mon compte, et disant que c'est pour moi pour ne pas prodiguer mon nom. Quand la cuisine est fini, il faut blanchir tout l'ancienne cuisine et autres endroits qui sont sur son niveau." . . .

In a letter from Latackia, 1st October, 1772, he speaks of projects promising great results; 'broad rivers' (he says) 'are the sum of narrow streams.' In a still later letter the project seems to refer to pearls and rich stuffs. The letter concludes thus :

" Je vous prie de me faire faire par Schieck Ali, un catalogue de tous mes livres Arabes, Turques, et Persans, qui sont manuscrits, et qu'il mette vis-à-vis de chacun le prix suivant qu'il les estime."

This indicates an approaching break up. The cause of it does not appear, except as far as can be made out in a letter from

" Alexandrie, 13 oct. 1772.
" . . . Je vois que M. Dormer veut rester à Rosette, et en ce cas je n'y resterai pas. J'ai dit autant à Madame, pour lui donner le tems de se retirer à Alexandrie avant mon arrivée. Je coucherai demain à Raimhé; dimanche à Aboukir, lundi à Etikon, et mardi, s'il plaît à Dieu, je serai à Rosette, et si j'y trouva M. Dormer je n'y resterai qu'autant qu'il faudra pour empaqueter quelque livres, car je ne veux pas rester dans la même ville avec M. Dormer. J'aurais été charmé de le voir ici, mais je ne veux pas le voir à Rosette; ainsi, mon chèr, persuadez le de partir immédiatement; car si je le trouve je n'y coucherai pas; cela est certain."

What the ground of dissension was that induced Montagu to declare that he would not remain in the same city with Dormer is not known. Whatever it was, the Egyptian home was broken up. The wife and her sister subsequently established themselves, temporarily, at Marseilles, definitively at Nancy. Montagu moved about the Continent in moody restlessness. In 1773 and the following year he settled for awhile in Venice. He lived in frequent retirement, and to all outward appearance in as truly a Turkish fashion as if he were a faithful child of Islam.

While Mr. Montagu was residing at Venice an illustrious traveller,

the Duke of Hamilton, arrived in that city, under the care of his
physician, Dr. John Moore, afterwards the author of ' Zeluco,' and the
father of a glorious son, Sir John Moore, the hero of Corunna.
The doctor had probably talked with his patron or ward about the
more eccentric traveller, of whom he had more to say than most
people as to the affair between Montagu and the Jew Payba, Moore
having been official medical man at the English Embassy in France,
when Lord Albemarle was ambassador, and Montagu was appealing to
him for aid and protection.   At Venice, the duke, according to Moore,
"had the curiosity " (he does not say the *courtesy*) " to wait on this
extraordinary man." " Montagu," says the Doctor, in his published
letters,

"met his Grace at the stair-head, and led us through some apartments furnished in the Venetian manner, into an inner room in quite a
different style.   There were no chairs, but he desired us to seat ourselves
on a sofa, whilst he placed himself on a cushion on the floor, with his legs
crossed in the Turkish fashion.   A young black slave sat by him, and a
venerable old man, with a long beard, served us with coffee.   After this
collation some aromatic gums were brought, and burnt in a little silver
vessel.   Mr. Montagu held his nose over the steam for some minutes, and
sniffed up the perfume with peculiar satisfaction; he afterwards endeavoured
to collect the smoke with his hands, spreading and rubbing it carefully
along his beard, which hung in hoary ringlets to his girdle. . . . We had
a great deal of conversation with this venerable looking person, who is, to
the last degree, acute, communicative, and entertaining, and in whose discourse and manners are blended the vivacity of a Frenchman with the
gravity of a Turk."

Moore does not say that Montagu had assumed the Mohammedan
faith, but simply that he considered the Turkish way of life to surpass
that of all other nations.   Indeed they deserved to be "the happiest
of mankind," if they were, as Montagu held them to be, distinguished
for integrity, hospitality and most other virtues.   Egypt was, in his
eyes, " a perfect paradise," to which he was longing to return; and
he was convinced that if the Israelites of old could have had their own
way they would have stuck to the land and the flesh-pots and driven
the Egyptians into Canaan.   But he added, with a fine sense of what
the occasion required, that " it had been otherwise ordered, for wise
purposes, of which it did not become us to judge."
Subsequently, Montagu returned the visit of the duke and his
medical guardian.   He seated himself on a sofa with his legs drawn
up under him, as the most natural and convenient position that a
gentleman could take.   Moore, in the course of the conversation
which ensued, slily adverted to the Mohammedan views with regard
to women.   The quasi Turk became Oriental to the very ends of his
fingers, and grew eloquent on this delicate question.   Of course, he
defended polygamy and concubinage, even as Solomon had wisely

observed it. Women liked neither, and but for this foolish objection they would have had influence enough to have spread Islam as one religion throughout Europe. The men hated Christianity on more valid ground. Auricular confession they abhorred. "No Turk of any delicacy would ever allow his wife (particularly if he had but one) to hold private conference with a man on any pretext whatever." When the Doctor (for the Duke seems to have been generally silent) insinuated that the Turks had not the same grounds to hate Protestantism, Montagu remarked that the Turks could not tolerate the Christian idea of the equality of women and men, nor accept the Christian view of an exceedingly dull heaven, where the souls of ordinary women were to be assembled, instead of the graceful bodies of Houris, who were to welcome the sons of Islam to a joyous paradise.

The self-exile continued to be the observed of all curious travellers; but he directed his steps at last in the direction of home, if with no decided resolution to return thither. The cause, perhaps, is found in a phrase of a letter from Mrs. Delany, written in February, 1776: "Mr. Wortley Montagu's wife is dead." This was the laundress, his only legitimate wife, who had married him in his youthful time. Her husband had recently been entertaining Romney, and Romney had painted the portrait of his friend in Turkish costume, which bespeaks the talent of the artist and the sad yet manly beauty of the friend. The latter had been the victim of more lies and jests than any man of his time, and these were multiplied now, but they are not worth repeating. The wanderer himself was near the end of his course. Two months subsequent to his lawful wife's decease he died, after a brief illness, at Padua. He is said to have expressed a hope that he should die as a good Moslem; but that he was held to have died in the Roman Catholic faith is best proved by the fact that he lies beneath a church roof in Padua, and with a Latin inscription over him, which describes him as "ubique civis," and which credits him with nearly all the qualities that can dignify humanity. If much eccentricity has been ascribed to him by the world, it is because his acts and words gave some warrant for it. There was scarcely any condition in life but in some country or another he had assumed it. He used to boast that he had never committed a *small* folly; and his gambling was certainly, at one time, of gigantic proportions. A memoir of him, published in Dublin two years after his death, reckoned among his boyish assumptions those of link-boy, chimney-sweep, and shoe-black! The same veracious volume numbered among his wives, with the English laundress, a Dutch Jewess, a Turkish lady, a Greek girl, a Circassian damsel, and an Arabian maiden. Even to the English laundress he is said to have been married by an official of the Fleet prison. His old tutor, Forster, claimed the merit of having written the work on Ancient Republics, but this claim, made when the author could not answer it, was universally scouted, as was the contemptible pretender. Lady Louisa Stuart, referring to the various ladies who assumed a right to bear his name, remarks:

"More than one lady took the title of his wife, with or without the pretext of a ceremony which, it is to be feared, he would not scruple to go through any number of times, if requisite for the accomplishment of his wishes. But the last person so circumstanced, and the loudest in asserting her claims, met him upon equal ground, having herself a husband living, from whom she had eloped; therefore, she at least could not complain of deception."

The above lady was the *ci-devant* Miss Dormer. She appeared in London soon after Edward Wortley Montagu's death; and in her family papers it is stated that she received one hundred pounds annually from Coutts's out of her alleged husband's estate. For a long period she resided at Nancy, and she may yet live in the recollection of not very old persons, English and others, who dwelt in that pleasant city in their youth, for the last of the wives of Wortley Montagu survived till January, 1821. She lived and died as Countess of Montagu, and her death finally closed a romance of real life, the unfortunate hero of which would probably have won honourable fame if he had been blessed with a mother of a different quality.

# Ten Minutes Late:

## A TALE WITHOUT A MORAL.

### DEDICATED TO UNPUNCTUAL PEOPLE.

I HAVE always been late all my life. I began it by being ten minutes late for a title and fortune. In this wise it happened : my mother, after ten years of marriage, during which time she had not made the slightest attempt at presenting my father with an heir, suddenly announced that she had great hopes of, in time, supplying him with the much desired blessing. Great hopes they proved themselves to be; for one lovely June morning she not only conferred on my father one son, but being determined to do nothing by halves, ten minutes afterwards a second made his appearance. The eldest son was at once proclaimed as such, and invested with a piece of blue ribbon—which I should think formed a pleasing contrast to the crimson wrist it adorned—that no mistake as to his identity should occur, while I, not being expected, came off second best in honour and attention, and went shares in all the goods the gods had provided for my brother, i.e., his food, his clothes, and his cradle. Of course we were the image of each other, and being strongly impressed with the fact we naturally grew up to admire each other intensely.

I never, however, quite forgave him for giving me the go-by in my entrance into life until he squared matters by outrunning me in another race which proved more to my advantage than the first. It is this adventure I am about to relate.

First it is necessary to tell you, that through a whim of my mother's we were christened by the respective names of Charles and Charlewood; my father's name was Manners; my mother having been an heiress of the name of Compton, had conferred it, with herself, on my grateful father, whose acres before his marriage were not equal to his ancestry, and whose baronetcy was bestowed upon him by an impoverished monarch, who received in exchange an equivalent, and rather more, in the coin of his realm. Such being the case, the double patronymic of Compton-Manners descended to the twin offspring of the illustrious couple afore-mentioned, and remained their undisputed possession, as my mother, after that supreme and highly-successful effort of maternity, rested on her laurels, so to speak, and no other child arrived to share my fortune as a younger son. I have mentioned that it was a whim of my mother's to call us both by Christian names beginning with the same letters, and the same whim caused her to increase if possible the likeness between us by dressing us exactly alike. Of course this occasioned endless confusion, but luckily when we had both attained the age of twelve years my hair grew rapidly darker, while my brother's retained its rich auburn colour. This at once, greatly to my mother's disgust, proclaimed a difference between us, though we possessed the same blue eyes, dark eyelashes, and regular features.

I pass over the school-days at Harrow, a year at Christ Church, and, finally, as we would have it so, our first separation, my brother Charley getting his commission in the Guards while I contented myself with one in the Rifle Brigade; and I had not been in that most edifying and steadiest of dear old regiments for a month before I became fully convinced that the Guards were nowhere as compared with it, and not for gold untold would I have exchanged my dark green—there is really as much green about it as there is in a London square—for the gaudier trappings of the Household troops.

When I was about two and twenty it chanced that my brother's battalion of the Guards and my battalion of the Rifle Brigade were ordered to Montreal, we preceding the Guards by a few weeks. It happened to be about the time that a certain political outbreak was feared, and soon after our arrival at Montreal I was sent on detachment to a country town to frighten the disaffected inhabitants into good behaviour. This proceeding, strange to say, gave great delight to some of them, though I fear it was only the female portion of the town of Agnesville, Canada West, who hailed our advent, not only as a protection, but as a break in the monotony of an otherwise decidedly dull country town.

I think it only fair to mention that I consider his Excellency was, for once in his life, wrong in the impression he received of the rebellious state of feeling at Agnesville. From my humble experience, which I believe would be endorsed by the bulk of my brother officers and signed by the Colonel himself, I should say we found far more affection than disaffection in that hospitable town; the only danger we ran was from the fire of the brightest eyes I ever remember. This fire we returned, as in duty bound, so as to keep up the name for gallantry we have always borne; not, however, that we all escaped scot-free; there were one or two of us, and perhaps more, who, I am ashamed to say, were taken prisoners after a very faint resistance, and who, being allowed their freedom on parol, acted very much as certain Continental neighbours lately did under similar circumstances.

You must know that in those days of youth and folly, dear reader, I prided myself on an unexceptionable taste in beauty, and to keep up my supposed credit for this I went systematically to work to ascertain who was the *belle par excellence* before I fixed on any one young lady as my "muffin" during our stay at Agnesville. For the first week I flirted generally; the second week I began to reduce the circle of my acquaintance; the third found me in a state of waver between two beauties; and by the end of the first month I was, figuratively speaking, on my knees before Miss Marguerite Duval, who, I had now quite made up my mind, was one of the most beautiful, as well as one of the most innocent and simple-minded, of her sex. Who could doubt the fact for an instant who had been permitted the felicity of gazing at her? When with her I felt inspired, like Montrose,

"To make her glorious by my pen, and famous by my sword."

When I was away from her I felt—don't be shocked, my sentimental reader—as if I had had nothing to eat for a fortnight, followed by an extraordinary tendency towards Villa Duval. This, I suppose, was sympathetical electricity.

Let me describe her; let me, in fact, make her glorious by my pen, as the substitute of a rifle, I fear, precludes the possibility of winning her fame by any other means. She was tall and slight—very slight. Now this slightness is, to my mind, almost a fault in a Canadian beauty, and it is in the one respect of figure that the maidens of England excel their Canadian sisters. Imploring your pardon for this digression, let me proceed with my portrait. Very slight, with a graceful, piquant head, crowned with quantities of silky hair massed in an extraordinary and mysterious way, all loops and twists and coils and sunshine. No; it was not dyed, and it was not bought. She fainted in my arms once, and though it came tumbling down in glorious and golden confusion it did not tumble off. These wonderful tresses were cut straight across the forehead à la Vandyke. I am aware that this way of arranging the hair is generally condemned as "bad style," but it was not so common then as it is now, and I boldly say nothing can be more becoming when it forms a fair and silken fringe over a soft young forehead and dark pencilled eyebrows. As for the eyes, it is simply impossible to describe them. They were "everything by turns and nothing long." Yes; they were always beautiful—melting, burning, laughing, loving, scorning. They were large, they were brown, with very large dilating irides, and they were guarded by a double file of lashes, long, soft, and almost black.

As I write these words in praise of those wonderful eyes, helping my memory with a glance at a vignette by Notman that does them but scant justice, if any, the recollection of them even now will stir the blood in my veins, and cause my heart to beat almost as tumultuously, as if I were once more gazing into their unfathomable depths in the conservatory, or, to use Maggie's own words, "the Flirtorium," at Villa Duval.

It must not be supposed that I was allowed undisputed possession of the first place in Miss Marguerite Duval's affections. Had that been

the case, I ask myself, looking back as I do now over an intervening
lapse of time, How long should I have valued such solitary possession ?
And I answer after reflection, and always taking the lapse of time into
consideration, Not an hour!  I should have certainly sent in my
resignation, which she on her side would have accepted as gracefully
as she did everything, from bouquets to bracelets, with a faint sigh
perhaps over the fickleness of mankind generally and soldierkind
individually.  But Miss Duval was never doomed to receive mortification at my hands; she had swarms of admirers, some of whom
were declared lovers, and I being, as I have before stated, very young
and very foolish and not a little vain, actually allowed myself to be
aggravated into love with her; I really cannot describe the process
in any other way, and the amount of excitement I went through in
keeping my place among my rivals and my anxiety always to be first
by her side almost cured me of my early failing.

When the Rifle Brigade, or to use the Agnesville abbreviation,
" the Brigade," had been quartered there two months, it was agitated
amongst us that a ball to our hospitable entertainers would not only .
be right and proper, but politic, in fact the only thing wanting to
restore completely and immediately that loyal state of feeling that
once existed in Agnesville.  We at once called a meeting to discuss
and settle this important matter without more delay, as we were in
fear of being recalled to headquarters immediately, now that the
Fenian panic seemed to have' abated.  After the question of funds
had been discussed and we had all declared our readiness to place our
enormous fortunes at the disposal of the mess committee, the next
question was mooted as to " when ?" and " where ?"

" When ?  Next week," was the answer from one of the younger
and more enthusiastic of the Prince Consort's Own.  " Where?  In
Aylmer's Hall, to be sure, not in this wretched rat's-hole, they call
a barrack."

The first part of this suggestion was negatived as impossible by
the steadier members of our council, the second was taken into
consideration and ultimately carried without a dissentient voice.
The ball was finally fixed for that day fortnight at Aylmer's Hall,
a tolerably good set of public reception rooms in the heart of the
little town, which were used for state affairs and small entertainments,
and called Aylmer's Hall, after a former Canadian governor of that
name who had passed through the town during its erection.

It was the day before that fixed for our ball, and when my arduous
duties were over, I drove out to Villa Duval to pay my respects to
la belle Marguerite.  It was lovely weather in early spring, and the
delicate tender green of grass and foliage was an inexpressible relief
after the endless wearying miles of snow we had been gazing on and
walking over for months.  The sun had already attained considerable

heat, and when I reached my destination I found the jalousies closed, the awnings spread over the balconies, and some of the inhabitants of the villa assembled under the sheltering colonnade, while the more venturesome were returning to croquet with all the zest that a long interval devoted to sleighing and toboggin was likely to inspire them with.

I was received with considerable enthusiasm, and a flattering increase of colour on Maggie's fair cheeks as she left her game and came forward, mallet in hand, to greet me. I was not a little annoyed, however, when I discovered in a young man who was her partner at croquet one of my brother officers, as I had hoped I should reign supreme on this occasion, and did not fancy the espionage now, and the chaff afterwards, that would most assuredly be my lot. I therefore rather surlily refused Marguerite's request that I would join their party on the lawn, and throwing myself lazily on a rug that was spread under the colonnade devoted myself to a younger sister of my enchantress, who, for her age, scarcely sixteen, had a very fair idea of flirting. Miss Eunice was kept as a rule in the background, and how heartily she enjoyed on this occasion being first instead of second, I could see by the dimples round the mouth and the quiver of the dark eyelashes, in spite of her efforts to look demure. My back was turned on the croquet party, but I could see the whole scene reflected panorama-like in the plate-glass of the window in front of me, and in spite of my *accès* of temper I was not a little amused at the evident pique which Maggie endeavoured to hide by apparent absorption in her game, and I was as usual irresistibly fascinated by her grace, and the perfect foot she displayed in the rapid movements entailed by the vagaries of croquet.

Meanwhile Eunice did *la belle ingénue* to perfection, and while her little white fingers moved rapidly through her tatting, or some such pretentious work she was engaged in, her eyes and tongue were not slothful.

" And you will, you promise me, won't you, Mr. Manners?" she said, ending with these words a torrent of vivacious nonsense about her first ball and her fears that I should be too grand to dance " with such a stupid little thing as me, you know."

" Yes, you poor little Cinderella, I will do anything in the world you like to please you," I replied, returning her soft glances with with interest and in absurdly tender tones ; for I could see in my impromptu looking-glass that Maggie was approaching and was probably within earshot.

Eunice, to do her justice, looked a little astonished, and, I fancy, received an admonishing look from her sister, for she got up and went into the house, saying something about ordering tea, and then Maggie and I were left to a certain extent alone. As the house was a square surrounded by a piazza, the step or two I had taken in rising had carried me round one corner of it, and a newly leafed and thickly growing Virginia creeper screened us from the rest of the party.

There was silence for a moment, and then she said, "Come and see the monkey."

Dear me! how many tête a tête visits we paid that monkey! and how very little attention that small representative of our former inglorious but untrammelled state ever received! In that day, Mr. Darwin's theory had not attained its present beautiful perfection; had such been the case, what inexhaustible resource of scientific argument would that little animal have suggested to us. As it was, in my foolish and I must add insolent ignorance of the close connection between ourselves and that little gibbering nutcracker, I wondered how God, who had created so frightful a parody on man, could have devised so beautiful a creature as the fair woman who stood beside me, holding out her delicate snow-white hand to be emptied of its treasure of nuts by a black paw with curved nails, and hairy cuticle.

Pardon this digression; perhaps the reason of our undue partiality for the monkey was, that he lived in a house, suitable as to size, at the end of a long avenue, which house by a fortunate coincidence, and a lucky contrivance of art and nature, was not visible from any window of the villa; moreover, by keeping under the piazza for a yard or so, we could diverge from thence into this avenue without any one on the other side being the wiser. After a moment spent in laying in a stock of nuts for Dolly we started cautiously and rapidly on our little excursion.

"We must not be long," said Maggie, "for tea will be ready directly, and I guess I shall be wanted."

"It may be the last time I shall ever see the monkey," I said pathetically, not the least seeing how ridiculous my remark must sound. I have since thought how well Maggie resisted the struggle to laugh that must have assailed her, for she had a strong sense of the ridiculous. She replied, without a muscle of her face moving:

"Captain Johnstone was telling us you expect to be recalled soon, but I hope it is only a false report. We should miss you all—really!"

"I don't suppose you'd care," said I, shaking the basket of nuts so energetically that two or three hopped out on to the gravel path and necessitated our both stooping to pick them up. If two faces *did* get close together for a second, what matter? There was only Dolly the monkey looking on, and he could not tell tales—luckily!

"I don't suppose you'd care?" said I, repeating my question and trying to get a peep at the eyes that were shaded by the envious straw hat.

She did not reply; she did far better, raised those darkly fringed lids and gazed full at me. Was there a tear trembling on the lashes?

There surely was, and the thought intoxicated me. I caught her round the waist and drawing her unresistingly towards me, began, "My darling!" In another moment I should have poured my love tale into her ear, when a rustling in the neighbouring bushes and a laugh startled me, and I had hardly time to release Marguerite when from behind the monkey house appeared Johnstone and *la belle ingénue*. Maggie, who had fled from my grasp like a startled fawn, had instantly regained her composure and began to feed poor neglected Dolly, who was chattering and grinning, and trying with his paw stretched to its utmost length to reach the nuts, talking to him as if she had but one thought in life and that thought giving a monkey nuts.

At that moment, balked as I was, I hated Eunice, Johnstone, the monkey, everything but Marguerite, whom I loved with a passion which astonished myself.

"I came for the keys," said Eunice, with an aggravatingly pert smile and know-all-about-it sort of look.

"And what did Captain Johnstone come for?" said Marguerite, bestowing her last nut on the monkey, and speaking in the sweetest tones imaginable.

"To see your charming monkey, Miss Duval," replied Johnstone, smiling, "and to assist your sister in the search for the key."

"Hang the keys!" said I, semi-audibly.

"Yes; but that's just what Marguerite won't recollect to do, though mamma has had a nail driven in for her and all," said Eunice, with delightful simplicity.

What the "all" was I was never fated to hear, for Marguerite made one effort to renew our tête-à-tête by despatching her sister to the house with the said keys, in great hopes that Captain Johnstone would think it necessary to escort her on her return journey; but she and I were doomed to be disappointed, for Johnstone stuck to us perseveringly from that moment until I took my leave. I only just managed, as I pressed her hand at parting, to whisper "Keep the first dance for me to-morrow night," and even this was overheard by Johnstone, who said:

"He'll not be there to claim it, Miss Duval. Don't you wait for him; he never was known to keep an appointment in his life;" and a good deal more in the same pleasant bantering strain. It was enough to try the patience of a saint, and as I never pretended to be worthy of canonical honours, my reader, unless she or he happens to be blest with a super-angelic nature, may easily picture to her or himself the horrible temper I was in when I mounted my dog-cart to return to the barracks in company with my interfering friend Captain

Johnstone. I had indeed almost descended to the petty revenge of refusing him the lift back that he had the audacity to demand, but the recollection that if I did so he would probably remain in my beloved's company until the next car passed made me deem it more prudent to comply.

Johnstone was really rather a friend of mine and a good fellow, but possessed, as I then thought, of no tact whatever. Directly we were off he began cheerily :

" What's the row, old fellow ?  Won't she have anything to say to you ? "

" I beg you will not make Miss Duval the subject of any foolish jesting," I replied with dignity.

He gave a whistle long and low. " Why, you don't mean to say, Charlie, it's as serious as all that ?  I am sorry I spoke."

I vouchsafed no reply, but gave the mare a savage cut.  My companion lit a cigar, and after a puff or two began :

" But seriously, Manners, I hope you are not caught.  You are far too young, and the girl has nothing but her looks; these, I admit, *are* good enough to turn an older head than yours; but still you'll be a great fool to give up all your future to a pair of fine eyes."

" What the d—— can it matter to you what I do ? " I retorted, further incensed by the contempt expressed for my two and twenty years.  " And I consider the expression you use with reference to ' being caught' extremely offensive, in the strongest sense of the word, to Miss Duval, whose name I again request may not be mentioned in my presence."

" Oh, these boys ! these boys ! " grumbled my adviser ; then laying his hand firmly on my shoulder, he said : " Now, look here, Manners, you are a capital good fellow—far too good a fellow to make a fool of yourself and quarrel with your best friend.  You are irritated just now, and not likely to take a favourable view of my conduct; some day you will thank me for the last hour's work.  I am many years older than you, and I have saved more than one youngster from marrying in haste and repenting at leisure ; and, by Jove ! I'll save you, whether you like it or no."

I was provoked at his obstinacy, but his good-tempered face and little twinkling eyes—not unlike the monkey we had just left—upset my gravity, and forgetting my dignity I burst into a hearty laugh.

" That's all right," said my unthwartable friend ; " I see I'm forgiven, Charlie.  I wish, at the same time, I could see any signs in your face of taking my advice and letting the matter drop, now and for ever."

I became grave again and replied stiffly, " I am obliged to you for your advice, Johnstone, and I am sure you mean it kindly ; but I consider I am compromised and bound in honour to propose to Miss

Duval; and moreover, I tell you frankly that I intend to do so to-morrow night at the ball."

Now, to tell truth, until that moment I had never quite made up my mind to take the final step; and as to being compromised, officers in the army, who are always running the blockade, so to speak, know a trick worth two of that. But I had recovered my temper a little, and with it a strong temptation had set in to defy my self-instituted mentor. The latter shrugged his shoulders, and merely remarking, "That being all settled, it is useless to discuss the subject further until the young lady has either accepted or rejected you," changed the topic, and we talked away amicably till we reached our quarters in time to dress for mess. After that convivial repast was over I beat a retreat to my own room, as I found the mess committee had by no means exhausted the subject of the coming ball. There had been a lull, and we thought that a calm had set in, and that those over-strained brains were going to give themselves and us a little rest; but consternation had fallen upon them owing to the non-arrival of a large instalment of champagne expected from Montreal, and their plaints were long and loud; so, inwardly anathematising them and their liquors, I left them and sought consolation and rest in a large and comfortable arm-chair in my own room, and as I sank into its calm embraceful arms I gazed round me with a sigh of contentment.

Now, from personal experience, I should say that a good dinner, a fair allowance of wine, a luxurious arm-chair, solitude, and a pipe, are to a man, however slightly in love, fuel to the flames; and if your experience tells you the same I need hardly say that, on this particular evening, under these particular circumstances, my thoughts had a decided leaning to one subject. Should I propose to Marguerite Duval or no? Prudence—that too often fatal enemy to the tender passion—said "No." Love contradicted her flatly and said "Yes." And Love, having the formidable allies before mentioned to strengthen his cause, was on the point of gaining a victory over his stern adversary, when I was recalled to a sense of my present position by the opening of the ante-room door, from whence distasteful sounds of mirth were borne on the tobacco-tainted air; then, as I feared, steps approached my door, which I had taken the precaution of locking. I paid no attention to a loud knocking, which was followed immediately by a violent wrench at the handle, and "I say, old fellow!"

"Well?" I growled surlily.

"I say, old fellow!"

"Well?" (still more surlily, and drawn out into a prolonged tone of irritation.)

"It's only me—Hood; I want to speak to you."

Here another voice chimed in: "Oh, leave him alone—he's a sulky brute—and come and have a game of pool." Then the speaker walked off, leaving Hood master of the position.

Hood, or as we generally called him, Robin, was a great ally of mine and as good a fellow as ever lived; so, repenting me of my ungraciousness, I opened my door cautiously and admitted him. Though I had yielded so far, I was too sulky to offer him my favourite arm-chair, but let him make himself as happy as he could in an American rocking-chair, with his feet up on another. Next came the inevitable question, "Got anything to drink?"

"What a bore you are!" I replied civilly, and dragging my weary limbs out of my chair, I produced from an oaken bureau some seltzer, brandy, champagne, and some old Venetian glasses, of which I was not a little proud.

"Why, old fellow, you have got an attack of blue devils to-night, and no mistake," said my companion, helping himself liberally to liquor. "I'll give you some of this delectable beverage, and you'll be all square in no time at all."

Having taken a dose of that remedy of the British sub. against all evils, I became more amiable, and we both began to smoke. At last Hood asked, as he knocked the ashes out of the top of his old gentleman's expansive head, and proceeded to refill it again from the contents of a small sealskin tobacco-pouch, "Any plans for to-morrow, Manners? I vote we get away from the busy haunts of men, especially committee men."

"No, I've no plans; and I perfectly agree with you that flight or suicide is the only course left open to us."

"Not going to see Mademoiselle Marguerite, eh?" This was said too gravely for me to take umbrage. I glanced at him to try and detect chaff, but his face was as sober as a judge's is popularly supposed to be, and wearing that peculiarly dreamy expression the physiognomy of man derives from the perfect enjoyment of a second pipe.

"No, I was there to-day," I said, conscious of a wretched failure in my attempted unconcern of tone.

Puff, puff, from Robin, and silence for a few seconds. "I am going to drive out to Nethercotes," he presently said, apparently regardless of my last remark. "Will you come? Let me see, do you know them?"

"I know the son, and between you and me, I think he is a bit of a cad."

"Not a bit of one, but the whole animal," replied Hood; "but the girls are pretty, and sing like syrens. By Jove," he added, waxing quite enthusiastic, "I could listen for ever to Pauline's voice."

"Are these young ladies Terpsichores, as well as Euterpes?" I asked sententiously.

"What the deuce do you mean?" said Robin, who was not well up in his classics, not having had the advantage of a college education. (?)

"Well, in plain English, are they dancers as well as musicians? And are they coming to our ball?"

"Decidedly. I have promised to dine there and escort them thither; and I have an invitation for you to do the same."

I was about to express my approval of the arrangement, for I had long wished to make the Miss Fanshaws' acquaintance, when my appointment with Marguerite flashed to my recollection, and I hesitated.

"I should like to go with you, of all things, Robin; but won't it make us late at our ball? For the Colonel expressed a hope we should be all there to receive our guests."

"Is that your only reason for wishing to be early? But I won't chaff you, my dear Charlie," replied Robin. "To relieve your mind, let me assure you you will be in ample time for the first dance. The Fanshaw girls have each a promising flirtation on hand, and are not likely to be late. So you come with me to Nethercotes; we'll drive out about four o'clock, and I promise you a very agreeable afternoon."

I consented, but not without some fears, for one well knows how difficult it is to start from a country house eight miles off so as to be in anything like time. The next day, at four o'clock, found me driving with Robin through Mr. Fanshaw's pretty pleasure ground, and approaching the large white verandah-guarded house. My friend was right; we had a very pleasant afternoon; the girls were large-eyed, large-limbed, and large-voiced, and sang to perfection. The dinner, also, when it arrived, was perfection; but it was unpunctual, and my fears were realised when, on the ladies leaving us, I looked at the clock and saw the hand fast approaching nine. The ladies had to dress, and I saw the gentlemen of the party intended to fortify themselves against the fatigues of the coming evening by a "big drink," and I reflected with the calm agony of despair, that if I were enabled to keep my appointment it must be by a miracle. However, I determined upon making an attempt, and leaning across the table, I said to Hood, "I must be off. Will you let me order the dogcart at once?"

"Couldn't be done, dear boy," he said, with provoking calmness; "I should have to pay a doctor's bill either for your neck or my horses' knees, to a dead certainty. No one but myself shall drive Semiramis; she takes after her beautiful namesake, who, by all accounts, was a rum one. Besides, I have promised to take Fanshaw over, and you are to cavalier the ladies."

There was nothing more to be said, and I wisely gave up the idea of being in time, and trusted to the chapter of accidents. And a very long chapter it was. It was exactly half-past ten when we got under

2 M 2

way, and it was not by any means plain sailing after that. What with a jibbing horse, a broken bolt, and something wrong with Hood's turn-out—he insisted on our waiting while he remedied it, it being, he said, so unsociable to divide parties—it was twelve o'clock before we reached Aylmer's Hall, and by that time the fun was raging fast and furious. Of course I was bound to dance with the Miss Fanshaws directly we got into the ball-room, and I did so with as good a grace as was compatible with the fact that the whole time I was looking eagerly about me for Marguerite. She was nowhere to be seen. There were gardens at the back of the Hall, and these were lit up for the occasion with coloured lamps, and there were seats placed at intervals for the comfort of exhausted dancers. Immediately on obtaining my release from the second Miss Fanshaw I went off on a systematic search for Marguerite, and this I prosecuted with unflagging perseverance, but with no success, for a quarter of an hour.

On my return to the Hall, and just as I entered an ante-room, almost dazzled with the full blaze of light, I saw my lost love approaching me; I did not notice her partner, who immediately disappeared to get her some tea, but greeting her eagerly, and pouring out apologies for my non-appearance before, I solicited the honour of a dance. To my astonishment she received me as if she had never seen me before, and regretted in the orthodox young lady style her inability to confer on me the desired favour as she was unfortunately engaged for the rest of the evening. Just then her partner returned, bearing a cup of tea, and to my further astonishment accosted me with a "Hollo! Charlie! how are you?" and there was my twin brother, whom I thought safe at Montreal, dressed in the Rifle Brigade uniform, and evidently carrying on a flirtation with my love.

"Why, when did you come, and why thus got up?" I questioned, having returned his greeting with brotherly affection.

"Too long a story to tell you now, old fellow," he replied, and murmuring something about "lost my luggage—borrowed your coat—rather a lark," rushed forward to relieve Miss Duval of her emptied cup, and taking her upon his arm again in another minute had disappeared from the room, leaving me in a state of mind in which mystification, anger, and astonishment struggled for the mastery. Indeed, I began to fancy that the fumes of Mr. Fanshaw's claret had turned my brain, and I betook myself to a distant part of the garden to collect my scattered senses. The fresh night air had the desired effect, and all became as clear as day. My brother, who was always up to some lark or another, and took especial delight in mystifying people with our extraordinary resemblance, had borrowed my uniform for that purpose, and had certainly succeeded with poor Marguerite. It was not a pleasant idea to think of the mistakes she might be guilty of in taking him for me. It was evidently impossible to enlighten her respecting the delusion she was under, and with a laugh at so ridiculous a dilemma I determined to go to her parents and explain the matter to them. I found my little friend Eunice doing wallflower between her father and mother, looking rather disconsolate, and being received with one of her prettiest smiles, I carried her off, nothing loth, to dance a quadrille which was just being formed near us. As luck would have it, her sister and my brother were *vis-à-vis*, and Marguerite, when she saw us, coloured up to the roots of her hair. Eunice looked puzzled, and kept on glancing from one to the other. "That's my twin brother, Miss Eunice," I said at last, "isn't he like me ?"

"Oh !" she exclaimed. "I never !"—her astonishment drawing forth her most nasal pronunciation. "Why did you never tell us ? And he is in the Brigade too."

"No, he is not; he is in the Guards; but lost his clothes and borrowed my uniform."

"But does Marguerite know ? She takes him for you, I really do believe, for that gentleman met us at the door and she laughed and said, 'Punctual, I do really declare.' "

"And what did he say," I asked, beginning to smell a rat.

"Oh, something smart about 'such an inducement,' you know," and then Marguerite thanked him for her flowers, and, oh ! what a deceiver he must be ! He said, 'They were the best he could get.' "

I saw it all now, and I was furious; when the dance was over, which I walked through like one in a dream, for I was almost motionless with anger, I took Eunice for a little walk and told her what I suspected; then, scrawling a note to Marguerite on a piece of old letter, explaining the trick of which she and I had been the victims, I gave it to the little sister to give her. This she promised, and having restored her to her parents, I went off to the barracks to prepare a tremendous burst of wrath against my brother and his colleagues Johnstone and Hood, who were evidently both in the plot. I had been caught in a trap, purposely prevented from proposing by Johnstone, purposely detained from keeping my appointment by Hood, and purposely personated by my brother. I need not trouble my readers with my note to Marguerite in detail, it was merely exposing the trick, and I concluded by offering her my heart, which I assured her had been her exclusive property for any number of weeks and months.

When I woke from my troubled sleep the following morning I found a note awaiting me, not from Marguerite, and it was as follows :

"RESPECTED SIR,—My daughter desires me to express the deep sense she has of the extreme and unmerited honour you have done her in offering her your hand, but she feels that with your habits of unpunctuality she could never be happy with you, and though far from being mercenary, she feels that she is not one who could exist without the amenities of life, that is to say, on love alone. She confesses that she allowed herself to become temporarily attached to you, sir, believing you to be one who could bestow on her the position her beauty should gain for her. She finds she has been deceived, and that your brother is the future possessor of the title she had reason to fancy would have been yours. Sir, she feels sure that such being the case, you will resign all pretensions to her hand. I entirely indorse my daughter's sentiments, and beg to subscribe myself

"Your obedient servant,<br>"ALFONSO DUVAL."

* * * * *

My brother was most agreeably astonished at his hearty welcome, when he appeared in the course of the morning, looking, to do him justice, extremely like a naughty boy. I handed him the elegant effusion above transcribed, and on mastering its contents he laughed till I was fearful of the consequences. He then, by my request, told me the whole story—how he had received a frantic note from Johnstone relative to my fool-hardy determination to fall into the trap laid for me, how he had run down to Agnesville, and he, Hood, and Johnstone had laid their heads together to save me.

Knowing that I was supposed by the Duval family to be the eldest son and heir, they arranged that he should personate me until he had become sufficiently acquainted with Marguerite to find out which way the land lay. In the course of the evening he had quietly told her that I was the younger son, and that he had personated me in order to make the acquaintance of one whose beauty was of world-wide renown. So well did he do this, and with such extraordinary tact, that he was immediately forgiven, and Mademoiselle Duval turned the whole battery of her charms on him, as representing the elder son. She flattered herself she had succeeded so well that, without hesitation, she gave me my *congé*. I need hardly say it was a case of the biter bit, and that my brother departed and was never more seen by the lovely eyes of *la belle* Marguerite; and when, after some months, I heard of the fickle beauty's marriage to a rich merchant it was without a regret, and with devout thankfulness that my dreadful habit of unpunctuality had for once saved me from a terrible error, and with a conviction that a man may do far worse things than commit the crime of being TEN MINUTES LATE.

# Roots.

Six months had passed away since the departure of Mary Stringer for Auckland, when, on a fine spring morning, I was startled from my work by the hoarse rattle of a chain in the landlocked harbour; and running down to the shore found myself close to the vessel that had just anchored, and on her deck saw, to my intense dismay, the young lady in question.

Beautiful, dangerous, reserved and cat-like as ever, she received all our greetings with the calmest self-possession, shook hands with my young friend as though he was the nearest acquaintance—an incident that, for some reason that I can't quite define, gave me a shiver of dread—asked if there was any chance of her father coming down the bay that afternoon, and if not, whether any one would be kind enough to row her and her luggage up to the head. Jack was there, and would be delighted, of course—Poor Jack!

The time that followed—the terrible catastrophe it ended in—I cannot yet dwell upon without almost unbearable pain, and so I shall describe what took place as shortly and as simply as I can.

Three days had not passed before Mary and my young friend had slipt back into their former positions of tutor and pupil, while Jack became a more infatuated and more hopeless worshipper than ever. A child might have foreseen that such a state of things would bring mischief and sorrow to some one of the three, and I made up my mind at last to interfere.

I first tried to do something through Dan, and was completely unsuccessful. In the first place, he looked on my young friend as the king who could do no wrong. Secondly, he, not without reason, declared that his daughter was so strong-willed and so reserved that an attempt on his part to remonstrate against anything she chose to do would be utterly futile. "As for Jack" said he, "I've got no patience with such as he. If the girl will have him, let him take her; if she won't, let him make his mind up to it like a man, instead of going tearin' and bellowin' an' moanin' about like a wild cow that's lost her calf. I do deride at such stuff."

And then I tried Mary herself, and found that Dan knew his daughter's character better than I expected. She was extremely civil, with the faintest dash of sarcasm in her civility. She utterly refused to be drawn into a discussion upon the subject, thanked me very coldly for the interest I had shown in her welfare; in fact,

somehow managed to put me in the wrong, and to make me leave
her baffled, humiliated and angry, both with myself and every one
else.

And then I did what I ought to have done at first: I spoke to my
young friend without reservation. He exasperated me at first more
than the others had done. " What a to do about nothing ! " cried he
laughing. " Why ! so far from there being any too great tenderness
between us, I have laughed at her innate tendency to flirtation till
she scarcely dares say good morning to me with decent civility for
fear of my tongue ! "

Oh, the blind idiotcy of the male mind ! Here was the whole
mischief laid bare to my feminine one in one sentence. If he had
been the most accomplished *roué* in the world he could not have
adopted a surer plan to break the vanity and win the heart of a vain,
wilful, passionate, half-educated girl like Mary.

" You silly boy," said I impatiently, " what do you suppose it is
that makes her receive your scoldings humbly, while she will fly out
at the most gentle reproof from any one else ? What is it that makes
her prefer your rudeness to any one else's flattery ? "

" Love of variety I suppose," said he doubtingly, and then held
his tongue to think. After a while he continued, " I begin to see
many little things in a new light, and believe you are right. What
shall I do ? "

" Do ? " cried I energetically. " Get away from the island at once,
and don't come back until I can get the girl sent back to her
relations in town again ;"—and I made a mental resolve that on this
occasion Miss Mary should find me as obstinate as herself. " My
husband is thinking of going to Taupo, to look at a run that is
offered for sale. You shall get instructions from him and go instead.
When will the cutter sail ? "

" She ought to have all her cargo on board by noon to-morrow,"
replied he, " and I will go in her. I do believe you're the best
hearted old woman that ever lived ! "—and I ran into the house
delighted; to mature my scheme.

To-morrow ! To-morrow ! I was one day too late.

The events that occurred before nightfall I will relate as they were
told me by the actors concerned.

On the very morning that this conversation with my young friend
took place Jack had gone up to Dan's hut, and pleaded his love to
Mary, for the third time. She, poor girl, was herself in a fretful
anxious state of mind, and he irritated her into dismissing him rudely
—almost insultingly. All the wild beast in his uneducated nature
was roused. He turned as he left her, and whispered hoarsely, " I
know who's the cause of this, curse him ! and if I don't pay him for
it "—I can't repeat the rest of the sentence.

"You had better not," replied the girl contemptuously, "if you care for your own life;" and poor Jack blundered out heedlessly into the bush, giddy and sick with rage. For some time he wandered about through the forest, trying to think, but one thought kept possession of his mind: "The infernal scoundrel! he has broken her heart and mine too, not because he cares a d—— for her, but just for amusement. Curse him! I'll pay him for it!" and then he directed his steps steadily in the direction of our bay. Straight over the hills and across the gullies he held his way, heedless of the chattering birds over head, heedless of the wild pig he startled from its lair, heedless of the little fish that darted wildly up and down the little creeks as he splashed through them, heedless of everything but his determination to find the man who had injured him, and to say and do—he knew not what.

Meanwhile my young friend, as soon as our conversation was over, had shouldered sack, a pick and a spade, and had marched off to a place about half a mile up the harbour, where he had discovered a splendid mine of *kauri-gum*, with the intention of digging up as much of it as he could, and taking it up with him to Auckland for sale, intending thereby to realise a couple of sovereigns; and having discovered the stick by which he had marked the spot he worked away till he had got as much as the sack would hold, and strolled to the edge of the cliff hard by, where he sat down to smoke his pipe and rest his aching back. It was a favorite spot of his—a network of branches over head, another below his feet growing out of the face of the cliff. Peering through the latter you could see the still water about thirty feet below, and in it generally a gigantic stingaree, lazily coasting around the black rocks. And as he lay there in peaceful solitude he subjected himself to a severe cross-examination about his behaviour to Mary. The more he examined it the worse he found it. He had been culpably thoughtless and thoughtlessly selfish. What possible right could he have had to dissect her mind as he would the body of a dead rat? What business was it of his to try and work her intellect up to a higher level than that of the people she belonged to? Had he done it for a good motive? Well, he had, partly. He had seen that unless her energies were directed to higher things they would devote themselves to low ones—that without education she promised fair to become a thoroughly mischievous dangerous woman, but his chief reason for doing it had been the interest and amusement the task brought him. He came to the conclusion that he had been a vain, meddlesome, selfish, thoughtless fool.

But I would beg those who read this, however much inclined they may be to agree with the poor boy's comments on his own conduct, not to judge him too hardly. Let them ask themselves how many young men they know who could withstand the subtle flattery conveyed in a beautiful fascinating wilful girl being soft to them and them only, obedient to their will and to none other. How many they know honourable enough never to use their influence for the slightest mischievous purpose?—honourable enough to cast that influence away without hesitation the moment they found the secret of its spell—above all, honourable and simple enough to be ashamed of having gained such influence, instead of triumphing in their power? Cast loose upon the world at the age of sixteen by an enraged Tractarian father, it is not to be wondered at that his life had been a wild and venturous though never a vicious one; and as he lay in the long grass and turned over his late conduct in his mind, he could not help being half amused at the serious way in which he was regarding what a year or so ago he would have called an unfortunate accident. He supposed that the pure solitude of his life had restored the sensitive innocence of his nursery days. Perhaps it had. Should he marry her? The fact of her being the daughter of a runaway sailor and a savage did not make much odds in the land he had resolved to stay in. But could he love her? Yes! in a kind of way he did already, but not as a young man should love the woman he marries. ; He loved her as he loved his pet dog; he could not look on her as a being to be respectfully and ecstatically worshipped. If he were ten years older, and had a little more romance kicked out him, it might do, but now—the best thing he could do for all parties was to vanish.

And as he came to this wise conclusion he heard the breaking of a stick, and turning himself on his elbow, found himself face to face with Jack. The two kept silence; Jack glaring at his foe with a kind of stony fury, the other noting the expression of his face with an honest pang of shame and remorse. There was no sound but the measured panting of Jack's lungs. Hop! pit! pat! A fearless little bird settled on the ground between them, picked up the fragment of a twig, and darted away; in the branches overhead a judicial-looking *caw-caw* established himself comfortably to watch the proceedings. . At last Jack cast his eyes down sullenly, and spoke:

" Master Charles, I've got an account to settle with you."

" Well, out with it," was the reply.

Jack's lips moved painfully and noiselessly for a few seconds: then thickly and slowly came, " Do you intend marryin' Mary Stringer?" and he held his breath, waiting for the reply.

" It's not your business, Jack; but I'll answer your question. No."

"Then," burst out the poor fellow, "you are an infernal scoundrel, and I'll thrash you within an inch of your —— life. Get on to your feet, you coward!"

My young friend never stirred.

"Calling me a coward," he said quietly, "is nonsense. You don't believe it yourself. We've got all the afternoon to fight in, if fight we must; for the present, just listen to me. You know I never tell lies; and I declare to you on my honour that I have never intentionally tried to stand between you and Mary, and have never in *any* way made love to her in my life."

It was a curious proof of the respect in which he was held that Jack, though naturally incapable of understanding the kind of friendship his rival felt towards the girl, though perfectly mad with fury, believed what he said unhesitatingly.

"Oh, no!" cried he, distorting his features into a hideous sneer. "You would'nt go to make love to her. You would'nt bemean yourself by doing nothin' so low and debasin' as that. But it's high old fun for you to go and turn the girl's head by filling it with a lot of rubbish, till she looks on all her old friends as the dirt beneath her feet. If the girl's fool enough to fall in love with you, that's her fault, in course; and if a poor devil like me breaks his heart about it, that's another unfortinit accident. You ain't done nothin' wrong in your little amusement!" And Jack laughed a short convulsive laugh, terrible to hear.

There was a leaven of truth in his sneer that went home to my young friend's heart, and he resolved to make another attempt at pacification.

"Look here, Jack. If what you have said is true I am very sorry. I am going to leave the island to-morrow, and shan't come back till Mary is gone or married."

"So you mean sneakin' off now, do you?" retorted Jack. "I'm d——d if you leave the island, or this spot either, before I've left my marks on you. Get up and fight—curse you! or I'll kick you up."

"All right," replied my young friend, getting up and preparing to fight, with that peculiar absence of anything like malice so characteristic of Englishmen; "I'm ready."

As far as strength and weight went there was not much to choose between them, but in temper and skill they were no match at all. Jack pushed in desperately to fight at close quarters, but he never had the slightest chance. At last, half stunned with blows that might have killed a weaker man, he charged furiously at his antagonist, who quietly waited for him, sprang lightly on one side, and putting his foot on a loose stone as he hit out, lost his balance, and crashing through the branches, fell with a dull thud on the rocks below.

For an instant Jack stood thunderstruck. And in that instant all the wrath and jealousy died out of his heart, and he thought of the man with the respect and love of the old days, before Mary came back from school. He peered down through the bushes, and saw the body lying motionless, half in half out of the water.

"Master Charles!" said he, hardly daring somehow to speak above his breath.

"It's no use your scrambling down here, Jack," answered a quiet voice. "Go round to the house bay and get a boat. Quick! for the tide's rising and I can't move."

There was no need to hurry poor Jack. In half an hour he had brought him home, and was running to our house for help. I sought the poor boy's cottage at once, with what anxiety and grief I need not say. No doctor could be fetched for two or three days; but it needed no doctor to tell us that the case was hopeless, for his back was broken. All he told us was that he had put his foot on a loose stone and fallen down the cliff; but Jack, in his sorrow and remorse, blurted out the true story at once. At last he said:

"If somebody must go for a doctor it had better be Jack. He can take the small life-boat, and sail at once. Yes, you must go, Jack, or there will be mischief between you and Dan. Don't blame yourself about this unlucky business, old fellow; it was all an accident, and I hope you forgive me for the trouble I have brought you. Good-bye."

And Jack took the proffered hand, and stared blankly at the smiling face, said "I wish I was dead!" and walked quietly out of the room.

Dan and Mary, as soon as they heard of what had occurred, took up their quarters at his cottage, and two kinder gentler nurses the poor boy could not have had.

In three days the doctor arrived—"the first of the vultures" as poor Charlie remarked, with one of his old quaint *moues*. They had a long talk together; and going into the room, I found, to my astonishment, the doctor doubled up with laughter in a chair by the bedside. On leaving it with me, his face saddened suddenly.

"What a pity! what a pity!" said the good old man, with real feeling. "One of the finest and pleasantest young fellows, both in mind or body, I ever met! How long will he live, madam? Upon my word, I can't tell you exactly; he may linger on for days, weeks, or perhaps even months. I wish I could do anything for him; but he has done with this world, poor boy."

And I grieved silently and bitterly, for I loved him as my own son. He had fallen amongst us homeless, friendless and lonely; and it is little wonder that all of us, but I more than all, learnt to love a character so gentle, so earnest, so clever, and yet so true. And so I felt my heart go out towards one who loved him even better than I—Mary Stringer. There was something terrible in her stoical fortitude. No tear was ever seen in her eyes, no tremor heard in her voice; the only signs she gave of a great grief were silence and immobility of countenance. Day after day she sat by the sick man's bed, with her head and her hands always ready to attend to his wants, keeping every one at a distance by her impenetrable reserve. I used to watch that pale motionless face for hour after hour, until I felt a terrified longing to see it as it looked alone; and one day this came to pass.

Being an artist in a humble way, I had acquired a habit, rather mechanical perhaps, if the truth were told, of noting the shape, colouring, and general effects of any scene before me, and it was one of the poor boy's whims after his fatal accident that I should go up every morning to Farewell Point, and come down and tell him what I had seen; and I went up there for another reason of my own, to have a quiet cry on the spot where all our pleasant talks had taken place, like a silly old woman that I was. Those who fancy that sentimental folly is confined to, or is even peculiar to, the young, know very little of human nature.

One warm bright morning I wended my way up to the Point with this rational purpose. The sun had not long been up, and had scarcely finished unveiling the calm oily-looking sea from its night mist shroud; the dew was still dropping from the bright fresh-looking leaves into the thirsty volcanic soil, and an obstinate *more-pork* was still declaring, in the teeth of all evidence, that the day had not yet commenced, when I gained the summit of the narrow ridge, and there, lying at full length on her face, amongst the luxuriant wild flowers, motionless, except with the convulsive twitching of her fingers, lay—Mary! Frightened, but still more interested, I approached her, but she neither heard nor saw. "Mary!" said I gently; and then she started up, with a face that shocked me—haggard, wild, despairing, and above all, defiant.

"I have been a little upset," said she slowly, "but it will pass away directly;" and whilst she spoke the human face seemed to transform itself into marble, as by sheer strength of will she veiled her features once more in their usual blank impenetrable calm.

"I don't want it to pass away like that!" cried I impulsively, seating myself beside her and drawing her close to me, without noticing whether she was angry or not. "My poor child, you will kill yourself, or go mad, if you let your sorrow eat into your heart as you do now. Can't you speak out, even to an old woman like me, who loves *him*, in a different way, almost as much as you do?"

My words seemed to soften her, but not in the way they would have softened an ordinary girl. She did not cry; she only said, "I can't talk," with a mind of hopeless bewildered misery, and laying her head on my shoulder closed her eyes wearily and was still. And then, after a minute had passed, she raised herself suddenly, scanned my sorrowful face with a wild eager scrutiny, pressed two or three fierce passionate kisses on my lips, and rising to her feet, wended her way, erect and alone, down towards the cottage.

And this was the beginning of a friendship—or, rather an affection, for friendship implies some sympathy in character, thought, or opinion—that will last, I firmly believe, till one of us has found rest in death.

A few days after this, as I was strolling towards the cottage with a bouquet of wild flowers, I noticed a strange boat hauled up on the beach, and on inquiry learnt that it belonged to the Rev. James Brown, of Mahurangi, who was indoors attending to my unfortunate young friend's soul at the very moment. Directly afterwards I met him returning to his boat.

My young friend used laughingly to declare that there were only two breeds of missionary : the lean, brown, dry ones, and the fat, white, damp ones ; the Rev. James Brown was of the latter strain. He answered my " Good morning " by an incoherent exclamation, and went his way gasping, and panting, like a wheezy pet spaniel that has just received its first lesson in swimming from some mischievous boy. The simile proved to be not inapt.

As I entered my young friend's room I perceived, by the half vexed half amused smile on his face, that there had been a passage of arms. " The second of the vultures," said he, " has come and gone, having received the dying donkey's last kick. I groaned in spirit when he was announced, for I knew what was coming. He sat himself down by my bed with a kind of gentle moan, and an unctuous leer on his face, intended, I believe, to express a holy pity, that almost tempted me to ask Mary to box his ears. He informed me that he had come to offer me the spiritual consolation of which I stood so much in need. I tried to save him by telling him that our opinions were probably so widely different on such matters that no good could come of our discussing them. But the self-satisfied well-meaning idiot wouldn't be saved. He said that he had heard of the infidelity of my opinions, but it was not too late for me to leave the paths of error and to return to Divine truth. I told him to remember that from my point of view I was not in error, and moreover could say with an honest conscience that I had sought Divine truth sedulously all my life. He asked me, with pompous dignity, whether he was to understand that I wilfully declined the light that had been graciously revealed.

" ' Which particular one of the countless so-called ' revelations' in the world do you refer to ? ' said I.

" ' The true one,' said he.

" ' They all call themselves the true one,' replied I mercilessly.

" ' Young man,' said he, ' you know very well which one I mean ; you are trifling with me.'

" ' Not the least,' replied I. ' I merely asked you the question to explain to you that the answer you shall hear directly applies to all of them, and not any one in particular ; ' and then I impaled the poor creature on the horns of that terrible humiliating truth that all the world so persistently shuts its eyes to: "As no man can possibly have a prior knowledge of God to enable him to know what God and his thoughts are, no man has a right to say that he is certain that any book, or opinion, or command, or theory, is absolutely God's truth; whence it follows that the truth or untruth of all opinions on supernatural things is a mere question of human judgment and belief; and as no man has a prior knowledge of God to justify him in transforming 'I believe' into 'I know this is Divine Truth,' it follows that you, whether you be a Christian, a Moslem, a Hindoo, a Buddhist, a Parsee, or a Fetish-worshipper, have no right whatever to assume that I am wilfully declining Divine truth when I happen to disagree with you about the unknowable."

"The scene that ensued is not easy to describe. He ranted, declaimed, tried to beg the question in every possible way, but I held his mental nose down to the unpalatable truth persistently, administering doses of it in fresh forms whenever he had a lucid interval, till he utterly lost his temper, likened me to an impenitent thief, told me the world I was about to go to (which would have been interesting, had the information been reliable), told me what God's opinions on my way of thinking were (which information had the same defect), and continued with volleys of contradictions and blasphemies till he had made me nearly sick and himself breathless. When he had recovered himself he asked me whether I felt no fear about my future life. I replied, that as I trusted God implicitly I did not. He stared blankly at hearing this, for the fact was, that like many another priest who raves fiercely and continuously from the pulpit against what he calls scepticism, rationalism, or freethinking, he was entirely ignorant of what it really is. I explained to him that men who have not the comforts of what is called revealed light are driven to trust God wholly and blindly; those who find it impossible to do this rush back into some dogmatic creed. But he did not choose to listen to this. He had found that he was a better hand at declamation than argument, and utterly ignoring, with the stern disingenuousness of a polemical theologian, all that had been proved five minutes before, rushed vehemently into the usual attacks upon scepticism, reviling its vain confidence in human reason, its conceit, &c.

"I was getting venomous. 'The less you say about conceit,' cried I, ' the better, considering that the sole difference between us lies in the fact that you consider your human judgment capable of deciding absolutely what theories and impressions are Divine and what are not, while I hold that all such things are beyond the reach of the human intellect. And I do wish that when you religious people of all creeds are abusing the unorthodox, the freethinkers—in short, every one who disagrees with you—you would remember that the men you respect

most, the founders of your creeds, were all unorthodox, and to a
greater or lesser extent freethinkers.'*

"At this awful speech he looked as if, like Mrs. Raddles in 'Pick-
wick,' he hoped he mightn't be tempted to forget his sex and strike
me; and whilst he stood facing me, opening and shutting his mouth
in silence, like some ingenious machine for cutting string, he was seized
upon by Mary, and firmly conducted out of the room on the ground
that I wasn't to be bothered."

He made one forget continually that his end was so near; for, living,
his spirit had been so thoughtful and earnest that it could scarcely
become more so as death approached, while his old love of humour
remained the same as ever.

"After all," said he, after a long pause, "it was very kind of him
to come all this way to try and do me good. I almost wish I had
allowed him to think he had converted me. It would have made the
worthy creature a proud and happy man, while I—I should have been
immortalised in ten thousand tracts. Just think of my humble self
contributing to the edification of any number of old ladies, not to
speak of their cats."

"I don't like to hear you speak like that," said I.

"I am very sorry," replied he; "but that well-meaning ass's blunders
reminded me bitterly how utterly I had wasted my life and its opportunities. I had a noble cause before me, and neglected it, because I
thought I might do more harm than good; but I begin to see now
that I was mistaken."

"Do you mean to say," cried I astonished, "that after all you have
told me you have come to the conclusion that it was your duty to have
set up a pulpit, and to have tried to instill your religion into the
world in general?"

"Certainly not," replied he. "I am no mad conceited enthusiast,
who fancies that his panacea is going to put the whole world straight,
without comparing it calmly and closely with what they already
possess, and judging which is likely to suit them best on the whole.
My creed is not narrow, exclusive, or conceited enough to be a pro-
selytising one, whether it is likely to do good or the reverse. Looking
as I do on all creeds as Divine instruments for the improvement of
humanity, I am not likely to try and force down men's throats what

* Freethinking does not necessarily lead to Rationalism; for what is
meant usually by that term is the offspring of our increased scientific
knowledge. But a certain amount of free thought, however distorted, has
been the cause of every new religion, and each at its birth claims to be
more rational, that is to say, more in accordance with man's impressions of
all around him, than its predecessor. And in judging this theory, please
remember that at the time most of the religions now holding sway in the
world were instituted, miracles and such like were looked upon as being no
more irrational and improbable than a thunderstorm.

is after all only my idea of more perfect truth, unless I am sure it would tend to make men better and happier; and you know that for several reasons I am pretty sure that it would not. Because I have had corns and have been forced to give up shoes, shall I try to force all mankind to do the same, whether they have corns or not? I may, with many others, believe that a time will come when such things will be found unnecessary; but the time is not come, as any one who chooses to study human thought and character may plainly see.

"If I preached a sermon to a mixed assemblage of all classes, religions and characters, it would be something of this kind: 'You who think and you who are frivolous, you whose time and thoughts are devoted to your business in life and you who are idle, you who are educated and you who are not, are met here to-day to hear me speak about my religious creed. I cannot teach it to you, and unless it is already born in your minds I doubt if I can even put you in the way of learning it; but I will try. You will have to devote many years to its study. Begin by travelling until your preconceived ideas about everything are thoroughly shaken. Try to learn meanwhile, at least, the general philosophical truths of science; examine carefully into the creeds of the various races you visit, and compare them with strict impartiality with the one you were brought up in; read a few books on every side of the religious question (if you have any brains it don't matter which), but above all observe and think; make the quest of truth your sole object, and shrink from no conclusions your reason may lead you to; argue on religion with any one who is fool enough to let you, for it is seldom that one man's mind clashes with another's without evolving some spark of new light, and argument makes a man think keenly and explodes fallacies. After a steady course of this kind, together with a mixture of solitude and contemplation of nature and men's minds, you will find your early prejudices considerably weakened; and to put a finishing touch to them, study such books as 'Aids to Faith' and any sermons about freethinking you can get hold of. About this period, if you have not had time and opportunity to become a monomaniac, if you have only read and not thought out things for yourself, if an earnest desire to learn a little of God's greatness is not rooted in your character, you will lapse into reckless despair, sceptical indifference, or violent superstition. If you are really in earnest you will tide over this time, but the more earnest you are the more miserable you will be. Keep on working at the philosophy of science, always remembering that you get nothing from reading without the help of reflection, and that it is the work of your own mind, not that of others, you must depend on. And then perhaps you may arrive at the glorious end that I am honestly proud of; that is to say, you will have lost all those comforting helpful dogmas of your old creed that it caused you such misery to leave, you will have gained (if you have escaped shipwreck) a higher, broader idea of Divinity and the universe, and your code of right and wrong will be pretty nearly the same as that you professed before, without the comforting feeling that you used to have, that it represented God's own ideas upon the subject. Now all you who came here to-day, not because you were dissatisfied with the form of belief you profess, but simply because you were curious to hear some new thing, don't you think you may as well go home again and stick to your old religions, which are more likely to keep you decent than any I can give you the key to? Are you prepared to devote all this time and trouble to the study of a religion which will teach you very little that is new practically, and which, as you are pretty well contented as you are, you can't really want? I have neither the wish nor the power to convert you; but if in the crowd here present there are any earnest sceptics—men who are unable to reconcile their creed with their consciences, I, and others far wiser and cleverer than I, will do our best to help them to work out their own salvation. I shall not attempt to destroy or supplant any portion of your various creeds except those dogmas which produce intolerance. On that subject I will preach through my whole life.' And so ends my imaginary sermon.

" And now you will guess what my purpose in life should have been: to do what little I could towards helping those floundering in the sea of thought like myself; and, as far as the world in general is concerned, to contribute my mite towards the suppression of intolerance in all creeds.

" The only way in which this can ever be done is by teaching mankind the mental foundations on which their belief is founded, and forcing them to see what the things they abuse really are. For as surely as conceit is the mother of intolerance, ignorance is the father. All the misery, the bitterness, the sorrow, the loneliness produced in so many families that I know by religious difference, have their real root in ignorance. For instance, a religious family look upon a sceptic amongst them as something wicked and horrible, simply because they don't know the mental grounds of their own belief or the nature of his. Every Sunday, in many a pulpit, an imaginary freethinker—a distorted, foolish, lying caricature—is stuck up, and of course triumphantly knocked down again, with the whole question begged; while we sceptics, fools that we are, smile at the preacher's ignorance or growl at his disingenuousness, seldom reflecting that the promulgation of such misstatements and slanders is the cause of the bitter loneliness of our lives. Unless we speak out plainly and fairly, how is this mass of lying and misconception to be cleared away?

" I tell you that if I could have persuaded half a dozen religious men that scepticism is born, not out of conceit in human judgment, but the

reverse: not out of indifference, but earnestness—not out of irreverence, but reverence for God—that far from being a vain glorification
of the human intellect, it claimed a narrower limit for its powers; if
I could have shown them the real grounds on which it differed from
religion—convinced them that the responsibility of what we believe or
disbelieve *must* rest upon our private human judgment, and that
therefore we should look upon differences in religion merely as differences in opinion and fallacies of thought—I should feel that I had
done my duty in my generation. The only way men can become
tolerant is by learning the roots, first of their own opinions, then of
those that disagree."

"But haven't you always told me," said I, "that what you called
'intolerance,' 'exclusiveness,' 'narrowness,' 'conceit,' in religious
thought, had a power for good over men's actions that seemed to
balance its evils?"

"It is a great problem," replied he slowly. "Complete intolerance
means fanatical persecution; complete tolerance (utterly impossible
to men as they are) would mean indifference. We must strike a
medium as well as we can—a medium that will change perpetually as
men change. Intolerance produced by a narrow exclusive view of
Divine favours seemed, to the best of my knowledge, to be intrinsically
wrong, and my scruples in attacking it were very absurd; something
like a child hesitating to pull off a piece of bark from a tree for fear it
should bring the tree down with a crash. I begin to think that without knowing it I have been a conceited fool. I can only say that I
acted according to my lights.

"But even if I could not have rid myself of the habit of looking at
everything from both sides of the hedge, I should have made public
my very hesitation and its reasons. For there is a kind of good, but
utterly illogical, tolerance gaining ground amongst mankind, the roots
of which require to be exposed, by showing the principles, the virtues,
and the vices of both tolerance and intolerance. It is a confused
feeling, more of the heart than the head, amongst those who unconsciously drop out of sight the exclusive and damnatory tenets of their
creeds. And unless this movement is looked fairly in the face, unless
religious tenets about God are made to keep pace with the development
of the human mind, there will come a time (I have seen signs of it
already) when a great mass of men will be startled to find themselves
positive disbelievers in the actual meaning of the dogmas they profess,
and will rush into infidelity, not because they are fit to accept a
natural religion void of dogma and superstition, but because they have
outgrown some of the articles of their creeds. The consequence of
this anarchy of thought will be to purify religions, but the process
will be dreadful—violent alternations between reckless atheism and
frantic superstition."

" I don't quite see," said I, after a long pause, "how you can reconcile the two purposes, of obtaining toleration by showing what scepticism
really is and of trying to give help and sympathy to sceptics, with your
determination not to preach your own religion."

"It all depends upon what you mean by preaching," replied he.
" You would not suspect a man who wrote an article in the 'Quarterly,'
showing fairly what Mohammedanism was, and how it differed from
Christianity, of trying to convert people to the faith of Mohammed.
What *I* understand by preaching a religion is trying by every possible
means to convert people from their faith to yours, trying to show your
faith in the most attractive light and to hide its practical deficiencies.
If you will think over our various conversations, you will not accuse
me of *that*. Besides, this scepticism has (at any rate apparently) none
of the comforts for which men value their religions. It has no attraction whatever, but the reverse. And men who have a religion that
contents them, may be converted to another faith by their feelings
and inclinations, but never by simple reasón, to a way of thinking
whose sole glory is a painful humble uncertainty on subjects they
could scarcely bear to doubt upon for a moment. I am past the folly
of thinking that I either would or *could* influence such men towards
anything except a little wider toleration.

"But to those who are not content—those who, either from the
greater earnestness, originality, or sensitiveness of their minds, or from
having the sleep of early prejudice destroyed by various causes, feel
the vivid common-sense reality of many things which to others convey
no startling meaning—those to whom many of the doctrines of the
creed they were brought up in seem perpetual offences against God
and their conscience, I would cry: Work out your own salvation! I
honestly believe it is their best path; for if they do not cast the
offending dogmas away and seek truth by honest fearless thought,
they either benumb themselves into a terrible indifference, or, having
forced themselves to believe in the tenets that caused them such
misery, they produce a ghastly caricature of their creed, with all its
worst points fanatically exaggerated, which shocks and astonishes their
fellow-believers, who have not experienced the phases of mind they
have passed through.

"You will say that the experiment is a dangerous one. I will not
deny it. The man accustomed to support life on stimulants and nar-
cotics may find a sudden change to a simple diet unpleasant, perhaps
fatal. But it saves them at least from the terrible spirit death, or
the no less terrible distortion of mind, that I have just spoken of. And
I think the danger is somewhat overdrawn. The man whose faith in
the religion of his birth is shaken only by the love of truth and reverence for God, is not likely to rush despairingly to lower things in his
search for a haven."

"Yes," continued he dreamily, "there *is* a haven, once we have passed through the bitter ordeal of finding some knowledge beyond our reach that we had been taught to think so near.

"If we can find peace for our consciences in no dogmatic creed we have God left to us, with all His universe, as the book to teach us a little of His ways. Every new discovery in science adds to our feeling of His omnipresent wonder, and places another stone in the walls of a temple of pure Monotheism.

"It was not always thus, and we should be thankful that we live as late as we do. There was a time when a man who, even from a spirit of reverence, doubted the religion of his day, had no refuge for his soul to flee to. Nature could then give him but little help; the foolish doctrine of entities was then in existence, and the false charge of Atheism, levelled to this day against free thought and infidelity, was then true. But science has done and is doing the great work. Stretching out its researches in all directions, showing the inscrutable mystery of all things, small and great, it is teaching us a universal God, unconfined within the pale of any human creed, and forcing us to believe in Him and trust Him.

"The old blank hopelessness of the earnest sceptic is passing away. When his faith in the theory he has been brought up in has broken down, he does not feel that God has gone with it. All around him testifies to Him, and he has now a power of realising the greatness and the marvel of His works, and of learning from that realisation an implicit trust in Him, that in a past age could scarcely have been more than a misty dream. Out of a bitter lesson of humility come first trust, and then peace."

He seemed exhausted and inclined to sleep, so I left him and went home.

Three days afterwards, as I was returning from my usual pilgrimage to Farewell Point, I met Dan seeking me, with his message written in his face. "It is coming," whispered he; and I followed him in silence to the cottage.

As I entered the room I saw Mary kneeling by the bedside, with her face buried in the pillow. I bent over the dying boy and kissed him, for I could not speak. He took my hand and laid it gently on Mary's head. She looked up, and he, touching her forehead with his lips, settled his face in the pillow, like a weary child falling asleep, and was still.

\* \* \* \* \* \*

"What is the object," may be asked, "of giving this eccentric young man's thoughts and opinions? Who can be any the better for reading them?"

In the first place, let me say that this eccentric boy's mind is a type of a class among the most earnest and thoughtful young men of the

day—far more common than is usually supposed, because, for obvious
reasons, they keep their opinions secret from all but their fellow-
sufferers.

My first object is, by showing what a sceptic really is when stripped
of the slanders constantly hurled against him, to plead to society in
general for a little more fairness and toleration towards him; for
though the strength and purity of my young friend's individual
character held him up, I *know* of many of his way of thinking who
have been driven into morbid vanity, indifference, and despair, entirely
by the narrow ignorant want of charity of the people about them.
I almost doubt sometimes whether the good people of this world
have not ruined as many souls as the wicked!

But I have another object: to teach (if possible) a lesson by
example to young freethinkers themselves. For there is another class
of earnest sceptics far more noisy, if not more numerous, I grieve to
say, than that represented by my young friend, who, though bearing a
general likeness to him in their general method of thought, are widely
different from him in several very important particulars. On entering
manhood, their second birth, their period of *Sturm und Drang*, as my
poor boy used to call it, comes suddenly upon them. They become
positively intoxicated all at once by the superb logic of the philosophical
writers of the day; and their conversion is generally extreme, because it
is sudden—shallow, because it has been developed more by quick external than gradual internal means. In religion and politics they are
equally radical; they are as bigoted as the opponents they hate and
despise most, for they cannot acknowledge the good worked by any
belief but their own. Both in religion and politics they would
destroy, if they had the power, everything that does not fit itself to
their ideas, without reflecting whether it does most harm or most
good, or whether they have anything equally serviceable to replace it;
and they will boldly defend this line of conduct by saying, "It is
not our business to calculate about the utility of anything: the
question is one of right or wrong. Has not the greatest thinker of
our day proved conclusively that we should be guided only by what
is right according to first principles, because no man can have a sufficient knowledge of other minds to justify him in neglecting abstract
right for what he considers utility? Read 'Social Statics,' &c.,
and they will teach you the *truth*, dear Mrs. ——, as they have
done me." Oh, pot and kettle! pot and kettle! as my young friend
would have said. Both these young fanatics, and often the idols
they worship, seem to forget entirely that men disagree as utterly
about the rectitude as they do about the utility of all things—religious, political, and social; and moreover, that no two of their
idolised philosophers, starting from the same first principle, arrive on
the whole at the same conclusions. To my young friend's serious

question, "Supposing that all the superstitions, the false claims to Divine knowledge, which exist now, could be abolished, what could you put in their places which would have an equal power for good over the actions of mankind? They have only the fanatical argument above quoted to answer with; a sophism which, a little caricatured, seems to be "You are utterly to discard your fallible knowledge of what is likely to do good, and to look on your opinion of what is abstract truth as infallible." The fact is, that this school manage, like their religious opponents, though in a different way, to look upon abstract truth and utility as identical, which, *when men are perfected*, they no doubt will be. To explain. The religious man says, "See how useful this dogma is in improving mankind; *therefore* it must be true." The other says, "See how incontestably true this conclusion is; *therefore* it *must* have a power for good over men's minds." My young friend would have said, "Both inferences are equally unjustifiable. Men being perfect, it is possible that absolute truth and what is best for them may be identical; but men being imperfect, an opinion may be too much before the age to be beneficial if spread, just as we see many opinions once useful now behind it; so, until we near the goal of perfection, we must remember that absolute truth and utility cannot be identical, and that moreover, we have no right to claim a knowledge of what absolute truth is. The essence, the glory, of the sceptic's creed, should be, the humility that is born of doubt—the doubt that is born of a broad wide power of acknowledging that all things equally are part of God's work. Directly we begin to claim absolute truth we become as bad as the bigots we despise; nay, worse; for they have been brought up to believe their creed an incontestable truth, and our training should have taught us more liberality." Whether my young friend's mind was one to be admired or despised, I leave it to my readers to decide.

# The Wooing O't.

## A NOVEL.

------

## CHAPTER XXII.

MAGGIE was fortunate in descending the stairs as the trio from the drawing-room crossed the hall.

"Just in time, Miss Grey," said Miss Grantham, as she followed Lady Dormer, who was leaning on the arm of a stout, square, elderly gentleman, with twinkling black eyes and a short throat.

"Glad to see you, Miss Grey," said Lady Dormer, with a kind little nod. "Miss Grey—Mr. Bolton," said the hostess. "Wheeler, has Mr. Trafford returned?"

"Yes'm. Just come in."

"Do you never take a gun now, Mr. Bolton?"

"No, my dear lady," in a rich, slightly choky voice. "I am quite content to eat the spoil of other people's."

"If I remember right, you used to shoot—when I was a little girl, I mean."

"I have had moments of folly," Mr. Bolton was beginning, when Mr. Trafford came in and took his place beside Maggie, and on Miss Grantham's right. He was immediately waited on by the three attendants with a subdued ardour very expressive to Maggie's observant optics.

"Well, Mr. Trafford, any sport?" asked Lady Dormer.

"Nothing startling—two brace and a half. I assure you, Margaret, your preserves are fearfully poached; and I suspect will be, till you turn sportswoman yourself. I wonder you don't. You have tried nearly everything. Why not a gun?"

"Nonsense. But I am vexed that Hood and his men are so careless. You must row them for me, Geoff."

Maggie fancied she observed a triumphant sort of twinkle in Mr. Bolton's eyes as Miss Grantham spoke.

"What have you been about? Perpetrated a murder or two, or made the virtuous hero whop the bad one?"

"Really, Geoffrey, your expressions are painfully low."

"You must know, Bolton," continued Trafford, "that Miss Grantham"——

"Pray, pray remember it is a secret!" cried that lady a little eagerly. "Do not be a traitor both to Miss Grey and myself."

"Oh! if it is a secret, that alters the case. Bolton shall not hear a word from me, not even if he tried, with the diabolical art of his profession, to bribe me."

"Really, Mr. Bolton," said Lady Dormer, apologetically, "young people indulge in strange language nowadays."

Miss Grantham laughed heartily, and Maggie joined. At the once familiar sound of her frank sweet laughter Trafford turned and offered her some grapes which stood before him, observing that "hunger and exercise had made him oblivious of every one's wants but his own." "It is a splendid day, Margaret," he continued. "Frost not too hard. We ought to start as soon as you can dress, and we may be able to get round through Southam before it is dark."

"Very well." Oh, by the way, I had a letter from poor dear Lady Brockhurst this morning. She writes in miserable spirits from Paris. Lord Brockhurst had just started for Algeria with his brother and a Doctor somebody. She is obliged to return on account of the boys' holidays, and will be at Southam next week. So much the better for me. But she seems terribly cut up."

"Hum!" said Trafford. "If she stays against her will, it is a new *rôle* for the fair viscountess. I suspect she considers poor Brockhurst a good riddance."

"What an ill-natured censorious creature you are, Geoffrey," cried Miss Grantham, rising. "Lady Dormer—Mr. Bolton, if you will excuse me, I will go and dress."

"May I come with you ?" said Maggie, in a low tone.

"Yes, certainly," in the most gracious voice ; and they left the room.

"Well, Mr. Trafford, if you and Mr. Bolton will excuse *me*, I will go to the drawing-room ; it is warmer."

Trafford and Bolton rose as her ladyship withdrew. Trafford nodded to the butler in token of dismissal. The two gentlemen were alone.

"Who is that quiet girl with the soft eyes and pleasant smile?" asked Bolton.

"That quiet girl with the soft eyes, as you discriminatingly remark," said Trafford, pouring out a bumper of sherry, and then looking straight at his companion, "is the young lady who objected to be Countess of Torchester."

"The deuce she is! How, in Heaven's name, does she come here ?"

"Answered Miss Grantham's advertisement for a secretary, and promises to be *l'enfant gâté* of the establishment."

"Secretary ! What does she want with a secretary ?"

"Literary undertakings of some magnitude."

"Literary bosh ! It is frightful to think of this noble property being in the hands of a fanciful inexperienced girl. She really ought to marry, Mr. Trafford."

"Why don't you tell her so ? You have rather more influence with her than most people."

"I fancy advice or suggestions, especially on *such* a subject, would be most acceptable from yourself. Really, Mr. Trafford, it is impious to throw aside the fortune that seems to court you."

"Court me! Pooh, Bolton! that is putting it rather strong." And Trafford's brow dropped rather sternly, which the careful man of business observing, he steered deftly away a point or two.

"Rather awkward, will it not be, when Lady Torchester and the Earl come?"

"Yes; and by Jove, my aunt will think I placed Miss Grey here," cried Trafford, with a sudden recollection of his intercession with the Countess, and speaking without thought.

"Why should she take up so extraordinary an idea?" asked Mr. Bolton, suspiciously; while Trafford cursed his own heedlessness.

"Oh! Lady Torchester was anxious to do something for Miss Grey, to show that she was pleased with her; and as I saw the poor girl was not very happily placed, I suggested that the Countess should write to her. She did, and Miss Grey never got the letter, so there was an end of it; and that's all. Pass the sherry, Bolton."

"Hum!" said the sage. "It's all very queer; and it will be uncommonly awkward. Could you suggest to Miss Grantham"——

"I will suggest nothing. And if you ever catch me meddling in any one's affairs—amorous or otherwise—you have my permission to put me in the parish stocks."

"Are you ready, Geoff?" said Miss Grantham, opening the dining-room door. Trafford rose very readily.

"And what are you going to do, Mr. Bolton?" continued the hostess. "Perhaps you would have come with Geoff and me if I had thought of it in time?"

"Indeed I should not, my dear young lady," said the old lawyer, with an exceedingly knowing smile. "Even in Lincoln's Inn we are aware that two are company and three are not."

Miss Grantham laughed and blushed, and frowned slightly. "What will you do then? Drive with Lady Dormer?"

"No, I am much obliged to you. I have work enough cut out in the library to fill up my time."

"Nevertheless, Mr. Bolton, your visit to Grantham must not be all work."

"Even that couldn't turn Bolton into a dull old boy," said Trafford, gaily. "Come, Miss Grantham, your steed and your humble servant wait."

Maggie had descended, by her mistress's invitation, to see her mount. "Now, if you want assistance in your notes and queries," continued Trafford to the lawyer, "ask Miss Grey to help you; our gracious hostess gives her a high character for skill and diligence."

"Yes, really, Mr. Bolton," said Miss Grantham, as she laid her hand on Trafford's shoulder to mount, "Miss Grey is the most perfect secretary in the world;" and Miss Grantham sprang lightly to her saddle.

"Much too perfect to be wasted on me," said Mr. Bolton, with an echo as of a growl in his voice. Maggie felt foolishly hurt at this rejection, and a little healthy stinging shoot of dislike put forth a germ in her heart.

"Dispose of yourselves as you will," said Miss Grantham pleasantly, and rode away. Trafford's horse, fresher and not so well tempered as his companion, pranced and tried to bolt, but was soon reduced to order; his rider smiled a kindly smile, and waved his hand to the quiet slender figure standing on the steps, and looking wistfully after them; so the equestrians passed out of sight.

Mr. Bolton made Maggie rather a grand bow, and stood aside to let her pass. After a moment's hesitation she went to Lady Dormer in the drawing-room, and found that excellent lady absolutely on her legs (to speak irreverently).

"Would you like to drive with me, Miss Grey? I am going now."

"Yes, very much, thank you."

"Then put on your bonnet; it is a lovely day."

Lady Dormer made some praiseworthy attempts at conversation during their tranquil drive, but on the whole Maggie had ample time for undisturbed reflection. And she thought very intensely of what was before her in the impending domestication with Lord Torchester and his mother. "I should not mind him so much as her, but she will be vexed to find me here, and afraid of Lord Torchester taking a fancy to me again. And then my having left her letter unanswered! I wish they were not coming! And Miss Grantham, I do not think she would like the idea of Lord Torchester's whim about me. I wish I could go away somewhere." Yet in her heart she was glad she could not. Still Grantham was wonderfully changed from the day before. There was no longer the sort of tranquillising hope, the consciousness of rest. No; there was instead a feverish mingling of dread and pleasure, which yet she did not like to resign. And Miss Grantham; inexperienced as she was, Maggie could not help thinking that Trafford possessed the long list of requirements which the beautiful heiress had declared essential in a husband. "I am afraid she loves him. Afraid—why? Because, whispered her inner conviction, I do not think he loves her; but he will, he must! she is so fair and kind and generous." At this point of her meditations Lady Dormer exclaimed, "I think that must be Miss Grantham and Mr. Trafford before us."

Maggie looked ahead and recognised the equestrians. They were proceeding leisurely at a foot pace, evidently in deep conversation, for Trafford's hand was on the crest of his companion's horse, and his face was turned towards her. They drew up to let the carriage pass, Lady Dormer inquired if they had had a pleasant ride, and if they were on their way back.

"We have had the most charming gallop over Southam Park,"

returned Miss Grantham, who looked radiantly handsome; "and we shall return by the Bridge and Hartley End."

"Why," cried Lady Dormer in some dismay, "you will not be back till dark!"

"Well, both Geoff and I know the country," returned Miss Grantham carelessly; then to Maggie, "So you left poor Mr. Bolton all alone, Miss Grey?"

"He did not want me," replied Maggie, laughing, and Lady Dormer was good enough to say she did.

The carriage rolled on, and in due course set down its freight considerably the fresher for their airing—Lady Dormer inviting Maggie to partake of afternoon tea with her, and in her own mind pronouncing her to be a remarkably nice, well bred, unobtrusive young person. Maggie was glad to escape as soon as she could from her ladyship's tea, and the threatened elucidation of another pattern, to her room, in order to fasten black ribbon bows on her white dress, for Miss Grantham had said, "I shall send for you this evening."

And Maggie was sent for, and found the heiress and her friends sipping their tea and coffee in another and a superb room, as it seemed to the little secretary. It was brilliantly lit by a large chandelier full of wax lights, and contained a grand piano, a harp, and some music stands.

Miss Grantham explained pleasantly that Miss Grey was going to try over some songs with her, but they were not accustomed to each other, &c. And then song after song succeeded. Mr. Bolton, who had almost as keen an appreciation of music as of claret and old port, listened and applauded heartily. Trafford lay back in an easy chair, from which he could see the performers if he chose to look, but his eyes seemed wholly or half closed, and he was so still that he looked more like a recumbent lay figure than a living man.

"Now Geoff! are you asleep?" asked Miss Grantham a little impatiently, after she had sung a *Schlummerlied*.

"No, no," said he; "only delightfully comfortable; pray go on." When it was over Mr. Bolton condescended to remark that Miss Grey accompanied very fairly; while Trafford said, "Rather more grateful work than running after Mrs. Berry's 'rapid acts'?—for I can think of no other term—eh, Miss Grey?"

"Very indeed," said Maggie. "I fancy if Miss Grantham allows me to accompany her I must succeed by-and-by, it is so delightful to me."

"You have improved marvellously," said Trafford to his cousin, "but it is a long time since you and I spent an evening at Grantham together."

Miss Grantham said something in a low voice, and as Trafford bent to hear it, Maggie discreetly turned away, and began to talk to Bolton, who appeared much more approachable than in the morning, though she could not help thinking his little twinkling eyes very searching.

Two more days passed very like the one just described. Miss Grantham was scarcely five minutes at a time anywhere, but on horseback—and Maggie went down regularly each evening to the music-room.

She scarce exchanged a word with Trafford, yet he never quite let her feel she was overlooked or neglected. He was rather silent, and accepted court from, rather than offered it to, his cousin. Indeed, Maggie thought that she, even as simple, humble, Maggie Grey, would have exacted more homage. "But they are related and understand each other, for it is impossible he can be indifferent; but he seems changed, he is not like the Mr. Trafford who danced with me at the ball."

"Miss Grey," said the mistress of the mansion, walking into her room one morning. "I want you to come over to Castleford with me immediately after breakfast. Geoffrey has absolutely persuaded Mr. Bolton to venture into the preserves, and I have a special errand to Castleford; pray wrap up, for it is very cold."

Trafford and Mr. Bolton were waiting to hand the ladies into Miss Grantham's special equipage.

"An early start! May I ask the object?" said the former.

"Mysteries of shopping, beyond your comprehension."

"Then there are shops in Castleford?"

"What disgraceful ignorance," said Bolton.

"Mr. Trafford is so provoking," said the fair charioteer, after having driven a little way in silence.

"Is he?" asked her companion.

"Yes, he is so indolent and apathetic. Mr. Bolton and I almost quarrelled with him at breakfast. He might be anything or do anything, but he won't. He ought to be in Parliament." A long pause.

"Miss Grey, do you know I am going into Castleford on your account?"

"On my account! How can that be?"

"Promise to take what I am going to say in good part, and not to be unkind or disagreeable."

"Unkind—me—to you? Impossible, in every way."

"Well, I have noticed that you very considerately wear black since you came down here, and I thought that as you are not wearing black on your own account you would not mind accepting a couple of dresses from me. We are on the way to order them."

"Miss Grantham! you are only too kind and considerate. I never dreamed of such a thing. If you really wish to give them to me I shall of course accept them as frankly as they are offered. But ought you not to wait and see if you continue"——

"What should I wait for? I am only so glad you are pleased and

do not try to do the grand. Poor dear Miss Colby would have made
me a speech a yard long; by-the-by, I must write to her, but I seem
never to have time for anything. Really to-morrow we must do
something to the story, and on Tuesday the Torchesters will be here,
and then Christmas."

"Yet it seems such a pity not to finish your story."

"Well, we must see about it. You never saw Lady Torchester?"

"Never."

"She is not handsome, but then she is very good. Tremendously
religious, and so fond of those wretched Low Church clergymen, who
look like Dissenters—so different from our rector." And Miss Grantham
talked pleasantly at intervals till they reached the little town of
Castleford, which was in its way a flourishing place. The grandest
shop in the principal street was Miss Moody's, where the wealthy
farmers' daughters thought fashion itself lay enshrined.

"What an awful name!" said Miss Grantham, laughing, as she
drew up at the door. "She ought to change it to Mademoiselle
Modiste."

The lady of Grantham was received with the most profound
deference, the most obsequious attention, and to do her justice she
gave no unnecessary trouble. A rick black silk was quickly chosen
and ordered to be made up, and then a thin black gauze or grenadine
was picked out, and some special directions given as to its being somewhat elaborately fashioned as a demi-toilette dress. "Mind, Miss
Moody, they must both be finished and ready for my messenger by
eight o'clock on Monday evening."

"Indeed, madam, this is a very busy time, and I almost fear"——

"Oh nonsense! If you cannot promise them on Monday we shall
retract the order and send to town for them. Come, you must promise
them on Monday and fulfil your promise."

"Well 'm, rather than disoblige you in any way I will put aside
other work. And though this is always a busy time it will not be quite
so busy as usual, on account of poor Mr. Burge's sad illness."

"Why! what is the matter with him?" asked Miss Grantham,
who was examining some bonnets with more curiosity than admiration.

"Some say apoplexy, and others congestion of the brain; but he
fell quite sudden at the Town 'All on Saturday, and they say has
not spoken since."

"I am sorry to hear it," returned the heiress thoughtfully. "Lord
Grantham had a great regard for him. Make haste and fit on Miss
Grey's dress, for I must drive round and inquire for him before we
go back."

"This Mr. Burge is the mayor and member for the town. I think
he was a tanner—a very clever man. He sometimes came to dine at
Grantham. I must call," said Miss Grantham, and fell into a fit of

musing which lasted till she had made her inquiries at Riversdale, a very pretty but highly tutored place on the outskirts of the town. The replies were not very encouraging. Mr. Burge had been attacked with congestion of the brain. Sir Savill Row had been telegraphed for and had given hopes of his restoration. Miss Grantham was exceedingly silent all the way back, but when about half way across the park she exclaimed: "I have been meditating a grand scheme; perhaps I shall tell you some day. When you take off your bonnet come into the study; I think I shall want you there."

As soon as she entered the hall Miss Grantham asked, "Has Mr. Bolton come in?"

"Yes, 'm, some time ago."

"Ask him to come to me in the library," said she, and walked away in the direction of that apartment.

Meantime Trafford had returned to the house with Mr. Bolton, who speedily discovered that the cold struck to his feet and would bring on gout. Finding no one in the drawing-room but Lady Dormer, dozing over her crochet, Trafford retired to his own room, and sitting down to his writing-table, wrote the day of the month rather slowly at the top of a sheet of note paper, and a little lower down, "My dear Lady Torchester." Then he leant back and thought for a while in a desultory manner. It was curious that his suspicions, roused by Miss Grantham's description of her delightful secretary, should have been verified—and that Maggie Grey should be domiciled under the same roof with him; curious, too, that she should have answered Miss Grantham's advertisement. Had she then rejected the ourang of a cousin? It was impossible she could ever have thought seriously of him. Yet certainly she had a tender recollection of him in Paris. Paris!—what an idiot he had made of himself there! Nevertheless, what pleasant hours he had spent in that cool shady *salon* of Mrs. Berry's! From his soul he wished himself back there with no thought for the morrow. It was strange how well that simple humbly-born little Maggie stood the contrast with her splendid patroness. "What is it in that girl that makes her an individual everywhere—herself always? But I had better write and tell Lady Torchester she is here. I wish I could speak a word or two first with Maggie—Miss Grey—and by Jove!" looking up out of the window which commanded the approach, "there come the white ponies. I'll go down to the study, ask for the precious MS., and try my luck."

When Maggie came into the room a few minutes after she found Mr. Trafford standing in one of the windows. She was quite composed, for the strange prescience with which she seemed gifted regarding him told her she would find him there.

"What have you done with Miss Grantham?"

"She has gone to talk to Mr. Bolton in the library."

"I was greatly surprised to find you here, Miss Grey," said

Trafford, taking his stand on the hearth-rug, as Maggie sat down by the large writing-table.

"I suppose you were."

"I supposed a very different destiny for you," looking intently at her; but she did not raise her eyes. "Forgive me," he went on, "if I use the privilege of an old acquaintance; are you happy here—happier than with Mrs. Berry?"

"I am not quite sure," returned Maggie, answering with a fuller truth than she spoke, even to her own heart, raising her eyes and looking straight into his. "Miss Grantham is so kind and generous and beautiful," she went on with enthusiasm, "it is delightful to be with her; but poor Mrs. Berry, she was my first friend. I knew I was useful, almost essential to her, and equality is a grand ingredient in friendship, affection, everything."

"Is it?" said Trafford mechanically, as she paused, for he was thinking of her eyes. They were not great blue orbs—that challenged instant admiration, like Miss Grantham's; they were merely grey, darkly fringed and full, generally very quiet restful eyes; but once they began to speak their own language to you you could not help feeling curious as to what they would say next. At this moment there was an earnest outlook in them as if she was thinking of her past more than her interlocutor.

"Now you know I cannot be of the smallest *real* use to Miss Grantham, but it is a great pleasure and advantage to be with her, and I consider it a wonderful piece of good fortune to have found her; so I will just try and enjoy the sunshine while I have it. Is that not true wisdom, Mr. Trafford?"—with a frank smile.

"Excellent philosophy. I always thought you a philosopher, Miss Grey." A slightly awkward pause, during which Trafford meditated how he could best introduce the Torchester topic, and not finding a way, exclaimed, "I suppose you have quite lost sight of that old Red Republican you secluded, *au cinquième?*"

"Oh yes, quite, I am afraid," with a sad little smile. "Poor Monsieur Duval!"

"I believe, in spite of all your enthusiasm for my charming kinswoman, you would rather read his papers to him than write her books."

"Just think what a treasure I should be to him. And do you know, he was very lovable?"

"In what does being lovable consist? I wish you would teach me," said Trafford, with his old smile and manner. Maggie felt a strange dull pang at her heart, but only smiled, and said, "I do not know myself."

"At all events," continued Trafford in an altered tone. "You have won Miss Grantham's heart; but you must remember that charming women have certain privileges of variability—so be prepared"——

"Miss Grantham will always be loyalty itself," interrupted Maggie.

"But if you mean to warn me that I must not count on too long a spell of rest and sunshine, I am quite aware of it. In the first place, Miss Grantham does not really want me, and in the second she will soon marry, and then, as with Mrs. Berry, my 'occupation' would be 'gone.'" She paused for a moment to gather courage, and turning her head slightly aside, presented Trafford with the side view of her face and throat and little pink ear, which he so well remembered, went on, blushing and hesitating. "There is one thing I wanted so much to say—to ask you about, just once. I have been quite uncomfortable ever since I heard that Lord Torchester and his mother were coming. Not about him," she went on hastily, for without seeming to look at Trafford, she was aware that a smile was stealing round the corners of his mouth; "but I do dread meeting Lady Torchester, and I do particularly wish that Miss Grantham should never know anything of her cousin's nonsense about me—she would not like, she would somehow be displeased with me, and I *do* want to rest here for a little while; so if you could just tell Lady Torchester not to say anything, I know Lord Torchester' will not."

"I shall do my best to carry out your wishes," said Trafford gravely.

"You do not think it false or wrong in any way?" asked Maggie simply. "You see I cannot help fancying that perhaps Miss Grantham was the young lady you once mentioned to me that Lady Torchester wished her son to marry, and it would never do for her to know "——

"That he was your rejected suitor? Certainly not. You reason shrewdly; but may he not become your suitor again?" put in Trafford as she paused.

"Oh, no!" with a sunny smile and shake of the head. "It is not in Lord Torchester. He will never quite forgive me for the mortification. Oh, I am not the least afraid of that!"

"And are you still quite content to have thrown over an earl and his rent-roll?"

"Quite, quite," said Maggie, leaning her elbows on the table and resting her chin on her clasped hands. "I have read that some wise old Greek used to write about the 'fitness of things,' and I am sure I am not at all fit to be a countess."

Trafford was too much occupied in observing the quiet grace of her attitude to reply. There was a something of sadness and resignation in it, but not the slightest tinge of an appeal for pity.

"No," she continued, for she had grown quite at ease while she talked, "all that is quite out of the question; but if you will tell Lady Torchester that Miss Grantham has no idea—that I am so anxious it should not be known. I should be so much obliged; it would secure me a little longer the quiet, the strengthening, of such a resting-place as this before I drift away to sea again. Not that I fear doing so," she added hastily, half frightened, half resentful at the look of tenderness and compassion that melted Trafford's dark eyes into unusual softness. "To bear is to conquer one's fate, you know," she added almost gaily.

"I feel quite sure your destiny is to 'conquer,'" replied Trafford, looking steadily away from her, for he felt he dared not trust his eyes. "But so far as the Torchester question is concerned, you may consider it settled; and if at any time there is anything else I can do for you, pray let me know."

"Thank you very much. It is not likely—what a long time Miss Grantham is with Mr. Bolton! I am sure the luncheon bell must have rung."

"And I must go," said Trafford regretfully. "By the way, I came to ask you for some of the novel; can you give me a specimen?"

"Certainly. Here are three chapters."

"Thank you," said Trafford, taking them; yet he lingered. "Does your cousin, Mr. John Grey, return soon to—Africa, Australia, wherever he came from?—or perhaps he has returned?"

"He does not go back till next spring."

"Oh, indeed! Very delightful to meet an old friend and champion again."

"Very," said Maggie with a sigh. After a moment's hesitation Trafford left the room, and Maggie immediately flew to her own.

The letter to Lady Torchester was finished in time for post. It was remarkably candid in tone. After a few preliminaries, he continued thus: "Fancy my astonishment at finding Tor's 'young lady,' Miss Grey, established here as secretary to our fair princess. We were equally surprised to see each other, as she had no idea that the houses of Torchester and Grantham were connected. I find she is greatly alarmed at the idea of encountering you, and equally fearful lest Margaret should discover your son's episode concerning her. I have therefore promised and vowed three things in your name. First, that you would not say a word respecting Torchester's temporary insanity; secondly, that you would be graciously pleased to accept the expression of her regret that she was, though unconsciously, the means of causing you temporary annoyance; and third, that you would be so good as to understand that the letter you had the kindness to write never reached her, and allow her to explain the same. Now, my dear aunt, I think you are bound to believe and do as I have promised for you. It is also the wisest course; and I fancy I have penetrated the secret of my young protégée's disinterested refusal of your son. She has been long attached and is now, I fancy, engaged to a cousin of her own, who is going out to the colonies somewhere, and she has probably taken the place of secretary here while waiting her intended's summons."

"There," said Trafford to himself, "I hope and believe this last piece of intelligence is an utter falsehood. Still I have every right to come to such a conclusion, nor am I bound to give the Countess the light of my inner consciousness."

A few gossiping lines to the same effect were directed to Lord Torchester, and Geoffrey went to luncheon with a lighter spirit.

The first moment Maggie could speak to Miss Grantham alone was in the drawing-room, after dinner.

"Mr. Trafford came to the study to-day while I was waiting for you, and asked for some of your manuscript. I suppose I was not wrong in giving it to him?"

"Oh, no. I am rather pleased he took the trouble, but you will see how he will cut it up. He does not believe in anything I do," said Miss Grantham with an impatient, petulant gesture.

"That is impossible," replied Maggie gravely. "But perhaps," smiling, "he wants you to be perfection."

"He had better by far be satisfied with what I am," said Miss Grantham haughtily; and then the object of their discussion joined them.

"So you are really reading my novel, Geoff? What do you think of it?" asked Miss Grantham in a careless manner; but Maggie could detect a suppressed anxiety in her voice.

"I shall not commit myself to any opinion till I have perused it with profound attention. The day after to-morrow I may pronounce judgment."

"Well, be sure you give me your real opinion, and be serious about it."

"Am I not always sober and serious?—melancholy with the weight of do-nothingness on my shoulders? Do you know, some old fellow-travellers of mine are talking of an expedition to search for the sources of the Nile, and I am strongly inclined to join them? I daresay, Miss Grey, your relative could give one some hints as to African travelling?"

"Perhaps so. He once went with some exploring party to look for diamonds."

"And found none, or I am sure you would be sparkling with them."

"Really, Geoffrey, there is plenty of work to be done at home if you would allow Mr. Bolton and me to cut it out for you," said Miss Grantham, rising to go into the music-room. Trafford made no answer, and as she passed the chair in which he was lounging she repeated her words, adding, "Do you hear me?" and laying her white hand on his shoulder.

"I do, fair queen," said he, turning his head and kissing the long taper fingers.

Miss Grantham blushed vividly and drew her hand away very

2 o 2

gently, while she exclaimed, "You are the most quietly audacious man in existence," but she spoke with a tender smile and melting glance. The whole was a complete revelation to the observant secretary, even as though both hearts were laid bare before her. The noble, beautiful heiress had given her whole soul to the plain, dark, gentleman-like kinsman, who treated her as a spoiled child, while the lazy kindliness of his caress bespoke in Maggie's estimation almost insulting indifference. What would she not give to warn her admired friend; to save her in some way from the pain and mortification she felt were before her!

<h2 style="text-align:center">CHAPTER XXIII.</h2>

THE almost dreaded Tuesday came on with terrible rapidity—for Maggie was kept tolerably well occupied in writing lists, respecting donations of coal and beef and blankets—which seemed to her on a scale of extraordinary magnificence. She also was constantly in attendance on Miss Grantham, who made frequent visits to those parts of Castleford which were occupied by her tenants, and showed a lively interest in their well-being. " You see we can have no festivities at Grantham this Christmas, so I must make up for it, somehow," she explained to Maggie.

But Maggie thought what was much more deserving of explanation was the extraordinary interest taken by Mr. Bolton in these benevolent proceedings, and the curiosity he evinced as to the politics of Castleford.

On Tuesday morning Maggie and Miss Grantham had been over to Castleford, and inquired, as they generally did, for Mr. Burge. He was considerably better, but the doctors had recommended complete rest and change to a warmer climate. On their return, Miss Grantham had flown away in search of Mr. Bolton, passing Trafford, who met them in the hall with a nod. So he had a moment to speak to Maggie : " I had a line from Lady Torchester, yesterday, and it is all right. Are you satisfied?"

" Quite satisfied; and oh, so much obliged to you !"

" By the way, I told Lady Torchester you had never received her letter, but that you would explain. Pray be sure to do so."

" I will; that is, I will try—if she is not very formidable."

" She is not, I assure you. I imagine Bolton and Miss Grantham have some secret, they are always in conclave."

" I have guessed it, and you will know, if you only ask, I imagine," said Maggie, laughing gaily, in her relief at Trafford's intelligence, and running away up-stairs.

Trafford looked after her. " She has come out of it unscathed," he thought; and then the memory of the little cold trembling hand he had taken that wretched evening, when he had bid her good-bye in

Paris—of the strained look of bewildered grief in those speaking eyes—came back to him, as it had often done before; for on that occasion only had Trafford caught a glimpse of Maggie's real feelings.

"Bah! it was only a feeling of her loneliness that affected her; at any rate, she was soon consoled by her polished relative in the blue satin tie! She has never denied any of my insinuations about 'Cousin John.' I am really sick of this place. I am in for the family gathering at Christmas; but by Heaven, as soon as that is over, I'll be off, unless indeed, I see any signs of Torchester tormenting her—and then —we'll see."

With no small trepidation, Maggie attired herself in her new dress, to make her appearance on the memorable Tuesday. Had it been only to meet Lord Torchester she would have been simply glad; but his mother—that was an ordeal. "If she is cold and disdainful, it will make me miserable, at least for a little while; for if she does not turn Miss Grantham against me why need I mind? Only I do not want Mr. Trafford to compassionate me, to look upon me as a pitiable object, as I fancy he does. Heigho! Oh! how I wish I could manage to fall in love with Cousin John! But it is quite, quite impossible. I wish he thought so. It is a long time since he has written."

And then she looked very closely to the details of her dress, and viewed herself critically in the glass. The thin gauzy black looked well over her white neck and arms, her smoothly-braided brown hair rolled up so neatly into a thick knot at the back, suited admirably the perfect outline of her head, her unpretending style.

"It is hardly worth thinking so much how I look, I shall be scarcely seen," she thought—smiling, not unpleased, at her own reflection. "But that does not trouble me. Yet how charming it must be to know that some one watches for you, and rejoices to see you look well. Ah what folly for me to think such things! But perhaps it may come to me some day, if I am a good girl—as the children say."

And she stole down to the drawing-room in good time, that she might be safely landed before the ladies came from the dining-room. She sat down, on a low chair at the further end of the room from the grand fire that blazed and glowed so gorgeously, and took up a newspaper; but she could not read; she was acting over again the scenes of her life in Paris. She saw Lord Torchester come into Mrs. Berry's saloon and say, "I have come for you, Miss Grey." What a delightful day it was at Versailles! How good Lord Torchester was! How long ago it seemed—how much older she seemed to herself now! And then that evening when Lord Torchester brought Mr. Trafford to her tea-table, and she felt half angry, half frightened, at his searching grave dark eyes; but the opening door roused her, her heart beat—a tall lady in black velvet and bugles, and a snowy-looking head-dress of white crêpe lisse, with jet ornaments, walked in, and straight up to the fire, without seeming to see that there was any one in the room. Lady Dormer and Miss Grantham followed.

The latter turned towards her secretary. " How nice you look ! " she said quickly, in a low voice. " The dress does admirably ; come, I must introduce you." Maggie, encouraged, though blushing vividly, followed her patroness. The Countess, still standing before the fire, was speaking slowly and emphatically to Lady Dormer, who had sunk into her usual arm chair :

" A more conscientious and truly Christian young man, I have never met, and if Margaret would only exert her "——

" Let me present my secretary, Miss Grey, to you, Lady Torchester," said the young hostess.

Lady Torchester made the slightest possible courtsey, and looked full into Maggie's face—but with a smile. Maggie thought that, apart from voice and manner, the Countess was rather a common-looking woman. " I am sure, my dear," she said to Miss Grantham, " I am quite puzzled what you can possibly have for a secretary to do. That you should have Miss Grey for a companion, seems perfectly natural ; but one associates a secretary with parliamentary business and blue books."

" I am quite willing that Miss Grey should be my companion. So call her which you like "——

"There is something rather masculine and pretentious in a ' secretary,' do you not think so yourself, Miss Grey ?"

" I am not sure ; a secretary is a person who writes, and I do write for Miss Grantham."

" And a ' companion ' suggests the idea of a charming victim to some Gorgon of an old maid with a vicious pug. Now Miss Grey may be ever so charming, but she is not a victim."

" No, indeed !" cried Maggie, with a gay laugh.

Lady Torchester looked at her with some interest, and then resumed the subject from which she had diverged ; this was a glowing eulogy on an admirable young curate for whom she wished to secure Miss Grantham's interest with the rector. The heiress listened weariedly, glancing sometimes at the door by which the gentlemen would enter ; and Maggie, taking up Lady Dormer's crochet, went on with it mechanically, while she contrived to study Lady Torchester's appearance. She was, of course, quite different from what her fancy had painted. The Countess was a large, solemn-looking woman, with a slightly wandering expression, which reminded Maggie of Lord Torchester, and conveyed the idea of being terribly in earnest ; yet she did not seem cold or unkindly ; rather unsympathetic from slowness of comprehension.

At last Miss Grantham rose from the sofa where she had been sitting beside the Countess, saying, " Well, I will speak to the Dean about him, but I do not think it will do much good," and walked into the next room.

When she was gone, Lady Torchester asked, "What is your work, Miss Grey?" slightly moving her dress as she did so, as if inviting her to her side.

Maggie immediately accepted the invitation. "It is Lady Dormer's, but I sometimes help her."

"Pretty," said Lady Torchester, carelessly, and then became silent.

Maggie nerved herself; now was the moment to speak to Lady Torchester about her letter, and have done with it. Blushing brightly, and in a low tremulous voice, Maggie began. "Mr. Trafford told me you had been so very good as to write to me, and I have been so anxious to tell you I never received the letter. It must have come to Paris after we left, and as I never thought of any one writing to me I left no address.

"I was sorry you did not get it, but as it has turned out it was of no consequence. You could not be better placed than with Miss Grantham."

"Oh no indeed! She is so good and so delightful. But I should like you to know how much obliged I am to you—how "——

"I understand," said Lady Torchester, smiling indulgently; and just then the door opened, and the Earl and Mr. Bolton entered together. The moment he crossed the threshold Maggie was conscious of a change in her former admirer. He looked older, browner, more erect and assured. An expression of amused surprise came into his face when his eyes fell on his former divinity sitting quietly by his lady mother, and smiled upon by the Countess. Trafford, and a tall, large, elderly, jovial looking man, with profuse reddish-grey moustaches and whiskers, whom Maggie had never seen before, followed.

"Miss Grey," said the Earl, walking straight up to her and shaking hands cordially, "I am very glad to see you. I never was more surprised than when Geoff Trafford told me you were here." Drawing a chair beside her, Lord Torchester sat down, while the lines of his mother's face gradually contracted into an expression of watchfulness and anxiety. "So you are Miss Grantham's secretary? What do you write about? Is she not a jolly girl?"

"How can you use such an expression?" cried Maggie, indignantly, all her old frank ease towards the Earl returning to her. "Miss Grantham is like a young princess."

"Well, there were lots of very jolly girls princesses at St. Petersburg."

"Not like our princess," cried Maggie; "I'm sure of that."

"Miss Grey is quite right," said the Countess, gravely. "It is a most objectionable and inappropriate expression, and I am sure Margaret would not like it."

"She scarcely ever likes anything I say; but I can't be dumb, for all that. Now what do you do with yourself all day?—not write letters?"

"A secretary is bound to keep the secrets of the cabinet," said Maggie.

The Countess looked a little aghast at the easy tone of this badinage.

"Look," said Trafford to Bolton, as they stood together, coffee-cups in hand, at the other end of the room. "Look at Lady Torchester's face. I must take Tor off somehow." Through the open door he saw Miss Grantham in the music-room, leaning against a high-backed chair, talking to the stout stranger. Trafford set down his cup, and coming up to the group on the sofa, said, "Excuse me, Torchester, but Miss Grantham wants Miss Grey's assistance in the music-room."

"Very well," she replied, rising, rolling up her work, and carefully depositing it in Lady Dormer's basket.

Trafford offered his arm. "I was afraid to trust you any longer," said he. "You must not delude Tor again."

"There is no danger; and I was so glad to see him. It quite took me back to Paris—dear Paris!"

"Yet you had not your cousin John there," and Trafford looked down to see how she would take the thrust.

Maggie, amused and a little nettled, looked up defiantly and replied, "No, but I had my idea of him."

"Which has, no doubt, been amply realised," added Trafford. But Maggie would not answer, either by lip or eyes. "We are famishing for a song," said Trafford, "so I have brought Miss Grey to deprive you of the shadow of an excuse."

"Oh! I shall be very happy; but, Colonel Molyneux, do go and ask the Countess to come. Say I want her opinion of my performance."

The whole party were soon assembled in the music-room, and Maggie thought she observed, through all the sparring that went on between the Earl and his cousin, a decided, though suppressed, admiration on his part for the beautiful *châtelaine*. She sang unusually well, as she was always excited by the chance of fresh triumphs, for even her adoring secretary was obliged to see that the joy of her heart was to win the admiration of every man, woman and child who approached her; and the individual who withheld that tribute was, *pro tem.*, the most important personage.

"I fear this is a great risk," said Lady Torchester to Trafford, under cover of an eager dispute between Miss Grantham, Lord Torchester, and the stout Colonel, as to the merits of Jenny Lind and Grisi. "You see he was instantly attracted."

"I think it would have been a worse symptom if he had avoided her. His ease and frankness are most reassuring, and what can't be cured, &c. Here we are, we must make the best of it," returned Trafford.

"Of course. She is really a nice girl; perfectly ladylike. If Torchester were married I think I should not mind having her for a companion myself. Her stay with Margaret is of course uncertain; but you think it not improbable Miss Grey is herself engaged?"

"Well, I have an idea she is—only an idea; of course Miss Grey does not make a confidant of me.  I have not spoken half-a-dozen words to her since I came into the house."

"Nevertheless, Geoffrey," said his aunt suspiciously, "you always seem to know more about her than any one else."

"Intuition, I suppose," carelessly.

"Don't you think it very wrong of Torchester to bring Colonel Molyneux down here?  He is a man I have a great objection to; not even good style."

"He is rather of the sounding-brass order, but not a bad sort of fellow, and I think it was rather a good idea of your son's, because a family party in a house without a male head, though charming in many ways, is *rather* slow."  The Countess shook her head.  "You know," continued Trafford, "Margaret rather took a fancy to him in Scotland."

"And what have you done with Mrs. Berry?" said Lord Torchester, who was leaning on the piano, to Maggie, who was sitting at it.

"She suddenly married Monsieur de Bragance, and has quite disappeared."

"What, that clever scamp?  Poor woman, won't he lick her!  I say, Molyneux, did'nt you know something of Bragance here—in London, I mean?"

"Yes, a long time ago—eight or nine years ago."

"What was he then?"

"Why, a distinguished foreigner."

The Colonel seemed rather reserved.  Soon after Lady Torchester said she was tired, and the party broke up.

The gentlemen kept together a while longer, and the Colonel was more communicative respecting M. de Bragance than he seemed disposed to be before the ladies.

"I'll come into your room, Geoff, and have a weed, before I retire," said the Earl.  "I want to talk to you."

"Enter then," returned his kinsman.

"How well Margaret Wallcourt is looking," said Lord Torchester, after smoking a few moment in silence.

"Very well."  A pause.

"She has turned out a much finer girl than I expected; but is always the same with the tongue, so deuced ready, she takes a fellow's breath away."

"She does rather."  Another pause.

"Still she does not mean the half she says."

"Very likely."

"Why, Geoff! you seem to think your words worth their weight in gold, you are so stingy of them.  Don't you see I want to talk?"

"Well, talk, for heaven's sake."

"Yes, but I want you to talk too.  What have you been doing since you came down?  You have been here ten days and more."

"Not much—shooting and arguing with old Bolton, riding and talking metaphysics with our beautiful cousin."

"Metaphysics! Making love, you mean? Well, there is no reason why you should not."

"Perhaps so," said Trafford, coolly; "but I am not inclined to do it. Margaret, in my opinion, will be a more lovable woman eight or ten years hence than she is now."

"By Jove, what a notion! Why she will be thirty by that time."

"It will take her that time to know herself and the life that is round her. At present she is like the juice of the grape in its first stage, with all its flavour and strength and richness in a ferment. You cannot tell what she will be; but she is a fine creature, though awfully overweighted with fortune."

"I think she is very fond of you Geoff?"

"She is rather, just now; she does'nt think she has reduced me to a proper state of subjection. If that could be accomplished, why I should fall rapidly in her estimation. However, I am really very fond of her."

"I thought so," said the Earl, puffing vigorously.

"I have a fatherly regard for her, and should be most happy to bestow a paternal blessing on her union with—yourself, for instance."

"Oh, you would! You are really not hit? Well I am not in love with her or any one, thank God, and don't intend to be."

"Right, most potent signor. It would hardly be decent to recover so quickly and plunge in *medias res* over again."

"Well, I was a great ass," said the Earl good-humouredly; "but I was a lucky one. What a nice little thing she is," he went on musingly. "I mean Miss Grey. Do you know, I was so glad to see her I felt inclined to give her a kiss. She is such a sensible true-hearted brick, and stuck so gallantly to the man she liked in spite of my rank and fortune and all that."

Trafford looked hard at the speaker, but all was honest and sincere in the expression of his frank commonplace countenance.

"What is this cousin of hers? Could one give him a lift any how?"

"I know nothing whatever of him. So you are perfectly reconciled to your loss, ready to resign the divine party to another's arms?"

"Yes," said the Earl placidly, and evidently quite reconciled to Maggie by the idea that her affections had been engaged before they had met. "I daresay though, if I had married her I should have been tremendously fond of her; but marriages of this sort are great folly. I seem to have come to my senses from the moment she refused me. I shall never forget opening the door to-night, and seeing her and my mother talking so sweetly together. What an extraordinary chance to find her here! I hope Margaret will never know what an ass I made of myself about her. Now Margaret is one of the disinterested ones—she *must* be, she has so much of her own, eh? Nearly all the women you meet are so disgustingly greedy about rank and settlements"—— the Earl looked at Trafford inquiringly.

" Margaret may be ambitious," he replied, chosing a fresh cigar. " But I should say perfectly disinterested."

"At any rate, Maggie Grey is. If one woman is, why shouldn't another?" resumed the Earl logically. "I remember the first day I ever saw her alone—wasn't it nice! You know Mrs. Berry's *salon* was so shady and cool and full of flowers ?"

" Yes ;" Trafford remembered it.

" Well, the first time I ever had a quiet talk with her she told me I reminded her of her cousin John."

" Then I wish to heaven you could see cousin John, and you would be flattered," said Trafford, with unusual energy.

" Why—how—have you seen him? You seem to know more of Miss Grey than I thought."

" I was trying that chestnut Molyneux persuaded me to buy in the Park the day before we started for St. Petersburg, when I met her walking with the said cousin, very lovingly, arm and arm."

" Well ?"

" She looked confused, blushed, and introduced the relative, who called me ' sir.'

" The deuce he did! So you think it is all fixed ?"

" I cannot possibly tell."

" I wonder you did not mention this to me before."

" Why, of course I thought it better not." Another pause, and then in an altered voice Trafford asked what horses the Earl had brought, as the Castleford hounds met constantly in the neighbour-hood. "I have sent for the chestnut and Prince Henry myself," continued Trafford, "and expect them to-morrow." The conversation then became of horses, horsey, and the Earl grew even more ani-mated than when the talk was on a nobler theme.

The following Saturday was Christmas Day, and the intervening time flew by with great rapidity. The lady of the house went out on two occasions to see the hounds throw off, and the gentlemen were quite animated in their evening discussions on the events in the field. Mr. Bolton took a quiet ride to and fro' cover with Miss Grantham, who spent some time one evening in the vain attempt to persuade her secretary to mount and ride. "You would soon learn," said the heiress, "and it would be very nice for me to have a lady with me."

"I should only be an incumbrance to you at present," urged Maggie, dreadfully confused to find herself the centre of a group, all waiting for her decision. "If you still wish it, and I am here in the spring, I will learn, provided the great Mr. Andrews will condescend to teach me."

"‚You were always shy of riding, Miss Grey," cried Lord Torchester. " Do you remember how I tried to persuade you in Paris?"

" Miss Grey is quite right, as I must say she generally is," said Lady Torchester quickly. " If you want a companion in your rides why do you not ask Alicia Longmore?"

" My dear Countess, how can you suggest such a thing! However, Lady Brockhurst will be here next week, and then I shall have an ally *par excellence*." Lady Torchester shook her head.

As Miss Grantham was dressing for dinner the day before Christmas Day Maggie tapped at her door.

" May I speak to you a moment?" she was a little confused, and blushing.

" Certainly, only pray don't tell me you are going away."

" No, no; but I have had a letter from my cousin John; he wants to come down to see me. Indeed I cannot prevent him, and I am afraid you may not like it."

" Yes, of course I shall. Ask him down, by all means. I will speak to nurse to look after him. Only mind, he must not take you away directly."

" I assure you, Miss Grantham, there is no likelihood of such a thing, not the least."

" Well, well, we will see. At any rate it will be nice for you to have one of your own people. Cecile, call nurse to me. When is your cousin coming, dear?"

And on the spot, Maggie's' right royal protectress gave orders for the honourable reception of Mr. John Grey, jun.

" Christmas is the time for cousins to crop up, as Geoffrey would say. Grantham Longmore arrived to-day while you were out with Aunt Dormer. It is wonderful how well you get on with the old ladies. The Countess declares you the very essence of prudence and common sense—that your being sent to a castaway like myself was a direct answer to prayer; but whose, she doesn't mention. Remember, you must dine with us to-morrow. I will sing ' Robert, toi que j'aime ' to-night. Geoff Trafford says it is only fit for the stage."

LONDON: PRINTED BY WILLIAM CLOWES AND SONS, STAMFORD STREET AND CHARING CROSS.

Lightning Source UK Ltd.
Milton Keynes UK
UKHW020820241218
334505UK00012B/966/P